"R. A. Salvatore makes a solid mark on the world of fantasy
writing. The characters are rich, vibrant, and full of life. The
story line is quick-paced and flowing."
—*Cryptych*

BOOKS BY R. A. SALVATORE

Forgotten Realms® Book Series
Author of more than 20 novels including:
The Crystal Shard
Homeland
The Two Swords
Promise of the Witch King

DemonWars Series
The Demon Awakens
The Demon Spirit
The Demon Apostle
Mortalis
Ascendance
Transcendence
Immortalis

The Highwayman

Spearwielder's Tale

Star Wars: Vector Prime

R. A. SALVATORE

THE CRIMSON SHADOW

FOR THE FIRST TIME IN ONE VOLUME...

THE SWORD OF BEDWYR
LUTHIEN'S GAMBLE
THE DRAGON KING

WARNER BOOKS

NEW YORK   BOSTON

The Sword of Bedwyr copyright © 1995 by R. A. Salvatore
Luthien's Gamble copyright © 1996 by R. A. Salvatore
The Dragon King copyright © 1996 by R. A. Salvatore
Compilation copyright © 2006 by R. A. Salvatore
All rights reserved.

Warner Books
Hachette Book Group USA
1271 Avenue of the Americas
New York, NY 10020

Visit our Web site at www.HachetteBookGroupUSA.com.

Printed in the United States of America

The Sword of Bedwyr, Luthien's Gamble, and *The Dragon King* were each originally published in hardcover by Warner Books.

First Compilation Edition: October 2006
10 9 8 7 6 5 4 3

Warner Books and the "W" logo are trademarks of Time Inc. or an affiliated company. Used under license by Hachette Book Group USA, which is not affiliated with Time Warner Inc.

LCCN: 2006926966
ISBN-13: 978-0-446-69850-4
ISBN-10: 0-446-69850-4

CONTENTS

THE CRIMSON
SHADOW

THE
SWORD OF
BEDWYR

To Betsy Mitchell, for all of her support and input,
for showing me new potential and new directions.
Enthusiasm truly is infectious.

And a special thank you to Wayne Chang,
Donald Puckey, and Nancy Hanger.
In a business as tough and competitive as this,
it's comforting to be working with
such talented and dedicated people.

PROLOGUE

THESE ARE THE AVONSEA ISLANDS, rugged peaks and rolling hills, gentle rains and fierce winds blowing down from the glaciers across the Dorsal Sea. They are quiet Baranduine, land of folk and Fairborn, land of green and rainbows. They are the Five Sentinels, the Windbreakers, barren peaks, huge, horned sheep, and multicolored lichen that grows eerily when the sun has set. Let all seafarers beware the rocks of the channels near to the five!

They are Praetoria, most populous and civilized of the islands, where trade with the mainland is the way and cities dot the countryside.

And they are Eriador, untamed. She is a land of war, of hardy folk as familiar with sword as with plow. A land of clans, where loyalties run as deep as blood and to fight a man is to fight all his kin.

Eriador, untamed. Where the clouds hang low over rolling hills thick with green and the wind blows chill, even in the height of summer. Where the Fairborn, the elves, dance atop secret hills and rugged dwarves forge weapons that will inevitably taste of an enemy's blood within a year.

The tales of barbarian raiders, the Huegoths, are long indeed, and many are the influences of that warlike people on the folk of Eriador. But never did the Huegoths hold the land, never did they enslave the folk of Eriador. It is said among the clans of both Eriador and the barbarian islands that one Eriadoran was killed for every slain Huegoth, a score that no other civilized people could claim against the mighty barbarians.

Down from the holes of the Iron Cross came the cyclopians, one-eyed brutes, savage and merciless. They swept across the land, burning and pillaging, murdering any who could not escape the thunder of their charge. And there arose in Eriador a leader among the clans, Bruce Mac-Donald, the Unifier, who brought together the men and women of the land and turned the tide of war. And when the western fields were clear, it is said that Bruce MacDonald himself carved a swath through the northern leg of the Iron Cross so that his armies could roll into the eastern lands and crush the cyclopians.

That was six hundred years ago.

From the sea came the armies of Gascony, vast kingdom south of the islands. And so Avon, the land that was Elkinador, was conquered and "civilized." But never did the Gascons claim rule of Eriador in the north. The great swells and breakers of the Dorsal Sea swept one fleet aground, smashing the wooden ships to driftwood, and the great whales destroyed another fleet. Behind the rallying cries of "Bruce MacDonald!" their hero of old, did the folk of Eriador battle every inch for their precious land. So fierce was their resistance that the Gascons not only retreated but built a wall to seal off the northern lands, lands the Gascons finally declared untamable.

And with Eriador's continued resistance, and with war brewing among some of the other southern lands, the Gascons eventually lost interest in the islands and departed. Their legacy remains in the language and religion and dress of the people of Avon, but not in Eriador, not in the untamable land, where the religion is older than Gascony and where loyalty runs as deep as blood.

That was three hundred years ago.

There arose in Avon, in Carlisle on the River Stratton, a wizard-king of great power who would see all the islands under his rule. Greensparrow was his name, is his name, a fierce man of high ambition and evil means. And evil was the pact that Greensparrow signed with Cresis who ruled the cyclopians, appointing Cresis as his first duke and bringing the warlike one-eyes into Greensparrow's army. Avon became his in a fortnight, all opposition crushed, and then did he turn his sights on Eriador. His armies fared no better than the barbarians, than the cyclopians, than the Gascons.

But then there swept across Eriador a darkness that no sword could cut, that no courage could chase away: a plague that whispers hinted was inspired by black sorcery. None in Avon felt its ravages, but in all of free Eriador, mainland and islands, two of every three perished, and two of every three who lived were rendered too weak to do battle.

Thus did Greensparrow gain his rule, imposing a truce that gave unto him all the lands north of the Iron Cross. He appointed his eighth duke in the mining city of Montfort, which had been called Caer MacDonald, in honor of the Unifier.

Dark times there were in Eriador; the Fairborn retreated and the dwarves were enslaved.

That was twenty years ago. That was when Luthien Bedwyr was born. This is his tale.

CHAPTER 1

ETHAN'S DOUBTS

ETHAN BEDWYR, eldest son of the Eorl of Bedwydrin, stood tall on the balcony of the great house in Dun Varna, watching as the two-masted, black-sailed ship lazily glided into the harbor. The proud man wore a frown even before the expected standard, crossed open palms above a bloodshot eye, came into view. Only ships of the king or the barbarians to the northeast would sail openly upon the dark and cold waters of the Dorsal Sea, so named for the eerie black fins of the flesh-eating whales that roamed the waters in ravenous packs, and barbarians did not sail alone.

A second standard—a strong arm, bent at the elbow and holding a miner's pick—soon appeared.

"Visitors?" came a question from behind.

Recognizing the voice as his father's, Ethan did not turn. "Flying the duke of Montfort's pennant," he answered, and his disdain was obvious.

Gahris Bedwyr moved to the balcony beside his son and Ethan winced when he looked upon the man, who appeared proud and strong, as Ethan distantly remembered him. With the light of the rising sun in his face, Gahris's cinnamon eyes shone brightly, and the stiff ocean breeze blew his thick shock of silvery white hair back from his ruddy, creased face, a face that had weathered under the sun during countless hours in small fishing craft out on the dangerous Dorsal. Gahris was as tall as Ethan, and that was taller than most men on Isle Bedwydrin, who in turn were taller than most other men of the kingdom. His shoulders remained broader than his belly, and his arms were corded from a youth spent in tireless work.

But as the black-sailed ship drifted closer to the docks, the coarse shouts of the brutish cyclopian crew urging the islanders into subservient action, Gahris's eyes betrayed his apparent stature.

Ethan turned his gaze back to the harbor, having no desire to look upon his broken father.

"It is the duke's cousin, I believe," Gahris remarked. "I had heard that he was touring the northern isles on holiday. Ah well, we must see to his pleasures." Gahris turned as if to leave, then stopped, seeing that stubborn Ethan had not loosed his grip on the balcony rail.

"Will you fight in the arena for the pleasure of our guest?" he asked, already knowing the answer.

"Only if the duke's cousin is my opponent," Ethan replied in all seriousness, "and the fight is to the death."

"You must learn to accept what is," Gahris Bedwyr chided.

Ethan turned an angry gaze on him, a look that might have been Gahris's own a quarter of a century before, before independent Eriador had fallen under the iron rule of King Greensparrow of Avon. It took the elder Bedwyr a long moment to compose himself, to remind himself of all that he and his people stood to lose. Things were not so bad for the folk of Bedwydrin, or for those on any of the isles. Greensparrow was mostly concerned with those lands in Avon proper, south of the mountains called the Iron Cross, and though Morkney, the duke of Montfort, had exacted rigid control over the folk of the Eriadoran mainland, he left the islanders fairly alone—as long as he received his tithes and his emissaries were granted proper treatment whenever they happened onto one of the isles.

"Our life is not so bad," Gahris remarked, trying to soothe the burning fires in his dangerously proud son. The eorl would not be shocked if later that day he learned that Ethan had attacked the duke's cousin in broad daylight, before a hundred witnesses and a score of Praetorian Guards!

"Not if one aspires to subservience," Ethan growled back, his ire unrelenting.

"You're a great-grand," Gahris muttered under his breath, meaning that Ethan was one of those throwbacks to the days of fierce independence, when Bedwydrin had fought against any who would call themselves rulers. The island's history was filled with tales of war—against raiding barbarians, cyclopian hordes, self-proclaimed Eriadoran kings who would have, by force, united the land, and even against the mighty Gascon fleet, when that vast southern kingdom had attempted to conquer all of the lands in the frigid northern waters. Avon had fallen to the Gascons, but the hardened warriors of Eriador had made life so miserable for the invaders that they had built a wall to seal off the northern province, proclaiming the land too wild to be tamed. It was Bedwydrin's boast during those valorous times that no Gascon soldier had stepped upon the island and lived.

But that was ancient history now, seven generations removed, and Gahris Bedwyr had been forced to yield to the winds of change.

"I am Bedwydrin," Ethan muttered back, as if that claim should explain everything.

"Always the angry rebel!" the frustrated Gahris snapped at him. "Damn the consequences of your actions! Your pride has not the foresight—"

"My pride marks me as Bedwydrin," Ethan interrupted, his cinnamon eyes, the trademark of the Bedwyr clan, flashing dangerously in the morning sunlight.

The set of those eyes forestalled the eorl's retort. "At least your brother will properly entertain our guests," Gahris said calmly, and walked away.

Ethan looked back to the harbor—the ship was in now, with burly, one-eyed cyclopians rushing about to tie her up, pushing aside any islanders who happened in their way, and even a few who took pains not to. These brutes did not wear the silver-and-black uniforms of the Praetorian Guards but were the house guard escorts kept by every noble. Even Gahris had a score of them, gifts from the duke of Montfort.

With a disgusted shake of his head, Ethan shifted his gaze to the training yard below and to the left of the balcony, where he knew that he would find Luthien, his only sibling, fifteen years his junior. Luthien was always there, practicing his swordplay and his archery. Training, always training. He was his father's pride and joy, that one, and even Ethan had to admit that if there was a finer fighter in all the lands, he had never seen him.

He spotted his brother immediately by the reddish tint of his long and wavy hair, just a shade darker than Ethan's blond locks. Even from this distance, Luthien cut an impressive figure. He stood two inches above six feet, with a broad chest and muscled arms, his skin golden brown, a testament for his love of the outdoors on this isle, which saw more rain than sun.

Ethan scowled as he watched Luthien easily dispatch his latest sparring partner, then pivot immediately and with a single thrust, twist, and leg-sweep maneuver take down the opponent who rushed in at his back, trying to take him by surprise.

Those warriors watching in the training yard gave a cheer of approval, and Luthien politely stood and bowed.

Yes, Ethan knew, Luthien would properly entertain their "guests," and the thought brought bile into the proud man's throat. He didn't really blame Luthien, though; his brother was young and ignorant. In Luthien's twenty years, he had never known true freedom, had never known Gahris before the rise of the Wizard-King Greensparrow.

Gahris walked out into the training yard, then, and motioned for

Luthien to join him. Smiling and nodding, the eorl pointed to the docks. Luthien responded with a wide smile and ran off, toweling his corded muscles as he went: always ready to please.

"My pity to you, dear brother," Ethan whispered. The sentiment was an honest one, for Ethan knew well that Luthien would one day have to face up to the truth of their land and the cowardice of their father.

A shout from the dock stole Ethan's attention, and he looked that way just in time to see a cyclopian smash an islander fisherman to the wharf. Two other cyclopians joined their comrade, and the three punched and kicked the man repeatedly, until he finally managed to scramble away. Laughing, the three went back to their duties tying up the cursed craft.

Ethan had seen enough. He spun away from the balcony and nearly crashed into two of his father's own one-eyed soldiers as they walked past.

"Heir of Bedwyr," one of the cyclopians greeted through smiling, pointy yellow teeth.

Ethan did not miss the condescension in the brute's tone. He was the heir of Bedwyr, true enough, but the title rang hollow to the cyclopians, who ultimately served only the king of Avon and his wizard dukes. These guards, these "gifts" from the duke of Montfort, were no more than spies, Ethan knew as everybody knew. Not a soul on Bedwyr mentioned that little fact openly though.

"Do your appointed rounds normally take you to the private quarters of the ruling family?" Ethan snapped.

"We have only come to inform the nobles that the cousin of the duke of Montfort has arrived," the other guard replied.

Ethan stared at the ugly creature for a long while. Cyclopians were not quite as tall as most men, but were much thicker, with even the smallest of the burly race weighing nearly two hundred pounds and the heavier brutes often passing three hundred. Their foreheads, slipping out of a tight patch of stringy hair, were typically sloped down to the bushy brow of the single, always bloodshot, eye. Their noses were flat and wide, their lips almost non-existent, offering a perpetual view of those animal-like yellow teeth. And no cyclopian had ever been accused of possessing a chin.

"Gahris knows of the arrival," Ethan replied, his voice grim, almost threatening. The two cyclopians looked at each other and smirked, but their smiles disappeared when they looked back at the fiery Ethan, whose hand had gone to the hilt of his sword. Two young boys, human servants of the noble family, had come into the hall and were watching the encounter with more than a passing interest.

"Strange to wear a sword in one's own private quarters," one of the cyclopians remarked.

"Always a wise precaution when smelly one-eyes are about," Ethan answered loudly, taking strength in the appearance of the two human witnesses. He more than matched the ensuing scowls of the guards.

"And not another word from your mouth," Ethan commanded. "Your breath does so offend me."

The scowls increased, but Ethan had called their bluff. He was the son of the eorl, after all, an eorl the cyclopians had to at least maintain the pretense of serving. The two soldiers turned about and stomped off.

Ethan glanced at the boys, who were running off, but undeniably smiling. They were the youth of Bedwydrin, the eldest son thought. The youth of a proud race. Ethan took some solace and some hope in their obvious approval of the way he had stood down the ugly cyclopians. Perhaps the future would be a better time.

But despite the fleeting hope, Ethan knew that he had given his father yet another reason to berate him.

CHAPTER 2

TWO NOBLES AND THEIR LADIES

A CYCLOPIAN SOLDIER, shield emblazoned with the bent arm and pick design of Montfort, entered the audience hall of Gahris Bedwyr's home a short while later. It was a large rectangular room, set with several comfortable chairs and graced by a tremendous hearth.

"Viscount Aubrey," the one-eyed herald began, "cousin of Duke Morkney of Montfort, sixth of eight, fourth in line to . . ." And so it went on for several minutes, the cyclopian rambling through unimportant, even minuscule details of this viscount's heritage and lineage, feats of valor (always exaggerated, and still seeming not so tremendous to Gahris, who had lived in the tough land of Bedwydrin for more than sixty years) and deeds of generosity and heroism.

A viscount, the island eorl mused, thinking that practically every fourth man in Eriador seemed to hold claim to that title, or to one of baron.

"And his fellow, Baron Wilmon," the cyclopian went on, and Gahris sighed deeply at the not-unexpected proclamation, his thoughts proven all too true. Mercifully, Wilmon's introductory was not nearly as long as

Aubrey's, and as for their female escorts, the cyclopian merely referred to them as "the ladies, Elenia and Avonese."

"Ellen and Avon," Gahris muttered under his breath, for he understood the level of pretension that had come to the normally level-headed people of the lands.

In strode the viscount and his entourage. Aubrey was a meticulously groomed, salty-haired man in his mid-forties, Wilmon a foppish and swaggering twenty-five. Both wore the weapons of warriors, sword and dirk, but when they shook Gahris's hands, he felt no callouses, and neither had a grip indicating that he could even swing a heavy sword. The ladies were worse yet, over-painted, over-perfumed creatures of dangerous curves, clinging silk garments, and abundant jewelry that tinkled and rattled with every alluring shift. Avonese had seen fifty years if she had seen a day, Gahris knew, and all the putty and paint in the world couldn't hide the inevitable effects of nature.

She tried, though—oh, how this one tried!—and Gahris thought it a pitiful sight.

"Viscount Aubrey," he said politely, his smile wide. "It is indeed an honor to meet one who has so gained the confidence of our esteemed duke."

"Indeed," Aubrey replied, seeming rather bored.

"May I inquire what has brought such an unexpected group so far to the north?"

"No," Aubrey started to answer, but Avonese, slipping out of Aubrey's arm to take hold of the eorl's, interrupted.

"We are on holiday, of course!" she slurred, her breath scented by wine.

"We are come now from the Isle of Marvis," added Elenia. "We were informed that none in all the northland could set a banquet like the eorl of Marvis, and we were not disappointed."

"They do have such fine wines!" added Avonese.

Aubrey seemed to be growing as tired of the banter as Gahris, though Wilmon was too engaged with a stubborn hangnail to notice any of it.

"The eorl of Marvis has indeed earned his reputation as a fine host," Gahris remarked sincerely, for Bruce Durgess was a dear friend of his, a common sufferer in the dark times of the wizard-king's rule.

"Fair," Aubrey corrected. "And I suppose that you, too, will treat us with renowned leek soup, and perhaps a leg of lamb as well."

Gahris started to reply, but wasn't sure what to say. The two dishes, along with a multitude of fish, were indeed the island's staple.

"I do so hate leek soup," Aubrey went on, "but we have enough provisions on board our vessel and we shan't be staying for long."

Gahris seemed confused—and that sincere expression hid well his sudden sense of relief.

"But I thought . . ." the eorl began, trying to sound truly saddened.

"I am late for an audience with Morkney," Aubrey said haughtily. "I would have bypassed this dreary little island altogether, except that I found the eorl of Marvis's arena lacking. I had heard that the islands were well-stocked with some of the finest warriors in all of Eriador, but I daresay that a half-crippled dwarf from the deepest mines of Montfont could have easily defeated any of the fighters we witnessed on the Isle of Marvis."

Gahris said nothing, but was thinking that Aubrey's description of Bedwydrin as a "dreary little island" would have cost the man his tongue in times past.

"I do so hope that your warriors might perform better," Aubrey finished.

Avonese squeezed Gahris's arm tightly, apparently liking the hardened muscles she felt there. "Warriors do so inspire me," she whispered in the eorl's ear.

Gahris hadn't expected a morning arena fight, but was glad to oblige. Hopefully, the viscount would be satisfied with the show and would be gone before lunch, saving Gahris the trouble of setting a meal—be it lamb or leek soup!

"I will see to the arrangements personally," Gahris said to Aubrey, smoothly pulling free of Avonese's nailed clutches as he spoke. "My attendants will show you to where you might refresh yourselves after the long journey. I will return in a few moments."

And with that he was gone, hustling down the stone corridors of his large house. He found Luthien just a short distance away, dressed in fine clothes and freshly scrubbed after his morning workout.

"Back to the yard with you," Gahris said to his son's confused expression. "They have come to see a fight and nothing more."

"And I am to fight?"

"Who better?" Gahris asked, patting Luthien roughly on the shoulder and quickly leading him back the way he had come. "Arrange for two combats before you take your turn—at least one cyclopian in each." Gahris paused and furrowed his brow. "Who would give you the best fight?" he asked.

"Ethan, probably," Luthien replied without hesitation, but Gahris was already shaking his head. Ethan wouldn't fight in the arena, not anymore, and certainly not for the entertainment of visiting nobles.

"Garth Rogar, then," Luthien said, referring to a barbarian warrior, a giant of a man. "He has been in fine form of late."

"But you will defeat him?"

The question seemed to sting the proud young warrior.

"Of course you will." Gahris answered his own question, making it seem an absurd thing to ask. "Make it a worthy fight, I beg. It is important that Bedwydrin, and you, my son, be given high praise to the duke of Montfort."

Gahris stopped then, and Luthien bounded away, brimming with confidence and with the sincerest desire to please both his father and the visiting nobles.

"How embarrassed will Luthien be to fail before his father and his father's honored guests?" the huge man bellowed to the approving laughter of many other fighters. They sat in the low and sweaty chambers off the tunnels that led to the arena, testing the feel of their weapons while awaiting their call.

"Embarrassed?" the young Bedwyr replied, as though he was truly stunned. "There is no embarrassment in victory, Garth Rogar."

A general, mocking groan rolled about the chamber as the other warriors joined in the mood.

The huge Rogar, fully a foot taller than Luthien's six feet two inches, with arms as thick as Luthien's legs, dropped his whetstone to the floor and deliberately rose. Two strides took him right up to the still-seated young Bedwyr, who had to turn his head perpendicular to his body to see tall Garth Rogar's scowl.

"You fall this day," the barbarian promised. He began a slow turn, shoulders leading so that his grim expression lingered on Luthien for a long moment. All the room was hushed.

Luthien reached up and slapped Garth Rogan across the rump with the flat of his sword, and howls of laughter erupted from the warriors, Garth Rogan included. The huge northman spun about and made a mock charge at Luthien, but Luthien's sword snapped out quicker than the eye could follow, its waving tip defeating the charge.

They were all friends, these young warriors, except for the few cyclopians who sat in a distant corner, eyeing the play disdainfully. Only Garth Rogar had not been raised on Bedwydrin. He had floated into Dun Varna's harbor on the flotsam of a shipwreck just four years previously. Barely into his teens, the noble young barbarian had been taken in by

the islanders and treated well. Now, like the other young men of Bedwydrin, he was learning to fight. It was all a game to the young rascals,
but a deadly serious game. Even in times of peace, such as they had
known all their lives, bandits were not uncommon and monsters occasionally crawled out of the Dorsal.

"I will cut your lip this day," Garth said to Luthien, "and never again
will you kiss Katerin O'Hale."

The laughter became a hush; Katerin was not one to be insulted. She
was from the opposite side of Bedwydrin, raised among the fisherfolk
who braved the more dangerous waters of the open Avon Sea. Tough indeed were the stock of Hale, and Katerin was counted among their
finest. A leather packet soared across the room to bounce off the huge
barbarian's back. Garth Rogar spun about to see a scowling Katerin
standing with her muscled arms crossed atop her sword, its tip resting
against the stone floor.

"If you say so again, I will cut something of yours," the fiery red-
haired young woman promised grimly, her green eyes flashing dangerously. "And kissing will then be the last thing on your small mind."

The laughter erupted once more, and Garth Rogar, red with embarrassment, knew that he could not win this war of insults. He threw up
his hands in defeat and stalked back to his seat to prepare his weapons.

The weapons they used were real, but blunted, and with shortened
tips that might pierce and sting, but would not kill. At least, not usually.
Several warriors had died in the arena, though none in more than a
decade. The fighting was an ancient and necessary tradition on Bedwydrin and in all of Eriador, and deemed worth the potential cost by
even the most civilized of men. The scars that young men and women
carried with them from their years training in the arena taught them well
the respect of weapons and enemies, and gave them a deep understanding of those they would fight beside if trouble ever came. Only three
years of training were required, but many stayed on for four, and some,
like Luthien, had made the training their life's endeavor.

He had been in the arena perhaps a hundred times, defeating every
opponent except for his first, his brother Ethan. The two had never re-
matched, for Ethan had soon left the arena, and while Luthien would
have liked to try again his skills against his undeniably talented brother,
he did not allow his pride to blemish his sincere respect and love for
Ethan. Now Luthien was the finest of the group. Katerin O'Hale was
swift and agile as any cat, Bukwo of the cyclopians could take a tremendous amount of punishment, and Garth Rogar was powerful beyond the
normal limitations of any human. But Luthien was a true warrior: fast

and strong, agile and able to bring his weapon to bear or to parry at any angle in the blink of a cinnamon-colored eye. He could take a hit and growl away any pain, and yet he carried fewer scars than any except the very newest of the warriors.

He was the complete fighter, the shining light in his father's aging eyes, and determined now to honor his father this day, to bring a smile to the face of a man who smiled far too little.

He brought a whetstone singing along the side of his fine sword, removing a burr, then held the weapon out in front of him, testing its balance.

The first fight, two cyclopians beating each other about the head and shoulders with light clubs, had already commenced when Gahris led his four visitors into the seats of honor at the front of the balcony directly opposite the tunnels that opened onto the circular fighting grounds of the arena. Gahris took his seat in the middle and was promptly sandwiched between Elenia and Avonese, squeezing in tight beside him, with their respective consorts flanking them on the outside. To increase the eorl's discomfort, three of Aubrey's personal cyclopian guards were close behind the seated nobles. One carried a crossbow, Gahris noted, an unusual sight among cyclopians. With only one eye, the brutes lacked depth perception and were normally not adept with distance weapons. This one seemed comfortable holding the crossbow, though, and Gahris noted that it had been fitted with a curious device, opposing and angled mirrors, atop its central shaft.

Gahris sighed when he noticed that only a handful of islanders were in attendance this day. He had hoped for a cheering crowd and wished that he had been given the time to assemble one.

But Aubrey was obviously impatient. The viscount was here only so that his pestering consort, Avonese, would stop her incessant nagging.

"Cyclopians?" Avonese whined. "If I wanted to watch cyclopians brawl, I would simply throw a piece of uncooked meat into their midst at Castle Montfort!"

Gahris winced—this wasn't going well.

"Surely you have better to offer than two cyclopians battering each other, Eorl Bedwyr," Aubrey put in, and his look to Gahris was both pleading and threatening. "My cousin Morkney, the duke of Montfort, would be so disappointed to learn that my journey to your island was not a pleasurable one."

"This is not the primary show," Gahris tried to explain against a rising chorus of groans. Finally, the eorl gave up. He signalled to the marshal of the arena, and the man rode out from a side stable and broke up the fight, ordering the two brutes back to the tunnel. The cyclopians gave their customary bow to the eorl's box, then walked away, and were promptly fighting again before they even got out of sight.

The next two combatants, red-haired Katerin and a young lass from across the island, a newcomer to the arena but with promising speed, had barely walked out of the tunnel when both Avonese and Elenia took up cries of protest.

Gahris silently berated himself for not anticipating this. Both women warriors were undeniably beautiful, full of life and full of health. Also, their warrior garb, cut so that they might have full freedom of movement, was something less than modest, and the looks upon the faces of Aubrey and Wilmon showed that they had been cooped up in the company of the two painted "ladies" far too long.

"This will not do!" Avonese cried.

"I do so want to see some sweating man-flesh," Elenia purred, and her ample fingernails drew little lines of blood on Wilmon's arm.

Gahris couldn't tell if it was Wilmon's anticipation of what the sight of sweating man-flesh would do to his eager escort, or if it was simply fear of Elenia that led him to demand that they move on to the next fight.

"We are pressed for time," Aubrey added sharply. "I wish to see a fight, a single fight, among the best warriors Bedwydrin can muster. Surely that task is not beyond the understanding of the eorl of Bedwydrin."

Gahris verily trembled, and it took every ounce of control he could muster to hold him back from throttling the skinny Aubrey. But he nodded his head and signaled to the marshal once more, calling out that it was time for Luthien and Garth Rogar.

On the tiered steps behind the eorl's viewing box, Ethan looked upon his cowed father and the pompous guests, his expression sour.

Both women simultaneously cooed when Luthien and Garth Rogar walked out of the tunnel, side by side, wearing little more than sandals, mailed gauntlets, loincloths, and a collar and bandolier device designed to protect their vital areas.

"Is there a bigger man alive?" Elenia gasped, obviously taken with the flaxen-haired barbarian.

"Is there a handsomer man alive?" Avonese retorted, turning her glower on her companion. She noticed Gahris then, took a deep look at him, then turned back to Luthien, intrigued.

"My son," the eorl proudly explained. "Luthien Bedwyr. And the giant is a Huegoth who floated to our shores as just a boy, as honorable a fighter as any. You will not be disappointed, Viscount."

It was obvious that Avonese and Elenia were in full agreement with the last statement. They continued to gawk and to toss snide comments back and forth, quickly drawing lines.

"The barbarian will crush him down," Elenia remarked.

"Those eyes are too wise to be caught in the primitive webs of a savage," Avonese countered. She jumped up from her seat suddenly and moved to the rail, throwing out her fine cambric handkerchief.

"Luthien Bedwyr!" she cried. "You fight as my champion. Fight well and you will savor the rewards!"

Gahris looked over to Aubrey, stunned by the woman's blunt forwardness and fearing that the viscount would be boiling with rage. It seemed to the eorl that Aubrey was more relieved than angry.

Elenia, not to be outdone, quickly rushed to the balcony and threw out her own kerchief, calling for the Huegoth to come and champion her cause.

Luthien and Garth Rogar walked over and took up the offered trophies, each tucking a kerchief into his belt.

"It shall not be so much as soiled," cocky Luthien said to Avonese.

"Bloodied, yes, soiled, no," Garth Rogar agreed, turning away from giggling Elenia.

Luthien quickly caught up to his opponent as Garth Rogar moved back toward the center of the arena, both of them putting on their helmets. "So the stakes are raised," the young Bedwyr remarked.

Garth Rogar scoffed at him. "You should not be thinking of pleasures with a fight before you," the barbarian said, and as soon as the marshal clapped his hands for the fight to begin, the barbarian charged forward, his long spear thrusting for Luthien's belly and a quick victory.

Luthien was taken off guard by the bold attack. He fell to the side and rolled away, but still took a stinging nick on the hip.

Garth Rogar stepped back and threw up his hands, as if in victory. "And so it is soiled!" he cried, pointing at Avonese's kerchief.

Elenia squealed with joy, oblivious to the dart-throwing gaze Avonese had turned on her.

Now Luthien went on the attack, scrambling forward in a crouch so low that he had to use his shield arm as a third support. His sword whipped across at Garth's legs, but the barbarian hopped back quickly enough. On came Luthien, knowing that if he let up the attack, his opponent, standing high above him, would surely pound him into the dirt.

But Luthien was quick, snapping his sword back and forth repeatedly, keeping Garth Rogar hopping. Finally, the barbarian was forced to stab his spear straight down to intercept a cut that would have cracked his knee. Up came Luthien fiercely, and though he could not realign his sword, he swung hard with his shield, slamming the barbarian in the chest and face.

Garth Rogar staggered backward; lines of blood ran from his nose and one side of his mouth. But he was smiling. "Well done!" he congratulated. As Luthien took an appropriate bow, the barbarian howled and charged back in.

Luthien was ready for the obvious move, though, and his sword flashed across, turning the spear out wide. The cunning Bedwyr rolled in behind the wide-flying weapon, again scoring a hit with his shield—just a glancing blow against Garth Rogar's powerful chest.

The barbarian countered quickly, though, hooking his free arm around the young fighter and driving his knee hard into Luthien's thigh. Luthien stumbled past, and Rogar would have had him, except that the young man was quick enough and wise enough to slice across with his sword, nicking his opponent's knee and stopping the charging giant short.

They squared up again and rushed right back in, fighting for pride and for the love of competition. Sword and spear crossed and parried; Luthien's shield rushes were countered by Rogar's punching fist.

Gahris had never seen his son, and especially Garth Rogar, fight better, and he was positively beaming with pride, for both Wilmon and Aubrey were fully entranced by the action, shouting out cheers for every cunning counter or last-second parry. The men could not match the squeals of Avonese and Elenia, though, as each cheered her champion on. These two were not as familiar with fighting styles as the others and many times thought the fight to be at its end, thinking that one or the other had gained an insurmountable advantage.

But these two fighters were well matched and well trained. Always the appropriate defenses were in place, always the men were balanced.

Garth Rogar started with a spear thrust, but as Luthien's sword parried, the barbarian unexpectedly heaved his weapon up high, taking Luthien's sword with it. Following his own building momentum, Garth lifted a foot for a well-aimed kick, slamming Luthien in the midsection and doubling him over, gasping for breath.

Luthien's shield came up at the last moment to stop the spear's butt end, aimed for his head, but he took another kick, this one on the hip, and went scrambling away.

"Oh, good!" cried Elenia, and only then did Gahris notice the scowl

Avonese threw the younger woman's way, and he began to understand that there might be serious trouble brewing.

Sensing the advantage, Garth Rogar roared in, hurling himself at his winded opponent.

Luthien's shield took the spear up high, Luthien ducking underneath and snapping a quick sword cut into the barbarian's lead hand. The mailed gauntlet allowed Garth Rogar to keep his fingers, but he howled anyway for the pain and let go with that hand.

Now Luthien pressed forward, keeping his shield in line as he charged so that Garth could not retract his spear for any parries. His sword cut in from the side, pounding hard against the barbarian's leather bandolier. Garth Rogar winced, but kept his focus, and as Luthien brought the sword back out, then reversed it for a second cut, Garth caught the blade in his mailed fist.

Luthien pressed forward, and Garth got his feet under him enough to press back—just as Luthien had anticipated. Suddenly, the young Bedwyr stopped and backpedaled, and Garth found himself overbalanced. Luthien fell into a backward roll and planted his feet in the barbarian's belly as Garth tumbled over him.

"Oh, send him flying away!" screamed Avonese, and Luthien did just that, pushing out with both feet so that Garth Rogar did a half somersault, landing heavily on his back.

Both men were up in an instant, weapons in hand, eyeing each other with sincere respect. They were weary and bruised, and both knew that they would be wickedly sore the next day, but this was competition at its finest and neither cared.

Across from Gahris, it was Elenia's eyes that were now throwing darts. "Crush him!" she cried out to Garth Rogar, so loudly that her call temporarily halted all the other cheering in the arena, and all eyes, Luthien's and Garth Rogar's included, turned to her.

"It would seem that you have made a friend," Luthien said to the barbarian.

Garth Rogar nearly burst out laughing. "And I would not want to disappoint her!" he said suddenly, and on he came, thrusting his spear. He pulled it up short and whipped it about instead, its butt end ringing loudly off of Luthien's shield. Luthien countered with a straight cut, but the barbarian was out of range. A second spear thrust slipped over Luthien's shield and nearly took his eye out, nicking his helm as he ducked, and the butt end whipped about again, banging both shield and Luthien's back.

That hit stung, but Luthien ignored it, understanding that he had to go to the offensive or be buried under the powerful man's attacks. He started to run with the momentum of the spear, then ducked under it and pivoted about, coming up under Garth's swinging arm. The edge of Luthien's shield hooked under the taller man's armpit, lifting him off balance. Again, Garth Rogar caught Luthien's swinging sword in his hand, but this time, his feet were tangled. When Luthien heaved suddenly, arms and legs wide, the barbarian's spear went flying and Rogar himself fell heavily to the ground.

"Get him! Get him!" Avonese cried.

"Fight back, you oaf!" screamed Elenia.

Luthien was just settling into his stance when Garth Rogar jumped up. Luthien thought Rogar would go for the fallen spear—and he would have let the worthy opponent retrieve it—but Garth, savagery coursing wildly within his barbarian blood, charged instead. Surprised, Luthien got his shield up, and then his whole arm fell numb under the sheer weight of the Huegoth's tremendous punch.

Luthien bounced back a full step, looked in amazement as his shield, one of its straps snapped by the blow, fell from his arm. He just managed to duck a second punch, one that he figured would have hurt him more than any spear could, and leaped back from a third, swinging his broken shield at his opponent as he went to keep the man back.

Garth Rogar smacked the metal shield away and came in, slowing only to dodge a short thrust from Luthien's sword. A second thrust turned him to the side, to Luthien's left, and Luthien's free hand was waiting, snapping a punch into the barbarian's already broken nose.

Garth Rogar tried to fake a smile, but he had to shake his head to clear away the dizziness.

"Do you yield?" Luthien politely asked, and they both heard Elenia's protesting scream from the stands, and Avonese's howls of victory.

Predictably, Garth Rogar charged. At the last instant, Luthien tossed his sword up into the air, right in the barbarian's face. Garth flinched, then jolted to a stop, his own momentum used against him, by a left-right punch combination that would have felled a small bull.

Luthien caught the sword in his left hand, moved it to Garth's neck to force a yield. Ferocious Garth caught its tip, tossed it out wide and clamped his hand on Luthien's forearm.

"Rip his arm off!" Elenia cried. Avonese leaned right across Gahris's lap to hiss at her.

Luthien's muscles flexed as he fell into a clinch with the larger and stronger man. Wilmon, and even Aubrey, scowled a bit at the ensuing sighs of their obviously enchanted consorts.

Luthien held well against Rogar, but knew that the man's sheer weight would soon overwhelm him. He pushed forward with all his might, then took a quick step backward, breaking one hand free, though Garth stubbornly held his sword arm. The combatants exchanged punches; Garth Rogar took a second, and a third, willingly, as he bent to clamp a hand under Luthien's crotch. A moment later, the young Bedwyr was rising helplessly into the air, the angle all wrong for him to get any weight behind a punch—and Garth Rogar's grip on his sword arm remained unrelenting.

Luthien head-butted the barbarian instead, forehead to face. The stunned Garth Rogar heaved him ten feet away, then focused on just keeping his balance. For the barbarian, the world would not stop spinning.

Luthien pulled himself up from the ground and cautiously stalked back in, looking for a clean opening between Garth's wild swings. Luthien was on the verge of exhaustion and feared that a single hit from his powerful enemy would send him spinning to the ground.

He waved his sword all about as he came in slowly, forcing the dizzy barbarian to keep up with its tantalizing movements. The thrust was a feint—Garth Rogar knew that—but so was the following right cross. Luthien pulled up short and fell to the ground, his legs sweeping across, kicking out both of Garth Rogar's knees. Down went the barbarian hard on his back, his breath coming out in one profound blast.

Luthien was up, quick as a cat, but Garth had not the strength to follow. Luthien planted a foot on the fallen man's chest, and his sword tip came to rest on the bridge of Garth Rogar's nose, right between his unfocused eyes.

The screams of Elenia and Avonese were surprisingly similar, but the expressions that each wore after the initial outburst certainly were not.

Gahris was truly pleased by the appreciation, even admiration, stamped upon Aubrey's face, but the eorl's smile disappeared as Avonese again leaned heavily across his lap, looking at the pouting Elenia with sparkling, wicked eyes.

"Pray offer the down-pointing thumb, Eorl Bedwyr," Avonese purred.

Gahris nearly choked. A down-pointing thumb meant that the loser should be killed. That was not the way on the islands: the fights were for sport and training alone!

Elenia cried out in outrage, which only spurred on the evil Avonese.

"Thumb down," she said again, evenly, looking to protesting Elenia all the while. It wasn't hard for Avonese to figure out what Elenia had in mind for the barbarian, and stealing her younger rival's pleasure felt wonderful indeed. "Your son was my champion, he wears my offered pennant, and thus, I am granted the decision of victory."

"But . . ." was all that stammering Gahris managed to get out before Aubrey reached across and put a hand on the eorl's shoulder.

"It is her right, by ancient tradition," the viscount insisted, not daring to displease his vicious companion.

"Garth Rogar fought valiantly," Gahris protested.

"Thumb down," Avonese said slowly, emphasizing each word as she shifted her gaze to look right into Gahris's cinnamon-colored eyes.

Gahris looked past her to see the viscount nodding. He tried to weigh the consequences of his actions at that moment. Avonese's claim was true enough—by the ancient rules, since Luthien had unwittingly agreed to be her champion, she had the right to decide the fate of the defeated man. If he refused now, Gahris could expect serious trouble from Montfort, perhaps even an invading fleet that would take his eorldom from him. Ever was Morkney looking for reasons to replace the often troublesome island eorls.

Gahris gently pushed Avonese aside and looked out to the arena, where Luthien was still poised above the fallen Garth Rogar, waiting for the signal to break and the applause both he and the barbarian so richly deserved. Great was Luthien's astonishment when he saw his father extend his hand, thumb pointing down.

Luthien stood confused for a long while, hardly hearing Avonese's calls for him to finish the task. He looked down at his friend; he could not comprehend the notion of killing the man.

"Eorl Gahris," prompted an increasingly impatient Aubrey.

Gahris called to the arena marshal, but the man seemed as transfixed as Luthien.

"Do it!" vicious Avonese snapped. "Aubrey?"

The viscount snapped his fingers at one of his cyclopian guardsman behind him, the one with the curious crossbow.

Luthien had stepped back by this point and extended his hand to his friend. Garth Rogar had reached up and taken that grasp, starting to rise, when there came the click of a firing crossbow. The barbarian jerked suddenly, clamping tightly on Luthien's hand.

Luthien did not at first understand what had just transpired. Then Garth Rogar's grip loosened, and time seemed to move in slow motion as the proud barbarian slowly slipped back to the dirt.

CHAPTER 3

FAREWELL, MY BROTHER

LUTHIEN STARED AT GARTH ROGAR in shocked silence, stared at the surprised expression on the flaxen-haired barbarian's rugged and bruised face. Surprised even in death or, perhaps, because of his death.

"Fly, Death!" Luthien wailed, throwing his sword aside and diving down to kneel beside the man. "Be gone from this place, for here you do not belong! Seek an aged man, or an infant with not the strength to survive in this cruel world, but take not this man, this boy, younger than I." Luthien grabbed up Garth Rogar's hand in his own and propped the barbarian's head with his other arm. He could feel the heat leaving Rogar's body, the sweat the barbarian had worked up in the fight becoming clammy. Luthien tried to stammer more protests, but found his tongue caught in his mouth. What might he say to Death, that most callous of spirits which does not care to hear? What use were words when the heat was fast leaving Garth Rogar's young and strong body?

Luthien looked back helplessly to the box, his expression a mixture of confusion and boiling rage. But Aubrey's party, Gahris included, was already gone from sight; further up the stands, Ethan, too, had fled the scene. Luthien's gaze darted all about. Many of the spectators had departed, but some remained, whispering and pointing incredulously to the man lying in the dirt, and the son of Bedwyr leaning over him.

Luthien turned back to Garth Rogar. He saw the back tip of the crossbow quarrel protruding from the man's side, between two ribs, and reached for it tentatively, as if he thought that pulling it free would give Garth Rogar back his breath. Luthien tried to touch the metal shaft, but found that his fingers would not close about it.

A cry made him lift his gaze to see the other warriors fast exiting the tunnel, led by Katerin. She skidded to her knees before the man, and after just an instant, reached up and gently closed his eyes. Her somber gaze met Luthien's and she slowly shook her head.

Up jumped Luthien, roaring, the cry torn from his heart. He looked around wildly, hands clenched at his side, then found a focus to his rage. He tore Avonese's kerchief from his hip and flung it to the ground, then stamped it into the dirt.

"On the death of Garth Rogar, friend and fellow," he began, "I, Luthien Bedwyr, do vow—"

"Enough," interrupted Katerin, rising beside him and taking his arm in hers. He looked at her incredulously, hardly believing that she would interrupt at so solemn a moment. When he stared into her face, though, he saw no apology for her unexpected action, only a pleading look.

"Enough, Luthien," she said softly, in full control. "Garth Rogar died as a warrior by the most ancient and hallowed rules of the arena of our people. Do not dishonor him."

Horrified, Luthien pulled away from Katerin. He stared at his fellows, at the fighters who had trained beside him for these last years, but found no support. He felt as though he was standing in a group of strangers.

And then Luthien ran, across the field and into the tunnel, out into the open area near to the harbor and north along the beach.

"It was unfortunate," Gahris began, trying to downplay the events.

"It was murder," Ethan corrected, and his father looked about nervously, as if he expected one of Aubrey's cyclopian guards to be lurking in the area.

"Strong words," Gahris whispered.

"Often strong is the ring of truth," Ethan said sternly and loudly, not backing off an inch.

"I'll have no more of it," Gahris demanded. Still he looked about, drawing a disdainful glare from his judgmental son. "No more, do you hear!"

Ethan snorted derisively and stared down at this man, this stranger who could be so cowed. He understood Gahris's tentative position quite well, understood the politics of the land. If Gahris took any action against Aubrey, or any of Aubrey's party, then the duke of Montfort would surely retaliate, probably with a fleet of warships. Ethan didn't care, though, and didn't sympathize. To the proud young Bedwyr, some things were worth fighting for, worth dying for.

"And what of the Lady Avonese?" Ethan asked, putting a sarcastic tone on his use of the word "lady."

Gahris sighed, seeming very small to his son at that moment, "Aubrey hints at leaving her behind," he admitted. "He thinks that her influence might be a positive thing for Bedwydrin."

"A new wife for Gahris," Ethan spat out sarcastically. "A spy for Morkney in the house of Bedwyr." His father did not reply.

"And what of this woman who would so readily change consorts?" Ethan asked loudly and venomously. "Am I, then, to call her mother?"

A spark of fury ignited within Gahris, and before he could control the emotion, his hand snapped out and slapped the impertinent Ethan across the face.

Ethan didn't retaliate other than to fix a glare on his father, his striking eyes narrowed.

Gahris had not wanted things to go this far, but there was a danger brewing here, for him and for all the folk of Bedwydrin. In the flash of a passing instant, the white-haired eorl remembered his wife, who died in the great plague, and remembered the free time before that, before Greensparrow. But those times were gone, and the thoughts, like the instant, were passing, stolen by an unrelenting stare that amply reflected what the pragmatic elder Bedwyr knew he had to do.

Luthien looked back from a high bluff toward the north side of the bay as the last lights went out in the town of Dun Varna. He still could not believe the events of this day, could not believe that Garth Rogar, his friend, was dead. For the first time, the sheltered young man tasted the rotten flavor of life under King Greensparrow and, inexperienced in anything beyond the arena, Luthien did not know what to make of it.

Might this be tied to Ethan's perpetually sour mood? he wondered. Luthien knew that Ethan held little respect for Gahris—something that the younger Bedwyr son, who saw his father as a bold and noble warrior, could not understand—but he had always attributed that to a flaw in Ethan's character. To Luthien, Gahris was above reproach, the respected eorl of Bedwydrin, whose people loved him.

Luthien did not know all the ancient rules of the arena, but he did understand that Gahris alone was overseer of the events. Garth Rogar was dead, and his blood was certainly on the hands of Gahris Bedwyr.

But why? Luthien could not understand the reason, the possible gain. He imagined all sorts of wild possibilities—perhaps word had come that the Huegoth barbarians were planning a raid upon Bedwydrin, and it had been learned that Garth Rogar had been acting as a spy. Perhaps Gahris had even uncovered a report that Garth Rogar was planning to assassinate him!

Luthien shook his head and discarded the ridiculous thoughts. He had known Garth Rogar for several years. The noble fighter was no spy and certainly no assassin.

Then why?

"Many in the town are worrying about you," came a quiet voice from behind. Luthien didn't have to turn to know that it belonged to Katerin O'Hale. "Your father among them, I would guess."

Luthien continued his silent stare across the still waters of the harbor toward the darkening town. He did not move even when Katerin came over to stand beside him and took his arm in her own, as she had done in the arena.

"Will you come back now?"

"Vengeance is not dishonor," Luthien replied with a growl. He deliberately turned his head to stare into Katerin's face, though he could barely see her in the gloom of the deepening night.

A long moment of silence passed before Katerin answered.

"No," she agreed. "But proclaiming vengeance openly, in the middle of the arena, against one who names the duke of Montfort as his friend and relative would be a foolish thing. Would you give the man an excuse to kill you, and replace your father, for a moment of outrage?"

Luthien pulled away from her, his anger now showing that he could not honestly disagree.

"Then I make the vow now," he said, "openly to you alone. On the grave of my dead mother, I'll repay he who killed Garth Rogar. Whatever the cost, whatever the consequences to me, to my father, to Bedwydrin."

Katerin could hardly believe what she had just heard, but neither could she rightly berate the man for his honorable words. She, too, burned with helpless rage, feeling like a captive for the first time in her life. She had been raised in Hale, on the open Avon Sea. Her life was spent in danger in small fishing craft braving the swells and the fierce whales, living on the very edge of disaster. But Hale was a private place and a self-sufficient one, rarely visited. Whatever the news of Bedwydrin, or of Eriador and Avon beyond that, Hale was oblivious; and so in their ignorance were the proud folk of Hale free.

But now Katerin had seen the politics of the land, and the taste in her mouth was no less bitter than the taste in Luthien's. She turned the young man toward her fully and moved closer to him, using the warmth of their bodies to ward off the chill winds of the August night.

On the morning winds of the next dawn, the black-sailed ship, proudly flying its pennants of Montfort and Avon, its prow lifting sheets of water high into the crystalline air, charged out of Dun Varna's harbor.

Katerin had returned to her barracks, but Luthien still watched from the wooded ridge. Long indeed would be his travels if he planned to keep his vow of revenge, he realized as the sails diminished. But he was a young man with a long memory, and up there on that ridge, watching the ship depart, Luthien vowed again that he would not forget Garth Rogar.

He would have liked to remain out of Dun Varna for many more days; he had no desire at all to face his father, for what explanation might the man offer? But Luthien was hungry and cold, and the nearest town, where he certainly would be recognized, was fully a day's march away.

He had barely walked through the doors of House Bedwyr when two cyclopians came upon him. "Your father would see you," one of them announced gruffly.

Luthien kept on walking, and nearly got past the two before they crossed their long halberds in his path. The young man's hand immediately went to his hip, but he wasn't wearing any weapons.

"Your father would see you," the cyclopian reiterated, and he reached up with his free hand and grabbed Luthien's upper arm hard. "He said to bring you, even if we have to drag you."

Luthien roughly pulled away and kept his unrelenting stare on the brute. He thought of punching the cyclopian in the face, or of just pushing through the two, but the image of him being dragged into his father's chambers by the ankles was not a pleasant one.

He was standing before Gahris soon after, in the study where Gahris kept the few books his family owned (some of the very few books on all the isle of Bedwydrin) along with his other heirlooms. The elder Bedwyr stood hunched at the hearth, feeding the already roaring fire as if a deep chill had settled into his bones, though it was not so cold this day. Mounted on the wall above him was his most-prized piece, the family sword, its perfect edge gleaming and its golden hilt lined with jewels and sculpted to resemble a dragon rampant with upraised wings serving as the formidable crosspiece. It had been cunningly forged by the dwarves of the Iron Cross in ages past, its blade of beaten metal wrapped tight about itself a thousand times so that the blade only sharpened with use. *Blind-Striker*, it was called, both for its balanced cut and the fact that it had taken the eye of many cyclopians in the fierce war six hundred years before.

"Where have you been?" Gahris asked calmly, quietly. He wiped his sooty hands and stood up straight, though he did not yet turn to face his son.

"I needed to be away," Luthien replied, trying to match his father's calm.

"To let your anger settle?"

Luthien sighed but did not bother to answer.

Gahris turned toward him. "That was wise, my son," he said. "Anger brews rash actions—oft with the most dire of consequences."

He seemed so calm and so logical, which bothered Luthien deeply. His friend was dead! "How could you?" he blurted, unconsciously taking a long stride forward, hands bunched into fists. "To kill . . . what were you . . ." His words fell away in a jumble, his emotions too heated to be expressed.

Through it all, the white-haired Gahris cooed softly like a dove and waved his hand in the empty air. "What would you have me do?" he asked, as though that should explain everything.

Luthien opened his hands helplessly. "Garth Rogar did not deserve his fate!" Luthien cried. "A curse on Viscount Aubrey and on his wicked companions!"

"Calm, my son," Gahris was saying, over and over. "Ours is a world that is not always fair and just, but—"

"There is no excuse," Luthien replied through gritted teeth.

"Not even war?" Gahris asked bluntly.

Luthien's breath came in short, angry gasps.

"Think not of bloodied fields," Gahris offered, "nor of spear tips shining with the blood of fallen enemies, nor turf torn under the charge of horses. Those are horrors that have not yet been reflected in your clear eyes, and may they never be! They steal the sparkle, you see," Gahris explained, and he pointed to his own cinnamon orbs. Indeed, those eyes did seem without luster this August morning.

"And were the eyes of Bruce MacDonald so tainted?" Luthien asked somewhat sarcastically, referring to Eriador's greatest hero.

"Filled with valor are the tales of war," Gahris replied somberly, "but only when the horrors of war have faded from memory. Who can say what scars Bruce MacDonald wore in his heavy soul? Who alive has looked into the eyes of that man?"

Luthien thought the words absurd; Bruce MacDonald had been dead for three centuries. But then he realized that to be his father's very point. The elder Bedwyr went on in all seriousness.

"I have heard the horses charge, have seen my own sword—" he glanced back at the fabulous weapon on the wall "—wet with blood. I have heard the stories—other's stories—of those heroic battles in which I partook, and I can tell you, in all honesty and with arrogance aside, that they were more horror than valor, more regret than victory. Am I to bring such misery to Bedwydrin?"

Luthien's sigh this time was more of resignation than defiance.

"Breathe out your pride with that sigh," Galiris advised. "It is the most deadly and most dangerous of emotions. Mourn your friend, but accept that which must be. Do not follow Ethan—" He broke off suddenly, apparently rethinking that last thought, but his mention of

Luthien's older brother, a hero to the youngest Bedwyr, piqued Luthien's attention.

"What of Ethan?" he demanded. "What part does he play in all of this? What has he done in my absence?"

Again Gahris was cooing softly and patting the air, trying to calm his son. "Ethan is fine," he assured Luthien. "I speak only of his temperament, his foolish pride, and my own hopes that you will temper your anger with good sense. You did well in walking out of House Bedwyr, and for that you have my respect. We are given a long rein from the duke of Montfort, and longer still from the throne in Carlisle, and it would be good to keep it that way."

"What did Ethan do?" Luthien pressed, not convinced.

"He did nothing, other than protest—loudly!" Gahris snapped back.

"And that disappoints you?"

Gahris snorted and spun back to face the fire. "He is my eldest son," he replied, "in line to be the eorl of Bedwydrin. But what might that mean for the folk?"

It seemed to Luthien that Gahris was no longer talking to him; he was, rather, talking to himself, as if trying to justify something.

"Trouble, I say," the old man went on, and he seemed very old indeed to Luthien at that moment. "Trouble for Ethan, for House Bedwyr, for all the island." He spun back around suddenly, one finger pointing Luthien's way. "Trouble for you!" he cried, and Luthien, surprised, took a step backward. "Never will stubborn Ethan come to learn his place," Gahris went on, muttering again and turning back to the fire. "Once eorl, he would surely facilitate his own death and bring ruin upon House Bedwyr and bring watchful eyes upon all of Bedwydrin. Oh, what a fool is a proud man! Never! Never! Never!"

Gahris had worked himself into quite a state, pumping his fist into the air as he spoke, and Luthien's first instincts were to go to him and try to calm him. Something held the young man back, though, and instead he quietly left the room. He loved his father, had respected him all of his life, but now the man's words rang hollowly in Luthien's ears—ears that still heard the fateful crossbow click and the pitiful wheeze of Garth Rogar's last breath.

CHAPTER 4

WET WITH THE BLOOD
OF A FALLEN ENEMY

WHAT MIGHT HAVE BEEN had the parents of a king not met? What might have been had a hero been cut down in his or her youth by an arrow that whizzed harmlessly past, cracking the air barely an inch away? Often does the simplest chance affect the history of nations, and so it was that August night, when Luthien walked out of House Bedwyr to the stables, where he found Ethan readying a horse, saddlebags stuffed with provisions.

Luthien moved near his brother, eyeing him curiously, letting his expression ask the obvious question.

"I have been sent away," Ethan answered.

Luthien seemed not to understand.

"I am to go to the south," Ethan went on, spitting out every word with disgust, "to travel with the king's soldiers who would go into Gascony and fight beside the Gascons in their war with the Kingdom of Duree."

"A noble cause," replied Luthien, too overwhelmed to consider his words.

"A mercenary cause," Ethan snarled back. "A mercenary cause for an unlawful king."

"Then why go?"

Ethan stopped tightening the saddlebags and turned an incredulous look upon his naive little brother. Luthien just shrugged, still not catching on.

"Because the eorl of Bedwydrin has ordered me to go." Ethan spelled it out plainly and went back to his work.

It made no sense to Luthien, and so he did not reply, did not even blink.

"It will bring honor to our family and to all Bedwydrin, so said Gahris," Ethan went on.

Luthien studied his brother carefully, at first jealous that Gahris had chosen Ethan for the campaign over him. "Would not *Blind-Striker* serve you better if you go for the honor of House Bedwyr?" he asked, noticing the unremarkable weapon sheathed on Ethan's belt.

Again came that disbelieving, condescending look. "Can you be so incredibly blind to the world?" Ethan asked, and he got his answer when Luthien winced.

"Gahris sends me," the elder son went on, "following the whispered suggestions of Aubrey. Gahris sends me to die."

The casual way Ethan spoke struck Luthien more than the words. He grabbed Ethan roughly by the shoulder and spun him away from his horse, forcing his brother to face him squarely.

"I am not his choice for the succession," Ethan spat out, and Luthien, remembering his earlier conversation with his father, could not disagree. "But the rules are clear. I am the eldest son, thus I am next in line as eorl of Bedwydrin."

"I do not challenge your right," Luthien replied, still missing the point.

"But Gahris does," Ethan explained. "And my reputation of disloyalty has gone beyond Bedwydrin, it would seem."

"So Gahris will send you out with the army to win glory and restore your reputation," Luthien reasoned, though he suspected his line of thought was still traveling the wrong direction.

"So Gahris has sent me out to die," Ethan reiterated firmly. "I am a problem to him—even Aubrey has heard of me and understands the difficulties of my potential ascension. Perhaps it is my arrogance, but I do not think Morkney's cousin's only purpose in coming to Bedwydrin was sport."

"You think Aubrey braved the breakers of the Dorsal, came all the way to Bedwydrin, merely to have you sent away?"

"Beyond that, my young brother," Ethan said, and for the first time, a ring of sympathy was evident in his harsh tones. "My young brother, who has never known freedom, who has lived all his life under the rule of Carlisle and Montfort."

Luthien crinkled his brow, now thoroughly confused.

"Aubrey toured the northern islands," Ethan explained. "Caryth, Marvis, Bedwydrin, even the Diamondgate on his return trip, to ensure that all was as it should be in the northland, to help secure Morkney's tethers. Politicians do not take 'holidays.' Ever they work, living to work, to heighten their power. That is their way and their lifeblood. Aubrey came to Bedwydrin in part to deal with me, and also because the duke has no eyes out here. That has been remedied." His work on the mount done, Ethan swung up into the saddle.

"You will have a new mother, Luthien," he went on. "Treat her with respect and fear." He started to walk the horse away, but Luthien, flustered and outraged, grabbed the bridle and held the beast in check.

"One who is known to you," Ethan went on. "One whose pennant you once carried into battle."

Luthien's eyes widened in shock. Avonese? This could not be true! "Never!" he protested.

"On Sunday's morn," Ethan assured him. "The duke has forced Gahris's hand," he explained. "Lady Avonese remains, the perfect spy, to wed Gahris. It is bait, you see, for the fall of the House of Bedwyr. Gahris will bend to the events, or Morkney will have the excuse he desires and will bid Greensparrow to fill the harbor with black sails."

"How can you leave?" Luthien cried out helplessly as all of his sheltered world appeared to be falling down around him.

"How can I stay?" Ethan corrected calmly. "Gahris has given his command." Ethan paused and stared hard at his brother, his intensity offering a calming effect to the excited young man.

"You know little beyond Bedwydrin," Ethan said sincerely. "You have not seen the eyes of the poor children starving in Montfort's streets. You have not seen the farmers, broken in spirit and wealth by demanded taxes. You have not seen the helpless rage of a man whose daughter was taken from him to 'serve' in the house of a noble, or heard the cries of a mother whose child has died in her arms for lack of food."

Luthien's grip on Ethan's saddle loosened.

"I do not accept the world as it is," Ethan went on. "I only know how it should be. And our father, lackey to an unlawful king, has not the strength nor the courage to stand up and agree with me."

Ethan recognized that his blunt accounting was finally beginning to sink into Luthien's naive skull. If he had hit Luthien with a dwarvish maul, he could not have stunned the man any more. Beyond all their differences, Ethan loved and pitied his brother, who had never known life before Greensparrow, the king who had subtly stolen away true freedom.

"Farewell, my brother," Ethan said solemnly. "You are all of my family that I will miss. Keep your eyes to the window and your ears to the door, and above all, beware the Lady Avonese!" A kick of his heels sent his horse leaping away, leaving the perplexed Luthien alone in the yard with his unsettling thoughts.

Luthien did not sleep that night and wandered the grounds alone all the next day, not even harking to a call from Katerin, who saw him from across a field. Again the next night, he did not sleep, thinking of Ethan, of Garth Rogar, of this new view of Gahris.

Most of all, Luthien thought of confronting his father, of calling

Gahris out on the accusations Ethan had boldly made. What might the other side of that tale be? he wondered.

But it was a false hope. Ethan's few words had opened Luthien's young eyes, and he did not believe that he could ever close them again.

And so, in the morning of the next day, he went to see Gahris, not to seek any explanation but to put in his own thoughts, to express his anger over the tragedy in the arena and the fact that this Avonese creature was apparently intended to become his mother.

He smiled when he considered how much like Ethan he would sound and wondered if his father would send him away to fight in a distant war, as well.

He entered the study without even knocking, only to find the room empty. Gahris had already left on his morning ride. Luthien started to leave, thinking to go down to the stables and take a horse of his own and ride off in pursuit of the man. He changed his mind almost immediately, though, realizing that Avonese might be riding beside his father, and the last thing in all the world that Luthien wanted was to see that woman.

He made himself comfortable in the study instead, perusing the books on the shelves, even starting a fire in the hearth. He was sitting back in the comfortable chair, feet propped on the desk and book in hand, when the door burst open and a burly guardsman rushed in.

"What are you about?" the cyclopian demanded, waving a trident dangerously. He remained near to the door, though, across the room from Luthien.

"About?" Luthien echoed incredulously, and then his face screwed up even more, for he did not recognize this guard—though he knew all of Gahris's contingent.

"About!" the brute roared back. "What business have you in the private quarters of the eorl and eorless of Bedwydrin?"

"Eorless?" Luthien muttered under his breath, and he nearly choked on the word.

"I asked you a question!" the cyclopian growled, waving its trident again.

"Who in the lava pits of the Five Sentinels are you to ask anything of me?" the young Bedwyr demanded.

"Personal guard of the eorless of Bedwydrin," the one-eyed soldier replied without hesitation.

"I am the son of the eorl," Luthien proclaimed.

"I know who you are, arena fighter," the cyclopian replied, snapping the trident aside. It was only then, as the brute jerked about and revealed a crossbow strapped to its wide back, that Luthien realized the creature's identity. He leaped up from his seat, dropping the book to the desk.

"You were not announced," the cyclopian continued undaunted. "So here you do not belong! Now be gone, before I teach you some of the proper etiquette of nobility!"

The cyclopian clutched the long trident close to its chest and slowly turned toward the door, keeping its bloodshot eye on Luthien for as long as possible.

Luthien stood transfixed, held in place by the enormity of the situation that had been unexpectedly dropped on his shoulders. He had vowed revenge, and now his sworn enemy, whom he had thought long gone on the black-sailed ship, stood before him. But what of the consequences? he had to wonder—and what purpose might be served to Aubrey by leaving this particular cyclopian behind? To leave Avonese behind was one thing—Luthien would not strike down a woman who was no warrior—but to allow this murderous brute to remain on Bedwydrin was beyond Luthien's comprehension. Surely the viscount must have known what would happen. . . .

Ethan's words about bait for the fall of House Bedwyr rang in Luthien's mind, and he knew that his decision now would follow him for the rest of his life.

"You will follow me," the cyclopian remarked, not looking back and giving Luthien a perfect view of the crossbow he had used to murder Garth Rogar.

"Tell me," Luthien began calmly, "did you enjoy killing a human while he lay helpless upon the ground?"

The cyclopian whirled about and faced the young man squarely, an evil smile widening upon its face, showing Luthien an array of pointy and yellow-stained teeth. "I always enjoy killing men," the cyclopian said. "Are you to leave, or learn that for yourself?"

His action purely reflexive, Luthien reached down and grabbed a stone that his father kept on the desk for holding parchments smooth and, in a swift motion, hurled it across the room, where it smacked off the dodging cyclopian's thigh. The creature groaned, then growled and leveled its trident Luthien's way.

"That was not among your brightest actions," Luthien said quietly to himself, taking the moment to realize that he wasn't even wearing a weapon. In stalked the one-eyed brute. Luthien scooped up a wooden chair to use as a shield, but the first powerful thrust of the trident shattered it to kindling and left Luthien scrambling.

He rolled from behind the desk to the hearth and grabbed up a long metal hook used for turning logs. He spun back and put his feet under him just in time to meet the second thrust. Fortunately, the sweeping hook caught the tip of the trident enough to deflect the weapon somewhat to the side, and agile Luthien twisted the other way. Still, he got a painful scratch on the side of his abdomen, a line of blood staining his torn white shirt.

The cyclopian licked its pointy teeth and smiled wide.

"I have no weapon!" Luthien protested.

"That makes it all the more fun," the cyclopian replied, and it started a straight thrust, then reversed its weapon and swung the butt end about in a low arc. Seeing the feint in time, Luthien managed to stop his dodging defense and leap straight up, over the swing. He landed and took one step forward, and poked his fingers straight ahead into the cyclopian's eye.

The powerful backswing of the trident stung the young man again, knocking him aside before he could do any real damage to the large, bloodshot orb, but he had dazed the cyclopian enough to break off combat.

And Luthien knew right where to run.

Back to the hearth he leaped, this time high on the balls of his feet. "You should have finished me while you could!" he cried, and grabbed the dragon-sculpted hilt of the fabulous Bedwyr sword. He laughed and yanked, and pulled the sword free—almost.

Now the cyclopian was laughing—and leveling that wicked trident once more.

Luthien had torn out the hook holding the hilt, but the second hook, near the sword's point, held stubbornly to the wall. The sword was angled far out, but its razor-edge tip was merely digging a line in the stone of the wall. Luthien heaved again to no avail; he rolled about to put all his weight behind the pull, and from that angle, he clearly saw the cyclopian's charge.

He shouted and heaved with all his might, and the sword snapped free of the hook and whipped around and down, smashing hard against the trident's tip just an instant before it would have plunged deeply into his chest. Both combatants were now off balance, their weapons out far too wide for any counter attacks, so Luthien planted one foot against the stonework of the hearth and rushed out at full speed, barreling into his opponent and sending them both tumbling to the floor.

Luthien was up, quick as a cat. He spun and launched a downward cut, but to his amazement, the trident came up and blocked him, the sword blade falling neatly into the groove between two of the weapon's three tips. With a growl, the cyclopian threw him to the side, fully defeating Luthien's attack.

"I am no child in an arena," the one-eye boasted. "I was a commander in the Praetorian Guard!" On the cyclopian came with a series of devilish thrusts and feints, half twists designed to make Luthien duck a second butt-end sweep, followed by reversed movements that again sent the trident straight out in front. The cyclopian worked the long weapon brilliantly, as though it was a small blade, keeping Luthien fully on the defensive.

But neither was the son of Bedwyr some "child in an arena." Luthien's parries were perfect; he reversed his intended dodges as quickly as the cyclopian reversed the attack. Not once did the trident so much as nick him.

Luthien knew that he was in a tough fight, though, and his respect for the cyclopian grew with each close pass. They worked around the room, Luthien, with the shorter weapon, inevitably backing and circling, and the cyclopian quick to press. Then Luthien scrambled behind a divan, an effective shield from the waist down.

He smiled as he easily knocked aside a high thrust, then chopped his blade down atop a lower cut, temporarily pinning the trident to the top of the divan. He could see the frustration building in the one-eye's expression, and he skittered back cautiously when the cyclopian came in a sudden charge, appearing as though it might bull its way right through the small couch.

The cyclopian wisely stopped before it crashed through, for it realized that it would not quickly catch up to the agile Luthien, and knowing that if the couch tangled its feet at all, the cunning young fighter and his sword would surely grab the advantage. The cyclopian then tried to push the piece of furniture aside, but Luthien, understanding that the divan offered him an advantage with his shorter weapon, rushed back in and sliced with the sword, almost taking off the cyclopian's hand and digging a deep slash into the padding of the couch in the process.

"Gahris will not be pleased," Luthien remarked, trying to sound supremely confident.

"Not when he buries his son!" the cyclopian roared, and on the brute came again, a powerful thrust leading the way. The soldier expected Luthien to chop down again, to try and pin the trident to the top of the divan, and if that had happened, the cyclopian intended to barrel through, pushing both Luthien and the couch closer to the wall.

But Luthien dropped straight to a crouch instead, and his parry came in exactly the opposite direction, sword straight across in front of him and going up, not down. Up, too, went the trident, and opportunistic Luthien went up behind the weapons, up and over the divan in a headlong roll. The cyclopian instinctively fell back, trying to realign his weapon, but Luthien came up under his reach, sword leading the way.

Blind-Striker's tip dug into the cyclopian's belly and ran its way up through the creature's diaphragm, cutting at the lungs and heart. The one-eye had the trident up above its head by that time, and angled down at Luthien, and for a horrifying second, Luthien thought the wicked prongs would dive down into him.

Then he saw the light go out of the cyclopian's eye, saw the strength drain from the dying brute's thick muscles. The trident fell to the floor, its dead owner sliding back off of Luthien's sword and falling over it.

Luthien tentatively regained his footing, staring down at the perfectly still cyclopian. His first kill. Luthien did not enjoy the sensation, not at all. He looked at the dead cyclopian and reminded himself many times that this had been the murderer of Garth Rogar, that this brute would have killed him if he had not proven the better warrior. And it was a cyclopian. Sheltered Luthien could not fully appreciate the significance of that fact, but he did understand that cyclopians were not human, in either appearance or temperament. The one-eyes were savage creatures, evil creatures, devoid of love and mercy. This knowledge alone saved the young man from his own conscience at that moment, and allowed Luthien to take heart. A deep breath helped steady the young warrior.

Luthien looked at the bloody sword. Its balance was perfect and its deadly cut incredible. Luthien could not believe how easily *Blind-Striker* had slid through the thick leather coat of the cyclopian and through the creature's body, as well. He had, with a simple cut, chopped more than half a foot into the well-constructed divan, taking out a few boards, he knew, on the way. Holding the sword now, his vow fulfilled, his friend avenged, he felt the blood of his proud ancestors pumping wildly through his veins.

Then Luthien calmed and realized that he had set many events into motion—events that would likely bury him if he remained in Dun Varna. But Luthien wept no tears of pity for his predicament. He had made his choice willingly when he had thrown the stone at the brute and forced the confrontation. There could be no excuses, not in Gahris's cowed eyes, he knew—if all that Ethan had said was true. Luthien now replayed his last meeting with his father, listened to Gahris's words in the new light of Ethan's revelations. His brother had not lied to him.

Luthien could hardly believe how much his life had so abruptly changed, and how it would continue to change as he, now obviously a criminal, made his way far from Dun Varna, far from Bedwydrin. He thought that he must catch up to Ethan on the road, for surely his brother would sympathize with his actions and help him along his way. Luthien cringed. Ethan had probably already reached the ferry to Eriador's mainland. Where would his brother go from there? To Montfort, perhaps? Or all the way around the Iron Cross to Carlisle?

Luthien looked out the room's one small window and could see that the sun was fast climbing in the east. His father would soon return; Luthien would have to find his answers along the road.

He thought of taking the sword—he had never felt such perfect craftsmanship. But *Blind-Striker* was not his, he knew, especially not now. Though he thought his actions justified and honorable, demanded by the death of his friend, in Luthien's young eyes, he had just brought shame upon House Bedwyr. He would not complicate that matter by stooping to common thievery.

He did not wipe the blood from the blade as he carefully replaced it above the hearth. He thought it fitting that Gahris should see what weapon had exacted revenge for the unfair death of Garth Rogar.

CHAPTER 5

WITHOUT LOOKING BACK

*L*UTHIEN LEFT DUN VARNA on the northern road soon after upon his favorite mount, Riverdancer. The steed was a Morgan Highlander, a short-legged, thickly muscled white stallion that could plow through the soft turf of Eriador's perpetually wet ground as well as any beast alive. The Highlander horses had been bred with long, shaggy coats to ward off the chill winds and drizzle. On many Highlanders, this hair was perpetually prickly and snarled, but Riverdancer's coat was smooth as fine silk and glistened with every movement, like the sparkles of a dancing river on a sunny spring day.

Riverdancer carried a heavy load this day, laden with the supplies Luthien would need for the road and, displayed more openly, with fishing gear, including heavy pole-nets. It was not an unusual thing for the young Bedwyr to go off in this fashion, especially considering there had been little training in the arena since the Garth Rogar incident. Certainly few in Dun Varna would expect Luthien to go right back to his fighting.

Few took notice of him as he walked his way through the dirt and cobblestone avenues. He did slow and speak with one man, a captain of a fishing boat, just to ask him what was running north of the bay and whether the sea was calm enough for the pole-nets or if he should try a long line. It was all very cordial, very normal. Just the way Luthien wanted it to be.

When he had gone beyond the bluffs, though, out of sight of the stone-and-thatch houses, he broke Riverdancer into a run. Five miles out of town, he veered down toward the shore to one of his favored fishing spots. There he left his gear, net and pole, and one of his wet boots lying on the stones right near the water. Better to give them as many riddles as possible, he thought, though he cringed when he considered his father's pain if Gahris truly thought he had been swept out into the fierce Dorsal.

It couldn't be helped, Luthien decided. Back on Riverdancer, he picked his way carefully among the stones, trying to leave as little visible trail as possible—he sighed deeply when the horse lifted its tail and dropped some obvious signs of passage.

Away from the shore, Luthien turned to the west, riding toward Hale, and then swung back to the south. By early afternoon, he was passing Dun Varna again, several miles inland and far out of sight. He wondered what commotion his actions had brought. What had Gahris and especially Avonese thought when they had gone into the study and found the dead cyclopian? Had Gahris noticed the bloodied sword on the wall?

Certainly by this time somebody had gone north in search of Luthien. Perhaps they had even found his gear and boot, though he doubted that word had gotten back to his father.

Again, the young Bedwyr decided that it couldn't be helped. He had followed the course his heart demanded. In truth, Luthien had only defended himself against the armed cyclopian. He could have stayed in House Bedwyr and been exonerated: even after all that Ethan had told him, Luthien did not believe that his father would turn against him. And so it was not actually fear of the law that sent Luthien away. He only realized that now, passing his home for what might be the very last time. Ethan had brought doubts to him, deep-rooted doubts that made Luthien question the worth of his very existence. What was the truth of the kingdom and the king? And was he truly free, as he had always believed?

Only the road could give him his answers.

The Diamondgate ferry was normally a three-day ride from Dun Varna, but Luthien thought he could make it in two if he pushed Riverdancer hard. The horse responded eagerly, happy for the run, as they charged down the island's central lowlands, and Luthien was far from Dun Varna when he broke for camp. It rained hard that first night. Luthien huddled under his blanket near a fire that was more hiss and spit than flame. He hardly felt the chill and the wetness, though, too consumed by the questions that rolled over and over in his thoughts. He remembered the salty smell of sweet Katerin and the look in her green eyes when they had made love. He should have told her, perhaps.

He did fall asleep sometime not long before the dawn, but he was up early anyway, greeted by a glistening sunny day.

It was a marvelous day, and Luthien felt delight in every bit of it as he mounted Riverdancer and started off once more. Not a cloud showed itself in the blue sky—a rare occurrence, indeed, on Bedwydrin!—and a sense of euphoria came over Luthien, a sense of being more alive than he had ever been. It was more than the sun, he knew, and the birds and animals skittering about on one of the last truly wondrous days before the gloomy fall and chill winter. Luthien had rarely been out of Dun Varna all his life, and then always with the knowledge that he would not be gone for long.

Now the wide road lay before him leading eventually to the mainland, to Avon, even to Gascony and all the way to Duree if he could catch up with his brother. The world seemed so much bigger and scarier suddenly, and excitement welled up in the young man, pushing away his grief for Garth Rogar and his fears for his father. He wished that Katerin was there beside him, riding hard for freedom and excitement.

He was more than two-thirds of the way to the ferry by midday, Riverdancer running easily, as though he would never tire. The road veered back toward the southeast, passing through a small wooded region and across the field just out the wood's southern end. There Luthien came upon a narrow log bridge crossing a strong-running river, with another small forest on the other side.

At the same time, a merchant wagon came out of the trees and upon the bridge from the other end. Its cyclopian driver certainly saw Luthien and could have stopped short of the bridge, allowing the horseman to scramble across and out of the way, but with typical cyclopian bravado and discourtesy, the brute moved the wagon onto the logs.

"Turn about!" the one-eye growled, as its team came face-to-face with Riverdancer.

"You could have stopped," Luthien protested. "I was onto the bridge

before you and could have gotten off the bridge more quickly than you!"
He noted that the cyclopian was not too well-armed and wearing no
special insignia. This brute was a private guard, not Praetorian, and any
passengers in the coach were surely merchants, not noblemen. Still,
Luthien had every intention of turning about—it was easier to turn a
single horse, after all, than a team and wagon.

A fat-jowled face, blotchy and pimpled, popped out of the coach's
window. "Run the fool down if he does not move!" the merchant ordered brusquely, and he disappeared back into the privacy of his coach.

Luthien almost proclaimed himself to be the son of the eorl of Bedwydrin, almost drew weapon and ordered the cyclopian to back the
wagon all the way to the ferry. Instead he wisely swallowed his pride, reminding himself that it would not be the smartest move to identify himself at this time. He was a simple fisherman or farmer, nothing more.

"Well, do you move, or do I put you into the water?" the cyclopian
asked, and it gave a short snap of the reins just to jostle its two-horse
team and move them a step closer to Riverdancer. All three horses
snorted uncomfortably.

Several possible scenarios rushed through Luthien's thoughts, most of
them ending rather unpleasantly for the cyclopian and its ugly master.
Pragmatism held, however, and Luthien, never taking his stare off the
one-eyed driver, urged Riverdancer into a slow backward walk, off the
bridge, and moved aside.

The wagon rambled past, stopping long enough for the fat merchant
to stick his head out and declare, "If I had more time, I would stop and
teach you some manners, you dirty little boy!" He gave a wave of his soft,
plump hand and the cyclopian driver cracked a whip, sending the team
into a charge.

It took many deep breaths and a count of fifty for Luthien to accept
that insult. He shook his head, then, and laughed aloud, reclaiming a
welcome sense of euphoria. What did it count for, after all? He knew
who he was, and why he had allowed himself to be faced down, and that
was all that truly mattered.

Riverdancer trotted across the bridge and along the road, which
looped back to the north to avoid a steep hillock, and Luthien quickly
put the incident out of his mind. Until a few minutes later, that is, when
he looked back across the river from higher ground down at the merchant's coach moving parallel to him and only a couple of hundred feet
away. The wagon had stopped again, and this time the cyclopian driver
faced the most curious-looking individual Luthien Bedwyr had ever
seen.

He was obviously a halfling, a somewhat rare sight this far north in Eriador, riding a yellow mount that looked more like a donkey than a pony, with an almost hairless tail sticking straight out behind the beast. The halfling's dress was more remarkable than his mount, though, for though his clothes appeared a bit threadbare, he seemed to Luthien the pinnacle of fashion. A purple velvet cape, which flowed back from his shoulders out from under his long and curly brown locks, was opened in front to reveal a blue sleeveless doublet, showing the puffy white sleeves of his silken undertunic, tied tightly at the wrists. A brocade baldric laced in gold and tasseled all the way crossed his chest, right to left, ending in more tassels, bells, and a loop on which to hang his rapier, which was now being held in readiness in one of his green-gauntleted hands.

His breeches, like his cape, were purple velvet, and were met halfway up the halfling's shin by green hose, topped with silk and tied by ribbons at the back of his calf. A huge hat completed the picture, its wide brim curled up on one side and a large orange feather poking out behind. Luthien couldn't make out all of his features, but he saw that the halfling wore a neatly trimmed mustache and goatee.

He had never heard of a halfling with face hair and had never imagined one dressed in that manner, or sitting on a donkey, or pony, or whatever that thing was, and robbing a merchant wagon at rapier point. He pulled Riverdancer down the bank, slipping in behind the cover of some low brush, and watched the show.

"Out of the way, I tell you, or I'll trample you down!" growled the burly cyclopian driver.

The halfling laughed at him, bringing a smile to Luthien's lips as well. "Do you not know who I am?" the little one asked incredulously, and his thick brogue told Luthien that he was not from Bedwydrin, or from anywhere in Eriador. From the halfling's lips, "you" sounded more like "yee-oo" and "not" became a two-syllable word: "nau-te."

"I am Oliver deBurrows," the halfing proclaimed, "highwayman. You are caught fairly and defeated without a fight. I will your lives give to you, but your co-ins and jew-wels I claim as my own!"

A Gascon, Luthien decided, for he had heard many jokes about the people of Gascony in which the teller imitated a similar accent.

"What is it?" demanded the impatient merchant, popping his fat-jowled head out of the coach. "What is it?" he asked in a different tone when he looked upon Oliver deBurrows, highwayman.

"An inconvenience, my lord," the cyclopian answered, staring dangerously at Oliver. "Nothing more."

"See to it, then!" cried the merchant.

The cyclopian continued to stare over its shoulder as the merchant pulled his head into the coach. When the brute did turn back, it came about suddenly and viciously, producing from nowhere, it seemed, a huge sword and cutting it in a wicked chop at the halfling's head. Luthien sucked in his breath, thinking this extraordinary Oliver deBurrows about to die, but quicker than he believed possible, the halfling's left hand came out, holding a large-bladed dagger with a protective basket hilt—a main gauche, the weapon was called.

Oliver snapped the main gauche in a circular movement, catching the sword firmly in its hilt. He continued the fast rotation, twisting the sword, and then with a sudden jerk, sent the weapon flying from the cyclopian's hand to land sticking point-first into the turf a dozen feet away. Oliver's rapier darted forward, its tip catching the top of the cyclopian's leather tunic. The blade bent dangerously, just an inch below the brute's exposed neck.

"Rodent," growled the impudent cyclopian.

The highwayman laughed again. "My papa halfling, he always say, that a halfling's pride is inversely proportional to his height," Oliver replied.

"And I assure you," the halfling continued after a dramatic pause, "I am very short!"

For once, the cyclopian driver seemed to have no reply. It probably didn't even understand what the halfling had just said, Luthien realized, squatting in the brush, trying hard not to burst out in laughter.

"How far do you think my so fine blade will bend?" Oliver asked with a short chuckle. "Now, I have won the day and your precious co-ins and jew-wels."

To Oliver's surprise, though, the single cyclopian guard became six, as soldiers burst out of the coach door and rolled from every conceivable nook in the large wagon, two even coming out from underneath. The highwayman considered the new odds, eased the pressure on his bending rapier, and gave a new finish to his previous thought.

"I could be wrong."

CHAPTER 6

OLIVER DEBURROWS

THE FASHIONABLE HIGHWAYMAN was about eye level with the cyclopian soldiers as he looked at them from atop his yellow mount. He parried a spear thrust from one direction, yanked the bridle to bring his mount back on two legs and swing the beast about just in time to defeat a slashing sword from behind. He was a flurry of activity, but the cyclopian driver, smiling wickedly, pulled out another weapon: a loaded crossbow.

That would have been the end of the legendary (at least in his own mind) Oliver deBurrows, but a short distance away, in the thicket across the river, young Luthien Bedwyr had found his courage and his heart. Luthien had never been fond of the ever-present greedy merchants, placing them in a category just above cyclopians. The halfling was a thief—that could not be denied—but to Luthien so was the merchant. He didn't acknowledge the emotions guiding his actions in that critical moment; he only did as his heart dictated.

He was no less surprised than the cyclopian driver when an arrow, Luthien's arrow, took the brute in the chest and pushed it back down in its seat, the crossbow slipping from its weakening grasp.

If Oliver even saw the shot, he didn't show it. "Yes, do come on, you with one eye who looks so much like the back end of a cat!" he bellowed at one cyclopian, spinning his rapier in such a dazzling (though totally ineffective) display that the cyclopian took two steps back from the yellow mount and scratched its sloped forehead.

Luthien walked Riverdancer out of the thicket and down the steep bank, the strong horse gaining enough momentum to leap out, barely touching the water, crossing with one running stride. Across the field charged Luthien, bow in hand, shooting as he went.

The cyclopians roared in protest. One gabbed a long halberd from the side of the coach and darted out to meet Luthien, then changed its mind amidst the stream of soaring arrows and slipped in behind the coach's horses instead. Oliver, entangled in fending attacks from three different positions, didn't even know what his enemies were yelling about. The halfling did note, though, that the cyclopian now behind his turning mount became distracted.

"Pardon," he said to the brute in front of him, and he hurled his main gauche so that the opponent had to fall back a step, getting tan-

gled but not hurt as it pushed away the halfheartedly tossed weapon. In
the same movement, Oliver swooped off his wide hat and placed it over
his mount's rump, and the pony responded immediately by rearing up
and kicking out, straight into the ribs of the distracted cyclopian behind. Oliver, meanwhile, now saw Luthien, riding and shooting. The
composed halfling simply shrugged and turned back to the more pressing situation.

It was still two against one, though, and the halfling found himself
immediately hard-pressed, even more so because now he held only one
weapon.

Another crossbowman, lying flat on top of the coach, changed its target from Oliver to the newest foe. The cyclopian leveled the weapon, but
could not get a clear shot as Luthien bent low to the side of his running
horse, using Riverdancer as a shield. The cyclopian fired and missed
badly, and Luthien came up high enough to return the shot, his arrow
knocking into the wood just below the prone cyclopian's face. Even on
the running mount, Luthien managed to reload before the cyclopian,
and his second shot, fired no more than twenty feet from the coach,
nailed the brute in the face.

Then a halberd was thrust in front of Luthien's face as the next soldier darted out from behind the horse team. The only defense offered to
Luthien was to fall back and to the side, right off of Riverdancer. He
landed hard, and only by reminding himself through every inch of the
brutal tumble that if he did not get right back up he would soon be
skewered did he manage to keep his wits about him. He also wisely held
onto the bow, and he whipped it across in front as he finally managed to
put his feet under him just in time to bat aside the next thrusting attack.

Oliver was able to line up his pony so that both remaining cyclopians
were facing him. His rapier snapped back and forth over the pony's low-
hung head, intercepting cut after cut. The halfling tried to appear non-
chalant, even bored, but in truth he was more than a little concerned.
These cyclopians were pretty good and their weapons finely made. Still,
Oliver had not survived two decades as a highwayman without a few
tricks up his puffy white sleeve.

"Behind you!" he cried suddenly, and one of the cyclopians almost fell
for the obvious ruse, almost turned its head to look over its shoulder—
not an easy feat when you have only one eye located in the middle of
your face!

The other cyclopian kept up its attack without a blink, and the foolish one came back doubly hard as soon as it realized how stupid it looked.

But not only did Oliver guess that the brutes wouldn't fall for the ruse, he hoped they wouldn't. "Behind you!" he cried again, just to egg them on a bit more, just to make them think that he thought they were stupid. Predictably, both cyclopians growled and pressed harder.

Oliver kicked his heels and his yellow pony leaped forward, right between the brutes. So intent were they on their offensive posture, the cyclopians didn't even mark Oliver's swift maneuver as the halfling let go the bridle and rolled off the back end of the pony, turning a complete somersault and landing easily on his feet. The cyclopians swung about as the horse cut between them, and Oliver promptly jabbed his rapier blade deep into the rump of one.

The cyclopian howled and whipped about, and a snap of Oliver's rapier sent the outraged brute's sword falling free.

"Foolish one-eyed sniffer of barnyard animals!" the halfling snorted, holding his hands out wide in disbelief. "I, polite Oliver deBurrows, even told you that it would come from behind!" The halfling then assumed his best fencing posture, free hand on hip. He yelled and leaped forward as if to strike, and the wounded cyclopian turned and fled, howling and fiercely rubbing its stuck butt.

The other cyclopian came on, though, viciously.

"You should be so wise as your friend," Oliver taunted, parrying one swing, ducking a second, and hopping over a third. "You are no match for Oliver deBurrows!"

In response, the cyclopian came on with such a vicious flurry that Oliver was put back on his heels, and though he could have poked his rapier home a dozen times, any offensive strike would surely have allowed the cyclopian a solid hit at him, as well. The creature was strong and its sword nearly as heavy as the halfling, and Oliver wanted no part of that trade.

"I could be wrong," the halfling admitted again, working furiously to keep the brute off of him. He gave a short and sharp whistle then, but the cyclopian took no note of it.

An instant later, Oliver's yellow pony slammed into the brute's back, throwing it facedown on the turf, and the pony continued forward, clambering atop the groaning cyclopian. The curious-looking and curiously trained pony then began hopping up and down, crunching bones with every short jump.

"Have you met my horse?" Oliver asked politely.

The cyclopian roared and tried to rise, but a hoof crushed the side of its face.

Luthien was hurt more than he cared to admit. The wounds wouldn't have been serious, except that he was engaged in a brutal fight at the moment and his head was pounding so badly that he could hardly see straight.

In fact, he saw not one but two halberd tips continually darting his way. He whipped the bow back and forth and backpedaled.

He walked right into a tree, and lost his breath in the surprise. The agile young Bedwyr fell to the side as the cyclopian, thinking him caught, jabbed straight ahead, the wicked halberd tip digging a fair-sized hole in the wood.

Luthien responded with a swing of his own, but he missed and cringed when he heard the bow crack as it struck the tree. He brought it back out in front of him: half of it was hanging by a splinter.

The cyclopian bellowed with laughter; Luthien threw the bow at it. The brute batted it aside and its laugh turned to a growl, but when it began to advance once more, the cyclopian found that its opponent now carried a sword.

Oliver's pony was still dancing atop the groaning cyclopian when the halfling swung into the saddle. He meant to turn about and go help the young man who had come to his aid, but he paused, hearing whispers from inside the coach.

"Shoot him!" he heard a woman say. "Are you a coward?"

Oliver nodded in confirmation, guessing that she was talking to the merchant. Most merchants were cowards, the halfling believed. He hopped to a standing position atop his saddle, turned his pony beside the coach, and stepped lightly onto its roof, nearly tripping over the body of a cyclopian, a long arrow stuck deep into its face. Oliver looked down at his shoe, streaked with the cyclopian's blood, and crinkled his face in disgust. A huge hand shot out suddenly, gabbing the halfling's ankle and nearly knocking him over.

The cyclopian driver held on stubbornly, despite the arrow sticking into his chest. Oliver whipped him atop the head with the side of his rapier blade, and when the brute let go of the halfling's ankle to grasp at its newest wound, Oliver kicked it in the eye. The cyclopian gurgled, trying to scream, and tumbled backward off its seat, falling in a heap behind the nervous horse team.

"Count your luck that you did not mess my fine and stolen clothes," the halfling said to him. "For then I would surely have killed you!"

With a derisive snort, the halfling picked his way to the other side of the coach's roof and knelt down on one knee. A moment later, the plump arms and head of the merchant appeared, holding a crossbow and pointing it in the general direction of Luthien and the last remaining soldier.

Something tapped the merchant on top of his head.

"I do not think that would be such a wise idea," he heard from above. Slowly the merchant turned his head upward to regard the halfling, on one knee still, with his elbow propped against his other knee, green-gloved hand, holding the rapier, against the side of his face, with his index finger tap-tapping against the side of his nose.

"I do not know for sure, of course," the halfling went on casually, "but I think he might be a friend of mine."

The merchant screamed and tried to wheel about and bring the crossbow to bear on this new foe. The rapier snapped suddenly, flashing before the fat man's eyes, and he froze in shock. As soon as his senses recovered and he realized that he hadn't been hit, he tried to finish the move, even going so far as to pull the crossbow's trigger, before he realized that the quarrel was no longer in place along the weapon's shaft, plucked cleanly away by the well-aimed rapier.

Oliver held out his hands and shrugged. "I am good, you must admit," he said. The merchant screamed again and disappeared into the coach, whereupon the woman set upon him, calling him "coward" repeatedly, and many other worse names.

Oliver sat in a comfortable crouch on the roof, enjoying it all thoroughly, and turned his gaze back to the continuing fight.

The cyclopian was working the long halberd fiercely, whipping it to and fro and straight ahead. The young man, to his credit, hadn't been hit, but he was tumbling wildly and snapping his blade all about, apparently unaccustomed to facing so long a weapon.

"You must move straight ahead when he moves ahead!" Oliver called out.

Luthien heard him, but the strategy made no sense. He had fought against spear wielders in the arena, but those weapons were no more than eight feet long. The shaft of this halberd nearly doubled that.

Luthien started forward, as instructed, on the cyclopian's next thrust, and he caught the tip of the halberd on his right shoulder for his effort. With a yelp, the young man fell back, grabbing his sword in his left hand and favoring the stung shoulder.

"Not like that!" Oliver scolded. "Do not thrust in an angle that is complementary to your enemy's line of attack!"

Still hard-pressed, Luthien and the cyclopian paused for an instant to wonder what in the world this curious halfling was talking about.

"Do not line up your body with the enemy's closest tip," Oliver instructed. "Only a silly viper snake would do that, and are you not smarter than a silly viper snake?" The halfling then launched into a long dissertation about the proper methods of parrying long weapons, and of fighting silly viper snakes, but Luthien was no longer listening. A sweeping cut forced him to spin away to the side; a straight thrust for his abdomen had him jerking his rump far out behind him, doubling over. The cyclopian retracted and poked ahead again, thinking he had the young man off balance. He did, indeed, except that Luthien hurled himself facedown to the ground right behind the retracting blade. The halberd's tip as it came jabbing back scratched Luthien's behind but caused no serious damage, and Luthien spun about on the ground and scrambled ahead, grabbing the halberd shaft in his right hand and pulling it down as his sword came whipping up. The long weapon cracked apart.

"Well done!" came the halfling's cry from the top of the coach.

The cyclopian was not unarmed, though, still holding a broken shaft that now effectively served as a spear. Oliver's cheer had barely left his mouth when the one-eyed brute growled and pushed ahead, catching Luthien as he tried to stand. Down went the young man, apparently impaled.

"Oh," the halfling groaned as the roaring cyclopian put his weight behind the spear and began to grind and twist it mercilessly. On the ground, Luthien squirmed and squealed.

Oliver put his grand hat over his heart and lowered his head in respect. But then the cyclopian jerked suddenly and straightened, letting go of his weapon. He stumbled backward several steps and tried to turn, and Oliver saw that he was grabbing his belly, trying to hold in his spilling guts. Back on the ground, Luthien's sword, the top half of the blade bloodied, was sticking straight up. Luthien sat up, tossing the spear aside, and Oliver laughed loudly as he recognized the truth of the matter. Luthien hadn't been impaled; he had caught the cyclopian's blade under his arm and rolled to the side as he fell to disguise the ruse.

"Oh, I do think that I am going to like this one," the halfling said, and he tipped his hat to the victorious Luthien.

"Now, cowardly fat merchant-type, will you admit that you are defeated?" Oliver called, rapping the coach door with his rapier. "You may get out now, or come out at the end of my so fine rapier blade!"

The door creaked open and the merchant came out, followed by a painted and perfumed lady wearing a low-cut-up-high and high-cut-down-low silken crimson gown. The woman eyed the halfling incredulously, but her expression changed when she noticed the handsome young Bedwyr as he walked over to join the group.

Luthien caught her lewd gaze and returned it with an incredulous smirk. He immediately thought of Avonese, and his left hand unconsciously tightened on the hilt of his bloody sword.

Three graceful hops—to the seat, to the horse's rump, and to the ground—brought Oliver down to them, and he walked around the two prisoners. A yank of his free hand took the merchant's belt purse, and a flick of his rapier took the woman's jeweled necklace over her head.

"Go and search the coach," he instructed Luthien. "I did not ask for your help, but I will graciously split the wealth." He paused and thought for a moment, counting kills. At first, he gave Luthien credit for three of the cyclopians, half the enemy, but then he convinced himself that the driver belonged to him. "You defeated two of the six," he announced. "So four of six items are mine."

Luthien stood up straight, indignant.

"You think you get half?" the highwayman balked.

"I am no thief!" Luthien proclaimed. All three—Oliver, the merchant, and the lady—looked about the carnage and the dead and wounded cyclopians lying in the muck.

"You are now," they all said together, and Luthien winced.

"The coach?" Oliver prompted after a long and silent minute slipped past. Luthien shrugged and moved by them, entering the coach. It had many compartments, most filled with food or handkerchiefs, perfume and other items for the journey. After some minutes of searching, though, Luthien found a small iron chest under the seat. He pulled it out to the open floor and hoisted it, then moved back outside.

Oliver had the merchant on his knees, stripped to his underwear and whimpering.

"So many pockets," the halfling explained to Luthien, going through the man's huge waistcoat.

"You may search me," the woman purred at Luthien, and he fell back a step, banging against the coach's open door.

"If you are hiding anything precious under there," the halfling said to her, indicating her skintight, revealing gown, "then you are not half the woman you pretend to be!"

He was laughing at his own joke until he noticed the iron box in Luthien's hands. Then Oliver's eyes lit up.

"I see that it is time to go," he said, and tossed the waistcoat away.

"What about them?" Luthien asked.

"We must kill them," Oliver said casually, "or they will bring the whole Praetorian Guard down upon us."

Luthien scowled fiercely. Killing armed cyclopians was one thing, but a defenseless man and woman, and wounded enemies (even if they were cyclopian) defeated on the field of honor, was something entirely different. Before the young man could begin to protest, though, the halfling moaned and slapped a hand across his face.

"Ah, but one of the one-eyes got away," Oliver said in feigned distress, "so we cannot eliminate all witnesses. It would seem, then, that mercy would serve us well." He looked around at the groaning cyclopians: the driver behind the team; the one trampled into the ground by Oliver's pony, propped on one elbow now and watching the proceedings; the one that Luthien had stabbed still kneeling and holding his belly; and the one that Oliver's horse had sent flying away standing again, though unsteadily, and making no move to come back near the robbers. With the one Oliver had sent running away, rubbing his behind, that left only the dead crossbowman atop the coach.

"Besides," the halfling added with a smirk, "you are the only one who actually killed anybody."

"Take me with you!" the lady screamed suddenly, launching herself at Luthien. She crashed into him, and Luthien dropped the iron box—right on both of his own feet. Inspired by the pain, the overpowering stench of the lady's perfume, and his memories of Avonese, Luthien growled and pushed her back, and before he could think of what he was doing, he punched her right in the face, dropping her heavily to the ground.

"We must work on your manners," Oliver noted, shaking his head. "And your chivalry," he remarked to the merchant, who made not the slightest protest about the punch.

"But that, like the chest of treasure, can wait," the halfling explained. "To the road, my friend!"

Luthien shrugged, not knowing what to do, not even understanding what he had done.

"Threadbare!" Oliver called, a fitting name if Luthien had ever heard one. Oliver's ugly yellow pony trotted around the coach horses and kneeled so that the halfling could better gain his seat.

"Put the chest upon your own horse," Oliver instructed, "and I will go and find my main gauche. And you," he said, tapping the quivering merchant atop the head with the side of his rapier blade. "Count as you would count your own co-ins. And do not stop until you have counted them, every one, a thousand times!"

Luthien retrieved Riverdancer and secured the chest behind the horse's saddle. Then he walked over and helped the woman back to her feet. He meant to offer a sincere apology—this was not Avonese, after all, and he and the halfling had just robbed her—but she immediately wrapped herself around him once more, biting at his earlobe. With great effort (and nearly at the cost of that ear), Luthien managed to pull her back to arm's length.

"So strong," she purred.

"Your lady?" Oliver began, walking Threadbare past the kneeling merchant.

"My wife," the merchant replied sourly.

"A loyal type, I can see," Oliver said. "But then, now we have the money!"

Luthien shoved off and ran away from the woman, getting into his saddle so quickly that he nearly tumbled off the other side. He kicked Riverdancer into a short gallop, seeing the woman running fast after him, and rushed right past Oliver, toward the bridge.

Oliver watched him with amusement, then wheeled Threadbare around to face the merchant and his woman. "Now you may tell all your fat merchant-type friends that you were robbed by Oliver deBurrows," he said, as though that should carry some significance.

Threadbare reared on his hind legs, and with a tip of his hat, Oliver was off.

CHAPTER 7

THE DIAMONDGATE FERRY

I AM OLIVER DEBURROWS," the halfling said, bringing his pony to a trot after the two had put more than a mile behind them. "Highwayman," he added, sweeping his hat off gracefully.

Luthien started to likewise introduce himself, but the halfling was not finished. "I used to say 'highwayhalfling,'" he explained, "but the merchants did not take that so seriously and I had to more often use my rapier blade. To make my point, if you understand my meaning." As he spoke, he snapped the rapier from the loop on his baldric and thrust it Luthien's way.

"I understand," Luthien assured him, gently pushing the dangerous weapon away. He tried to introduce himself but was promptly cut off.

"And this is my fine horse, Threadbare," Oliver said, patting the yellow pony. "Not the prettiest, of course, but smarter than any horse, and most men, as well."

Luthien patted his own shaggy mount and started to say, "Riverda—"

"I do appreciate your unexpected help," Oliver went on, oblivious to Luthien's attempt to speak. "Of course, I could have defeated them by myself—there were only six, you see. But take help where you find help, my papa halfling always say, and so I am grateful to . . ."

"Luth—" Luthien began.

"Of course, my gratitude will not carry beyond the split of the profits," Oliver quickly added. "One in four for you." He eyed Luthien's rather plain dress with obvious disdain. "And that will probably be more wealth than you have ever seen."

"Probably," the son of the eorl of Bedwydrin said immediately, trying to hide his smirk. Luthien did realize, though, that he had left his home without taking much in the way of wealth. He had enough to cross on the ferry and support himself for a few days, but when he had left Dun Varna, he hadn't really thought much beyond that.

"Not in debt, then," Oliver said, barely pausing for a breath, before Luthien, for the fourth time, could offer his name. "But I will allow you to ride beside me, if you wish. That merchant-type was not surprised to see me—and he knew all along that he could have kept me away by showing his six guards openly. Yet he hid them," the halfling reasoned, seeming as if he was speaking to himself. Then he snapped his fingers and looked straight at Luthien so quickly that he startled the young man.

"I do think that he hid the one-eyes in the hopes of luring me in!" Oliver exclaimed. He paused for just an instant, stroking his goatee with one of his green-gloved hands.

"Yes, yes," he went on. "The merchant-type knew I was on the road— this is not the first time I have robbed him at rapier point. I got him outside of Princetown once, I do believe." He looked up at Luthien, nodding his head. "And of course, the merchant-type would have heard my name in any case. So you may ride with me," he offered, "for a while. Until we are beyond the traps this merchant-type has no doubt set."

"You think that the danger is not behind us?"

"I just said that."

Luthien again hid his smirk, amazed at how the little one had just pumped himself up to be some sort of legendary highwayman. Luthien had never heard of Oliver deBurrows before, though the merchants traveling to his father's house in Dun Varna often brought tales of thieves along the road.

"I assure you," Oliver began, but he stopped and looked at Luthien curiously. "You know," he said, seeming somewhat perturbed, "you really should properly introduce yourself when traveling beside someone you have never met. There are codes of etiquette, particularly for those who would be known as proper highwaymen. Ah well," he finished with a great sigh, "perhaps you will learn better in your time beside Oliver deBurrows."

"I am Luthien," the young Bedwyr shouted quickly, before Oliver could interrupt him once more. He wondered if he should, perhaps, go by an alias. But he couldn't think of one at that moment, and he really didn't see the point. "Luthien Bedwyr of Dun Varna. And this is Riverdancer," he added, giving the horse another pat.

Oliver tipped his hat, then pulled up short on his pony. "Bedwyr?" he asked, as much to himself as to Luthien, as though he wanted to hear the ring of the name again. "Bedwyr. This name is not unknown to me."

"Gahris Bedwyr is the eorl of Bedwydrin," Luthien said.

"Ah!" Oliver agreed, pointing one finger up into the air and smiling widely in recognition. That smile went away in an incredulous blink. "Family?"

"Father," Luthien admitted.

Oliver tried to respond, but nearly choked instead. "And you are out here on the road—for sport!" the halfling reasoned. In Gascony, where Oliver had spent most of his life, it was not uncommon for the rowdy children of nobles to get into all sorts of trouble, including ambushing merchants on the road, knowing that their family connections would keep them free. "Draw your sword, you silly little boy!" the halfling cried, and out whipped his rapier and his main gauche. "I so much do not approve!"

"Oliver!" Luthien replied, swinging Riverdancer about to put some ground between himself and the fuming halfling. "What are you talking about?" As the halfling turned his pony to pursue, Luthien grudgingly drew his weapon.

"You bring disgrace to every reputable highwayman in all the land!" the halfling went on. "What need have you of co-ins and jew-wels?" Threadbare sidled up close to Riverdancer, and the halfling, though he was sitting at only about half Luthien's height and could barely reach the man's vital areas, thrust forward his rapier.

Luthien's sword intercepted the weapon and turned it aside. Oliver countered with a rapid series of thrusts, feints and cuts, even slipping in a deceptive jab with the main gauche.

Skilled Luthien defeated every move, kept his balance perfect and his sword in proper defensive posture.

"But it is a game for the son of an eorl," Oliver remarked sarcastically. "He is too bored in his daily duties of cowering his subjects." The thrusts became fiercer still, Oliver apparently going for a kill.

That last line got to Luthien, though, insulted him and insulted his father, who had never acted in such a way. He rocked back in his saddle, letting Oliver play out his fury, then came on with an attack routine of his own, slapping the rapier out wide and swiping his sword across fiercely. Oliver's main gauche intercepted, and the halfling squealed, thinking that he could send Luthien's weapon flying, as he had done to the cyclopian.

Luthien was quicker than that brute, and he turned his blade before Oliver could twist the trapping dagger, nearly taking the main gauche from the halfling's hand and freeing the sword so that it could complete its swing.

Oliver's great hat fell to the ground, and both the halfling and Luthien knew that Oliver's head would have still been inside if Luthien had so desired.

A tug on the reins sent Threadbare back several feet, putting some distance between the combatants. "I could be wrong," the halfling admitted.

"You are wrong," Luthien answered sternly. "You could find fault with Gahris Bedwyr, that I do not doubt. He does not follow his heart if that course would go against the edicts of King Greensparrow, or the duke of Montfort, or any of the duke's many emissaries. But on pain of death, never again speak of Gahris as a tyrant!"

"I said I could be wrong," Oliver replied soberly.

"As for me . . ." Luthien went on, his voice subdued, for he was not sure of how to proceed. What of me? he wondered. What had happened this day? It all seemed a surrealistic blur to the suddenly confused Luthien.

For once, Oliver remained silent and let the young man sort out his thoughts, understanding that whatever Luthien might have to say could be important—both to Oliver and to Luthien.

"I no longer claim any of the rights that accompany the name of Bedwyr," Luthien said firmly. "I have fled my house, leaving the corpse of a cyclopian guardsman behind. And now I have chosen my course." He held his sword up before him, letting its fine blade shine in the sun, though it was still a bit stained with the blood of the merchant's guard. "I am as much an outlaw as are you, Oliver deBurrows," Luthien proclaimed. "An outlaw in a land ruled by an outlaw king. Thus will my sword swing for justice."

Oliver raised his own rapier in like salute and outwardly proclaimed his agreement. He thought Luthien a silly little boy, though, who didn't understand either the rules or the dangers of the road. Justice? Oliver nearly laughed aloud at the thought. Luthien's sword might swing for justice, but Oliver's rapier jabbed for profit. Still, the young man was a mighty ally—Oliver couldn't deny that. And, Oliver mused, lending some credibility to the smile he was showing to Luthien, if justice was truly Luthien's priority, then more of the profits might fall Oliver's way.

Suddenly, the highwayhalfling was beginning to think that this arrangement might not be so temporary. "I accept your explanation," he said. "And I apologize for my too rash actions." He went to tip his hat again, then realized that it was lying on the ground. Luthien saw it, too, and started to move for it, but Oliver waved him back. Leaning low off the side of his saddle, the halfling tipped his rapier low, slipping the point in under the hat. A flick and twist brought the hat spinning atop the rapier's tip as Oliver lifted the weapon. He thrust it up, then jerked his rapier away, and the hat dropped in a spin, landing perfectly atop the halfling's head.

Luthien sat amazed, answering Oliver's smug smile with a shake of his head.

"But we are not safe on the island, fellow outlaw," Oliver said, his expression turning serious. "That merchant-type knew me, or of me, and expected me. He was probably on his way to your own father to organize a hunt for Oliver deBurrows." The halfling paused and snorted. He looked at Luthien and his chuckle became a full-blown laugh.

"Oh, wonderful irony!" Oliver cried. "He goes to the eorl for assistance, while the eorl's own son comes to my assistance!" Oliver's laughter continued to grow, and Luthien joined in, more to be polite than with any real feelings of mirth.

They did not make the ferry that afternoon, as Luthien had hoped. He explained to Oliver that the ferries would not cross the choppy seas at night. In the darkness, the island spotters could not see if any dorsal whales had come into the narrow channels. A description of the ten-ton man-eaters was all that Oliver needed to be convinced that they should forgo plans to be off the island that same day and set up their camp.

Luthien sat up long into the night in the drizzle beside the hissing and smoking low campfire. To the side, Threadbare and Riverdancer stood quietly, heads bowed, and across the fire, Oliver snored contentedly.

The young man huddled under his blanket, warding off the chill. He still could not believe all that had happened over the last few days: Garth Rogar, his brother, the cyclopian guardsman, and now the attack on the merchant wagon. It remained unreal to Luthien; he felt as if he had fallen into a river of uncontrollable events and was simply being swept along in their tide.

No, not uncontrollable, Luthien finally decided. Undeniable. The world, as it turned out, was not as he had been brought up to expect it to be. Perhaps his last actions in Dun Varna—his decision to leave and his fight with the cyclopian—had been some sort of passage into adulthood, an awakening for the naive child of a noble house.

Perhaps, but Luthien knew that he still had no solid answers. He knew, too, that he had followed his heart both in Dun Varna and when he had seen Oliver's fight with the merchant's guards. He had followed his heart, and out there, on the road, in the drizzle of a chill August night, Luthien had little else to guide him.

The next day was similarly gray and wet, but the companions made good time out of their encampment. Soon the smell of salt water filled their nostrils and put a tang in their mouths.

"If the day was clear," Luthien explained, "we could see the northern spurs of the Iron Cross from here."

"How do you know?" Oliver asked him sarcastically. "Have you ever had a clear day on this island?" The banter was light and so were their hearts (Oliver's always seemed to be!). Luthien felt somehow relieved that day, as though he would find his freedom when he crossed the narrow channel and stepped onto Eriador's mainland. The wide world beckoned.

But first, they had to get across.

From the top of a rocky bluff, the two got their first view of the Diamondgate Ferry, and of the mainland across the narrow channel. The place was called Diamondgate for a small, diamond-shaped isle, a lump of wet black rock in the middle of the channel, halfway between the shores.

Two flat, open barges sat at the ends of long wooden wharves whose supporting beams were as thick as ancient oaks. Off to the side loomed the remains of the older wharves, equally well constructed, their demise a testament to the power of the sea.

The barges, including the two now moored across the channel, had originally been designed and built by the dwarves of the Iron Cross more than three hundred years before, and had been meticulously maintained (and replaced, when the rocks or the currents or a dorsal whale took one) by the islanders ever since. Their design was simple and effective: an open, flat landing for cargo and travelers, anchored at each corner by thick beams that arched up to a central point ten feet above the center of the landing. Here the beams connected to a long metal tube, and through this ran the thick rope that guided the ferry back and forth. A large gear showed on each side of the tube, its notches reaching in through slits along the tube's side. A crank on the deck turned a series of gears leading to these two, which in turn caught the knots on the rope and pulled the ferry along the taut cord's length. The beauty of the system was that, because of the marvelous dwarven gearing, a single strong man could pull the ferry even if it was heavily laden.

But still the crossing was always dangerous. The water this day, as every day, showed white tips on its bouncing waves and abundant rocks, especially near to Diamondgate, where the ferries could dock if they encountered any trouble.

One of the barges was always inoperable, taken down so that its guide rope could be replaced, or when its floor planking needed shoring up. Several dozen men worked long days at Diamondgate just to keep the place in operation.

"They are planning to shut down that one," Luthien, familiar with the operation, informed Oliver, pointing to the barge on the north. "And it seems as if the other is about to leave. We must hurry, or wait perhaps hours for the next barge to cross over." He gave a ticking sound to Riverdancer, and the horse started down the path leading to the landings.

A few minutes later, Threadbare pranced up alongside and Oliver grabbed Luthien's arm, indicating that he should slow the pace.

"But the ferry—" Luthien started to protest.

"There is an ambush about," Oliver explained.

Luthien stared at him incredulously, then looked back to the landing. More than a score of men moved down there, but just a pair of cyclopians, these showing no weapons and appearing as simple travelers waiting to cross. This was not common, Luthien knew, for there were few cyclopians on Bedwydrin, and those were only merchant guards or his father's own. Still, under the edicts of King Greensparrow, cyclopians were allowed free passage as citizens of Avon, and affairs at Diamondgate did not seem so out of place.

"You have to learn to smell such things," Oliver remarked, recognizing the young man's doubts. Luthien shrugged and gave in, moving along the path at as fast a pace as Oliver would allow.

The two cyclopians, and many of the men, spotted the companions when they were about a hundred feet from the landing, but none made any gestures or even called out to indicate that the two might have been expected. Oliver, though, slowed a bit more, his eyes darting this way and that from under the brim of his hat.

A horn blew, indicating that all should move back from the end of the wharf as the barge was about to pull out. Luthien started forward immediately, but Oliver held him in check.

"They are leaving," Luthien protested in a harsh whisper.

"Easy," Oliver implored him. "Make them think that we intend to simply wait for the next crossing."

"Make who think?" Luthien argued.

"You see those barrels along the wharf?" Oliver asked. Luthien swung his gaze about and Oliver squeezed hard on his forearm. "Do not be so obvious!" the halfling scolded softly.

Luthien sighed and subtly looked at the casks Oliver had mentioned. There was a long line of them; they had probably come from the mainland and were waiting for a caravan to claim them.

"They are marked with an X," Oliver remarked.

"Wine," Luthien explained.

"If they are wine, then why do so many have open bungholes?" the alert halfling asked. Luthien looked more closely, and sure enough, saw that every third barrel had a small, open hole in it, minus its bung.

"And if those cyclopians on the landing are simply travelers," Oliver went on, "then why are they not on the departing barge?"

Luthien sighed again, this time revealing that he was starting to follow, and agree with, the halfling's line of reasoning.

"Can your horse jump?" Oliver asked calmly.

Luthien noted that the barge was slowly moving away from the wharf and understood what the halfling was thinking.

"I will tell you when to break," Oliver assured him. "And do kick a barrel into the water if you get the chance as you pass!"

Luthien felt his adrenaline building, felt the same tingling and butterflies in the stomach that he got when he stepped into the arena. There was little doubt in the young man's mind that life beside Oliver deBurrows would not be boring!

They walked their mounts easily onto the boards of the thirty-foot wharf, passing two workers without incident. A third man, one of the cargo workers, approached them smiling.

"Next barge is an hour before the noon," he explained cheerily, and he pointed to a small shed, starting to explain where the travelers could rest and take a meal while they waited.

"Too long!" Oliver cried suddenly, and off leaped Threadbare, Riverdancer charging right behind. Men dove out of the way; the two visible cyclopians shouted and scrambled, producing short swords from under their cloaks. As Oliver had predicted, every third barrel began to move, lids popping off and falling aside as cyclopians jumped out.

But the two companions had gained surprise. Riverdancer sprang past Oliver's pony and blasted past the two cyclopians, hurling them aside. Oliver moved Threadbare to the edge of the wharf, along the row of barrels, and managed to bump more than a few as he rushed by, spinning them into the drink.

The slow-moving ferry was fifteen feet out when Luthien got to the end of the wharf, no great leap for powerful Riverdancer, and the young man held on tight as he soared across.

Oliver came next, sitting high and waving his hat in one hand as Threadbare flew across, coming to a kicking and skidding stop, banging into Riverdancer atop the smooth wooden barge. Back on the wharf, a dozen cyclopians shouted protests and waved their weapons, but Oliver, more wary than his less-experienced companion, paid them no heed. The halfling swung down from his mount, his weapons coming out to meet the advance of a cyclopian that suddenly appeared from among the piles of cargo.

The rapier and main gauche waved in a dizzying blur, a precise and enchanting dance of steel, though they seemed to come nowhere near to hitting the halfling's opponent. The cyclopian gawked at the display, sincerely impressed. But when the flurry was done, the brute was not hurt at all. Its one eye looked down to its leather tunic, though, and saw that the halfling had cut an "O" into it in a fine cursive script.

"I could write my whole name," Oliver remarked. "And I assure you, I have a very long name!"

With a growl of rage, the cyclopian lifted its heavy ax, and Oliver promptly dove forward, running right between its wide-spread legs and spinning about to poke the brute in the rump with his rapier.

"I would taunt you again," the halfling proclaimed, "but I see that you are too stupid to know that you are being taunted!"

The cyclopian howled and turned, then instinctively looked ahead again just in time to see Luthien's fist soaring into its face. Oliver meanwhile had retracted the rapier and rushed ahead, driving his shoulder into the back of the cyclopian's knees. Over went the brute, launched by Luthien's punch, to land heavily, flat on its back. It struggled for just a moment, then lay still.

A splash made Luthien turn around. The cyclopians on the wharf had taken up spears now and were hurling them out at the barge. "Tell the captain to get this ferry moving," Oliver said calmly to Luthien as he walked past. He handed Luthien a small pouch of coins. "And do pay the man." Oliver walked to the stern of the ferry, apparently unconcerned with the continuing spear volley.

"You sniffers of barnyard animals!" he taunted. "Stupid oafs who poke their own eyes when trying to pick their noses!"

The cyclopians howled and picked up their throwing pace.

"Oliver!" Luthien cried.

The halfling turned to regard him. "They have but one eye," he explained. "No way to gauge depth. Do you not know that cyclopians cannot throw?"

He turned about, laughing, then shouted, "Hello!" and jumped straight up as a spear stuck into the deck right between his legs.

"You could be wrong," Luthien said, imitating the halfling's accent and stealing Oliver's usual line.

"Even one-eyes can get lucky," the halfling replied indignantly, with a snap of his green-gloved fingers. And to prove confidence in his point, he launched a new stream of taunts at the brutes on the wharf.

"What is this about?" an old, weather-beaten man demanded, grabbing Luthien by the shoulder. "I'll not have—"

He stopped when Luthien handed him the pouch of coins.

"All right, then," the man said. "But tether those horses, or it's your own loss!"

Luthien nodded and the wiry old man went back to the crank.

The ferry moved painfully slowly for the anxious companions, foot by foot across the choppy dark waters of the channel where the Avon Sea met the Dorsal. They saw cyclopians scrambling back on the wharf, trying to get the other ferry out of its dock and set off in pursuit. Luthien wasn't too concerned, for he knew that the boats, geared for solid and steady progress across the dangerous waters, could not be urged on any faster. He and Oliver had a strong lead on their pursuers, and Riverdancer and Threadbare would hit the ground across the way running, putting a mile or more behind them before the cyclopians stepped off their ferry.

Oliver joined Luthien beside the horses, limping and grumbling as he approached.

"Are you injured?" a concerned Luthien asked.

"It is my shoe," the halfling answered, and he held his shoe out for Luthien to see. It seemed intact, though quite dirty and quite wet, as if Oliver had just dipped his leg into the water.

"The stain!" Oliver explained, pushing it higher, near to Luthien's face. "When I crossed the roof of the merchant-type coach, I stepped in the blood of the dead cyclopian. Now I cannot get the blood off!"

Luthien shrugged, not understanding.

"I stole this shoe from the finest boarding school in Gascony," Oliver huffed, "from the son of a friend of the king himself! Where am I to find another in this too wild land you call your home?"

"There is nothing wrong with that one," Luthien protested.

"It is ruined!" Oliver retorted, and he crossed his arms over his chest, rocked back on one heel, his other foot tap-tapping, and pointedly looked away.

Luthien did well not to laugh at his pouting companion.

A few feet away, the downed cyclopian groaned and stirred.

"If he wakes up, I will kick him in the eye," Oliver announced evenly. "Twice."

Oliver snapped his glare up at Luthien, whose chest was now heaving with sobs of mirth. "And then I will write my name, my whole name, my very long whole name, across your ample buttocks," the halfling promised.

Luthien buried his face in Riverdancer's shaggy neck.

The ferry was well over a hundred yards out by then and nearing Diamondgate Isle, the halfway point. It seemed as if the friends had made their escape, and even pouting Oliver's mood seemed to brighten.

But then the guide rope jerked suddenly. Luthien and Oliver looked back to shore and saw cyclopians hanging from the high poles that held the ropes, hacking away on the rope with axes.

"Hey, don't you be doing that!" the captain of the ferry cried out, running back across the deck. Luthien was about to ask what problems might arise if the guide rope was cut down behind them when the rope fell free. The young man got his answer as the ferry immediately began to swing to the south, toward the rocks of the island, caught in the current of the channel.

The captain ran back the other way, screaming orders to his single crewman. The man worked frantically on the crank, but the ferry could not be urged any faster. It continued at its snail pace and its deadly swing to the south.

Luthien and Oliver grabbed hard to their saddles and tried to find some secure footing as the ferry bounced in. The boat scraped a few smaller rocks, narrowly missed one huge and sharp jag, and finally crashed into the rocks around a small and narrow inlet.

Cargo tumbled off the side; the cyclopian, just starting to regain its footing, went flying away, smacking hard into the barnacle-covered stone, where it lay very still. One of the other passengers shared a similar fate, tumbling head over heels into the water, coming up gagging and screaming. Threadbare and Riverdancer held their ground stubbornly, though the pony lurched forward a bit, stepping onto Oliver's unshod foot. The halfling quickly reconsidered his disdain over his dirty shoe and took it out of his pocket.

More swells came in under them, grinding the ferry against the stone, splintering wood. Luthien dove to the deck and crawled across, grabbing hold of the fallen man and pulling him back up out of the water. The captain called for his crewman to crank, but then spat curses instead, realizing that with the other end of the guide rope unsecured, the ferry could not possibly escape the current.

"Bring Riverdancer!" Luthien called to Oliver, understanding the problem. He scrambled to the back of the raft and took up the loose guide rope, then looked about, finally discerning which of the many stones would best hold the rope. He moved to the very edge and looped up the rope, readying his throw.

A swell nearly sent him overboard, but Oliver grabbed him by the belt and held him steady. Luthien tossed the rope over the rock and pulled the loop as tight as he could. Oliver scrambled onto Riverdancer's back and turned the horse around, and Luthien came up behind, tying off the rope onto the back of the saddle.

Gently, the halfling eased the horse forward and the rope tightened, steadying the rocking ferry. Oliver kept the horse pressing forward, taking up any slack, as Luthien tied off the guide rope. Then they cut Riverdancer free and the cranking began anew, easing the ferry out of the inlet and back out from the rocks. A great cheer went up from the captain, his crewman, and the four other passengers.

"I'll get her into Diamondgate's dock," the captain said to Luthien, pointing to a wharf around the outcropping of rocks. "We'll wait there for a ferry to come for us from the other side."

Luthien led the captain's gaze back into the channel, where the other ferry, teeming with armed cyclopians, was now working its way into the channel.

"All the way across," the young Bedwyr said. "I beg."

The captain nodded, looked doubtfully to the makeshift guide rope, and moved back to the front of the ferry. He returned just a few moments later, though, shaking his head.

"We have to stop," he explained. "They're flying a yellow flag on the Diamondgate dock."

"So?" put in Oliver, and he did not sound happy.

"They have spotted dorsals in the other side of the channel," Luthien explained to the halfling.

"We cannot take her out there," the captain added. He gave the pair a sincerely sympathetic look, then went back to the bow, leaving Luthien and Oliver to stare helplessly at each other and at the approaching boatload of cyclopians.

When they reached the Diamondgate dock, Luthien and Oliver helped everyone to get off the ferry. Then the halfling handed the captain another sack of coins and moved back to his pony, showing no intention of leaving the boat.

"We have to go on," Luthien explained to the gawking man. They both looked out to the two hundred yards of choppy dark water separating them from Eriador's mainland.

"The flag only means that dorsals have been spotted this morning," the captain said hopefully.

"We know that the cyclopians are very real," Luthien replied, and the captain nodded and backed away, signaling for his crewman to do likewise, surrendering his craft to Luthien and Oliver.

Luthien took the crank and set off at once, looking more to the sides than straight ahead. Oliver remained in the stern watching the cyclopians and the curiously forlorn group they had just left at the dock. Their expressions, truly concerned, set off alarms in the normally unshakable halfling.

"These dorsals," Oliver asked, moving up to join Luthien, "are they very big?"

Luthien nodded.

"Bigger than your horse?"

Luthien nodded.

"Bigger than the ferry?"

Luthien nodded.

"Take me back to the dock," Oliver announced. "I would fight the cyclopians."

Luthien didn't bother to respond, just kept cranking and kept look-ing from side to side, expecting to see one of those towering and omi-nous black fins rise up at any moment.

The cyclopians passed Diamondgate, dropping two brutes off as they passed. Oliver groaned, knowing that the cyclopians would inevitably try to cause mischief with the guide ropes once more. But the halfling's fears soon turned to enjoyment. The ropes were suspended quite high over the Diamondgate docks, and the cyclopians had to build a make-shift tower to get anywhere near them. Worse, as soon as the ferry with its cyclopian load had moved out a safe distance, the captain of Luthien's ferry, his crewman, and the other passengers—even the injured one Luthien had pulled from the cold water—set on the two cyclopians, pushing them and their tower over the edge of the wharf and into the dark water.

At Oliver's cheer, young Luthien turned and saw that spectacle and marked it well, though he had no idea then of how significant that little uprising might later prove.

Oliver did a cartwheel, leaped and spun with joy, and came down frozen in place, looking out to the north side, to the open channel and the tall fin—thrice his height, at least—that had come up through the dark waves.

Luthien's smile disappeared as he considered his friend's sudden ex-pression, then shifted his gaze to consider its source.

The dorsal fin sent a high wake in its speeding path, dropped to half its height, then slipped ominously under the water altogether.

Luthien, trying to remember all the advice his local fishermen had ever given to him, stopped the crank, even back-pulling it once to halt the ferry's momentum.

"Crank!" Oliver scolded, running forward, but Luthien grabbed him and held him steady and whispered for him to be quiet.

They stood together as the water around them darkened and the ferry shifted slightly to the south, nearly snapping its guide rope, moved by the passage of the great whale as it brushed under them. When the whale emerged on the other side, Oliver glimpsed its full forty-foot length, its skin patched black and white. Ten tons of killer. The halfling would have fallen to the deck, his legs no longer able to support him, but Luthien held him steady.

"Stay calm and still," the young Bedwyr whispered. Luthien was counting on the cyclopians this time. They were beasts of mountain holes and surely knew little about the habits of dorsal whales.

The long fin reappeared starboard of the craft, moving slowly then, as if the whale had not decided its next move.

Luthien looked behind at the eagerly approaching cyclopians. He smiled and waved, pointing out the tall dorsal fin to them.

As Luthien expected, the cyclopians spotted the great whale and went berserk. They began scrambling all about the deck of their ferry; the one on the crank began cranking backward, trying to reverse direction. A few of the brutes even climbed up to their guide rope.

"Not such a bad idea," Oliver remarked, looking at his own high rope.

Luthien turned his gaze instead to their loyal mounts, and Oliver promptly apologized.

Then Luthien looked back to the great whale, turning now, as he had expected. The cyclopians kept up their frenzy, disturbing the water, inadvertently calling the whale to them.

When the behemoth's course seemed determined, Luthien went back to the crank and began easing the ferry ahead slowly, so as not to attract the deadly whale's attention.

With typical cyclopian loyalty, the cyclopians chose one from their own ranks and threw the poor brute into the water ahead of the approaching whale, hoping that the behemoth would take the sacrifice and leave the rest of them alone.

They didn't understand the greedy nature of dorsal whales.

The black-and-white behemoth slammed the side of the cyclopians' ferry, then, with a flick of its powerful tail, heaved itself right across the flat deck, driving half of the pitifully small craft under water. Cyclopians flew everywhere, flailing and screaming. The dorsal slipped back under the water, but reappeared on the ferry's other side. The whale's head came right out of the water, a cyclopian in its great maw up to the waist, screaming and slapping futilely at the sea monster.

The whale bit down and slid back under, and the severed top half of the one-eye bobbed in the reddening water.

Half a cyclopian would not satisfy a dorsal whale, though. The beast's great tail slapped the water, launching two cyclopians thirty feet into the air. They splashed back in and one was sent flying again; the other was bitten in half.

The frenzy went on for agonizing minutes, and then, suddenly, the dorsal fin appeared again, cutting a fast wake to the north.

"Luthien," Oliver called ominously.

Several hundred yards away, the whale breached, slamming back down into the water, using the jump to pivot about.

"Luthien," Oliver called again, and the young Bedwyr didn't have to look north to know that the whale had found another target.

Luthien realized at once that he could not make the mainland dock, fully fifty yards away. He jumped up from the crank and ran about, thinking, searching.

"Luthien," Oliver said again, frozen in place by the approaching specter of doom.

Luthien ran to the stern of the ferry and called across the water to the shouting people of the Diamondgate dock: "Cut the rope!"

At first, they didn't seem to hear him, or at least, they seemed not to understand, but then Luthien called it again and pointed above himself at the guide rope. Immediately the captain signaled to his crewman, and the agile man put a large knife between his teeth and scrambled up the pole.

Luthien went to stand beside Oliver, watching the whale's approach.

A hundred yards away. Eighty.

Fifty yards away. Luthien heard Oliver muttering under his breath—praying, the young man realized.

Suddenly, the ferry lurched to the side and began a hard swing. Luthien pulled Oliver over to their mounts. Both Riverdancer and Threadbare were standing nervously, nickering and stamping their hooves as if they understood their peril. Luthien quickly tied off the end of the loose rope so that the ferry could not slip down along its length.

The dorsal fin angled accordingly, keeping the pursuit, closing.

Thirty yards away. Oliver could see the whale's black eye.

The ferry was speeding along quite well by then, caught in the deceivingly swift currents, but the whale was faster still.

Twenty yards away. Oliver was praying loudly.

The ferry jolted, skidding off a rock, and when Oliver and Luthien managed to tear their stares from the whale, they realized that they were very near the rock coastline. They looked back just in time to see the dorsal fin veer away, stymied by the shallows.

The companions' relief was short-lived, though, for they were moving at a wild clip, much faster than when they had been cut free near to Diamondgate, and were coming up on a sheer cliff of jagged rock.

CHAPTER 8

A ROAD WELL TAKEN

ET ON YOUR HORSE! Get on your horse!" Oliver cried as he mounted Threadbare, holding the reins hard to keep the nervous beast from stumbling.

Luthien followed the command, not really knowing what Oliver had in mind, but with no better plan of his own. As soon as he was astride Riverdancer, he saw Oliver lining up the pony exactly opposite from where the ferry would likely hit, and then the young man began to catch on.

"You must time the jump well!" the halfling called. The ferry lurched suddenly as it grazed across more rocks; the plank furthest aft broke apart and was left drifting in the speeding craft's wake.

"Jump?" Luthien cried back. The approaching wall of stone was only a few feet high, and Luthien held no doubts that Riverdancer could make the leap if they were on solid ground. But the bouncing raft could not be considered solid ground, and even worse, Luthien was not sure of what was on the other side of that wall. He knew what would happen if he did not make the jump, though, and so when Oliver kicked Threadbare into a short run across the ferry, Luthien and Riverdancer followed.

Luthien buried his head in the horse's shaggy mane, not daring to look as he lifted away, propelled by the momentum of the ferry. He heard the explosion of wood on the rocks behind him, knew an instant later that he had cleared the wall.

He looked up as Riverdancer touched down in a short trot on a grassy knoll. Threadbare stood to the side, riderless and with a small cut on her foreleg. For a moment, Luthien feared that Oliver had toppled in the middle of the jump and had been slammed against the stones. Then he spotted the halfling lying in the wet grass and laughing wildly.

Oliver hopped to his feet and scooped up his fallen hat. He looked back to Diamondgate and waved frantically, wanting those who had helped him to know that he and Luthien had survived.

Luthien walked Riverdancer to the edge of the knoll and looked down at the smashed ferry. Twenty yards out, the fierce dorsal whale reappeared, circling the flotsam.

"That was not so bad," Oliver remarked.

Luthien didn't know whether to jump down and punch the halfling, or to throw him into the air in victory. His blood was coursing mightily through his veins, his heart pumping strongly. He felt more alive than ever before, more sheer elation than any victory in the arena could ever have afforded him.

But if Oliver spoke the truth, then what else might the young Bedwyr face beside the halfling? What worse?

Despite his primal joy, a shudder ran along Luthien's spine.

"They are coming to congratulate our quick thinking," Oliver said, drawing Luthien's attention and leading his gaze north along the knoll, back toward the ferry docks on this side of the channel. Two dozen men were running at them, calling out and waving tools.

"To congratulate?" Luthien asked.

Oliver looked down to the smashed ferry. "You think they might want us to pay for that?"

Luthien's shrug sent the halfling running to his mount.

He swung up into his saddle and bowed from a sitting position, sweeping his great hat low along the pony's side. "I do so appreciate your applause," he called to the approaching mob. "But now, I fear, the curtain is closed!"

And off they ran, side by side, the foppish halfling swashbuckler on his ugly yellow pony and the son of Bedwyr on his glistening white stallion.

The next few days proved quite uneventful for the weary companions. They traveled easily south through the Eriadoran farmlands, taking food and lodging where they found it. This was not too difficult, for the farmers of northern Eriador were a friendly folk, and more than willing to share a meal and a place in their barns in exchange for news of the outside world.

Oliver always dominated the conversations on such occasions, telling Luthien and the farmers grand tales of his times in Gascony, telling of adventures far beyond the scope of the "minor inconveniences" he and Luthien had been through since the fight with the merchant wagon.

Luthien listened to all the tales without reply, though he knew that Oliver was three parts bluster and one part truth (and allowing him that formula, Luthien figured, was being generous). The young man saw no harm in the halfling's outrageous claims, and Oliver seemed to entertain the farmers well enough, though none of the farmers were able to provide any information about Ethan. Every morning, when Luthien and Oliver left a farm, they were seen off by an entire family, and sometimes neighbors as well, smiling and waving and calling out for their good fortunes.

Luthien had too much on his mind to worry about any lies or exaggerations the halfling might spout. The young man still could not sort through all of his confusing thoughts and events of the last week, but he knew that he was comfortable with all that he had done. Even when he thought of the cyclopian in his father's house, or the one atop the merchant's wagon, or those in the overturned boat, Luthien held no remorse and took heart that if the identical situation were to come upon him again, he would react in the very same way.

He took heart, too, in his companion. Every day that passed, Luthien found that he liked Oliver's company more and more. This halfling, admittedly a thief, was not an evil person. Far from it. From his actions and the tales of his past (those parts that Luthien decided might have a ring of truth), Luthien could see that Oliver held himself up to some very high principles. The halfling would only steal from merchants and nobles, for example, and despite his suggestions when they had the merchant and his wife helpless on the road, from what Luthien could discern, Oliver was reluctant to kill anything except cyclopians.

And so Luthien, with no idea of how to locate his brother, decided to simply ride along the course beside the highwayhalfling, wherever it might lead, and let the fates guide him.

They moved south for several days, then veered to the east, crossing fields of tall, blowing wheat and high stone walls. "We will go between the mountains," Oliver explained one afternoon, pointing to a wide gap between the main bulk of the Iron Cross and a northern string of peaks. "My boat left me off on the road to Montfort and I have not been this way."

"Bruce MacDonald's Swath," Luthien replied, offering the name given to that particular gap.

Oliver slowed Threadbare and spent a moment in thought. "And will this Bruce MacDonald expect from us a toll?" he asked, putting a protective hand on his jingling pouch.

"Only if he comes from the grave," Luthien replied with a laugh. He went on to explain the legend of Bruce MacDonald, Eriador's greatest hero of old, who drove the attacking cyclopians back into their mountain holes. According to the tales, Bruce MacDonald cut the swath through the mountains, thus crossing more easily and gaining a surprise on the main cyclopian force, who did not expect his army before the spring cleared the mountain passes.

"And now the one-eyes are your friends?" Oliver asked. "We have no cyclopians in Gascony," he bragged. "At the least, we have none who dare to stick their ugly noses out of their dirty mountain holes!" The halfling went on, taking the tale from Luthien, and explained how Gascons dealt with the one-eyed brutes, telling of great battles—far greater, of course, than any Bruce MacDonald might have fought.

Luthien let the halfling ramble and, in fact, faded out of the conversation altogether, considering instead his own retelling of the MacDonald tale and how his blood stirred whenever he spoke of the legendary hero. Suddenly, the young Bedwyr was beginning to understand his own actions and feelings. He knew then why he was not so badly bothered by killing in his father's house. He thought of his feelings for the first cyclopian who had been tossed overboard on the ferry. Luthien had not gone to his aid, but he had rushed to help the man who had similarly been thrown.

Luthien had never realized before how deeply his hatred of cyclopians ran. In realizing the truth, he came to understand Ethan better. He knew then why his brother had quit the arena as soon as the cyclopian guards had been given to Gahris by the duke of Montfort, several years before. A rush of other memories came over the young man as he explored these new emotions: childhood tales he had been told by his father and others detailing the atrocities of the cyclopians before Bruce MacDonald had put them down. Other vicious raids had occurred even more recently, usually against helpless farm families.

Luthien was still deep in his contemplations when Oliver stopped Threadbare and looked all about. The young Bedwyr and his horse continued on, oblivious to the halfling, and would have kept going had not Oliver whistled.

Luthien turned around, eyeing the halfling curiously. Seeing the sincere concern on Oliver's face, he waited until he had walked Riverdancer back beside the yellow pony before he quietly asked, "What is it?"

"You have to learn to smell these things," Oliver whispered in reply.

As if on cue, an arrow cut through the air, well above the companions' heads.

"Cyclopians," Oliver muttered, noting the terrible shot.

Again, as if on cue, the wheat to either side of the road behind them began to shake and whip about and cyclopians crashed out onto the road, riding fierce ponypigs, ugly but muscular beasts that looked like a cross between a shaggy horse and a wild boar.

Luthien and Oliver swung about and kicked their mounts ahead, but out of the wheat came two more cyclopians, one appearing right next to Oliver, and one further down the road.

Oliver reared Threadbare and turned the pony to the side as the cyclopian mount bore down upon him. The intelligent yellow pony kicked out with its forelegs, smacking the cyclopian's arms and sword. Threadbare did no real damage, but did distract the brute, and Oliver, lying low in the saddle, slipped his rapier in under the pony's kicking feet.

The engaged cyclopian never saw the blade coming. It squealed and tried to move away, but the rapier had already done its business. The ponypig continued past Oliver and Threadbare, and Oliver, just to make sure, caught the cyclopian's sword with his main gauche and tossed it away.

The cyclopian was oblivious to that move, though, slumping forward in its saddle, darkness filling its eye.

Further down the road, Luthien angled Riverdancer for a close pass at the charging ponypig. Luthien lifted his sword; the cyclopian leveled a spear.

The one-eye seemed to have the advantage with its longer weapon, and thought it would score a solid hit as the two began their pass.

But Luthien's sword came down, around and inside the tip of the spear. The rolling motion brought the spear out wide, and then high, leaving Luthien's sword across the neck of the snorting ponypig. The young warrior reversed his grip suddenly, turning the blade in line, and its fine edge gashed the cyclopian's forearms and forced the brute to fall back as the two passed.

Luthien kept the pressure firm, forcing the cyclopian right over backward, to land heavily on the dirt road. The brute looked up just in time to see Oliver bearing down on it, and it dropped its face and covered its head with its wounded arms, expecting to be trampled.

Oliver had no time to finish the job, though. With a score of cyclopians bearing down from behind, the halfling could not risk getting tangled in this one's breaking limbs. With a bit of urging, Threadbare cleared the prone cyclopian and thundered on down the road in Riverdancer's wake.

The chase was on, with arrows flying everywhere, and though Oliver's claims about a cyclopian's ability to judge distance were certainly true, the simple rules of chance told both the halfling and Luthien that they were in trouble.

Luthien felt Riverdancer stumble for just a moment and knew that the horse had taken an arrow in the rump. Another bolt came dangerously close, nicking the young man's shoulder.

"Off the road?" Luthien cried out, wondering if he and Oliver should take to the high wheat stalks for cover. Oliver shook his head, though.

Horses, even a pony such as Threadbare, could outrun ponypigs on clear ground, but the grunting cyclopian mounts could plow through brush faster than any creature. Besides, the halfling pointed out to Luthien, wheat stalks on both sides of the road were already whipping violently as more cyclopians joined in the chase.

"This merchant-type," Oliver called out, "he really cannot take a joke!"

Luthien had no time to respond, seeing a cyclopian coming out of the tall wheat ahead on his side of the road. He ducked low along Riverdancer's muscled neck and urged the horse forward. Riverdancer lowered his head, too, and gave a short burst of speed. Luthien felt the wind of a waving sword, but he was by the cyclopian too fast for the brute to score a hit.

Then the young man let up a bit and allowed Oliver to catch up beside him. They were in this together, Luthien decided, but he didn't see how either one of them was going to get out of it. More cyclopians were coming out onto the road ahead, and any delay at all would allow those behind the companions to overtake them.

Luthien looked over at Oliver—and nearly laughed aloud, seeing an arrow sticking through the halfling's great hat.

"Farewell!" the young Bedwyr cried, to which Oliver only smiled.

But both of them gawked when they looked ahead once again, for a translucent field of shimmering blue light had appeared on the road before them. Both the halfling and Luthien cried out in surprise and terror, thinking this some sort of devilish cyclopian magic, and tried to turn their mounts aside. Oliver plucked his great hat from his head and held it over his face.

They were too close, their momentum too great, and Riverdancer, and then Threadbare, plunged into the light.

All the world changed.

They were in a corridor of light now, everything appearing dreamlike to Luthien, as though he and Oliver were moving in slow motion. But when the young man looked at the world around or the ground below, he saw that he was moving at tremendous speed—every one of Riverdancer's slow-moving strides took him across great distances.

The corridor of light veered off the road, turning south across the wheat fields, though the passing of the two mounts did not disturb the grain. It was as if they were running in the air, or on a cushion of light, not touching the ground at all, and their mounts' hooves made not a sound. They came upon a wide river and moved across it, above it, without a splash. In a few seconds, the mountains loomed much closer, and then they were speeding up the slopes, crossing ravines as though the great valleys were but cracks in a stone.

A sheer cliff loomed ahead of them suddenly, and Luthien cried out again, though his words were lost behind him as they left his mouth. Straight up the cliff Riverdancer and Threadbare ran, cresting its top a thousand feet up and running across the broken boulder-strewn ground, through a copse of small trees too tightly packed for any horse to pass. Yet they did pass—without shaking a twig or leaf.

Soon Luthien saw another cliff face looming before them, and the light tunnel seemed to end there, with swirling patterns of blue and green dancing on the cliff wall. Before Luthien could even react, Riverdancer crossed into the stone.

Luthien felt the pressure building all about him: an uncomfortable, suffocating feeling. He could not cry out, could not even draw breath in that supremely enclosed place, and he thought he would surely perish.

But then, suddenly and without warning, Riverdancer came through the other side of the rock wall, stepping lightly into a torchlit cave, the horse's hooves clacking loudly on the hard stone.

Threadbare came out right behind, slowed and stopped beside the white horse, and Oliver, after a moment, dared to lower his great hat from his face and look around. He looked behind, too, staring incredulously at the stone wall as the swirling glow dissipated. The halfling turned to Luthien, who seemed as if he was about to speak.

"I do not even want to know," Oliver assured the young man.

CHAPTER 9

BRIND'AMOUR

IT APPEARED TO BE A NATURAL CAVE, somewhat circular and perhaps thirty feet in diameter. The walls were rough and uneven, and the ceiling dipped and rose to varying heights, but the floor was smooth and fairly level. There was one door, wooden and unremarkable, across the way and to the left of the companions. Next to that stood a wooden table with many parchments, some in silvery tubes, some loose but rolled, and others held flat by strangely sculpted paperweights that resembled little gargoyles. Further to the left stood a singular pedestal with a perfect ball of pure and clear crystal resting atop it.

A chair rested against the wall to the companions' right in front of an immense desk with many shelves and cubbies rising above it. Like the table, it was covered with parchments. A human skull, a twisting treelike candelabra, a chain strung of what looked like preserved cyclopian eyes, and dozens of inkwells, vials, and long, feathery quills completed the image and told both friends beyond any doubt that they had come into a wizard's private chambers.

Both dismounted, and Oliver followed Luthien to have a look at Riverdancer's rump. The young Bedwyr breathed a sincere sigh of relief to learn that the arrow had only grazed his valued horse and had not caused any serious wound.

He nodded to Oliver that the horse was all right, then started off toward the intriguing crystal ball while his halfling companion scampered for the desk. "No mischief," Luthien warned, for he had heard many tales of dangerous wizards in his youth and figured that any magician powerful enough to create the light tunnel that brought them here would not be a wise choice for an enemy.

Luthien's wonderment at the strange turn of events only heightened when he looked into the crystal ball. There he was! And Oliver, too, moving about the cave. He saw Threadbare and Riverdancer standing easily, resting from their long run. At first, Luthien thought it was merely a reflection, but he realized that the perspective was all wrong. He seemed to be looking down upon himself from the ceiling.

Over at the desk, Oliver slipped a vial into his pocket.

"Put it back!" Luthien scolded, seeing the halfling's every move within the crystal ball.

Oliver regarded him curiously—how could he know?

"Put it back," Luthien said again when the halfling made no move. He glared over his shoulder.

"Are you so quick to give up such treasures?" Oliver asked, reluctantly taking the small vial from his pocket and holding it up before his eyes. "The ingredients could be most exotic, you know. This is a wizard's house, after all."

"A wizard who saved us," Luthien reminded the thief.

With a deep sigh, Oliver placed the vial back in its place atop the desk.

"Your gratitude is appreciated," came a voice from right beside Luthien. He stared at the empty spot in amazement, then fell back a step as a pattern of the wall seemed to shift. Out from the stones stepped the wizard, his color at first the exact hue of the stone, but gradually reverting to pale flesh tones.

He was old, as old as Luthien's father at least, but held himself straight and with a grace that impressed the young Bedwyr. His thick and flowing robes were rich blue in color, and his hair and beard were white—snowy white, like Riverdancer's silken coat—and flowing all about his shoulders. His eyes, too, were blue, as deep and rich as the robe, and sparkling with life and wisdom. Crow's feet angled out from their corners—from endless hours of poring over parchments, Luthien figured.

When he finally managed to tear his gaze from the robed man, Luthien looked back to see that Oliver was similarly impressed.

"Who are you?" the halfling asked.

"It is not important."

Oliver plucked his hat from his head, beginning a graceful bow. "I am—"

"Oliver Burrows, who calls himself Oliver deBurrows," the wizard interrupted. "Yes, yes, of course you are, but that, too, is not important." He looked at Luthien, as if expecting the young man to introduce himself, but Luthien just crossed his arms resolutely, even defiantly.

"Your father misses you dearly," the wizard remarked, breaking down Luthien's fabricated defenses with a simple statement.

Oliver skipped up beside Luthien, lending support and needing it as well.

"I have been watching the two of you for some time," the wizard explained, slowly moving past them toward the desk. "You have proven yourselves both resourceful and courageous, just the two characteristics I require."

"For what?" Oliver managed to ask. The wizard turned toward him, hand outstretched, and with a shrug to Luthien, the halfling tossed the repocketed vial to him.

"For what?" Luthien asked immediately, impatiently, not wanting to get sidetracked and wanting to keep the dangerous wizard's mind off of Oliver's trickery.

"Patience, my boy!" the robed man replied lightheartedly, seeming not at all offended by the halfling's attempted theft. He stared at the vial for a moment, then offered a smirk at the halfling.

Oliver sighed and shrugged again, then took a similar vial out of his pocket and tossed it to the wizard.

"I always keep spares," the halfling explained to a confused Luthien.

"Several, it would seem," the wizard said, somewhat sharply, holding his hand out once more.

A third sigh came from Oliver, and this time the proper vial was flipped across the room. With a quick glance, the wizard replaced it on the desk and pocketed Oliver's other vials.

"Now," he said, rubbing his hands together and approaching the pair, "I have a proposition for you."

"In Gascony, we do not take well to wizard-types," Oliver remarked.

The wizard stopped and considered the words. "Well," he replied, "I did save your life."

Luthien started to agree, but Oliver cut him off short.

"Bah!" the halfling snorted. "They were only one-eyes. Those we could not outrun would have felt the very wicked sting of my rapier blade!"

The wizard gave Luthien a skeptical look; the young man had no reply.

"Very well," said the wizard. He motioned to the wall and the swirling blue light began anew. "On your mounts, then. It has only been a minute or two. The cyclopians will likely still be about."

Luthien scowled at Oliver, and when the halfling shrugged in defeat, the wizard smiled and dispelled the magical portal.

"I was only bargaining for the best price," the halfling explained in a whisper.

"Price?" balked the wizard. "I just plucked you from certain doom!" He shook his head and sighed. "Very well, then," he said after a moment of thought. "If that is not enough for your service, I will give to you passes into Montfort and information that might keep you alive once you get there. Also, I think that I might be able to convince this merchant you robbed that his continued pursuit of you would not be worth the trouble. And the favor I ask, though undoubtedly dangerous, will not take so long."

"Explain it," Luthien said firmly.

"Over dinner, of course," the wizard replied, motioning to the wooden door.

Oliver rubbed his hands—now the man was talking in terms that he could agree to—and turned for the door, but Luthien stood resolute, arms crossed over his chest and jaw firm.

"I'll not dine with one who will not give his name," the young Bedwyr insisted.

"More for me," Oliver remarked.

"It is not important," the wizard said again.

Luthien didn't blink.

The wizard moved to stand right before him, staring him in the eyes, neither man blinking. "Brind'Amour," the robed man said, and the gravity of his tone made Luthien wonder if he should know that name.

"And I am Luthien Bedwyr," the young man replied evenly, his eyes staring intently as if daring the wizard to interrupt.

Brind'Amour did not, though, allowing the young man the honor of a proper introduction.

The table in the adjoining room was simply spectacular, set for three, including one place with a higher chair.

"We were expected," Oliver remarked dryly, but as he aproached the table and saw the display set out, he had no further demeaning comments. Fine silverware and crystal goblets, cloth napkins, and plates fine and smooth were set and ready for the meal. Oliver was, too, judging from the way he hustled over and hopped up into the high seat.

Brind'Amour moved to the side of the room, an artificial chamber with bricked walls, very different from the one they had left behind. He opened several secret cupboards, their doors blending perfectly with the bricks, and brought out the courses—roasted duck and several exotic vegetables, fine wine, and clear, cold water.

"Surely a wizard could have conjured a servant," Luthien remarked after he had taken his seat, "or clapped his hands and let the plates float across to the table."

Brind'Amour chuckled at the notion. "I may have need of my powers later this day," he explained. "The use of magical energy is taxing, I assure you, and it would be a pity indeed if our quest failed because I was too lazy to walk over and bring out the food!"

Luthien let the explanation go at that. He was hungry, and besides, he realized that any important conversation he might now hold with Brind'Amour would only have to be repeated for Oliver's sake. The halfling was practically buried in a bowl of turnips at the moment.

By the time he lifted his glass of wine for a final sip, Luthien had to admit that Brind'Amour had set the finest table he had ever known.

"Perhaps we in Gascony should give another look to our wizard-types," Oliver remarked, patting his fattened belly in whole-hearted agreement with Luthien's thoughts.

"Yes, you could appoint them chefs in every town," Brind'Amour replied with good-hearted sarcasm. "What else would a wizard have to do?" he asked of Luthien, trying to draw the young Bedwyr into the casual conversation.

Luthien nodded but remained distant from the banter as Oliver and Brind'Amour went back and forth, with Oliver recounting the tale of an adventure he had experienced in a wizard's tower, and Brind'Amour adding some detail to Oliver's descriptions and generally nodding and gasping at the appropriately polite places. Now that the meal was done and the formal introductions were at their end, Luthien was anxious to focus on the task at hand. Brind'Amour had saved them from the cyclopians, and passes to Montfort (the last chance he figured he might have of ever catching up with Ethan), as well as getting that merchant off their backs, was a reward the young man could not ignore.

"You mentioned a task," Luthien was finally able to interject. The ease of the conversation disappeared in the blink of a halfling's eye. "Over dinner, I believe you said, but now dinner is over."

"I did not think that I could get my words in above the clamor of an eager halfling guest," Brind'Amour said with a strained smile.

"Oliver is done," the stern and determined Luthien remarked.

Brind'Amour sat back in his chair. He clapped his hands and a long-stemmed pipe floated out of a cubby, lighting as it approached the man, then settling gently into his waiting hand. Luthien understood that the magical display was for his benefit, a subtle reminder that Brind'Amour was in control here.

"I have lost something," the wizard said after several long draws on the pipe. "Something very valuable to me."

"I do not have it," Oliver remarked, clapping his hands.

Brind'Amour gave him a friendly gaze. "I know where it is," he explained.

"Then it is not lost." This time, the halfling's humor did not evoke any appreciative response from Brind'Amour or from Luthien. The young Bedwyr could see the pain on the old man's wizened face.

"It is in a great sealed cave complex not so far from here," he said.

"Sealed?" Luthien asked.

"By myself and several companions," Brind'Amour answered, "four hundred years ago, before the Gascons came to the Avonsea Islands, when the name of Bruce MacDonald was still prominent on every tongue in Eriador."

Luthien started to respond, then stopped, stunned by the implications of what he had just heard.

"You should be dead," Oliver remarked, and Luthien scowled fiercely at him.

Brind'Amour took no offense, though. He even nodded his agreement with the halfling. "All of my companions are long buried," he explained. "I live only because I have spent many years in magical stasis." He waved his hands suddenly, wildly, indicating that he needed a change of subject, that they had gotten off the issue at hand.

Luthien could see that the man was plainly uncomfortable.

"The world might be a simpler place if I was dead, Oliver Burrows," Brind'Amour went on. "Of course, then you two would also be dead," he pointedly reminded them, drawing a tip of the hat from Oliver.

"My task for you is simple," the wizard explained. "I have lost something—you are to go to the caves and retrieve it."

"It?" both friends asked together.

The wizard hesitated.

"We must know what we are looking for," Luthien reasoned.

"A staff," Brind'Amour admitted. "My staff. As precious as anything I own."

"Then how did you come to leave it in this cave?" Oliver wondered.

"And why did you seal the cave?" Luthien added.

"I did not leave it in the cave," Brind'Amour replied rather sharply. "It was stolen from me and placed there not so long ago. But that is another story, and one that does not concern you in the least."

"But . . ." Oliver began, but he quieted as soon as Brind'Amour's dangerous scowl settled on him.

"As for the cave, it was sealed to keep its inhabitants from roaming Eriador," the wizard said to Luthien.

"And what were they?" Luthien pressed.

"The king of the cyclopians and his mightiest warriors," Brind'Amour replied evenly. "We feared that he would ally with the Gascons, since we knew that they would soon be on our shores."

Luthien stared hard at the old man, not sure he believed the explanation. Oliver was even more doubtful. Gascons hated cyclopians more than did Eriadorans, if that was possible, and any potential alliance between the people of the southern kingdom and the one-eyes seemed unlikely at best.

Also, Luthien could not begin to fathom why such extreme measures would have been taken against a race that had been savaged not so long before that. Bruce MacDonald's victory had been complete, bordering on genocide, and as far as the young Bedwyr knew, the cyclopian race hadn't fully recovered to this day.

"Now, with any luck, the cave is uninhabited," Brind'Amour said hopefully, obviously trying to press on past that last point.

"Then why do you not go there and retrieve your so precious staff?" Oliver asked.

"I am old," Brind'Amour replied, "and weak. I cannot hold open the portal from here, my source of power, if I go through the tunnel to that other cave. And so I need your help—help for which you have already been, and will yet be, well paid."

Luthien continued to study the wizard for some time, sensing that what the man had said was not true, or not the whole truth. Still, he had no more specific questions to ask, and Oliver simply sat back in his chair and patted his tummy. They had ridden far that day, fought on the road, and eaten well.

"I offer you now the comfort of warm and soft beds," Brind'Amour promised, sensing the mood. "Rest well. Our business can wait until the morn."

The companions readily accepted, and after a quick check on Threadbare and Riverdancer, who had been put in an empty chamber to the side of the library, they were soon nestled comfortably in featherbeds, and Brind'Amour left them alone.

"Four hundred years old?" Oliver asked Luthien.

"I do not question the words and ways of wizards," Luthien replied.

"But does not this magical stasis intrigue you?"

"No." It was a simple and honest answer. Luthien had been raised among pragmatic and solid fisherfolk and farmers. The only magic prominent at all on Bedwydrin were the herbs of healing women and premonitions of weather conditions offered to the captains of fishing boats by the dock seers. Even those two rather benign magic-using groups made Luthien uncomfortable—a man like Brind'Amour put the young man totally out of his element.

"And I do not understand why a cave holding nothing more than a cyclopian—"

Luthien cut Oliver off with a wave of his hand.

"And who would steal a wizard's staff?" Oliver put in quickly, before Luthien waved his words away once more.

"Let us just be done with this task and be on with our—" Luthien began, and then he paused at an obvious impasse.

"With our what?" Oliver prompted, and wondered, and young Luthien wondered, too.

What would he and Oliver Burrows, who called himself Oliver deBurrows, get on with? Their quest? Their lives? The road to continued thievery and, perhaps, worse?

The young Bedwyr had no answers—either for what would come, or for what had just passed. Ever since the arrival of Viscount Aubrey and his entourage in Dun Varna, Luthien's world had been turned upside down. He had left Dun Varna in search of his brother, but now he was beginning to get a feel of just how big the world truly was. Over the last couple of days, Oliver had explained to him that ships left the Avonsea Islands for Gascony by a dozen different ports, from Carlisle on the Stratton River to Montfort. And Gascony was a bigger place than Avon, Oliver assured his unworldly companion, with hundreds of cities larger than Dun Varna and scores larger even than Carlisle. And Duree, the land of the war Ethan was supposedly going off to fight, was over a thousand miles south of Gascony's northern coast.

A thousand miles!

How could Luthien hope to catch up to Ethan when he didn't know what course his brother might take?

Luthien never answered Oliver's question, and the halfling, soon snoring contentedly, didn't seem anxious to know.

CHAPTER 10

WHITE LIES?

THE FIRST THING THAT OLIVER and Luthien noticed when they exited Brind'Amour's new magical tunnel was that the cave they had entered was uncomfortably warm. And it was huge. Luthien's torch reflected off of one wall only, the one they had exited, and the two could barely see the crystalline glimmer of the sharp-tipped, long stalactites hanging ominously far above their heads.

There came a flash from behind them, and they turned to see Brind'Amour's portal beginning to shrink. At first, the two scrambled for the light, thinking the wizard meant to desert them. The swirl continued, diminished to the size of a fist, but its light was no less intense.

"He only wishes to make sure that no cyclopians, if they live, could come through," a relieved Oliver remarked.

"Or to make sure that we do not come through until we have found the staff," Luthien added. "He has that crystal ball and will watch our every move."

Luthien moved over to the wall again as he spoke, studying its curious texture. He hadn't been in many caves—only the wizard's and the sea caves along the rocky coast near Dun Varna—but still, this one seemed somehow strange to him. The rock of the walls was coppery in color and rough, as Luthien would expect, but interwoven with it were lines of a darker hue, smooth to the touch.

"Melted ore," Oliver explained, coming to join him. The halfling looked up and all around. "Copper, I would guess. Separated from the stone by some very large heat."

Luthien, too, studied the area. "This must be where the wizards sealed the cave," he decided. "Perhaps they used magical fires to create the avalanche." It seemed to be as much a question as a statement.

"That must be it," Oliver agreed, but he, too, did not sound convinced. He tapped the stone gently with the pommel of his main gauche, trying to gauge its density. From what he could tell, the wall was very thick. That, in turn, led him to the conclusion that something on this side of the wall had caused the heat, but he kept his thoughts private.

"Come along," the halfling muttered. "I do not wish to be in here any longer than is necessary." He paused and looked at Luthien, who was still studying the melted ore, and got the feeling that the intelligent young man's reasoning was following the same trail as had his own. "Not with so many fattened purses awaiting my eager grasp in Montfort," he added a bit too loudly, for echoes came back at him from several directions. His words took Luthien's thoughts from the wall, though, as he had hoped.

No sense in worrying, Oliver believed.

The floor was uneven and dotted by rows of stalagmites, many taller than Luthien. Even though this area was a single chamber, at times it seemed to the two as if they were walking along narrow corridors. Shadows from Luthien's flickering torch surrounded them ominously, keeping them tense, continually glancing from side to side.

They came to a steeply sloping area, and in the open area below they could see that a path had been made through the stalagmites—trampled, it seemed, with great hunks of broken stone scattered all about.

"The traveling will be easier," Luthien remarked hopefully. He gingerly started down the slope, leaning back so far that he was practically sitting down.

Oliver grabbed him by the shoulder and tugged hard.

"Do you not even wonder what broke those things?" the halfling asked grimly.

It was a question that Luthien preferred not to answer, not even to think about. "Come along," was all that he replied, and he resumed his controlled slide to the lower level.

"Wizard-types," Oliver muttered under his breath, and with a last look back to the now-distant wall and the wizard's portal, he shrugged and followed the young man.

When Oliver stopped his descent and looked up once more, he found Luthien standing very still, staring off to the side, looking over one broken stalagmite.

"What . . ." the halfling started to ask, but he got his answer as he came up beside Luthien. Pieces of skeletons lay broken behind the rocky pile. Both the friends looked about nervously, as if expecting some horrid and powerful monster to rush out and squash them.

"Human," Oliver remarked as he moved over to investigate, holding up a skull that showed two eye sockets. "Not cyclopian."

They pieced together three bodies in all, but only two skulls, for the third had apparently been smashed into a thousand pieces. There was little more than whitened bone, but it didn't seem to either of the companions that these corpses had been here for all that long, certainly not four hundred years. One of the legs, buried under some rock, showed ligaments and pieces of skin, and the clothing, though tattered, was not so rotted.

"We might not be the first group Brind'Amour has sent in search of his staff," Luthien remarked.

"And whatever was in here lives still," Oliver added. He looked around at the toppled stalagmites and the crushed skull. "I do not think cyclopians could have done this," he reasoned. "Not even a cyclopian king."

First the melted ore along the wall, then the line of broken rock mounds, and now this. A sense of dread dropped over the companions. Luthien replayed Brind'Amour's words about the cave in his mind. In light of these new discoveries, it seemed to Luthien that the wizard was indeed lying, or not telling the whole truth.

But what could Luthien and Oliver do now? The portal offered them no escape unless Brind'Amour widened it, and Luthien knew that the wizard would not do that until they had recovered his lost staff.

"If the staff is so valuable, then we should expect to find it among the treasures of whatever rules this place," Luthien said determinedly. "And this trail of rubble should lead us to it."

"How fine," Oliver replied.

The trail soon led them out of the vast chamber and they moved down a wide corridor. Both walls were within the area of torchlight then, and they could see the ceiling as well. That offered them little comfort, though, for whatever had come through this passage had not only flattened stalagmite mounds but had broken short the hanging stalactites, as well.

The air seemed to be growing even warmer in here, and the walls shone a deep crimson. After a few hundred yards, the corridor dipped suddenly, turning almost vertical for a few feet, until it widened into a chamber on a more level but still descending slope. Luthien skidded down first, Oliver coming close behind.

They had come to the banks of an underground pool, its still waters shimmering a dull red and orange in the reflections of the light. The torch seemed much brighter in here, for the walls were lined with quartz and other crystals. Across the pool, the companions could see the entrance to another corridor, running generally along the same direction they had been traveling.

Luthien bent low over the water and reached out his hand slowly, tentatively. He could feel the heat of the rising steam, and he dared to gently touch the pool, retracting his hand immediately.

"Why is it so very hot?" Oliver asked. "We are high up in the mountains—there is snow on peaks not so far from here."

"Are we?" Luthien replied, reminding the halfling that they really didn't know where the wizard's tunnel had led them.

Oliver stared at the lake. It was only a hundred feet across and perhaps twice that wide, but it seemed at that moment to be an impenetrable barrier. Perhaps even the end of the road, for it filled the floor of the chamber, and the halfling, who was not so fond of water in the first place, had no intention of swimming across.

"There is a way around," Luthien noticed. He pointed to the left to a ledge running along the wall about ten feet above the water level.

Oliver did not seem thrilled by the prospect of the narrow ledge. He dropped his traveling pack to the ground and fumbled with its straps, ignoring the questions Luthien put his way. A few moments later, the halfling produced a long, thin, almost translucent cord and a three-pointed grappling hook.

The ceiling was not so high in here, no more than thirty feet in most areas, and it was broken and uneven, full of jags and cracks. Oliver put the grappling hook into a spin at the end of the rope, then sent it flying away, high over the lake. It banged against the ceiling, but found no hold and dropped into the water with a resounding *ka-thunk*.

Luthien stared hard at the halfling as the echoes of the splash died away, neither companion daring to move for several seconds.

"I only thought—" Oliver started to explain.

"Get it back," Luthien interrupted, and Oliver began slowly reeling in the line. It came easily, and Oliver explained that he wanted it up on the ceiling so that he could carry the end as he crossed the ledge—in case one of them slipped, or they were forced to get away quickly.

The reasoning seemed sound to Luthien, and it appeared as if Oliver's errant throw had not done any damage. The rope was still coming easily, and the grappling hook couldn't be very far from shore. Then it stopped suddenly, resisting Oliver's strongest tugs.

Luthien and the halfling looked at each other curiously, then Luthien took hold and pulled, too. The rope held fast seeming as though the grappling hook had snared on something along the lake bottom.

"Cut the line and let us be on our way," Luthien offered, and Oliver, though he prized that fine and light cord and hated to lose any part of it, reluctantly reached for his main gauche.

Suddenly the halfling was jerked forward. He instinctively grabbed the rope in both hands, then, realizing that he could not resist the pull and would be taken into the lake, loosened his grasp. Only Oliver's well-made leather gauntlets saved him from serious rope burns as the cord whipped along. The halfling looked back at the coiled and rapidly diminishing pile and began hopping all about, calling for Luthien to do something.

But what could Luthien do? He braced himself and bent low, as if trying to catch the flying rope, but never took the chance, knowing that he could not possibly break its tremendous momentum.

Oliver had started with over a hundred feet of the cord, and it was nearly gone. But then, without warning, the furious pulling suddenly stopped.

The halfling stopped, too, and stood staring at Luthien and at the cord.

"Big fish in this pond," the halfling remarked.

Luthien had no answer, just stood staring out over the lake as the waters flattened to stillness once more. Finally, the young Bedwyr mustered the nerve to reach down and grab the cord. He pulled gently, taking in the rope hand over hand, expecting it to be pulled away again at any moment.

His surprise (and Oliver's, as well) was complete when the grappling hook appeared, covered with brown and red weeds. Luthien lifted it up and cleaned it so that he and Oliver could inspect it. One of the prongs was bent a bit, but it showed no other marks and no sign of flesh or scales or anything else that might indicate what had taken it.

"Big fish who do not so much like the taste of iron," Oliver said with a halfhearted chuckle. "Let us get to the ledge and along our way."

But now Luthien wasn't so sure of that course. He eyed the ceiling and, seeing a spot where two stalactites were joined, forming an inverted arch, he spun the grappling hook above his head.

"Do not lose my so fine rope!" Oliver protested, but before he finished his thought, Luthien let it fly. The hook soared through the gap and came back down on the other side, and when Luthien pulled the cord taut, the hook stuck firmly.

"Now we can go across," Luthien explained.

Oliver shrugged and let Luthien lead the way.

The path along the edge of the lake took them right to the ledge, and soon they were moving steadily, if slowly, along the ledge, ten feet up from the water. The lake remained quiet for a short while, but then Oliver noticed subtle ripples lapping gently against the base of the stone wall.

"Faster," the halfling whispered, but Luthien was already moving as fast as he could. The ledge was no more than a foot wide in many places, and the wall behind it was uneven, sometimes forcing Luthien to arch his back so that he could slip around thick jags.

A moment later, Oliver's urgency was reaffirmed as the two heard the water lapping harder at the base of the wall, and then a spot perhaps thirty feet out from the wall began to churn and bubble.

"What?" Oliver asked incredulously as a column of water rose half a dozen feet into the air, as though something beneath the surface was displacing a tremendous amount of the lake.

And then it smoothed, or seemed to smooth, until the halfling and Luthien realized that they were staring not at the surface of the lake but rather at the curving shell of a gigantic turtle.

The halfling squeaked, and Luthien tried to pick up the pace as the giant glided in. Its head, with a mouth big enough to swallow poor Oliver whole, lifted high out of the water eyeing the scrambling companions dangerously.

Ten feet from the ledge, the head shot forward suddenly on an impossibly long neck. Oliver cried out again and fell back, poking with his rapier. The turtle missed, biting instead a piece of the ledge, and actually chipping the stone!

The great reptilian body turned to keep pace with the halfling. It came forward again, and Oliver started to dodge, but he was grabbed suddenly as Luthien ran back the other way and scooped him into his strong arms.

The ledge was too narrow for such tactics, but Luthien had no intention of even trying to keep his balance. He leaped off and out, just in front of the rushing turtle head, holding tight to Oliver and holding tight to the rope. The turtle whipped its head to the side, but the angle for the snapping maw was not right, and though the head banged hard against Luthien pushing the companions on, the turtle could not bite down.

"Lucky turtle!" Oliver cried, braver now that he was fast swinging out of the monster's reach. "I would make of you a fine soup, such as we have in Gascony!"

They swung in a wide arc, circling close to where they had first come down to the lake, then onward in a loop that took them all the way to the other side. Luthien was no novice with such rope swings; as a boy on Bedwydrin, he had spent his summers swinging out across the sheltered bays near to Dun Varna. He had wisely grabbed the rope up as high as he could before leaping from the ledge, but still the two would have dipped into the water if they had come near to the spot directly below the grappling hook. Only the momentum inadvertently given to them by the banging turtle head saved them from that fate, and still Luthien had to tuck his feet up to keep them clear.

As they rose on the backswing, Luthien slid a bit down the cord, extending their range. He had to let go altogether, taking a screaming Oliver with him, as they fell the dozen feet to splash into the shallow waters near to the yellowish spongy ground on the lake's opposite shore.

Luthien scrambled up first, grabbing the rope and taking it with him as far as its length would allow. He tripped and almost lost it, instinctively swinging it hard toward a cluster of large rocks. Luck was with the young man, for the rope looped about these rocks enough so that it did not slide back into the water. Luthien regained his footing and his composure and went for the rope as Oliver ran past him toward the back exit.

Luthien skidded to an abrupt halt, though, as the turtle's head came back out of the water not so far away. To the young man's utter amazement, the creature opened wide its maw and breathed out a cloud of steam.

Luthien fell back to the ground, saved only by the surrounding boulders that protected him from the full force of the scalding breath. He came up sweating, his face bright red, and ran toward Oliver, who was signaling frantically from the exit. Into the corridor they ran, pausing just inside to look back toward the water.

The pond was still once more, with no sign of the giant turtle.

"My rope?" Oliver asked, looking at the cord, which was securely looped about the rock.

"On the way out," Luthien replied.

"We may need it."

"Then you go get it."

Oliver looked doubtfully at the cord and at the deceptively quiet lake. "On the way out," he agreed, even though both he and Luthien hoped to find a different way back to the wizard's tunnel.

The halfling's demeanor changed considerably when the two companions had put the lake farther behind them. The going was easier on this side, with the cave floors relatively flat and clear of stalagmites and rubble.

"Now we know what caused the problems to those who came before us," Oliver insisted hopefully, even cheerily "And we have left the beast in a lake behind us."

"A lake that we will have to cross once more," Luthien reminded him.

"Perhaps," Oliver conceded, "perhaps not. Once we have found the wizard-type's most valuable staff, he will come to get us, do not doubt."

"Have you considered that the staff might be in the lake?" Luthien had to ask. He did not think this the time for celebration or that all of the dangers had passed.

Oliver did not answer the pragmatic young man directly. He just began muttering about "lying wizard-types" and scoffing at the notion that this cave had been sealed to entrap a cyclopian king. The quiet tirade went on for many minutes as the friends crossed through several unremarkable chambers and adjoining corridors. Oliver even expanded his grumbling to include "merchant-types," "king-types," and several other types that Luthien had never heard of. The young Bedwyr let the halfling ramble, knowing that he really could do little to stop Oliver's momentum.

But the sight that greeted the two as they entered one large, domelike chamber certainly did.

Oliver stood as if stricken, Luthien, too, as the torchlight was reflected back at them from a pile of gold and silver, gems and jewels, beyond anything either of them had ever seen before. One mound of silver and gold was as high as two tall men, dotted with glittering crystals and precious artifacts—goblets and jeweled serving utensils—probably dwarvish in make. As if in a trance, the two moved into the chamber.

Oliver shook the stunning surprise out of his head and ran toward the pile, stuffing his pockets, tossing coins into the air and climbing around with unbridled glee.

"We have come for something specific," Luthien reminded him, "and we will never get out of here carrying much of this."

Oliver didn't seem to care, and Luthien had to admit that this all seemed too good to pass up. There were no other apparent exits from the room, and they had traveled along the most open and easily accessible trail. It seemed that this was either the turtle's hoard—and the turtle showed no indication of following them—or the hoard of a long-dead king, perhaps the cyclopian Brind'Amour had spoken of. But "duty first," Luthien's father had always told him, and that advice seemed pertinent now with so many obvious distractions lying about.

"The staff, Oliver," he called out once more. "Then you can have your play."

From the top of the largest mound of coins, Oliver, the world's happiest thief, stuck his green-gloved thumbs in his ears, waggled his fingers and stuck out his tongue in Luthien's direction.

Luthien was about to scold him once more, but something caught the young man's attention. He noticed a large cloth sack off to the right of where he was standing, on the lower slope of another of the mounds. Luthien was certain that the sack hadn't been there a moment ago.

He looked up the mound, up to the ceiling above it, searching for some perch from which it might have fallen. Nothing was evident. Luthien was not surprised, for if it had fallen, or slid down the mound of coins, he certainly would have heard the movement. With a shrug, he walked the few feet and bent over the sack. He poked at it with his sword, then hooked the weapon into the drawstring, working it back and forth. Convinced that the sack wasn't trapped, Luthien lay his torch on the pile, grabbed the sack's top and pulled it open.

He found a beautiful crimson cape, richer in color, even in the dim torchlight, than anything the young Bedwyr had ever seen. With it was a rectangular piece of wood: two sticks side by side, curving at the ends in opposite directions. As soon as be took the piece out and saw that it was hinged, Luthien recognized it as a bow. He unfolded it, aligned the pieces, and found a pin hanging from a string on it that settled into a central notch and secured the weapon. A small compartment on one end concealed the bowstring of fine and strong gut.

Luthien drew out the silken cape and draped it around his shoulders, even putting up the hood. He picked the sack up next, inspecting it carefully to see if it held any more remarkable items.

It was truly empty, but Luthien then noticed a quiver beneath it, small and sleek and on a belt that would indicate it should be worn on the hip, not on the back. It contained only a handful of arrows. There was one more longer arrow lying next to it, a curious sight indeed, for the last few inches of the shaft, just below the small head, were cylindrical and nearly as thick as Luthien's forearm. Surprisingly, the arrow still seemed somewhat balanced when Luthien picked it up. He studied it more closely and found that the notched end, near the fletching, was metallic, not wood, a counterbalance to the thick end near to the tip. Even with its balance, though, Luthien doubted that he could shoot the weighty and less-than-sleek arrow very far.

"You mean this very same wizard-type's staff?" he heard Oliver shout out, drawing him from his contemplations. "Luthien?"

Luthien pushed back the cape's hood and rushed to the large mound as Oliver slid the oaken staff down its side.

"Ah, there you are," the halfling remarked. He eyed Luthien suspiciously. The young Bedwyr put one arm on his hip, held the strange bow in the other and posed in the new cloak.

Oliver held his hands up, not knowing what he should say. "Now I might play," he replied instead, and he skittered down to the floor some distance to Luthien's left.

Oliver stopped abruptly, staring down at the floor, caught by what appeared to be the shadows of a group of men, their arms held up in front of them as though warding away some danger. Oliver bent to touch the shadowy images, discovering to his horror that they were comprised of ashes.

"You know," the halfling began, standing straight and looking back at Luthien, "in Gascony we have tales of treasures such as this, and every time, they are accompanied by . . ."

The great mound of silver and gold shifted suddenly and fell apart, coins rattling and bouncing to every part of the large chamber. Oliver and Luthien looked up into the slitted eyes of a very angry dragon.

"Yes," the halfling finished, pointing at the great beast, "that is it."

CHAPTER 11

BALTHAZAR

*L*UTHIEN HAD LIVED HIS LIFE beside the oceans of the great whales, had seen the bodies of giants taken down from the mountains by his father's soldiers, had nearly been bitten apart by the monstrous turtle in the other room. And he, like every other youth in Eriador and Avon, had heard many tales of the dragons and the brave men who slew them. But none of that could have prepared the young Bedwyr for this sight.

The great wyrm slowly uncoiled—was it a hundred feet long?—and rose up on its forelegs, towering over poor Oliver. Its yellow-green eyes shone like beacons, burning with inner fire, and its scales, reddish gold in hue and flecked with many coins and gemstones, which had become embedded during the beast's long sleep, were as solid as a wall of iron. How many weapons did this monster possess? Luthien wondered, awe-stricken. Its claws appeared as though they could rend the stone, its abundant teeth gleamed like ivory, as long as Luthien's sword, and its horns could skewer three men in a line. Luthien had heard tales of a dragon's fiery breath. He knew then what had melted the ore in the walls near where he and Oliver had entered, and knew, too, that it wasn't the turtle that had destroyed those stalagmites. The dragon had been there, four hundred years ago, and had taken out its frustration at being imprisoned.

And now it stood before Oliver, seething with rage.

"YOUR POCKETS BULGE WITH MY JEWELS, LITTLE THIEF!" the beast roared, the sheer strength of its voice blowing Oliver's hat to the back of his head.

Oliver unconsciously dropped his hands into his pockets. He kept his wits enough to slip aside from the ashen remains, away from the one spot in this chamber that was relatively clear of dragon treasure.

Luthien stood open-mouthed, amazed that this reptilian beast had spoken. Of course, the dragons of the ancient tales spoke to the heroes, but Luthien had considered that an embellishment on the part of the tale-teller. To hear such a monster, a giant winged lizard, speaking the language of the land was perhaps the most amazing thing of all.

"WELL?" the beast went on, still looking only at Oliver, as though it hadn't yet even noticed Luthien. "DO YOU NOT WISH TO BEG MIGHTY BALTHAZAR FOR YOUR PITIFUL LIFE?"

"I only wish to stare at the magnificence before me," Oliver replied suddenly. "I came in to find, so I thought, only the treasure, and that was magnificent indeed. So very magnificent."

Luthien could hardly believe that the halfling would make any references to the treasure, especially with so much of it obviously in his pockets. He could hardly believe that Oliver found any voice at all in the face of that wyrm!

"But it was not thoughts of your treasure that brought me here, mighty Balthazar," the halfling went on, trying to appear at ease. "It was to beg sight of you, of course. To let my eyes bask in the magnificence of the legend. You have slept away the centuries—there are not so many dragons about these days."

"IF THERE WERE MORE DRAGONS, THEN THERE WOULD LIKELY BE FEWER THIEVES!" the dragon answered, but Luthien noticed that there was some measure of calm in the monster's voice this time, as though Oliver's compliments were having some minor effect. The young Bedwyr had heard, too, of the vanity of dragons—and by the tales, the greater the dragon, the greater its conceit.

"I must humbly accept your description," Oliver admitted, and began emptying his pockets. Coins and jewels bounced on the floor at his feet. "But I did not know that you were still to be about. I only found a turtle—in a lake not so far away. Not so great a beast, but since I have never seen a dragon, I thought that it might be you."

Luthien's eyes widened, as did the dragon's, and the young man thought the wyrm would snap its serpentine neck forward and swallow the halfling whole.

"You can imagine my great disappointment," Oliver went on, before the wyrm could move to strike. "I had heard so very much about Balthazar, but if that turtle was you, then I did not think you worthy of such a treasure. Now I see my error, of course." The halfling stuck his hand deep into a pocket and produced a large gem, as if to accentuate his point, and calmly tossed it onto the nearest pile of treasure.

Balthazar's head swayed back and forth slowly, as if the beast was unsure of how to react. It stopped the motion briefly and sniffed the air, apparently catching a different scent.

"I do not wish to disturb your treasure and did not wish to disturb your sleep," Oliver said quickly, his facade of calm somewhat stripped away. "I only came to look upon you, that I might view the magnificence of a true dragon once in my—"

"LIAR!" Balthazar boomed, and Luthien's ears hurt from the volume. "LIAR AND THIEF!"

"If you breathe at me, you will surely ruin so very much of your gold!" Oliver cried back, skittering to the coin pile. "Am I worth such a price?"

But Balthazar didn't seem too worried about his treasure. It looked to Luthien as if the reptilian beast was actually smiling. It turned its head to put its huge maw directly in line with the halfling and hunched its armored shoulders so that its neck was partially coiled.

Then the beast straightened suddenly and sniffed again, and its great head snapped about—so quickly that the movement stole the strength from Luthien's knees—and dropped its lamplight vision over the young man.

Luthien stood perfectly still, frozen with the most profound terror he had ever known. This was the fabled dragon-gaze, a spellbinding fear that often fell over those who looked into the eyes of such a beast, but like the tales of a dragon's ability to speak, the young Bedwyr hadn't fully appreciated the notion.

He appreciated it now, though. His mind screamed at him to throw aside his weapons and run away, and truly he wanted to, but his body would not move, could not move.

The dragon looked away, back to Oliver, who was staring in Luthien's direction curiously.

"WHO IS WITH YOU?" the beast demanded.

"Not a one," Oliver answered firmly.

Luthien did not understand what they were talking about—they had both just looked right at him!

"LIAR!" Balthazar growled.

"You have already said that," Oliver replied. "Now, what are we to do? I have given back your treasure and I have gazed upon your magnificence. Are you to eat me, or am I to leave and tell all the world what a most magnificent dragon you truly are?"

The dragon backed off a bit, seeming perplexed.

"They have not seen you in four hundred years," Oliver explained. "The tales of Balthazar grow less, do not doubt. Of course, if I were to be gone from here, I could renew the legends."

Crafty Oliver! Luthien thought, and his admiration for the halfling increased a hundredfold in that moment. The mere fact that Oliver could speak under that terrible gaze impressed Luthien, whose own mouth was still cotton dry from fear.

The dragon issued a long and low growl. It sucked in its breath forcefully, straightening Oliver's hat on his head.

"Ah, ah," the halfling teased, wagging a finger in the air before him. "Do not breathe or you will ruin so very much of your gold and silver co-ins."

Luthien could hardly believe it, but the halfling seemed to have this situation in hand. The young man drew strength from that fact and found that he could move his limbs once more.

But appearances could be deceiving when dealing with dragons. Balthazar was weighing the situation carefully, even considering the halfling's offer to go out and spread anew the legend. Such tales would no doubt inspire others to come to the lair, would-be heroes and treasure seekers. The dragon wondered if that might be the way in which it would at last end its imprisonment and be free to fly about the land once more, feasting on whole villages of men.

In the end, though, lazy Balthazar decided that it really didn't want to have to continually wake up and deal with upstart heroes. And Balthazar had already determined that this foppish halfling was a liar and a thief.

The wyrm's head snapped forward, so quickly and terribly that Luthien cried out, thinking Oliver surely eaten. Up came the bow, Luthien nocking the strange arrow as he raised it.

Worldly Oliver, who had studied fighting tactics in the finest schools of Gascony, including tactics used against legendary beasts, was not caught unawares. He dove forward as the dragon's head came down, drawing his rapier as he rolled. When he regained his feet, he prodded the blade straight up, but sighed resignedly as the slender blade bent nearly in half with no chance of penetrating the dragon's armor.

Up reared Balthazar, swishing its great tail, beating its leathery wings so fiercely that the wind from them halted Oliver's advance. Purple cape flying behind him, the halfling squinted against the onslaught and put his free hand on his hat to hold it in place.

That would have been the end of Oliver deBurrows, taken in the bite of a dragon's mouth, but Luthien let fly the arrow, hoping and praying that it was something special.

It arced for the beast, then was deflected by the tremendous wind and seemed as if it would hit nothing but the floor. It never made it that far, exploding unexpectedly in midair.

Rockets squealed and bursts of multicolored sparkles filled the chamber. Balls of sizzling light whooshed out in wobbling lines, one heading straight for Balthazar's face and forcing the dragon to dodge to the side. A red flare rocketed straight up and blew apart with a tremendous, resounding explosion that shook the chamber, rattled the coins and gems and nearly knocked Luthien from his feet.

Balthazar's protesting roar joined in the echoes and squeals.

Oliver had the presence of mind to run off under that cover, thinking quickly enough to bend and scoop Brind'Amour's oaken staff as he passed it. He ran straight for Luthien and would have run by, but the young man reached out and grabbed the staff, which was nearly twice the stumbling halfling's height.

Oliver cried out as if struck, then opened his eyes wide, realizing that it was only Luthien. He willingly gave over the staff and ran on, grabbing the torch, the young man right beside him.

Balthazar roared again as the two exited the chamber, and loosed a line of fiery breath.

Luthien and Oliver were around the corner in time, but deflected flames licked at their backsides and prodded them along; the stone of the corner crackled and melted away. Luthien couldn't resist the urge to look back and see the bared fury of the mighty dragon. Oliver tugged him along fiercely, suspecting that even the slightest delay would put them right in the middle of Balthazar's next flaming blast.

The rocket fanfare continued in the treasure chamber. Above it, the fleeing companions heard the scraping tumult of the dragon's stubborn pursuit.

"THERE IS NOWHERE TO RUN, THIEVES!" Balthazar roared. The great wyrm entered the corridor, claws digging into the stone so that it could pull its huge mass along and breathing forth its deadly breath once more.

Luthien and Oliver were long gone, down the passage and through the next chamber. Luthien thought of turning with the bow and putting a few shots behind him, but he scowled at his own stupidity, wondering what those little arrows were supposed to do against the likes of the armored dragon. He popped the pin out of the bow instead, folded it, and tucked it into his new belt, near the small quiver.

The companions continued to widen their lead, the dragon's bulk working against it in the narrow corridors, but then they came to the one barrier—the underground pool—where Balthazar would have a tremendous advantage.

Luthien started to the right, toward the ledge, though he knew that they could not possibly get all the way along its narrow length before the dragon caught up to them. He saw that the rope was still on this side, still loosely looped about the boulders, and so he turned and went for that instead.

Rope in one hand, Brind'Amour's staff in the other, he climbed the highest rock he could find and bade Oliver to scramble atop his shoulders.

"You will have to get up higher if you wish to swing across!" the halfling pointed out, and Luthien, looking all about for sight of the turtle, handed the staff to the halfling. The young man reached up as high as he could along the rope's length, bent his knees and tensed his legs.

A roar from the corridor behind them launched Luthien into action. He leaped from the rock as high as he could, scrambled hand over hand to get as high a grip on the rope as possible, and tucked his legs under him as he and Oliver swung out over the pool.

They weren't even near the middle when the drag on the trailing rope slowed them and Luthien's legs splashed into the water. Knowing what was to come, the desperate man climbed, hand over hand, to pull himself out of the hot pool, then kept climbing, remembering the awful reach of the giant turtle.

The weight as they came out of the water halted their swing altogether, and the two began to rotate slowly as the rope untwisted.

"I do not so much like this," Oliver remarked.

"Give me the staff," Luthien replied, and the halfling gladly handed it over, using the opportunity of two free hands to scramble a bit higher on Luthien's shoulders. Oliver was already thinking that if the turtle snapped at Luthien, he might be able to leap atop the thing's back and run toward the far shore, then spring out and swim for his life.

He hated the notion of leaving Luthien behind, though, for he had taken a sincere liking to this brave young human.

Luthien, hooking his ankles around the rope and hanging on with one free hand, unexpectedly began to loop himself about the rope, increasing the swing and nearly dislodging Oliver from his shoulders.

"What are you doing?" the halfling demanded.

"At least this will be safe," Luthien answered, and as he came around, he used the momentum of the swing to aid his throw and hurled Brind'Amour's staff toward the far shore. It skipped off the last few feet of water and settled, floating near the bank.

"I thought you meant to try to use the silly thing!" Oliver protested. He ended with a squeal as a loud roar told him that Balthazar was entering the chamber.

"How would I know how to use a wizard's staff?" Luthien quipped back.

"You would not," came an unexpected answer from the shore. The two hanging companions looked over to see Brind'Amour calmly bending over the water to retrieve his valued item. As the rope rotated, the two then saw Balthazar come up to the other shoreline.

"Caught in line between a wizard and a dragon," Oliver remarked. "This is not my very best day."

Luthien grabbed on tight and tried to steady the rope, looking from one powerful adversary to the other. Balthazar issued a long, low growl at the sight of the wizard, and Luthien did not doubt that the dragon remembered well that day four hundred years before, when Brind'Amour and his cohorts had sealed the cave.

"In Gascony, we have always found wizard-types to be amusing, if a bit benign," Oliver remarked, seeming not so optimistic despite Brind'Amour's appearance.

"Go back to your hole!" Brind'Amour called to the wyrm.

"WITH YOUR BONES!" came the not-surprising reply.

Brind'Amour thrust his staff before him, and crackling bolts of black energy shot out from its end. Luthien and Oliver both cried out, thinking that they would be caught in the barrage, but the wizard's bolts arced around them and sizzled unerringly into the dragon and the stones around the beast.

The dragon roared in protest; rocks exploded, and parts of the ceiling fell in, engulfing Balthazar in a cloud of dust and debris.

"In Gascony, we could be wrong," Oliver admitted, and both he and Luthien dared to hope that Brind'Amour had won the day.

Neither of them had dealt with a dragon before. As soon as the energy was expended, the debris settling to the floor, Balthazar reared up and shook himself free of it, looking more angry than ever but hardly wounded. If he had not been so amazed, Luthien would have let go of the rope and let himself and Oliver splash into the protection of the pool, but he was too entranced to move as Balthazar's great head shot forward and his mouth opened wide, sending out a line of white-hot flames.

Brind'Amour had already enacted his next spell, though, and like a great rolling wave, the water between the companions and the wyrm rose up suddenly in a blocking wall.

Fires hissed in protest and clouds of steam rose about the lake. Hot droplets splattered back from the force of the breath, nipping at Oliver and Luthien, who could only close their eyes and hold on.

It went on for what seemed like minutes, Balthazar's unending breath drawing Brind'Amour's powers out to their limits. When Luthien dared to peek out, it seemed to him as though the watery wall was inevitably thinning. Then it fell flat suddenly, and Luthien thought he was surely doomed.

But ended, too, was the dragon's breath, and Luthien could hardly see the massive wyrm through the cloud of thick steam. He heard splashing, though, as Balthazar steadily advanced.

"What are you doing to my rope?" he heard Oliver gasp. He looked at the halfling, then followed Oliver's incredulous gaze to the water and the loose end of the rope. Luthien's eyes widened as well when he saw the spectacle: Brind'Amour had somehow transformed that end of the rope into a living serpent, which was now swimming toward the far bank and the wizard.

The water then churned under the companions—they had almost forgotten about the turtle!

The snake/rope crawled onto the shore and, following Brind'Amour's frantic directions, looped itself about a rock and began to tighten, pulling the companions up at an angle away from the water and the turtle.

Oliver looked back and nearly fainted dead away, staring into the evil and angry eyes of the dragon not more than a dozen feet away. The halfling tried to speak, but got his lips all tied together, and instead began tapping Luthien frantically on the shoulder.

"HELLO, THIEF AND LIAR," Balthazar said calmly. Luthien didn't have to look back to know that he was about to become lunch.

The dragon jerked suddenly; there came a huge splash from below. Oliver looked down as Balthazar looked down—to see the snapping maw of the turtle tightly clamped on the dragon's great leg.

The rope was taut, then, and Luthien began half crawling, half sliding toward the far shore.

Hot water splashed over the companions as the behemoths battled in the lake. The dragon roared and breathed forth and a new cloud of steam joined the first, and the agonized shriek of the startled and wounded turtle cut the air. Luthien finally let go of the rope altogether as they neared the shore and dropped onto the beach, Oliver still clutched tightly to his back and neck.

"Run on!" Brind'Amour prodded them. The wizard understood that the turtle would not last long against the likes of Balthazar. He looked back to the lake one final time, sent forth another black-crackling bolt of energy, and ran after Luthien. Then he produced a magical light, for Oliver had left the still-burning torch on the far bank.

The three had barely exited the chamber, climbing back into the corridor strewn with broken stalagmites, when they heard Balthazar splash ashore, calling out, "THIEVES!" and "LIARS!"

Now the landscape favored the wyrm, with the three companions having to scramble over and around the tumbled blocks. Luthien finally spotted the fist-sized swirl of blue glowing energy, but he heard the dragon right behind them and did not think he had any chance of making it.

Brind'Amour, chanting wildly, grabbed the young man's shoulder suddenly—Oliver's, as well—and all three took off from the ground, flying, speeding for the wall.

Balthazar roared and loosed another line of flames. Oliver screamed and covered his head, thinking that he would smash into the stone. The lights of the tunnel expanded, as if to catch them, and the dragon's breath was licking again at their backsides as they entered the wizard's tunnel.

CHAPTER 12

TALES FROM BETTER DAYS

SMALL WISPS OF SMOKE ROSE from their clothes as they tumbled back into the wizard's cave, all three in one ball. Brind'Amour, showing surprising agility, extracted himself first and rose laughing.

"Old Balthazar will be steaming about that one for a hundred years!" the wizard roared.

Luthien eyed him, stone-faced, his stern gaze diminishing the wizard's howls to a coughing chuckle.

"Young Bedwyr," Brind'Amour scolded. "Really, you must learn to laugh when the adventure is at its end. Laugh because you are alive, my boy! Laugh because you stole an item from a dragon's hoard . . ."

"More than one," Oliver corrected, producing several gemstones from his seemingly bottomless pockets.

"All the more reason to laugh!" Brind'Amour cried. Oliver began juggling three of the stones, admiring their glitters in the flickering torchlight, and Brind'Amour raised his fist in a salute to the halfling.

Luthien did not crack the slightest hint of a smile. "Balthazar?" he asked.

"Balthazar?" Brind'Amour echoed.

"You called the dragon Balthazar," Luthien explained. "How did you know?"

Brind'Amour seemed uneasy for just a moment, as though he had been caught in a trap. "Why, I watched you through my crystal ball, of course," the wizard replied so suddenly and exuberantly that Luthien knew he was lying. "The dragon named himself—to Oliver, of course."

"He did," Oliver remarked to an obviously unconvinced Luthien.

"You knew the name before the dragon declared it," Luthien pressed grimly. He heard a clinking sound as Oliver stopped his juggling, one gem falling to the stone floor. And Brind'Amour stopped his chuckling, as well, in the blink of an eye. The atmosphere that only a moment ago seemed to Oliver and the wizard to be a victory celebration now loomed thick with tension. It almost appeared to Oliver that Luthien would strike out at Brind'Amour. "Your tale of a cyclopian king was a lie."

Brind'Amour gave a strained smile. "Dear young Luthien Bedwyr," he began solemnly, "if I had told you that a dragon awaited you at the other end of the magical tunnel, would you have gone through?"

"Very good point," Oliver conceded. He looked up at Luthien, hoping that his friend would just let the whole thing go at that.

"We could have been killed," Luthien said evenly. "And you sent us in there, expecting us to die."

Brind'Amour shrugged, seeming unimpressed by that statement. The wizard's casual attitude only spurred Luthien on. A barely perceptible growl escaped the young Bedwyr's lips; his fists were clenched tightly at his sides.

"Luthien," Oliver whispered, trying to bring him back to a rational level. "Luthien."

"Am I to apologize?" Brind'Amour spat suddenly, incredulously, and his unexpected verbal offensive set Luthien back on his heels. "Are you so selfish?"

Now Luthien's face screwed up with confusion, not having any idea of what the wizard might be talking about.

"And do you believe that I would have allowed the two of you to walk into such danger unless there was a very good reason?" Brind'Amour went on, snapping his fingers in the air in front of Luthien's face.

"And your 'very good reason' justifies the lie and is worth the price of our lives?" Luthien snapped back.

"Yes!" Brind'Amour assured him in no uncertain terms. "There are more important things in the world than your safety, dear boy."

Luthien started to react with typical anger, but he caught a faraway look in Brind'Amour's blue eyes that held his response in check.

"Do you not believe that I grieve every day for those men who went in search of my staff before you and did not return?" the wizard asked somberly. A great wash of pity came over Luthien, as if somehow the gravity of the wizard's words had already touched his sensibilities. He looked at Oliver for support, honestly wondering if he had been caught by some sort of enchantment, but the halfling appeared similarly overwhelmed, similarly caught up in the wizard's emotions.

"Do you know from where a wizard gains his power?" the man asked, and Brind'Amour suddenly seemed very old to the companions. Old and weary.

"His staff?" Oliver answered, a perfectly reasonable assumption given the task he and Luthien had just completed.

"No, no," Brind'Amour replied. "A staff is merely a focus for the power, a tool that allows a wizard to concentrate his energies. But those energies," he went on, rubbing his thumb across his fingertips in front of his face as though he could feel the mysterious powers within his hand. "Do you know where they come from?"

Luthien and Oliver exchanged questioning expressions, neither having any answers.

"From the universe!" Brind'Amour cried abruptly, powerfully, moving both of the friends back a step. "From the fires of the sun and the energy of a thunderstorm. From the heavenly bodies, from the heavens themselves!"

"You sound more like a priest," Oliver remarked dryly, but his sarcasm was met with unexpected excitement.

"Exactly!" Brind'Amour replied. "Priests. That is what the ancient brotherhood of wizards considered themselves. The word 'wizard' means no more than 'wise man,' and it is a wise man indeed who can fathom the complete realities of the universe, the physical and the spiritual, for the two are not so far apart. Many priests do not understand the physical. Many of our recent inventors have no sense of the spiritual. But a wizard . . ." His voice trailed away, and his blue eyes sparkled with pride and that faraway look. "A wizard knows both, my boys, and always keeps both in mind. There are spiritual consequences to every physical act, and the physical being has no choice except to follow the course of the soul.

"Who do you think built the great cathedrals?" Brind'Amour asked, referring to the eight massive structures that dotted the islands of Avonsea. Six were in Avon, the largest in Carlisle and a similar one in Princetown. The Isle Baranduine, to the west, had only one, and Eriador had one located in Montfort. Luthien had never been into Montfort, but he had passed by the city along the foothills of the Iron Cross. From that perspective, all the buildings of Montfort (and many were large and impressive), and even the one castle of the city, seemed to be dollhouses of children under the long shadows of the towering spires and huge stone buttresses of the massive cathedral. It was called simply the Ministry, and it was one of the greatest sources of pride for the people of Eriador. Every family, even those of the islands, had an ancestor who had worked on the Ministry, and that heritage inspired Luthien to respond now through gritted teeth:

"The people built them," he answered grimly, as if daring Brind'Amour to argue.

The wizard nodded eagerly.

"In Gascony, too," Oliver promptly put in, not wanting his homeland to be left out of any achievement. The halfling had been to Montfort, though, and he knew that the cathedrals of Gascony, though grand, could not approach the splendor of those on the islands. The Ministry had taken the halfling's breath away, and by all accounts, at least three of the cathedrals south of the Iron Cross were even larger.

Brind'Amour acknowledged the halfling's claims with a nod, then looked back at Luthien. "But who designed them?" he asked. "And who oversaw the work, supervising the many hardy and selfless people? Surely you do not believe that simple farmers and fishermen, noble though they might be, could have designed the flying buttresses and great windows of the cathedrals!"

Luthien took no offense at the wizard's words, in full agreement with the logic. "They were an inspiration," he explained, "from God. Given to his priests—"

"No!" The sharpness of the wizard's tone stopped the young man abruptly. "They were an inspiration of the spirit, from God," Brind'Amour conceded. "But it was the brotherhood of wizards who designed them, not the priests who later, with our profound blessings, inhabited them." The wizard paused and sighed deeply before continuing.

"We were so powerful then," he went on, his tone clearly a lament. "It was not so long after Bruce MacDonald had led the rout of the cyclopians, you see. Our faith was strong, our course straight. Even when the great army of Gascony invaded, we held that course. It saw us through the occupation and eventually forced the Gascons back to their own land." Brind'Amour looked straight at Oliver, not judging the halfling but simply explaining. "Your people could not break our faith in ourselves and in God."

"I was told that we had other business to the south," Oliver replied, "and could not keep so many soldiers in Avonsea."

"Your people had no heart to remain in Avonsea," Brind'Amour said calmly. "There was no point, no gain to Gascony. They could never take Eriador, that much was conceded, and with the disarray in the north . . . Well, let us just agree that your king was having little fun in holding the reins about the spirited Avonsea Islands."

Oliver nodded his concession to the point.

"It is ironic indeed that the greatest canker began to grow during the peace that ensued after the Gascons departed," Brind'Amour said, turning his attention back to Luthien. The young Bedwyr got the distinct feeling that this history lesson was almost exclusively for his benefit.

"Perhaps we were bored," the wizard remarked with a chuckle, "or perhaps the lure of the greater powers prodded us on too far. Wizards had always used minor creatures of the lower planes—bane midges and the lesser demons—as servants, calling on them, with their knowledge of other planes of existence, to find answers to those questions we could not discern from within our earthly mantles. Until that time not so long ago, though, our true powers came from the pure energies: fires and lightning, the cold winds of the northern glaciers and the strength of an ocean swell. But then some in the brotherhood, including our present king, Greensparrow"—he spat the name with obvious disdain—"forged evil pacts with demons of great power. It took many decades for their newfound and ill-gotten powers to come to true fruition, but gradually they drove the goodly wizards, like myself, from their ranks." He ended with a sigh and looked down, seeming thoroughly defeated.

Luthien stared long and hard at Brind'Amour, his thoughts whirling down many newly opened avenues. Nothing Brind'Amour had said to him, up until the last couple of sentences, had gone against the precepts he had been taught as a child, the basis for his entire perception of the world. The news that wizards, not priests, had inspired the great cathedrals was only a minor point. But what Brind'Amour had just said rocked the young man profoundly. Brind'Amour had just accused Luthien's king, the man to whom his father owed fealty, of severe crimes—terrible crimes!

Luthien wanted to lash out at the wizard, punch the lying old man in the face. But he held steady and quiet. He felt Oliver's stare upon him and guessed that the halfling understood his turmoil, but be did not return the look. He could not, at that moment.

"My greatest lament," Brind'Amour said softly—and truly, he seemed sincere—"is that the magnificent cathedrals of Avonsea, the dominant structures of every large city in the land, have become so perverted, have become the houses of Greensparrow's eight dukes, the newest generation of perverted wizards. Even the Ministry, which I, Brind'Amour, as a young man, helped to design."

"How old are you?" Oliver asked, but the wizard seemed not to hear.

"Once they stood as a tribute to man's spirituality and faith, a place of holy celebration," the wizard went on, still eyeing Luthien directly. The weight of his tone dissipated the budding rage in Luthien, forced him to hear the man out. "Now they are no more than gathering places where the tax rolls might be called."

The last statement stung, for it rang of truth. Luthien's father had been called to Montfort on several occasions, and he had spoken of walking into the Ministry not to pray or celebrate God but to explain a discrepancy in the tithe sent to Duke Morkney from Bedwydrin.

"But let that not be your concern," Brind'Amour said, his cheery tone obviously forced, "neither of you!"

The way Brind'Amour made the assertion made Luthien wince. The proud young man had a strange feeling that what Brind'Amour had just told him would make a profound difference in his life, would change the very way he looked at the world. What scared Luthien was that he wasn't yet sure what that meant.

"And you both have earned your freedom from my . . . interference and have earned my friendship, whatever that may be worth." The cloud of pained memories had flown clear of the wizard's face. A wistful look came into his eye as he took a moment to fully regard Luthien.

"That cape fits you well," the wizard remarked.

"I found it in the dragon cave," Luthien started to explain, but he stopped, catching the mischievous twinkle in the wizard's blue eyes and remembering the circumstances under which he had come upon the leather sack. "You put it there," he accused.

"I meant to give it to you after you returned with my staff," Brind'Amour admitted. "I would have hated to lose those items—the cape and the folding bow—to Balthazar, as well! But you see, I held faith in you, in both of you, and I thought you might be able to make use of them where you were."

Oliver cleared his throat loudly, interrupting the conversation and drawing looks from both men. "If you could drop us such toys, then why did you not just get us out of there?" the halfling demanded of Brind'Amour. "I had your staff already—it would have been so much easier."

The wizard looked at Luthien but didn't find much support there, for Oliver's line of reasoning had obviously set off some doubts in the young man's mind. "The enchantment was not potent enough," Brind'Amour stammered, trying to figure out how he might begin to explain. "And I didn't know where you were, exactly, and what you might soon be facing."

"Shooting blind?" Oliver asked both incredulously and suspiciously. "Then your aim, it was not so bad."

Brind'Amour began waving his hands, as if to indicate that the companions simply did not understand. "Of course I was able to locate you with a simple spell, though I didn't know where that was, if you understand what I mean. And then to get the items to you was another spell, a fairly simple transference, but certainly no open gate like the one that got you to the lair and got you back from the lair. No, no."

Oliver and Luthien looked at each other, and after a moment, Oliver gave a shrug. Brind'Amour's explanation was acceptable.

"And what of that strange arrow?" Luthien asked, getting back to the original conversation.

"Harmless, really," Brind'Amour said with a chuckle. "I didn't even intend to put it there—it was merely lying beside the belt quiver and just got caught up in the spell! Those types of arrows are called 'fireworks' and were used for celebrations in the happier days before Greensparrow. I must say, you were very resourceful in putting it to such valuable use."

"I was lucky," Luthien corrected. "I had no idea of what the arrow might do."

"Never underestimate the value of luck," Brind'Amour replied. "Was it anything more than luck that brought you to Oliver in his time of need? If not for that chance happening, would the halfling be alive?"

"I had my rapier blade," Oliver protested, drawing out the weapon and holding it directly in front of his face, its side against his wide nose.

Brind'Amour looked at him skeptically and began to chuckle.

"Oh, you have so wounded me!" Oliver cried.

"No, but the merchant's cyclopians surely would have!" the wizard replied with a hearty laugh, and Oliver, after a moment's thought, nodded and replaced his weapon in its sheath, trying futilely to hide his own chuckles.

Brind'Amour's demeanor changed again, suddenly, as he looked at Luthien. "Do not openly wear that cape," he said seriously.

Luthien looked at the shimmering, crimson material cascading down from his broad shoulders. What was the man talking about? he wondered. He wondered, too, what use a cape would be if it could not be worn.

"It belonged to a thief of some renown," Brind'Amour explained. "The bow, too, was his, and those folding bows are outlawed in Avon, since they are the weapons of underground bands, threats to the throne."

Luthien looked at the cape and the bow and continued to ponder the value of such items. Were these gifts Brind'Amour had given to him, or burdens?

"Just keep them away and keep them safe," Brind'Amour said, as if reading Luthien's thoughts. "You might find a use for them, and then again, you might not. Consider them, then, trinkets to spur your memories of your encounter with a dragon. Few in all the world can claim to have seen such a beast, for those that have are likely dead. And that encounter, too, must remain a secret," Brind'Amour said almost as an afterthought, though he seemed deadly serious.

Luthien nearly choked on the request and turned his continuing incredulous look upon Oliver. The halfling put a finger over his pursed lips, though, and shot Luthien a sly wink. The young Bedwyr got the message that worldly Oliver understood this better than he and would explain it to him later.

They said nothing more about the dragon, the gifts, or even about

Brind'Amour's history lesson for the rest of that evening. Again, the wizard set a fabulous table before the companions and offered them another comfortable night on the soft beds, which they eagerly accepted.

Brind'Amour came to Oliver later that night, woke him and motioned for him to exit the room. "Watch over him," the wizard explained to the sleepy-eyed halfling.

"You expect great things from Luthien Bedwyr," Oliver reasoned.

"I fear for him," Brind'Amour replied, dodging the question. "Just two weeks ago, he fought friendly jousts in the secure arena of his father's protective home. Now he has become an outlaw, a thief and a warrior . . ."

"A murderer?" Oliver remarked, wondering if Brind'Amour thought the correction appropriate.

"He has killed cyclopians—who meant harm to him, or to you," Brind'Amour replied firmly. "A warrior." He looked back to the closed door of Luthien's room, and he seemed to Oliver a concerned parent.

"He has suffered many adventures all at once," Brind'Amour went on. "Has faced a dragon! That might not seem like much to the likes of Oliver deBurrows—"

"Of course not," the halfling interrupted, and since Brind'Amour was not looking at him, he rolled his eyes, nearly gagging on that claim.

"But no doubt it is traumatic to young Luthien," the wizard finished. "Watch over him, Oliver. I beg you. The very foundation of his world has become, or will likely soon become, as loose sand, shifting under his feet."

Oliver put a hand on his hip and leaned back, putting his weight on one foot, the other tapping impatiently on the floor. "You ask much," he remarked when the wizard turned to regard him. "Yet all the gifts you have offered have been to Luthien, not me."

"The pass into Montfort is more valuable to you than to Luthien," Brind'Amour was quick to point out, knowing Oliver's recent history in the city—and knowing the reputation the halfling thief left behind with some fairly influential merchants.

"I do not have to go into Montfort," the halfling replied casually, lifting one hand before his face to inspect his manicured fingernails.

Brind'Amour laughed at him. "So stubborn!" the wizard remarked jovially. "But would this buy the favor?" From a cupboard to the side of the room, the wizard produced a large leather harness. Oliver's eyes widened as he regarded the device. Among the thieves of any city's alleys, it was commonly called a "housebreaker." Links of leather strapping se-

cured it to a burglar, and other straps—and small pouches, in the case of
the more elaborate designs—held many of the tools of the trade.

"This one is special," Brind'Amour assured Oliver. He opened a
pouch on one of the shoulder straps, and from it, though it was much
too small to hold such an item, took out a curious-looking device: a
black, puckered ball affixed to a fine cord. "A cord much finer than the
one you were forced to leave in Balthazar's cave," the wizard explained.
"And this grapnel will secure itself to the smoothest of walls." To demon-
strate, Brind'Amour casually tossed the ball against the nearest wall and
pulled the rope tightly. "It will hold three large men," the wizard assured
Oliver.

"Three quick tugs," Brind'Amour went on, jerking the rope, "will release the hold." Sure enough, on the third pull, the grapnel popped free
of the wall.

Brind'Amour replaced the item and opened another pouch, this one
along the harness's belt strap. He held the housebreaker up close to
Oliver's face so the halfling could look inside.

Oliver gawked and blinked. The area inside the open flap was much
larger than it appeared from the outside—extradimensional, Oliver realized—and within was the most complete set of tools, files and lock
picks, fine wire and even a glass cutter, that Oliver had ever seen.

"Just think about the item you desire," Brind'Amour explained. "It
will come to your waiting grasp."

Oliver did not doubt the wizard's words, but he dearly wanted to see
a demonstration. He held his hand near to the open pouch and silently
mouthed, "Skeleton key," then nearly jumped out of his nightshirt when
a long-handled key appeared suddenly in his hand.

Recovered from the shock, Oliver turned a devious look on
Brind'Amour.

"We have a deal?" the wizard asked, smiling widely.

"I never once thought to walk away from Luthien," Oliver assured the
man.

The next morning, as promised, Brind'Amour produced the passes
into Montfort—valuable items, indeed. When the three entered the
room where Riverdancer and Threadbare had been stabled, they found
Brind'Amour's magic already at work. A glowing door swirled upon the
wall, the tunnel that would place the friends on the road outside of
Montfort.

The farewell was short and friendly, except from Luthien, who remained cautious and suspicious. Brind'Amour accepted the young man's
light handshake and tossed a knowing wink at Oliver.

With his crystal ball, Brind'Amour watched the friends as they exited the magical tunnel and stepped onto the road to Montfort. The wizard would have liked to keep his protective gaze over them at all times. He had taken a great chance by giving the cape and bow to young Luthien, and honestly, he did not know whether faith or simple desperation had guided his actions.

Whatever the reason, Brind'Amour had to leave events to the friends now. He could not emerge from his secret cave, not even look out from it in the direction of Montfort, or anywhere that one of Greensparrow's wizard-dukes might sense his magical gaze and trace the energies to the outlaw wizard.

If King Greensparrow even suspected that Brind'Amour was alive, then doom would surely fall over the wizard, and over Luthien and Oliver as well.

Brind'Amour waved his hand and the crystal ball went dark. The hermit wizard walked slowly out of the chamber and to his bedroom, falling listlessly onto his soft bed. He had set the events into motion, perhaps, but now all that he could do was sit by and wait.

CHAPTER 13

MONTFORT

RIVERDANCER SEEMED TRULY GLAD to be back out on the open road. The shaggy white stallion, coat glistening in the typical morning drizzle, strode powerfully under Luthien. Riverdancer wanted to run, but Luthien kept him in check. The terrain here was more broken than back in the northern fields. They were approaching the foothills of the Iron Cross, and even though they would have the better part of a day's ride to get into Montfort and the rockier mountains, the ground here was strewn with boulders.

"I wish that he had put us closer to the city," Luthien remarked, anxious to see the place. "Though I think Riverdancer could use the run." He patted the horse's muscled flank as he spoke and eased the reins a bit, allowing Riverdancer to spring ahead. Oliver and Threadbare were up beside them again in a moment.

"The wizard, he put us as close as he could," Oliver replied. He noticed Luthien's quizzical look, not unexpected since Oliver was beginning to understand just how sheltered the young Bedwyr truly was. Oliver remembered Brind'Amour's plea to him to watch over Luthien, and he nodded. "Whoever it is that keeps the wizard up in his secret cave is likely in Montfort," he explained.

Luthien thought about it for a moment. "Morkney," he reasoned. Brind'Amour had mentioned that Greensparrow's dukes had been corrupted by demonic powers, as had the king, so the reasoning seemed logical enough.

"Or one of his captains," Oliver agreed.

"Then I should not complain," Luthien said. "Brind'Amour proved a fine friend, and I forgive him his lie about the dragon cave in full—he did come to us in our time of need, after all."

Oliver shrugged in halfhearted agreement. "If he had come sooner, then we might have enjoyed the spoils of a dragon's treasure," the halfling said, and he sighed profoundly at that thought.

"We got our gifts," Luthien replied and patted his saddlebags. He chuckled as he said it, for a cape and folding bow, in truth, did not seem like much of a reward for invading a dragon's lair. But Oliver did not share the young man's mirth, and Luthien was surprised when he looked upon the halfling's cherubic face to see a most serious expression there.

"Do not underestimate that which you have been given," the halfling said solemnly.

"I have never seen such a bow," Luthien began.

"Not the bow," Oliver interjected. "It is valuable enough, do not doubt. But that which I speak of, that which was the greatest gift, was the crimson cape."

Luthien looked at him doubtfully, then looked at his saddlebags as though he expected the cape to slip out and rise up in defense of itself. Truly it was a beautiful cape, its crimson coloring so rich that it invited the eye into its depths and shimmered in the slightest light as though it was alive.

"You do not know, do you?" Oliver asked, and Luthien's expression went from doubtful to curious.

"Did you notice anything so very strange about the dragon's reaction toward you when we were in the treasure cave?" Oliver asked slyly. "And about my own reaction when you met me on the hasty flanking maneuver?"

Hasty flanking maneuver? Luthien pondered for just an instant, but then he realized that to be Oliver's way of saying "desperate retreat." Indeed, Luthien had given some thought to the matter of the halfling's question. In the treasure cave, the dragon had ignored him—even seemed as if it hadn't noticed that Oliver had a companion.

"A dragon's eyes, they are finer than an eagle's," Oliver remarked.

"He never noticed me," Luthien said, knowing that to be the answer Oliver was looking for, though Luthien didn't think as much of that fact as Oliver obviously did.

"Because of the cape," Oliver explained. Luthien was shaking his head before the expected response even came forth.

"But it is true!" Oliver told him. "I, too, did not see you, and almost ran over you."

"You were intent on the dragon behind you," Luthien rationalized. "And Balthazar was intent on you, especially since your pockets were so stuffed with his treasures!"

"But I did not see you even before we found the dragon," Oliver protested. Now Luthien looked at him with more concern.

"When I first found the staff, I turned about and called down to you," Oliver went on. "I thought you had left or gone behind one of the piles, and only when you pulled back your hood was I able to see you."

"A trick of the light," Luthien replied, but now it was Oliver who was shaking his head.

"The cape is red, but the floor behind you was gray stone and gold co-ins."

Luthien looked back at the saddlebags once more and rubbed his hand across his stubbly chin.

"I have heard of such items," Oliver said. "You will find the cape a handy tool in the streets of Montfort."

"It is the tool of a thief," Luthien said disdainfully.

"And you are a thief," Oliver reminded him.

Luthien held his next thoughts silent. Was he a thief? And if not, what exactly was he, and why was he riding along the road into Montfort beside Oliver deBurrows? The young Bedwyr laughed aloud, preferring that reaction to having to face up to his course thus far. Events had taken him, not the other way around; if Oliver deBurrows called him a thief then who was he to argue?

Montfort came into sight around the next bend, nestled among the rocky cliffs and outcroppings of the northern slopes of the Iron Cross. The companions saw many buildings set in straight rows along the slopes of the foothills and spreading down into the valley, but most of all, they saw the Ministry.

It seemed more a part of the majestic mountains than a man-made creation, as though the hand of God had squared and shaped the stone.

Two square-topped towers, each rising more than a hundred feet into the air, flanked the front of the building, and a much taller spire was centered on the back. Huge, arching buttresses lined the sides from the peaked roof to the rows of smaller steeples, accepting the tremendous weight of the stone and channeling it to the ground. Stone gargoyles leaned out from every side of these smaller towers to leer at passersby, and great colored windows depicted a myriad of scenes and free-flowing designs.

Even from this distance, Luthien was overwhelmed by it all, but his spirits never lifted from the ground as he recalled Brind'Amour's lament about the present purpose of the cathedrals. Again the young Bedwyr felt the foundation of his life shifting underneath him, and he almost expected the ground to crack open and drop him into a horrific abyss.

Like most towns near to the wild Iron Cross, Montfort was surrounded by two walls both manned by many grim-faced cyclopians. Two came down to the gate to meet Oliver and Luthien. At first, they seemed suspicious and clutched their weapons tightly, particularly when they glanced upon the outrageous halfling. Luthien expected to be turned away, at the very least, and honestly wouldn't have been surprised if the crossbowmen atop the wall opened fire.

One of the cyclopians moved toward Riverdancer's saddlebags, and Luthien held his breath.

"You have no cause!" Oliver protested firmly.

Luthien glanced at the halfling in disbelief. Certainly he and Oliver might find some trouble if the cyclopian found the folded bow, but that trouble could not compare to the potential repercussions of Oliver's boldness.

The other cyclopian eyed the halfling dangerously and took a step toward him, and was met by Oliver's hand thrusting forward the wizard-forged passes. The cyclopian opened the parchment and looked at it carefully. (Luthien knew that the brute couldn't read it, though, particularly since the pass was upside down at the time.) Still, the cyclopian's expression brightened considerably, and it called its companion to its side.

This cyclopian was smarter, even turned the parchment right-side up after a moment's thought. But the cyclopian's expression, like that of its companion, was soon beaming. The brute looked up to the wall and waved the crossbowmen away, and seemed almost thrilled to let the two riders enter Montfort—the two cyclopians even bowed low as Luthien and Oliver rode past them!

"Oh, this wizard-type, he is very good!" Oliver laughed when they had put the gate behind them. "Very good!"

Luthien did not reply, too entranced by the sheer enormity of Montfort. The largest city the young Bedwyr had ever been in was Dun Varna, and he saw now that Dun Varna could fit into Montfort twenty times over.

"How many people?" he numbly asked Oliver.

"Twenty thousand, perhaps," the halfling replied, and from his tone, Luthien gathered that Oliver was not so impressed.

Twenty thousand people! All of Isle Bedwydrin, a place of five thousand square miles, boasted barely more than a quarter of that. The sheer enormity of Montfort, and the way people were jammed in so tightly together, stunned the young man, and made him more than a little uncomfortable.

"You will get used to it," Oliver assured him, apparently sensing his confusion.

From this vantage point, Luthien noticed an inner wall, anchored at one point by the Ministry, ringing the higher section of the city. Montfort, flanked by many mines rich in various ores, was a prosperous place, but Luthien could see now that, unlike the communities of Bedwydrin, where the wealth was pretty much evenly divided, Montfort was more like two separate cities. The lower areas consisted of many markets and modest houses and tenements, many no more than shacks. As they walked their mounts along the cobblestone streets, Luthien saw children at play with makeshift toys, swinging broken branches like swords or tying sticks together to roughly resemble a doll. The merchants and craftsmen he saw were a hard-working lot, their backs bent under the weight of toil, their hands sooty and calloused. They were friendly enough, though, and seemingly content, tossing a wave or a smile at the two rather unusual visitors.

Luthien didn't have to go up through the inner wall to imagine the types of people he would meet within its confines. Grand houses peeked over the wall, some with spires soaring up into the sky. He thought of Aubrey and Avonese, and suddenly he had no desire to go up into the higher section at all. What he did notice, though, and it touched him as more than a little curious, was that more guards walked the inner wall than both of the outer walls combined.

The young Bedwyr didn't understand it at that time, but what he was getting was his second taste of a society sharply divided by its economic classes.

Oliver led the way into the shadow of a cliff, Montfort's southeastern section, and to a stable. He knew the hands well there, it seemed to Luthien, and tossed the stablemaster an ample pouch of coins. With no bartering and no exchange of instructions, just a friendly greeting and small conversation, Oliver handed over Threadbare's reins and bade Luthien do the same with Riverdancer. Luthien knew how much Oliver cared for his exceptional, if ugly, pony, and so he held no reservations. Oliver had obviously boarded the pony here before to his complete satisfaction.

"On to the Dwelf," the halfling announced when they departed, Luthien carrying the saddlebags over one shoulder.

"The Dwelf?"

Oliver didn't bother to explain. He led on to a seedier section of town, where the eyes of the waifs in the streets showed a hard edge, and where every door seemed to belong to a tavern, a pawn shop, or a brothel. When Oliver turned toward one of these doors, Luthien understood it to be their destination, and in looking at the sign over the place, he understood the name Oliver had given to it. The painting on the sign depicted a sturdy, muscular dwarf and a Fairborn elf, leaning back to butt, each smiling widely and hoisting drinks—a mug of ale for the dwarf and a goblet, probably of wine, for the elf. "THE DWELF, FINE DRINK AND TALK FOR DWARF AND ELF," the words proclaimed, and underneath them someone had scribbled, "Cyclopians enter at your own risk!"

"Why the Dwelf?" Luthien asked, stopping Oliver short of the door.

Oliver nodded down the street. "What do you see at the other taverns?" he asked.

Luthien didn't understand the point of the question. All the places seemed equally busy. He was about to respond when he realized Oliver's intent: all the patrons at the doors to the other bars were either human or cyclopian.

"But you are neither dwarf nor elf," Luthien reasoned. "Nor am I."

"The Dwelf caters to men as well and, mostly, to all who are not men," Oliver explained.

Again, Luthien had a hard time comprehending that point. While there were few Fairborn and even fewer dwarves on Bedwydrin, they were in no way segregated from the general community. A tavern was a tavern, period.

But Oliver seemed determined, and the halfling certainly knew his way around Montfort better than Luthien, so the young Bedwyr offered no further protests and willingly followed Oliver into the tavern.

He nearly choked as he entered, overwhelmed by a variety of smells, ale and wine and exotic weeds the most prominent among them. Smoke hung thick in the air, making the crowd seem even more ominous to Luthien. He and Oliver picked their way through clusters of tables, most surrounded by groups of huddled men, or huddled dwarves, or huddled elves—there didn't seem to be much mingling between the races. Five cyclopians, silver-and-black uniforms showing them to be Praetorian Guards, sat at one table, laughing loudly and casually tossing out insults to anyone near to them, openly daring someone to make trouble.

All in all, it seemed to Luthien as if the whole place was on the verge of an explosion. He was glad he had his sword with him, and he clutched the saddlebags protectively as he bumped and squeezed his way to the main bar.

Luthien began to better appreciate the allure of this place to some of the nonhumans when he saw that many of the bar stools were higher than normal, with steps leading up to them. Oliver perched himself comfortably on one, easily able to rest his elbows on the polished bar.

"So they have not yet hung you, eh, Tasman," the halfling remarked. The barkeep, a rough-looking, though slender character, turned around and shook his head as he looked upon Oliver, who returned the look with a huge smile and a tip of his great hat.

"Oliver deBurrows," Tasman said, moving over and wiping the bar in front of the halfling. "Back in Montfort so soon? I had thought your previous antics would have kept you away through the winter at least."

"You are forgetting my obvious charms," the halfling replied, none too worriedly.

"And you're forgetting the many enemies you left behind," Tasman retorted. He reached under the bar and produced a bottle of dark liquor and Oliver nodded. "Let's hope that they've also forgotten you," the barkeep said, pouring Oliver a drink.

"If not, then pity them," Oliver replied, lifting his glass as though the words were a toast. "For they will surely feel the sting of my rapier blade!"

Tasman didn't seem to take well to the halfling's cavalier attitude. He shook his head again and stood a glass in front of Luthien, who had retrieved a normal-sized stool to put next to Oliver's.

Luthien put his hand over the mouth of the glass before Tasman could begin to pour. "Just some water, if you please," the young man said politely.

Tasman's steel gray eyes widened. "Water?" he echoed, and Luthien flushed.

"That is what they call light ale on Bedwydrin," Oliver lied, saving his friend some embarrassment.

"Ah," Tasman agreed, though he didn't seem to believe a word of it. He replaced the glass with a flagon topped by the foam of strong ale. Luthien eyed it, and eyed Oliver, and thought the better of protesting.

"I . . . we, will be in need of a room," Oliver said. "Have you any?"

"Your own," Tasman replied sourly.

Oliver smiled widely—he had liked his old place. He reached into a pocket and counted out the appropriate amount of silver coins, then started to hand them over.

"Though I suspect it will need a bit of cleaning up," Tasman added, reaching for the coins, which Oliver promptly retracted.

"The price is the same," Tasman assured him sharply.

"But the work—" Oliver began to protest.

"Is needed because of your own antics!" Tasman finished.

Oliver considered the words for a moment, then nodded as though he really couldn't argue the logic. With a shrug, he extended his arm once more and Tasman reached for the payment.

"Throw in a very fine drink for me and my friend," Oliver said, not letting go.

"Done, and you're drinking them," Tasman agreed. He took the money and moved off to the side.

When Oliver looked back to Luthien, he found the young man eyeing him suspiciously. The halfling let out a profound sigh.

"I was here before," he explained.

"I figured that much," Luthien replied.

Oliver sighed deeply again. "I came here in the late spring on a boat from Gascony," Oliver began. He went on to tell of a "misunderstanding" with some of the locals and explained that he had gone north just a few weeks before in search of honest work. All the while, Tasman stood off to the side, wiping glasses and smirking as he listened to the halfling, but Luthien, who had seen firsthand the reason Oliver, the highway-halfling, had gone north, didn't need Tasman's doubting expression to tell him that Oliver was omitting some very important details and filling in the holes with products of his own imagination.

Luthien didn't mind much, though, for he could guess most of the truth—mainly that Oliver had probably been run out of town by some very angry merchants and had willingly gone north following the cara-vans. As he came to know the halfling, the mystery of Oliver deBurrows was fast diminishing, and he was confident that he would soon be able to piece together a very accurate account of Oliver's last passage through Montfort. No need to press the issue now.

Not that Luthien could have anyway, for Oliver's tale ended abruptly as a shapely woman walked by. Her breasts were rather large and only partially covered by a low-cut, ruffled dress. She returned the halfling's smile warmly.

"You will excuse me," Oliver said to Luthien, never taking his eyes from the woman, "but I must find a place wherein to warm my chilly lips." Off the high stool he slid, and he hit the ground running, cornering the woman a few feet down the bar and climbing back up onto a stool in front of her so that he would be eye-to-eye with her.

Eye-to-chest would have been a better description, a fact that seemed to bother Oliver not at all. "Dear lady," he said dramatically, "my proud heart prompts my dry tongue to speak. Surely you are the most beautiful rose, with the largest . . ." Oliver paused, looking for the words and unconsciously holding his palms out in front of his own chest as he spoke. "Thorns," he said, poetically polite, "with which to pierce my halfling heart."

Tasman chuckled at that one, and Luthien thought the whole scene perfectly ridiculous. Luthien was amazed, though, to find that the woman, nearly twice Oliver's size, seemed sincerely flattered and interested.

"Any woman for that one," Tasman explained, and Luthien noticed sincere admiration in the gruff barkeep's voice. He looked at the man skeptically, to which Tasman only replied, "The challenge, you see."

Luthien did not "see," did not understand at all as he turned back to observe Oliver and the woman talking comfortably. The young Bedwyr had never looked at women in such an objectified way. He thought of Katerin O'Hale and imagined her turning Oliver upside down by his ankles and bouncing his head off the ground a few times for good measure if he had ever approached her in such a bold manner.

But this woman seemed to be enjoying the attention, however shallow, however edged by ulterior motives. Never had Luthien felt so out of place in all his young life. He continued to think of Katerin and all his friends. He wished that he was back in Dun Varna (and not for the first or the last time), beside his friends and his brother—the brother that Luthien was resigning himself to believe he would never see again. He wished that Viscount Aubrey had never come to his world and changed everything.

Luthien turned back to the bar, staring at nothing in particular, and drank down the ale in a single swig. Sensing his discomfort, Tasman, who was not a bad sort, filled the flagon once more and slid it in front of Luthien, then walked away before the man could either decline the drink or offer payment.

Luthien accepted the gift with an appreciative nod. He swung about on the stool, looking back at the crowd: the thugs and rogues, the cyclopians, itching for a fight, and the sturdy dwarfs, who appeared to be more than ready to give them one. Luthien didn't even realize his own movements as his hand slipped to the pommel of his sword.

He felt a slight touch on that arm, and jerked alert to find that a woman had come over and was half sitting, half standing on the stool Oliver had vacated.

"Just into Montfort?" she asked.

Luthien gulped and nodded. Looking at her, he could only think of a cheaper version of Avonese. She was heavily painted and perfumed, her dress cut alluringly low in the front.

"With lots of money, I would bet," she purred, rubbing Luthien's arm, and then the young man began to catch on. He felt suddenly trapped, but he had no idea of how he might get out of this without looking like a fool and insulting the woman.

A yell cut through the din of the crowd, then, silencing all and turning their heads to the side. Luthien didn't even have to look to know that Oliver was somehow involved.

Luthien leaped from his seat and rushed past the lady before she could even turn back to him. He pushed his way through the mob to find Oliver standing tall (for a halfling) before a huge rogue with a dirty face and threadbare clothing, an alley-fighter sporting a metal plate across his knuckles. A couple of friends flanked the man, urging him on. The woman Oliver had been wooing also stood behind the man, inspecting her fingernails and seeming insulted by the whole incident.

"The lady cannot make up her own mind?" Oliver asked casually. Luthien was surprised that the halfling's rapier and main gauche were still tucked securely in their sheaths; if this large and muscular human leaped at him, what defense could the little halfling offer?

"She's mine," the big man declared, and he spat a wad of some chewing weed to the floor between Oliver's widespread feet. Oliver looked down at the mess, then back at the man.

"You do know that if you had hit my shoe, you would have to clean it," Oliver remarked.

Luthien rubbed a hand across his face, stunned by the halfling's stupidity, stunned that Oliver, outnumbered at least three to one, and outweighed at least ten to one, would invite such a lopsided fight.

"You speak as if she was your horse," Oliver went on calmly. To Luthien's amazement, the halfling then spoke past the man to the woman who had been the subject of the whole argument. "Surely you deserve better than this oaf, dear lady," the halfling said, sweeping off his hat as he spoke.

On came the growling man, predictably, but Oliver moved first, stepping into rather than sidestepping the charge and snapping his head forward and down, a head butt that caught the bullish man right between the pumping thighs and stopped him dead in his tracks.

He straightened, his eyes crossed, and he reached down over his flattened crotch with two trembling hands.

"Not thinking of any ladies now, are you?" Oliver taunted.

The man groaned and toppled over, and Oliver slipped to the side. One of the man's companions was there to take his place, though, with dagger drawn. The weapon started forward, only to be intercepted right over Oliver's head by Luthien's sword and thrown out wide. Luthien's free hand struck fast, a straightforward punch that splattered the man's nose and launched him toward the floor.

"Ow!" Luthien cried, flapping his bruised knuckles.

"Have you met my friend?" Oliver asked the downed man.

The remaining thug came forward, also holding a dagger, and Luthien stopped his flapping and readied his sword, thinking that another fight was upon him. Oliver leaped out instead, drawing rapier and main gauche.

The crowd backed away; Luthien noticed the Praetorian Guards looking on with more than a passing interest. If Oliver killed or seriously wounded the man, Luthien realized, he would likely be arrested on the spot.

A gasp arose as the man lunged with the dagger, but Oliver easily dodged, moved aside, and slapped the man on the rump with the side of his rapier. Again the stubborn thug came on, and again Oliver parried and slapped.

The man Luthien had hit was starting to get up again, and Luthien was about to jump in to meet him, but the woman, charmed by Oliver's attention, was there first. She neatly removed one shoe, holding it up protectively in front of her, seeming the lady all the while. Then her visage turned suddenly savage and she launched a barrage of barefooted kicks on the man's face so viciously that he fell back to the ground, squirming and ducking.

That brought cheers from the onlookers.

Oliver continued to toy with the thug for a few passes, then went into a wild routine, his blades dancing every which way, crossing hypnotically and humming as they cut the air. A step and a thrust brought the main gauche against the man's dagger, and a twist of Oliver's wrist sent the weapon spinning free.

Oliver jumped back and lowered his weapons, looking from the stunned thug to the fallen dagger.

"Enough of this!" the halfling shouted suddenly, quieting the whispering and gasping crowd.

"You are thinking that you can get to the weapon," Oliver said to the man, locking stares with him. "Perhaps you are correct." The halfling tapped the brim of his hat with his rapier. "But I warn you, sir, the next time I *disarm* you, you may take the word as a literal description!"

The man looked at the dagger one last time, then rushed away into the crowd, bringing howls of laughter. Oliver bowed gracefully after the performance and replaced his weapons, gingerly stepping by the original rogue, who was still prone and groaning, clutching at his groin.

Many of the dispersing group, particularly the dwarves, chose a path that took them close enough so that they could pat the daring and debonair halfling on the back—salutes that Oliver accepted with a sincere smile.

"Back five minutes and already there's trouble!" Tasman remarked when the halfling and Luthien returned to their seats at the bar. It didn't seem to Luthien, however, that the man was really complaining.

"But sir," Oliver replied, seeming truly wounded, "there was the reputation of a lady to consider."

"Yeah," Tasman agreed. "A lady with large . . . thorns."

"Oh!" the halfling cried dramatically. "You do so wound me!"

Oliver was laughing again when he returned his gaze to Luthien, sitting open-mouthed and amazed by it all.

"You will learn," Oliver remarked.

Luthien wasn't sure if that was a promise or a threat.

CHAPTER 14

THE FIRST JOB

*L*UTHIEN THOUGHT "TINY ALCOVE" the most ridiculous name he had ever heard for a street—until Oliver, leading him through the shabby avenues of dilapidated wooden buildings, turned a corner and announced that they were home. Tiny Alcove was more an alley than a street, barely eight feet wide and shrouded in the shadows of tall buildings whose main entrances were on other fronts.

The two walked down through the gloom of a moonless night, gingerly stepping over the bodies of those drunken men who had not made it to their own doors, or had no doors to call their own. A single street lantern burned in the lane above a broken railing and chipped stairs that led down to an ironbound door. As they passed, Luthien noticed other lights burning within and the huddled shadows of people moving about.

"Thieving guild," Oliver explained in a whisper.

"Were you a member?" Luthien thought the question perfectly reasonable, but the look Oliver gave to him showed that the halfling apparently did not share his feelings.

"I?" Oliver asked imperiously, and he chuckled and walked on, out of the lamplight and into the gloom.

Luthien caught up to him across the lane and four doors down, on the top step of another descending stone stairway that ended in a narrow, but long landing and a wooden door. Oliver paused there for a long, long while, studying the place quietly, stroking his neatly trimmed goatee.

"This was my house," he whispered out of the corner of his mouth.

Luthien did not reply, caught up in the halfling's curious posture. Oliver was tentative, seemed almost afraid.

"We cannot go down there," the halfling announced.

"One must learn to sense these things?" Luthien asked, to which Oliver only smiled and turned, stepping back up to the street level. The halfling stopped abruptly and snapped his fingers, then spun back and whipped his main gauche down the stairs. It hit the door with a loud thump and hung quivering.

Luthien started to ask what the halfling thought he was doing, but the young man was interrupted by a dozen rapid clicking noises, the sound of stone scraping stone, and a sudden hiss. He spun back toward the door, then hopped up next to Oliver as darts ricocheted off the stone stairs. The bottom of the landing burned with a hot fire, and as Luthien stared on in disbelief, a large block of stone slid out from above the doorway, crashing down into the flames.

As though a giant had peeked over the edge of the stairs and puffed out a candle, the flames suddenly disappeared.

"Now we can go down there," Oliver said, and hooked his fingers into his wide belt. "But do watch where you put your feet. The darts were likely poisoned."

"Somebody does not like you," the stunned Luthien remarked, slowly following the halfling.

Oliver grabbed the hilt of the main gauche and gave a great tug, but it did not pull free from the door. "That is only because they never came to know my most charming personality," he explained. He stood straight, hands on hips, and eyed the weapon as though it were a stubborn enemy.

"Too bad you don't have your main gauche," Luthien quipped behind him, seeing his dilemma. "You could disarm the door."

Oliver turned a not appreciative glare on his friend. Luthien reached over the halfling for the stuck dagger, but Oliver slapped his arm away. Before Luthien could protest, Oliver leaped up, grabbed the hilt of the main gauche in both hands, and planted his feet on the door on either side of it.

A heave brought the blade free, and sent Oliver, and Oliver's great hat, flying. He did a backward somersault, landing nimbly on his feet, and caught his hat as he slipped the main gauche back into its scabbard.

"My most charming personality," he announced again, quite pleased with himself, and Luthien, though he hated to admit it to Oliver, was quite pleased as well.

The halfling bowed and swept his arm out toward the door, indicating that Luthien should go first. The young Bedwyr almost fell for it, dipping a similar bow and stepping for the door. He reached for the handle, but then straightened and looked back at Oliver.

"It was your house," he said, stepping to the side.

Oliver brushed his cloak back from his shoulders and boldly strode past Luthien. With a single steadying breath, he yanked the door open. A smell of soot assaulted both the friends, and though the light was practically nonexistent, they could see that the inside wood of the door was blackened. Oliver huffed and took a tentative step over the threshold, then quickly retracted his foot.

A double-bladed pendulum swung past, just inside the door jamb. Its supporting beam creaking, it swung back and forth several times, finally coming to a halt in a vertical position directly centering the door.

"Someone really did not like you," Luthien said again.

"Not true," Oliver quickly replied, and he gave Luthien a mischievous smile. "This trap was my own!" Oliver tipped his hat and gingerly stepped past the pendulum.

Luthien smiled and started to follow, but stopped when he realized the implications of Oliver's game. Oliver had bade him to go first, but the halfling had obviously known about the pendulum trap! Muttering with every step, Luthien entered the apartment.

Oliver was over to the left, fidgeting with an oil lamp. The halfling added some oil and finally got it going, though its glass was gone and its frame had been bent and charred.

Something powerful had hit the place. Every piece of furniture was smashed down and blackened, and the layers of carpets had been burned away to clumps of worthless rags. Smoke hung thickly in the stagnant air, though no traces of any heat remained.

"A magical fireball," Oliver remarked casually. "Or an elvish hot wine."

"Elvish hot wine?"

"A bottle of potent oils," the halfling explained, kicking aside the remains of what looked to have been a chair. "Topped with a lighted rag. So very effective."

Luthien was amazed at how well Oliver seemed to be taking the disaster. Though the light from the battered lamp was dim, it was obvious to Luthien that nothing remained of the place's contents, and obvious, too, that some of those contents had been quite valuable.

"We will find no sleep this night," Oliver said. He opened one of his saddlebags and fished out a plain, less expensive suit of clothing.

"You mean to start cleaning right away?" Luthien asked.

"I do not wish to sleep out in the street," Oliver replied matter-of-factly. And so they went to work.

It took two days of hard labor to clean out the debris and air out the smoke. The friends left periodically during that time, back to the Dwelf for meals, and to the stables to check on their mounts. Each time, they found groups of children hovering about and in their apartment when they returned—curious waifs, half-starved and dirty. Luthien didn't miss the fact that Oliver always brought back a good part of his own meal for them.

Tasman offered them a much-needed bath at the Dwelf that second night, and afterwards, Oliver and Luthien donned their better clothes again and went to the place that they could now rightly call their home.

Bare walls and a rough wooden floor greeted them. Oliver had at least purchased a new lantern, and they had retrieved their bedrolls from the stable.

"Tomorrow night, we begin our furnishing," the halfling announced as he crawled into his bedroll.

"How fare our funds?" Luthien asked, noticing that Oliver's pouches seemed to be getting inevitably smaller.

"Not well," the halfling admitted. "That is why we must begin to-morrow night."

Then Luthien understood, and his expression aptly reflected his dis-appointment. Oliver wasn't planning on *buying* anything. They were to live the lives of thieves from the outset.

"I had planned a burglary on a certain merchant-type's house," the halfling said. "Before events put me out on the road. The merchant-type's guards remain the same, I am sure, and he has not moved his valuables."

Luthien continued to scowl.

Oliver paused and stared at him, the halfling's mouth turning up into a wry smile. "The life does not please you," he stated as much as asked. "You do not think thieving an honorable profession?"

The question seemed ridiculous.

"What do you know of the law?" Oliver asked.

Luthien shrugged as though the answer should have been obvious—at least as far as stealing was concerned. "To take another man's property is against the law," he answered.

"Aha!" the halfling cried. "That is where you are wrong. Sometimes to take another man's property is against the law. Sometimes it is called business."

"And is what you do 'business'?" the young Bedwyr asked sarcastically.

Oliver laughed at him. "What the merchant-types do is business," he replied. "What I do is enforce the law. Do not confuse the law with jus-tice," Oliver reasoned. "Not in the time of King Greensparrow." With that, the halfling rolled over, ending the conversation. Luthien remained awake for some time, considering the words but uneasy nonetheless.

They made their way across the rooftops of the grand houses in Montfort's upper section, Luthien in his cape and Oliver wearing a tight-fitting but pliable black outfit and the harness Brind'Amour had given him underneath his purple cape. Cyclopians, mostly Praetorian Guards, walked every street, and a couple were up on the roofs as well, but Oliver knew the area and guided Luthien safely.

They came to a waist-high ledge, three stories above the street. Oliver smiled wickedly as he peeked over, then he looked back to Luthien and nodded.

Luthien, feeling vulnerable, feeling like a naughty child, glanced around nervously and pulled his crimson cape up higher about his shoulders.

Oliver took the small puckered ball and the fine line out of his shoulder pouch, stringing the cord through his hands as he went. He popped the unusual grapnel against the ledge and pulled the cord tight.

"Be of cheer, my friend," Oliver whispered. "This night, you learn from the master." Over the side went Oliver, slipping silently down the cord. Luthien watched as the halfling stopped in front of a window, opened another pouch, and took out some small instrument that the young man could not discern. He figured out what it was soon enough when Oliver placed it against the window and cut a wide circle, gently popping out the cut piece of glass. With a quick look around, the halfling disappeared into the room.

As soon as the cord came back out, Luthien slipped over the ledge and eased his way down to Oliver's side.

The halfling held a small lamp, its directional beam focused tightly. Luthien's eyes widened as Oliver shifted that light about the room. Though his father was an eorl, and well to do by Bedwydrin standards, Luthien had never seen such a collection! Intricate tapestries lined every wall, thick carpets covered the floor, and a myriad of artifacts—vases, statues, decorative weapons, even a full suit of plate mail armor—littered the large room.

Oliver placed the lamp on the chamber's sole piece of furniture, a huge oaken desk, and rubbed his plump hands together. He began an inspection, using hand signals to Luthien to let him know what was most valuable. The trick of burglary, Oliver had previously explained, was in knowing what to take, both by its value and its size. One could not go running through the streets of Montfort with an open armload of stolen goods!

After a few minutes of inspection, Oliver lifted a handsome vase of blue porcelain trimmed in gold. He looked at Luthien and nodded, then froze in place.

At first, Luthien didn't understand, and then he, too, heard the heavy footsteps coming down the hall.

The friends got to the window together, Luthien inadvertently stepping on the circle of cut glass that Oliver had laid to the side. Both cringed at the sound of the breakage and looked back nervously to the door. The vase still under his arm, Oliver jumped out to the cord and swung to the side.

Luthien had no time. He looked to the door and saw the handle turn—and only then remembered that the lamp was still perched upon the desk! The young man leaped across the room and blew out the flame, then fell back against the wall and stood perfectly still as two cyclopians entered the room.

The brutes sniffed the air as they moved in, milling about curiously. Only their own lantern offered Luthien any hope that they would not detect the smelly wick of the extinguished lamp. One of the brutes actually sat on the desk barely two feet from Luthien.

Luthien held his breath, put his hand to the hilt of his sheathed sword, and nearly drew it out when the cyclopian turned toward him.

Nearly drew it out, but did not, for the brute, though it was obviously looking right at Luthien, did not appear to notice him at all.

"I do like the pictures of cyclopian victories!" the one-eye laughed to its friend, and Luthien realized that he was standing right in front of a tapestry depicting such a scene. But the cyclopian, though it continued to stare, did not seem to notice any incongruity within the picture.

"Come on," the other cyclopian said a moment later. "No one's here. You heard wrong."

The cyclopian on the desk shrugged and hopped to its feet. It started to leave, but glanced back over its shoulder and stopped suddenly.

Peeking out under the cowl of his hood, Luthien realized that, as chance would have it, the brute had spotted the broken glass. The cyclopian slapped its companion hard on the shoulder, and together they ran to the window.

"The roof!" one of them cried, leaning out and looking up. Again Luthien reached for his sword, but his instincts told him to hold back and avoid a fight at any cost.

The cyclopians ran out of the room, and Luthien went for the window—to be met by Oliver, swinging back in. The halfling slipped down and pivoted on the rope, gave three quick tugs on the line, and hauled in the magical grapnel. He started to set it on the windowsill so that they could slip down to the street, but the sound of more approaching footsteps stopped him.

"No time," Luthien remarked, grabbing Oliver's arm.

"I do so hate to have to fight," Oliver replied, cool as always.

Luthien moved back to the wall, pulling Oliver with him. He flattened his back against the tapestry and opened his cape, indicating that his little friend should slip under its camouflage. Oliver found little choice as the door began to open.

Luthien peeked from under the cowl, Oliver from a tiny opening in the folds, as a wiry man in a nightshirt and cap, obviously the merchant, and several more cyclopians, all bearing lanterns, entered the room.

"Damn!" the man spat out as he looked around and spotted the lamp on the desk, the broken window, and the empty pedestal where the vase had been. He went to the desk at once and fit a key into the top drawer, pulling it open, then gave a relieved sigh.

"Well," the man said, his tone changing, "at least all they took was that cheap vase."

Luthien looked under the neck of his cape, and the halfling, glancing up at him, only shrugged.

"They did not take my statue," the merchant went on, obviously relieved, looking at a small figure of a winged man perched upon the desk. He dropped a hand into the drawer and the friends heard the tinkling of jewels. "Or these." The merchant shut the drawer and locked it.

"Conduct a search of the area," the merchant ordered the cyclopians, "and report the theft to the city watch." He looked back over his shoulder and scowled; both Luthien and Oliver held their breath, thinking they had been bagged. "And see to it that the windows are barred!" the man growled angrily.

Then he left, taking the cyclopians with him, even obliging the friends by locking the room's door behind him.

Oliver came out from under the cloak, rubbing his greedy hands. He went right for the desk—the merchant had conveniently left the lamp sitting upon it.

"That drawer is locked," Luthien whispered, coming up beside the halfling as Oliver fumbled with yet another pouch on the harness. The halfling produced several tools and laid them out on the desk.

"You could be wrong!" he announced a moment later, eyeing Luthien proudly as he pulled open the drawer. A pile of jewels awaited them: gem-studded necklaces and bracelets, and several golden rings. Oliver emptied the contents in a flash, stuffing them into a small sack, which he produced from yet another pouch in the incredible harness. The halfling was truly beginning to appreciate the value of Brind'Amour's gifts.

"Do get the statue," he said to Luthien, and he walked across the room and put the vase back where it belonged.

They waited by the window for half the night, until the clamor of rushing cyclopians outside died away. Then Luthien easily swung the grapnel back up to the roof, and away they went.

The light in the room had been dim, and the friends did not notice the most significant mark they had left behind. But the merchant most certainly did, cursing and wailing when he returned the next day to find that his more valuable items had been stolen. In his rage, he picked up the vase Oliver had returned and heaved it across the room, to shatter against the wall beside the desk. The merchant stopped his yelling and stared curiously at the image on the wall.

On the tapestry, where Luthien had first hidden from the cyclopians, loomed the silhouette of a caped man—a crimson-colored shadow somehow indelibly stained upon the images of the tapestry. No amount of washing could remove it; the wizard the merchant later hired only stared at it helplessly after several futile attempts.

The crimson shadow was forever.

CHAPTER 15

THE LETTER

*L*UTHIEN SAT BACK in his comfortable chair, bare feet nestled in the thick fur of an expensive rug. He squirmed his shoulders, crinkled his toes in the soft fur and yawned profoundly. He and Oliver had come in just before dawn from their third excursion into the merchant section this week, and the young man hadn't slept very well, awakened soon after the dawn by the thunderous snoring of his diminutive companion. Luthien had gotten even, though, by putting Oliver's bare foot into a bucket of cold water. His next yawn turned into a smile as he remembered Oliver's profane shouts.

Now Luthien was alone in the apartment; Oliver had gone out this day to find a buyer for a vase they had appropriated three days before. The vase was beautiful, dark blue in color with flecks of gold, and Oliver had wanted to keep it. But Luthien had talked him out of it, reminding him that winter was fast approaching and they would need many supplies to get through comfortably.

Comfortably. The word rang strangely in Luthien's thoughts. He had been in Montfort for just over three weeks, arriving with little besides Riverdancer to call his own. He had come into a burned-out hole in the street that Oliver called an apartment, and truly, after the first day or two of smelling the soot, Luthien had seriously considered leaving the place, and Montfort, altogether. Now looking around at the tapestries on the walls, the thick rugs scattered about, the floor, and the oaken desk and other fine furnishings, Luthien could hardly believe that this was the same apartment.

They had done well and had hit at the wealthy merchants in a frenzy of activity. Here were the spoils of their conquests, taken directly or appropriated in trades with the many fences who frequented Tiny Alcove.

Luthien's smile sank into a frown. As long as he looked at things in the immediate present, or in the recent past, he could maintain that smile, but inevitably, the young and noble Bedwyr had to look farther behind, or farther ahead. He could be happy in the comforts he and Oliver had found, but could not be proud of the way he had come into them. He was Luthien Bedwyr, son of the eorl of Bedwydrin and champion arena warrior.

No, he decided. He was just Luthien, now, the thief in the crimson cape.

Luthien sighed and thought back to the days of his innocence. He longed now for the blindness of sheltered youth, for those days when his biggest worry was a rip in his fishing net. His future had seemed certain then.

Luthien couldn't even bear to look into his future now. Would he be killed in the house of a merchant? Would the thieves guild across the lane grow tired of the antics, or jealous of the reputations, of the two independent rogues? Would he and Oliver be chased out of Montfort, suffering the perils of the road in harsh winter? Oliver had only agreed to sell the vase because it seemed prudent to stock up on winter supplies— and Luthien knew that many of the supplies the halfling would stockpile would be in preparation for the open road. Just in case.

A burst of energy brought the troubled young man from his seat. He moved across the small room to a chair in front of the oaken desk and smoothed the parchment on its top.

"To Gahris, Eorl of Bedwydrin," Luthien read his own writing. Gingerly, the young man sat down and took quill and inkwell from the desk's top drawer.

Dear Father, he wrote. He smirked sarcastically to think that, in the span of a few seconds, he had nearly doubled all the writing on the parchment. He had begun this letter ten days ago, if a scribbled heading could be called a beginning. And now, as then, Luthien sat back in the chair, staring ahead blankly.

What might he tell Gahris? he wondered. That he was a thief? Luthien blew a loud sigh and dipped the quill in the inkwell determinedly.

I am in Montfort. Have taken up with an extraordinary fellow, a Gascon named Oliver deBurrows.

Luthien paused and chuckled again, thinking that he could write four pages just describing Oliver. He looked at the small vial on the desk beside the parchment and realized he didn't have that much ink.

I do not know why I am writing this, actually. It would seem that you and I have very little to say to each other. I wanted you to know that I was all right, and doing quite well.

That last line was true, Luthien realized as he gently blew upon the letter to dry the ink. He did want Gahris to know that he was well.

Again came the smile that dissipated into a frown.

Or perhaps I am not so well, Luthien wrote. *I am troubled, Father, by what I have seen and what I have learned. What is this lie we live? What fealty do we owe to a conquering king and his army of cyclopian dogs?*

Luthien had to pause again. He didn't want to dwell on politics that he hardly understood, despite Brind'Amour's emphatic lessons. When the quill ran again over the rough parchment, Luthien guided it in a direction that he was beginning to know all too well.

You should see the children of Montfort. They scramble about the gutters, seeking scraps or rats, while the wealthy merchants grow wealthier still off the labors of their broken parents.

I am a thief, Father. I AM A THIEF!

Luthien dropped the quill to the desk and stared incredulously at the parchment. He hadn't meant to reveal his profession to Gahris. Certainly not! It had just come out of its own accord, the result of his mounting anger. Luthien grabbed the edge of the parchment and started to move to crumble it. He stopped at once, though, and smoothed it out again, staring at those last words.

I AM A THIEF!

To the young Bedwyr, it was like looking into a clear mirror, an honest mirror of his soul and his troubles. The image did not break him, though, and stubbornly, against his weakness, he picked up the quill, smoothed the parchment again, and continued.

I know there is a terrible wrong in the land. My friend, Brind'Amour, called it a canker, and that description seems fitting, for the rose that was once Eriador is dying before our very eyes. I do not know if King Greensparrow and his dukes are the cause, but I do know, in my heart, that any who would ally himself with cyclopians would favor the canker over the rose.

This infestation, this plague, lies thick behind Montfort's inner wall, and there I go in the shadows of night, to take what little vengeance my pockets will hold!

I have wetted my blade in the blood of cyclopians, but I fear that the plague is deep. I fear for Eriador. I fear for the children.

Luthien sat back again and spent a long while staring at his words. He felt an emptiness in his breast, a general despair. "What little vengeance my pockets will hold," he read aloud, and to Luthien Bedwyr, who thought the world should be different, it seemed a pittance indeed.

He dropped the quill on the desk and started to rise. Then, almost as an afterthought, amply wetted the quill's tip with ink and scratched a thick line across the letter's heading.

"Damn you, Gahris," he whispered, and the words stung him profoundly, bringing moisture into his cinnamon-colored eyes.

Luthien was fast asleep on the comfortable chair when Oliver entered the little apartment. The halfling skipped in gaily, a bag of golden coins tinkling at his belt. He had done well with the vase and was busy now thinking of the many enjoyable ways he might spend the booty.

He moved toward Luthien, thinking to wake the young man that they might get to market before all the best items were bought or stolen, but he noticed the parchment lying flat on the desk and slipped quietly that way instead.

Oliver's smile disappeared as he read the grim words, and the gaze he leveled Luthien's way was sincerely sympathetic.

The halfling sauntered over to stand before the troubled young man, forced a smile once more and woke Luthien by jingling the coins in his face.

"Do open your sleepy eyes," the halfling bade cheerily. "The sun is high and the market awaits!"

Luthien groaned and started to turn over, but Oliver grabbed him by the shoulder and, with surprising strength for one so little, turned him back around. "Do come, my less-than-sprightly friend," Oliver bade. "Already this northern wind carries the bite of winter and we have so many things to buy! I will need at least a dozen more warm coats to be properly attired!"

Luthien peeked out from under one droopy eyelid. A dozen more coats? his mind echoed. What was Oliver talking about?

"A dozen, I say!" the halfling reiterated. "So I might properly choose which among them is most fitting for one of my reputation. The others, *ptooey*," he said with a derisive spit. "The others, I discard to the street."

Luthien's face screwed up with confusion. Why would Oliver throw perfectly fine coats out into the street?

"Come, come," the halfling chattered, moving impatiently toward the door. "We must get to market before all the rotten little children steal away the goods!"

The children. Discard the coats to the street indeed! Oliver would throw them out, where those same children Oliver had just complained about, most of them approximately the halfling's size, might pick them up. Luthien had his answer, and the understanding of Oliver's secret generosity gave him the strength to leap out of his chair.

A new spring in his step, a new and valuable purpose, showed clearly to Oliver as they made their way to Montfort's lower central area, a wide and open plaza, lined by kiosks and some closed tents. Corner performers were abundant, some singing, others playing on exotic instruments, others juggling or performing acrobatics. Luthien kept his hand against his purse whenever he and Oliver passed anywhere near these people—the first lesson Oliver had given him about the market plaza was that almost all of the performers used their acts to cover their true profession.

The market was bustling this bright day. A large trading caravan, the last major one of the year, had come in the previous night, traveling from Avon through Malpuissant's Wall and all the way around the northern spurs of the Iron Cross. Most goods came in through Port Charley, to the west, but with the Baranduine pirates running the straits, the largest and wealthiest of the southern merchant caravans sometimes opted for the longer, but safer, overland route.

The two friends milled about for some time. Oliver stopped to buy a huge bag of hard candies, then stopped again at a clothier's kiosk, admiring the many fur coats. The halfling made an offer on one, half the asking price, but the merchant just scowled at him and reiterated the full price.

The impasse continued for a few minutes, then Oliver threw up his hands, called the merchant a "barbarian," and walked away briskly.

"The price was fair," Luthien remarked, running to catch up with his brightly dressed companion.

"He would not bargain," Oliver replied sourly.

"But the price was already fair," Luthien insisted.

"I know," Oliver said impatiently, looking back at the kiosk. "Barbarian."

Luthien was about to reply, but changed his mind. He had limited experience at the market, but had come to know that most of the goods could be bought at between fifty and seventy-five percent of the obviously inflated asking price. It was a game merchants and buyers played, a bargaining session that, as far as Luthien could tell, was designed to make both parties feel as though they had cheated each other.

At the next stop, another clothier, Oliver and the merchant haggled vigorously over a garment similar to the one the halfling had just passed up. They came to terms and Oliver handed over the money—fully five silver coins more than the other coat had been priced. Luthien thought of pointing this out to Oliver as they walked away with their latest purchase, but considering the halfling's smug smile, he didn't see the point.

And so their morning went: buying, bartering, watching the performers, tossing handfuls of hard candy to the many children running about the crowd. It was truly an unremarkable morning, but one that heightened Luthien's sagging spirits considerably and made him feel that he was doing a bit of good at least.

By the time they were ready to leave, Luthien carried a tremendous sack over his shoulder. Oliver flanked him defensively as they pushed back through the mob, fearing sharp-knived cutpurses. The halfling was turning his head slowly, regarding one such shady-looking character, when he walked headfirst into Luthien's sack. Oliver bounced back and shook his head, then stooped to retrieve his fallen hat. The rogue he had been watching openly laughed, and Oliver thought he might have to go over and inscribe his name on the man's dirty tunic.

"You silly boy," the embarrassed halfling snarled at Luthien. "You must tell me when you mean to stop!" Oliver batted his hat against his hip and continued his scolding until he finally realized that Luthien wasn't even listening to him.

The young Bedwyr's eyes were locked straight ahead in an unblinking stare. Oliver started to ask what he found so enthralling, but following Luthien's line of vision, it wasn't really very hard for the halfling to figure it out.

The lithe woman was beautiful—Oliver could see that despite the threadbare and plain clothes she wore. Her head was bowed as she walked, her long and thick wheat-colored hair cascading down her cheeks and shoulders—was that the tip of a pointed ear that Oliver saw peeking from within its lustrous strands? Huge eyes, bright and compelling green, peeked out from under those tresses and showed an inner strength that belied her obviously low station in life. She was at the head of a merchant's procession, her sharp-featured master a few paces behind her. Oliver thought the man looked remarkably like a buzzard.

Oliver walked up beside his companion and nudged Luthien hard in the side.

Luthien didn't blink, and Oliver sighed, understanding that his friend was fully stricken.

"She is a slave girl," Oliver remarked, trying to draw Luthien's attention. "Probably half-elven. And that merchant-type would not sell her to you for all the gold in Eriador."

"Slave?" Luthien remarked, turning his confused stare upon Oliver as if the concept was foreign to him.

Oliver nodded. "Forget her now," the halfling explained.

Luthien looked back to find that the woman and her procession had disappeared from sight into the crowd.

"Forget her," Oliver said again, but Luthien doubted that to be an option.

The companions went back to their little apartment and dropped off their goods, then, at Oliver's insistence, went to the Dwelf. Luthien's thoughts lingered on the woman, and the implications of his strong feelings, as they sat by the bar in the familiar place.

He thought of Katerin, as well, the love of his youth. "Of my youth," he mumbled under his breath, considering how curious that thought sounded. He had been with Katerin O'Hale just weeks before, but that life, that innocent existence on Bedwydrin, seemed so far removed to him now, seemed another life in another world, a sweet dream lost in the face of harsh reality.

And what of Katerin? he wondered. Surely he had cared for her, perhaps had even loved her. But that love had not fired him, had not set his heart to pounding, as had the mere glimpse of the beautiful slave girl. He couldn't know, of course, whether that fact should be attributed to honest feelings for the slave, or to the general changes that had occurred in Luthien's life, or to the simple fact that he was now living on the edge of catastrophe. Had all of his emotions been so amplified? And if Katerin walked into the Dwelf at that moment, how would Luthien have felt?

He did not know and could no longer follow his own reasoning. All that Luthien understood was the lifting of his heart at the sight of the fair slave, and that was all he truly wanted to understand. He focused his thoughts on that look again, on the bright and huge green eyes peeking out at him from under those luxurious wheat-colored tresses.

Gradually the image faded, and Luthien again considered his present surroundings.

"Many of the Fairborn are held as slaves," Oliver was saying to him. "Especially the half-breeds."

Luthien turned a fierce look upon the halfling, as though Oliver had just insulted his love.

"Half-breeds," the halfling said firmly. "Half elf and half human. They are not so rare."

"And they are held as slaves?" Luthien spat.

Oliver shrugged. "The pure Fairborn do not think highly of them, nor do the humans. But if you wish to cry tears for any race, my naive young friend, then cry for the dwarves. They, not the elves or the half-elves, are the lowest of Avon's hierarchy."

"And where do halflings fit in?" Luthien asked, somewhat nastily.

Oliver ran his hands behind his head, through his long and curly brown hair. "Wherever we choose to fit in, of course," he said, and he snapped his fingers in Luthien's face, then called for Tasman to refill his empty flagon.

Luthien let the discussion go at that and turned his private thoughts back to the woman and to the issue of slavery in general. There were no slaves on Bedwydrin—at least, none that Luthien knew of. All the races were welcomed there, in peace and fairness, except for the cyclopians. And now, with the edicts coming from Carlisle, even the one-eyes could not be turned away from the island's borders. Cyclopians on Bedwydrin would not find themselves welcomed at every door—even keepers of public inns had been known to tell them lies about no open rooms.

But slavery? Luthien found the whole issue thoroughly distasteful, and the thought that the woman he had spied, the beautiful and inno-cent creature who had so stolen his heart with just a glance, was a slave to a merchant filled his throat with a bitterness that no amount of ale could wash down.

Several drinks later, Luthien was still sitting at the bar grumbling openly to himself about injustice and, to Oliver's disdain, vengeance.

Oliver elbowed Luthien hard, spilling the meager remaining contents of the young man's flagon down the front of Luthien's tunic. Fuming, Luthien turned a sharp gaze on his friend, but before he could speak out, Oliver was motioning for him to remain silent, and nodding for him to train his eyes and ears to a discussion going on between two roguish-looking men a few stools down.

"It's the Crimson Shadow, I tell ye!" one of them proclaimed. "'E's back, and Duke Morkney and his thievin' merchants'll get it good, don't ye doubt!"

"How can ye make the claim?" the other rogue asked, waving the no-tion away. "How long do Crimson Shadows live? What say you, Tasman? Me friend 'ere thinks the Crimson Shadow's come back from the dead to haunt Montfort."

"They seen the shadows, I tell ye," the first rogue insisted. "A slave friend told me so! And no wash'll take 'em off, and no paint'll cover 'em!"

"There are whispers," Tasman interjected, wiping down the bar in front of the two slovenly rogues. "And if they are true," he asked the first rogue, "would you think it a good thing?"

"A good thing?" the man slurred incredulously. "Why I'd be glad in-deed to see those fattened piggy merchants get theirs, I would!"

"But wouldn't your own take be less if this Crimson Shadow hits hard at the merchants?" Tasman reasoned. "And won't Duke Morkney place many more guards on the streets of the upper section?"

The rogue sat silent for a moment, considering the implications. "A good thing!" he declared at last. "It's worth the price, I say, if them fatted swine get what's coming to them!" He swung about on his stool, nearly tumbling to the floor, and lifted his spilling flagon high in the air. "To the Crimson Shadow!" he called out loudly, and to Luthien's surprise, at least a dozen flagons came up in the toast.

"A thief of some renown, indeed," Oliver mumbled, remembering Brind'Amour's description when he had given Luthien the cape and bow.

"What are they talking about?" Luthien asked, his senses too dulled to figure it out.

"They are talking of you, silly thief," Oliver said casually, and he drained his flagon and hopped down from his stool. "Come, I must get you back to your bed."

Luthien sat quite still, staring dumbfoundedly at the two rogues, still not quite comprehending what they, or Oliver, were talking about.

He was thinking of the slave girl, then, all the way home, and long after Oliver dropped him onto his cot.

The second rogue, the doubtful one in the discussion of the Crimson Shadow, watched Oliver and Luthien leave the Dwelf with more than a passing interest. He left the tavern soon after, running a circuitous route along the streets to a secret gate in the wall to the upper section.

The cyclopian guards, recognizing the man but obviously not fond of him, watched him suspiciously as he crawled out the other side. He flashed them his merchant seal and ran on.

He had much to report.

CHAPTER 16

THE PERILS OF REPUTATION

"*Y*OU SHOULD BE THINKING of the task at hand," Oliver remarked in uncomplimentary tones as he and Luthien wove their way through the darkened streets toward Montfort's inner wall.

"I do not even think we should be going," Luthien replied. "We have more than enough money . . ."

Oliver spun in front of the young Bedwyr, stopping him with a pointing finger and a vicious scowl. "Never," Oliver said slowly and deliberately. "Never, never say such a stupid thing."

Luthien flashed a disgusted expression and ignored the halfling, but when he tried to continue walking, Oliver grabbed him and held him back.

"Never," Oliver said again.

"When is enough enough?" Luthien asked.

"Bah!" the halfling snorted. "I would steal from the merchant-types until they became pauper-types, giving their riches to the poor. Then I would go to the poor who were no longer poor, and steal the wealth again and give it back to the merchant-types!"

"Then what is the point?" Luthien asked.

"If you were truly a thief, you would not even have to ask," Oliver said, snapping his fingers in Luthien's face, a habit that had become quite regular over the last few days.

"Thank you," Luthien replied without missing a beat, and he forced his way around Oliver.

The halfling stood in the deserted street for some time, shaking his head. Luthien had not been the same since that day a week before in the market. He was thrilled when Oliver had discarded those coats he did not deem appropriate—and the children of Tiny Alcove had fallen upon them like a pack of ravenous wolves—but Luthien's mood had become generally surly, even despondent. He ate little, talked less, and had found an excuse to prevent him from going to the inner section of the city on every occasion Oliver had proposed an excursion.

This time, though, Oliver had insisted, practically dragging Luthien out of the apartment. Oliver understood the turmoil that had come over the proud young Bedwyr, and truthfully, the rapidly growing reputation of the Crimson Shadow added an element of danger to any intended burglaries. Rumors along the seedy streets near Tiny Alcove hinted that many of Montfort's thieves had cut back on activities for a while, at least until the merchants' panic over this Crimson Shadow character died away.

But Oliver knew that it was neither confusion nor fear that held Luthien back. The man was smitten—it was written all over his somber face. Oliver was not coldhearted, considered himself a romantic, even, but business was business. He skittered up beside Luthien.

"If I looked into your ear, I would see an image of a half-elven slave girl," he said, "with hair the color of wheat and the greenest of eyes."

"You aren't big enough to look into my ear," Luthien coldly reminded him.

"I am smart enough so that I do not have to," Oliver quipped in reply. The halfling recognized that this conversation was seriously degenerating, something he did not want with a potentially dangerous job ahead of them, so he jumped out in front again and brought the impatient Luthien to a stop.

"I am not cold to the ways of the heart," the halfling asserted. "I know you are in pain."

Luthien's defenses melted away. "In pain," he whispered, thinking those words a perfect description. Luthien had never known love before, not like this. He could not eat, could not sleep, and all the time his mind was filled, as Oliver had said, with that image of the half-elven woman. A vivid image; Luthien felt as if he had looked into her soul and seen the perfect complement of his own. He was normally a pragmatic sort, and he knew that this was all completely irrational. But for being irrational, it hurt all the more.

"How beautiful is the wildflower from across the field," Oliver said quietly, "peeking at you from the shadows of the tree line. Out of reach. More beautiful than any flower you have held in your hand, it seems."

"And what happens if you cross the field and gather that wildflower into your hand?" Luthien asked.

Oliver shrugged. "As a gentlehalfling, I would not," he replied. "I would appreciate the glimpse of such beauty and hold the ideal in my heart forevermore."

"Coward," Luthien said flatly, and for perhaps the first time since the children had gathered around Oliver's discarded coats, the young Bedwyr flashed a sincere smile.

"Coward?" Oliver replied, feigning a deep wound in his chest. "I, Oliver deBurrows, who am about to go over that wall into the most dangerous section of Montfort to take whatever I please?"

Luthien did not miss Oliver's not-so-subtle reminder that they had more on their agenda this night than a discussion of Luthien's stolen heart. He nodded determinedly to the halfling and the two moved on.

An hour later, the friends managed to find enough of a break in the patrol routes of the plentiful cyclopian guards to get over the wall and up onto a roof in the inner section, along the southern wall under the shadows of great cliffs. They had barely scampered over the lip when yet another patrol came marching into view. Oliver scrambled under Luthien's crimson cape and the young man ducked his face low under the hood.

"So fine a cape," Oliver remarked as the cyclopians moved away, oblivious to the intruders.

Luthien looked about doubtfully. "We should have waited," he whispered, honestly amazed by the number of guards.

"We should be flattered," Oliver corrected. "The merchant-types show us—show the Crimson Shadow—true respect. We cannot leave now and let them down."

Oliver crept along the rooftop. Luthien watched him, thinking perhaps that the impetuous halfling was playing this whole thing too much like a game.

Oliver swung his grapnel across an alley to another roof and secured the line with a slipknot. He waited for Luthien to catch up, looked around to make certain that no other cyclopians were in the area, then crawled across to the other roof. Luthien came next, and Oliver, after some effort, managed to work the rope free.

"There are arrows that bite into stone," the halfling explained as they made their way across another alley. "We must get you some for that bow of yours."

"Do you have any idea of where we are going?" Luthien asked.

Oliver pointed north to a cluster of houses with slanting rooftops. Luthien looked from the halfling to the houses, then back to the halfling, blinking curiously. Always before, the two had hit the southern section. With its flat roofs and the darkness offered by the sheltering mountain walls, it was ideal for burglars. He understood the halfling's reasoning, though; with so many cyclopians in this area, the less accessible houses would not be so heavily guarded.

Still, Luthien could not get rid of a nagging sensation of danger. The less accessible houses were the domains of the richest merchants, even the members of Duke Morkney's extended family. Luthien figured that Oliver knew what he was doing, and so he kept quiet and followed, saying nothing even when the cocky halfling led the way back down to the streets.

The avenues were wide and cobblestoned, but up above them the second stories of the houses were built tightly together. No building fronts were flat, rather they were curving and decorated, with jutting rooms and many alcoves. Teenagers milled about, along with a smattering of cyclopian guards, but between Luthien's cape and the many nooks, the companions had little trouble in avoiding detection.

Oliver paused when they came to one intersection, the side lane marked by a sign that proclaimed it the Avenue of the Artisans. Oliver motioned to Luthien, leading the young man's gaze to a group of cyclopians milling about a block from the intersection and calmly approaching them, apparently in no hurry.

"I'm thinking that tonight we do not go down from a roof," the halfling whispered with a wistful smile, rubbing his eager hands together.

Luthien caught on quickly and eyed the halfling doubtfully. One of the first rules that Oliver had taught him about cat-burglary in Montfort was that the wealthy shops of the inner section were best left alone. The proprietors up here often employed wizards to put up magical wards to watch over their stores. The obvious disinterest of the patrolling cyclopians did lend some hope, but again, that nagging sensation of danger tugged at Luthien.

Oliver grabbed him by the arm and slithered into the avenue. Luthien followed, again trusting the judgment of his more experienced companion. A short while later, the two were standing in the shadows of an alcove between two shops, Oliver admiring the goods displayed in the side panels of their large front windows.

"This one has the more valuable items," the halfling said, speaking more to himself than to Luthien and eyeing the fine china and crystal goblets on display. "But these," he turned about to regard the many pewter figurines and art in the other window, "will be the easier to be rid of."

"And I do so like the statue of the halfling warrior," he remarked. It was obvious that Oliver's mind was made up. He looked all about to make sure that no cyclopians were in the immediate area, then reached under his gray cloak to a pouch on the housebreaker and brought forth the glass cutter.

Luthien stared at the figurine Oliver had noted. It was a fine representation of a halfling in pewter, standing boldly, cape billowing out behind him and sword drawn, its tip to the ground beside bare, hair-topped feet. A fine work indeed, but Luthien couldn't help but notice how it paled compared with the larger, gem-studded statues in the window beside it.

Luthien grabbed Oliver by the arm, just as the halfling placed the glass cutter on the window.

"Who put it there?" Luthien asked.

Oliver looked at him blankly.

"The statue," Luthien explained. "Who put it on such prominent display?"

Oliver looked at him doubtfully, then turned to regard the statue. "The proprietor?" he asked more than stated, wondering why the answer didn't seem obvious to his companion.

"Why?"

"What are you whispering about?" the halfling demanded.

"Bait for a halfling thief?" Luthien asked.

Again Oliver looked at him doubtfully.

"You must learn to smell such things," Luthien replied with a smile, perfectly mimicking Oliver's accent.

Oliver looked back to the statue, and for the first time noticed how out of place it truly seemed. He turned and nodded grimly to Luthien. "We should be leaving."

Luthien felt the hairs standing up on the back of his neck. He leaned out of the alcove, looking one way and then the other, and his expression was grave when he slipped back in beside Oliver.

"Cyclopians at both ends of the lane," he explained.

"Of course," Oliver replied. "They were there all alo—" The halfling stopped in mid-sentence, suddenly viewing things with the same suspicion as Luthien.

"They were indeed," the young Bedwyr remarked dryly.

"Have we been baited?" Oliver asked.

In answer, Luthien pointed upwards. "The rooftops?"

Oliver replaced his tools and had the grapnel out in an instant, twirling it about and letting fly. Once secured, he handed the rope to Luthien and said politely, "After you."

Luthien took the rope and glared at Oliver, knowing that the reason the halfling wanted him to go first was so that Oliver could be hauled up and wouldn't have to climb.

"And do look about before you bring me up," the halfling remarked.

With a resigned sigh, the young man began the arduous task of climbing hand over hand. Oliver snickered when Luthien was out of the way, noticing that the young man's crimson-hued shadow had been left behind on the pewter store's window.

Luthien did not take note of Oliver's movements as he went up, reminding himself that he shouldn't be surprised when he pulled the halfling up a few minutes later to find Oliver carrying a sack filled with china plates and crystal goblets.

"I could not let all our work this night go to waste," the sly halfling explained.

They set off among the steeply pitched rooftops, often walking in gullies between two separate roofs. Unlike the city section near the dividing wall, all the buildings here were joined together, making the whole block one big mountainlike landscape of wooden shingles and poking chimneys. Scrambling along, Luthien and Oliver were often separated, and only luck prevented Luthien from whispering to a shadowy form that appeared in a gully ahead of him.

The form moved before Luthien could speak, and that movement showed it to be several times the size of the halfling.

Cyclopians were on the roofs.

Luthien fell flat on his belly, thanking God once more for his crimson cape. He glanced about, hoping that Oliver would amble up beside him, but had a feeling that the halfling had gone beyond this point along the other side of the angled roof to Luthien's left. He could only hope that Oliver was as wary, and as lucky, as he.

Faced with a dangerous decision, Luthien took out his bow and unfolded it, popping the pin into place. The cyclopian in the gully ahead continued to mill about, apparently not yet sensing that it was not alone. Luthien knew he could hit it, but feared that if the shot was not a clean and swift kill, the brute would bring half the Praetorian Guards in Montfort down upon him.

His decision was made for him a moment later when he heard a cry and a crash, accompanied by the unmistakable sound of a certain halfling's taunts.

Oliver had not been caught unawares. Moving along the gutter overlooking the avenue, the halfling had noted a movement near the peak of the high roof. For a fleeting instant, he thought it to be Luthien, but he realized that his companion was not so stupid as to be up high where he might be spotted a block away.

Oliver then pressed on, looking for a more defensible position. If those were indeed cyclopians up there, they could dislodge him from his precarious perch simply by sliding down the steep roof into him. The halfling came to a break and started to turn right, but stopped, noticing the same cyclopian Luthien was watching. Fortunately, the dull-witted cyclopian hadn't noticed Oliver, and so the halfling ran on along the gutter, taking some consolation in the fact that this next roof was not nearly as steep.

He was hoping that he could get around this roof, too. Then he could swing back around to come at the cyclopian in the gully from the opposite side of Luthien.

He never made it that far.

A cyclopian came at him from over the rooftop, half running, half bouncing its way down, sword waving fiercely. Oliver dropped his sack of booty to the roof and drew rapier and main gauche, settling into a defensive crouch. When the cyclopian came upon him, predictably leading with its outstretched sword, the halfling dodged aside and hooked the blade with his shorter weapon.

He tugged fiercely and the dumb cyclopian, not wanting to lose its weapon, held on stubbornly. Its momentum, coupled with Oliver's tug, proved too much, though, and over the edge the brute pitched, getting a kick in the rump from Oliver as it went tumbling past. The cyclopian yelped through the twenty-five-foot drop, then quieted considerably when it smacked the cobblestones face first. Its arm twisted underneath as it hit, and its own sword drove up through its chest and back to stick garishly into the air.

"Fear not, stupid one-eye," Oliver taunted. He knew he should be quiet, but he just couldn't resist. "Even my main gauche could not now take your precious sword from you!"

Oliver spun about—to see three more cyclopians coming down at him from the rooftop. Figuring to go out in style, the halfling swashbuckler removed his great hat from one of the housebreaker's many magical pouches, slapped it against his hip to get the wrinkles out, and plopped it onto his head.

The cyclopian in the gully jumped straight up at the sound, then shuddered suddenly as Luthien's arrow drove into its back. Luthien started to jump up, thinking to run to Oliver's aid, but he flattened himself again, hearing the distinctive clicks of crossbows from the top of the steep roof to his left.

They were firing blindly, unable to penetrate the crimson cape's camouflage, but they had an idea of where to shoot. Luthien nearly wet his pants as three quarrels drove into the wood, one barely inches from his face.

Luthien was not so blind to the archers, though, seeing their black silhouettes clearly against the cloudy gray sky. He knew that there must be magic in the folding bow (or he must have been blessed with an inordinate amount of luck), for his next shot was too perfect as he shifted to the side and awkwardly fired off the arrow.

One of the cyclopians was jolted upright and tilted back its thick head—Luthien could see the thin black line of his arrow sticking from the creature's forehead. The brute reached up and grabbed the quivering shaft, then fell backward, dead, and slid halfway down the other side of the roof.

The other two cyclopians disappeared behind the roof peak.

Oliver's rapier darted left, then right, his main gauche slashing out to the side, intercepting one attack, his spinning rapier defeating another. Down ducked the halfling as a cyclopian sword swooped over his head.

Then he sneaked in a counter, jabbing his rapier into the leg of one of the brutes just above the knee. The one-eye howled in pain.

"Ha, ha!" Oliver cried, as though the score was a foregone conclusion, hiding his honest surprise that, in his wild flurry, he had managed to hit anything. He brought his rapier up to the brim of his cap in victorious salute, but was put back on his heels, spinning and dodging, even whimpering a bit, as the wounded cyclopian responded with a vicious flurry of its own.

The halfling felt his heels hanging over open air. His blades went into another blinding spin, keeping the cyclopians at bay long enough for him to skitter along the roof's edge. The maneuver allowed him to regain secure footing, though the cyclopians kept pace every step, and the halfling quickly came to the realization that fighting with three-to-one odds, with his back leaning out over a long drop, was not such a smart thing to do.

The two cyclopians, their crossbows reloaded, popped up over the roof peak again. They glanced all about, cursing the crafty thief and his concealing cloak, then fired at the spot where they suspected Luthien had been.

Luthien, having slipped around the roof, looked up the slope, past the dead cyclopian, to the backs of his remaining adversaries. Up came the bow and he let fly his arrow, hearing the grunt as one of the brutes caught it full in the back. The other cyclopian regarded its companion curiously for just a moment, then snapped its terrified gaze about. It scrambled up the last few steps of the roof and leaped over the peak, but took Luthien's next flying arrow right in the belly.

Groaning, the brute disappeared over the peak.

Luthien readied another arrow, amazed, for the cyclopian that had taken the shot in the back staggered down the peak at him. The brute picked up momentum and speed with every stride, and Luthien soon realized that it was running completely out of control, blinded by pain and rage. It fell far short of Luthien and slid down to the roof's rough shingles on its face.

Oliver's only saving grace was the fact that the three cyclopians had never learned to fight in harmony. Their lumbering strikes did not complement each other, and for Oliver, it seemed more as though he was fighting one fast, long-armed opponent than three.

Still, the halfling was in a precarious position, and it was only the cyclopians' clumsiness, and not his own skills with the blade, that gained him a temporary advantage. One of the brutes lunged forward only to be intercepted by the cyclopian standing beside it, also lunging forward. The two got tangled together, and one actually fell on its rump to the roof. The third cyclopian, also coming straight forward in a thrusting maneuver, became distracted, turning its gaze to the side.

Oliver's main gauche took the weapon from the brute's hand.

"What will you do now?" the halfling taunted his disarmed opponent. The cyclopian stared dumbfoundedly at its empty hand as though it had been betrayed.

The angry brute snarled, curled its fingers, and punched out, and Oliver, caught by surprise, barely ducked in time. The halfling had to bend at the waist, then wave his arms frantically to regain his balance. He came up straight and slashed across with his shorter blade, forcing the advancing cyclopian back at the last desperate instant.

"I had to ask," Oliver scolded himself.

His slip had given the edge back to the cyclopians, all three standing straight and untangled once more. The one who had lost its sword grinned wickedly, drawing out a long curved dagger.

Oliver was back on his heels in an instant. "This is not going well at all," he admitted, and gave a profound sigh.

One of the brutes lunged for him again, and Oliver's rapier turned the attack aside. Then, to Oliver's surprise, the cyclopian kept going forward, pitching right off the ledge—and Oliver noticed an arrow sticking from its back. The halfling glanced up past the cyclopians to see Luthien running over the peak, bow in hand and readying another arrow.

"I love this man," Oliver said, sighing.

One of the cyclopians charged up to intercept Luthien before he could ready another arrow.

Luthien shrugged and smiled agreeably, dropping the bow to the roof and whipping out his sword. In came the brute, standing somewhat below the young man, and down snapped Luthien's blade, diagonally across the cyclopian's sword.

Luthien brought his sword back up, turning it as he went so that its tip sailed further ahead, nicking the cyclopian on the cheek. Up came the cyclopian's blade as well, stubbornly aimed for Luthien's chest.

But Luthien was quick enough to bring his sword ringing down on the thrust once again, this time turning his blade under his own arm as he slapped the cyclopian's sword out to the side. Continuing the subtle twist of the wrist, Luthien straightened his elbow suddenly, snapping the sword tip ahead.

The cyclopian grimaced and took a quick step back, sliding Luthien's blade out of its chest. It looked down to the wound, even managed to get a hand up to feel the warmth of its spilling blood, then slumped face-down on the roof.

The cyclopian remaining against Oliver, wielding only the dagger, used sheer rage to keep the halfling on the defensive. It sliced across, back and forth, and Oliver had to keep hopping up on his toes, sucking in his ample stomach as the blade zipped past. The halfling held his rapier out in front to keep the cyclopian somewhat at arm's length and kept hurling taunts at the brute, goading it into making a mistake.

"I know that one-eye is not a proper description," the halfling said, laughing. "I know that cyclopians have two eyes, and the brown one on their backsides is by far the prettier!"

The brute howled and whipped its arm above its head, cutting down with the dagger as if it meant to split Oliver down the middle. In stepped the halfling and up came his arms in a cross above his head, catching and cradling the heavy blow, though his little legs nearly buckled under the tremendous weight.

Oliver spun about to put his back toward his opponent, which further extended the cyclopian's arm and forced the brute to lean forward. Before the cyclopian could react, Oliver reversed his grip on his main gauche and brought it swinging down, like a pendulum, to rise behind him and move in the general direction of the cyclopian's groin.

Up went the squealing cyclopian on its toes and higher, and Oliver aided the momentum by bending at the waist and throwing his weight backward into the brute's rising shins.

Then the cyclopian was flying free, turning a half somersault. It hit the cobblestones flat on its back and lay very still.

"It is not so bad," Oliver called after it. "While you are down there, you might retrieve your sword!"

"More are coming," Luthien started to explain as he joined Oliver by the sack of booty. He understood his point was moot when Oliver reached into the sack, drew out a plate and whipped it sidelong up the roof. Luthien turned about to see the spinning missile shatter against the bridge of a cyclopian's nose as the beast came over the peak.

Luthien looked back to Oliver in disbelief.

"That was an expensive shot," the halfling admitted with a shrug.

Then the two were running along the uneven roofs, and when they ran out of rooftops, they descended to the street. They heard the pursuit—so much pursuit—and found themselves surrounded.

Oliver started for an alcove, but Luthien cut him off. "They will look down there," the young man explained, and instead, he put his back against the plain wall to the side of the shadowy alcove's entrance.

Oliver heard cyclopians turning into the lane all about him and promptly dove under the folds of the cloak.

As Luthien had predicted, the one-eyes flushed out every alcove in the area, then many ran off, grumbling, while others began checking all the houses and shops nearby. It was a long, long while before Luthien and Oliver found the opportunity to run off again, and they cursed their luck, seeing that the eastern horizon was beginning to glow with the onset of dawn.

Soon they found cyclopians on their trail again, particularly one large and fast brute that paced them easily. With the rising sun, they couldn't afford to stop and try to hide again, and they found the situation growing more and more desperate as the stubborn beast on their heels called out directions to its trailing and flanking companions.

"Turn and shoot it! Turn and shoot it!" Oliver shouted, sounding as winded and exasperated as Luthien had ever heard him. Luthien thought the reasoning sound, except for the fact that he did not have the time to turn around for any kind of a shot.

Then the city's dividing wall was in sight across Morkney's Square, a wide plaza centered by a tremendous fountain and flanked by many craft shops and fine restaurants. The square was quiet in the early light; the only movements were that of a dwarf chipping away at a design on the newly built fountain and a few merchants sweeping their store fronts, or setting up fruit and fish stands.

The friends ran past the seemingly ambivalent dwarf, Oliver taking the effort to quickly tip his hat to his fellow short-fellow.

The large cyclopian came running right behind, howling with glee, for it was sure that it could get the little one, at least, before Oliver got over the wall.

The distracted cyclopian never saw the dwarf's heavy hammer, only saw the stars exploding behind its suddenly closed eyelid.

Oliver looked back from the wall, grabbed Luthien and bade him do likewise. They nodded their appreciation to the dwarf, who didn't acknowledge it, just patiently reeled in his hammer (which was on the end of a long thong) and went back to his work before the other cyclopians flooded the square.

Back at their apartment, the morning bloom in full, Luthien grumbled considerably about how dangerously close they had come that day, while Oliver, fumbling in his sack, grumbled about how many of the plates and goblets he had broken in their wild flight.

Luthien eyed him with disbelief. "How could you even think of stealing anything at that time?"

Oliver looked up from the sack and shot Luthien a wistful smile. "Is that not the fuel of excitement and courage?" he asked, and he went back to his inspection, his frown returning as he pulled a large chip of yet another plate out of the sack.

The halfling's mouth turned up into that mischievous smile again a moment later, though, and Luthien eyed him curiously as he reached deeply into his sack.

Oliver shot Luthien a sly wink and took out the pewter figurine of a halfling warrior.

CHAPTER 17

OUTRAGE

THE FRIENDS SPENT the next few days in or near their apartment, making small excursions to the Dwelf mostly to hear the chatter concerning the mysterious Crimson Shadow. The last daring hit, raiding two shops and taking out several cyclopian guards in the face of an apparent conspiracy of several merchants, had heightened the talk considerably, and Oliver thought it prudent, and Luthien did not disagree, that they lie low for a while.

Oliver accepted the self-imposed quarantine in high spirits, glad for the rest and thrilled to be a part of the growing legend. Luthien, though, spent most of the days sitting quietly in his chair, brooding. At first, Oliver thought he was just nervous about all the attention, or simply bored, but then the halfling came to understand that Luthien's sorrows were of the heart.

"Do not tell me that you are still thinking of her," Oliver remarked one rare sunny day. The halfling had propped the door half open, letting the remarkably warm September air filter into the dark apartment.

Luthien blinked curiously when he looked at Oliver, but it didn't take the young man long to realize that Oliver had seen through his sad frown.

He looked away quickly, and that nonverbal response told Oliver more than any words ever could.

"Tragic! Tragic!" the halfling wailed, falling into a chair and sweeping his arm over his eyes dramatically. "Always this is tragic!" His movements shifted the chair, knocking it against a pedestal, and Oliver had to react quickly to catch the pewter halfling figurine as it started to tumble to the floor.

"What are you speaking of?" Luthien demanded, not in the mood for any cryptic games.

"I am speaking of you, you silly boy," Oliver replied. He paused for a few moments, dusting off the pedestal and replacing his trophy. Then, with no response apparently forthcoming, he turned a serious expression upon Luthien.

"You have been searching for the meaning of life," Oliver stated, and Luthien eyed him doubtfully. "I only lament that you choose to find it in the form of a woman."

Luthien's expression became a fierce scowl. He started to respond, started to rise up from his chair, but Oliver waved a hand at him absently and cut him off.

"Oh, do not deny it," the halfling said. "I have seen this very thing too many times before. Courtly love, we call it in Gascony."

Luthien settled back down in the chair. "I have no idea of what you are talking about," he assured Oliver, and to emphasize his point, he looked away, looked out the partially opened door.

"Courtly love," Oliver said again, firmly. "You have seen this beauty and you are smitten. You are angry now because we have not returned to the market, because you have not had the opportunity to glimpse her beauty again."

Luthien bit hard on his lip, but did not have the conviction to deny the words.

"She is your heart's queen, and you will fight for her, champion any cause in her name, throw your cloak over a puddle of mud in her path, throw your chest in front of an arrow racing toward her."

"I will throw my hand into your face," Luthien answered seriously.

"Of course you are embarrassed," Oliver replied, seeming not at all concerned, "because you know how stupid you sound." Luthien looked at him directly, an open threat, but still the halfling was undeterred. "You do not even know this woman, this half-elf. She is beautiful, I would not argue, but you have imagined everything, every quality you desire, as part of her, when all you really know is her appearance."

Luthien managed a slight chuckle; the halfling was right, he knew. Logically, at least, Luthien was acting ridiculous. But he couldn't deny his feelings, not in his heart. He had seen the green-eyed half-elf for perhaps a minute, and yet that vision had been with him ever since, in waking hours and dreams alike. Now, discussed openly in the bright air of a shining morning, his obsession sounded ridiculous.

"You seem to possess a great deal of knowledge on this subject," Luthien accused, and Oliver's mouth turned up into a wistful smile. "Personal knowledge," Luthien ended wryly.

"Perhaps," was the strongest admission Oliver would offer.

They let it go at that, Luthien sitting quietly and Oliver busying himself in rearranging the many trophies they had acquired. Luthien didn't notice it, but many times that morning, Oliver's expression would brighten suddenly, as though the halfling was reliving fond memories, or Oliver would grimace in heartfelt pain, as though some of the memories were, perhaps, not so pleasant.

Sometime later, Oliver tossed his winter coat across Luthien's lap. "It is ruined!" he wailed and lifted up one sleeve to show Luthien a tear in the fabric.

Luthien studied the cut carefully. It had been made by something very sharp, he knew, something like Oliver's main gauche, for instance. The weather had been unseasonably warm the last few days, even after sunset, and as far as Luthien could remember, the halfling had not worn this coat at all. Curious that it should be torn, and curious that Oliver should find that tear now, with the sun bright and the air unseasonably warm.

"I will throw it out to the greedy children," the halfling growled, hands on hips and face turned into one of the most profound pouts Luthien had ever witnessed. "Of course, this weather will not hold so warm. Come along, then," he said, grabbing his lighter cloak and moving for the door. "We must go back to market that I might buy another one."

Luthien didn't have to be asked twice.

They spent the day in the bustling market, Oliver perusing goods and Luthien, predictably, watching the crowd. The thief of the young man's heart did not show herself, though.

"I have found nothing of proper value," Oliver announced at the end of the day. "There is one merchant-type who will be in a better bargaining mood tomorrow, though. Of this much, I am sure."

Luthien's disappointment vanished, and as the young man followed his halfling friend out of the market, his expression regarding the halfling was truly appreciative. He knew what Oliver was up to, knew that the halfling was truly sympathetic to his feelings. If Luthien had held any doubts that Oliver's lecture concerning "courtly love" was founded in personal experience, they were gone now.

They went through a similar routine at the market the next day, breaking for lunch at one of the many food kiosks. Oliver carried on a light conversation, mostly about the shortcomings of merchant-types: winter was near at hand and he had found little luck in reducing any of the prices for warm coats.

It took the halfling some time to realize that Luthien wasn't listening to him at all and wasn't even eating the biscuit he held in his hand. The halfling studied Luthien curiously and understood before he even followed the young man's fixed stare across the plaza. There stood the half-elven slave girl, along with her merchant master and his entourage.

Oliver winced when the half-elf looked up from under her wheat-colored tresses, returning Luthien's stare, even flashing a coy smile the young man's way. The worldly halfling understood the implications of that response, understood the trials that might soon follow.

Oliver winced again when the merchant, noticing that his slave had dared to look up without his permission, stepped over and slapped the back of her head.

The halfling jumped on Luthien before he even started to rise, blurting out a dozen reasons why they would be foolish to go over to the merchant at that time. Fortunately for the halfling, several of the people nearby knew him and Luthien from the Dwelf and quickly came over to help out, recognizing that trouble might be brewing.

Only when a group of Praetorian Guards came over to investigate did the fiery young Bedwyr calm down.

"All is well," Oliver assured the suspicious cyclopians. "My friend, he found a cock'a'roach in his biscuit, but it is gone now, and cock'a'roaches, they do not eat so much."

The Praetorian Guards slowly moved away, looking back dangerously with every step.

When they were out of sight, Luthien burst free of the many hands holding him and stood up—only to find that the merchant and his group had moved along.

Oliver had to enlist the aid of the helpful men to "convince" Luthien, mostly by dragging him, to go back to the apartment. But after the helpful group had gone, the young Bedwyr stormed about like a caged lion, kicking over chairs and banging his fists on the walls.

"I really expected much better from you," Oliver remarked dryly, standing by the pedestal to protect his treasured halfling warrior figurine from the young man's tirade.

Luthien leaped across the room to stand right in front of the halfling. "Find out who he is!" the young Bedwyr demanded.

"Who?" Oliver asked.

Luthien's arm flashed forward, snapping up the figurine, and he cocked his arm back as if he meant to throw the statue across the room. The sincerely terrified expression on Oliver's face told him that the halfling would play no more coy games.

"Find out who he is and where he lives," Luthien said calmly.

"This is not so smart," Oliver replied, tentatively reaching for the figurine. Luthien jerked his arm up higher, moving the trophy completely out of the little one's reach.

"It might even be a trap," Oliver reasoned. "We have seen that many merchant-types wish us captured. They might suspect that you are the Crimson Shadow, and might have found the perfect bait."

"Bait like this?" Luthien replied, indicating the statue.

"Exactly," Oliver said cheerily, but his bright expression quickly descended into gloom when he realized Luthien's point. The previous danger hadn't stopped Oliver from lifting the bait from the hook.

The halfling threw his hands up in defeat. "Lover-types," he grumbled under his breath, storming out of the apartment and pointedly slamming the door behind him. But Oliver was truly a romantic, and he was smiling again by the time he climbed the stairs back to the street level.

CHAPTER 18

NOT SO MUCH A SLAVE

J CANNOT TALK YOU OUT OF THIS?" Oliver asked when he returned late that afternoon to find Luthien pacing the small apartment anxiously.

Luthien stopped and fixed a determined stare upon the halfling.

"Stealing co-ins and jew-wels is one thing," the halfling went on. "Stealing a slave is something quite different."

Luthien didn't blink.

Oliver sighed.

"Stubborn fool," the halfling lamented. "Very well, then. We are in some luck, it would seem. The merchant-type's house lies in the north-western section of town, just south of the road to Port Charley. There are not so many guards up there and the wall has not yet even been completed about these new houses. Lesser merchant-types, mostly. But still they will have guards, and you can be death-sure that, in stealing a slave, you will put Duke Morkney and all of his Praetorian Guards on our tail. When we go . . ."

"Tonight," Luthien clarified, and again, the defeated halfling sighed.

"Then tonight might be our last night in the hospitable city of Mont-fort," Oliver explained. "And we will be on the road with winter licking at the backs of our boots."

"So be it."

"Stubborn fool," Oliver grumbled, and he moved across the floor to his bedroom and slammed the door behind him.

They got to the alley beside the merchant's house, a fine two-story L-shaped stone structure with many small balconies and windows, without incident. Oliver continued to express his doubts and Luthien continued to ignore him. The young man had found a purpose in life, something that went beyond discarding winter coats where the poor children of Tiny Alcove might find them. He thought himself the proverbial knight in shining armor, the perfect hero who would rescue his lady from the evil merchant.

He never thought to ask if she needed rescuing.

The house was quiet—all the area was quiet, for few thieves bothered to come this way and thus few guards patrolled the streets. A single candle showed through one of the house's windows, on the short side of the "L." Luthien led Oliver to the wall of the darker section, the main section.

"I cannot talk you out of this?" Oliver asked one final time. When Luthien scowled at him, he tossed his magical grapnel, which caught above a balcony and just below the roof. This time Oliver went first, fearing to let the anxious Luthien up on that balcony without him. The way the young man was behaving, Oliver feared he would crash through the doorway, slaughter everybody in the house, then walk up to the Ministry, woman in arms, and demand that Duke Morkney himself pronounce them married!

The halfling made the balcony and slipped over to the door. Confident that no one was about, he came back to the rail to signal for Luthien to follow.

Oliver wasn't really surprised to see the young Bedwyr already halfway up and climbing furiously.

He would have hissed out a scolding at his impetuous companion, but something else caught the halfling's attention. Looking across the courtyard to a window showing the flicker of a candle, Oliver saw a woman—the beautiful slave, he knew from her long tresses, shining lustrously even in the dim light. The halfling watched curiously as the woman tucked that hair up under a black cap, then picked up a bundle, blew out the candle, and moved for the window.

Luthien's hand came over the top of the railing and the young Bedwyr began to pull himself up. He was stopped as he straddled the railing by the smiling halfling, Oliver motioning for him to look over his shoulder.

A makeshift rope, a line of tied bedsheets, hung from window to ground, and a lithe form, dressed in gray and black, similar to Oliver's thieving clothes, nimbly made its way down.

Luthien's lips tightened into a grimace. Some thief had dared to break into the house of his love!

Oliver didn't miss the expression and understood where the anger was coming from. He put a hand on Luthien's shoulder, turning the young man to face him, then put a finger over his pursed lips.

The lithe form dropped to the ground and slipped off into the shadows.

"Well?" Oliver asked, indicating the rope.

Luthien didn't understand.

"Are you going back down?" the halfling asked. "We have no more business here."

Luthien looked at him curiously for a moment, then blinked in amazement and snapped his gaze across the small courtyard. When he looked back to Oliver, the halfling was smiling widely and nodding.

Luthien slid down the rope, and Oliver followed quickly, fearing that the young man would run off into the night. Oliver's humor about the unexpected turn of events faded quickly as he began to understand that even though this slave was apparently not what she appeared to be, this might be a long and difficult evening.

The halfling hit the ground, gave three tugs to retrieve his grapnel, and ran off after Luthien, catching the man two blocks away.

Luthien stood at a corner, peeking around the stone into an alley. Oliver slipped in between his legs and peeked around from a lower vantage point.

There stood the half-elven slave—there could be no doubt now, for she had removed the cap and was shaking out her wheat-colored tresses. With her were two others, one as tall as Luthien but much more slender, the other the woman's size.

Luthien looked down at Oliver at the same time the halfling turned his head to look up at Luthien.

"Fairborn," the halfling mouthed silently, and Luthien, though he had little experience with elves, nodded his agreement.

Luthien let Oliver, more versed in the ways of trailing, lead as they followed the group to the richer section of Montfort. The young Bedwyr could not deny the obvious, but still he was surprised when the three elves slipped into a dark alley, set a rope and quietly entered the second-story window of a dark house.

"She does not need your help," Oliver remarked in Luthien's ear. "Leave this alone, I beg."

Luthien could not find the words to argue against Oliver's solid logic. The woman did not need his help, so it appeared, but he would not, could not, leave this alone. He pushed Oliver away and kept his gaze locked on the window.

The three came back out in a short time—they were efficient at their craft—one of them carrying a sack. Down to the alley they went, and the slave woman gave a deft snap of the rope that dislodged the conventional grappling hook.

Oliver dove into the fold of Luthien's cape, and Luthien fell back motionless against the wall as the three came rushing out, passing barely five feet from the friends. Luthien wanted to reach out and grab the half-elf, confront her there and then. He resisted the urge with help from Oliver, who apparently sensing his companion's weakness, had prudently grabbed a tight hold on both of Luthien's hands. As soon as the three elven thieves were safely away, Oliver and Luthien took up the chase all the way back to the northwestern section.

The three parted company in the same place they had met the other two taking the sack and the slave heading back for her master's house.

"Leave this alone, I beg," Oliver whispered to Luthien, though the halfling knew beyond doubt that his plea was falling on deaf ears. Luthien didn't have to trail the woman now, knowing her destination, so he slipped ahead instead. He ducked behind the last corner before the merchant's house, melted under the folds of his cape and waited.

The woman came by, perfectly silent, walking with the practiced footsteps of a seasoned thief. She moved right past the camouflaged Luthien, glanced both ways along the street and started across.

"Not so much a slave," Luthien remarked, lifting his head to regard her.

He nearly jumped out of his boots at the sheer speed of the half-elf's movements. She whipped about, a short sword coming out of nowhere, and Luthien shrieked and ducked the metal blade clicking off the stone above his head. Luthien tried to move to the side, but the woman paced him easily, her sword flashing deftly.

In the blink of an eye, Luthien was standing straight again, his back to the wall, the tip of a sword at his throat.

"That would not be so wise," came Oliver's comment from behind the woman.

"Perhaps not," came a melodic, elven voice from behind the halfling.

Oliver sighed again and managed a glance over his shoulder. There stood one of the woman's companions, grim-faced, sword in hand and its tip not so far from the halfling's back. A bit to the side, further down the alley, stood the other female, bow in hand, an arrow trained upon Oliver's head.

"I could be wrong," the halfling admitted. He slowly slid his rapier back into its sheath, then even more slowly, allowing the elf to watch his every move, reached for a pouch and produced his hat, fluffing it and plopping it on his head.

The woman's green eyes bored into Luthien's stunned expression. "Who are you to follow me so?" she demanded, her jaw firm, her expression grave.

"Oliver," Luthien prompted, not knowing what he should say.

"He is a stubborn fool," the halfling gladly put in.

Luthien's expression turned sour as he regarded his loyal companion.

The woman prodded slightly with the sword, forcing Luthien to swallow.

"My name is Luthien," he admitted.

"State your business," she demanded through gritted teeth.

"I saw you in the market," the young man stammered. "I . . ."

"He came for you," Oliver put in. "I tried to tell him better. I tried!"

The woman's features softened as she regarded Luthien, and a note of recognition came into her eyes. Gradually, she eased her sword away. "You came for me?"

"I saw him hit you," Luthien tried to explain. "I mean . . . I could not . . . why would you allow him to do that?"

"I am a slave," the woman replied sarcastically. "Half-elven. Less than human." Despite her bravado, a certain tinge of anger and frustration became evident in her tone as she spoke.

"We are standing in the street," the male elf reminded them, and he motioned for Oliver to get back into the alley. To the halfling's relief, the thief put up his sword and the other one eased her bowstring back and removed the arrow.

The half-elf bade Luthien to follow, but hesitated as he walked by, looking curiously at the shadowy image he had left behind on the wall. Smiling with a new perspective, she followed Luthien into the alley.

"You are all half-elven," Oliver remarked when he had the moment to study the three.

"I am full Fairborn," the woman with the bow answered. She looked at the male, an unmistakable connection between them. "But I do not desert my elven brethren."

"The Cutters," Oliver remarked offhandedly, and all three of the elven thieves snapped their surprised looks upon him.

"A notorious thieving band," Oliver explained calmly to Luthien, who obviously had no idea of what was going on. "By reputation, they are all of the Fairborn."

"You have heard of us, halfling," the woman with Luthien said.

"Who in Montfort has not?" Oliver replied, and that seemed to please the three.

"We are not all elves," the half-elven woman answered, looking back over her shoulder at Luthien, a look that truly melted his heart.

"Siobhan!" the male said sternly.

"Do you not know who we have captured?" the woman asked easily, still looking at Luthien.

"I am Oliver deBurrows," the halfling cut in, thinking that his reputation had preceded him. To Oliver's disappointment, though, none of the three even seemed to take note that he had spoken.

"You have left a curious shadow behind," Siobhan remarked to Luthien. "Out in the street. A crimson shadow."

Luthien looked back that way, then turned to Siobhan and shrugged apologetically.

"The Crimson Shadow," the male half-elf remarked, sounding sincerely impressed. He slid his sword completely away then, nearly laughing aloud.

"And Oliver deBurrows!" the halfling insisted.

"Of course," the male said offhandedly, never taking his gaze from Luthien.

"Your work is known to us," Siobhan remarked, her smile coy. Luthien's heart fluttered so badly he thought it would surely stop. "Indeed," she continued, looking to her friends for confirmation, "your work is known throughout Montfort. Truly you have put the merchants on their heels, to the delight of many."

Luthien was sure that he was blushing a deeper red than the hue of his cape. "Oliver helps," he stuttered.

"Do tell," the deflated halfling muttered under his breath.

"I would have thought you a much older man," Siobhan went on. "Or a longer-living elf, perhaps."

Luthien eyed her curiously. He remembered Brind'Amour's words that the cape had belonged to a thief of high renown, and it seemed that Siobhan had heard of the cape's previous owner, as well. Luthien smiled as he wondered what mischief the first Crimson Shadow might have caused in Montfort.

"It grows late," remarked the elven woman from further down the alley. "We must go, and you," she said to Siobhan, "must get back inside your master's house."

Siobhan nodded. "We are not all of the Fairborn," she said again to Luthien.

"Is that an invitation?" Oliver asked.

Siobhan looked to her companions, and they, after a moment, nodded in reply. "Consider it so," Siobhan said, looking back directly at Luthien, making him think, in the secret hopes of his heart, that the invitation was more than to join the thieving band.

"For you and for the esteemed Oliver deBurrows," she added, her tone revealing that extending the invitation to Oliver, however kindly phrased, had come more as an afterthought.

Luthien looked over her shoulder to Oliver, and the halfling gave a slight shake of his head.

"Consider it," Siobhan said to Luthien. "There are many advantages to being well connected." She flashed her heart-melting smile one last time, as if confirming to the stricken Luthien that she had more than a thieving agreement in mind. Then, with a nod to her departing companions, she started across the street toward her impromptu rope.

Luthien never blinked as he watched her graceful movements, and Oliver just shook his head and sighed.

CHAPTER 19

IN HALLOWED HALLS

FEIGNING INTEREST, Duke Morkney leaned forward in his wooden chair, his skinny elbows poking out of his voluminous red robe, hands set on his huge desk. Across from him, several merchants spoke all at once, the only common words in their rambling being "theft" and "Crimson Shadow."

Duke Morkney had heard it all before from these same men many times over the last few weeks, and he was truly growing tired of it.

"And worst of all," one merchant cried above the tumult, quieting the others, "I cannot get that damned shadow stain off of my window! What am I to reply to the snickers of all who see it? It is a brand, I say!"

"Hear, hear!" several others agreed.

Morkney raised one knobby hand and thinned his lips, trying to bite back his laughter. "He is a thief, no more," the duke assured them. "We have lived with thieves far too long to let the arrival of a new one—one that conveniently leaves his mark—bother us so."

"You do not understand!" one merchant pleaded, but his face paled and he went silent immediately when Morkney's withered face and bloodshot amber eyes turned upon him, the duke scowling fiercely.

"The commoners may help this one," another merchant warned, trying to deflect the vicious duke's ire.

"Help him what?" Morkney replied skeptically. "Steal a few baubles? By your own admission, this thief seems no more active than many of the others who have been robbing you of late. Or is it just that his calling card, this shadowy image, stings your overblown pride?"

"The dwarf in the square . . ." the man began.

"Will be punished accordingly," Morkney finished for him. He caught the gaze of a merchant at the side of his desk and winked. "We can never have too many dwarvish workers, now can we?" he asked slyly, and that seemed to appease the group somewhat.

"Go back to your shops," Morkney said to them all, leaning back and waving his bony arms emphatically. "King Greensparrow has hinted that our production is not where it should be—that, I say, is a more pressing problem than some petty thief, or some ridiculous shadows that you say you cannot remove."

"He slipped through our trap," one of the merchants tried to explain, drawing nods from three of the others who had been in on the ambush at the Avenue of the Artisans.

"Then set another trap, if that is what needs be done!" Morkney snapped at him, the duke's flashing amber eyes forcing the four cohorts back a step.

Grumbling, the merchant contingent left the duke's office.

"Crimson Shadow, indeed," the old wizard muttered, shuffling through the parchments to find the latest word from Greensparrow. Morkney had been among that ancient brotherhood of wizards, had been alive when the original Crimson Shadow had struck fear into the hearts of merchants across Eriador, even into Princetown and other cities of northern Avon. Much had been learned of the man back in those long-past days, though he had never been caught.

And now he was back? Morkney thought the notion completely absurd. The Crimson Shadow was a man—a long-dead man by now. More likely, some petty thief had stumbled across the legendary thief's magical cape. The calling card might be the same, but that did not make the man the same.

"A petty thief," Morkney muttered, and he snickered aloud, thinking of the tortures this new Crimson Shadow would surely endure when the merchants finally caught up to him.

"I work alone," Oliver insisted.

Luthien stared at him blankly.

"Alone with you!" Oliver clarified in a huffy tone. The halfling stood tall (relatively speaking) in his best going-out clothes, his plumed chapeau capping the spectacle of Oliver deBurrows, swashbuckler. "It is very different being a part of a guild," he went on, his face sour. "Sometimes you must give more than half of your take—and you may only go where they tell you to go. I do not like being told where to go!"

Luthien didn't have any practical arguments to offer; he wasn't certain that he wanted to join the Cutters anyway, not on any practical level.

But Luthien did know that he wanted to see more of Siobhan, and if joining the thieving band was the means to that end, then the young Bedwyr was willing to make the sacrifice.

"I know what you are thinking," Oliver said in accusatory tones.

Luthien sighed deeply. "There is more to life, Oliver, than thievery," he tried to explain. "And more than material gain. I'll not argue that joining with Siobhan and her friends may lessen our take and our freedom, but it might bring us a measure of security. You saw the trap the merchants set for us."

"That is exactly why you cannot join *any* band," Oliver snapped at him.

Luthien didn't understand.

"Why would you so disappoint your admirers?" Oliver asked.

"Admirers?"

"You have heard them," the halfling replied. "Always they talk of the Crimson Shadow, and always their mouths turn up at the edges when they speak the name. Except for the merchant-types, of course, and that makes it all the sweeter."

Luthien shook his head blankly. "I will still wear the cape," he stammered. "The mark . . ."

"You will steal the mystery," Oliver explained. "All of Montfort will know that you have joined with the Cutters, and thus you will lower your budding reputation to the standards of that band. No, I say! You must remain an independent rogue, acting on your own terms and of your own accord. We will fool these silly merchant-types until they grow too wary, then we will move on—the Crimson Shadow will simply disappear from the streets of Montfort. The legend will grow."

"And then?"

Oliver shrugged as if that did not matter. "We will find another town—Princetown in Avon, perhaps. And then we will return to Montfort in a few years and let the legend grow anew. You have done something marvelous here, though you are not old enough to understand it," the halfling said. It seemed to Luthien that this was about as profound and intense as he had ever heard Oliver. "But you, the Crimson Shadow, the one who has fooled the silly merchant-types and stolen their goods from under their fat noses, have given to the people who live on the lower side of Montfort's wall something they have not had in many, many years."

"And that is?" Luthien asked, and all the sarcasm had left his voice by this point.

"Hope," Oliver answered. "You have given hope to them. Now, I am going to the market. Are you coming?"

Luthien nodded, but stood in the room for several minutes after Oliver had departed, deep in thought. There was a measure of truth in what the halfling had said, Luthien realized. By some trick of fate, a chance gift after a chance meeting with an eccentric wizard, and that after a chance meeting with an even more eccentric halfling, he, Luthien Bedwyr, had found himself carrying on a legend he had never heard of. He had been thrust into the forefront of the common cause of those who had been left out of King Greensparrow's designs for wealth.

"A peasant hero?" remarked the young man who was not a peasant at all. The furious irony, the layers of pure coincidence, nearly over-whelmed Luthien, and though he was truly confused by it all, an unmis-takable spring was evident in his step as he ran out to catch up with Oliver.

The day was cold and gray—typical for the season—and the market was not so crowded. Most of the worthy goods had been bought or stolen and no new caravans had come in, or would for many months.

It didn't take long for Luthien and Oliver to wish that more people were at the plaza. The two, particularly Oliver, were quite a sight, and more than a few cyclopians, including one who wore a thick bandage around his bruised skull, took note of the pair.

They stopped at a kiosk and bought some biscuits for lunch, chatting easily with the proprietor about the weather and the crowd and anything else that came to mind.

"You should not be out here," came a whisper when the proprietor shuffled away to see to another customer.

Luthien and Oliver looked at each other, and then at a slender figure, cloaked and hooded, standing beside the kiosk. He turned to face them more squarely and peeked up from under the low hood, and they recog-nized the male half-elf they had met the previous night.

"Do they know?" Oliver asked quietly.

"They suspect," the half-elf answered. "They'll not openly accuse you, of course, not with witnesses about."

"Of course," Oliver replied. Luthien continued to stare off noncom-mittally, not wanting to give away the secret conversation and not un-derstanding much of what the half-elf and Oliver were talking about. If the brutish cyclopians suspected him and Oliver, then why didn't they simply walk over and arrest them? Luthien had been in Montfort long enough to know that the law here required little evidence to haul some-one away—gangs of Praetorian Guards were commonplace in the area near to Tiny Alcove and usually left with at least one unfortunate rogue in tow.

"There is news," the half-elf continued.

"Do tell," Oliver started to say, but he quieted and looked away as a group of cyclopians ambled past.

"Not now," came the half-elf's whisper as soon as the cyclopians had moved off a short distance. "Siobhan will be behind the Dwelf at the rise of the moon."

"We will be there," Oliver assured him.

"Just him," came the reply, and Oliver looked over at Luthien. When Oliver turned his curious glance back the half-elf's way, he found that the thief had moved along.

With a sigh, the halfling turned back again, toward Luthien and the open plaza, and then he understood the half-elf's sudden departure. The cyclopian group was returning, this time showing more interest in the pair.

"My papa halfling, he always say," Oliver whispered to Luthien, "a smart thief can make his way, a smarter thief can get away." He started off, taking Luthien's arm, but was forced to stop as the cyclopians rushed in suddenly, encircling the pair.

"Cold day," one of them remarked.

"Buying the last things for winter?" asked another.

Oliver started to respond, but bit back his retort as Luthien broke in suddenly, looking at the cyclopian directly.

"That we are," he replied. "Montfort's winter is colder for some than for others."

The cyclopian didn't seem to understand that remark—Oliver wasn't sure that he did, either. Though Oliver didn't know it, his last remarks at the apartment had put a spark into the young Bedwyr, had touched a chord in Luthien's heart. He was feeling quite puffed at this moment—feeling the part of the Crimson Shadow, the silent speaker for the underprivileged, the purveyor of coats for cold children, the thorn in the rich man's side.

"How long've you been in Montfort?" the brute eyeing Luthien asked slyly, fishing for clues.

Now Oliver stepped forward and wrapped his arm about Luthien's waist forcefully. "Since the day my son was born," the halfling proclaimed, to the wide-eyed stare of Luthien. "Alas, for his poor mother. She could not accept the size of this one."

The cyclopians looked at each other in confusion and disbelief. "He's your father?" the one addressing Luthien asked.

Luthien draped his arm about Oliver's shoulders. "My papa halfling," he answered, imitating Oliver's thick accent.

"And what business—" the cyclopian began to ask, but a comrade of his grabbed his arm and interrupted, motioning for him to drop the matter.

The cyclopian's fierce scowl diminished as he glanced around the marketplace. Dozens of men, a couple of dwarves, and a handful of elves were watching intently—too intently—their faces grim and more than one of them wearing a dirk or short sword at his belt.

The cyclopian group was soon on its way.

"What happened?" Luthien asked.

"The cyclopians just met people who have found their hearts," Oliver answered. "Come along and be quick. The Cutter was right—we should not be about this day."

"Kiss me." Her melodic tones caught the young man off guard, and the unexpected request nearly buckled his knees.

Luthien froze in place, staring blankly at Siobhan, having no idea of what to do next.

"You want to." She stated the obvious.

"I came because I was told that there was some news," Luthien informed her. He wished that he hadn't said that as soon as the words left his mouth; what a stupid time to be changing the subject!

The half-elf seemed even more alluring to poor Luthien as she stood in the silver moonlight in the shadowy alley behind the Dwelf. She gave a coy smile and pushed her long tresses back from her fair face. Luthien glanced back over his shoulder, as though he expected Oliver to be standing nearby watching him. The halfling had gone into the Dwelf and told Luthien to meet him there when he finished his business with Siobhan.

Luthien looked back to see that Siobhan's smile had already disappeared without a trace.

"The dwarf—" she began grimly, but she stopped suddenly as Luthien leaped up to her and kissed her full on the lips. The embarrassed young man hopped back immediately, searching Siobhan's expression for some hint of a reaction.

But it was Luthien, and not Siobhan, who seemed most ill at ease. The half-elf only smiled and shook the hair back from her face, seemingly composed. "Why did you ask me to do that?" Luthien asked bluntly.

"Because you wanted to," Siobhan replied.

Luthien's proud shoulders slumped visibly.

"And I wanted you to do it," Siobhan admitted. "But I thought we should be done with it."

"Be done with it?" Luthien echoed. That did not sound promising.

Siobhan took a deep breath. "I only thought that you and Oliver should know . . ." she began to explain. She paused, as if the words were hard to come by.

Luthien was beginning to get more than a little alarmed. "Know what?" he prompted, and stepped toward Siobhan, but she put up a defensive hand and took a step back.

"The dwarf," she went on. "The dwarf who helped you in Morkney Square. He has been taken by the Praetorian Guard and locked in a dungeon to await trial."

Luthien's expression went grave, his hands clenched anxiously at his sides. "Where?" he asked determinedly. Siobhan had no doubt he meant to run off that very moment and rescue the dwarf.

Her helpless shrug, accompanied by a sincere expression, thoroughly deflated him. "The Praetorian Guards have many dungeons," she said, shaking her head. "Many dungeons. The dwarf will be tried in the Ministry on the morrow, along with so many others," Siobhan quickly added. "He will be sentenced to the mines, no doubt."

Luthien didn't understand. He stood in quiet thought for a moment, trying to sort some things out, then looked curiously at Siobhan. How could she possibly know about the dwarf in Morkney Square? he wondered, and it seemed as if she was reading his thoughts, for that coy smile returned to her face.

"I told you there were benefits to being well connected," she said, answering his unspoken question. "And I thought that you should know."

Luthien nodded.

Almost as an afterthought, Siobhan added, "The dwarf, Shuglin by name, knew that he would be caught, of course."

"Was he part of your band?"

Siobhan shook her head. "He was a craftsman and no more."

Luthien nodded knowingly, but he didn't *know* anything at all. Why would this craftsman dwarf help him, fully understanding that he would likely be captured and punished?

"I must be going," Siobhan said, looking up at the position of the moon.

"When will I see you again?" Luthien asked anxiously.

"You will," Siobhan promised, and started to fade into the shadows.

"Siobhan!" Luthien called, more loudly than he had intended, his desires getting the best of his judgment. The fair maiden stepped back near to him, an inquisitive look on her face.

Staring into the green glow of her eyes, Luthien could not find any words. His expression said it all.

"One more kiss?" she asked. She barely had the words out before Luthien was up against her, his lips soft against hers.

"You will see me again," she teased again, pulling back. And then she was gone, a shadow among the shadows.

"It is all a game," Oliver complained when he and Luthien were walking home later that night, the young man with a few too many ales in him. "Surely you are not so stupid that you cannot understand that."

"I do not care!" It was a determined statement, if a bit slurred.

"Dwarves are always being accused, tried, and sentenced to hard work in the mines," Oliver went on stubbornly. "Legal and unarguable slavery. That is how Montfort has become so wealthy, can you not see?"

"I do not care."

Oliver was afraid Luthien would say that.

Before the next dawn, the two companions were creeping along the city's dividing wall at the base of the Ministry. They got over the divider easily enough, and Oliver, knowing the routine, positioned them in the shadows of the cathedral's northern wing: a transept, one of two armlike sections of the long building that gave it the general shape of a cross. Few buildings were close to the cathedral on this side, forming an open plaza. "We must go in the west end," Oliver explained, peeking around the edge of the huge transept wall, and he told Luthien to put away the cape.

Luthien did as instructed, but he was hardly conscious of the act. This was the closest he had been to the Ministry, and how small the young Bedwyr felt! He looked straight up the side of the building's wall to the tremendous flying buttresses and many gargoyles hanging out over the edge to look down upon puny humans such as he. Ominous and imposing was Montfort's Ministry in the growing light of predawn.

Soon after the sun came up, the plaza was buzzing with many people, merchants and craftsmen, and quite a few Praetorian Guards, as well. Luthien noted that many of the people had brought their children along with them.

"The last day of the week," Oliver explained, and Luthien nodded, realizing that another week, and the whole month of September, had indeed passed them by. "Tax day. They bring their children in the hope of mercy." Oliver's ensuing snicker showed that he did not think mercy a likely thing for any of them.

They waited inconspicuously behind the transept as the Ministry's tall and narrow oaken doors were unlocked and opened at the west end, and the procession made its way into the giant structure, one group at a time. Burly cyclopians stood to either side of the doors, asking questions, herding the men and their families as they would sheep.

Oliver pulled Luthien further back into the shadows of the wall as a caravan of ironbound wagons rolled up to the side door in the middle of the transept's north-facing wall, another impressive portal, though not as huge as the cathedral's towering western doors. Many Praetorian Guards came out of the cathedral to meet the transported prisoners—four men, three women, and two dwarves, all dressed in loose-fitting gray robes, mostly open at the front. Luthien recognized the one who had helped him and Oliver immediately, from the dwarf's bushy blue-black beard poking out under the cowl of his robe, and by his clothes, the same sleeveless leather tunic he had been wearing that morning in Morkney Square.

"Shuglin," the young Bedwyr mouthed silently, remembering the name Siobhan had told him.

He motioned to Oliver, but the halfling held him back firmly. Luthien threw a plaintive look at the halfling.

"Too many," Oliver mouthed, and pointed to a structure across the plaza from the prisoner wagons. Luthien noticed several forms milling about this smaller building and a couple sitting on the cobblestones like the beggars who were more common to the city's lower section. They were fully cloaked, their faces hidden, but scrutinizing them more closely now, Luthien understood his partner's concern.

Each one of them was broad-shouldered like a warrior, or like a cyclopian.

"Do they expect us?" Luthien whispered in Oliver's ear.

"It would be an easy trap," the halfling replied. "An easy way to be rid of a growing problem. Perhaps they understand how stupid you can be."

Luthien glared at him, but standing beside that tremendous structure, the day brightening around them, the streets and cathedral teeming with Praetorian Guards, Luthien couldn't honestly refute the halfling's insult. He didn't want to leave, but instead wondered what in the world he might do.

When he looked back at Oliver, his expression went from crestfallen to curious. The halfling had tucked his dark jacket, his black shoes and his hat away in pouches, had rolled his pant legs up even higher, and was in the process of slipping into the printed dress of a young girl. That done, Oliver produced a horse-hair wig, long and black (where he had gotten that, Luthien had no idea), then wrapped veils about his head, strategically covering his mustache and goatee.

Good old Oliver, Luthien thought, and he had to fight hard to keep his laughter from bursting forth.

"I am your virgin daughter, merchant-type," the halfling explained, handing Luthien a pouch that jingled with coins. Luthien opened it and peeked in, and his eyes went wide to see that the coins were gold.

Oliver took him by the arm and led him boldly around the corner of the transept. They gave the prisoner wagons and the cyclopians a wide berth, moving near the center of the plaza as they made their way up to the Ministry's western door.

That western wall held Luthien's attention all the way to the door. It was not flat, but rather filled with niches, and in these were beautiful, brightly painted statues. These were the figures of Luthien's religion: the heroes of old, the shining lights of Eriador. He noted that they had not been maintained of late, their paint chipping and peeling, and the nests and droppings of many birds evident in nearly every niche.

The young Bedwyr was beginning to work himself into quite a state, but Oliver's unexpected outburst broke into his private thoughts.

"I told you that we would be late, Papa!" the halfling wailed in a high-pitched voice.

Luthien glanced incredulously the halfling's way, but straightened immediately and eyed the two amused cyclopian guards. "Are we too late?" he asked.

"'E's afraid of the mines for missing the tax call," one of the brutes remarked, and it blinked lewdly as it regarded Oliver. "Or might be that Morkney'll take his little daughter." The wicked laughter that followed made Luthien want to go for his hidden sword, but he held steady.

Oliver nudged him hard, and when he looked at the halfling, Oliver motioned fiercely for the pouch.

Luthien nodded and grabbed a few gold coins. He'd owe Oliver dearly for this; he knew how hard it was to part the halfling from his ill-gotten gains!

"Are you sure that I am late?" Luthien asked the cyclopians. They looked at him curiously, their interest apparently piqued by his sly tone.

Luthien looked up and down the near-empty plaza, then inched his coin-filled hand toward them. The dimwitted cyclopians caught on.

"Late?" one asked. "No, you're not late." And the brute stepped aside and drew open one of the tall doors, while its companion eagerly scooped up the bribe.

Luthien and Oliver entered a small and high foyer, barely a five-foot square, with doors similar to the outside pair looming directly before them. They both breathed easier when the cyclopians shut the outside doors behind them, leaving them alone for the moment.

Luthien started to reach for the handle of an inside door, but Oliver stopped him and put a finger to pursed lips. They moved their ears against the wood instead, and could hear a strong baritone voice calling out names—the tax roll, Luthien realized.

They had come this far, but what were they to do now? he wondered. He looked to Oliver, and the halfling nodded in the direction over Luthien's shoulder. Following the gaze, Luthien noticed that the foyer was not enclosed. Ten feet up the middle of both side walls were openings leading straight in, to concealed corridors that ran south along the front wall of the structure.

Out came the magical grapnel, and up they went. They passed several openings that led onto a ledge encircling the cathedral's main hall, and came to understand that this corridor was the path used by the building's caretakers to clean the many statues and stained-glass windows of the place.

They went up a tight stairway, and then up another, and found a passage leading to an arched passageway that overlooked the cathedral's nave fully fifty feet up from the main area's floor.

"The triforium," Oliver explained with a sly wink, apparently believing that they would get a good view of the proceedings in relative safety.

They were fifty feet up from the floor, Luthien noted, and barely halfway to the network of huge vaulting that formed the structure's incredible roof. Again the young Bedwyr felt tiny and insignificant, overwhelmed by the sheer size of the place.

Oliver was a couple of steps ahead of him by then, and turned back, realizing that Luthien wasn't following.

"Quickly," the halfling whispered harshly, drawing Luthien back to the business at hand.

They scampered along the back side of the triforium wall. On the front side of the passageway, centering every arch, was a relatively new addition to the cathedral, a man-sized, winged gargoyle, its grotesque and horned head looking down over the ledge, looking down upon the gathering. Oliver eyed the statues with obvious distaste, and Luthien heartily concurred, thinking the gargoyles a wretched stain upon a holy church.

They crept along quietly to the corner of the triforium, where the passageway turned right into the southern transept. Diagonally across the way, Luthien saw the pipes of a gigantic organ, and beneath them the area where the choir had once stood, singing proud praises to God. Now cyclopians milled about in there.

The altar area was still perhaps a hundred feet away, tucked into the center of a semicircular apse at the cathedral's eastern end. The bulk of this apse was actually in Montfort's lower section, forming part of the city's dividing wall.

Luthien's eyes were first led upward by the sweeping and spiraling designs of the apse, up into the cathedral's tallest spire, he realized, though from this angle, he could not see more than halfway up the towering structure. He shook his head and looked lower to the great tapestries of the apse, and to the altar.

There, Luthien got his first good look at the infamous Duke Morkney of Montfort. The old wretch sat in a comfortable chair directly behind the altar, wearing red robes and a bored expression.

At a podium at the corner of the apse stood the roll-caller, a fierce-looking man flanked by two of the largest cyclopians Luthien had ever seen. The man read a name deliberately, then paused, waiting for the called taxpayer—a tavern owner in the lower section whom Luthien recognized—to shuffle out of one of the high-backed wooden pews in the nave and amble forward with his offering.

A sour taste filled Luthien's mouth when the summoned man handed a bag of coins over to a cyclopian. The merchant stood, head bowed, while the bag was emptied onto the altar, its contents quickly counted. The amount was then announced to Morkney, who paused a moment—just to make the merchant sweat, Luthien realized—then waved his arm absently. The merchant verily ran back to his pew, gathered up the two children who had come in with him, and scooted out of the Ministry.

The process was repeated over and over. Most of the taxpayers were allowed to go on their way, but one unfortunate man, an old vendor from a kiosk in the market, apparently had not given enough to suit the greedy duke. Morkney whispered something to the cyclopian at his side, and the man was promptly dragged away. An old woman—his wife, Luthien assumed—leaped up from a pew, wailing in protest.

She was dragged off also.

"Pleasant," Oliver muttered at Luthien's side.

About halfway through the tax call, two hours after Luthien and Oliver had found their high perch, Morkney raised one skinny hand. The man at the lectern stepped down and another took his place.

"Prisoners!" this new caller yelled, and a group of cyclopians rose and stepped out from the first pew, pulling the chained men, women, and dwarves along with them.

"There is our savior," Oliver remarked dryly, noting the bushy-haired dwarf. "Have you any idea of how we might get near to him?"

The obvious sarcasm in Oliver's tone angered Luthien, but he had no response. To his dismay, it seemed that the halfling was right. There was nothing he could do, nothing at all. He could see at least two-score cyclopians in the cathedral and did not doubt that another two-score were nearby, not counting the ones in the wagons beyond the door of the north transept. That, plus the fact that Morkney was reputedly a powerful wizard, made any plan to spring Shuglin seem utterly ridiculous.

Charges were read and the nine prisoners were given various punishments, various terms of indenture. The four men would accompany a caravan to Princetown—likely to be sold off to the army once they reached the Avon city, Oliver informed Luthien. The three women were sentenced to serve as house workers for various merchants, friends of the duke—Oliver did not have to explain their grim fate. And the dwarves, predictably, were given long terms at hard labor in the mines.

Luthien Bedwyr watched helplessly as Shuglin was pulled away down the north transept and out the side door to a waiting wagon.

The tax call soon began anew, and Oliver and the fuming Luthien made their way back along the triforium to the hidden corridor and down to the ledge overlooking the foyer. They let one released merchant go out, then slipped down into the small narthex. Oliver retrieved his grapnel and slipped it away, then adjusted his veils and motioned for Luthien to lead the way.

The cyclopian guards made some nasty comment as the "merchant" and his virgin daughter stepped between them, but Luthien was hardly listening. He didn't say a word all the way back to Tiny Alcove, and then paced the apartment like a caged dog.

Oliver, still in his maiden's garb, remarked that midday was almost upon them and the Dwelf would soon be open, but Luthien gave no indication that he heard.

"There was not a thing you could do!" Oliver finally shouted, hopping up to stand on a chair in Luthien's pacing path so that he could shout in the man's face. "Not a thing!"

"They took him to the mines," the burdened young man remarked, turning back on his heels and ignoring the ranting halfling. "Well, if they took Shuglin to the mines, then I go to the mines."

"By all the virgins of Avon," Oliver muttered under his breath, and he sat forcefully down in the chair and pulled the long black hair of his wig over his eyes.

CHAPTER 20

THE VALUE OF A KISS

OLIVER AND LUTHIEN waited for more than an hour, crouched among a tumble of boulders in the rocky foothills just a quarter of a mile outside Montfort's southern wall, overlooking the narrow trail which led to the mines. Riverdancer and Threadbare, glad to be out of the city, grazed in a small meadow not far away. Oliver had explained that the slaver wagon would not leave the city until the tax calls were completed—in case Morkney found some other "volunteers" who preferred to work in the mines rather than pay their heavy tithes.

Luthien had planned to hit the wagon here, long before it got to the mine; Oliver knew better.

The young Bedwyr's expression fell considerably when the wagon came bouncing along, escorted by a score of cyclopians riding fierce ponypigs.

"Now can we go to the Dwelf?" the weary halfling asked, but from the determined way angry Luthien stormed off to retrieve his mount, Oliver guessed the answer.

They trotted along the road a good distance behind the wagon, but sometimes catching sight of it far ahead on the rocky trail as it came out along an open ledge.

"This is not so smart a thing," Oliver said many times, but Luthien didn't reply. Finally, with more than three miles of trail behind them, the halfling stopped Threadbare. Luthien went on for about twenty yards, then turned Riverdancer about and looked back accusingly at his friend.

"The dwarf—" he began, but stopped immediately as Oliver threw his hand up. The halfling sat with his eyes closed, his head tilted back, and it seemed to Luthien that he was sniffing the air.

Threadbare leaped at Oliver's command, crashed through the brush at the side of the road and disappeared. Luthien eyed Oliver incredulously for just a moment, then heard the rumble of rushing ponypigs not so far up the road.

He had no time to escape to where Oliver had gone! Head down over the horse's thick mane, Luthien kicked Riverdancer into a dead run, back toward Montfort. A mile passed before he found a place where he could get off the road, and he and his horse skidded into a shallow gully and banged roughly off a stone wall. Luthien dropped from the saddle and grabbed Riverdancer's bridle, trying to soothe and quiet the nervous beast.

He needn't have worried, for the cyclopian band passed by at a full gallop, the thunder of their heavy mounts and the empty wagon bouncing behind them burying any other sounds.

After a few deep breaths, Luthien walked Riverdancer back to the road, waited a moment to make sure that all the one-eyes had passed, then galloped back the other way. He found Oliver right where he had left him.

"Is about time," the halfling complained. "We must get to the dwarf before they bring him to the lower mines. Once he is down there . . ." Oliver didn't bother finishing the thought, since Luthien was long past him by then.

The mine entrance was little more than an unremarkable hole in the side of a mountain, its sides propped with heavy timbers. The friends tethered their horses far to the side of the trail and crept to a vantage point behind some brush. They saw no cyclopians milling about; saw no movement at all.

"It is not well guarded," Luthien remarked.

"Why would it be?" Oliver asked him.

Luthien shrugged and started out from their hiding place. Oliver grabbed his arm, and when he looked back, the halfling directed his gaze along the mountain wall to another opening at the right of the mine entrance.

"It could be the barracks," the halfling whispered. "Or it could be where they keep the prisoners before they send them down."

Luthien looked from one entrance to the other. "Which one?" he finally asked, turning back to Oliver.

Oliver held his hands out wide and finally pointed to the main mine. "Even if this dwarf, Shuglin, is not in there, that is the way they must get him down."

Luthien moved up to the wall, Oliver right behind. He put the cowl of his crimson cape low and inched along, pausing at the entrance. The tunnel was dark, very dark, and Luthien had to pause until his eyes adjusted to the gloom. Even then, he could hardly make out the shapes within.

He lifted a fold in his cloak and Oliver scooted under, then Luthien inched his way around the corner and into the mine. They went around one bend—a side passage broke off to the right, possibly leading to tunnels within the other mine opening. Further down the passageway they were traveling, though, they saw the flicker of a torch and heard the foot-steps of approaching cyclopians.

Into the side passage the friends skittered, taking up a position so they could continue to watch down the tunnel. Luthien had his bow out and assembled in an instant, while Oliver, flat on the floor, peeked around the corner.

The torchlight grew; two cyclopians rounded the next bend, talking lightly. Oliver held two fingers up in the air for Luthien to see, then kept his hand up high, ready to signal the attack.

Luthien drew back his bowstring. The light intensified, as did the sound of heavy cyclopian footsteps. Oliver's hand snapped down and Luthien leaped by the prone halfling into the tunnel, bow bent and arrow ready to fly.

The cyclopians were barely a dozen feet away, leaping wildly in surprise.

Luthien missed.

He could hardly believe it, but as one of the cyclopians jumped and twisted in fright, its arm waving high, his arrow sliced in below the crea-ture's armpit, grazing it but doing no real damage.

Luthien stood staring blankly, holding his bow as if it had deceived him. On came the growling cyclopians, and if Oliver hadn't slid out to intercept, Luthien would have surely been cut down.

Rapier and main gauche whipped in a wild dance, Oliver scoring a wicked hit in the ribs of the closest brute and nicking the second before they even realized he was there.

The wounded cyclopian, weapon arm tight against its side, clubbed at the halfling with its torch. Its companion fell back a step, then came on, throwing curses and waving a heavy club.

Oliver rolled left, back toward the tunnel. Luthien, sword drawn, dove ahead behind the halfling. The club wielder, its bulbous eye follow-ing Oliver's movement, gawked in surprise as the young man's sword ex-ploded into its chest.

Oliver came up short, halfway through the roll, and fell forward in-stead, inside the arc of the down-swinging torch. The halfling's rapier plunged ahead once, and then again, and the cyclopian staggered back-ward, eyeing little Oliver with sheer disbelief.

Then it fell dead.

Taking only the moment to put out the torch (and for Oliver to ask, "How did you miss?"), the two friends moved on more urgently now. Soon more torchlight loomed up ahead.

The tunnel ended at a ledge forty feet above the floor of a large, roughly oval chamber. Five cyclopians were in here and, to the friends' relief, two dwarves, including one with a bushy, blue-black beard and a sleeveless leather tunic. Both were shackled at the wrists and ankles, surrounded by their cyclopian captors. The group stood near the opposite end of the chamber in front of a large hole cut into the floor. Suspended above the hole was a block and tackle, with one thick rope going to a cranking mechanism on the chamber's floor at the side of the hole and two other ropes disappearing beneath the floor.

One cyclopian leaned over the hole, loosely holding the side rope and looking down, while another worked the crank.

Luthien crouched and nocked another arrow, but Oliver looked at him doubtfully, pointing to one side and then the other of the well-lit room. At least three tunnels came into this chamber at the floor level.

Luthien understood the halfling's concerns. This higher region of the complex was likely for the guards, and those three tunnels, and the one Luthien and Oliver had just come down, might quickly fill with cyclopians at the first sounds of battle.

But Luthien did not miss the significance of the crank. Those two ropes supported a platform, he figured, and once Shuglin and the other dwarf went down, they would be lost to him forever.

The cyclopian leaning over the hole nodded stupidly and called down. The brute was answered by another cyclopian, and then another, not far below the rim.

The first cyclopian jerked suddenly, then fell headlong into the hole. Four other cyclopians, seeing the arrow in their companion's back, looked across the room and up to the ledge, to see Luthien fire off another arrow, then take a rope from Oliver. The arrow skipped harmlessly off the cranking mechanism, but the cyclopian working it fell back and shrieked.

Oliver, his adhering grapnel set against the ceiling far out from the ledge, jumped onto Luthien's back and as soon as Luthien packed his folding bow away, the two swung down, crimson and purple capes billowing behind them. Luthien angled the jump toward the crank: the most important target, he figured.

Oliver's calculations in setting the grapnel were not far off, and Luthien let the halfling down as they came to the low point of the swing, the halfling falling the last three feet to the floor, landing in a headlong roll, one somersault after another.

Luthien continued on toward the cyclopian near the crank. The young Bedwyr kicked out, trying to knock the brute aside, but he went up too high as he passed, kicking at empty air when the cyclopian ducked. The brute's distraction cost it dearly, though, for when it looked back down, it saw Oliver, or more specifically the tip of Oliver's rapier, coming toward it. The fine blade pierced the cyclopian's belly and sliced upward into its lungs, and it fell aside, gasping for breath that would not come.

Luthien, spinning in tight circles from the momentum of his kick, swung right over the shaft. As he had figured, he saw a large platform holding half a dozen yelling cyclopians fifteen feet below the rim. But the far edge of the hole was still out of reach when his momentum played out and the rope began its inevitable swing the other way—where three armed cyclopians waited.

Luthien wisely jumped free, flailing his arms wildly. He banged his shin hard against the lip of the shaft and nearly fell in. With a groan and a roll, he cleared the drop and regained his footing, drawing his sword. With a quick look, he rushed to the far side of the rim. One of the cyclopians went for the halfling; the others shoved past the dwarves and went to the corner to meet the circling Luthien.

And all of them were screaming for help, screaming that "the Crimson Shadow" was upon them!

"I see the biggest came for me," Oliver remarked, and he wasn't idly bantering. The brute facing him was among the largest and ugliest cyclopians Oliver had ever seen. Worse still, the cyclopian wore heavy padded armor—Oliver doubted that his rapier could even get through it—and wielded a huge double-bladed battle-ax.

Down came the weapon in an overhead chop, and Oliver darted forward, rolling right through the brute's widespread legs. He looked back to see sparks flying as the weapon took a chunk of stone out of the floor.

Oliver dove and rolled back the other way as the cyclopian roared and swung about. Then they were facing each other squarely again, Oliver with his back to the crank and the shaft beyond.

Luthien charged in bravely, daring the odds. These two brutes were also well armored, and they wielded fine swords that accepted the heavy hits of the young Bedwyr's first flurry and turned his blade aside.

Luthien lunged straight forward; a sword chopped his blade's tip to the stone, while the other brute thrust ahead, forcing Luthien to twist violently to the side to avoid being impaled. He got his weapon back in line quickly and slapped the stubborn cyclopian's sword away, then countered viciously.

But the attack was again defeated.

Oliver's rapier jabbed into the front of the cyclopian's armor three times in rapid succession, but the blade only bent and would not penetrate. The halfling had hoped to tire the heavy-muscled brute, but it was he who was soon panting, diving this way and that to avoid the mighty battle-ax.

He glanced all about, searching for a new tactic, a chink in the cyclopian's armor. What he found instead was a ring of keys tagged onto the brute's belt. Instinctively, the halfling glanced over at Luthien, and continued to watch the young man out of the corner of his eye, waiting for the right moment.

Luthien was hard-pressed but fought back valiantly, fiercely, keeping the cyclopians in place. Looking past his adversaries, he saw the two dwarves untangle themselves from the chain that hooked them together at the ankles, saw them line up, and could guess well enough what they had in mind.

Luthien's sword snapped left and right, left and right, routines easily defeated, but demanding his opponents' complete attention.

The charging dwarves hit the cyclopians in the back of the legs, heaving them forward.

Luthien's sword snapped right, turning down the blade of that brute. The young Bedwyr then spun fast to the left, tucking his shoulder so that the cyclopian would not ram him and so the brute would slip behind him. And Luthien's sword flashed left, not only defeating the attack of that stumbling cyclopian, but knocking its sword to the stone.

He heard Oliver call out his name and spun around once more, jamming an elbow into the ribs of the cyclopian behind him and knocking the unfortunate brute down the shaft. Then Luthien rushed forward out of the tumbling cyclopian's desperate reach.

In one fluid motion, Oliver's rapier darted at his adversary and slipped to the side, through the loop of the key ring. Out to the right went the blade, snapping the keys from the jailor's belt, then high and back to the left, the key ring slipping free and flying through the air.

Into Luthien Bedwyr's waiting hand.

Luthien slid down to the floor, knowing the most important shackle to be the one binding the dwarves together. He was lucky—the second key fit—and the lock clicked open, and Luthien jumped back up to meet the remaining cyclopian, its sword back in its hand.

For all the advantage the friends had apparently gained, though, none were breathing easier. Torchlight flickered from two of the side tunnels, and yells and heavy footsteps echoed down one. The soldiers on the platform below the room were not content to sit back and wait, either. A one-eyed face came above the lip, and then another to the side; the brutes were climbing the guide ropes.

The jailor roared to see its keys go flying away and on the monster came, its huge ax thrashing back and forth. Oliver twisted and darted, making no attempt to get a weapon up to block the battle-ax, knowing that either of his blades would be snapped in half or taken from his hand by the sheer force of the jailor's blows.

The ax chopped down, and Oliver skipped left, near the crank. Up he hopped, atop the spindle and heavy rope. Then he hopped straight up again, desperately tucking his little legs under him as the ax swished across. The powerful cyclopian broke its momentum in mid-swing and curved the ax up high, over its head.

Down it came, and Oliver leaped and rolled to the right. The ax smashed onto the spindle, bit hard into the rope. The dimwitted jailor blinked in amazement as the frayed hemp unraveled and snapped, then watched helplessly as the rope's severed end soared off toward the block and tackle, and the platform (and a dozen cyclopians) fell away!

"I do thank you," Oliver remarked.

The jailor roared and swung about, overbalancing with the unbridled strength of the blow. The cyclopian never came close to hitting the halfling, though, for Oliver was on his merry way back toward the crank even as the ax came across the other way. Up again, Oliver poked straight out, his rapier's tip scoring a hit into the cyclopian's big eye.

The blinded jailor slashed wildly, this way and that, banging his ax off the stone, off the crank. Oliver tumbled and rolled, thoroughly enjoying the spectacle (as long as the ax didn't get too near to him!), and gradually, by calling out taunts, he managed to get the jailor near the edge of the hole.

On a nod from Oliver, Shuglin barreled into the backside of the jailor, launching the brute over the side.

"Should've kept the ax," the dwarf grumbled as the jailor, and the battle-ax, plummeted from sight.

One on one, Luthien had little trouble in parrying the vicious strokes of his cyclopian adversary. He let the one-eye play out the rage of its initial attack routine and gradually turned the tide against it, setting it on its heels with one cunning thrust after another.

Understanding that it could not win, the beast, with typical cyclopian bravery, turned and fled—to join its companions who were then entering the chamber from the side passages.

And so the forces faced off for several tense seconds, the cyclopian ranks swelling to a dozen or more. Oliver looked back into the shaft doubtfully, for it dropped out of sight into the gloom and he did not even have his grapnel and line. Luthien managed to get the shackles off of Shuglin, then went to work on the other dwarf, while Shuglin ran over and retrieved the sword from the first cyclopian Oliver had killed.

Still the cyclopians did not advance, and Luthien understood that they were allowing their enemies to prepare themselves only because they expected more reinforcements to enter the room.

"We must do something," Oliver reasoned, apparently having the same grim thoughts.

Luthien slipped his sword in its scabbard and took out his bow, popping it open, pinning it, and setting an arrow in one fluid motion. The cyclopians understood then what this man with the curious stick was doing, and they fumbled all over themselves trying to get out of harm's way.

Luthien shot one in the neck, and it went down screaming. The others screamed, too, but they did not run for cover. Rather, they charged before Luthien could set another arrow.

"That was not what I had in mind," Oliver remarked dryly.

In the ensuing tumult, the desperate companions did not hear the twang of bowstrings, and all four of them looked on curiously as several of the charging brutes lurched weirdly and tumbled to the stone. Seeing arrows protruding from their backs, the friends and the cyclopians looked back to the room's ledge and saw a handful of slender archers— elves, probably—their hands moving in a blur as they continued to rain death on the cyclopians.

The one-eyes scrambled and fled, many running with one or two arrows sticking from them. In response, arrows and spears came whistling out of the side passages, and though Oliver's claims about a cyclopian's lack of depth perception held true once more, the sheer numbers of flying bolts presented a serious problem.

"Run on!" came a cry from the ledge, a voice Luthien knew.

"Siobhan," he said to Oliver, pulling the halfling along as he made for the wall.

Luthien grabbed Oliver's rope and gave three quick tugs, releasing the magical grapnel from the ceiling. Siobhan's group already had one rope down to them, and Shuglin's companion grabbed on and began climbing swiftly, hand over hand. An arrow thunked into the dwarf's heavily muscled shoulder, but he only grimaced and continued on his determined way.

Luthien set Oliver's rope, heaving the grapnel onto the wall up beside the ledge, and he handed the rope over to Shuglin. The dwarf bade Oliver to grab on to his back, and up they went, Luthien shaking his head in amazement at how quickly the powerful dwarf could climb.

A spear skipped across the stone between Luthien's legs; cyclopians came out of all three passages, the lead ones carrying large shields to protect them from the archers on the ledge.

Luthien had wanted to wait and let Shuglin and Oliver get off the rope, not knowing how much weight the small grapnel would support, but he had run out of time. He leaped up as high as he could, grabbing the rope (and tucking its end up behind him), and began pulling himself up, hand over hand, trying to steady his feet against the wall so that he could walk along.

It wasn't as easy as the powerful dwarves made it look. Luthien made progress, but he would have surely been caught, or prodded by long spears, except that Shuglin shrugged Oliver off as soon as they made the ledge, and he and his dwarven companion took up the rope and began to methodically haul it in.

Arrows whizzed down past Luthien's head, and even more alarmingly, arrows and spears came up from below. He felt a bang against his foot and turned his leg to see an arrow sticking from the heel of his boot.

Then rough hands grabbed his shoulders and he was hauled over the ledge, and on the group ran. They passed several dead cyclopians, including the two Luthien and Oliver had killed, and came out of the tunnel, hearing that the cyclopians had gained the ledge behind them and were once again in pursuit.

"Our horses are there!" Luthien explained to Siobhan, and she nodded and kissed him quickly, then pushed him along to catch up with Oliver. She and her Cutter companions, along with Shuglin and the other dwarf, went the other way, disappearing into the brush.

"I cannot believe they came for us," Luthien remarked as he caught up to the halfling, Oliver with one foot already in Threadbare's stirrup.

"You must be a good kisser," the halfling answered. Then Threadbare leaped away, Riverdancer pounding right behind, back out onto the road.

The cyclopian horde exited the mine, howling with outrage, but all they heard was the pounding of hooves as Luthien and Oliver charged away.

CHAPTER 21

UNWANTED ATTENTION

*L*UTHIEN CASUALLY WALKED into the Dwelf sometime after Oliver, as the halfling had instructed. Oliver had grown very cautious in the week since the escape at the mines and had gone out of his way so that he and Luthien were not viewed as an inseparable team. Luthien didn't really understand the point; there were enough halfling rogues in this area of Montfort to more than cover their tracks. If the Praetorian Guard was searching for a human and his halfling sidekick, they would have dozens of possibilities to sift through.

Luthien didn't argue, though, thinking the halfling's demands were prudent.

The Dwelf was packed, as it had been every night that week. Elves and dwarves, halflings and humans filled every table—except one. There in the corner sat a group of cyclopians, Praetorian Guards, brimming with fine weapons and wearing grim, scowling expressions.

Luthien pushed his way through the crowd and found, conveniently, an empty stool at the bar near Oliver.

"Oliver!" he said, overly excited. "So good to see you again! How long has it been? A month?"

Oliver turned a skeptical look upon the exuberant young man.

"You were both in here the night before last," Tasman remarked dryly, walking past.

"Oops," Luthien apologized, giving a weak smile and a shrug. He looked around at the throng. "The crowd is large again this night," he remarked.

"Good gossip brings them in," Tasman replied, walking past the other way and sliding an ale across the counter to Luthien as he went off to see to another thirsty customer.

Luthien hoisted the mug and took a hearty swig, then noticed Oliver's profound silence, the halfling wearing an expression which showed him to be deep in contemplation.

"Good gossip—" Luthien started to say. He was going to ask what the patrons might be talking about, but in just deciphering the small patches of conversation he caught out of the general din about him, he knew the answer. They were talking about the Crimson Shadow—one scruffy-looking human even shuffled his drunken way near the cyclopians' table and muttered, "The Shadow Lives!" and snapped his fingers under their noses. One of the brutes started up immediately to throttle the rogue, but its comrade grabbed it by the arm and held it firmly in place.

"There is sure to be a fight," Luthien said.

"It will not be the first this week," Oliver replied glumly.

They remained in the Dwelf for more than an hour, Luthien taking in all the excited chatter and Oliver sitting with a single ale, mulling over the situation. A general chorus of dissatisfaction sounded behind every story, and it seemed to Luthien as if the legend he had become had given the poor of Montfort a bit of hope, a rallying point for their deflated pride.

His step was light when Oliver left the Dwelf, signaling him to follow.

"Perhaps we should stay a while," Luthien offered when they walked out into the crisp night air. "There may be a fight with the cyclopians, and the brutes are better armed than the Dwelf's patrons."

"Then let the patrons learn their folly," Oliver retorted.

Luthien stopped and watched the halfling as Oliver continued on his way. He didn't know exactly what was bothering Oliver, but he understood that it probably had something to do with the increased attention.

Oliver was indeed worried, fearful that this whole "Crimson Shadow" business was quickly getting out of control. It did not bother the halfling to hear the populace speaking out against the tyrannies of Morkney and his pompous merchant class—those wretches had it coming, the halfling figured. But Oliver did harbor a thief's worst fear: that he and Luthien were attracting too much unwanted attention from powerful adversaries. The halfling loved being the center of attention, oftentimes went out of his way to be the center of attention, but there were reasonable limits.

Luthien caught up to him quickly. "Have you planned an excursion into the upper section this night?" the young man asked, and it was plain from his tone that he hoped Oliver had not.

The halfling turned his gaze upon Luthien and cocked an eyebrow as if to mock the question. They had not pulled any jobs since springing Shuglin, and Oliver had explained that they likely wouldn't go into the upper section again for at least a month. He knew why Luthien was asking, though.

"You have plans," he stated as much as asked. Oliver could guess the answer readily enough. Luthien was ready for another tryst with Siobhan.

"I will meet with the Cutters," Luthien answered, "to check on Shuglin and his companion."

"The dwarves fare well," Oliver said. "Elves and dwarves get on well, since they share persecution at the hands of the humans."

"I just want to check," Luthien remarked.

"Of course," Oliver said with a wry smile. "But perhaps you should come this night back to the apartment. The air is chill and the Dwelf will likely see trouble before the moon is set."

The deflated look that washed over Luthien nearly pulled a burst of laughter from Oliver's serious expression. Oliver didn't harbor any intentions of keeping Luthien from his meeting, he just wanted to make the young man squirm a bit. In the halfling's view, love should never be an easy thing: sweeter tasting is the forbidden fruit.

"Very well," the halfling said after a long and uncomfortable moment. "But do not be out too late!"

Luthien was off and running, and Oliver did chuckle. He smiled all the way back to the apartment, his worries brushed aside by his romantic nature.

Candles burned long into the night in the private chambers of Duke Morkney's palace. A group of merchants had demanded an audience, and the duke, so busy with the approaching end of the trading season, could find no time to accommodate them earlier in the day.

Morkney could easily guess the topic of this meeting—all of Montfort was buzzing about the break at the mines. Morkney was not so concerned with the news—this wasn't the first time a prisoner had escaped, after all, and it wouldn't likely be the last. But these merchants, standing before the duke's fabulous desk, their grim features set with worry, obviously were more than a little concerned.

The duke sat back in his chair and listened attentively as the merchants complained and whined, their stories always connected to this mysterious Crimson Shadow figure.

"They're painting red shadows all over my store!" one man grumbled.

"And mine," two others said at the same time.

"And nearly every street in Montfort bears the words 'The Shadow Lives!'" offered another.

Morkney nodded his understanding; he, too, had seen the annoying graffiti. He understood, too, that this Crimson Shadow wasn't doing the painting. Rather, others were taking up the call of this mysterious figure-head; and that, Morkney was wise enough to realize, was more dangerous indeed.

He listened to the rambling merchants for another hour, politely, though he heard the same stories over and over again. He promised to take the matter under serious consideration, but secretly, Morkney was hoping that this minor annoyance would simply go away.

King Greensparrow was complaining again about the size of Montfort's tithe, and by all the words of the local seers, the winter would be a cold one.

And so the duke of Montfort was more than a little relieved when the captain of his Praetorian Guard interrupted his breakfast the next morning to inform him that the wagon caravan which had set out for Avon— the caravan carrying the four men who had been sentenced the same day as the dwarf, Shuglin—had been attacked on the road.

The captain of the guard produced a tattered red cloak, its material taking on the darker hue of dried blood in many places.

"We got the bloke," the cyclopian said. "No more Crimson Shadow. And we got the halfling 'twas said to be traveling in the shadow's shadow! And seven others"—he held up six fingers—"that were with them."

"And the caravan?"

"On its merry way," the cyclopian replied happily. "I lost four, but we got two more prisoners now, and the Crimson Shadow and the halfling're dead and dragging by ropes behind."

Morkney took the torn cloak and promised the soldier that he and his troops would be properly rewarded, then dismissed the cyclopian and found that his breakfast suddenly tasted better.

Later, though, on a sudden discomforting hunch, Morkney took the torn cloak into his private study. He searched his library for a specific tome, then fumbled through his desk drawers to find the proper components for a spell. The Crimson Shadow had left telltale signs behind him on his thieving adventures, silhouettes magically created against walls and windows, and by Morkney's reasoning, this cloak was likely the source.

The duke sprinkled exotic herbs and powders over the tattered cloth and read the enchantment from his book. The components eerily glowed a silvery blue hue, then went dark.

Morkney waited quietly for another minute, then another. Nothing happened. The bloodstained cloak was not magical and had never been enchanted.

Like the vandals painting walls throughout the city, this attempted raid had not been the handiwork of the real Crimson Shadow, but rather the lame attempt of an upstart glory-seeker.

Duke Morkney settled back into a large chair and put his old and shaky hand up to his chin. The Crimson Shadow was fast becoming a real problem.

*   *   *

The Dwelf was subdued that day and that night, sobered by news that a halfling named Stumpy Corsetbuster and a human rogue by the name of Dirty Abner had been killed out on the road east of Montfort. The Crimson Shadow was dead, said the rumors—rumors that Oliver deBurrows did not seem so unhappy to hear when he entered the tavern to join Luthien sometime after sundown.

"Yep, the Crimson Shadow's no more, so it's said," Tasman remarked to them, filling their mugs.

It occurred to Luthien that the barkeep's expression was not in accord with the gravity of his words. And how long had it been, Luthien wondered, since Tasman had asked him or Oliver for any payment? Or were free drinks a benefit of renting an apartment from the barkeep?

Tasman walked away to see to another customer, but he let his stare—his knowing stare, Luthien realized—linger long on the young man and the halfling sitting beside him.

"A pity about Stumpy," Oliver remarked. "A fine halfling-type, with a fine fat belly." As with Tasman, though, Luthien didn't think Oliver's emotions agreed with his words.

"You're not bothered by this," the young man accused. "Some men—and your fine halfling-type—are dead."

"Thieves are killed every day in Montfort's streets," Oliver remarked, and he looked directly into Luthien's cinnamon-colored eyes. "We have to consider the benefits."

"Benefits?" Luthien nearly choked on the word.

"Our money will not last the winter," Oliver explained. "And I do not like the prospects of wandering the open road with so cold snowflakes coming down around me."

Luthien figured it out. He settled back over his mug of ale, his expression forlorn. The whole affair left a sour taste in his mouth.

"Now if we could only coax your remarkable cape to stop leaving its mark behind," Oliver added.

Luthien nodded grimly. There was a price in all of this less-than-honorable life, he decided, a price paid for by his conscience and his heart. People had died in the name of the Crimson Shadow, impersonating the Crimson Shadow, and now he and Oliver would use that grim fact for their benefit. Luthien drained his mug and motioned for Tasman to get him another.

Oliver tugged on his arm and nodded to the Dwelf's door, then whispered that they would be wise to take their leave.

A group of Praetorian Guards entered the tavern, smug looks on their ugly faces.

Soon after Luthien and Oliver got back to their apartment, a fight erupted in the Dwelf. Three men and two cyclopians were killed, many others wounded, and the Praetorian Guards were driven back into the upper section.

Duke Morkney was again awake late that night. Midnight was the best hour for what he had in mind, the time when magical energies were at their peak.

In his private study, the duke moved to one wall and slid a large tapestry aside, revealing a huge golden-edged mirror. He settled into a chair directly in front of it, read from a page in another of his magical tomes and tossed a handful of powdered crystal at the glass. Almost immediately, the reflections in the mirror disappeared, replaced by a swirling gray cloud.

Morkney continued his arcane chant, sending his thoughts— thoughts of the Crimson Shadow—into the mirror. The gray cloud shifted about and began to take form, and Morkney leaned forward in his chair, thinking that he would soon learn the identity of this dangerous rogue.

A wall of red came up suddenly across the mirror, blotting out everything within its enchanted confines.

Morkney's eyes widened in amazement. He took up the chant again for nearly an hour, even sprinkled the mirror several more times with the valuable crystalline powder, but he could not break through the barrier.

He went back to his desk and the pile of books and parchments he had pored over all day. He had found several references to the legendary Crimson Shadow, a thief who had terrorized the Gascons in their days of occupation. But these written tidbits were as vague as the clues left by the man now wearing the mantle. One reference had spoken of the crimson cape, though, and told of its magical dweomer designed to shelter its possessor from prying eyes.

Morkney looked back to the red mirror; apparently the cloak could shelter its possessor from magical prying, as well.

The duke was not too disappointed, though. He had learned much this night, gaining confirmation that the rogues on the road were impostors and that the real Crimson Shadow was indeed still alive. And wise Morkney, who had lived through centuries, was not too upset that the cloak had blocked his scrying attempt. He could not get the image of the

Crimson Shadow into his mirror, but perhaps he could locate someone else, some tear in this crafty thief's disguise.

CHAPTER 22

BAIT

OLIVER WENT INTO THE DWELF alone a couple of days later. As usual, the place was crowded, and as usual, most of the talk centered on the continuing antics of the Crimson Shadow. One group of dwarves at a table near the bar where Oliver was sitting whispered that the Crimson Shadow had been killed out on the road, trying to free four enslaved men. The muscular, bearded dwarves lifted their flagons in toast to the memory of the gallant thief.

"He's not dead!" a human at a nearby table protested vehemently. "He pulled a job last night, he did! Got himself a merchant on the way." He turned to the other men at the table, who were nodding in complete agreement.

"Skewered the bloke right 'bout here," one of them added, poking a finger into the middle of his own chest.

Oliver was not surprised by any of the outrageous claims. He had witnessed similar events back in Gascony. A thief would rise to a level of notoriety and then his legend would be perpetuated by imitators. There was more than flattery involved here; often lesser thieves could pull jobs more easily, frightening their targets by impersonating a notorious outlaw. Oliver sighed at the thought that someone had died playing the Crimson Shadow, and the possibility that he and Luthien, if caught, might now be charged with murdering a human merchant did not sit very well. Pragmatically, though, all the talk was good news. Imitators would blur the trail behind Oliver and Luthien; if the merchant-types thought the Crimson Shadow dead, they would likely relax their guard.

The contented halfling tuned out the conversations and took a look around the Dwelf, searching for a lady to court. The pickings seemed slim this night, so Oliver went back to his ale instead. He noticed Tasman then, standing a short distance down the bar, wiping out glasses and eyeing him grimly. When Oliver returned the look, the wiry barkeep eased his quiet way down to stand before the halfling.

"You came alone," Tasman remarked.

"Young Luthien cannot control his heart," Oliver answered. "He goes

again this night to meet with his love—a moonlight tryst on a rooftop."
The halfling spoke wistfully, revealing that he was beginning to approve
of the lovers. Oliver was indeed a romantic sort, and he remembered his
days back in Gascony when he had left one (at least) broken heart behind him in every town.

Tasman apparently was not sharing the halfling's cozy feelings. His expression remained grim. "He'll be back at the apartment soon, then," he
said.

"Oh, no," Oliver began slyly, misunderstanding Tasman's meaning.
As he continued to study the grim-faced barkeep, Oliver began to
catch on.

"What do you mean?" he asked bluntly.

Tasman leaned over the bar, close to Oliver. "Siobhan, the half-elf,"
the barkeep explained. "She was taken this day for trial in the morning."

Oliver nearly fell off his stool.

"She was accused for the escape at the mines," Tasman explained.
"Her merchant master walked her into Duke Morkney's palace this very
afternoon—apparently she didn't even know that she was to be arrested."

Oliver tried to digest the information and to fathom its many implications. Siobhan arrested? Why now? The halfling could not help but
think that the half-elf's professional relationship with the Crimson
Shadow had played a part in this. Perhaps even her personal relationship
with Luthien had come into play. Was the wizard-duke onto Luthien's
true identity?

"Some are even saying that she's the Crimson Shadow," Tasman went
on, and Oliver winced at hearing that, certain then that Siobhan's arrest
was no simple coincidence. "They're sure to be asking about that in the
Ministry tomorrow morning."

"How do you know all this?" the halfling asked, though he realized that
Tasman had keen ears and knew many things about Montfort's under-
world. There was a reason that Oliver and Luthien had enjoyed free drinks
and meals for the last weeks. There was a reason that wise Tasman seemed
as amused as Oliver by the many tales of phony Crimson Shadows.

"They're making no secret of it," the toughened barkeep replied.
"Every tavern's talking about the half-elf's arrest. I'm surprised that you
hadn't heard of it before now."

Suspected thieves were arrested almost every day in Montfort, Oliver
knew, so why was this one being made so public?

Oliver thought he knew the answer. The word "bait" kept popping
into his mind as he skittered out of the Dwelf.

*   *   *

Oliver lost his "little-girl" smile as soon as he and Luthien walked between the Praetorian Guards outside the Ministry's great front doors the next morning. In the foyer, the halfling looked disdainfully at his disguise, wondering why he kept winding up in this place. Of course, Oliver had known the night before, when he had told forlorn Luthien of Siobhan's arrest, that he would find himself in the Ministry once more.

But he didn't have to like it.

"We might be causing her harm," Oliver reasoned, and not for the first time, as he set the magical grapnel on the passageway's entrance high above the room. Luthien took the rope in hand and verily ran up the wall, then hoisted Oliver behind him.

"Morkney might only suspect that she has knowledge of the Crimson Shadow," Oliver went on when he got into the hidden passage. "If we are caught here this day, it could weigh badly on the one you love." To say nothing of how it would weigh on the two of them! Oliver reasoned, keeping the thought private. The flustered halfling pushed the long black hair of his wig out of his face and roughly rearranged his printed dress, which had gotten all twisted up in the climb.

"I have to know," Luthien answered.

"I have seen many traps baited like this before," Oliver said.

"And have you ever left a love behind?" Luthien asked.

Oliver didn't answer and made no further remarks. The question had stung, for Oliver had indeed left a lover behind—a halfling girl of eighteen years. Oliver was very young, living in a rural village and just beginning his career as a thief. The local landowner (the only one in town worth stealing from) could not catch up to Oliver, but he did find out about the halfling's romance. Oliver's lover was taken and Oliver had run off, justifying his actions as in his lover's best interest.

He never found out what happened to her, and many times, in hindsight, he wondered if his "tactical evacuation" had been wrought of pure cowardice.

So now he followed Luthien up to the higher levels, as they had gone on their first excursion into the great cathedral. Oliver noticed that there seemed to be more cyclopians about this day than on that previous occasion, and many more villagers, as well. Morkney was planning a show, the halfling mused, and so the wicked duke wanted an audience.

Oliver grabbed Luthien by the shoulder and bade the man to put on the crimson cape—and Oliver wrapped his own purple cape over the print dress, and plopped his hat, which had gotten more than a little rumpled, atop his head—before they crept out onto the gargoyle-lined triforium fifty feet up from the floor.

They went out quietly and without interruption, ending at the corner of the south transept, where Luthien crouched behind a gargoyle, Oliver behind him.

The scene was much the same as the first time the friends had ventured into the majestic building. Red-robed Duke Morkney sat in a chair behind the great altar at the cathedral's eastern end, appearing quite bored as his lackeys called the tax rolls and counted the pitiful offerings of the poor wretches.

Luthien watched the spectacle for only a moment, then focused his attention on the front pews of the cathedral. Several people were sitting in line, wearing the gray hooded robes of prisoners and guarded by a group of cyclopians. Only one was a dwarf, yellow haired, and Luthien sighed in relief that it was not Shuglin. Three others were obviously men, but the remaining three appeared to be either younger boys or women.

"Where are you?" the young Bedwyr whispered, continuing his scan through long minutes. One of the forms in the prisoner line shifted then, and Luthien noted the end of long wheat-colored hair slipping out from under her hood. Instinctively, the young man edged forward as if he would leap off of the ledge.

Oliver took a tight hold on Luthien's arm and did not blink when the young man turned to him. The halfling's expression reminded Luthien that there was little they could do.

"It is just as it was with the dwarf," Oliver whispered. "I do not know why we are here."

"I have to know," Luthien protested.

Oliver sighed, but he understood.

The tax rolls went on for another half hour, everything seeming perfectly normal. Still, Oliver could not shake the nagging feeling that this was not an average day at the Ministry. Siobhan had been taken for a reason, and spreading the news about the arrest had been done deliberately, the halfling believed. If Shuglin had been arrested to send a clear message to the Crimson Shadow, then Siobhan had been taken to lure the Crimson Shadow in.

Oliver looked disdainfully at Luthien, thinking how much the young man resembled a netted trout.

The man calling the roll at the lectern gathered up his parchments and moved aside, and a second man took his place, motioning for the Praetorian Guards to prepare the prisoners. The seven gray-robed defendants were forced to stand and the man called out a name.

An older man of at least fifty years was roughly pulled out from the pew and pushed toward the altar. He stumbled more than once and would have fallen on his head, except that two cyclopians flanking him caught him and roughly stood him upright.

The accusation was a typical one: stealing a coat from a kiosk. The accusing merchant was called forward.

"This is not good," Oliver remarked. The halfling nodded toward the merchant. "He is a wealthy one and likely a friend of the duke. The poor wretch is doomed."

Luthien's lips seemed to disappear into his frustrated scowl. "Is anyone ever found innocent in this place?" he asked.

Oliver's reply, though expected, stung him profoundly. "No."

Predictably, the man was declared guilty. All of his belongings, including his modest house in Montfort's lower section, were granted to the wealthy merchant, and the merchant was also awarded the right to personally cut off the man's left hand that it might be displayed prominently at his kiosk to ward off any future thieves.

The older man protested weakly, and the cyclopians dragged him away.

The dwarf came out next, but Luthien was no longer watching. "Where are the Cutters?" he whispered. "Why aren't they here?"

"Perhaps they are," Oliver replied, and the young man's face brightened a bit.

"Only to watch, as are we," the halfling added, stealing Luthien's glow. "When thieves are caught, they are alone. It is a code that the people of the streets observe faithfully."

Luthien looked away from the halfling and back to the altar area, where the dwarf was being pronounced guilty and sentenced to two years of labor in the mines. Luthien could understand the pragmatism of what Oliver had just explained. If Duke Morkney believed that a thieving band would try to come to the rescue of one of its captured associates, then his job in cleaning out Montfort's thieves would be easy indeed.

Luthien was nodding his agreement with the logic—but if that was truly the case, then why was he perched now, fifty feet above the Ministry's floor?

It worked out—and Oliver was sure that it was no coincidence—that Siobhan was the last to be called. She moved out of the pew, and though her hands were tied in front of her, she proudly shook off the groping cyclopians as they prodded her toward the lectern.

"Siobhan, a slave girl," the man called loudly, glancing back to the duke. Morkney still appeared bored with it all.

"She was among those who attacked the mine," the man declared.

"By whose words?" the half-elf asked sternly. The cyclopian behind shoved her hard with the shaft of its long pole-arm, and Siobhan glanced back wickedly, green eyes narrowed.

"So spirited," Oliver whispered, his tone a clear lament. He was holding firmly to Luthien's crimson cape then, half-expecting the trembling young man to leap down from the ledge.

"Prisoners speak only when they are told to speak!" the man at the podium scolded.

"What worth is a voice in this evil place?" Siobhan replied, drawing another rough shove.

Luthien issued a low and guttural growl, and Oliver shook his head resignedly, feeling more than ever that they should not be in this dangerous place.

"She attacked the mine!" the man cried angrily, looking to the duke. "And she is a friend of the Crim—"

Morkney came forward in his chair, hand upraised to immediately silence his impetuous lackey. Oliver didn't miss the significance of the movement, as though Duke Morkney did not want the name spoken aloud.

Morkney put his wrinkled visage in line with Siobhan; his bloodshot eyes seemed to flare with some magical inner glow. "Where are the dwarves?" he asked evenly.

"What dwarves?" Siobhan replied.

"The two you and your . . . associates took from the mines," Morkney explained, and his pause again prodded Oliver into the belief that this entire arrest and trial had been put together for his and Luthien's benefit.

Siobhan chuckled and shook her head. "I am a servant," she said calmly, "and nothing more."

"Who is the owner of this slave?" Morkney called out. Siobhan's master stood from one of the pews near the front and raised his hand.

"You are without guilt," the duke explained, "and so you shall be compensated for your loss." The man breathed a sigh of relief, nodded and sat back down.

"Oh, no," Oliver groaned under his breath. Luthien looked from the merchant to the duke, and from the duke to Siobhan, not really understanding.

"And you," Morkney growled, coming up out of his chair for the first time in the two hours Oliver and Luthien had been in the Ministry. "You are guilty," Morkney said evenly, and he slipped back down into his seat, grinning wickedly. "Do enjoy the next five days in my dungeons."

Five days? Luthien silently echoed. Was this the sentence? He heard Oliver's groan again and figured that Morkney was not quite finished.

"For they will be your last five days!" the evil duke declared. "Then you will be hung by your neck—in the plaza bearing my own name!"

A general groan rose from the gathering, an uneasy shuffling, and cyclopian guards gripped their weapons more tightly, glancing from side to side as if they expected trouble. The sentence was not expected. The only time during Morkney's reign that a sentence of death had ever been imposed was for the murder of a human, and even in such an extreme case, if the murdered human was not someone of importance, the guilty party was usually sentenced to a life of slavery.

Again the word "bait" flitted through Oliver's thoughts. His mind careened along the possible trials he and his cohort would soon face, for Luthien would never allow such an injustice without at least a try at a rescue. The halfling figured that he would be busy indeed over the next five days, making connections with the Cutters and with anyone else who might help him out.

The distracted halfling figured differently when he looked back to Luthien, standing tall on the ledge, his bow out and ready.

With a cry of outrage, the young Bedwyr let fly, his arrow streaking unerringly for the chair and Duke Morkney, who glanced up to the triforium in surprise. There came a silvery flash, and not one arrow, but five, crossed the opening to the north transept. Then came a second flash, and each of those five became five; and a third, and twenty-five became a hundred and twenty-five.

And all of them continued toward the duke, and Luthien and Oliver looked on in disbelief.

But the volley was insubstantial; the dozens of arrows were no more than shadows of the first, and all of them dissipated into nothingness, or simply passed through the duke as he leaned forward in his chair, still grinning wickedly and pointing Luthien's way.

Luthien felt himself an impetuous fool, a thought that did not diminish when he heard Oliver's remark behind him.

"I do not think that was so smart a thing to do."

CHAPTER 23

TELL THEM!

*L*UTHIEN FELL BACK from the ledge as the gargoyle statue writhed to life. He whipped his bow across, breaking it on the creature's hard head, and started to call out for Oliver. But he soon realized that the halfling, now with his great hat upon his head, was already hard-pressed as the sinister statues all along the triforium animated to the call of their wizard master.

"Why do I always seem to find myself fighting along a ledge?" the halfling whined, ducking a clawed hand and jabbing ahead—only to sigh as his slender rapier bowed alarmingly, barely penetrating the gargoyle's hard skin.

All gathered in the cathedral had, by this time, learned of the tumult along the arched passageway. Cyclopians shouted out commands; the duke's man at the lectern called for the "death of the outlaws!" and then made the profound mistake of altering his cry to, "Death to the Crimson Shadow!"

"The Crimson Shadow!" more than one curious commoner shouted from the pews, pointing anxiously Luthien's way. The timing was perfect for the young Bedwyr, for at that moment, he landed a clean strike on the gargoyle, his sword slashing down across the creature's neck and biting deep into the hard wing. Luthien bulled ahead and the gargoyle fell from the ledge, flapping its wings frantically, though with the wound, it could not sustain itself in the air and spiraled down to the floor.

"The Crimson Shadow!" more people called out, and others screamed in terror as they came to recognize the living gargoyle.

Chased by two of the winged monsters, Oliver skittered behind Luthien to the edge of the corner where the triforium turned into the south transept. Frantically the halfling fumbled out his grapnel and rope, but he did not miss the significance of the growing tumult below.

Luthien's sword sparked as it cut a ringing line across one gargoyle's face. The young Bedwyr fought fiercely, trying to hold the powerful creatures at bay. He knew that he and Oliver were in trouble, though, for more monsters were coming along the arched passageway from the other way, and still others had taken wing and were slowly drifting across the open area of the transept.

Cyclopians were fast organizing down below, trying to corral the increasingly agitated crowd—many people, gathering their children in their arms, had run screaming for the western doors. One cyclopian reached for Siobhan and promptly got kicked in the groin. The other brute flanking her had even less luck, taking an arrow in the ribs (shot from somewhere back in the pews) as it tried to grab ahold of the fiery half-elf.

And still other people stood staring blankly, pointing to the triforium and calling out for the mysterious thief in the crimson cape.

Oliver, rope and grapnel free by then, did not miss the significance of it all.

"Yes!" he cried as loudly as he could. "The Crimson Shadow has come! Your hour of freedom is upon you, good people of Montfort."

"For Eriador!" Luthien cried, quickly catching on to the halfling's plan. "For Bruce MacDonald!" In lower, more desperate tones, he quickly added, "Hurry, Oliver!" as the gargoyles pressed ahead.

"Brave people of Montfort, to arms!" shouted the halfling, and he sent his grapnel spinning above his head and launched it to the base of the vaulting above and out a bit from the triforium. "Freedom is upon you. To arms! Now is the moment for heroes. Brave people of Montfort, to arms!"

Luthien groaned as a heavy gargoyle arm clubbed him across the shoulders. He went with the weight of the blow, spinning into a stumbling step and falling over Oliver. Scooping the halfling in one arm, the young Bedwyr wrapped himself about the rope and leaped out.

The spectacle of Luthien and Oliver, crimson and purple capes flying behind them, swinging from the triforium, sliding down the rope inexorably toward the altar and the tyrant duke, replaced panic with courage, gave heart to the enslaved people of Montfort. Fittingly, a merchant with a large bag of coins, his taxes for the day, struck the first blow, smacking that same bag across the face of the nearest Praetorian Guard and laying the cyclopian out. The mob fell over the brute, one man taking its weapon.

Near to the side, another cyclopian was pulled down under a thrashing horde.

And from the back, Siobhan's allies, the Cutters, drew out their concealed weapons and bows and drove hard into a line of charging cyclopians.

Siobhan's accuser rushed around the podium, dagger in hand, apparently meaning to strike the half-elf down. He changed his mind and his direction, though, as the dwarven prisoner barreled forward to the half-elf's side. Down the north transept went the man, screaming for Praetorian Guards.

Siobhan and the dwarf glanced all about, saw their jailor go down near one of the front pews, and rushed for the spot, seeking the keys to their shackles.

Oliver and Luthien got more than halfway to the floor, and to the apse, before they were intercepted by a gargoyle. Luthien let go his hold on Oliver and freed up his sword hand, hacking wildly as the rope spun in a tight circle.

Oliver understood their dilemma, understood that more gargoyles were coming in at them. By the halfling's estimation, even worse was the fact that they were hanging in the air, open targets for the angry wizard-duke. The halfling looked to the floor and sighed, then gave three sharp tugs on the rope.

The gargoyle latched on to Luthien, and all three dropped the fifteen feet to the floor. On the way down, the halfling kept the presence of mind to scramble above the gargoyle, even to put the tip of his main gauche against the engaged creature's scalp, and when they hit, the force of the landing drove the weapon right through the animated monster's head.

Luthien was up first, whipping his sword back and forth to keep the nearest cyclopians at bay. Intent on him, the brutes didn't react to an approaching group of men, but the gargoyles flying down found good pickings. One man was lifted into the air, his head wrapped in gargoyle arms, his hands of little use against the hard-skinned monster.

All the nave was wild with the riot, all the people fighting with whatever weapons they could find, and many calling out, "The Crimson Shadow!" over and over.

Duke Morkney clenched his bony fists in rage when the troublesome Oliver and Luthien dropped into the throng, and he stopped the chanting that would have sent a bolt of energy out at the duo. When he looked around, Morkney realized that focusing on the two might not be so wise; the people in the cathedral far outnumbered his cyclopians, and to the duke's surprise, quite a few of them had apparently brought in weapons. Morkney's gargoyles were formidable, but they were not many, and they were slow to kill.

Another arrow whistled the duke's way, but it, too, hit his magical barrier, multiplying and diminishing in substance, until the images were no more than mere shadows of the original.

Morkney was outraged at the riot, but he was not worried. He had known that this scenario would come to pass sooner or later, and he had prepared well for it. The Ministry had stood for hundreds of years, and over that time, hundreds, mostly those who had helped construct the place or had donated great sums to the church, had been interred under its stone floor and within its thick walls.

Duke Morkney's thoughts slipped into the spirit world now, reached out for those buried corpses and called them forth. The Ministry's very walls and floor shuddered. Blocks angled out and hands, some ragged with rotting skin, others no more than skeletal remains, poked out.

"What have we started?" Luthien asked when he and Oliver got out of the immediate battle and found a moment to catch their breath.

"I do not know!" the halfling frankly admitted. Then both fell back in horror as a gruesome head, flesh withered and stretched thin, eyeballs lost in empty sockets, poked up from a crack in the floor to regard them.

Luthien's sword split the animated skull down the middle.

"There is only one way!" Oliver shouted, looking toward the apse. "These are Morkney's creatures!"

Luthien took off ahead of the halfling. Two cyclopians intercepted. The young Bedwyr's sword thrust forward, then whipped up high and to the side, taking one of the brutes' swords with it. Luthien followed straight ahead, his fist slamming the cyclopian in the face and knocking it over backward.

Down Luthien dropped, purely on instinct, barely ducking the wicked cut of the second brute's blade. He turned and slashed, disemboweling the surprised cyclopian.

Oliver came by him in a headlong roll, somehow launching his main gauche as he tumbled, the dagger spinning end over end and nailing the next intercepting Praetorian Guard right in the belly. The brute lurched and howled, a cry that became a gurgle as Oliver's rapier dove through its windpipe.

Luthien barreled past Oliver, throwing the dying guard aside. Another cyclopian was in line, its heavy sword defensively raised before it.

Luthien was too quick for the brute. He slashed across, deflecting the cyclopian's sword to his left, then continued the spin, turning a complete circuit and lifting his foot to slam the brute in the ribs, under its high-flying arm. The cyclopian fell hard to the side. It was stunned, but not badly wounded. It did not come back at Luthien and Oliver, though. Rather, it scrambled away to find someone easier to fight.

The friends were at the altar, at the edge of the apse, with no enemies between them and Duke Morkney, who was now standing before his comfortable chair.

Oliver went under the altar, Luthien around to the left. The duke snapped his arm out toward them suddenly, throwing a handful of small pellets.

The beads hit the floor all around the altar and exploded, engulfing the friends in a shower of sparks and a cloud of thick smoke. Oliver cried out as the sparks stung him and clung to his clothes, but he kept the presence of mind to dart under Luthien's protective cape. Choking and coughing, the two pushed their way through—only to find that Duke Morkney was gone.

Oliver, always alert, caught a slight motion and pointed to a tapestry along the curving wall of the apse. Luthien was there in a few quick strides and he tore the tapestry aside. He found a wooden door, and beyond it, a narrow stone stairway rising inside the wall of the Ministry's tallest tower.

Siobhan and the eight Cutters in the cathedral split ranks, each going to a different area to try and calm the frenzied mob, to try and bring some semblance of order to the rioting citizens. One of the Cutters tossed the half-elf his bow and quiver, then drew out his sword and rushed two cyclopians. Only one was there to meet the charge, though, as Siobhan quickly put the bow to good use.

The cyclopians were not faring well, but their undead and gargoyle allies struck terror into the hearts of all who stood before them.

One woman, using her walking stick as a club, knocked the head off a skeleton, and her eyes widened in shock as the disgusting thing kept coming at her. She would have surely been killed, but the dwarven prisoner, free of his shackles, slammed into the headless thing and brought it down to the floor under him, thrashing about and scattering the bones.

Siobhan looked all about and saw a woman and her three children trying to duck low under a pew as a gargoyle hovered above them, slashing with its claws. The half-elf put an arrow into the gargoyle, then another, and as the monster turned toward her, a group of men leaped up from the pews and grabbed it, pulling it down under their weight.

Siobhan realized that any way she ran would be as good as another; the fighting was throughout the nave. She headed for the apse, thinking to find Luthien and Oliver and hoping for a shot at Duke Morkney. She emerged from the throng just as the tapestry swung back behind her departing lover and his halfling sidekick.

The stair was narrow and curving, circling the tower as it climbed, and Luthien and Oliver were afforded a view only a few feet in front of them as they ran upward in pursuit of the duke. They passed a couple of small windows with thick stone sills sporting small statues, and Luthien prudently kept his sword in line with these, expecting them to writhe to life and take up the fight.

About seventy steps up, Luthien pulled up short and turned to regard Oliver, who was distracted as he continued to coil the line of his magical grapnel. Luthien bade him to hold a moment and listen carefully.

They heard chanting not so far ahead on the winding stair.

Luthien dove flat to the stone and tried to pull Oliver down behind him. Before the startled halfling could react, there came a rapid series of explosions rocketing down the stairs, a bolt of lightning ricocheting off the stone. It sizzled past—Luthien felt its tingling sting along his backbone—and then it was gone. Luthien looked up, expecting to find Oliver's blackened body.

The halfling was still standing, trying to straighten his dishevelled hat and fix the broken orange feather.

"You know," he said nonchalantly, "sometimes is not so bad to be short."

Luthien jumped up and on they ran, the young Bedwyr leaping two stairs at a time, trying to get at the duke before he could cause more mischief.

Luthien could not ignore the deep gouges in the stone wall at every point where the bolt had struck, and he wondered then what in the world he was doing. How had it come to this? How was it that he, the son of the eorl of Bedwydrin, was now chasing a wizard-duke up the tallest spire of Eriador's greatest building?

He shook his head and charged on, without a clue.

Around the endless spiral, the young Bedwyr's eyes widened in surprise and terror, and he ducked, crying out as a heavy ax chipped the stone above his head. Two cyclopians blocked the stairs, one behind the other.

Luthien pressed quickly with his sword, but the cyclopian had a large shield and the advantage of the higher ground, and the young Bedwyr had little to hit at. More dangerous was the cyclopian's ax, chopping down whenever Luthien got too near, forcing him back on his heels, driving him back down the stairs.

"Fight through!" Oliver cried behind him. "We must get to the wizard-type before he can prepare another surprise!"

Easier said than done, Luthien knew, for he could not offer any solid attacks against his burly and well-protected foe. On even ground, he and

Oliver would already have dispatched the two cyclopians, but in the stair, it seemed utterly hopeless to Luthien.

He was even considering turning back, joining the ruckus in the nave, where he and Oliver could at least do some good.

An arrow skipped off the wall above Luthien's head, angled upward. The cyclopian, shield down low to block the continuing sword blows, caught it full in the chest and staggered backward.

Up came the brute's shield reflexively; Luthien didn't miss the opportunity to thrust his sword into the cyclopian's knee. The brute fell back on the stairs, helpless, and the second cyclopian promptly took flight.

Oliver's flying dagger got the other monster in the back, two steps up.

Luthien had finished off the first cyclopian and the second turned with a howl—just in time to catch a second rebounding arrow.

Luthien and Oliver figured it out as Siobhan came around the bend behind them.

"Run on!" Oliver bade Luthien, knowing that the lovesick young man would likely stop and make sweet eyes at their rescuer for eternity. To Luthien's credit, he was already in motion, bounding past the fallen brutes and up the winding stair. "We must get to the wizard-type . . ."

"Before he can prepare another surprise!" Luthien finished for him.

They put two hundred steps behind them, and Luthien's legs ached and felt as though they would buckle beneath him. He paused for a moment and turned to regard his halfling friend.

"If we wait, the wizard-type will have a big boom waiting for us, I am sure," Oliver said, brushing the thick wig hair back from his face.

Luthien tilted his bead back and took a deep breath, then ran on.

They put another hundred steps behind them and then saw the unmistakable glow of daylight. They came to a landing, then up five more stairs to the very roof of the tower, a circular space perhaps twenty-five feet in diameter that was enclosed by a low battlement.

Across from them stood Duke Morkney, laughing wildly, his voice changing, growing deeper, more guttural and more ominous. Luthien leaped to the platform, but skidded to a quick stop and looked on in horror as the duke's body lurched violently, began twisting and bulging.

And growing.

Morkney's skin became darker and hardened to layered scales along his arms and neck. His head bulged weirdly, growing great fangs and a forked and flicking tongue. Soon Morkney's face resembled that of a giant snake, and great curving horns grew out from the top of his head. His red robes seemed a short skirt by then, for he was twice his original height, and his chest, so skinny and weak before, was now massive, stretching his previously voluminous robes to their limits. Long and powerful arms reached out of those sleeves, clawed fingers raking the air as the duke continued his obviously agonizing transformation.

Drool dripped off the front of the serpentine face, sizzling like acid as it hit the stone between the monster's three-clawed feet where Morkney's boots lay in tatters. With a shrug, the beast brushed free of the red robe, great leathery wings unfolding behind it, its black flesh and scales smoking with the heat of the Abyss.

"Morkney," Luthien whispered.

"I do not think so," Oliver replied. "Perhaps we should go back down."

CHAPTER 24

THE DEMON

J AM MORKNEY NO MORE," the beast proclaimed. "Gaze upon the might of Praehotec and be afraid!"

"Praehotec?" Luthien whispered, and he was indeed afraid.

"A demon," Oliver explained, gasping for breath—from more than the long run up the stairs, Luthien knew. "The clever wizard-type has lent his material body to a demon."

"It is no worse than the dragon," Luthien whispered, trying to calm Oliver and himself.

"We did not beat the dragon," Oliver promptly reminded him.

The demon looked around, its breath steaming in the chill October air. "Ah," it sighed. "So good to be in the world again! I will feast well upon you, and you, and upon a hundred others before Morkney finds the will to release me to the Abyss!"

Luthien didn't doubt the claim, not for a minute. He had seen giants as large as Praehotec, but nothing, not even Balthazar, had radiated an aura as powerful and as unspeakably evil. How many people had this demon eaten? Luthien wondered, and he shuddered, not wanting to know the answer.

He heard movement on the steps behind him and glanced back just in time to see Siobhan come up onto the lower landing, bow in hand.

Luthien took a deep breath and steadied himself. In his love-stricken heart, it seemed as if the stakes had just been raised.

"Come with me, Oliver," he said through gritted teeth, and he clutched his sword tightly, meaning to charge into the face of doom.

Before the halfling could even turn his unbelieving stare on his taller friend, Praehotec reached out a clawed hand and clenched its massive fist.

A tremendous wind came up suddenly from over the battlement to their left, assaulting the companions. At the same moment, Siobhan let fly her arrow, but the gust caught the flimsy bolt and tossed it harmlessly aside.

Luthien squinted and raised an arm defensively against the stinging wind, his cape and clothes whipping out to the right, buffeting Oliver. The halfling's hat pulled free of his head; up it spiraled.

Instinctively, Oliver leaped up and caught it, dropping his rapier in the process, but then he was flying, too, bouncing head over heels in a soaring roll. As he came back upright, he went high into the air, right over the battlement. Stunned Oliver was fully a dozen feet out from the ledge when Praehotec's snakelike face turned up into a leering grin and the demon released the wind.

Oliver let out a single shriek and dropped from sight.

Crying out for his lost friend, Luthien charged straight in, sword slashing viciously. Siobhan's arrows came in a seemingly continuous line over his head, scoring hit after hit on the beast, though whether or not they even stung the great Praehotec, Luthien could not tell.

He scored a slight nick with his sword, but the blade was powerfully batted away. Luthien dropped to one knee, ducking a slashing claw, then came right back to his feet and hopped backward, sucking in his belly to avoid the demon's swiping arm.

An arrow nicked Praehotec's neck and the demon hissed.

In came Luthien with a straightforward thrust that cut the fleshy insides of the demon's huge thigh. The young Bedwyr whipped his head safely to the side as the fanged serpent head rocketed past, but a swiping claw caught him on the shoulder before he could regain his balance, gouging him and heaving him aside.

He kept the presence of mind to slash once more with his blade as he fell away, scoring a hit on Praehotec's knuckle.

Luthien knew that last cut had hurt the demon, but he almost regretted that fact as Praehotec turned on him, reptilian eyes flaring with simmering fires of rage.

He saw something else, then, a flicker in the demon's fiery eyes and a slight trembling on the side of the beast's serpentine maw.

An arrow razored into the demon's neck.

That flicker and trembling came again, and Luthien got the feeling that Praehotec was not so secure in this material body.

The demon straightened, towering above Luthien, as if to mock his suspicions. It shifted its furious gaze, and from its eyes came two lines of crackling red energy, joining together inches in front of the demon's face and sizzling across the tower's top to slam into Siobhan, throwing her back down the stairs.

Luthien's heart seemed to stop.

Hanging from the tower's side, Oliver plopped his hat on his head once more. The thing was on fairly straight, but the wig underneath it had turned fully about, and the long black tresses hung in front of his face, obscuring his vision. His legs and one hip ached from his swinging slam into the stone, and his arms ached, too, as he clung desperately to the rope of his magical grapnel.

The horrified halfling knew that he could not simply hang there forever, so he finally found the courage to look up, shaking the hair out of his face. His grapnel—that beautiful, magical grapnel!—had caught a secure hold on the curving stone, but it was not close enough to the tower's rim for the halfling to climb over it, and Oliver didn't have nearly enough rope to get down the side to the street below.

He spotted the depression of a window a bit above him and to his left.

"You are so very brave," he whispered to himself, and he brought his legs up under him and stood out from the wall. Slowly, he walked himself to the right, then, when he figured that he had the rope stretched far enough, he half ran, half flew back to the left, like a pendulum. Diving at the end of his swing, he just managed to hook the fingers of one hand over the lip of the window, and with some effort, he wriggled himself onto the ledge.

Oliver grumbled as he considered the barrier before him. He could break through the stained glass, but the window opening was crossed by curving metal that would certainly bar his entrance to the tower.

The grumbling halfling glanced all about, noticed that a crowd was gathering down below, many pointing up his way and calling out to their compatriots. In the distance, Oliver could see a force of Praetorian Guards making their way along the avenues, coming to quell the rioting in the cathedral, no doubt.

The halfling shook his head and straightened his hat, then gave three quick tugs to release the grapnel. He might be able to set the magical thing below him and get down the tower in time to escape, he realized, but to his own amazement, the halfling found himself swinging the item up instead, higher on the wall and near to another window.

Bound by friendship, Oliver was soon climbing, to the continuing shouts of the crowd below.

"Sometimes I do not think that having a friend is a good thing," the halfling muttered, but on he went, determinedly.

Inside the cathedral, the riot had turned into a rout. Many cyclopians were dead and the remaining brutes were scattered and under cover, but the crowd could not stand against Morkney's horrifying undead brigade and the wicked gargoyles. The Cutters worked to herd the frantic people now, to put them together that they might bull their way to an entrance.

All that mattered to the rioters at this point was escape.

The cyclopians seemed to understand, the gargoyles, too, and whichever way the mob went, barriers were thrown up in their path.

And the horrid undead monsters dogged their every step, pulling down those who were not fast enough to dodge the clawing, bony hands.

A primal scream of outrage accompanied Luthien's bold charge. The young Bedwyr wanted only to strike down this foul beast, caring not at all for his own safety. Two clawed hands reached out to grasp him as he came in, but he worked his sword magnificently, slapping one and then the other, drawing oozing gashes on both.

Luthien ducked his shoulder and bore in, slashing, even kicking, at the huge monster.

The demon apparently understood the danger of this one's fury, for Praehotec's leathery wings began to flap, lifting the creature from the tower.

"No!" Luthien protested. He wasn't even thinking of the dangers of letting Praehotec out of his sword's range; he was simply enraged at the thought that the murderous monster might escape. He jumped up at the beast, sword leading, accepting the inevitable clawing hit on his back as he came in close.

He felt no pain and didn't even know that he was bleeding. All that Luthien knew was anger, pure red anger, and all of his strength and concentration followed his sword thrust, plunging the weapon deep into Praehotec's belly. Smoking greenish goo poured from the wound, covering Luthien's arm, and the stubborn young Bedwyr roared and whipped the sword back and forth, trying to disembowel the beast. He looked Praehotec in the eye as he cut and saw again that slight wavering, an indication that the demon was not so secure in the wizard's material form.

Praehotec's powerful arm slammed down on his shoulder, and suddenly, Luthien was kneeling on the stone once more, dazed. Up lifted the demon, wings wide over Luthien like an eagle crowning its helpless prey.

From somewhere far away, the young Bedwyr heard a voice—Siobhan's voice.

"You ugly bastard!" the half-elf growled, and she let fly another arrow.

Praehotec saw it coming, all the way up to the instant it drove into the beast's reptilian eye.

Siobhan! Luthien realized, and instinctively the young Bedwyr braced himself and thrust his sword up above his head.

Praehotec came down hard, impaling itself to the sword's crosspiece. The demon began to thrash, but then stopped and looked down curiously at Luthien.

And Luthien looked curiously at his sword, its pommel pulsing with the beating of the beast's great heart.

With a roar that split stone and a violent shudder that snapped the blade at the hilt, Praehotec flung itself back against the parapet.

Siobhan hit it with another arrow, but it didn't matter. The demon thrashed about; red and green blood and guts poured down the creature.

Luthien stood tall before it, fought away his dizziness and pain and looked into the eyes of the monster he thought defeated.

He recognized the simmering fires a moment too late, tried to dodge as lines of red energy again came from the demon, joining in a single line and blasting out.

Luthien went tumbling across the tower top, and Siobhan once more disappeared from sight, this time to roll all the way to the bottom and land hard on the lower landing, where she lay, groaning and helpless.

Luthien shook his head, trying to remember where he was. By the time he managed to look back across the tower, he saw Praehotec standing tall, laughing wickedly at him.

"You believe that your puny weapons can defeat Praehotec?" the beast bellowed. It reached right into the garish wound in its belly and, laughing all the while, extracted Luthien's slime-covered blade. "I am Praehotec, who has lived for centuries untold!"

Luthien had no more energy to battle the monster. He was defeated; he knew that, and knew, too, that if Greensparrow had indeed made such allies as Praehotec, as Brind'Amour had claimed, and as Morkney had apparently proven true, then a shadow might indeed soon cover all of Eriador.

Luthien struggled to his knees. He wanted to die with dignity, at least. He put one foot under him, but paused and stared hard at the monster.

"No!" Praehotec growled. The demon wasn't looking at Luthien; it was looking up into the empty air. "The kill is rightfully mine! His flesh is my food!"

"No," came Duke Morkney's voice in reply. "The sweet kill is mine!"

Praehotec's serpentine face trembled, then bulged weirdly, reverting to the face of Duke Morkney. Then it returned to Praehotec, briefly, then back to Duke Morkney.

The struggle continued, and Luthien knew that the opportunity to strike would not last long. He staggered forward a bit, trying to find some weapon, trying to find the strength to attack.

When he glanced back across the tower top, he saw not Praehotec but Duke Morkney's skinny and naked body, the duke bending low to retrieve his fallen robe.

"You should be dead already," Morkney said, noticing that Luthien was struggling to stand. "Stubborn fool! Take pride in the fact that you fended off the likes of Praehotec for several minutes. Take pride and lie down and die."

Luthien almost took the advice. He had never been so weary and wounded, and he did not imagine that death was very far away. Head down, he noticed something then, something that forced him to stand straight once more and forced him to remember the losses he had suffered.

Oliver's rapier.

To Duke Morkney's mocking laughter, the young Bedwyr stepped over and picked up the small and slender blade, then stood very still to find his balance and stubbornly rose up tall. He staggered across the tower top, toward his foe.

Morkney was still naked and still laughing as Luthien staggered near, rapier aimed for the duke's breast.

"Do you believe that I am not capable of defeating you?" the duke asked incredulously. "Do you think that I need Praehotec, or any other demon, to destroy a mere swordsman? I sent the demon away only because I wanted your death to come from my own hands." With a superior growl, Morkney lifted his bony hands, fingers clawed like an animal, and began to chant.

Luthien's back arched suddenly and he froze in place, eyes wide with shock and sudden agony. Tingling energy swept through him, back to front and right out of his chest. It seemed to him, to his ultimate horror, that his own life energy was being sucked out of him, stolen by the evil wizard!

"No," he tried to protest, but he knew then that he was no match for the powers of the wicked duke.

Like a true parasite, Morkney continued to feed, taking perverse pleasure in it all, laughing wickedly, as evil a being as the demon he had summoned.

"How could you ever have believed that you could win against me?" the duke asked. "Do you not know who I am? Do you now understand the powers of Greensparrow's brotherhood?"

Again came the mocking laughter; the dying Luthien couldn't even speak out in protest. His heart beat furiously; he feared it would explode.

Suddenly, a looped rope spun over the duke's head, drawing tight about his shoulders. Morkney's eyes widened as he regarded it, and he followed its length to the side to see Oliver deBurrows, crawling over the battlement.

The halfling shrugged and smiled apologetically, even waved to the duke. Morkney growled, thinking to turn his wrath on this one, thinking that he was through with the impudent young human.

The instant he was free, Luthien jerked straight, and the motion brought the deadly rapier shooting forward, its tip plunging into the startled duke's breast.

They stood face to face for a long moment, Morkney staring incredulously at this curious young man, at this young man who had just killed him. The duke chuckled again, for some reason, then slumped dead into Luthien's arms.

Down below, in the nave, the gargoyles turned to stone and crashed to the floor, and the skeletons and rotting corpses lay back down in their eternal sleep.

Oliver looked far below to the now huge crowd and the large force of Praetorian Guards coming into the plaza beside the Ministry.

"Put him over the side!" the quick-thinking halfling called to Luthien.

Luthien turned curiously at Oliver, who was now scrambling all the way over the battlement and back to the tower's top.

"Put him over the side!" the halfling said again. "Let them see him hanging by his skinny neck!"

The notion horrified Luthien.

Oliver ran up to his friend and pushed Luthien away from the dead duke. "Do you not understand?" Oliver asked. "They need to see him!"

"Who?"

"Your people!" Oliver cried, and with a burst of strength, the halfling shoved Morkney over the battlement. The lasso slipped up from the duke's shoulders and caught tight about his neck as he tumbled, his skinny, naked form coming to a jerking stop along the side of the tower a hundred feet above the ground.

But the poor people of Montfort, under this one's evil thumb for many years, surely recognized him.

They did, indeed.

Out of the north transept came the victorious mob from the cathedral, taking their riot to the streets, sweeping up many onlookers in their wake.

"What have we done?" the stunned young Bedwyr asked, staring down helplessly at the brutal fight.

Oliver shrugged. "Who can say? All I know is that the pickings should be better with that skinny duke out of the way," he answered, always pragmatic and always opportunistic.

Luthien just shook his head, wondering once more what he had stumbled into. Wondering how all of this had come to pass.

"Luthien?" he heard from across the tower top, and he spun about to see Siobhan, leaning heavily on the battlement, her gray robe in tatters.

But smiling.

Epilogue

The snow lay thick along the quiet streets of Montfort, nearly every street lined with the red stains of spilled blood. Luthien sat atop the roof of a tall building in the lower section, looking out over the city and the lands to the north.

The people of Montfort were in full revolt, and he, the Crimson Shadow, unwittingly had been named their leader. So many had died, and Luthien's heart was often heavy. But he gathered strength from those who savagely fought on for their freedom, from those brave people who had lived so long under tyranny and now would not go back to that condition, even at the price of their lives.

And, to Luthien's amazement, they were winning. A powerful and well-armed cyclopian force still controlled the city's inner section beyond the dividing wall, protecting the wealthy merchants who had prospered under Duke Morkney. Rumors said that Viscount Aubrey had taken command of the force.

Luthien remembered the man well; he hoped the rumors were true.

The fighting had been furious in the first weeks following the duke's death, with hundreds of men, women, and cyclopians dying every day. Winter had settled in quickly, slowing the fighting, forcing many to think merely of keeping from freezing or starving. At first, the cold seemed to favor the merchants and cyclopians in their better quarters within the city's higher section, but as time went on, Luthien's people began to find the advantage. They controlled the outer wall; they controlled any goods coming into the city.

And Siobhan's group, along with a number of ferocious dwarves, continued to wreak havoc. Even now, plans were being laid for a full-scale raid upon the mines to free the rest of Shuglin's enslaved people.

But Luthien could not shake his many doubts. Were his actions truly valuable, or was he walking a fool's parade? How many would die because he had chosen this course, because at that fateful moment in the Ministry, the Crimson Shadow had been revealed and the people had rallied behind him? And even with their astonishing initial victories, what hope could the future hold for the beleaguered people of Montfort? The winter would be a brutal one, it seemed, and the spring would likely bring an army from Avon, King Greensparrow's forces coming to reclaim the city.

And punish the revolutionaries.

Luthien sighed deeply, noticing another rider galloping out from Montfort's northern gate, riding north to spread the news and enlist help—in the form of supplies, at least, from nearby villages. There was word of some minor fighting in Port Charley to the east, but Luthien took little heart in it.

"I knew you would be up here," came a voice from behind, and Luthien turned to see Oliver climbing up onto the roof. "Surveying your kingdom?"

Luthien's scowl showed that he did not think that to be funny.

"Ah, well," the halfling conceded, "I only came to tell you that you have a visitor."

Luthien cocked a curious eyebrow as a woman climbed over the roof's edge. Her eyes were green as Siobhan's, the young Bedwyr realized, somehow surprised by that fact, but her hair was red, fiery red. She stood tall and proud, holding something wrapped in a blanket before her, locking stares with her old friend.

"Katerin," Luthien whispered, hardly able to get words out of his suddenly dry mouth.

Katerin walked across the roof to stand before the man and handed him the item.

Luthien took it gingerly, not understanding.

His eyes went wide when he slipped off the blanket and saw *Blind-Striker*, his family's treasured sword.

"From Gahris, your father and the rightful eorl of Bedwydrin," Katerin O'Hale explained, her tone stern and determined.

Luthien looked searchingly into her green eyes, wondering what had happened.

"Avonese is in chains," Katerin said. "And there is not a living cyclopian on Isle Bedwydrin."

Luthien found breath hard to come by. Gahris had followed his lead, had taken up the war! The young man glanced all about, from the smiling Katerin, to the smiling Oliver, to the snow-covered rooftops of the quiet city.

He was faced with a decision then, Luthien knew, but this time, unlike the many events that had led him to this fateful point, he was making it consciously.

"Go out, Oliver," the young man said. "Go out and tell the people to take heart. Tell them that their war, the war for their freedom, has begun." Luthien again locked stares with the proud woman from Hale.

"Go out, Oliver," he said again. "Tell them that they are not alone."

LUTHIEN'S GAMBLE

To Diane, and to Bryan, Geno, and Caitlin

PROLOGUE

$\mathcal{J}$T WAS A TIME in Eriador of darkness, a time when King Greensparrow and his wizard-dukes blanketed all the Avonsea Islands in a veil of oppression and when the hated cyclopians served as Praetorian Guard, allied with the government against the common folk. It was a time when the eight great cathedrals of Avonsea, built as blessed monuments of spirituality, the epitome of homage to higher powers, were used to call the tax rolls.

But it was a time, too, of hope, for in the northwestern corner of the mountain range called the Iron Cross, in Montfort, the largest city in all of Eriador, there arose cries for freedom, for open revolt. Evil Duke Morkney, Greensparrow's pawn, was dead, his skinny body hanging naked from the tallest tower of the Ministry, Montfort's great cathedral. The wealthy merchants and their cyclopian guards, allies of the throne, were sorely pressed, bottled up in the city's upper section, while in the lower section, among the lesser houses, the proud Eriadorans remembered kings of old and called out the name of Bruce MacDonald, who had led the victory in the bitter cyclopian war centuries before.

It was a small thing really, a speck of light in a field of blackness, a single star in a dark night sky. A wizard-duke was dead, but the wizard-king could easily replace him. Montfort was in the throes of fierce battle, rebels pitted against the established ruling class and their cyclopian guards. The vast armies of Avon had not yet marched, however, with winter thick about the land. When they did come on, when the might that was Greensparrow flowed to the north, all who stood against the wizard-king would know true darkness.

But the rebels would not think that way, would fight their battles one at a time, united and always with hope. Such is the way a revolution begins.

Word of the fighting in Montfort was not so small a thing to the proud folk of Eriador, who resented any subjugation to the southern kingdom of Avon. To the proud folk of Eriador, uttering the name of Bruce MacDonald was never a small thing—nor were the cries for Eriador's newest hero: the slayer of Morkney, the unwitting leader of a budding revolution.

Cries for the Crimson Shadow.

CHAPTER 1

THE MINISTRY

THE REVOLT HAD BEGUN HERE, in the huge nave of the Ministry, and the dried blood of those killed in the first battle could still be seen, staining the wooden pews and the stone floor, splattered across the walls and the sculpted statues.

The cathedral was built along the wall separating the city's merchant class from the common folk, and thus held a strategic position indeed. It had changed hands several times in the weeks since the fighting began, but so determined were the revolutionaries that the cyclopians still had not held the place long enough to climb the tower and cut down Duke Morkney's body.

This time, though, the one-eyed brutes had come on in full force, and the Ministry's western doors had been breached, as well as the smaller entrance into the cathedral's northern transept. Cyclopians poured in by the score, only to be met by determined resistors, and fresh blood covered the dried blood staining the wooden pews and the stone floor.

In mere seconds, there were no obvious battle lines, just a swarming mob of bitter enemies, hacking at each other with wild abandon, killing and dying.

The fighting was heard in the lower section of the city, the streets belonging to the rebels. Siobhan, half-elven and half-human, and her two-score elvish companions—more than a third of all the elves in Montfort—were quick to answer the call. A secret entrance had been fashioned in the wall of the great cathedral, which it shared with lower Montfort, cut by cunning dwarfs in those rare times when there was a lull in the fighting. Now Siobhan and her companions rushed from the lower section of town, scrambling up preset ropes into the passageway.

They could hear the fighting in the nave as they crawled along the crude tunnel. The passage split, continuing along the city's dividing wall, then curving as it traced the shape of the cathedral's apse. The dwarfs had not had a hard time fashioning the passage, for the massive wall was no less then ten feet thick in any place, and many tunnels were already in place, used by those performing maintenance on the cathedral.

Soon the elves were traveling generally west. They came to an abrupt end in the tunnel at a ladder that led them up to the next level. Then they went south, west again, and finally north, completing the circuit of the southern transept. Finally Siobhan pushed a stone aside and crawled out onto the southern triforium, an open ledge fifty feet up from the floor that ran the length of the nave, from the western door all the way to the open area of the crossing transepts. The beautiful half-elf gave a resigned sigh as she brushed the long wheat-colored tresses from her face and considered the awful scene below.

"Pick your shots with care," Siobhan instructed her elven companions as they crowded out behind her and filtered along the length of the ledge. The command hardly seemed necessary as they viewed the jumble of struggling bodies below. Not many targets presented themselves, but few archers in all of Avonsea could match the skill of the elves. The great longbows sang out, arrows slicing through the air unerringly to take down cyclopians.

A quarter of the elvish force, with Siobhan in the lead, ran along the triforium all the way to its western end. Here a small tunnel, still high above the floor, ran across the western narthex and crossed the nave, opening onto the northern triforium. The elves rushed among the shadows, around the many statues decorating that ledge, to its opposite end, the base of the northern transept. More cyclopians poured in through the door there, and there were few defenders to stem their flow in this area. The ten elves bent their bows and fired off arrow after arrow, devastating the invading cyclopians, filling the northern transept with bodies.

Below in the nave, the tide seemed to turn, with the cyclopians, their reinforcements dwindling, unable to keep up the momentum of their initial attack.

But then there came an explosion as a battering ram shattered the doors at the end of the southern transept, destroying the barricades that had been erected there. A new wave of cyclopians charged in, and neither the archers on the triforium nor the men fighting in the nave could slow them.

"It is as if all the one-eyes of Montfort have come upon us!" the elf standing behind Siobhan cried out.

Siobhan nodded, not disagreeing with the assessment. Apparently Viscount Aubrey, the man rumors named as the new leader of the king's forces in Montfort, had decided that the Ministry had been in enemy hands long enough. Aubrey was a buffoon, so it was said, one of the far too many fumbling viscounts and barons in Eriador who claimed royal blood, lackeys all to the unlawful Avon king. A buffoon by all accounts, but nevertheless Aubrey had taken control of the Montfort guards, and now the viscount was throwing all of his considerable weight at the rebel force in the cathedral.

"Luthien predicted this," Siobhan lamented, speaking of her lover, whom the fates had chosen as the Crimson Shadow. Indeed, only a week before, Luthien had told Siobhan that they would not be able to hold the Ministry until spring.

"We cannot stop them," said the elf behind Siobhan.

Siobhan's first instinct was to yell out at the elf, to berate him for his pessimism. But again Siobhan could not disagree. Viscount Aubrey wanted the Ministry back, and so he would have it. No longer was their job the defense of the great building. Now all they could hope to do was get as many allies out alive as possible.

And, in the process, inflict as much pain as possible on the cyclopians.

Siobhan bent her bow and let fly an arrow that thudded into the chest of a one-eyed brute an instant before it thrust its huge sword into a man it had knocked to the floor. The cyclopian stood perfectly still, its one large eye staring down at the quivering shaft, as though the brute did not understand what had happened to it. Its opponent scrambled back to his feet and brought his club in a roundhouse swing that erased the dying brute's face and hastened its descent to the floor.

The man spun and looked to the triforium and Siobhan, his fist raised in victory and in thanks. Two running strides put him in the middle of yet another fight.

The cyclopians advanced in a line along the southern end of the swarming mob, linking up with allies and beating back resisters.

"Back to the southern triforium," Siobhan ordered her companions. The elves stared at her; if they rejoined their kin across the way, they would be surrendering a valuable vantage point.

"Back!" Siobhan ordered, for she understood the larger picture. The nave would soon be lost, and then the cyclopians would turn their eyes upward to the ledges. The only escape for Siobhan's group was the same route that had brought them in: the secret passage that linked the far eastern wall with the southern triforium. The half-elf knew that she and her companions had a long way to go, and if that small tunnel above the western doors was cut off by the cyclopians, the northern ledge, and Siobhan's group, would be completely isolated.

"Run on!" Siobhan called, and her companions, though some still did not understand the command, did not pause to question her.

Siobhan waited at the base of the northern triforium looking back across the nave as her companions rushed by. She remained confident that her elven band, the Cutters by name, would escape, but feared that not a single man who was now defending the nave would get out of the Ministry alive.

All the elves passed her by and were moving along the tunnel. Siobhan turned to follow, but then looked back, and a wave of hope washed over her.

As she watched, a small, perfectly squared portion of the back end of the cathedral, directly below the secret tunnel that her group had used to enter the Ministry, fell in. Siobhan expected a resounding crash, and was surprised to see that the wall did not slam to the floor but was supported by chains, like some drawbridge. A man rushed in, scrambling over the angled platform, his crimson cape flowing behind him. He leaped to the floor, and two short strides brought him to the altar, in the center of the apse. Up he leaped, holding high his magnificent sword. Siobhan smiled, realizing that those cunning dwarfs had been at work on more than the secret entrance. They had fashioned the drawbridge, as well, probably at Luthien's bidding, for the wise young man had indeed foreseen this dangerous day.

The defenders of the Ministry fought on—but the cyclopians looked back and were afraid.

The Crimson Shadow had come.

"Dear Luthien," Siobhan whispered, and she smiled even wider as Luthien's companion, the foppish halfling Oliver deBurrows, rushed to catch up to the man. Oliver held his huge hat in one hand and his rapier in the other, his purple velvet cape flowed out behind him. He got to the altar and leaped as high as he could, fingers just catching the lip. Kicking and scrambling, the three-foot-tall Oliver tried desperately to clamber up beside Luthien, but he would not have made it except that Luthien's next companion rushed up behind, grabbed the halfling by the seat of his pants, and heaved him up.

Siobhan's smile faded as she regarded the newcomer, though surely the half-elf was glad to see Luthien in such strong company. This one was a woman, a warrior from Luthien's home island of Bedwydrin, tall and strong and undeniably beautiful, with unkempt red hair and eyes that shone green as intensely as Siobhan's own.

"Well met, Katerin O'Hale," the half-elf whispered, putting aside the moment of jealousy and reminding herself that the appearance of these three, and of the three-score warriors that poured over the drawbridge behind them, might well be the salvation of those trapped defenders in the nave.

Crossing the tunnel within the west wall was no easy task for the elves, for Siobhan's fears that the cyclopians would cut them off were on the mark, and the one-eyed brutes were waiting for them in the crawl spaces above the western narthex. The defense had not yet been organized, though, and the elves, with help from their kin from the southern tunnel, fought their way through to the southern triforium with only a few minor injuries

Coming out onto that ledge, Siobhan saw that the fighting below had shifted somewhat, with the defenders gradually rolling toward the east, toward the escape route that Luthien and his force had opened.

"Fight to the last arrow," Siobhan told her companions. "And prepare ropes that we might go down to the southern wing and join with our allies."

The other elves nodded, their faces grim, but truly they could not have expected such an order. The Cutters were quick-hitters: in, usually with their bows only, and out before the enemy could retaliate. This was the Ministry, though, and it was about to be lost, along with many lives. Their usual tactics of hit and retreat be damned, Siobhan explained hurriedly, for this battle was simply too important.

Luthien was in the fighting now, his great sword *Blind-Striker* cutting down cyclopians as he spearheaded a wedge of resistance. Oliver and Katerin flanked him, the halfling—tremendous hat back upon his long and curly brown locks—fighting with rapier and main gauche, and the woman deftly wielding a light spear. Oliver and Katerin were formidable fighters, as were the men holding the lines behind them, a wedge of fury working out from the semicircular apse, felling enemies and enveloping allies in their protective shield.

For the cyclopians, though, the focus of the march was Luthien, the Crimson Shadow, slayer of Morkney. The one-eyes knew that cape and they had come, too, to know the remarkable sword, its great golden and jewel-encrusted hilt sculpted to resemble a dragon rampant, outspread wings serving as the secure crosspiece. Luthien was the dangerous one: he was the one the Eriadorans rallied behind. If the cyclopians could kill the Crimson Shadow, the revolt in Montfort might quickly be put down. Many cyclopians fled the determined stalk of the mighty young Bedwyr, but those brave enough put themselves in Luthien's way, eager to win the favor of Viscount Aubrey, who would likely be appointed the next duke of the city.

"You should fight with main gauche," Oliver remarked, seeing Luthien engaged suddenly with two brutes. To accentuate his point, the halfling angled his large-bladed dagger in the path of a thrusting spear, catching the head of the weapon with the dagger's upturned hilt just above the protective basket. A flick of Oliver's deceptively delicate wrist snapped the head off the cyclopian's spear, and the halfling quick-stepped alongside the broken shaft and poked the tip of his rapier into the brute's chest.

"Because your left hand should be used for more than balance," the halfling finished, stepping back into a heroic pose, rapier tip to the floor, dagger hand on hip. He held the stance for just a moment as yet another cyclopian came charging in from the side.

Luthien smiled despite the press, and the fact that he was fighting two against one. He felt a need to counter Oliver's reasoning, to one-up his diminutive friend.

"But if I fought with two weapons," he began, and thrust with *Blind-Striker*, then brought it back and launched a wide-arcing sweep to force his opponents away, "then how would I ever do this?" He grabbed up his sword in both hands, spinning the heavy blade high over his head as he rushed forward. *Blind-Striker* came angling down and across, the sheer weight of the two-handed blow knocking aside both cyclopian spears, severing the tip from one.

Around went the blade, up over Luthien's head and back around and down as the young man advanced yet again, and again the cyclopian spears were turned aside and knocked out wide.

Blind-Striker continued its furious flow, following the same course, but this time the young man reversed the cut, coming back around from the left. The tip drew a line of bright blood from the closest cyclopian's shoulder down across its chest. The second brute turned to face the coming blade, spear held firmly in front of its torso.

Blind-Striker went right through that spear, right through the brute's armor, to sink deeply into its chest. The cyclopian staggered backward and would have fallen, except that Luthien held the sword firmly, and the blade held the brute in place.

The other cyclopian, wiping away its own blood, fell back and scrambled away, suddenly having no desire to stand against this young warrior.

Luthien yanked his sword free and the cyclopian fell to the floor. He had a moment before the next cyclopian adversary came at him, and he couldn't resist glancing back to see if he had taken the smile from Oliver's face.

He hadn't. Oliver's rapier was spinning circles around the tip of a cyclopian sword, the movement apparently confusing the dim-witted brute.

"Finesse!" the halfling snorted, his strong Gascony accent turning it into a three-syllable word. "If you fought with two weapons, you would have killed them both. Now I might have to chase the one you lost and kill the most ugly thing myself!"

Luthien sighed helplessly and turned back just in time to lift *Blind-Striker* in a quick parry, intercepting a wicked cut. Before Luthien could counter, he saw a movement angle in under his free hand at his left. The cyclopian jerked suddenly and groaned, Katerin O'Hale's spear deep in its belly.

"If you fought more and talked less, we'd all be out of here," the woman scolded. She tugged her spear free and swung about to meet the newest challenge coming in at her side.

Luthien recognized her bluster for what it was. He had lived and trained beside Katerin for many years, and she could fight with the best and play with them, too. She had taken an immediate liking to Oliver and his swaggering bravado, an affection that was certainly mutual. And now, despite the awful battle, despite the fact that the Ministry was about to fall back into Aubrey's dirty hands, Katerin, like Oliver, enjoyed the play.

At that moment, Luthien Bedwyr understood that he could not be surrounded by better friends.

A cyclopian roared and charged in at him, and he went into a crouch to meet the rush. The brute jerked weirdly, though, and then crashed onto its face, and Luthien saw an arrow buried deep in its skull. He followed the line of that shot, up and to the left, fifty feet above the floor, to the triforium and to Siobhan, who was eyeing him sternly—and he got the distinct feeling that she was not pleased to see him at play beside Katerin O'Hale.

But that was an argument for another day, Luthien realized as yet another brute came on, and several more beside it. The wedge had passed out of the apse and crossed the open transept areas by this point, and the narrow formation could effectively go no farther, for now Luthien and his companions were fighting on three sides. Many of the trapped defenders of the Ministry had joined their ranks, but one group of a half-dozen was still out of reach, only thirty feet ahead of where Luthien stood.

Only thirty feet, but with at least a dozen cyclopians between them and the rescuers.

"Organize the retreat," Luthien called to Katerin, and as soon as she looked back to him she knew what he meant to do. It seemed overly daring, even suicidal, and Katerin's instincts and her love of Luthien made her want to try the desperate charge beside the man. She was a soldier, though, duty-bound and understanding of her role. Only Luthien or Oliver or she could lead the main group back across the apse and through the breached eastern wall, back into the streets of the lower section, where they would scatter to safety.

"Oliver!" Luthien yelled, and then was forced to fight off the attack of a burly and ugly cyclopian. When he heard a weapon snap behind him, he knew that Oliver had heard his call. With a great heave, Luthien sent the cyclopian's arms and weapon up high. At the same time, the young warrior hopped up on his toes and spread his legs wide.

Oliver rolled through, coming back over to his feet with his rapier tip angled up. This was a tall cyclopian, and short Oliver couldn't make the hit as he had planned, driving his rapier up through the brute's diaphragm and into its lungs . . . but he settled for a belly wound instead, his fine blade sliding all the way in until it was stopped by the creature's thick backbone.

Luthien pushed the dying brute aside.

"You are sure about this?" Oliver asked, seeing the barrier between them and the trapped men. The question was rhetorical, and merely for effect, for the halfling waited not for an answer but leaped ahead into the throng of cyclopians, weaving a dance with his blade that forced the attention of the nearest two down to his level.

"You have met my fine friend?" the halfling asked as *Blind-Striker* swept in just above his head and above the defenses of the two brutes, slashing them away. Oliver shook his head incredulously at the continued stupidity of cyclopians. He and Luthien had used that trick twenty times in the last two weeks alone, and it hadn't failed yet

Back at the main group, Katerin, too, shook her head, amazed once again at the fighting harmony Luthien and Oliver had achieved. They complemented each other perfectly, move for move, and now, despite all odds, they were making fine progress through the cyclopians, down the middle aisle between the high-backed pews.

Up on the triforium ledge, Siobhan and her cohorts realized what Luthien and Oliver were trying to do and understood that the only way the young warrior and his halfling friend, along with the six trapped men, could possibly escape was if they got support from the archers. Katerin had the main group in organized retreat by then, fighting back across the open transept area and fast approaching the apse, so Siobhan and her friends concentrated their fire directly before, and behind, Luthien and Oliver.

By the time the two companions got to the pews where the fighting continued, only four of the men were left standing. One was dead; another crawled along the wooden bench, whimpering pitifully, his guts torn.

A cyclopian leaned over the back of the high pew behind him, spear poised to finish the job. Luthien got there first, and *Blind-Striker* lived up to its name, slashing across the brute's face.

"Run on! To the breach!" Oliver instructed, and three of the four men gladly followed that command, skittering behind the halfling. The fourth turned and tried to follow, but got a spear in his back and went down heavily.

"You must leave him!" Oliver cried out to Luthien as cyclopians closed all around them. "But of course you cannot," the halfling muttered, knowing his friend. Oliver sighed, one of his many sighs for the duties of friendship, as Luthien beat back another brute, then dropped to his knees, hauling the wounded man up onto his free shoulder.

The two got back out of the pew easily enough, but found the aisle fully blocked with so many cyclopians in front of them they couldn't even see the three retreating men who had come out just before them.

"At least he will serve as a shield," Oliver remarked, referring to the man slung over Luthien's shoulder.

Luthien didn't appreciate the humor, and he growled and rushed ahead, amazed when he took down the closest cyclopian with a single feint-thrust maneuver.

But it was blind luck, he realized, as the next cyclopian came in, pressing him hard. Unbalanced, he had to fight purely defensively, his sword barely diverting each savage thrust. Luthien understood the danger of delay, knew that time was against him. Cyclopians were coming out of the pews to either side and charging down the aisle behind him. Grabbing the wounded man had cost him his life, he suddenly realized, but still, Luthien Bedwyr didn't regret the decision. Even knowing the result, if the situation was before him again, he would still try to save the wounded man.

His vision impeded by the rump of the unconscious man, Luthien could hardly see his opponent when the brute dodged to the left. Had the cyclopian been smart enough to rush in from that angle, it surely would have cut Luthien down. But it came back out to the right, and Luthien saw, though the cyclopian did not, a slender blade following its path. The cyclopian stopped and cut back to the left again, right into Oliver's rapier.

That deadly rapier blade angled down for some reason that Luthien did not understand. He turned to regard Oliver, and found the halfling balancing on top of the pew back.

"Follow me!" Oliver cried, hopping ahead to the next high back, thrusting as he landed to force the nearest cyclopian to give ground.

"Behind you!" Luthien cried, but Oliver was moving before he ever spoke the words, turning a perfect spin on the narrow plank. The halfling leaped above a sidelong cut and struck as he landed, again with perfect balance, his rapier tip poking a cyclopian in the eye.

The brute threw its weapon away and fell on its back to the bench, grasping at its torn eye with both hands.

"So sorry, but I have no time to kill you!" Oliver yelled at it, and the halfling waved to Luthien and rushed to the side, down the pew instead of down the aisle.

Luthien wanted to follow, but could not, for a horde of cyclopians beat him to the spot, and he could feel the hot breath of many more at his heels. He roared and slashed wildly, expecting to feel a spear tip at any moment.

The tumult that suddenly erupted about him sounded like a swarm of angry bees, buzzing and whipping the air every which way. Luthien yelled out at the top of his lungs and continued to strike blindly throughout the terrifying moment, not really understanding.

And then it was over, as abruptly as it had begun, and all the cyclopians near the young man lay dead or dying, stung by elvish arrows. Luthien spared no time to glance back to the triforium; he skittered along between the pews in fast pursuit of Oliver.

When they exited the other end, along the northern wall of the cathedral, they were glad to see that the three men they had rescued were beyond the altar, clambering over the tip of the angled drawbridge, where Katerin and others waited.

Oliver and Luthien made the edge of the northern transept, and saw Katerin holding her ground as cyclopians scrambled to close the escape route.

Few cyclopians blocked the way to the apse, and those fled when one was taken down by Siobhan's last arrow. On ran the two companions, Luthien still carrying the wounded man.

The altar area teemed with one-eyed brutes, and the allies holding the breach were overwhelmed and forced to fall back.

"No way out," Oliver remarked.

Luthien growled and sprinted past the halfling, to the base of the apse, then up the few stairs to the semicircular area. He didn't go straight for the altar, though, but veered to the left, toward the arched northern wall. "Close it!" he yelled to his friends at the drawbridge.

After a moment of stark horror and shock, Oliver calmed enough to figure out Luthien's reasoning. The halfling quickly gained the angle that would put him ahead of his encumbered friend. He made the wall, ripping aside an awkwardly hanging torn tapestry to reveal a wooden door.

Another barrage of arrows from the triforium kept the path clear momentarily as Oliver stood aside and let Luthien lead the way into the narrow passage, a steeply angled and curving stair that wound its way up the Ministry's tallest tower, the same stair the two companions had chased Morkney up before their fateful encounter. Oliver slammed the door behind him, but cyclopians soon tore it from its meager hinges and took up the chase.

The first thing Luthien noticed when he went into the dark stair was how very cold it was. Twenty steps up, the young man came to understand why the cyclopians, on those few occasions since the uprising when they had occupied the Ministry, had not cut down the body of their fallen leader. The normally treacherous steps and the curving walls were thick and slick with ice, snow, and water no doubt pouring into the tower from the open landing at its top.

In the darkness, Luthien had to feel his way. He put one foot up after the other, as quickly as he could go, more often than not leaning heavily against the man he carried, who was, in turn, wedged against the frozen wall.

Then Luthien slipped and stumbled, banging his knee hard against the unyielding stone. He felt movement to his side and saw the halfling's silhouette as Oliver passed, low to the floor, using his main gauche as an impromptu ice pick, stabbing it, setting it, and pulling himself along.

"Yet another reason to fight with both hands," the halfling remarked in superior tones.

Luthien grabbed Oliver's cape and used it to regain his balance. He heard the cyclopians right behind, struggling, but coming on determinedly.

"Care!" Oliver warned as one block of ice cracked free of a step, sliding down past his friend and nearly taking Luthien with it.

Luthien heard a commotion behind him, just around the bend, and knew that the closest cyclopian had gone down.

"Leave a rope end," the young warrior instructed when he came up to the cleared step.

Oliver immediately tugged his silken rope from his belt and dropped one end close to Luthien, then pressed up the stairs with all speed.

Luthien didn't dare lay the unconscious man on the floor, fearing he would slide away to his doom. He turned on the cleared step and braced himself, readying his sword.

He couldn't see the cyclopian's look of horror, but could well imagine it, when the first creature stumbled around the bend right below him, only to find that the quarry was no longer in flight!

Blind-Striker hit hard and the brute went down. Luthien stumbled as he struck, falling against the wall, and he winced when he heard the agonized groan of the unconscious man.

Down the dying brute slid, taking out the next in line, and the next behind that, until all the cyclopians were in a bouncing descent down the curving stair.

Luthien shifted the man to a more secure position on his shoulder, took up the rope, waited for Oliver to tighten the other end about a jag in the uneven wall, and began his determined climb. It took the companions more than half an hour to get up the three hundred steps to the small landing just a few steps below the tower's top. There they found the way blocked by a wall of snow. Behind them came the pounding footsteps of cyclopians closing in once more.

Oliver dug into the snow with his main gauche, the dagger's thick blade chipping and cutting away the solid barrier. Half frozen, their hands numb from the effort, they finally saw light. Dawn was just beginning to break over Montfort.

"Now what are we to do?" Oliver yelled through chattering teeth and the howling, biting wind as they pushed through to the tower's top.

Luthien laid the unconscious man down in the snow and tried to tend his wound, a wicked, jagged cut across his abdomen.

"First we are to be rid of those troublesome one-eyes," Oliver answered his own question, while he searched about the tower top until he found the biggest and most solid block of ice.

He pushed it to the top of the stairwell and shouldered it through the opening with enough force so that it slid down the five steps and across the landing, then down the curving stairwell below that. A moment later, Oliver's efforts were rewarded by the screams—rapidly diminishing screams—of surprised cyclopians.

"They will be back," Luthien said grimly.

"My so young and foolish friend," Oliver replied, "we will be frozen stiff before they ever arrive!"

It seemed a distinct possibility. Winter was cold in Montfort, nestled in the mountains, and colder still three hundred feet up atop a snow-covered tower, with no practical shielding from the brutal northern winds.

Luthien went to the tower's side, to the frozen rope Oliver had tied off weeks ago around one of the block battlements. He shielded his eyes from the stinging wind and peered over, down the length of the tower, to the naked body of dead Duke Morkney, visible, though still in shadow, apparently frozen solid against the stone.

"You have your grapnel?" Luthien asked suddenly, referring to the enchanted device the wizard Brind'Amour had given to the halfling: a black puckered ball which once had been affixed to the now frozen rope.

"I would not leave it up here," Oliver retorted. "Though I did leave my fine rope, holding the dead duke. A rope you can replace, you see, but my so fine grapnel . . ."

"Get it out," Luthien shouted, having no patience for one of Oliver's legendary orations.

Oliver paused and stared hard at the young man, then cocked an eyebrow incredulously. "I have not enough rope to get us down the tower," the halfling explained. "Not enough rope to get us halfway down!"

They heard the grunts of approaching cyclopians from the entrance to the stairwell.

"Get it ready," Luthien instructed. As he spoke, he tugged hard on the frozen rope along the tower's rim, freeing some of it from the encapsulating ice.

"You cannot be serious," Oliver muttered.

Luthien ran back and gingerly lifted the wounded man. Another cyclopian growl emanated from the curving tunnel, not so far below.

Oliver shrugged. "I could be wrong."

The halfling got to the frozen rope first. He rubbed his hands together vigorously, blowing on them several times, and into his green gauntlets, as well, before he replaced them. Then he took up his main gauche in one hand and the rope in the other, and went over the side without hesitation. He worked his way down as quickly as he could, using the long-bladed dagger to free up the rope as he went, knowing that Luthien, with his heavy load, would need a secure hold.

Oliver grimaced as he came down to the rope's end, gingerly setting his foot atop the frozen head of the dead Duke Morkney. Settling in, he glanced all about in the growing light trying to find a place where he could use his magical grapnel, a place that could get him to another secure footing.

Nothing was apparent, except one tiny window far below. To make matters worse, Oliver and Luthien were coming down the northern side of the Ministry. The courtyard below was on the wrong side of the dividing wall and was fast-filling with cyclopians, looking and pointing up.

"I have been in worse places," Oliver said flippantly as the struggling Luthien joined him, the poor wounded man slipping in and out of consciousness and groaning with every bounce.

Luthien braced himself, putting one foot on Morkney's frozen shoulder. He turned so that he could clench the rope with the same hand that held the unconscious man, and tugged his other hand free.

"There was the time that you and I hung over the lake," Oliver went on. "A so huge turtle below us, a dragon to our left, and an angry wizard to our right . . ."

Oliver's story trailed off in a sympathetic "Ooh," when Luthien held up his hand to show that the rope had cut right through his gauntlet and into his skin as well. He would have been bleeding, except that what little blood had come out had already darkened and solidified on his palm.

Cyclopians gained the tower top just then and hung over the edge, leering down at Luthien and Oliver.

"We have nowhere to go!" the frustrated Oliver cried suddenly.

Luthien considered the apparent truth of the words. "Throw your grapnel around to the east," he instructed.

Oliver understood the wisdom—around the eastern corner would put them back on the right side of Montfort's dividing wall—but still, the command seemed foolish. Even if they swung around that way, they would be hanging more than two hundred feet above the street, with no practical way to get down.

Oliver shook his head, and both friends looked up to see a spear hanging down from the tower's lip, then rapidly dropping their way.

Luthien drew out *Blind-Striker* (and nearly tumbled away for the effort) and lifted the solid blade just in time to deflect the missile.

Cyclopians howled, both above and below the companions, and Luthien knew that the parry was purely lucky and that sooner or later one of those dropped spears would skewer him.

He looked back to Oliver, meaning to scold him and reiterate his command, and found that the halfling had already taken out the curious grapnel and was stringing out the length of rope. Oliver braced himself and flung the thing with all his strength, out to the northwest. As the rope slipped through his fingers, Oliver deftly applied enough pressure and brought himself around toward the east, turning the angle of the flying ball.

A final twist slapped Oliver's hand against the icy wall to the east, and the smooth-flying ball disappeared around the bend.

Neither companion dared to breathe, imagining the ball striking sidelong against the eastern wall.

The rope didn't fall.

Oliver tugged gingerly, testing the set. They had no way of knowing how firmly the grapnel had caught, or if turning its angle as they swung around would free it up and drop them to their deaths.

Another spear fell past them, nearly taking the tip from Luthien's nose.

"Are you coming?" the halfling asked, holding the rope up so that Luthien could grab on.

Luthien took it and hugged it closely, securing himself and the unconscious man, and looping the rope below one foot. He took a deep breath—Oliver did, too.

"You have never been in a worse place," Luthien insisted.

Oliver opened his mouth to reply, but only a scream came out as Luthien slipped off the frozen duke, his weight taking the surprised halfling along for the ride.

An instant later, a better-aimed cyclopian spear buried itself deeply into the top of Duke Morkney's frozen head.

The trio slid along and down the icy-smooth tower wall, flying wide as they swung around the abrupt corner, and crashed back hard, sliding to a jerking stop forty feet below the enchanted grapnel.

They found no footing, and looked down, way down, to yet another gathering below, this one of their allies. Even as they watched, the last of the Cutters came out of the secret eastern door, using a rope to descend the twenty feet to the ground, past the drawbridge, which had been closed and secured. There was no way for those allies to help them, no way for Katerin, or even the agile elves, to scale the icy tower and get to them.

"This is a better spot," Oliver decided sarcastically. "At least our friends will get to see us die."

"Not now, Oliver," Luthien said grimly.

"At least we have no spears falling at our heads," the halfling continued. "It will probably take the dim-witted one-eyes an hour or more to figure out which side of the tower we are now on."

"Not now, Oliver," Luthien said again, trying to concentrate on their predicament, trying to find a way out.

He couldn't see even a remote possibility. After a few frustrating moments, he considered just letting go of the rope and getting the inevitable over with.

A spear plummeted past, and the pair looked up to see a group of brutes grinning down at them.

"You could be wrong," Luthien offered before Oliver could say it.

"Three tugs will free the grapnel," Oliver reasoned, for that indeed was the only way to release the enchanted device once it had been set. "If I was quick enough—and always I am—I might reset it many feet below."

Luthien stared at him with blank amazement. Even the boastful Oliver had to admit that his plan wasn't a plan at all, that if he pulled free the grapnel, he and Luthien, and the wounded man as well, would be darker spots on a dark street, two hundred feet below.

Oliver said no more, and neither did Luthien, for there was nothing more to say. It seemed as though the legend that was the Crimson Shadow would not have a happy ending.

Brind'Amour's grapnel was a marvelous thing. The puckered ball could stick to any wall, no matter how sheer. It was stuck now sidelong, the eye-loop straight out to the side and the weighted rope hanging down.

Luthien and Oliver felt a sudden jerk as their weight finally made the ball half-turn on the wall and straighten out, shifting so that it was in line above the hanging rope. Then, suddenly and unexpectedly, the pair found themselves descending, the ball sliding along the icy surface.

Luthien cried out. So did Oliver, but the halfling kept the presence of mind to jab at the stone with his main gauche. The dagger's tip bit into the ice, threw tiny flecks all about, drawing a fine line as the descent continued.

Up above they heard cyclopian curses, and another spear would have taken Oliver had he not thrust his main gauche above his head, knocking it away. Down below, they heard cries of "Catch them!"

Luthien kicked at the wall, tried to scratch at the ice with his boot heels, anything to maintain some control along the sliding descent. He couldn't tell how high he was, how far he had to go. Every so often, the puckered ball came to a spot that was not so thick with ice and the momentum of the slide was lessened. But not completely stopped. Down went the friends, sometimes fast and sometimes slow, screaming all the way. Luthien noted the secret door forty feet to the side and an instant later he felt hands reaching up to grab his legs, heard groans all about him as comrades cushioned the fall and the ground rushed up to swallow him.

Then he was down, in a tumble, and Oliver was above him, the halfling's fall padded by Luthien's broad chest.

Oliver leaped up and snapped his fingers. "I told you I have been in worse places," he said, and three tugs freed his enchanted grapnel.

A moment later, thunderous pounding began at the closed drawbridge, the cyclopians outraged that they had lost their prize. Blocks split apart and fell outward, the brutes using one of the many statues within the cathedral as a battering ram.

Luthien was helped to his feet; the wounded man was scooped up and carried away.

"Time to go," said Katerin O'Hale, standing at the stunned young Bedwyr's side, propping him by the elbow.

Luthien looked at her, and at Siobhan standing beside her, and let them pull him away.

In the blink of a cyclopian eye, the Eriadorans disappeared into the streets of Montfort's lower section, and the cyclopians, standing helplessly as they finally breached the wall, didn't dare to follow.

Some distance away, Oliver pulled up short and bade his companions to wait. They all looked back, following the halfling's gaze up the side of the Ministry's tower. The ice-covered eastern wall shone brilliantly in the morning light, and the image the halfling had spotted was unmistakable, and so fitting.

Two hundred feet up the wall loomed a red silhouette, a crimson shadow. Luthien's wondrous cape had worked another aspect of its magic, leaving its tell-tale image emblazoned on the stones, a fitting message from the Crimson Shadow to the common folk of Montfort.

CHAPTER 2

TO THE BITTER END

*Y*OU SHOULD NOT BE UP HERE," Oliver remarked, his frosty breath filling the air before him. He grabbed the edge of the flat roof and pulled himself over, then hopped up to his feet and clapped his hands hard to get the blood flowing in them.

Across the way, Luthien didn't reply, other than to nod in the direction of the Ministry. Oliver walked up beside his friend and noted the intensity in Luthien's striking cinnamon-colored eyes. The halfling followed that gaze to the southwest, toward the massive structure that dominated the Montfort skyline. He could see the body of Duke Morkney still frozen against the cathedral wall, the spear still stuck in the dead man's head. The rope around his neck, however, now angled out from the building, its end pushed away from the buttress where it had been tied.

"They cut the rope," the halfling howled, thinking the garish scene perfectly outrageous. "But still the dead duke stays!" Indeed the cyclopians had cut the rope free from the tower top, hoping to dislodge Morkney. Farther down the tower side, though, the rope remained frozen and so the cyclopians had done nothing more than create what looked like a ghastly antenna, sticking up from Morkney's head as if he were some giant bug.

Luthien jutted his chin upward, toward the top of the tower, and shifting his gaze, Oliver saw cyclopians bumbling about up there, cursing and pushing each other. Just below the lip, the tower glistened with wetness and some of the ice had broken away. The halfling realized what was happening a moment later when the cyclopians hoisted a huge, steaming cauldron and tipped it over the edge. Boiling water ran down the side of the tower.

One of the cyclopians slipped, then roared in pain and whirled away, and the hot cauldron toppled down behind the water. It spun along its descent, but stayed close to the wall, and slammed into the butt of the spear that was embedded in Morkney's head. On bounced the cauldron, bending the spear out with it, and the soldiers on the roof winced as Morkney's head jerked forward violently, nearly torn from his torso. The spear did come free, and it and the cauldron fell to the courtyard below, to the terrified screams of scrambling cyclopians and the derisive hoots from the many common Eriadorans watching the spectacle from the city's lower section.

The pushing atop the tower became an open fight and the offending cyclopian, still clutching the hand he had burned on the cauldron, was heaved over the battlement. His was the only scream from that side of the dividing wall, but the hoots from the lower section came louder than ever.

"Oh, I do like how they bury their dead!" Oliver remarked.

Luthien didn't share the halfling's mirth. The Ministry had been lost to Aubrey, and it was Luthien's decision to let the viscount keep it, at least for the time being. The cost of taking the building back, if they could indeed roust the cyclopians from the place, would not be worth the many lives that would be lost.

Still, Luthien had to wonder about the wisdom of that decision. Not because he needed the cathedral for strategic purposes—the huge building could be defended, but the open courtyards surrounding it made it useless as a base of offensive operations—but because of its symbolic ramifications. The Ministry, that gigantic, imposing temple of God, the largest and greatest structure in all of Eriador, belonged to the common folk who had built it, not to the ugly one-eyes and the unlawful Avon king. The soul of Montfort, of all of Eriador, was epitomized by that cathedral; every village, no matter how small or how remote, boasted at least one family member who had helped to build the Ministry.

The next cauldron of boiling water was dumped over the side then, and this time, the cauldron itself was not dropped. The hot liquid made it all the way down to the duke, and the rope, freed of its icy grasp, rolled over and hung down. A few seconds later, the upper half of Morkney's frozen torso came free of the wall and the corpse bent out at the waist.

The two friends couldn't see much on the top of the tower, of course, but after a long period when no cyclopians appeared near the edge, Luthien and Oliver surmised that the brutes had run out of hot water.

"Is a long way to climb with a full cauldron," the halfling snickered, remembering the winding stair, a difficult walk even without the cold and the ice.

"Aubrey believes that it is worth the effort," Luthien said, and his grim tone tipped Oliver off to his friend's distress.

Oliver stroked the frozen hairs of his neatly trimmed goatee and looked back to the tower.

"We could take the Ministry back," he offered, guessing the source of Luthien's mood.

Luthien shook his head. "Not worth the losses."

"We are winning this fight," Oliver said. "The merchant-types are caught in their homes and not so many cyclopians remain." He looked at the wall and imagined the scene in the northern courtyard. "And one less than a moment ago," he said with a snort.

Luthien didn't disagree. The Eriadorans were close to taking back their city—Caer MacDonald, it had been called—from Greensparrow's lackeys. But how long would they hold it? Already there were reports of an army coming from Avon to put down the resistance, and while those were unconfirmed and possibly no more than the manifestation of fears, Luthien couldn't deny the possibility. King Greensparrow would not tolerate an uprising, would not easily let go of Eriador, though he had never truly conquered the land.

Luthien thought of the plague that had ravaged Eriador some twenty years before, in the very year that he had been born. His mother had died in that plague, and so many others as well, nearly a third of the Eriadoran populace. The proud folk could no longer continue their war with Greensparrow's armies—forces comprised mostly of cyclopians—and so they had surrendered.

And then another plague had come over Eriador: a blackening of the spirit. Luthien had seen it in his own father, a man with little fight left in him. He knew it in men like Aubrey, Eriadorans who had accepted Greensparrow with all their heart, who profited from the misery of the commonfolk.

So what exactly had he and Oliver started that day in the Ministry when he had killed Morkney? He thought of that battle now, of how Morkney had given over his body to a demon, further confirmation of the wickedness that was Greensparrow and his cronies. The mere thought of the evil beast, Praehotec by name, sent shudders coursing through Luthien, for he would not have won that fight, would not have plunged Oliver's rapier through the duke's skinny chest, had not Morkney erred and released the demon to its hellish home, the human thinking to kill the battered Luthien on his own.

Looking back over the events of these last few weeks, the blind luck and the subtle twists of fate, Luthien had to wonder, and to worry—for how many innocent people, caught up in the frenzy of the fast-spreading legend of the Crimson Shadow, would be punished by the evil king? Would another plague, like the one that had broken the hearts and will of Eriador when Greensparrow first became king of Avon, sweep over the land? Or would Greensparrow's cyclopian army simply march into Montfort and kill everyone who was not loyal to the throne?

And it would go beyond Montfort, Luthien knew. Katerin had come from Isle Bedwydrin, his home, bearing his father's sword and news that the uprising was general on the island, as well. Gahris, Luthien's father, had apparently found his heart, the pride that was Eriador of old, in the news of his son's exploits. The eorl of Bedwydrin had declared that no cyclopian on Isle Bedwydrin would remain alive. Avonese, once Aubrey's consort and passed on by Aubrey to become the wife of Gahris, was in chains.

The thought of that pompous and painted whore brought bile into Luthien's throat. In truth, Avonese had begun all of this, back in Bedwydrin. Luthien had unwittingly accepted her kerchief, a symbol that he would champion her in the fighting arena. When he had defeated his friend, Garth Rogar, the wicked Avonese had called for the vanquished man's death.

And so Garth Rogar had died, murdered by a cyclopian that Luthien later slew. While the ancient rules gave Avonese the right to make such a demand, simple morality most definitely did not.

Avonese, in pointing her thumb down, in demanding the death of Garth Rogar, had set Luthien on his path. How ironic now that Aubrey, the man who had brought the whore to Bedwydrin, was Luthien's mortal enemy in the struggle for Montfort.

Luthien wanted Aubrey's head and meant to get it, but he feared that his own, and those of many friends, would roll once King Greensparrow retaliated.

"So why are you sad, my friend?" Oliver asked, his patience worn thin by the stinging breeze. No more cyclopians had appeared atop the tower, and Oliver figured that it would take them an hour at least to descend, fill another cauldron, and haul the thing up. The comfort-loving halfling had no intention of waiting an hour in the freezing winter wind.

Luthien stood up and rubbed his hands and his arms briskly. "Come," he said, to Oliver's relief. "I am to meet Siobhan at the Dwelf. Her scouts have returned with word from the east and the west."

Oliver hopped into line behind Luthien, but his step quickly slowed. The scouts had returned?

The worldly Oliver thought he knew then what was bothering Luthien.

The Dwelf, so named because it catered to nonhumans, particularly to dwarfs and elves, was bustling that day. It was simply too cold outside to wage any major battles, and many of the rebels were using the time to resupply their own larders and relax. Located in one of Montfort's poorest sections, the Dwelf had never been very popular with any except the nonhuman residents of Montfort, but now, as the favored tavern of the Crimson Shadow, the hero of the revolution, it was almost always full.

The barkeep, a slender but rugged man (and looking more fearsome than usual, for he hadn't found the time to shave his thick black stubble in nearly a week), wiped his hands on a beer-stained cloth and moved up to stand before Oliver and Luthien as soon as they took their customary seats at the bar.

"We're looking for Siobhan," Luthien said immediately.

Before Tasman could answer, the young Bedwyr felt a gentle touch on his earlobe. He closed his eyes as the hand slid lower, stroking his neck in the sensuous way only Siobhan could.

"We have business," Oliver said to Tasman, then looked sidelong at the couple. "Though I am not so sure which business my excited friend favors at this time."

Luthien's cinnamon eyes popped open and he spun about, taking Siobhan's hand as he turned and pulling it from his neck. He cleared his throat, embarrassed, to find that the half-elf was not only not alone, but that one of her companions was a scowling Katerin O'Hale.

The young man realized then that the gentle stroke of his neck had been given for Katerin's benefit.

Oliver knew it, too. "I think that the war comes closer to my home," he whispered to Tasman. The barkeep snickered and slid a couple of ale-filled mugs before the companions, then moved away. Tasman's ears were good enough to catch everything important that was said along his bar, but he always tried to make sure that those conversing didn't know he was in on the discussion.

Luthien locked stares with Katerin for a long moment, then cleared his throat again. "What news from Avon?" he asked Siobhan.

Siobhan looked over her left shoulder to her other companion, an elf dressed in many layers of thick cloth and furs. He had rosy cheeks and long eyelashes that glistened with crystals of melting ice.

"It is not promising, good sir," the elf said to Luthien, with obvious reverence.

Luthien winced a bit, still uncomfortable with such formal treatment. He was the leader of the rebels, put forth as the hero of Eriador, and those who were not close to him always called him "good sir" or "my lord," out of respect.

"Reports continue that an army is on the way from Avon," the elf went on. "There are rumors of a great gathering of cyclopian warriors—Praetorian Guard, I would assume—in Princetown."

It made sense to Luthien. Princetown lay diagonally across the Iron Cross to the southeast. It was not physically the closest to Montfort of Avon's major cities, but it was the closest to Malpuissant's Wall, the only pass through the great mountains that an army could hope to navigate, even in midsummer, let alone in the harsh winter.

Still, any march from Princetown to Montfort, crossing through the fortress of Dun Caryth, which anchored Malpuissant's Wall to the Iron Cross, would take many weeks, and the rate of attrition in the harsh weather would be taxing. Luthien took some comfort in the news, for it didn't seem probable that Greensparrow would strike out from Princetown until the spring melt was in full spate.

"There is another possibility," the elf said grimly, seeing the flicker of hope in the young Bedwyr's eyes.

"Port Charley," guessed Katerin, referring to the seaport west of Montfort.

The elf nodded.

"Is the rumor based in knowledge or in fear?" Oliver asked.

"I do not know that there is a rumor at all," the elf replied.

"Fear," Oliver decided, *and well-founded*, he silently added. As the realities of the fighting in Montfort had settled in and the rebels turned their eyes outside the embattled city, talk of an Avon fleet sailing into Port Charley abounded. It seemed a logical choice for Greensparrow. The straits between Baranduine and Avon were treacherous in the winter, and icebergs were not uncommon, but it was not so far a sail, and the great ships of Avon could carry many, many cyclopians.

"What allies—" Luthien began to ask, but the elf cut him short, fully expecting the question.

"The folk of Port Charley are no friend of cyclopians," he said. "No doubt they are glad that one-eyes are dying in Montfort, and that Duke Morkney was slain."

"But . . ." Oliver prompted, correctly interpreting the elf's tone.

"But they have declared no allegiance to our cause," the elf finished.

"Nor will they," Katerin put in. All eyes turned to her, some questioning, wondering what she knew. Luthien understood, for he had often been to Hale, Katerin's home, an independent, free-spirited town not so different from Port Charley. Still, he wasn't so sure that Katerin's reasoning was sound. The names of ancient heroes, of Bruce MacDonald, sparked pride and loyalty in all Eriadorans, the folk of Port Charley included.

"If a fleet does sail, it must be stopped at the coast," Luthien said determinedly.

Katerin shook her head. "If you try to bring an army into Port Charley, you will be fighting," she said. "But not with allies of Greensparrow."

"Would they let the cyclopians through?" Oliver asked.

"If they will not join with us, then they will not likely oppose Greensparrow," Siobhan put in.

Luthien's mind raced with possibilities. Could he bring Port Charley into the revolution? And if not, could he and his rebels hope to hold out against an army of Avon?

"Perhaps we should consider again our course," Oliver offered a moment later.

"Consider our course?" Katerin and Siobhan said together.

"Go back underground," the halfling replied. "The winter is too cold for much fighting anyway. So we stop fighting. And you and I," he said to Luthien, nudging his friend, "will fly away like wise little birds."

The open proclamation that perhaps this riot had gotten a bit out of hand sobered the mood of all those near to the halfling, even the many eavesdroppers who were not directly in on the conversation. Oliver had reminded them all of the price of failure.

Siobhan looked at her elvish companion, who only shrugged helplessly.

"Our lives were not so bad before the fight," Tasman remarked, walking by Luthien and Oliver on the other side of the bar.

"There is a possibility of diplomacy," Siobhan said. "Even now. Aubrey knows that he cannot put down the revolt without help from Avon, and he dearly craves the position of duke. He might believe that if he could strike a deal and rescue Montfort, Greensparrow would reward him with the title."

Luthien looked past the speaker, into the eyes of Katerin O'Hale, green orbs that gleamed with angry fires. The notion of diplomacy, of surrender, apparently did not sit well with the proud warrior woman.

Behind Katerin, several patrons were jostled and then pushed aside. Then Katerin, too, was nudged forward as a squat figure, four feet tall but sturdy, sporting a bushy blue-black beard, shoved his way to stand before Luthien.

"What's this foolish talk?" the dwarf Shuglin demanded, his gnarly fists clenched as though he meant to leap up and throttle Luthien at any moment.

"We are discussing our course," Oliver put in. The halfling saw the fires in Shuglin's eyes. Angry fires—for the dwarf, now that he had found some hope and had tasted freedom, often proclaimed that he would prefer death over a return to subjugation.

Shuglin snorted. "You decided your course that day in the Ministry," he roared. "You think you can go back now?"

"Not I, nor Luthien," the halfling admitted. "But for the rest . . ."

Shuglin wasn't listening. He shoved between Luthien and Oliver, grabbed the edge of the bar, and heaved himself up to stand above the crowd.

"Hey!" he roared and the Dwelf went silent. Even Tasman, though certainly not appreciating the heavy boots on his polished bar, held back.

"Who in here is for surrendering?" Shuglin called.

The Dwelf's crowd remained silent.

"Shuglin," Luthien began, trying to calm his volatile friend.

The dwarf ignored him. "Who in here is for killing Aubrey and raising the flag of Caer MacDonald?"

The Dwelf exploded in cheers. Swords slid free of their sheaths and were slapped together above the heads of the crowd. Calls for Aubrey's head rang out from every corner.

Shuglin hopped down between Oliver and Luthien. "You got your answer," he growled, and he moved to stand between Katerin and Siobhan, his gaze steeled upon Luthien and muscular arms crossed over his barrel chest.

Luthien didn't miss the smile that Katerin flashed at the dwarf, nor the pat she gave to him.

Of everything the dwarf had said, the most important was the ancient name of Montfort, Caer MacDonald, a tribute to Eriador's hero of old.

"Well said, my friend," Oliver began. "But—"

That was as far as the halfling got.

"Bruce MacDonald is more than a name," Luthien declared.

"So is the Crimson Shadow," Siobhan unexpectedly added.

Luthien paused for just an instant, to turn a curious and appreciative look at the half-elf. "Bruce MacDonald is an ideal," Luthien went on. "A symbol for the folk of Eriador. And do you know what Bruce MacDonald stands for?"

"Killing cyclopians?" asked Oliver, who was from Gascony and not Eriador.

"Freedom," Katerin corrected. "Freedom for every man and woman." She looked to Siobhan and to Shuglin. "For every elf and every dwarf. And every halfling, Oliver," she said, her intent gaze locking with his. "Freedom for Eriador, and for every person who would live here."

"We talk of halting what we cannot halt," Luthien put in. "How many merchants and their cyclopian guards have been killed? How many Praetorian Guards? And what of Duke Morkney? Do you believe that Greensparrow will so easily forgive?"

Luthien slipped off his stool, standing tall. "We have begun something here, something too important to be stopped by mere fear. We have begun the freeing of Eriador."

"Let us not get carried away," Oliver interjected. "Or we might get carried away . . . in boxes."

Luthien looked at his diminutive friend and realized how far Oliver—and many others, as well, given the whispers that had reached Luthien's ears—were sliding backward on this issue. "You are the one who told me to reveal myself in the Minisiry that day," he reminded the halfling. "You are the one who wanted me to start the riot."

"I?" Oliver balked. "I just wanted to get us out of there alive after you so foolishly jumped up and shot an arrow at the Duke!"

"I was there to save Siobhan!" Luthien declared.

"And I was there to save you!" Oliver roared right back at him. The halfling sighed and calmed, patted his hand on Luthien's shoulder. "But let us not get carried away," Oliver said. "In boxes or any other way."

Luthien didn't calm a bit. His thoughts were on destiny, on Bruce MacDonald and the ideals the man represented. Katerin was with him, so was Shuglin, and so was his father, back on Isle Bedwydrin. He looked toward Siobhan, but could not read the feelings behind the sparkle of her green eyes. He would have liked something from her, some indication, for over the past few weeks she had quietly become one of his closest advisors.

"It cannot be stopped," Luthien declared loudly enough so that every person in the Dwelf heard him. "We have started a war that we must win."

"The boats will sail from Avon," Oliver warned.

"And so they will be stopped," Luthien countered, cinnamon eyes flashing. "In Port Charley." He looked back out at the crowd, back to Siobhan, and it seemed to him as if the sparkle in her eyes had intensified, as if he had just passed some secret test. "Because the folk of that town will join with us," Luthien went on, gathering strength, "and so will all of Eriador." Luthien paused, but his wicked smile spoke volumes.

"They will join us once the flag of Caer MacDonald flies over Montfort," he continued. "Once they know that we are in this to the end."

Oliver thought of remarking on just how bitter that end might become, but he held the thought. He had never been afraid of death, had lived his life as an ultimate adventure, and now Luthien, this young and naive boy he had found on the road, had opened his eyes once more.

Shuglin thrust his fist into the air. "Get me to the mines!" he growled. "I'll give you an army!"

Luthien considered his bearded friend. Shuglin had long been lobbying for an attack on the Montfort mines, outside of town, where most of his kin were imprisoned. Siobhan had whispered that course into Luthien's ear many times, as well. Now, with the decision that this was more than a riot, with the open declaration of war against Greensparrow, Luthien recognized that action must be taken swiftly.

He eyed the dwarf directly. "To the mines," he agreed, and Shuglin whooped and hopped away, punching his fist into the air.

Many left the Dwelf then, to spread the word. It occurred to Oliver that some might be spies for Aubrey and were even now running to tell the viscount of the plan.

It didn't matter, the halfling decided. Since the beginning of the revolt in the city's lower section, Aubrey and his forces had been bottled up within the walls of the inner section and could not get word to those cyclopians guarding the Montfort mines.

"You are crazy," Siobhan said to Luthien, but in a teasing, not derisive, manner. She moved near to the man and put her lips against his ear. "And so exciting," she whispered, but loud enough so that those closest could hear. She bit his earlobe and gave a soft growl.

Looking over her shoulder, glimpsing Katerin's scowl, Luthien recognized again that Siobhan's nuzzle, like her earlier display of affection, was for the other woman's sake. Luthien felt no power, no pride, with that understanding. The last thing the young Bedwyr wanted to do was bring pain to Katerin O'Hale, who had been his lover—and more than that, his best friend—those years on Isle Bedwydrin.

Siobhan and her elvish companion left then, but not before the half-elf threw a wink back at Luthien that changed to a superior look as she passed Katerin.

Katerin didn't blink, showed no expression whatsoever.

That alone made Luthien nervous.

Not so long afterward, Luthien, Oliver, and Katerin stood alone just inside the door of the Dwelf. It was snowing again, heavily, so many of the patrons had departed to stoke the fires in their own homes.

The talk between the three was light, but obviously strained, with Oliver pointedly keeping the subject on planning the coming assault on the Montfort mines.

The tension between Luthien and Katerin did not diminish, though, and finally Luthien decided that he had to say something.

"It is not what it seems," he stammered, interrupting the rambling Oliver in midsentence.

Katerin looked at him curiously.

"With Siobhan, I mean," the young man explained. "We have been friends for some time. I mean . . ."

Luthien found no words to continue. He realized how stupid he must sound; of course Katerin—and everyone else!—knew that he and Siobhan were lovers.

"You were not here," he stuttered. "I mean . . ."

Oliver groaned, and Luthien realized that he was failing miserably and was probably making the situation much worse. Still, he could not bring himself to stop, could not accept things as they were between him and Katerin.

"It's not what you think," he said again, and Oliver, recognizing the scowl crossing Katerin's face, groaned again.

"Siobhan and I . . . we have this friendship," Luthien said. He knew that he was being ultimately condescending, especially considering the importance of the previous discussion. But Luthien's emotion overruled his wisdom and he couldn't stop himself. "No, it is more than that. We have this . . ."

"Do you believe that you are more important to me than the freedom of Eriador?" Katerin asked him bluntly.

"I know you are hurt," Luthien replied before he realized the stupidity of his words.

Katerin took a quick step forward, grabbed Luthien by the shoulders and lifted her knee into his groin, bending him low. She moved as if to say something, but only trembled and turned away.

Oliver noted the glisten of tears rimming her green eyes and knew how profoundly the young man's words had stung her.

"Never make that mistake about me again," Katerin said evenly, through gritted teeth, and she left without turning back.

Luthien gradually straightened, face white with pain, his gaze locked on the departing woman. When she disappeared into the night, he looked helplessly at Oliver.

The halfling shook his head, trying not to laugh.

"I think I'm falling in love with her," Luthien said breathlessly, grimacing with the effort of talking.

"With her?" Oliver asked, pointing to the doorway.

"With her," Luthien confirmed.

Oliver stroked his goatee. "Let me understand," he began slowly, thoughtfully. "One woman puts her knee into your cabarachees and the other puts her tongue into your ear, and you prefer the one with the knee?"

Luthien shrugged, honestly not knowing the answer.

Oliver shook his head. "I'm very worried about you."

Luthien was worried, too. He didn't know what he was feeling, for either Katerin or for Siobhan. He cared for them both—no man could ask for a dearer friend or lover than either woman—and that made it all the more confusing. He was a young man trying to explore emotions he did not understand. And at the same time, he was the Crimson Shadow, leader of a revolution . . . and a thousand lives, ten thousand lives, might hinge on his every decision.

Oliver started for the door and motioned for Luthien to follow. The young man took a deep and steadying breath and readily complied.

It was good to let someone else lead.

CHAPTER 3

BREAKOUT

ALF A DOZEN CYCLOPIANS, the leaders of the operation at the Montfort mines, turned dumbfounded stares to the door of their side cave—a door that they thought had been locked—when the man and the halfling casually strode in, smiles wide, as though they had been invited. The two even closed the door behind them, and the halfling stuck a pick into the lock opening and gave a quick twist, nodding as the tumblers clicked again.

The closest brute scrambled for its spear, which was lying across hooks set into the squared cave's right-hand wall, but faster than its one eye could follow, the man hopped to the side, whipped a magnificent sword from its sheath on his hip, and brought it swinging down across the spear shaft, pinning the weapon. The cyclopian shifted, meaning to run the man down. But it paused, confused, at the sight of the man standing calmly, unthreateningly, his hand held up as though he wanted no fight.

Before another cyclopian could react, the halfling rushed between the closest two chairs and leaped atop the table, rapier in hand. He didn't threaten any of the brutes, though. Rather, he struck a heroic pose.

A chair skidded from behind the table and one cyclopian, the largest of the group, stood tall and ominous. Like Luthien over to the side, Oliver waved his hand in the air as though to calm the brute.

"Greetings," the halfling said. "I am Oliver deBurrows, highway-halfling, and my friend here is Luthien Bedwyr, son of Eorl Gahris of Bedwydrin."

The cyclopians obviously didn't know how to react, didn't understand what was going on. The Montfort mines were some distance south of the city itself, nestled deep in the towering mountains. The place was perfectly secluded; the brutes didn't even know that the battle for Montfort was raging, for they had heard nothing from the city since before the first snows. Except for the prisoner caravans, which wouldn't resume until the spring melt, no one visited the Montfort mines.

"Of course, you would know him better as the Crimson Shadow," Oliver went on.

The large cyclopian at the end of the table narrowed its one eye dangerously. There had been a breakout at the mines just a few months before, when two invaders, rumored to be a human and a halfling, had slipped in, killed more than a few cyclopians, and freed three dwarven prisoners. The entire group of guards in this small side room had been on a shift far underground on that occasion, but these two certainly fit the descriptions of the perpetrators. The cyclopian and its allies couldn't be sure of anything, though, for this sudden intrusion was too unexpected, too strange.

"Now I wanted for me and my friend here, and for our two hundred other friends outside"—that turned more than one cyclopian's head toward the closed door—"to just come in here and kill you very dead," Oliver explained. "But my gentle friend, he wanted to give you a chance to surrender."

It took a moment for the words to register, and the large cyclopian caught on first. The brute roared, overturning the table.

Oliver whirled away from the brute on his heel, expecting the move. He scrambled and leaped, flicking his rapier to the left, then to the right, slicing the two closest cyclopians across their faces.

"I will consider that a no," the halfling said dryly, falling into a roll as he landed and turning a complete somersault to find his center of balance.

The cyclopian nearest to Luthien growled and lowered its shoulder to charge, but Luthien pointed toward the trapped spear. "Look!" the young Bedwyr cried.

The stupid brute complied, turning to see Luthien's sword rapidly ascending, as Luthien snapped a wicked backhand. *Blind-Striker's* heavy, fine-edged blade cracked through the brute's forehead.

Luthien leaped over the corpse as it crumbled.

"I told you they would not surrender!" yelled Oliver, who was engaged with two cyclopians, including one of the two he had stabbed in the face. The halfling's aim on the other had been better, his rapier taking the creature directly in the eye. Like its companion, the brute had stumbled out of its chair, but had then tripped over the chair, and it squirmed about on the floor, flailing its arms wildly.

Luthien charged the side of the tipped table, lowering his shoulder as though he meant to ram it and knock it into the cyclopian across the way. The one-eye, outweighing the man considerably, likewise dropped its massive shoulder, more than willing to oblige. At the last moment, Luthien cut to the side, behind the upturned table, and the brute hit the furniture alone. Overbalanced, the cyclopian came skidding by, and Luthien hardly gave it a thought as he snapped *Blind-Striker* once to the side, into the cyclopian's ribs.

The young Bedwyr cleared the jumble and squared his footing, facing evenly against the largest brute, who had retrieved a huge battle-ax.

"One against one," he muttered, but in truth Luthien figured that this particular cyclopian, seven feet tall, at least, and weighing near to four hundred pounds, counted for one and a half.

The two facing Oliver, neither holding any weapon, gingerly hopped and skittered from side to side, looking for an opening so that they could grab the miserable rat and his stinging blade.

Oliver casually shifted and turned, poking his rapier's tip into grasping hands and seeming as though he was truly enjoying every moment of this fight.

"And I haven't even drawn my second blade," the halfling taunted. One of the cyclopians lurched for him, and he responded by sinking his rapier through its palm, the tip sliding several inches deep into the brute's forearm.

The cyclopian howled and grasped its wrist, falling to its knees with the pain, and the movement temporarily trapped the rapier. Quick-thinking, Oliver drew out his main gauche, but he found that the other cyclopian was not coming for him. The brute had rushed to the side to retrieve a nasty-looking ax.

In it charged, and Oliver sprang atop the shoulders of the kneeling cyclopian and squared to meet the attack, eyes-to-eye.

The halfling sprang away, though, as the kneeling cyclopian reached up to grab at his feet and the charging brute launched a wicked overhead chop.

The descending ax missed—missed Oliver, at least—and the attacking cyclopian groaned as the head of its kneeling fellow split apart.

"Oh, I bet that hurt," the fleeing halfling remarked.

Luthien pivoted to retreat from a sidelong swipe. He went right down to one knee and lurched forward in a thrust, scoring a hit on the advancing brute's thigh.

It was a grazing blow, though, and did not halt the giant cyclopian's charge; Luthien had to dive forward in a headlong roll to avoid the next swipe.

He came up to his feet, spiraling back the other way, and scored another hit on his opponent, this time slashing the one-eye's rump. The monster growled and spun, and the heavy ax knocked *Blind-Striker* aside.

"Remember not to parry," Luthien told himself, his hand stinging from the sheer weight of the hit. He raised his sword in both hands then, and hopped back into a defensive crouch.

"We told you that you should surrender," Luthien teased, and in looking around at the carnage, the large brute could hardly argue. Three of its comrades were dead or dying, a fourth was blinded, struggling to regain its feet and swiping wildly at the empty air. Even as the largest brute started to yell out a warning, Oliver stuck the blind cyclopian in the butt as he rushed past.

The blind brute wheeled, turning the wrong way around, and was promptly knocked flat by the cyclopian chasing Oliver. The charging brute stumbled over its falling companion, but lurched forward in an impromptu attack, swinging with all its might.

Oliver skipped aside and the ax drove deep into the upturned table.

On its knees, off balance and fully extended, with its blind comrade grabbing at its waist, the outraged cyclopian had no leverage to extract the stuck blade.

"Do let me help you," Oliver offered, rushing up and slipping his main gauche into his belt. He reached for the ax, but shifted direction and thrust his rapier through the cyclopian's throat instead.

"I changed my mind," Oliver announced as the gurgling cyclopian slipped to the floor.

Luthien's sword went up high as his monstrous opponent brought its ax overhead. The young man rushed forward, knowing that he had to move quickly before the huge one-eye gained any momentum. He slammed hard into his adversary. *Blind-Striker* struck against the ax handle and took a finger from the brute's right hand, and the attack was stopped before it ever truly began.

Still clutching the sword hilt in both hands, Luthien spun to his right and took a glancing blow on the hip from a thrusting knee. Luthien kept his back in close to the brute as he rotated; he knew that this routine would bring victory or defeat, and nothing in between. He dropped his blade over his right shoulder and bent low, then came up straight hard, slicing his blade right to left.

Blind-Striker caught the one-eye under its upraised left arm, tearing muscle and bone and nearly severing the limb.

The cyclopian's ax banged off its shoulder and fell to the floor. The brute stood a moment longer, staring blankly at its wound and at

Luthien. Then it staggered a step to the side and fell heavily against the wall, its lifeblood pouring freely.

Luthien turned away to see Oliver tormenting the blind cyclopian, the halfling darting this way and that, poking the helpless creature repeatedly.

"Oliver!" Luthien scolded.

"Oh, very well," the halfling grumbled. He skipped in front of the brute, waited for its flailing arms to present an opening, then rushed in with a two-handed thrust, his rapier sliding between cyclopian ribs to find the creature's heart, his main gauche scoring solidly on its neck.

"You really should grow another eye," Oliver remarked, skipping back as the brute fell headlong, dead before it hit the floor.

Oliver looked at Luthien almost apologetically. "They really should."

A hundred feet east along the mountain wall from the side cave Luthien and Oliver had entered, Katerin O'Hale came running out of a tunnel in full flight, more than a dozen drooling cyclopians close behind.

The woman, her sword dripping blood from her first kill inside, started as though she meant to run down the road toward Montfort, but turned instead and rushed at a snow berm.

A spear narrowly missed her, diving deep into the snow, and Katerin was glad that cyclopians, with one eye and little depth perception, were not good at range weapons. Elves were much better.

Over the berm she went, diving headlong, the brutes howling only a couple of dozen feet behind her.

How they skidded and scrambled when Siobhan and the rest of the Cutters popped up over the lip of that banking, their great longbows bent back! Like stinging bees, the elvish arrows swarmed upon the cyclopians; one fell with eight arrows protruding from its bulky chest. A handful managed to turn and run back toward the mine entrance, but more arrows followed to strike them.

Only one cyclopian limped on, several arrows sticking from its back and legs. Another bolt got it in the back of the shoulder as it neared the cave, but it stubbornly plowed on and got inside.

Shuglin the dwarf and a host of rebels, mostly human, but with several other drawfs among them, were fast in pursuit. Soon after the blue-bearded Shuglin dashed into the cave, the wounded cyclopian shrieked a death cry.

Behind the berm, Katerin squinted against the glare off the white snow and looked to the west. The door of the side cave was open again, just a bit, and an arm waved up and down, holding Oliver's huge hat.

"No need to fear for those two when they are together," Siobhan remarked, standing at Katerin's side.

Katerin looked at the half-elf, her rival for Luthien's attention. She was undeniably beautiful, with long and lustrous wheat-colored hair that made Katerin self-conscious of her own red topping.

"They have more than their share of skill, and more than their share of luck," Siobhan finished, flashing a disarming grin. There was something detached about her, Katerin recognized, something removed and superior. Still, Katerin felt no condescension directed toward her personally. All the elves and half-elves shared that cool demeanor, and Siobhan was among the most outgoing of the lot. Even their obvious rivalry over Luthien seemed less bitter than it could have been, or would have been, Katerin knew, had her rival been another proud woman from her homeland.

Siobhan and her band filtered over the snow berm, following the others into the mine entrance. Siobhan paused and waited, looking back at Katerin.

"Well done," the half-elf said as she stood among the cyclopian corpses, her sudden words catching Katerin off guard. "You baited the brutes perfectly."

Katerin nodded and rolled over the banking, sliding to her feet on the other side. She hated to admit it, but she had to, at least to herself: she liked Siobhan.

They went into the cave side by side.

Much farther down the tunnel, Shuglin and his charging band had met with stiff resistance. A barricade was up, slitted so that crossbows could be fired from behind it. Cyclopians were terrible shots, but the tunnel was neither high nor wide, and the law of averages made any approach down the long and straight run to the barricade treacherous.

Shuglin and his companions crouched around the closest corner, angered at being bottled up.

"We must wait for the elven archers," one man urged.

Shuglin didn't see the point, didn't see what good Siobhan's band might do. The cyclopians were too protected by their barricade; one or two shots might be found, but even skilled elves would not do much damage with bows.

"We got to charge," the dwarf grumbled, and the chorus around him was predictably grim.

Shuglin peeked around the bend, and nearly lost his nose to a skipping bolt. By the number of quarrels coming out and the briefness of the delay between volleys, he figured that there must be at least a dozen cyclopians on the other side of the barrier. Three times that number of fighters stood beside the dwarf, and twenty times that number would soon filter in, but the thought of losing even a few allies here, barely into the mines, didn't sit well.

The dwarf pushed his way back from the corner, coming up to a man who carried a great shield. "Give it to me," Shuglin instructed, and the man eyed him curiously for only a moment before he complied.

The shield practically covered the dwarf from head to toe. He moved back to the corner, thinking to spearhead the charge.

A cyclopian groaned from behind the barrier. Then another.

Shuglin and his allies looked to each other, not understanding.

Then they heard the slight twang of a bow, far down the tunnel ahead of them, and behind the barrier another one-eye screamed out.

Shuglin's powerful legs began pumping; he verily threw himself around the corner. His allies took up the battle cry and the charge.

"Silly one-eye," came a voice with a familiar Gascon accent from beyond the barrier. "One poke of my so fine rapier blade and you cannot see!"

A quarrel skipped off Shuglin's shield. A man flanking him took a hit in the leg and went down.

Hearing swords ringing, the dwarf didn't pause long enough to look for an opening. He lowered his strong shoulder and plowed into the barricade. Wood and stone shook loose. Shuglin didn't get through, but his allies used him as a stepping-stone and the barrier was quickly breached. By the time the dwarf regained his wits and clambered over the rubble, the fight was over, without a single rebel killed or even seriously wounded.

Luthien pointed to a fork in the passage, just at the end of the lamplight. "To the left will take you to the lower levels and your enslaved kin."

Shuglin grunted; Luthien knew where the fighting dwarf wanted to be. Shuglin had been in the mines before, but for only a short while. The dwarf had been taken prisoner in Montfort for aiding Luthien and Oliver in one of their many daring escapes. He had been sentenced to hard labor in the mines as all convicted dwarfs were, along with two of his fellows. But Oliver, Luthien, and the Cutters had rescued the three dwarfs before the cyclopians had had the chance to take them down to the lower levels.

"And where are you off to?" Shuglin wanted to know, seeing that Luthien and Oliver weren't moving to follow him.

Luthien shrugged and smiled, and turned to leave. Oliver tipped his

hat. "There are many smaller side tunnels," the halfling explained.
"Look for us when you need us most!"

With that heroic promise, Oliver scampered off after Luthien, the two
of them going right at the fork, back to the narrow passage that had led
them here from the guard room. They had indeed found many tunnels
leading off that passage, several of which sloped steeply down. The main
entrance to the lower mines, where the dwarfs were kept as slaves, was to
the left at the fork, as Luthien had told Shuglin, but Luthien and Oliver
figured that if they could get down lower in secret, they could rouse the
enslaved dwarfs and strike at the cyclopian guards from behind.

They did make their way down and in the lower tunnels found a score
of dirty, beleaguered dwarfs for every cyclopian guard. Though battered
and half-starved, the tough bearded folk were more than ready to join in
the cause, more than ready to fight for their freedom. Pickaxes and shovels that had been used as mining tools now served as deadly weapons as
the growing force made its way along the tunnels.

Shuglin's group, rejoined with the rest of their allies, including Katerin and the Cutters, found their reception exactly the opposite. The
main entrance to the lower mines also housed the largest concentration
of cyclopians. They fought a bitter battle in the last room of the upper
level, and predictably, the large platform that served as an elevator to the
lower level was destroyed by the cyclopians.

Using block and tackle and dozens of ropes, Shuglin and his dwarfs
quickly constructed a new transport. Getting down was a different matter, and many were lost in the first assault, despite the fine work of the
elvish archers. Once the lower chamber was secured, the group faced a
difficult, room-to-room march, and there were at least as many well-
armed cyclopians as there were rebels.

But there were as many dwarf slaves as both forces combined, and
when Luthien and Oliver and their makeshift army showed up behind
the cyclopian lines, the defense of the mines fell apart.

That same night, the dwarfs crawled out of the Montfort mines,
many of them looking upon stars for the first time in more than a
decade. Almost without exception, they fell to their knees and gave
thanks, cursing King Greensparrow and singing praises to the Crimson
Shadow.

Shuglin put a strong hand on Luthien's shoulder. "Now you've got
your army," the blue-bearded dwarf promised grimly.

With five hundred powerful dwarfs camped about him, Luthien
didn't doubt those words for a moment.

Standing off to the side, Oliver's expression remained doubtful. He had previously offered to Luthien that perhaps the dwarfs should run off into the mountains, and that he and Luthien and whoever else would come could ride north, into the wilder regions of Eriador, where they might blend into the landscape, so many more rogues in a land of rogues. Despite the victorious and heartwarming scene around him now, Oliver seemed to be holding to those thoughts. The pragmatic halfling understood the greater nations of the wider world, including Avon, and he could not shake the image of Greensparrow's army flowing north and crushing the rebels. Many times in the last few weeks, Oliver had pondered whether Avon used the gallows or the guillotine.

Oliver the highwayhalfling longed for his life out on the road, an outlaw, perhaps, but not so much an outlaw that an entire army would search for him!

"We cannot flee," Luthien said to him, recognizing the forlorn expression and understanding its source. "It is time for Montfort to fall."

"And for Caer MacDonald to rise," Katerin O'Hale quickly added.

CHAPTER 4

A WISE MAN'S EYES

THE MANY WINTERS had played hard on the old wizard Brind'Amour's broad shoulders, and the crow's-feet that creased his face were testament to his many hours of study and of worry. No less were his worries now—indeed, he suspected that Eriador, his beloved land, was in its most critical time—but his shoulders were not stooped, and anyone looking at the wizened face would likely not notice the crow's-feet, too entranced by the sheer intensity of the old man's deep blue eyes.

Those eyes sparkled now, as the wizard sat in the high-backed chair before his desk in a roughly circular cave, its perfectly smooth floor the only clue that this was no natural chamber. A single light, sharp like a spark of lightning, illuminated the room, emanating from a perfectly round crystal ball sitting atop the desk between a human skull and a tall, treelike candelabra.

Brind'Amour leaned back in his chair as the light began to fade and considered the images that the enchanted ball had just shown to him.

The dwarfs were free of the Montfort mines and had come into the city beside Luthien and Oliver.

The dwarfs were free!

Brind'Amour stroked his snow-white beard and brushed his hand over his white hair, which he had tied back in a thick ponytail. He could trust these images, he reminded himself, because he was looking at things as they were, not as they might be.

He had done that earlier, looked into the future. A risky business, and an exhausting one. Of all the magical enchantments a wizard might cast, prophesying was perhaps the most troublesome and dangerous, for looking into the future involved more than harnessing simple energies, such as a strike of lightning, and more than sending one's consciousness to another real-time place, as in simple scrying. Looking into the future meant bringing together all the known elements of the present in one place, a crystal ball or a mirror, then forcing logical conclusions to each, as well as resultant new conflicts. Truly such prophesying was a test of a wizard's intelligence and intuition.

Brind'Amour rarely dared such prophesying because, despite his curiosity, he realized that the future was not dependable. He could cast the spell over his crystal ball, huddle close, and study the fleeting images—and they were always fleeting, flickers, and partial pictures—but he could never know which were true and which were only possibilities. And of course, the mere fact that some prying wizard had glimpsed into the potential future made it more likely that the natural outcome would be altered.

Brind'Amour hadn't been able to resist a quick glance this one day, and he had come away with one image that seemed plausible, even likely: a man atop a tall tower in Montfort. Brind'Amour had a general idea of the current events in the city—he had visited Montfort mentally on a couple of occasions, looking through the eyes of a half-elf—and though he didn't recognize the man on the tower, he knew from the rich clothes and ample jewelry that this was obviously one of Greensparrow's supporters.

The wizard leaned back in his chair. A man atop a tower, he thought. Taunting the populace. A leader, a symbol of what remained in Montfort of King Greensparrow. Something would have to be done about that, Brind'Amour mused, and he knew that he could work this change himself, without great expense and no risk at all. Perhaps his journey into the realm of what might be had been worth the cost this time.

The cost . . . he remembered the many warnings his masters of centuries ago had given him concerning prophesying. The risk . . .

Brind'Amour shook all that from his mind. This time was different. This time he had not looked primarily at what might be, but at what *was*. And "what was" was a full-scale revolt in Montfort, one that might turn into a revolution for all of Eriador. In a roundabout way, Brind'Amour had begun it. He was the one who had given the crimson cape to Luthien Bedwyr; he was the one who had set the Crimson Shadow and his halfling cohort on the road to Montfort. At that time, Brind'Amour had only hoped Luthien could cause some mischief, perhaps renewing the whispered legend of the Crimson Shadow, hero of old. Brind'Amour had dared to hope that in the years to come he might build upon the whispers surrounding Luthien to gradually diminish Eriador's acceptance of wicked King Greensparrow.

Fate had intervened to rush events much more quickly than the old wizard had anticipated, but Brind'Amour was not saddened by that fact. He was excited and hopeful. Above all else, Brind'Amour believed in Eriador and her sturdy folk, Luthien Bedwyr among them.

His divining had shown him that several villages, including Luthien's own of Dun Varna on the Isle Bedwydrin, had taken up the cause. Just that morning a fleet, mostly converted fishing boats, had put out from Dun Varna, braving the icy waters of the Dorsal on the short trip to neighboring Isle Marvis. Aboard were reinforcements for the eorl of Marvis as he, like Gahris, eorl of Bedwydrin, tried to rid his land of the hated cyclopians.

Brind'Amour whispered a few words and snapped his fingers three times, and the many tips of the candelabra flickered to flaming life. He rose from his chair, smoothing his thick and flowing blue robes as he made his way near a table that lay deeply buried under a pile of parchments. Brind'Amour shuffled them about, finally extracting a map of the Avonsea Islands. Thousands of colored dots, green and red and yellow, covered the map, representing concentrations of people and the sides they represented in the conflict. South of the mountains, in Avon proper, those dots were nearly all green, for those loyal to the throne, or yellow, indicating a neutral bent. North of the mountains showed many green concentrations, as well—the merchant section of Montfort remained one green blob—and most of the others were yellow still. But the red dots, symbolizing the rebels, were growing in number.

The wizard held the map up before him and closed his eyes, reciting the words of another spell. He recalled everything the crystal ball had just shown him, the new events in Montfort and the fleet in the north, and when he opened his eyes, the map now indicated the changes, with a wave of red flowing toward Isle Marvis and a red wall thickening about Montfort's entrapped merchant quarter.

"What have I begun?" the old wizard mused, and he chuckled. He hadn't anticipated this, not for another hundred years, but he believed that he was ready for it, and so was Eriador. Luthien had retrieved Brind'Amour's staff from the lair of the dragon Balthazar, and now Luthien, with handy Oliver beside him, and a growing number of other leaders surrounding them both, was showing remarkable progress.

Brind'Amour replaced the map on the table and pinned down its corners with paperweights that resembled little gargoyles. He sighed deeply and looked back to the immense desk and the dancing flames of the candelabra, throwing more light than normal candles ever could. The crystal ball tugged at his curiosity, as it had for many weeks, not to look at Eriador, but to explore beyond the land's southern borders to see what was brewing in Avon.

Brind'Amour sighed again and realized he was not prepared for that dangerous venture. Not yet. He needed to rest and gather his strength, and let the budding rebellion grow to full bloom. Briefly, he regretted having looked upon the future earlier, for the present continued to call out to him and he was too tired to answer. Scrying the future was taxing, but for a wizard in Brind'Amour's secret position, sending his magical energies over the miles to view the present events of the wide world was simply dangerous. Such energies could be detected by Greensparrow and his dukes, and since few wizards remained in the world, any of Brind'Amour's scrying attempts could be traced to this most secret of caves in the Iron Cross.

The wizard spoke a word of magic and gently puffed, and the flames atop the candelabra flickered wildly, then blew out. Brind'Amour turned and went through the door, down a narrow passage which led to his bedchamber. He had one more thing to accomplish before he could lie down for a well-deserved sleep. He trusted in his vision of what might soon come in Montfort, of Greensparrow's man standing atop that tall tower, and he knew what to do about it.

He stopped at a side room along the corridor, a small armory, and searched among the hodgepodge of items until he located a specific, enchanted arrow. Then he delivered it—a simple magical spell, really—to a certain beautiful half-elf in Montfort, one who always seemed to be in the middle of the trouble.

The wizard went to his rest.

*   *   *

Luthien woke with a start. He spent a long minute letting his eyes adjust to the dim lighting and looking about his small room, making sure that all was aright. The fireplace glowed still—it could not be too late—but the flames were gone, the pile of logs consumed to small red embers, watchful eyes guarding the room.

Luthien rolled out of bed and padded across the floor. He sat on the stone hearth. Its warmth felt good against his bare flesh. He moved the screen aside, took up the poker and stirred the embers, hardly considering the movements, for he was too filled with a multitude of emotions that he did not understand. He put a couple of logs on the pile and continued blowing softly until the flames came up again.

He watched them for some time, allowing their tantalizing dance to bring him back to Bedwydrin, back to Dun Varna and a time before he had taken this most unexpected road. He remembered the first time he and Katerin had made love on the high hill overlooking the city and the bay.

Luthien's smile was short-lived. He reminded himself that he needed his sleep, that the next day, like all the others, would be filled with turmoil, with fighting and decisions that would affect the lives of so many people.

Luthien replaced the poker in its iron stand near the hearth and stood up, brushing himself off. As he approached the bed, the light greater now that the fire was up once more, he paused.

The covers had rolled over when he got up, the thick down blanket bunched up high, and beneath it he could see Siobhan, lying naked on her belly, fast asleep. The young man gently sat down on the edge of the bed. He put his hand under the edge of the cover, on the back of Siobhan's knee, and ran it up slowly, feeling every inch of her curving form until he got to her neck.

Then he spread his fingers in her lustrous hair. Siobhan stirred, but did not wake.

She was so smooth, so beautiful, and so warm. Luthien couldn't deny the half-elf's overwhelming allure; she had captured his heart with a single glance.

Why, then, had he just been thinking of Katerin?

And why, the young man wondered as he crawled back under the covers, snuggling close to Siobhan, was he feeling so guilty?

In the days she had been in Montfort, Katerin had given no sign that she wanted to be back together with Luthien. She had not uttered a single word of disapproval about the relationship Luthien had fostered with Siobhan.

But she did disapprove, Luthien knew in his heart. He could see it in her green eyes, those beautiful orbs that had greeted him at dawn after the night he had become a man, on a hill in Dun Varna, in a world that seemed so many millions of miles and millions of years away.

It was all lace and frills, niceties and painted ladies who served the court well. The sight revealed in the crystal ball turned Brind'Amour's stomach, but at the same time, it gave him hope. Carlisle on Stratton, in Avon far to the south of Eriador, had been built for war, and by war, centuries before, a mighty port city bristling with defenses. Greensparrow had come to the throne ruthlessly, in a bloody and bitterly fought battle, and the first years of his reign had been brutal beyond anything the Avonsea Islands had seen since the Huegoth invasions of centuries before.

But now Carlisle was lace and frills, an overabundance of sweetened candies and carnal offerings.

Brind'Amour's magical eye wove its way through the palace. The wizard had never before been so daring, so reckless, as to send his mind's eye so near to his archenemy. If Greensparrow detected the magical emanations . . .

The thick stone walls of Brind'Amour's mountain hideaway would be of little defense against Greensparrow's allies, mighty demons from the pits of hell.

The sheer bustle of the palace amazed the distant wizard. Hundreds of people filtered through every room on the lower level, all drinking, all stuffing their faces with cakes, many stealing away to whatever darkened corner they could find. Burly cyclopians lined the walls of every room. How ironic, the wizard mused; many of the one-eyes stood before tapestries that depicted ancient battles in which their ancestors were defeated by the men of Avon!

The eye moved along, the images in the crystal ball flitting past. Then Brind'Amour felt a sensation of power, a magical strength, and for a moment, he thought that Greensparrow had sensed the intruding energy and he nearly broke the connection altogether. But then the old wizard realized that this was something different, a passive energy: the strength of Greensparrow himself, perhaps.

Brind'Amour leaned back and considered that point. He recalled Luthien's battle with the wizard Duke Morkney atop the tower of the Ministry. Morkney had called in a demon, Praehotec, and had given the beast his own body to use. In watching that battle, Brind'Amour had felt this very same sensation, only it was stronger here.

The old wizard understood, and he was filled with revulsion. With a low growl, he leaned forward, throwing all his concentration into the divining device and moving the eye along, following the beacon of Greensparrow's energy. It sailed up the back stairs of the palace, to the second floor where there weren't so many people, though even more one-eyed Praetorian Guards. It went down a maze of thickly carpeted hallways and came to a closed door.

Brind'Amour felt a jolt as the eye came up to that door. He tried to force it through, but found that a barrier was in place: the room had been magically sealed.

Greensparrow was behind that door. Brind'Amour knew it, but knew, too, that if he sent enough of his own energy to break through the blocking ward, the wizard-king would surely sense it.

Suddenly, the image in the crystal ball went dark as a huge cyclopian passed through the insubstantial eye. The door opened, and Brind'Amour was quick to urge his eye to follow the brute through.

The room beyond was relatively empty, considering the lavish furnishings throughout the rest of the palace. A single throne was centered in the square chamber, atop a circular dais, two steps up from the floor, and while the chair was ornate, decorated with glittering gemstones of green and red and violet, the floor was bare, except for narrow strips of red carpeting running from each of the room's four doors to the dais.

Greensparrow—Brind'Amour knew it was the wretch, though he hadn't seen the man in centuries, and had never known him well—lounged in the throne, fiddling with a huge ring upon the middle finger of his left hand. His hair was long and black and curly, and his face was painted and caked, though the makeup did little to hide the obvious toll his years of study and dealings with demons had taken. He appeared foppish, but Brind'Amour was not fooled. When Greensparrow looked out to regard the approaching cyclopian, his amber-colored eyes flickered with intelligence and intensity.

Brind'Amour wisely kept his magical eye near the cyclopian, hoping the strength of the imposing brute would somewhat mask the magical energy.

"What news, Belsen'Krieg?" the king asked, seeming bored.

Brind'Amour dared to move his magical eye out enough to get a good look at the brute. Belsen'Krieg was among the sturdiest and ugliest cyclopians the old wizard had ever seen. Rotting tusks stuck up over Belsen'Krieg's upper lip, which had been split in half diagonally just below its wide, flattened nose. The brute's eye was huge and bloodshot and a thick brow hung out over it like an awning on a storefront. Scars crossed both of Belsen'Krieg's cheeks, and his neck, as thick as a child's chest, seemed to be a yellow-green blob of scar tissue. His black-and-silver Praetorian Guard uniform, though, was perfectly neat, with gold brocade stitched on both shoulders and an assortment of medals and ribbons making his massive chest seem huger still.

"We have heard nothing from Montfort, my King," the cyclopian snorted, his diction impressive for one of his race, but his articulation difficult to understand due to his almost constant snuffling.

"Morkney's other cannot get back into the city," Greensparrow said, more to himself than to Belsen'Krieg.

"Morkney's other?" Brind'Amour whispered, thinking the choice of words odd. Was the wizard-king implying that all of his dukes had personal relationships with specific demons?

"So we must assume that the fool duke is dead," Greensparrow went on.

"A minor inconvenience," Belsen'Krieg offered.

"Is my ship ready to sail?" Greensparrow asked, and Brind'Amour held his breath, thinking that the king meant to go to Eriador personally to put down the revolt. If that happened, the old wizard knew, Luthien and his friends didn't have a chance.

"The waters are clear of ice all the way to Chaumadore Port," Belsen'Krieg replied immediately.

Gascony? Brind'Amour's heart leaped with sudden hope. Greensparrow was going to Gascony!

"And the waters to the north?" the king asked, and again, Brind'Amour held his breath.

"Less so, by all reports," the cyclopian answered.

"But you can get through," Greensparrow replied, and the words were not a question but a command.

"Yes, my King."

"Such silly business." Greensparrow shook his head as though the whole affair was thoroughly distasteful. "We must show them their folly," he went on, and rose from his chair, straightening his fine purple baldric and the thick and ruffled cloak. "Kill every man, woman, and child associated with the rebels. Make an example of them that Eriador will not forget for centuries to come."

He had said it so casually, so ruthlessly.

"Yes, my King!" came the predictably eager reply. No cyclopian ever questioned an order to slaughter humans.

"And I warn you," Greensparrow added, just before exiting the chamber through the back door, "if my vacation is interrupted, I will hold you personally responsible."

"Yes, my King," Belsen'Krieg responded, and the cyclopian didn't seem to be worried. Indeed, to the fearful old wizard watching from more than five hundred miles away, the cyclopian seemed to be rejoicing.

Brind'Amour cut the connection and leaned back in his chair. The crystal ball went dark, and so did the room, but the wizard didn't command his enchanted candelabra to light.

He sat in the dark, considering the connection his enemies held with demons, a relationship that was apparently still very strong. Brind'Amour thought of the fateful decision of the brotherhood those many, many years ago. The cathedrals had been built, the islands knew peace, and few cared much for the wizards, old men and women all. Their time had passed, the brotherhood had decided—even the great dragons had been put down, destroyed or imprisoned in deep caves, as Brind'Amour and his fellows had sealed up Balthazar. Brind'Amour had lost his staff in that encounter, and so convinced was he that his time was ended, that he did not even try to regain it.

All of the brotherhood had gone to sleep, some to eternal rest. Others, such as Brind'Amour, sent themselves into a magical stasis in private castles or caves. All of them . . . except for Greensparrow. He had been only a minor wizard in the old days, but one who had apparently found a way to extend the time of wizards.

Brind'Amour had chosen stasis over death because he believed that one day he might be useful to the world once more. Thus, when he had gone to his magical slumber, he had enacted spells of alarm that would call to him when the day was dark. And so he had awoken, just a few years before, to find Greensparrow seated as king of Avon and deep in unholy alliances with demons.

Brind'Amour sat in the dark considering his enemies, both human and fiend. He sat in the dark, wondering if he had been wise to set Luthien, and Eriador, on such a collision course against such an enemy as this.

CHAPTER 5

INCH BY INCH

"IT IS NOT SO DEEP," Shuglin grumbled, the end of his blue beard slick with slime.

"I am not so tall," Oliver retorted without hesitation.

The frustrated dwarf looked over to Luthien, who promptly hoisted the complaining halfling under one arm and struggled on through the ice and the muck.

"Oliver deBurrows, walking a sewer!" Oliver grumbled. "If I had known how low I would sink beside the likes of you . . ."

His complaint became a muffled groan as Luthien pitched suddenly to the side, slamming them both against the wall.

They came up apart, Oliver hopping to his feet and slapping at the muck on his blue pantaloons, crying "Ick! Ick! Ick!"

"We're under the merchants," Shuglin put in, his gravelly voice thick with sarcasm. "You probably should be quiet."

Oliver cast a hopeless glance at Luthien, but he knew that his friend was more amused than sympathetic. And he knew, too, that his complaints were minor; in light of the importance of this day, even Oliver could not take them seriously. Only a week after the opening of the mines, the rescued dwarfs had shown their value, repairing old weapons and armor, fashioning new equipment, and opening up the sewers under the embattled merchant quarter. Now Luthien and Oliver, Shuglin and three hundred of his bearded kin, were creeping along several parallel routes and would come up right in the midst of their enemies.

Still, the halfling figured that he didn't have to enjoy the journey. The lanterns lit the tunnels well enough, but they did nothing to ward off the dead cold. Ice lined the sewer tunnels and was thick about the floor's rounded center, but there was fresh waste above the ice and it would take more than a freeze to defeat the awful stench of the place.

"They had barricaded the openings," Shuglin explained, "but we got through in more than a dozen and killed four cyclopians who were nearby in the process."

"None escaped to warn of our approach?" Luthien asked for the tenth time since the expedition had set out from the city's lower section.

"Not a one," Shuglin assured him, also for the tenth time.

"I would so enjoy marching through this muck only to find the enemy waiting for us," Oliver added sarcastically.

Shuglin ignored him and took up the march again, moving swiftly down the straight tunnel. A few moments later, the dwarf stopped and signaled for those following to do likewise.

"We are found," the dismal halfling said.

Shuglin took the lantern from another dwarf and held it high in front of the mouth of the passage. He nodded as a like signal came from across the intersection, and he poked his stubby thumb upward. "All in time," the dwarf remarked, motioning for the others to move along once more.

They came into a small cubby at the side of the passage. A ladder— of new dwarfish construction—was secured against one wall, leading up a dozen feet to a wooden trapdoor.

Luthien motioned to Oliver. It had been agreed that the stealthy halfling would lead them out of the sewer, and Oliver was happy to oblige, happy to be out of the muck even if the entire cyclopian force was waiting for him above. He sprang nimbly and silently to the ladder and started up.

Before he neared the top, the trapdoor creaked open. Oliver froze in place and those down below went perfectly silent.

"Oh, no," the halfling moaned as a naked pair of cyclopian buttocks shifted over the hole. Oliver buried his face in his arms, hoping his wide-brimmed hat would protect him. "Oh, please shoot him fast," he whispered, not thrilled with the possibilities.

He breathed easier when Luthien's bow twanged and he felt the rush of air as an arrow whipped past. He looked up to see the bolt bury itself deep in the unwitting cyclopian's fleshy bottom. The brute howled and spun, and took a dwarfish crossbow quarrel right in the face as it foolishly leaned over the opening. The screaming went away and the friends heard the cyclopian fall dead on the floor of the small room above.

Oliver adjusted his hat and looked to the upturned faces below. "Hey," he called out softly, "the one-eyes, they look the same from both ends!"

"Just go on!" Luthien scolded.

Oliver shrugged and scampered up the ladder, coming into a small, square room, where the smell was nearly as bad as down below. Some brute was knocking on the door.

"Bergus?" it called.

Oliver turned back, putting his face over the opening, lifting his finger over pursed lips and motioning for the others to clear out of the way. Then he padded silently to the door. It rattled as the brute outside jostled it, for only a small hook held it closed.

"Bergus?" the brute growled again, and Oliver could tell that it was fast growing impatient.

The door shook as the cyclopian hit it harder, perhaps with his shoulder. Oliver looked to the dead cyclopian and considered the angle.

"You all right?" came a call, and the door shook again. Oliver slipped to the side of it and drew out his rapier.

Three loud knocks.

"Bergus?"

"Help me," Oliver grunted softly, trying to imitate the low tones of a cyclopian and to sound as though he was in trouble. As soon as he spoke the words, he brought his rapier flicking up, unhooking the latch. An instant later the cyclopian hit the door shoulder first, barreling through, and Oliver stung the inside of its knee with his rapier point, then kicked the brute's back foot in behind its leading one.

The overbalanced cyclopian pitched right over its fallen companion. Oliver was quick in the chase, guiding its flight so that it nearly tumbled right into the hole. A strong arm lashed out to the side, though, and the brute was able to hold itself up, with only its head and shoulders and one arm going over the lip.

Oliver jumped back and moved to strike, but he heard a twang from below and the cyclopian jerked violently, then went still. The halfling rushed back to the door and closed it once more, checking to ensure that no one else was around. Then he went to the cyclopian and heaved the creature into the hole.

"Good shot," he said to Luthien when he saw the man step over the body to get to the ladder. "But do you know which end of the thing you hit?"

Luthien didn't even look up. He didn't want to encourage Oliver, didn't want the halfling to see his amused smile.

All across the quiet upper section of the city, the invaders filtered out of several such outhouses and other privies located inside merchant dwellings. The air was still cold and dark before the dawn, and they could hear fighting over at the wall, near the Ministry.

"Right on time," Oliver said, for the diversion—an attack by forces from the lower section—was not unexpected.

Luthien nodded grimly. Right on time. Everything was going according to plan. He looked about, his eyes adjusting to the dim light, and he nodded, seeing lines of grim-faced dwarfs, who had lived for years as slaves under the tyranny of Greensparrow, filtering into nearly every shadow.

The young Bedwyr started off, Oliver in tow, heading in the general direction of the fighting. They quick-stepped along the shadows of one lane, coming to an abrupt stop at a corner when they heard footsteps fast approaching from the other way.

A cyclopian skidded around the bend, its one eye going wide with surprise.

"This is too easy," the halfling complained, and stuck his rapier into the monster's chest. A second later, *Blind-Striker* split the brute's skull down the middle.

Luthien started to answer, but both he and Oliver jumped and spun as a fight exploded behind them. A group of cyclopians had rushed out of a side avenue, also heading for the fight, but they found battle sooner than expected as two bands of dwarfs, Shuglin among them, caught them in a squeeze, overwhelming them in the street.

Skirmishes erupted all across the merchant section, and the fighting increased when the sun broke the horizon, sending slanting rays into the turmoil of war. Luthien and Oliver encountered only minimal resistance—two cyclopians, which they quickly defeated—on their way to the wall near the Ministry, where they would link with their allies, but found that a number of dwarfs had beaten them to the spot. Already the cyclopians holding the position were hard-pressed.

"Keep alert!" Luthien ordered the halfling. The young man took out his folded bow, opened and pinned it in a single movement and had an arrow ready to fly. While Oliver guarded his back and flanks, he picked his shots, one by one.

Grappling hooks came sailing over the wall, and with the dwarfs engaging the defenders on this side, others roaming the streets to cut off any reinforcements, the cyclopians could not resist. Elves and men streamed up and over the wall, joining the fighting throng.

Luthien tried to put an arrow up quickly, seeing one man slip down and a cyclopian moving in, sword high for the kill.

"Damn!" the young Bedwyr shouted, knowing he could not make the shot in time.

The cyclopian halted suddenly. Luthien didn't understand why, but didn't question the luck as he finally got his arrow sighted.

The brute fell headlong before he could let fly, two arrows protruding from its back. Following their line, back along the wall, Luthien spotted a familiar figure, beautiful and lithe, with the angular features of a half-elf.

"Siobhan," Oliver said behind him, the halfling obviously pleased and inspired by the fine figure she cut, standing tall atop the wall in the shining morning light.

Before Luthien remembered that he had a bow of his own, the half-elf held hers up again and fired, and another cyclopian fell away.

"Are you going to watch or play?" Oliver cried, running by the young man. Luthien looked back to the main fight, which was on in full now, at the wall and in the courtyard beside the towering Ministry. He slung his bow over his shoulder and drew out *Blind-Striker*, running to catch up with his friend.

Both spotted Katerin, leaping down off the wall into the middle of the fray, right in between two cyclopians.

Oliver groaned, but Luthien knew the sturdy woman of Hale better than to be afraid for her.

Back and forth she worked her spear, parrying and slapping at the surprised brutes. She thrust forward viciously, driving the spear tip into one's belly, then tore it free and shifted her angle as she reversed direction, the spear's butt end slamming the other cyclopian in the face. Katerin twirled the weapon in her hands and jabbed the tip the other way, slicing the brute's throat, then rotated it again and came back furiously, finishing the one that was holding its spilling guts.

Luthien, obviously pleased, looked at Oliver. "Two to two," he remarked.

"Say that five times fast," the halfling replied.

Before Luthien could begin to respond, Oliver poked his finger back toward the wall, and Luthien turned just as Siobhan felled another brute from the wall with her deadly bow.

"One up," Oliver said smugly, and it seemed to the two as if they had unintentionally taken sides.

"Not so!" Luthien was quick to call, and Oliver turned to see Katerin running full out. She skidded down into a crouch and hurled her spear, catching a fleeing cyclopian right in the back of the neck, dropping it to skid across the cobblestones on its ugly face.

"It would seem as if they were evenly matched," Oliver said, and his sly tone made Luthien realize that he was talking about more than fighting.

Luthien didn't appreciate the comment; Oliver saw that as soon as he had uttered the words. He rushed off, rapier held high. "Are you to watch or to play?" he cried again.

Luthien let go of his anger, put aside his confusion and all thoughts of the two wonderful women. Now wasn't the time for deep thinking. He caught up to Oliver and together they rushed headlong into the battle.

Merchant houses were raided by the dozen that fateful morning in

Montfort and scores of slaves were freed, most of whom gladly joined in the fight. Hundreds of cyclopians were beaten down.

The human merchants, though, were not summarily killed, except for those who fought back against the rebels and would not surrender. Giving them the option to surrender was Luthien's doing, the first order he had given to his rebels before the assault had begun. Luthien did not comfortably assume the role of leadership, but in this matter he was as forceful as anyone had ever seen him, for the young man believed in justice. He knew that not all of Montfort's merchants were evil men, that not all of those who had prospered during Greensparrow's time necessarily adhered to or agreed with the wicked king's edicts.

The final fight for the city was a bitter one, but in the end the cyclopian guards, city and Praetorian, were simply overwhelmed and the taking of Montfort was completed.

Except for the Ministry. The rebels had avoided attacking the place until all else was accomplished because it was too defensible. The five doors which led into the cathedral, including the secret one that had been cut in the eastern wall and the broken section of that same wall, had been secured and braced and could withstand tremendous punishment.

But now the Ministry was all that remained as a bastion for those loyal to the king of Avon. And with the mines taken, those brutes bottled up inside could not look anywhere close for support

Luthien and Oliver headed back for the place after a tour of the conquered merchant quarter. Luthien had hoped to find Viscount Aubrey alive, but had seen no sign of him. He wasn't surprised; vermin like Aubrey had a knack for survival and Luthien suspected that he knew exactly where to find the man.

The two companions joined the bulk of their army, which had gathered in the courtyards about the great structure of the Ministry, hurling taunts, and occasionally an arrow, at any cyclopian that revealed itself in any window or atop the smaller towers.

"We can get in there!" Shuglin the dwarf declared, running up and grabbing Luthien by the arm.

"They have nowhere to run," Luthien assured him, his voice soothing in its tone of complete confidence. "The battle is over."

"There could be near to five hundred of them in there," Katerin O'Hale interjected doubtfully, joining the three.

"Better reason to stay outside and wait," Luthien was quick to reply. "We cannot afford the losses."

The friends moved about the courtyard, helping out with the tending of the wounded and trying to organize the forces. Now that the cyclopian threat was ended, a myriad of other problems presented themselves. There was looting by many of the frustrated commonfolk who had lived so long with so little, and more than one merchant house had been set ablaze. Skirmishes took place between dwarfs and men, two races who had not lived beside each other in any numbers since Morkney had shipped most of the dwarfs off to the mines, and decisions still had to be made concerning the fate of the captured merchants.

Early that afternoon, Luthien finally caught sight of Siobhan again, the half-elf walking determinedly his way.

"Come with me," she ordered, and Luthien recognized the urgency in her voice.

From across the courtyard, Katerin and Oliver watched him go.

"It is business, that is all," Oliver said to the woman.

Katerin scowled at him. "What makes you believe that I care?" she asked, and walked away.

Oliver shook his head, and admired Luthien more at that moment than ever before.

"This is the most dangerous time," Siobhan said to Luthien after she had escorted him far away from the crowd. She went on to tell of the looting and of dissatisfied murmurs among the rebels.

Luthien didn't understand the seemingly illogical reactions, but he saw what was happening around him and could not deny Siobhan's fears. This should have been their moment of glory, and indeed it was, but mingled with that glory was a tumult of confusing emotions. The rebel mob did not move with a unified purpose, now that the actual battle had ended.

"The fighting will ebb for many weeks perhaps," Siobhan said.

"Our only strength is in unity," Luthien replied, beginning to catch on to her reasoning. Their goals had been met; even the Ministry could hold out only as long as the food inside lasted. The cyclopians bottled within the massive cathedral could not threaten them in any substantial way, for the rebels held strong defensive positions across the open plazas that surrounded the Ministry. If the cyclopians came charging out, their numbers would be decimated by archers before they ever engaged in close combat.

So Montfort had been taken, but what did that mean? In the weeks before the final attack, Luthien and the other leaders had clearly defined the goal, but they had not devised a plan for what would follow.

Luthien looked away from the open plaza, westward over the merchant section, and the plume of black smoke from the torched houses showed him beyond doubt that this was indeed a dangerous time. He understood the responsibilities before him and realized that he had to act quickly. They had taken Montfort, but that would mean nothing if the city now fell into disarray and anarchy.

The young Bedwyr inspected himself carefully, noted the muck from the sewer and the blood of enemy and friend alike. The magnificent crimson cape, though, showed no stains, as if its magic would tolerate no blemishes.

"I have to clean up," Luthien said to Siobhan.

She nodded. "A washbasin and a clean change of clothes have already been prepared."

Luthien looked at her curiously. Somehow he was not surprised.

Less than an hour later, with less time to prepare than he would have liked, but with the breakdown of order growing among the celebrating populace, Luthien Bedwyr walked out into the middle of the plaza in front of the Ministry. The young man's head swirled as he considered the mass of onlookers: every one of his rebel warriors, every one of Shuglin's kin, the Cutters, and thousands of others, had all come to hear the Crimson Shadow, all come to learn their fate, as though Luthien served as the mouth of God.

He tried not to look at their faces, at the want and need in their eyes. He was not comfortable in this role and hadn't the slightest idea of how or why this responsibility had befallen him. He should get Oliver to address them, he thought suddenly. Oliver could talk, could read the needs of an audience.

Or Siobhan. Luthien looked at her closely as she guided him along to the steps of a gallows that was under construction for those captured cyclopians or merchants who were deemed worthy of such an end. Perhaps he could get Siobhan to speak.

Luthien dismissed the thought. Siobhan was half-elven and more akin to elves than to men. Yet if ten thousand people were now gathered about the plaza, watching from the streets, the wall, and no doubt even below the wall in the lower section, where they could not see but could hear the relayed whispers, not seven hundred of them had any blood other than human.

He walked up the steps beside Siobhan and took some comfort in the familiar faces of Oliver, Katerin, and Shuglin standing in the front row. They looked expectant and confident; they believed in him.

"Do not forget the city's true name," Siobhan whispered in his ear, and then she stepped to the side of the platform. Luthien, the Crimson Shadow, stood alone.

He had prepared a short speech, but the first words of it would not come to him now. He saw cyclopians in the windows of the Ministry, staring down at him as eagerly as the gathered crowd, and he realized that their fate, and the fate of all Eriador and all of Avon, was held in this moment.

That notion did little to calm the young man.

He looked to his friends below him. Oliver tipped his monstrous hat, Katerin threw Luthien a wink and a determined nod. But it was Shuglin, standing patiently, almost impassive, burly arms across his chest and no telling expression on his bearded face, who gave Luthien the heart he needed. Shuglin, whose people had suffered so horribly in slavery under the tyranny of Duke Morkney. Indomitable Shuglin, who had led the way to the mines and would hear no talk of ending the fight for Montfort until the job was done.

Until the job was done.

His cinnamon eyes steeled, Luthien looked out to the crowd. No longer did he try to recall the words of his speech, rather he tried to decipher the feelings in his heart.

"My allies!" he shouted. "My friends! I see before me not a city conquered."

A long pause, and not a whisper rippled about the gathering.

"But a city freed!" Luthien proclaimed, and a huge roar went up. While he waited for the crowd to quiet, Luthien glanced over at Siobhan, who seemed perfectly at ease, perfectly confident.

"We have taken back a small part of what is rightfully ours," the young Bedwyr went on, gaining momentum, gaining heart. He held up his hand, thumb and finger barely an inch apart. "A small part," he reiterated loudly, angrily.

"Montfort!" someone yelled.

"No!" Luthien quickly interjected, before any chant could begin.

"No," the young Bedwyr went on. "Montfort is just a place on a map, a map in the halls of King Greensparrow." That name brought more than a few hisses. "It is a place to conquer, and to burn." Luthien swept his hand around to the plume of smoke behind him, diminished now, but still rising.

"What gain in taking Montfort and burning Montfort?" he called out above the confused murmurs. "What gain in possessing buildings and items, in holding things, simple things, that Greensparrow can come back and take from us?

"No gain, I say," Luthien continued. "If it was Montfort that we conquered, then we have accomplished nothing!"

A thousand shrugs, a thousand whispers, and a thousand curious questions filtered back to Luthien as he paused and held his conclusion, baiting the crowd, building their anxiety.

"But it was not Montfort!" he cried at last, and the whispers diminished, though the curious, confused expressions did not. "It was nothing that King Greensparrow—no, simply Greensparrow, for he is no king of mine—can take from us. It was not Montfort, I say. Not something to conquer and to burn. It was Caer MacDonald that we took back!"

The plaza exploded in roars, in cheers—for Luthien, for Caer Mac-Donald. The young Bedwyr looked at the beaming Siobhan. Remember the city's true name, she had coached him, and now that he had spoken the words, Siobhan looked different to Luthien. She seemed as if the cloud had passed from her face, she seemed vindicated and confident. No, more than confident, he realized. She seemed secure.

Siobhan, who had been a merchant's slave, who had fought secretly against the ruling class for years and who had stood beside Luthien since his rise in the underground hierarchy, seemed free at last.

"Caer MacDonald!" Luthien yelled when the gathering had quieted somewhat. "And what does that mean? Bruce MacDonald, who fought the cyclopians, what did he fight for?"

"Freedom!" came a cry directly below the platform, and Luthien did not have to look down to know that it was the voice of Katerin O'Hale.

The call was echoed from every corner of the plaza, around the city's dividing wall, and through the streets of the city's lower section. It came to the ears of those who were even then looting the wealthiest houses of the city, and to those who had burned the merchants' houses, and they were ashamed.

"We have taken back not a place, but an ideal," Luthien explained. "We have taken back what we were, and what we must be. In Caer Mac-Donald, we have found the heart of our hero of old, but it is no more than a small piece, a tiny gain, a candle's flicker in a field of darkness. And in taking that, in raising the flag of Caer MacDonald over the Ministry once more . . ." He paused, giving the crowd the moment to glance at the great structure's tall tower, where some figures were stirring.

"And we shall!" Luthien promised them when they looked back, and he had to pause again until the cheering died down.

"In taking back this piece of our heritage, we have accepted a responsibility," he went on. "We have lit a flame, and now we must fan that flame and share its light. To Port Charley, in the west. To the isles, Bedwydrin, Marvis, and Caryth, in the north. To Bronegan, south of the northern range, and to Rrohlwyn and their northern tip. To Chalmbers

and the Fields of Eradoch in the east and to Dun Caryth, until all the
dark veil of Greensparrow is lifted, until the Iron Cross and Malpuissant's Wall divide more than land. Until Eriador is free!"

It was the perfect ending, Luthien thought, played to the perfect syllable and perfect emphasis. He felt exhausted but euphoric, as tired as if
he had just waged a single-handed battle against a hundred cyclopians,
and as satisfied as if he had won that fight.

The thrill, the comradery, was back within the swelled ranks of the
rebels. Luthien knew, and Siobhan knew, that the danger had passed at
least for the moment.

The armies of Greensparrow would come, but if Luthien and his
friends could maintain the sense of higher purpose, could hold fast to
the truths that lay in their hearts, they could not lose.

Whatever ground Greensparrow reclaimed, whatever lives his army
claimed, they could not lose.

The rally did not lose momentum as the minutes slipped past; it
would have gone on all the day, it seemed, and long into the night. But
a voice sounded from the top of the Ministry, an answer to the claims of
Luthien Bedwyr.

"Fools, all!" cried a figure standing tall atop the tower's battlements,
and even from this distance, some four hundred feet, Luthien knew it to
be Viscount Aubrey. "What have you taken but a piece of land? What
have you won but a moment's reprieve and the promise of swift and terrible vengeance?"

That stole more than a little of the mirth and hope.

Luthien considered the man, his adversary. Even with all that had
transpired, Aubrey appeared unshaken, still meticulously groomed and
powdered, still the picture of royalty and strength.

Feigned strength, the battle-toughened Luthien pointedly told himself, for though Aubrey wore the weapons and ribbons of a warrior, he
was better at ducking a fight than waging one.

Luthien hated him, hated everything he stood for, but could not deny
the man's influence over the crowd, which did not recognize the ruse for
what it was.

"Do you think that you can win?" Aubrey spat with a derisive snicker.
"Do you think that King Greensparrow, who has conquered countries,
who even now wages war in lands south of Gascony, and who has ruled
for twenty years, is even concerned? Fools, all! Your winter snows will
not protect you! Bask in the glories of victory, but know that this victory
is a fleeting thing, and know that you, every one, will pay with your very
souls for your audacity!"

Oliver called up to Luthien, getting the man's attention. "Tell him that he was stupid for not better blocking the sewers," the halfling said.

Luthien understood Oliver's motives, but doubted the value of his methods. Aubrey had a powerful weapon here, a very real fear among the rebels that they had started something they could not hope to finish. Montfort—Caer MacDonald—was free, but the rest of their world was not, and the force they had beaten in this city was a tiny fraction of the might Greensparrow could hurl at them.

They all knew it, and so did confident Aubrey, standing tall atop the impervious tower, apparently beyond their reach.

When Luthien did not move to answer, Oliver did. "You talk so brave, but fight so stupid!" the halfling yelled out. A few half-hearted cheers arose, but did not seem to faze the viscount.

"He didn't even block the sewers," Oliver explained loudly. "If his king fights with equal wisdom, then we will dine in the palace of Avon by summer's end!"

That brought a cheer, but Aubrey promptly quenched it. "The same king who conquered all of Eriador," he reminded the gathering.

It could not go on, Luthien realized. They could gain nothing by their banter with Aubrey and would only continually be reminded of the enormity of the task before them. Oliver, sharp-witted as he was, had no ammunition to use against the viscount, no verbal barbs which could stick the man and no verbal salves to soothe the fears that Aubrey was inciting.

Luthien realized then that Siobhan had moved to stand beside him.

"Finish your speech," the half-elf said to him, lifting a curious arrow out of her quiver. It looked different from her other bolts, its shaft a bright red hue, its fletching made not of feathers but of some material even the half-elf did not know. She had discovered the arrow that morning, and as soon as she had touched it, it had imparted distinct telepathic instructions, had told her its purpose, and for some reason that she did not understand, the telepathic voice seemed familiar to her.

With her elven blood, Siobhan understood the means and ways of wizards, and so she had not questioned the arrow's presence or its conveyed message, though she remained suspicious of its origins. The only known wizards in all of the Avonsea Islands, after all, were certainly not allies of the rebels!

Siobhan kept the arrow with her, though, and now, seeing this situation, the exact scene which had been carried on telepathic waves, her trust in the arrow and in the wizard who had delivered it to her was complete. A name magically came into her head when Luthien took the arrow from her, a name that the half-elf didn't recognize.

Luthien eyed the bolt. Its shaft was bright red, its fletchings the whitish yellow of a lightning bolt. It possessed a tingle within its seemingly fragile shaft, a subtle vibration that Luthien did not understand. He looked at Siobhan, saw her angry glower turned to the tall tower, and understood what she meant for him to do.

It struck Luthien then how influential this quiet half-elf had been, both to him and to the greater cause. Siobhan had been fighting against the merchants and the cyclopians, against the reign of Greensparrow, much longer than Luthien. Along with the Cutters, she had been stealing and building the network that became Luthien's army. Siobhan had embraced Luthien, the Crimson Shadow, and had prodded him along. It was she, Luthien recalled, who had informed him that Shuglin had been captured after the dwarf had helped Oliver and Luthien escape a failed burglary. It was Siobhan who had pointed Luthien toward the Ministry, and then to the mines, and the Cutters had arrived at those mines when Luthien and Oliver went to rescue Shuglin.

It was Siobhan's own trial that had brought Luthien to the Ministry again, on that fateful day when he killed Duke Morkney, and she had followed him all the way up the tower in pursuit of the evil man.

And now Siobhan had given Luthien this arrow, which he somehow knew would reach its mark. Siobhan had led him to his speech and now she had told him to end that speech. Yet she carried a longbow on her shoulder, a greater bow than Luthien's, and she was a better archer than he. If this arrow was what Luthien suspected, somehow crafted or enchanted beyond the norm, Siobhan could have made the shot easier than he.

That wasn't the point. There was more at stake here than the life of a foolish viscount. Siobhan was propagating a legend; by allowing Luthien to take the shot, she was holding him forward as the unmistakable hero of the battle for Caer MacDonald.

Luthien realized then just how great a player Siobhan had been in all of this, and he realized, too, something about his own relationship with the half-elf. Something that scared him.

But he had no time for that now, and she wouldn't answer the questions even if he posed them. He looked back at the crowd and Aubrey and focused on the continuing banter between the viscount and Oliver.

Oliver drew occasional laughter from those around him with his taunts, but in truth, he had no practical responses to the fears that

Aubrey's threats inspired. Only a show of strength now could keep the rebels' hearts.

Luthien pinned open his folding bow, a gift from the wizard Brind'Amour, and fitted the arrow to its string. He brought it in line with Aubrey and bent the bow back as far as it would go.

Four hundred feet was too far to shoot. How much lift should he allow over such a distance and in shooting at such a steep angle? And what of the winds?

And what if he missed?

"For the heart." Siobhan answered his doubts in an even, unshakable tone. "Straight for the heart."

Luthien looked down the shaft at his foe. "Aubrey!" he cried, commanding the attention of all. "There is no place in Caer MacDonald for the lies and the threats of Greensparrow!"

"Threats you should heed well, foolish son of Gahris Bedwyr!" Aubrey retorted, and Luthien winced to think that his true identity was so well-known.

He had a moment of mixed feelings then, a moment of doubt about killing the man and the role he had unintentionally assumed.

"I speak the truth!" Aubrey shouted to the general gathering. "You cannot win but can, perhaps, bargain for your lives."

Just a moment of doubt. It was Aubrey who had come to Isle Bedwydrin along with that wretched Avonese. It was Aubrey who had brought the woman who had called for Garth Rogar's death in the arena, who had changed Luthien's life so dramatically. And now it was Aubrey, the symbol of Greensparrow, the pawn of an unlawful king, who stood as the next tyrant in line to terrorize the good folk of Montfort.

"Finish the speech," Siobhan insisted, and Luthien let fly.

The arrow streaked upward and Aubrey waved at it, discarding it as a futile attempt.

Halfway to the tower the arrow seemed to falter and slow, losing momentum. Aubrey saw it and laughed aloud, turning to share his mirth with the cyclopians standing behind him.

Brind'Amour's enchantment grabbed the arrow in mid-flight.

Aubrey looked back to see it gaining speed, streaking unerringly for the target Luthien had selected.

The viscount's eyes widened as he realized the sudden danger. He threw his hands up before him frantically, helplessly.

The arrow hit him with the force of a lightning stroke, hurling him back from the battlement. He felt his breastbone shatter under the weight of that blow, felt his heart explode. Somehow he staggered back to the tower's edge and looked down at Luthien, standing atop the gallows.

The executioner.

Aubrey tried to deny the man, to deny the possibility of such a shot. It was too late; he was already dead.

He slumped in the crenellations, visible to the gathering below.

All eyes turned to Luthien; not a man spoke out, too stunned by the impossible shot. Even Oliver and Katerin had no words for their friend.

"There is no place in Caer MacDonald for the lies and threats of Greensparrow," Luthien said to them.

The hushed moment broke. Ten thousand voices cried out in the exhilaration of freedom, and ten thousand fists punched the air defiantly.

Luthien had finished his speech.

CHAPTER 6

OUT OF HIS ELEMENT

WE COULD TAKE IT DOWN on top of them," Shuglin offered. The dwarf continued to study the parchment spread wide on the table before him, all the while stroking his blue-black beard.

"Take it down?" Oliver asked, and he seemed as horrified as Luthien.

"Drop the building," the dwarf explained matter-of-factly. "With all the stones tumbling down, every one of those damned one-eyes would be squashed flat."

"This is a church!" Oliver hollered. "A cathedral!"

Shuglin seemed not to understand.

"Only God can drop a church," the halfling insisted.

"That's a bet I would take," Shuglin grumbled sarcastically under his breath. The place was strongly built, but the dwarf had no doubt that by knocking out a few key stones . . .

"And if God had any intention of destroying the Ministry, he would have done so during Morkney's evil reign," Luthien added, his sudden interjection into the conversation taking Shuglin away from his enjoyable musings.

"By the whales, aren't we feeling superior?" came a voice from the door, and the three turned to see Katerin enter the room in Luthien and

Oliver's apartment on Tiny Alcove, which still served as headquarters for
the resistance even though great mansions and Duke Morkney's own
palace lay open for the taking. Staying on Tiny Alcove in one of the
poorest sections of Montfort was Luthien's idea, for he believed that this
was a cause of the common folk, and that he, as their appointed leader,
should remain among them, as one of them.

Luthien eyed Katerin carefully as she sauntered across the room. The
apartment was below ground, down a narrow stair from the street, Tiny
Alcove, which was, in truth, no more than an alleyway. Luthien could
see the worn stairs rising behind Katerin and the guards Siobhan had
posted relaxing against the wall, taking in the warm day.

Mostly, though, the young Bedwyr saw Katerin. Only Katerin. She
was one to talk about feeling superior! Ever since the incident in the
Dwelf, Katerin had taken on cool airs whenever she was around Luthien.
She rarely met his eyes these days, seemed rather to look past him, as
though he wasn't even there.

"Of course we are," Oliver answered with a huff. "We won."

"Not superior," Luthien corrected, his tone sharp—sharper than he
had intended. "But I do not doubt the evil that was Morkney, and that
is Greensparrow. We are not superior, but we are in the right. I have
no—"

Katerin's expression grew sour and she held up her hand to stop the
lecture before it had even begun.

Luthien winced. The woman's attitude was getting to him.

"Whatever you intend to do with the Ministry, you should do it
soon," Katerin said, suddenly grim. "We have news of a fleet sailing off
the western coast, south of the Iron Cross."

"Sailing north," Oliver reasoned.

"So say the whispers," Katerin replied.

Luthien was not surprised; he had known all along that Greensparrow
would respond with an army. But though he understood that the war
was not ended, that Greensparrow would come, the confirmation still
hit him hard. Caer MacDonald wasn't even secured yet, and there were
so many other tasks before the young man, more decisions each day than
he had made in his entire life. Fifteen thousand people were depending
on him, looking to him to solve every problem.

"The weather-watchers believe that the warm will stay," Katerin said,
and though that sounded like good news to the winter-weary group, her
tone was not light.

"The roads from Port Charley will be deep with mud for many
weeks," Luthien reasoned, thinking he understood the woman's dismay.

The snow was not so deep, but traveling in the early spring wasn't much better than a winter caravan.

Katerin shook her head; she wasn't thinking at all of the potential problems coming from the west. "We have dead to bury," she said. "Thousands of dead, both man and cyclopian."

"To the buzzards with the cyclopians!" Shuglin growled.

"They stink," Katerin replied. "And their bloated corpses breed vermin." She eyed Luthien squarely for the first time in several days. "You must see to the details. . . ."

She rambled on, but Luthien fell back into a chair beside the small table and drifted out of the conversation. He must see to it. He must see to it. How many times an hour did he hear those words? Oliver, Siobhan, Katerin, Shuglin, and a handful of others were a great help to him, but ultimately the last say in every decision fell upon Luthien's increasingly weary shoulders.

"Well?" Katerin huffed, drawing him back to the present conversation. Luthien stared at her blankly.

"If we do not do it now, we may find no time later," Oliver said in Katerin's defense. Luthien had no idea what they were talking about.

"We believe that they are sympathetic to our cause," Katerin added, and the way she spoke the words made Luthien believe that she had just said them a minute ago.

"What do you suggest?" the young Bedwyr bluffed.

Katerin paused and studied the young man, as though she realized that he hadn't a clue of where the discussion had led. "Have Tasman assemble a group and go out to them," Katerin said. "He's knowing the farmers better than any. If there's one among us who can make certain that food flows into Caer MacDonald, it is Tasman."

Luthien brightened, glad to be back in on the conversation and that this was one decision he didn't have to make alone. "See to it," he said to Katerin.

She started to turn, but her green eyes lingered on Luthien for a long while. She seemed to be sizing him up, and . . .

And what? Luthien wondered. There was something else in those orbs he thought he knew so well. Pain? Anger? He suspected that his continuing relationship with Siobhan did hurt Katerin, though she said differently to any who would listen.

The red-haired woman turned and walked out of the room, back up the stairs past the elven guards.

Of course, the proud Katerin O'Hale would never admit her pain, Luthien reasoned. Not about anything as trivial as love.

"We'll find no volunteers to bury one-eyes," Oliver remarked after a moment.

Shuglin snorted. "My kin will do it, and me with them," the dwarf said, and with a quick bow to Luthien, he, too, turned to leave. "There is pleasure to be found in putting dirt on top of cyclopians."

"More pleasure if they are alive when you do," Oliver snickered.

"Think on dropping that building," the dwarf called over his shoulder, and he seemed quite eager for that task "By the gods, if we do it, then the cyclopians inside will already be buried! Save us the trouble!"

Shuglin stopped at the door and spun about, his face beaming with an idea. "If we can get the one-eyed brutes to take their dead inside, and then we drop the building . . ."

Luthien waved at him impatiently and he shrugged and left.

"What *are* we to do about the Ministry?" Oliver asked after moving to the door and closing it.

"We have people distributing weapons," Luthien replied. "And we have others training the former slaves and the commoners to use them. Shuglin's folk have devised some defenses for the city, and I must meet with them to approve the plans. Now we have dead men to bury and food to gather. Alliances to secure with neighboring farm villages. Then there is the matter of Port Charley and the fleet that is supposedly sailing north along the coast. And, of course, the dead cyclopians must be removed."

"I get the point," Oliver said dryly, his Gascon accent making the last word into two syllables, "po-went."

"And the Ministry," exasperated Luthien went on. "I understand how important it is that we clear that building before Greensparrow's army arrives. We may have to use it ourselves, as a last defense."

"Let us hope the Avon soldiers do not get that far inside the city," Oliver put in.

"Their chances of getting in will be much greater if we have to keep a quarter of our forces standing guard around the cathedral," Luthien replied. "I know it, and know that I must come up with some plan to take the place."

"But . . ." Oliver prompted.

"Too many tasks," Luthien answered. He looked up at Oliver, needing support. "Am I to be the general, or the mayor?"

"Which would you prefer?" Oliver asked, but he already knew the answer: Luthien wanted to fight against Greensparrow with his weapons, not his edicts.

"Which would be the better for the cause of Eriador?" the man replied.

Oliver snorted. There was no doubt in the halfling's mind. He had seen Luthien lead the warriors, had watched the young man systematically free Montfort until it became Caer MacDonald. And Oliver had observed the faces of those who fought beside Luthien, those who watched in awe his movements as he led them into battle.

There came a knock on the door, and Siobhan entered. She took one look at the pair, recognizing the weight of their discussion, then excused herself from those who had come with her, waving them back out into the street and closing the apartment door. She moved quietly to the table and remained silent, deferring to the apparently more important discussion. This was not an unusual thing, Siobhan had a way of getting in on most of Oliver and Luthien's conversations.

"I do not think the Crimson Shadow would be such a legend if he was the mayor of a town," the halfling answered Luthien.

"Who then?" Luthien wanted to know.

The answer didn't come from Oliver, but, unexpectedly, from the half-elf, who had already surmised the problem. "Brind'Amour," she said evenly.

As soon as the weight of that name registered, both the friends nearly fell over with surprise—Luthien would have had he not been sitting already.

"How do you know that name?" Oliver, finding his voice first, wanted to know.

Siobhan put on a wry smile.

Oliver looked at Luthien, but the young Bedwyr shrugged, for he had not mentioned the old wizard to anybody in the city.

"You know of Brind'Amour?" Luthien asked her. "You know who he is and where he is?"

"I know of a wizard who lives still, somewhere in the north," Siobhan answered. "I know that it was he who gave to you the crimson cape, and the bow."

"How do you know?" Oliver asked.

"It was he who gave to me the arrow that you used to slay Viscount Aubrey," Siobhan went on, and that was explanation enough.

"Then you have spoken to him?" Luthien prompted.

The half-elf shook her head. "He has . . ." She paused, trying to find the right way to put it. "He has looked at me," she explained. "And through my eyes." She noted the surprise—hopeful surprise—on both her companions' faces. "Yes, Brind'Amour understands what has happened in Montfort."

"Caer MacDonald," Luthien corrected.

"In Caer MacDonald," Siobhan agreed.

"But will he come?" Oliver wanted to know, for the suggestion seemed perfect to the halfling. Who better than an old wizard to see to the day-to-day needs of a city?

Siobhan honestly did not know. She had felt the presence of the wizard beside her and had feared that presence, thinking that Greensparrow was watching the movements of the rebels. Then Brind'Amour had come to her in a dream and had explained who he was. But that was the only contact she had made with the old wizard, and even it was foggy, perhaps no more than a dream.

Although, considering the arrow she had found in her quiver, and Luthien and Oliver's confirmation of the existence of such a man, she now knew, of course, that it had been much more than a dream.

"Do you know where he is?" Luthien asked her.

"No."

"Do you know how to speak with him?"

"No."

At a loss, Luthien looked to Oliver.

"He is a fine choice," the halfling said, the exact words Luthien wanted to hear.

Luthien knew that the wizard's cave was somewhere within the northernmost spurs of the Iron Cross, to the north and east of Caer MacDonald, on the southern side of a wide gap called Bruce MacDonald's Swath. The young Bedwyr had been there only once, along with Oliver, but unfortunately on that occasion neither of them had found the chance to spy out the locale. A magical tunnel had brought them into the cave, whisking them off the road right in the midst of cyclopian pursuit. The pair had left via a magical tunnel, as well, Brind'Amour setting them down on the road to Montfort. Judging from where they were taken by the wizard, and where he had dropped them off, Luthien could approximate the location, and he knew that Brind'Amour's sight was not limited by stone walls.

Within the hour, the eager young man selected messengers, a dozen men he sent out from the city with instructions to ride to the northern tips of the Iron Cross, separate, and find high, conspicuous perches, and then read loudly from parchments Luthien gave to each of them, a note that the young man had written for the old wizard.

"He will hear," Luthien assured Oliver when the two saw the dozen riders off.

Oliver wasn't sure, or that the reclusive Brind'Amour would answer the call if he did hear. But Oliver did understand that Luthien, weary of the business of governing, had to believe that relief was on the way, and so the halfling nodded his agreement.

"So bids Luthien Bedwyr, present Lord of Caer MacDonald, which was Montfort," the young man called out, standing very still, very formal and tall, on a flat-topped hillock.

Some distance away, another man slipped off his horse and unrolled a parchment similarly inscribed. "To the wizard Brind'Amour, friend of those who do not call themselves friends of King Greensparrow . . ."

And so it went that morning in the northernmost reaches of the Iron Cross, with the twelve messengers, two days out from Caer MacDonald, each going his own way to find a spot which seemed appropriate for such a call into the wind.

Brind'Amour woke late that morning, after a refreshing and much-needed rest: twelve solid hours of slumber. He felt strong, despite his recent journeys into the realm of magic, always a taxing thing. He did not know yet that Viscount Aubrey was dead, slain by the arrow he had delivered into Siobhan's quiver, for he had not peered into his crystal ball in many days.

He still wasn't certain of Luthien and the budding revolt, of how long Montfort could hold out against the army that would soon sail up the coast, or about his own role in all of this. Perhaps this was all just a prelude, he had told himself the night before as he crawled into his bed. Perhaps this rumbling in Eriador would soon be quieted, but would not be forgotten, and in a few decades . . .

Yes, the old wizard had decided. In a few decades. It seemed the safer course, the wiser choice. Let the tiny rebellion play itself out. Luthien would be killed or forced to flee, but the young Bedwyr had done his part. Oh, yes, the young warrior from Isle Bedwydrin would be remembered fondly in the years to come, and the next time Eriador decided to test the strength of Avon's hold, Luthien's name would be held up beside that of Bruce MacDonald. And Oliver's, too, and perhaps that would inspire some help from Gascony.

Yes, to wait was the wiser choice.

When first he woke, feeling lighthearted, almost jovial, Brind'Amour told himself that he was happy because he was secure now with his decision to stay out of the fight and let it play out to the bitter end. He had chosen the safe road and could justify his inaction by looking at the greater potential for Eriador's future. He had done well in giving Luthien the cape; Luthien had done well in putting it to use. They had all done well, and though Greensparrow would not likely grow old—the man had lived for several centuries already—he might become bored with it all. After twenty years, Greensparrow's grip had already loosened somewhat on Eriador, else there never could have been such a rebellion in Montfort, and who could guess what the next few decades would bring? But the people of Eriador would never forget this one moment and would crystallize it, capture it as a shining flicker of hope, frozen in time, the legend growing with each retelling.

The old wizard went to cook his breakfast full of euphoria, full of energy and hope. He might do a bit more, perhaps when the battle was renewed in Montfort. Maybe he could find a way to aid Luthien, just to add to the legend. Greensparrow's army would no doubt regain the city, but perhaps Luthien could take on that ugly brute Belsen'Krieg and bring him to a smashing end.

"Yes," the wizard said, congratulating himself. He flicked his wrist, snapping the skillet and sending a pancake spinning into the air.

He heard his name and froze in place, and the pancake flopped over the side of the skillet and fell to the floor.

He heard it again.

Brind'Amour hustled down the passageways of his cavern home, into the room he used for his magic. He heard his name again, and then again, and each time he heard it, he tried to move faster, but only bumbled about.

He thought it was Greensparrow come calling, or one of the king's lesser wizards, or perhaps even a demon. Had he erred in sending his sight out to the palace in Carlisle? Had Greensparrow postponed his announced vacation in Gascony to deal first with troublesome Brind'Amour?

Finally, the old wizard got the thick cloth off of his crystal ball, put the item on the desk in front of him, and calmed himself enough to look into its depths.

Brind'Amour sighed loudly, so very relieved when he learned that the call was not from a wizard but from a mere man, apparently a messenger.

Relief turned to anger as Brind'Amour continued to seek and he came to know that there were several men calling for him.

"Fool!" Brind'Amour grumbled at Luthien as soon as he realized exactly what was going on. "Daring fool," he whispered. This was not

Montfort; these lands were still in the hands of cyclopians and others loyal to Greensparrow. No open revolt had come, at least not as far as Brind'Amour knew.

And to speak Brind'Amour's name so clearly, so loudly, where Greensparrow's ears might hear! If the king of Avon realized that Brind'Amour was somehow connected to the revolt in Montfort, if he knew that Brind'Amour was even awake from his centuries-long sleep, then his eyes would surely focus more closely on Eriador; he would not go to vacation in Gascony and would turn all of his attention north instead. The cause would be crushed.

The cause.

For a long, long time, Brind'Amour, ever cautious, had tried to convince himself that the cause was not so important, that the fight in Montfort was just a prelude to what might happen many decades down the road. But now, fearing that all of the rebellion was in jeopardy, considering the deep feelings rushing through him, he had to wonder if he had been fooling himself. He might justify letting this rebellion die in Montfort, but only for a short while. When it was done, when the blood had washed from the fields and the city's walls, Brind'Amour would lament the return of Greensparrow, the opportunity for freedom—for freedom *now*—lost.

Whatever course he now considered, Brind'Amour knew that he had to silence those silly boys with their silly scrolls. He felt strong indeed this morning and discovered that he dearly wanted to test his magic.

The wizard moved to the side of his desk, opened a drawer, and took out a huge, black leather-bound book, gently opening it. Then he began to chant, falling into the archaic runes depicted on the pages, falling deeper into the realm of magic than he had gone for nearly four hundred years.

The twelve men on their twelve hills had been reading and rereading their scrolls for more than two hours. But their instructions had been to read on from sunrise to sunset, day after day, until their call was answered.

Now their call *was* answered, but not in any way they, or Luthien, had anticipated.

A sudden black cloud rolled over the peaks of the Iron Cross, south of the readers. The blackest of clouds, a ball of midnight against the blue sky. A stiff wind kicked up, ruffling the parchments.

All twelve of the men held stubborn, loyal to Luthien and convinced of the importance of their mission.

On came the cloud, dark and ominous, blocking out the sun, except for twelve tiny holes in the blackness, twelve specific points that caught the rays of day and focused them through a myriad of ice crystals.

One by one, those holes released the focused ray of light under the cloud, and each of those beams, guided by a wizard looking into a crystal ball in a cave not so far away, found its mark, shooting down from the heavens to strike unerringly at the unfurled parchments.

The brittle paper ignited and burned, and one by one, the readers dropped the useless remnants and ran to their nearby mounts. One by one, they emerged from the foothills at a full gallop. Some linked up, but those who had charged out first did not stop and look back for their companions.

In the cave, Brind'Amour settled back and let the crystal ball go dark. Only a few minutes earlier he had felt refreshed and full of vigor, but now he was tired and old once more.

"Foolish boy," he muttered under his breath, but he found that he did not believe the words. Luthien's judgment in sending out callers might have been amiss, but the young man's heart was true. Could Brind'Amour say the same for himself? He thought again of the uprising, of its scale and of its importance, of his own insistence that this was just a prelude.

Was he taking the safe route or the easy one?

CHAPTER 7

THE CRIMSON SHADOW

COULD WE NOT HAVE GONE in the lower door?" Oliver asked, thoroughly cold and miserable and with still more than a hundred feet of climbing looming before him.

"The door is blocked," Luthien whispered, his mouth close to Oliver's ear, the cowl of his crimson cape covering not only his head but the halfling's as well. "You did not have to come."

"I did not want to lose my rope," the stubborn halfling replied.

They were scaling the eastern wall of the Ministry, more than halfway up the tallest tower. The night air was not so cold, but the wind was stiff this high up, biting at them and threatening to shake them free. Luthien huddled tight and checked the fastenings of his magical cape. He couldn't have it blowing open up here, leaving him and Oliver exposed halfway up the wall!

He had been wearing his cape daily since the rebellion began, for it was the symbol that the common folk of the city had rallied behind. The Crimson Shadow, the legend of old come to life to lead them to freedom. But the cape was much more than a showpiece. Cloistered within its protective magics, the cape tight about him and the cowl pulled low, Luthien was less than a shadow, or merely a shadow blended into other shadows—for all practical measures, completely invisible. He had only used the cape in this camouflaging manner a couple of times during the weeks of fighting to go over the wall and scout out enemy positions. He had thought of trying to find Aubrey, to kill the man in his house, but Siobhan had talked him out of that course, convincing him that the bumbling viscount was, in reality, a blessing to the rebels.

This time, though, Luthien would not be talked out of his plan; in fact, he had told no one except Oliver of his intentions.

So here they were, in the dark of night, almost up the Ministry's tallest wall. There were cyclopians posted up there, they both knew, but the brutes were likely huddled close around a fire. What would they be on watch against, after all? They could not see the movements of men on the streets below, and they certainly did not expect anyone to come up and join them!

Oliver's last throw had been good, heaving the magical grapnel up to the end of the rope, but after climbing the fifty feet to the puckered ball, the companions found few places to set themselves. There were no windows this high up on the tower, and the stones had been worn smooth by the incessant wind.

Luthien hooked his fingers tight into a crack, his feet barely holding to a narrow perch. "Hurry," he bade his companion.

Oliver looked up at him and sighed. The halfling, his feet against the wall, was tucked in tight against Luthien's belly—the only thing holding Oliver aloft was Luthien. Oliver fumbled with the rope, trying to loop it so that he could fling it up the remaining fifty feet, all the way to the tower's lip.

"Hurry," Luthien said more urgently, and Oliver understood that the young man's hold was not so good. Muttering a curse in his native Gascon tongue, the halfling reached out and tossed the magical grapnel as high as he could. It caught fast, no more than twenty feet above them.

Again came that whispered Gascon curse, but Luthien dismissed it, for he saw something that the halfling did not.

Oliver quieted and held on tight to Luthien, who took up the rope and climbed only a few feet, coming to a stop atop a jutting stone.

"Make the next throw the last throw," Luthien whispered, planting himself firmly.

Oliver tugged three times on the rope, the signal for the grapnel to loosen. It slipped down silently and Oliver reeled it in. Now, since Luthien had solid footing, so did Oliver, and the halfling took his time and measured his throw.

Perfect: the grapnel hit the wall with the slightest of sounds just a foot below the tower's lip.

Again Oliver grabbed on and Luthien took up the rope, ready to climb. Oliver grabbed his wrist, though, and when Luthien paused, he, too, heard the movement up above.

Luthien ducked low under the protective cape, sheltering himself and Oliver. After a long moment, the young Bedwyr dared to look up and saw the silhouette of a cyclopian peering over the wall down at him.

Luthien thought the game was up, but the brute made no move and no sound, gave no indication at all that it had seen the companions.

"Nothing," the cyclopian grumbled, and walked away from the rim, back to the warmth of the fire.

Oliver and Luthien shared a sigh, and then the young Bedwyr hauled them both up the rope to the tower's lip.

They heard the cyclopians—three, at least—about a dozen feet away.

Oliver's head came over the lip first, and he confirmed the number and the distance. Luck was with the halfling, then, for he noted, too, the movement of a fourth brute, milling about on the landing just a few stairs down from the tower's top.

Oliver signaled his intent to Luthien, and then, like a weasel slipping along a riverbank, the halfling picked his way along the top of the wall, around and over the battlements without a sound.

Luthien silently counted; Oliver had asked for a count of fifty. That completed, the young Bedwyr pulled himself up to the tower's lip, peering at the three brutes huddled about their small fire. Luthien slid up to sit on the wall, gently rolled his legs over, and put a hand to his sword's hilt. He would have to strike fast and hard and could only hope that Oliver would take care of the one by the stairs—and hopefully, there was only one at the stairs!

No time for those thoughts now, Luthien scolded himself. They were three hundred feet up the tower and fully committed. He slipped down off the wall, took a deep breath as he set his feet firmly, then charged, drawing his blade.

Blind-Striker hit the first cyclopian where it crouched, slashing diag-onally across the back of the brute's shoulder, severing the backbone. The cyclopian fell without a sound, and Luthien whipped the sword across as the second leaped up, spinning to face him. His blade got the creature through the chest—two dead—but snagged on a rib and would not immediately come free at Luthien's desperate tug.

The third cyclopian did not charge, but turned and fled for the stairs. It jerked weirdly halfway there, then stopped altogether, went to its knees, and fell over on its back, dead. Luthien noted Oliver's main gauche embedded deeply in its chest, a perfect throw.

Oliver came out of the stairwell and casually stepped over and re-trieved his thrown weapon. "What were they eating?" the halfling in-quired, walking past the kill toward the small fire. He picked up a stick, a chunk of cooking mutton on its other end.

"Ah, so fine," the halfling said, delighted, and sat down.

A few moments went by before Oliver looked up to see Luthien star-ing at him incredulously. "Do hurry," the halfling bade the young man.

"You are not coming?" Luthien asked.

"I said I would get you up the tower," Oliver replied, and went back to the mutton feast.

Luthien chuckled. He pulled off his pack and dropped another silken cord, this one as long as the tower was tall, at Oliver's feet. "Do prepare the descent," he bade the halfling.

Oliver, face deep in the mutton, waved him away. "Your business will take longer than mine," he assured Luthien.

Luthien snickered again and started away. It made sense of course, that he should go down alone. Once inside the Ministry, he would have to move quickly, and he could not do that with Oliver tucked under the folds of his cape.

He found the fourth cyclopian, dead of a rapier thrust, on the land-ing just below the tower level. An involuntary shudder coursed Luthien's spine as he recognized how efficient his little friend could be. All for the good cause, he reminded himself, and started down the longer, curving stair. He met no resistance all the three hundred steps to the floor, and to his relief found that the door at the bottom of the stair, along the curving wall of the cathedral's eastern apse, was ajar.

Luthien peered into the vast nave. A few torches burned; he heard the snores of dozens of cyclopians stretched out on the many benches. Only a few of the brutes were up, but they were in groups, talking and keep-ing a halfhearted watch.

They were confident, Luthien realized. The cyclopians were convinced that the rebels wouldn't accept the losses they would no doubt suffer if they attacked the fortified Ministry. A good sign.

Luthien came out of the door and crept among the shadows, silent and invisible. He noted more cyclopians milling about on the triforium ledges, but they, too, were not paying much attention. Luthien went right, to the north, and scouted out the transept. The doors down there were heavily barricaded, as expected, and a group of cyclopians sat in a circle before them, apparently gambling.

They were bored and they were weary—and soon they would have nothing to eat.

Luthien thought of going all around the transept, back into the nave and down to the west. He changed his mind and went back to the apse instead, then around the semicircle and into the southern transept.

Halfway down, he found what he was looking for: a huge pile of foodstuffs. The young Bedwyr smiled wickedly and moved in close. He took out a small black box, which Shuglin had designed for him, and then six small pouches, filled with a black powder that the dwarfs used in their mining. He considered the pile for a few moments, placing the pouches strategically. He set two between the three kegs of water he found on one side of the pile, probably the only drinking water the brutes had.

Next came some flasks of oil, wrapped in thick furs so that they would not clang together. Carefully, the invisible intruder doused the pile of provisions. One of the cyclopians near to the southern transept's door sniffed the air curiously, but the smell of Luthien's oil was not easily detected over that of the lanterns already burning throughout the Ministry.

When the cyclopian went back to its watch at the door, Luthien huddled under his cape with the black box, perfectly square and unremarkable, except that the top had a small hole cut into it. Luthien carefully opened the box. He tried to study Shuglin's design to see what was inside, but in the dim light he could make out little. There were two small glass vials, that much he could see, and the strike plate and wick were in between them.

Luthien looked up, glanced around to make sure that no cyclopians were nearby. Then he huddled low beside the pile, making sure that his cape and the piled provisions shielded the box. He flicked the strike plate. It sparked, but the wick did not catch.

Luthien glanced about again, then repeated the motion.

This time, the wick lighted, burning softly. Now Luthien could see Shuglin's design, the amber liquid in one glass, the reddish liquid in the other, and the leather pouch below, probably filled with the same black powder.

Intriguing, but Luthien had no time to study it further; Shuglin guaranteed him a count of twenty-five, no longer. He closed the box and crept away, back into the shadows, back into the apse, through the door and onto the lowest stairs. There, he paused, watching.

With a hiss and a sputter, the black box exploded, igniting the pile. Cyclopians hooted and shouted, charging in all directions.

A second explosion sounded, and then a third and a fourth, close together, and the water kegs burst apart.

Luthien turned and sprinted up the stairs, smiling as he heard four more distinctive blasts.

"I take it that we are done," Oliver remarked between bites of mutton when the young man, huffing and puffing, stumbled out onto the tower's top.

"We have to go and tell the guards around the plaza to be alert," Luthien replied. "The cyclopians will try to break out soon."

Oliver took one last bite, wiped his greasy hands on the furred cape of one of the dead cyclopians, and moved to the wall, where the grapnel and rope were already fastened to the longer cord that reached all the way to the street, ready to take them down.

Inside the Ministry, the cyclopians found most of their provisions ruined and nearly all of their potable water lost. They jostled and fought amongst themselves, every one blaming another, until one brute found the answer in the form of a crimson shadow of a caped man, indelibly stained on the wall of the eastern apse.

Luthien's enchanted cape had left its mark.

Word raced up Avon's western coast, across the mountains into Eriador, and from village to village, to Caer MacDonald and beyond. A great fleet was sailing, bracing the freezing waters: at least fifty Avon ships, enough to carry more than ten thousand Praetorian Guards. And those ships were low in the water, said the rumors, low and brimming with soldiers.

The news was received stoically at the Dwelf. Luthien and his companions had expected the army, of course, but the final confirmation that it was all more than rumor, that Greensparrow was indeed aware of the rebellion and responding with an iron fist, sobered the mood.

"I will set out for Port Charley in the morning," Luthien told his gathered commanders. "A hard ride will get me there before the Avon fleet arrives."

"You cannot," Siobhan replied simply, with finality.

Luthien looked hard at her, as did Oliver, who was about to volunteer to ride off beside his friend (all the while hoping that he might turn Luthien north instead, back into hiding in the wilds).

"You govern Caer MacDonald," the half-elf explained.

"Do not leaders often sally forth from the place they lead?" Oliver remarked.

"Not when that place is in turmoil," the half-elf answered. "We expect a breakout from the Ministry any day."

"The one-eyes will be slaughtered in the open plaza," Oliver said with all confidence, a confidence that was widespread among all the rebels.

"And Luthien Bedwyr must be there," Siobhan went on without hesitation. "When that fight is done, the city will be ours, wholly ours. It would not be appropriate for that important moment to pass with the leader of the rebellion halfway to Port Charley."

"We cannot underestimate the importance of Port Charley," Luthien interjected, feeling a little left out of it all, as if he weren't even in the room, or at least as though he didn't have to be in the room. "Port Charley will prove critical to the rebellion and to Caer MacDonald. Even as we sit here bantering, Shuglin's people work frantically to prepare the defenses of the city. If the whispers speak truly, then an army equal in size to our own force will soon march upon our gates."

"Equal odds favor the defense," Katerin O'Hale remarked.

"But these are Praetorian Guards," Luthien emphasized. "Huge and strong, superbly trained and equipped, and no doubt the veterans of many campaigns."

"You doubt our own prowess?" Katerin wanted to know, her tone sharply edged with anger.

"I want the best possible outcome," Luthien firmly corrected. In his heart, though, he did indeed doubt the rabble army's ability to hold against ten thousand Praetorian Guards, and so did everyone else in the room, proud Katerin included.

"Thus, Port Charley is all-important," Luthien went on. "They have not declared an alliance, and as you yourself have pointed out," he said to Katerin, "they will not be easily convinced."

The red-haired woman leaned back in her chair and slid it out from the table, visibly backing off from the conversation.

"We must bottle that fleet up in the harbor," Luthien explained. "If the folk of Port Charley do not allow them to pass, they will have to sail on, and might waste many days searching for a new place to land."

"And every day they are at sea is another day they might encounter a storm," Oliver said slyly.

Luthien nodded. "And another day that they will tax their provisions and, knowing cyclopians, their patience," he agreed. "And another day that Shuglin and his kin have to complete their traps around the outer walls of Caer MacDonald. The fleet must be kept out. We cannot fail in this."

"Agreed," Siobhan replied. "But you are not the one to go." Luthien started to respond, but she kept on talking, cutting him off. "Others are qualified to serve as emissaries, and it will not look as good as you believe to have the leader of the rebellion walking into Port Charley, to say nothing of the reaction from the cyclopians already in that town.

"You think that you will impress them with your presence," Siobhan went on, brutally honest, but her tone in no way condescending. "All that you will impress them with is your foolishness and innocence. Your place is here—the leaders of Port Charley will know that—and if you show up there, you will not strike them as a man wise enough for them to follow into war."

Luthien, slack-jawed, his shoulders slumped, looked over at Oliver for support.

"She's not so bad," the halfling admitted.

Luthien had no way to disagree, no arguments against the simple logic. Again he felt as if Siobhan, and not he, was in control, as if he were a puppet, its strings pulled by that beautiful and sly half-elf. He didn't like the feeling, not at all, but he was glad that Siobhan was at his side, preventing him from making foolish mistakes. Luthien thought of Brind'Amour then, realizing more clearly than ever that he was out of his element and in desperate need of aid.

"Who will go, then?" Oliver asked Siobhan, for Luthien, by his expression alone, had obviously conceded the floor to her on this matter. "Yourself? I do not think one who is half-elven will make so fine an impression."

Oliver meant no insult, and Siobhan, concerned only for the success of the rebellion, took none.

"I will go," Katerin promptly put in. All eyes turned her way, and Luthien leaned forward again on his stool, suddenly very interested and worried.

"I know the people of Port Charley better than anyone here," Katerin stated.

"Have you ever been there?" Oliver asked.

"I am from Hale, a town not so unlike Port Charley," Katerin answered. "My people think the same way as those independent folk. We have never succumbed to the rule of Greensparrow. We have never succumbed to any rule save our own, and tolerate kings and dukes only because we do not care about them."

Luthien was shaking his head. He wasn't sure that he wanted to be away from Katerin right now. And he didn't want her riding off alone to the west. Word of the fight in Caer MacDonald had spread throughout the southland of Eriador, and none of them knew what dangers might await any emissary on the road.

"There is another reason you cannot go," Katerin said to Luthien. "If the men of Port Charley do not join in our alliance, they will have all the ransom they need for Greensparrow with the Crimson Shadow delivered into their hands."

"You doubt their honor?" Luthien asked incredulously.

"I understand their pragmatism," Katerin replied. "They care nothing for you, not yet."

Katerin's point did not make Luthien feel any better about letting her go. She, too, would prove a fine bartering point with the king of Avon!

"Katerin is right," came word from an unexpected ally for the woman of Hale. "You cannot go, and she can accomplish what we need better than anyone in Caer MacDonald," Siobhan reasoned.

Katerin looked hard at the half-elf, suspicious of her rival's motives. For an instant she wondered if Siobhan wanted her to go so that she would perhaps be killed or taken prisoner, but looking into the half-elf's green eyes—sparkling, intense orbs so like her own—Katerin saw no animosity, only genuine hope and even affection.

Luthien started to protest, but Siobhan stopped him short. "You cannot let your personal feelings block the path to the general good," the half-elf scolded, turning to glare at the young man. "Katerin is the best choice. You know that as well as anyone." Siobhan looked back to Katerin, smiled, and nodded, and the woman of Hale did likewise. Then Siobhan turned back to Luthien. "Do I speak truly?"

Luthien sighed, defeated once more by simple logic. "Take Riverdancer," he bade Katerin, referring to his own horse, a shining highland Morgan, as fine a steed as could be found in all of Eriador. "In the morning."

"Tonight," Katerin corrected grimly. "The Avon fleet does not drop sail when the sun sleeps."

Luthien did not want her to go. He wanted to run across the room and wrap her in a tight hug, wanted to protect her from all of this, from all the evils and all the dangers in the world. But he realized that Katerin and Siobhan were right. Katerin was the best choice, and she needed no protection.

Without another word, she turned and left the Dwelf.

Luthien looked to Oliver. "I will return when I return," the halfling explained with a tip of his hat, and he moved to follow Katerin.

Luthien eyed Siobhan, expecting her to stop the halfling, dissuade him as she had Luthien.

"Ride well," was all the half-elf said, and Oliver tipped his hat to her as well, and then he, too, was gone.

Those remaining in the Dwelf had many other things to discuss that night, but they sat quietly, or in small, private conversations. Suddenly a man rushed in.

"The Ministry!" he cried.

It was all he had to say. Luthien leaped down from his stool and practically stumbled headlong for the door. Siobhan caught him by the arm and supported him, and he paused, straightening, and eyed her directly.

Her smile was infectious, and Luthien knew that, despite the fact that Oliver and Katerin were likely already on the road, he would not fight alone this night.

The desperate cyclopians charged out of the Ministry through the north, west, and south doors, roaring and running, trying to get across the plaza and into the shadows of the alleyways. Swarms of arrows met them from every side, and then the rebels didn't even wait for the cyclopians to charge; they rushed out to meet them, matching desperation with sheer fury.

Luthien and the others from the Dwelf did not go over the wall. Rather, they pounded their way through the eastern wall, where it had been breached before, up from the city's lower section and back into the Ministry once again. As the slaughter continued in the plaza, more than a few cyclopians thought to turn and flee back into the cathedral. There was still some food remaining, after all, and they figured that if they could get back in and barricade the doors once more, there would be fewer of them left to share it.

But Luthien's small group met them and kept the cathedral's main door thrown wide so that rebels, too, could get inside. Once more the hallowed floor of the great cathedral ran deep with blood. Once more a place of prayer became a place of cries, shouts of anger, and shrieks of the wounded.

It was finished that night. Not a single cyclopian remained alive in the city of Caer MacDonald.

CHAPTER 8

PORT CHARLEY

ORT CHARLEY WAS A HUDDLED VILLAGE, white-painted homes built in tight, neat rows up a series of cut steps along the foothills of the Iron Cross and overlooking the tumultuous Avon Sea. It was said that on the clearest of days the shining white and green cliffs of Baranduine, far to the west, could be seen from those highest perches, beckoning the souls of men. Port Charley was a dreamy place, and yet cheery on those rare days that the sun did shine, bouncing gaily off the white-faced houses, off the white fences outlining every yard and bordering each of the city's tiers.

Such was the day, bright and sunny and cheery, when Oliver and Katerin came in sight of the village. They noted that there was no snow in or about the town, just windblown rock, white and gray streaks amidst the squared and neat cottages. Splotches of green and brown dotted the landscape, and a few trees stood bare, poking high and proud between cottage and stone.

"Too early to bloom," Oliver remarked. He kicked Threadbare, his yellow pony, to a faster trot.

Katerin spurred Riverdancer on, the powerful white stallion easily pacing the smaller pony.

"I have been here in the spring," Oliver explained. "You really should see Port Charley in the spring!" The halfling went on to describe the blossoming trees and the many flowers peeking from sheltering crevices in the stones and from the many, many windowboxes, but Katerin only half-listened, for she needed no descriptions. To her, Port Charley was Hale, on a larger scale, and the young woman remembered well the land of her youth, the wind blowing off the cold waters, the spattering of bright color, purple mostly, against the gray and white. She heard the sound of the tide, that low rumble, the growl of the earth itself, and she remembered Isle Bedwydrin and taking to the sea in a craft that seemed so glorious and huge tied up at the wharf, but so insignificant and tiny once the land became no more than a darker line on the gray horizon.

And Katerin remembered the smell, remembered that most of all, heavy air thick with salt and brine. Heavy and healthy, primal somehow. Port Charley and Hale, these were places to be most alive, where the soul was closest to the realities of the tangible world.

Oliver noted the dreamy, faraway look in the woman's green eyes and went quiet.

They came in from the northeast, down the single road that forked, going right to the dunes and the sea, and left to the lowest section of the village. Oliver started left, but Katerin knew better.

"To the wharves," she explained.

"We must find the mayor," Oliver called after her, for she did not slow.

"The harbormaster," Katerin corrected, for she knew that in Port Charley, as in Hale, the person who controlled the docks controlled the town as well.

Their mounts' hooves clattered loudly on the wooden boardwalk that snaked through the soft sandy beach to the wharves, but once they approached those docks, where water lapped loudly and many boats bumped and banged against the wooden wharf, the sound of their mounts became insignificant. Gulls squawked overhead and bells sounded often, cutting the air above the continual groan of the rolling surf. One boat glided toward the docks at half-sail, a swarm of gray and white gulls flapping noisily above it, showing that the crew had landed a fine catch this day.

Squinting, Oliver could see that a man and a woman were at work on the deck of the boat, chopping off fish heads with huge knives and then tossing the unwanted portions into the air straight overhead, not even bothering to look up, as if they knew that no piece would ever find its way through the flock to fall back down.

Katerin led the way up a ramp to the long boardwalk that fronted the village. Seven long spurs jutted out into the harbor, enough room for perhaps two hundred fishing boats, five times Hale's modest fleet. An image of those small boats darting in and around massive war galleons flashed in Katerin's mind. She hadn't seen many ships of war, just those that occasionally docked in Dun Varna, and one that had passed her father's boat out on the open sea off Isle Bedwydrin's western coast; she had no idea what one of those ships could do. She could well imagine their power, though, and the image sent a shudder along her spine.

She shook the disturbing thoughts away and looked at the harbor. She hoped it had a shallow sounding, too shallow for the great ships to put in. If they could get the enemy into smaller landing craft, the fishermen of Port Charley would make a landing very difficult indeed.

Katerin realized that she was getting ahead of herself. Formulating battle plans by the folk who knew these waters best would come later. Right now, Katerin and Oliver merely had to convince the folk of Port

Charley to stand against the invading force and keep Greensparrow's army out in the harbor.

Riverdancer's hooves clomped along the boardwalk, Threadbare right behind. Katerin understood the wharf's design, similar to the one in Hale, and so she made her way to the fourth and central pier.

"Should we not walk the horses?" Oliver asked nervously, his gaze locked on the slits in the boardwalk, and the spectacle of the dark water far below them. The tide was out and soon Oliver and Katerin were a full thirty feet above the level of the water.

Katerin didn't answer, just kept her course straight for the small cottage built beside the pier. Only a couple of boats were in—it was still early in the afternoon—and a few crusty old sea dogs waddled along the various piers, turning curious glances at the strange newcomers, particularly at the foppish halfling, so colorful and out of place in the wintry village.

An old woman, her face brown and cracked and her white hair thin, as though the incessant sea breeze had blown half of it away, came out to greet them before they reached the cottage.

She nodded at them as they dismounted, and smiled, showing more gum than tooth: her few remaining teeth were crooked and stained. Her eyes were the lightest of blue, almost washed of color, and her limbs and fingers, like the teeth, were crooked and bent in awkward angles, with knuckles and joints like knobby bumps on her old frame.

But she was not an unattractive sight. There was a goodness about her, a genuinely noble and honest soul, someone who had walked a straight path despite the crooked limbs.

"Yer won't find passage south fer another two-week," she said in nasal tones. "And not fer north fer another two-week after that."

"We do not seek passage at all," Katerin replied. "We seek the harbormaster."

The old woman spent a long moment regarding Katerin, studying the hard texture of her hands and the way she held herself straight despite the stiff breeze. Then she extended her arm warmly. "Yer found her," she said. "Gretel Sweeney."

"Katerin O'Hale," the young woman replied, and her mention of the port town to the north brought a smile and a nod of recognition from Gretel. The old harbormaster recognized a fellow seagoer when she saw one. She didn't know what to make of Oliver, though, until she thought back across the years. Gretel had been Port Charley's harbormaster for nearly two decades, and she made it a point of watching every foreign ship dock and unload. Of course she did not remember everyone who passed through her village, but Oliver was one who was hard to forget.

"Gascon," she said, shifting her arm toward the halfling.

Oliver took the offered hand and brought it to his lips. "Oliver de-Burrows," he introduced himself, and when he let go of Gretel's hand, he dipped into a sweeping bow, his hat brushing the wooden decking.

"Gascon," Gretel said again to Katerin with a wink and a nod.

Katerin got right to the point. "You have heard of the fighting in Montfort?" she asked.

Gretel's almost white eyes twinkled with comprehension. "Strange to make a Gascon an emissary," she said.

"Oliver is a friend," Katerin explained. "A friend to me and a friend to Luthien Bedwyr."

"Then it's true," the old woman said. "The son of Bedwydrin's eorl." She shook her head, her expression sour. "To be sure, he's a long way from home," she remarked, as Katerin and Oliver looked to each other, each trying to gauge Gretel's reaction. "As are yerselves!"

"Trying to make that home whole again," Katerin was quick to respond.

Gretel didn't seem impressed. "I've got tea a'brewing," she said, turning toward the cottage. "Ye've got much to tell me, and no doubt to offer me, so we may as well be comfortable during the talking."

Oliver and Katerin continued to look at each other as Gretel disappeared into the cottage.

"This will not be easy," Oliver remarked.

Katerin slowly shook her head. She had known that the folk of Port Charley wouldn't be impressed with any rebellion. The place was so much like Hale. Why should they rebel, after all, when they were already free? The fisherfolk of Port Charley answered to no one but the sea, and with that as their overlord, Luthien and his fight in Montfort, and indeed, even King Greensparrow himself, did not seem so important.

A young boy bounded out of the cottage, running down the boardwalk and toward the town as the two friends tied up their mounts.

"Gretel is calling in some friends," Katerin explained.

Oliver's hand immediately and instinctively went to the hilt of his rapier, but he pulled it away at once, remembering the noble look in Gretel's eye and feeling foolish for entertaining such a fear even for a moment.

"Tea?" Katerin asked resignedly. She was thinking of the task before her, of convincing Gretel and her compatriots of the importance of the rebellion, of asking these people to risk their lives in a fight they likely cared nothing at all about. Suddenly she felt very tired.

Oliver led the way into the cottage.

Gretel would hear nothing of the troubles in Montfort, which Katerin insisted on calling Caer MacDonald, and nothing of the old legends come to life until the others arrived.

"Old fisherfolk," the harbormaster explained. "Too old for the boats and so we of Port Charley use their wisdom. They know the sea."

"Our troubles do not concern only the sea," Oliver politely reminded the woman.

"But the sea be our only concern," Gretel said, a stinging retort that reminded Oliver and especially Katerin of just how difficult this mountain would prove to climb.

Gretel wanted to talk about Hale; she knew some of the northern village's older fisherfolk, had met them at sea during the salmon runs many years before, when she was young and captained her own boat. Though she was an impatient sort, a woman of action and not idle talk (especially not with cyclopian ships sailing fast for Eriador's coast!), Katerin obliged, and even found that she enjoyed Gretel's stories of the mighty Avon Sea.

Oliver rested during that time, sipping his tea and taking in the smells and sounds of the seaside cottage. The other old sea dogs began arriving presently, one or two at a time, until Gretel's small cottage was quite filled with brown, wrinkled bodies, all smelling of salt and fish. The halfling thought he recognized one of the men, but couldn't quite place him, his suspicions only heightened when the fellow looked Oliver's way and gave a wink. Perhaps this had been one of the crew on the boat that had taken Oliver into Port Charley several years before, or one of the others at the boardinghouse where Oliver had stayed until he had grown bored of the port and departed for Montfort.

After a moment of studying the old creature, tucked protectively, even mysteriously, under a heavy blanket, even though he was sitting near the burning hearth, Oliver shrugged and gave it up. He couldn't place the man.

Despite that, Oliver thought it a perfectly grand gathering, and Katerin felt at home, more so than she had since she had left Hale at the age of fourteen to go into training in the arena at Dun Varna.

"There, then," Gretel announced after one particularly bawdy tale concerning ships that didn't quite make it past each other in the night. "Seems we've all gathered."

"This is your ruling council?" Oliver asked.

"These are all the ones too old to be out in the boats," Gretel corrected. "And not old enough yet to be stuck lying in their beds. Them soon returned with the day's catch will hear what we've to say."

She looked at Katerin and nodded, indicating that the floor was hers.

Katerin rose slowly. She tried to remember her own proud village and the reactions of her people if they were faced with a similar situation. The folk of Hale didn't much care for Greensparrow, didn't talk much about him, didn't waste many words on him—neither did the folk of Port Charley—but what she needed here and now was action, and ambivalence was a long way from that.

She rose slowly and moved to the center of the room, leaning on the small round table for support. She thought of Luthien in Caer MacDonald and his stirring speech in the plaza beside the Ministry. She wished that he was here now, dashing and articulate. Suddenly she blamed herself for being so arrogant as to think to replace him.

Katerin shook those negative thoughts from her mind. Luthien could not reach these folk—Katerin's folk. His words were the sort that stirred people who had something to lose, and whether it be Greensparrow, or Luthien or anyone else claiming rulership of Eriador, and thus, of Port Charley, the folk here recognized only one king: the Avon Sea.

Katerin continued to hesitate, and the fisherfolk, men and women who had spent endless hours sitting quiet on open, unremarkable waters, respected her delay and did not press her.

The young woman conjured an image of Port Charley, considered the neat rows and meticulous landscaping, a pretty village cut from the most inhospitable of places. So much like Hale.

But not so much like most of the more southern Eriadoran towns, Katerin realized, especially those in the shadows of the Iron Cross. The young woman's face brightened as she realized the course of her speech. The folk of Port Charley cared little for the politics of the land, but they, as much as any group in Eriador or Avon, hated cyclopians. By all accounts, very few of the one-eyes lived in or near Port Charley; even the merchants here usually kept strong men as guards, not the typical cyclopian escort.

"You have heard of the rebellion in Caer MacDonald," she began. She paused for a moment, trying to gauge the reaction, but there was none.

Katerin's eyes narrowed; she stood straight and tall away from the table. "You have heard that we killed many cyclopians?"

The nods were accompanied by grim, gap-toothed smiles, and Katerin's course lay open before her. She spoke for more than an hour before the first questions came back at her, then answered every one, every concern.

"All we need is time," she finally pleaded, mostly to Gretel. "Keep the Avon fleet bottled in your harbor for a week, perhaps. You need not risk the life of a single person. Then you will see. Caer MacDonald will fend off the attack, destroy Greensparrow's army in the field, and force a truce from the southern kingdom. Then Eriador will be free once more."

"To be ruled by . . . another king," one man interrupted.

"Better he, whoever it may be," Katerin replied, and she thought she knew who the next king of Eriador would be, but saw no sense in speaking of him specifically at this time, "than the demon-allied wizard. Better he than the man who invites cyclopians into his court and appoints them as his personal Praetorian Guard."

The heads continued to nod, and when Katerin looked at Oliver, she found that he, too, was nodding and smiling. Quite pleased with her performance, the young woman turned directly to Gretel, her expression clearly asking for an answer.

At that moment, a middle-aged man, his hair salt-and-pepper, his face ruddy and showing a few days of beard, burst into the cottage, wide-eyed and out of breath.

"Ye've seen them," Gretel stated more than asked.

"Anchorin' five miles to the south," the man explained.

"Too close in to sail through the dark."

"Warships?" Katerin asked.

The man looked at her, and then at Oliver, curiously. He turned his gaze to Gretel, who motioned that he should continue.

"The whole damned Avon fleet," he replied.

"As many as fifty?" Katerin needed to know.

"I'd be puttin' it more at seventy, milady," the man said. "Big 'uns, too, and low in the water."

Katerin looked again at Gretel, amazed at how composed the old woman, indeed the whole gathering, remained in light of the grim news. Gretel's smile was perfectly comforting, perfectly disarming. She nodded, and Katerin thought she had her answer.

"The two of yer will stay with Phelpsi Dozier," Gretel said. "On the *Horizon*, a worthy old tub."

Dozier, the oldest man at the gathering, perhaps the oldest man Katerin had ever seen, stepped up and tipped his woolen cap, smiling with the one tooth remaining in his wide mouth. "She's mostly at the docks nowadays," he said, almost apologetically.

"I'll have my boy see to yer horses," Gretel continued, and her tone seemed to indicate that the meeting was at its end. Several of those gathered stood up and stretched the soreness out of their muscles and headed for the door. Night had fallen by then, dark and chill, the wind groaning off the sea.

"We have many preparations," Katerin tried to put in, but Gretel hushed her.

"The folk of Port Charley've made them preparations before yer were even born, dear girl," the old harbormaster insisted. "Yer said yer needing a week, and we're knowing how to give it to yer."

"The depth of the harbor?" Katerin asked, looking all around. She didn't doubt Gretel's words, but could hardly believe that seventy Avon warships could be taken this lightly.

"Shallow," answered the old man by the hearth, the one Oliver thought he recognized. "The ships will have only the last forty feet of the longest two piers beside which to dock. And that section can be easily dropped."

The halfling noted then that the man's accent didn't match the salty dialect of the others, but that clue only left Oliver even more befuddled. He realized that he should know this man, but for some reason, as though something had entered his brain and stolen away a memory, he could not call him to mind.

He dismissed it—what else could he do?—and left with Katerin and Phelpsi Dozier. They found the *Horizon* tied up near to shore on the next pier in line and Phelpsi let them into the hold, surprisingly well furnished and comfortable, considering the general condition of the less-than-seaworthy old boat.

"Get yer sleep," old Dozier invited them, tossing pillows out to them from a closet. He nodded and started for the door.

"Where are you going?" Oliver was confused, for he thought that this was the man's home.

Dozier wheezed out a somewhat lewd laugh. "Gretel's to let me stay with her this night," he said. He tipped his wool hat once more. "See yer at the dawn."

Then he was gone, and Oliver tipped his hat toward the door, hoping that he would possess such fires when he was that old. The halfling kicked off his high boots and fell back onto one of the two cots in the tiny hold, reaching immediately to turn the lantern down low. He noted Katerin's look of a caged animal and hesitated.

"I thought you would be at home in such a place," he remarked.

Katerin's eyes darted his way. "Too much to be done," she replied.

"But not by us," Oliver insisted. "We have ridden a hard and long road. Take the last offered sleep, silly girl, for the road back is no shorter!"

Katerin remained uneasy, but Oliver turned down the lantern anyway. Soon Katerin was lying back on her cot, and soon after that, the gentle rhythm of the lapping waves carried her away into dreams of Hale.

A stream of light woke her, and Oliver, too: the first ray of dawn. They heard the outside commotion of people running along the wooden pier and realized that the fleet was probably in sight. Together, they jumped from their cots, Katerin rushing for the door while Oliver pulled on his boots.

The door was locked, barred from the other side.

Katerin put her shoulder against it hard, thinking it stuck.

It would not budge.

"What silliness is this?" Oliver demanded, coming up to her side.

"No silliness, my halfling hero," came a voice from above. The two looked up to see a hatch swinging open. They had to squint against the intrusion of sudden light, but could see that the opening was barred. Gretel knelt on the deck above, looking down at them.

"You promised," Katerin stuttered.

Gretel shook her head. "I said that we could give yer a week if we had a mind to. I didn't say we had a mind to."

For a moment, Katerin thought of grabbing the main gauche off of Oliver's belt and whipping it the old harbormaster's way.

But Gretel smiled at her, as though she read the dangerous thoughts completely. "I, too, was young, Katerin O'Hale," the old woman said. "Young and full of the fight. I know the fire that burns in yer veins, that quickens the beat of yer heart. But no more. My love fer the sword's been tempered by the wisdom o' years. Sit quiet, girl, and hold faith in the world."

"Faith in a world filled with deceit?" Katerin yelled.

"Faith that yer don't know everything," Gretel replied. "Faith that yer own way might not be the best way."

"You will let the one-eyes through Port Charley?" Oliver asked bluntly.

"Two of the Avon ships have already put in," Gretel announced. "Move them along, so we decided. In one side and out the other, and good riddance to them all!"

"You damn Caer MacDonald!" Katerin accused.

Gretel seemed pained by that for a moment. She dropped the hatch closed.

Katerin growled and threw herself at the door once more, to no avail. It held tight and they were locked in.

Soon they heard the unified footsteps and drum cadence of the first cyclopian troops marching in from the pier. They heard one brutish voice above the others, surprisingly articulate for one of the one-eyed race, but neither of them knew of Belsen'Krieg.

Belsen'Krieg the Terrible had come with nearly fifteen thousand hardened warriors to crush the rebellion and bring the head of Luthien Bedwyr back to his king in Carlisle.

CHAPTER 9

PREPARATIONS

*L*UTHIEN WALKED the length of the Caer MacDonald line, the area beyond the city's outer wall. Caer MacDonald had three separate fortifications. The tallest and thickest wall was inside the city, dividing the wealthy merchant section from the poorer areas. Next was the thick, squat fortification that surrounded the bulk of the city, and finally, fifty feet out from that, the outer defense, a bare and thin wall, half again a short man's height, and in some places no more than piled stones.

Beyond this outer wall, the land was open, with few trees or houses. Sloping ground, good ground to defend, Luthien thought. The cyclopians would have to come in a concentrated formation—en masse, as Oliver had called it—for the city could only be attacked from the north or the west. East and south lay the mountains, cold and deep with snow, and though a few of the one-eyes might swing around that way, just to pressure the defenders, the main group would have to come uphill, across open ground.

And that ground was being made more difficult by Shuglin's industrious dwarfs. Every one of them greeted Luthien as he walked past, but few bothered to look up, would not interrupt this most vital of jobs. Some dug trip trenches, picking through the still-frozen earth inch by inch. These were only about two feet deep and fairly narrow, and would afford little cover, but if a charging cyclopian stumbled across one, his momentum would be halted; he might even break his leg. Other dwarfs took the trip trenches one step further, lining the ridge closest to the city with sharp, barbed pickets.

Luthien grew hopeful while watching the quiet, methodical work, but, in truth, there were few dwarfs on the field. Most were over by the wall, and that was where the young Bedwyr found Shuglin.

The blue-bearded dwarf stood with a couple of friends by a small table, poring over a pile of parchments and every so often looking up toward the wall and grunting, "Uh huh," or some other noise. Shuglin was pleased to see Luthien, though he didn't even notice the man's approach until Luthien dropped a hand on his shoulder.

"How does it go?" the young Bedwyr asked.

Shuglin shook his head, didn't seem pleased. "They built this damned wall well," he explained, though Luthien didn't quite understand the problem. Wasn't a well-built wall a good thing for defenders?

"Only eight feet high and not so thick," Shuglin explained. "Won't stop the cyclopians for long. A ponypig could knock a hole in the damned thing."

"I thought you just said they built it well," Luthien replied.

"The understructure, I mean," said Shuglin. "They built the understructure well."

Luthien shook his head. Why would that matter?

Shuglin paused and realized it would be better to start from the beginning. "We decided not to hold this wall," he said, and pointed up Caer MacDonald's second wall.

"Who decided?"

"My kin and me," Shuglin answered. "We asked Siobhan and she agreed."

Again Luthien felt that oddly out-of-control sensation, like Siobhan was tugging hard at those puppet strings. For an instant, the young man was angry at being left out of the decision, but gradually he calmed, realizing that if his trusted companions had to come to him for approval on every issue, the whole of them would be bogged down and nothing important would ever get done.

"So we're thinking to fight from here, then retreat back to the city," Shuglin continued.

"But if the cyclopians gain this wall, they'll have a strong position from which to reorganize and rest up," Luthien reasoned.

The dwarf shrugged. "That's why we're trying to figure out how to drop this damned wall!" he grumbled, his frustration bubbling over.

"What about that powder you put in the box?" Luthien asked after a moment's thought. "The box I used to destroy the supplies in the Ministry."

"Not nearly enough of the stuff!" Shuglin huffed in reply, and Luthien felt foolish for not realizing that the cunning dwarfs would have considered the powder if it was a practical option. "And hard to make," Shuglin added. "Dangerous."

The dwarf finally looked up from the parchments, running his stubby fingers through his bushy blue-black beard. He reminded himself then that Luthien was only trying to help, and was even more desperate about the defense of Caer MacDonald than were Shuglin's folk.

"We'll use some of the powder," the dwarf elaborated, "on the toughest parts of the wall, but damn, they built it well!"

"We could knock it down now and just begin our defense from the second wall," Luthien offered, but Shuglin began shaking his head before the young man even finished the thought.

"We'll get it down," the dwarf assured Luthien. "The trick is to get it to fall *out*, on top of the stupid one-eyes."

Shuglin went back to his parchments; another dwarf asked him a question. Luthien nodded and walked away, reassured by the competence of those around him. Shuglin and his kin were trying hard to steal every advantage from their enemies, to hurt the cyclopians at every turn.

They would have to, Luthien knew. They would have to.

The two trapped friends sat glumly, listening to the passage all morning long. Marching feet, thousands of them, the clanking and bristling of heavy armor and shields, and the clomp of hooves: ponypigs, the cyclopians' favorite mount, smaller than horses and not as swift, but thicker and more muscular. The two heard the caissons roll, packed with weapons, no doubt, and food.

It went on, and on, and on, and Katerin and Oliver could do nothing to stop it. Even if they found some way out of the *Horizon*'s hold, there was nothing they could do anymore to slow the Avon army, nothing anyone could do.

"When they are gone, we will be freed," Oliver reasoned, and Katerin agreed, for it seemed to her that Gretel and the people of Port Charley held no grudge against the rebels. They merely wanted no trouble in their town. To proud Katerin, though, that position was not acceptable. The war had come, and in her mind, any Eriadoran that did not join them was, at best, a coward.

"Then we must ride so swiftly," Oliver went on. "North and east around the army, to warn our friends." He almost said "our friends in Caer MacDonald," but at that moment, with the unending, unnerving rumble of the army on the dock above him, it seemed to the halfling that the city in the mountains might soon be known as Montfort again.

"For whatever good that will do," Katerin replied, her tone bitter. She pounded a fist against the unyielding door and slumped back on her cot.

The procession outside continued, all through the morning and into the early hours of afternoon. Oliver's mood brightened when he found some food in a compartment under his cot, but Katerin wouldn't even eat, her mouth too filled with bitterness.

Finally, the clamor outside began to lessen somewhat. The solid rumble became sporadic and the voices of cyclopians were fewer, much fewer. And then, at last, a knock on the door.

It swung open before either could respond, and Gretel entered, her face somber but without apology.

"Good," she said to Oliver, "I see ye've found the food we left yer."

"I do so like my fish!" the happy halfling replied. "Oh," he said, his eyes cast down when he noticed the scowl Katerin was aiming at him.

"You promised," Katerin growled at Gretel.

The old woman held up her hand, waving away the remark as though it was insignificant. "We do what we must," she said. "We do what we must."

"Even if that means dooming fellow Eriadorans?" Katerin retorted.

"It was in all our best interests fer us to let the cyclopians pass, to treat them as friends," Gretel tried to explain.

But Katerin wasn't hearing it. "Our only hope was to bottle the fleet in the harbor, to keep them off-shore until the defense of Caer MacDonald could be completed and support could be mustered throughout the land," she insisted.

"And what would yer have us do?"

"Deny the docks!" the woman of Hale yelled. "Drop the outer piers!"

"And then what?" Gretel wanted to know. "The brutes'd sit in the harbor, whittling sticks? Yer smarter, girl. They'd've gone to the north and found a beach o' their own, and put in, and we could not have stopped them!"

"It would have bought us time," Katerm answered without hesitation.

"We are a town o' but three thousand," Gretel explained. "We could not have stopped them, and if they then marched back to Port Charley . . ."

She let the words hang unfinished in the air, dramatic and ominous, but still Katerin didn't want to hear the reasoning.

"The freedom of Eriador is all that matters," she said through gritted teeth, green eyes flashing dangerously. She flipped her fiery hair back from her face so that Gretel could see well her unrelenting scowl.

"Gretel echoes my own words," came a voice from just outside the door, and an old man walked into the small room. His hair and beard were snowy white, hair tied back in a ponytail, and his robes, rich and thick, were bright blue.

Oliver's mouth drooped open, and he realized then who the man at the meeting, the man at the hearth, had been. Clever disguise!

"I do not know you," Katerin said, as if to dismiss him, though from his clothing, and indeed his demeanor, he was obviously a man of some importance. She feared for a moment that he might be one of Greensparrow's remaining dukes.

"Ah, but I know you, Katerin O'Hale," the old man said. "The best friend Luthien Bedwyr ever had."

"Oh?" said Oliver, hopping up from his cot.

Katerin looked to the halfling, and then to the old man, and saw that there was recognition between them, smiles friends might exchange. It hit her suddenly.

"Brind'Amour?" she breathed.

The old man fell into a graceful, sweeping bow. "Well met, Katerin O'Hale, and long overdue," he said. "I am an old man," he winked at Oliver, "and getting older every day, but still I can appreciate such beauty as yours."

Katerin's first instinct was to punch him. How dare he think of such an unimportant thing at this time? But she realized that there was no condescension in his tone, realized somehow that the beauty he referred to was much more than the way she looked. He seemed to her, all at once, like a father, a wise overseer of events, watching them and measuring them, like the old fisherfolk of Hale who trained the novices in the ways of the sea. Brind'Amour was akin to those old fisherfolk, but the training he offered was in the way of life. Katerin knew that instinctively, and so when she realized what he had first said in support of Gretel's words, she found some comfort and began to hope that there was some other plan, some better plan, in motion.

"We must let the brutes through Port Charley," Brind'Amour said to the pair, mostly to Katerin, as though he realized that she would be the hardest to convince. "We must let them, and Greensparrow, think that the revolt in Montfort—"

"Caer MacDonald," Katerin corrected.

"No," said Brind'Amour. "Not yet. Let them think that the revolt in Montfort is a minor thing, an isolated thing, and not desired by any outside of that one city. We must plan long term."

"But the defenses will not be completed in time!" Katerin replied, her pleading voice almost a wail.

"Long term!" Brind'Amour said sharply. "If Eriador is indeed to be free, then this one force of cyclopians will prove the least of our troubles. Had we kept them out of the harbor, had we shown them that Eriador was in general revolt, they would have simply sent one of their ships sailing back to the south to inform Greensparrow and return with reinforcements. In the meantime, those cyclopians remaining would have overrun Port Charley and secured the defenses of this city, giving Greensparrow an open port north of the Iron Cross."

"How many warriors do you think Luthien would lose in trying to uproot fourteen thousand Praetorian Guards from Port Charley?" the old wizard asked grimly, and Katerin's sails had no more wind. She hadn't seen that possibility—neither had Luthien apparently—but now that Brind'Amour spoke, it seemed perfectly logical and perfectly awful.

"We are not ye enemies, Katerin O'Hale," Gretel put in.

Katerin looked hard at her, the young woman's expression clearly asking the question that was on her mind.

"But we are enemies of the one-eyes," Gretel confirmed. "And whoever rules Eriador should be of Eriador, not of Avon."

Katerin recognized the sincerity in the old woman's face and understood that Port Charley had indeed joined the alliance against Greensparrow. Again because of her knowledge of her own town, Katerin understood that Gretel would not have made such a bold and absolute statement if she didn't have the backing of her townsfolk.

"I still think that it would have been easier to keep them out of the docks," Katerin had to say. "Perhaps we might have even sunk one or two of their ships, taking half a thousand cyclopians to the bottom with them!"

"Ah, yes," Brind'Amour agreed. "But then they would have kept those ships we did not sink." Katerin and Oliver looked at the old man, his face widening with a wicked grin. "Not tomorrow night, but the night after that," he said, and he and Gretel exchanged a serious nod.

Brind'Amour turned back to the expectant companions. "The night after next will be a dark one," he explained. "Dark enough for us to board the Avon ships. In two nights, Eriador will have a fleet."

The wizard's smile was infectious. The halfling spoke for Katerin and himself: "I do like the way you think."

CHAPTER 10

MOSQUITOES

T HE WORD RAN AHEAD of the marching force like windswept fire, crossed from town to town, raced along the roads and the mountain trails, and came to Caer MacDonald before the whole of the Praetorian Guard had even marched out beyond Port Charley's eastern borders.

Luthien took the news stoically, putting on a bold face for his companions, telling them that the cyclopians' passage through the port city had been expected, and though he had hoped for more time, the defenses would be ready. A rousing cheer accompanied his every remark: after the victory in Caer MacDonald and the raising of Eriador's ancient flag over the Ministry—the decorated mountain cross, its four equal arms flared at their corners, on a green field—the rebels were ready for a fight, eager to spill more cyclopian blood.

Luthien appreciated that attitude and took heart in it, joining in the "celebration" Shuglin began in the Dwelf, the theme of the party giving praise for so many one-eyes to kill. The young Bedwyr left early, though, explaining that he had much to do the next day and reminding them that many small villages, most of them not shown on any maps or even named by any but those who lived there, lay between Caer MacDonald and Port Charley. When he left the Dwelf, the young Bedwyr did not go back to his apartment in Tiny Alcove. Rather, he slipped around to the back of the tavern and climbed the rain gutter to the roof.

"What have we begun?" Luthien asked the starry night. The air was crisp, but not too cold, and the stars glistened like crystalline ornaments. He considered the news from the west; the cyclopians hadn't even been slowed in Port Charley, and that could only mean that the folk of the port town had not embraced the rebellion.

"We need them all," Luthien whispered, needing to hear his thoughts aloud. He felt as if he was preparing a speech, and considering the way things had gone, he knew that he might well be. "All of Eriador. Every man, every woman. What good may our efforts be if those we seek to free do not take up arms in their own defense? What worth is victory if it is not a shared win? For then, I do not doubt, those who are free because of our sacrifice will not embrace that which we have accomplished, will not see the flag of Eriador as their own."

Luthien moved to the western edge of the roof, kicked away a piece of hardened snow and knelt upon the bare spot. He could see the massive silhouette of the Ministry, where so many brave folk had died. The Ministry, built as a symbol of man's spirit and love of God, but used by Greensparrow's pawn as a house of tax collection, and as a courtroom. Not even a courtroom, Luthien mused, for under Morkney, the Ministry was a place of condemnation and not of justice.

Stars twinkled all about the tallest tower, as though the structure reached right up into the heavens to touch the feet of God. Truly it was a beautiful night, calm and quiet. Few lights burned in the city, and the streets were quiet, except right in front of the Dwelf, where the impromptu celebration continued and an occasional soul wandered outside. Beyond the city's wall, Luthien could see the fires of the dwarven encampment. Some were blazing, but most had burned down to low embers, an orange glow in the darkened field.

"Sleep well," the young Bedwyr whispered. "Your work is not yet done."

"Nor is our own," Luthien heard behind him, and he turned to see Siobhan's approach, her step so light and quiet that she wasn't leaving an impression in the hardened snow that covered most of the roof.

Luthien looked back to the Ministry and the stars. He did not flinch, did not tense at all, as Siobhan put her hand under his ear and ran it gently down his neck to his shoulder.

"Katerin and Oliver have failed," Luthien said, bitter words indeed. "We have failed."

Siobhan cleared her throat, and it sounded to Luthien as more of a snicker than a cough. He turned to regard her.

How beautiful she appeared in the quiet light of evening; how fitting she seemed to the time of starlight, her eyes twinkling like those stars in the heaven above, her skin pale, almost translucent, and her hair flowing thick and lustrous, in such contrast to the delicate and sharp angles of her elven features.

"You declare defeat before the battle is even begun," Siobhan answered, her voice calm and soothing.

"How many cyclopians?" Luthien asked. "And they're not ordinary tribe beasts, but Praetorian Guard, the finest of Greensparrow's army. Ten thousand? Fifteen? I do not know that we could hold back half that number."

"They will not be as many when they get to Caer MacDonald," Siobhan assured him. "And our own numbers will grow as villagers flock in from the western towns." Siobhan slid her hand down Luthien's shoulder, across his chest, and leaned close, kissing him on the temple.

"You are the leader," she said. "The symbol of free Eriador. Your will must not waver."

Once more Luthien Bedwyr felt as if he had become a pawn in a game that was much too large for him to control. Once more he felt himself in the embrace of the puppeteer. Siobhan. Beautiful Siobhan. This time, though, Luthien did not resist that touch, the pulling of his strings. This time the presence of the half-elf, a tower of strength and determination, came as a welcome relief to him.

Without Siobhan beside him, behind him, Luthien believed that he would have broken that night, would have lost his purpose as he lost his hope. Without Siobhan, his guilt for those who would soon die, and who had already died, would have overwhelmed the prospects of the future, for with such a tremendous force marching toward the liberated city, the thought of a free Eriador seemed a fleeting, twinkling fantasy, as unreachable as the stars that flanked the tower of the Ministry.

Siobhan led him from the roof and back to the apartment in Tiny Alcove.

Katerin did not sleep well that night, too worried for her homeland, but she heard Oliver's contented snores in the room next to hers, comfortable quarters at a small inn high up the levels of Port Charley. The next morning, though, the woman of Hale was not tired, too excited by the sight of the departing army as she and Oliver joined Brind'Amour near to the eastern road.

The main body of the Avon force was long out of sight, several miles from the town already, and now came the supporting troops, mostly driving wagons loaded with provisions. Gretel directed its departure, working side by side with one of the largest and ugliest cyclopians either Katerin or Oliver had ever seen.

"The very ugliest!" Oliver assured his companions. "And I have seen many cyclopians!"

"Not as many as I," Brind'Amour interjected. "And Belsen'Krieg, for that is the brute's name, is truly the most imposing."

"Ugly," Oliver corrected.

"In spirit as well as in appearance," Brind'Amour added.

"He will ride out soon to join with his force." Katerin's tone was anxious.

"Belsen'Krieg will lead them, not follow," Brind'Amour confirmed. The wizard motioned to a powerful ponypig, heavily armor plated, with sharpened spikes protruding from every conceivable angle. Just looking at the monstrous thing, both Oliver and Katerin knew that it was

Belsen'Krieg's. Only the most ugly cyclopian would choose such a grue-some and horrible mount.

"As soon as Belsen'Krieg and his soldiers are away, we can stop the wagons," Katerin reasoned, her face brightening suddenly. That light dimmed, though, as she regarded the old wizard.

"The wagons will roll throughout the day," Brind'Amour explained. "And a smaller group will depart tomorrow. But all the food that leaves with that second group will be tainted, and their drinking supply will be salted with water from the sea. That should give Belsen'Krieg enough good supplies to get him more than halfway to Montfort, fully commit-ted to his march. Above all else, we must prevent him from turning back to Port Charley. Let them reach their goal, hungry and weary, and not ready for the fight, with Luthien before them and our army on their heels."

Both Oliver and Katerin looked curiously at the wizard, reacting to that last remark.

"Yes," Brind'Amour explained. "Port Charley will send a fair force after the cyclopians, and the one-eyes will be pecked every mile of their march, for every village between here and Montfort has joined in our cause."

Katerin was no longer arguing with the wizard, though she wasn't sure if he was stating fact or hope. Her instincts, her anger, continually prompted her to act, to strike out in any way she could find against the cyclopians and the foreign King Greensparrow. Already Brind'Amour had earned her trust. She realized that he, and not she, had brought Port Charley into the rebellion, before she and Oliver had even arrived. If the wizard's claim was correct, he had also secured alliance with the other southern Eriadoran villages, and if the wizard was right about Port Charley, Eriador would soon possess a fleet of great warships that was probably nearly as large as Greensparrow's remaining fleet in Avon.

Still, Katerin could not forget the army marching east, marching to Caer MacDonald and her beloved Luthien. Could Caer MacDonald hold?

She had to admit, to herself at least, that Brind'Amour was right as well in his argument about letting the cyclopians march upon that city. In the larger picture, if Eriador was indeed to be free, this force led by Belsen'Krieg—a mere token of what Greensparrow could ultimately hurl at them—might be among the least of their troubles.

That truth brought little comfort to Katerin O'Hale and sent a shud-der along her spine.

*   *   *

Siobhan's predictions were proven accurate the very next day, when villagers from the towns nearest Caer MacDonald began flocking into the city. Mostly, it was the young and the old who came in, in orderly fashion and all carrying provisions, ready to fight if necessary, to hold out against the wicked king of Avon to the last. And every group that came in spoke of their hardiest folk, who were moving to the west to meet with and hinder the approach of the cyclopian force.

Luthien didn't have to ask to know that this was somehow Siobhan's doing, that while he sat up on the roof, mulling over what seemed like an assured defeat, the half-elf and her stealthy cohorts were out and about, rousing the towns, telling them that the time for their independence had come.

The response from those towns was overwhelming. That day and the next, Luthien watched his garrison within the city grow from six thousand to ten thousand, and though many of the newer soldiers were elderly and could not match a powerful cyclopian in close combat, they had grown up on the Eriadoran plains hunting deer and elk, and they were skilled with their great yew bows.

So also were those younger warriors that went out in bands from the smaller villages, and Belsen'Krieg's army found itself under assault barely two days and ten miles out from Port Charley.

The damage to the massive force was not excessive. Every once in a while a cyclopian went down, usually wounded, but sometimes killed, and flaming arrows whipped into the supply wagons, causing some excitement. More important, though, was the effect of the skirmishers on the army's morale, for the cyclopians were being hindered and stung by an enemy that hit fast from concealment, then flittered away like a swarm of bees in a swift wind—an enemy they could not see and could not catch.

Belsen'Krieg kept them together and kept them marching straight for Montfort, promising them that once the city was overrun, they could slaughter a thousand humans for every dead cyclopian.

Oliver looked out at the heavy fog that came up that night, the third after the cyclopians had put into Port Charley, and he knew that this was no natural event. Since he had met up with Brind'Amour, the wizard had constantly complained about how weakened magic had become, but Oliver thought this enchantment wonderful, the perfect cover for this night's business.

Seventy ships from Avon lay anchored out in the harbor, great warships, many with catapults or ballistae set on the poop deck. In studying those magnificent vessels that day, Oliver and Katerin had agreed that it was a good thing Brind'Amour had intervened in Port Charley. Had they followed their original plan and tried to keep the cyclopians out in the water, this picturesque and enchanting town would have been reduced to piles of rubble.

Katerin, Brind'Amour, and Gretel joined Oliver at the dock a short while later. Immediately, the young woman scowled at Oliver, and the halfling pretended that he did not understand.

Katerin grabbed the plumed hat off his head and ruffled his purple cape. "Could you not have dressed better for the occasion?" she grumbled.

Oliver pulled the hat back from her and put his free hand over his heart, as though she had just mortally wounded him. "But I am!" he wailed. "Do you not understand the value of impressing your enemy?"

"If we are successful this night," Brind'Amour put in, "then our enemy will never see us."

"Ah, but they will," Oliver assured him. "I will wake at least one and let him see his doom before my rapier blade pierces his throat."

Katerin smiled. She loved the halfling's accent, the way he made rapier sound like "rah-pee-yer." She wasn't really angry with Oliver's dress; she was just teasing him a bit to get the edges off her own nerves. Katerin was a straightforward fighter, an arena champion, and this stealthy assassination technique was not much to her liking.

There was no other choice, though, and she understood that. Seventy ships, nearly a thousand cyclopian crewmen. There could be no mistakes; not a ship could escape to sail south and warn Greensparrow.

Port Charley was bustling that night. Many of the cyclopian sailors were ashore, even most of those who were supposed to be on watch out at the boats, lured in by the promise of fine food and drink, and other, more base, pleasures. The town's three taverns were bursting with excitement, and so were the more than a dozen private homes that had been opened up to accommodate the crews.

The killing would begin at midnight, when most of the one-eyes were too drunk to realize what was happening. By that time, a hundred small boats would be well on their way through the fog, out to the anchored ships.

"The signal!" Gretel motioned toward a flickering light to the north. She held up her own lantern to the south, unhooded it for just a moment, then again, and the message was relayed all down the line.

Brind'Amour, Oliver, and Katerin stepped into their small boat along with two of Port Charley's folk, a husband and wife.

"In Gascony we have such bugs as we are this night," Oliver said to them, quieting his tone as both Brind'Amour and Katerin *shhh*'d him. "They come from Espan, mostly, and so does their name," the halfling continued in a whisper. "Mosquitoes. Clever bugs. You hear them in your ear and swat at them, but they are not there. They are somewhere else on your body, taking drops of your blood.

"We are mosquitoes," the halfling decided. "Mosquitoes on Greensparrow."

"Then let us hope that enough mosquitoes can suck a body dry," Brind'Amour remarked, and they all went silent, drifting out from the docks, the oars barely touching the water, for stealth and not speed was the order of business this night.

Oliver was first up the anchor rope of the first ship they came upon, the halfling swiftly climbing hand over hand to the rail. He paused there, and then, to everyone's disbelief, he began talking.

"Greetings, my one-eyed, bow-legged, wave-riding, so ugly friend," he said, and reached under his cloak and produced a flask. "You are missing all the fun, but fear not, I, Oliver deBurrows, have brought the fun to you!"

Most alarmed were the villagers in the rowboat, but Katerin, who was beginning to figure this strange halfling out (and was beginning to understand why Luthien liked Oliver so much), stood up and steadied herself in the boat, taking the longbow from her shoulder.

They couldn't see what was transpiring beyond the rail, just Oliver's back, his purple cape fluttering in the breeze. "I have brought you a woman, as well," the halfling said. "But that will cost you a few of your so fine Avon gold pieces."

Predictably, the eager cyclopian leaned over the rail to get a look at the goods, and Katerin wasted no time in putting her arrow into the brute's head.

Even as the bolt struck the mark, Oliver grabbed the cyclopian by the collar and heaved. The one-eye hit the water between the ship and the rowboat, bobbing facedown after the initial waves had settled.

Brind'Amour wanted to call up and scold Oliver, for the noise was too great. Suppose other cyclopians were about on the deck? But Oliver was out of sight.

There was indeed another cyclopian awake and roaming the deck, but by the time Katerin, the next up the rope, had made the rail, it was already dead, Oliver standing atop its massive chest, wiping his blood-stained rapier blade on its cloak.

"Mosquitoes," the halfling whispered to her. "Buzz buzz."

And so it went up and down the line, with every ship boarded and taken.

Back on shore, the killing commenced as well, and in only two of the twelve houses and one of the taverns did the cyclopians have enough wits about them to even put up a struggle.

When the wizard's fog cleared later that night, nearly twenty of Port Charley's folk were dead, another seven wounded, but not a cyclopian remained alive in the town, or in the harbor, and the rebels now possessed a fleet of seventy fine warships.

"It was too easy," Brind'Amour said to Oliver and Katerin before the three retired that night.

"They did not expect any trouble," Katerin replied.

Brind'Amour nodded.

"They underestimate us," Oliver added.

Still the wizard nodded. "And if that truth holds, Montfort will not be taken," he said. The wizard dearly hoped he was right, but he remembered the image of mighty Belsen'Krieg, sophisticated, yet vicious, and doubted that the days ahead would be as easy as this night.

Late the next morning, so that the mosquitoes had the time for a good night's rest, the town of Port Charley organized its own force, nearly a thousand strong. With Katerin upon Riverdancer, Oliver on Threadbare, and Brind'Amour on a fine roan stallion, joining old Phelpsi Dozier—who had been a commander in the first war against Greensparrow twenty years before—at the head of the column, the soldiers started out toward the east.

Heading for Montfort, which Brind'Amour would not yet let them call Caer MacDonald.

CHAPTER 11

TAINTED

BELSEN'KRIEG, his ugly face a mask of outrage, pulled the cord from one of the sacks piled in the back of the wagon and reached inside with his huge hand. Those terrified cyclopians around him didn't have to wait for their general to extract the hand to know what would be found.

"Tainted!" the ugly general bellowed. He yanked his hand from the sack and hurled the worthless supplies—part foodstuffs, but mostly fine beach sand—high into the air.

Montfort was only thirty miles from Port Charley, as the bird flies, but given the rough terrain and the season, with some trails blocked by piled snow and tumbled boulders and others deep with mud, the cyclopian general had planned on a five-day march. The army had done well; as far as Belsen'Krieg could determine, they had crossed the halfway point early that morning, the third day out. And now their route could be directly east, sliding away from the mountains to easier ground for more than half the remaining distance.

But they were nearly out of food. The soldiers had left Port Charley with few supplies, the plan being that the wagons would continually filter in behind them on the road. So it had gone for the first two days, but when the wagons had left the afternoon of that second day to go back to Port Charley and resupply, they had been attacked and burned.

Belsen'Krieg had promptly dispatched a brigade of a thousand of his finest troops to meet the next east-moving train. Despite a few minor skirmishes with the increasing numbers of rebels, that caravan had gotten through, to the cheers of the waiting army. Those cheers turned to silent frowns when the soldiers discovered they had been deceived, that the supplies which had gone out of the port city on the second day were not supplies at all.

The cyclopian leader stood and stared back to the west for a long, long time, fantasizing about the torture and mayhem he would wreak on the fools of Port Charley. Likely it was a small group of sympathizers for the rebels—the fact that the wagons got out of the town at all made Belsen'Krieg believe that the criminals in Port Charley were few. That wouldn't hinder Belsen'Krieg's revenge, though. He would flatten the town and sink all of their precious fishing boats. He would kill . . .

The cyclopian dismissed the fantasy. Those were thoughts for another day. Right now, Belsen'Krieg had too many pressing problems, too many decisions. He considered turning the force back to Port Charley, crushing the town and feasting well, maybe on the meat of dead humans. Then he looked back to the east, to the easier ground, the rolling fields of white and brown that lay before them. They were more than halfway to Montfort, and of the twelve or so miles remaining, at least ten of them would be away from the treacherous mountains. With a good hard march, the army could reach Montfort's walls by twilight the next day. They might even happen upon a village or two, and there they could resupply.

There they could feast.

The cyclopian began to nod his huge head, and those around him stared hopefully, thinking that their magnificent leader had found a solution.

"We have two more hours of good light," Belsen'Krieg announced. "Double-step!"

A couple of groans emanated from the gathering about the general, but Belsen'Krieg's scowl silenced them effectively.

"Double-step," he said again, calmly, evenly. Had this been an ordinary cyclopian tribe, one of the wild groups that lived in the mountains, Belsen'Krieg's life would likely have been forfeit at that moment. But these were Praetorian Guards; most had spent their entire lives in training for service to Greensparrow. The grumbling stopped, except for the unintentional rumblings of empty stomachs, and the army resumed its march and gained another two miles before the sun dipped below the horizon and the chill night breeze came up.

Belsen'Krieg's advance scouts came back to the army soon after it had pitched camp, reporting that they had discovered a village ahead, not far off the trail, only a few miles to the north of Montfort. The place was not deserted, the scouts assured Belsen'Krieg, for as dusk fell, lamps were lit in every house.

The brutish cyclopian leader smiled as he considered the news. He still did not know what to make of this rebellion, did not know how widespread it might be. Going into a small village might be risky, might incite more Eriadorans to join in the fight against Greensparrow. Belsen'Krieg considered his own soldiers, their morale dwindling with their supplies. They would go into the town, he decided, and take what they needed, and if a few humans were killed and a few buildings burned, then so be it.

That rumor spread through the cyclopian encampment quickly, eagerly, and the soldiers bedded down with hope.

As the darkness settled in deep about the camp though, the night, like the one before, became neither quiet nor restful, and hope shifted to uneasiness. Bands of rebels circled the camp, peppering the brutes with arrows, some fire-tipped, others whistling invisibly through the dark to thud into the ground or a tree, a tent pole or even a cyclopian, surprising and unnerving all those around. At one point, a volley of nearly a hundred burning bolts streaked through the night sky, and though not a single cyclopian was slain in that barrage, the effect on the whole of the army was truly unsettling.

Belsen'Krieg realized that the small rebel bands would do little real damage, and he knew that his soldiers needed to rest, but for the sake of morale, he had to respond. So bold an attack could not go unanswered. Companies were formed up and sent out into the darkness, but they saw nothing among the snowy and muddy fields and heard nothing except the taunts of the elusive Eriadorans, who knew this ground, their home ground.

One company, returning to the encampment, was attacked openly, if only briefly, as they neared the crest of a small hill. A group of men sprang up from concealment atop that hillock and charged down through the cyclopian ranks, swatting at the brutes with clubs and old swords, poking at them with pitchforks and slicing with scythes. They ran right through the cyclopians with no intention of stopping for a pitched fight, and rushed out, disappearing into the darkness. A few seconds of frenzy, another small thorn poked into the side of the huge army.

In truth, only a dozen Praetorian Guards were killed that long night, and only a score or so were wounded. But few of the brutes slept, and those who did, did not sleep well.

"The bait is set?" Luthien asked Siobhan soon before dawn of the next day, an overcast, rainy, and windswept day. He looked out from Caer MacDonald's northern wall, across the lightening fields and hedgerows. He noted the lighter shade of gray, the last remnants of snow, clinging to the dark patches, losing the battle with spring.

"Felling Downs," the half-elf replied. "We had fifty soldiers in there all the yesterday, and burned the lights long into the night." Siobhan chuckled. "We expected to be attacked by the cyclopians' advance scouts, but they stayed out."

Luthien glanced at her sidelong. He had wondered where she had been the previous night, and now he thought himself foolish for not realizing that Siobhan would personally lead the group out to the small village north of Caer MacDonald as bait. Wherever the fighting might be, Siobhan would find her way to the front. Even Shuglin and the other dwarfs, so tortured under Greensparrow's rule, were not as fanatical. Everything in Siobhan's life revolved around the rebellion and killing cyclopians.

Everything.

"How many have gone?" Luthien asked.

"Three hundred," came the quick reply.

Again Luthien looked at the half-elf. Three hundred? Only three hundred? The cyclopian force numbered fifty times that, but they were supposed to go out and deal the brutes a stinging blow with only three hundred warriors? His expression, eyebrows arching high over his eyes, clearly asked all of those questions.

"We cannot safely cover more in the ground to the north," Siobhan explained, and from her tone it was obvious that she wished they could send out the whole of their force. She, perhaps even more than Luthien, wanted to hit hard at the cyclopian army. "We cannot risk many lives on the open field."

Luthien nodded. He knew the truth of what Siobhan was saying; in fact, he had initially argued against going out from Caer MacDonald at all. But the ambush plan was a good one. For the cyclopians to take the easiest and most logical route into Caer MacDonald, they would have to cross a small river west of Felling Downs, then turn south, through the town and straight to the foothills and the walled city. There was only one real bridge across that river anywhere in the vicinity, northwest of Felling Downs, but Luthien and his cohorts could cross the water in the rougher ground just to the west of Caer MacDonald. They would then strike out to the north and take up a secretive position in the hedgerows and other cover just south of the bridge—a bridge which Shuglin's folk had already rigged for collapse. When the bulk of the enemy army got across, heading out for Felling Downs, that bridge would be taken down and those cyclopians caught on the western side would face the wrath of Luthien's marauders.

"Know this as an important day," the young Bedwyr remarked. "The first true test of Avon's army."

"And of our own," Siobhan added.

Luthien started to argue, was going to remark that the taking of Montfort had been their first test, but he stopped, admitting the truth of Siobhan's words. This would be the first time the rebels battled with a large contingent of Praetorian Guards, a trained and prepared army.

"The group is away?" Luthien asked.

Siobhan nodded, and unconsciously looked to the west.

"And you will soon set out to join with them?" Luthien asked. The question was rhetorical, for of course Siobhan would rush to catch up with those who would soon see battle. "Then we must hurry," the young Bedwyr quickly added.

The fact that he had suddenly included himself in the ambush was not lost on Siobhan. She stared long and hard at Luthien, and he could not determine if her look was approving or not.

"You are too valua—" came the beginning of her response.

"We are all too valuable," the young Bedwyr said, determined that he would not be turned away this time. Lately, every time Luthien included himself in plans that would likely lead to fierce combat, someone, usually Siobhan, would pipe in that he was too valuable to risk himself so.

Siobhan knew better than to argue. She could convince Luthien of many things, could guide him through many decisions, but she had learned during the taking of Montfort that no amount of coercion would keep the brave young man out of harm's way.

"This is the test of Avon's army," Luthien explained. "And I must see how they respond."

Siobhan thought of several arguments against that course, primarily that the defense of Caer MacDonald, and the morale of the rebels, would be weakened indeed if Luthien Bedwyr, the Crimson Shadow, was killed before the cyclopians even reached the city walls. She kept her doubts private, though, and decided to trust in Luthien. He had been in on every major skirmish within the city, and whether it was skill or just dumb luck, he had come through it all practically unscathed.

They set out together almost immediately, running west and then north, along with a few elven archers. Less than an hour after the dawn, the three hundred warriors, hand-picked for this important battle, lay in wait within a mile south of the bridge over the small river known as Felling Run. Across the water to the east, the marauders could see the plumes of smoke rising from the chimneys of Felling Downs, more bait for the cyclopians.

And soon after, to the north, they caught their first glimpse of Avon's army, a huge black and silver mass, tearing up the turf, shaking the ground as they stomped determinedly on. Luthien held his breath for many moments after he realized the extent of that force. He thought of Oliver and the halfling's plan to abandon the rebellion and flee to the northland, and he wondered, for the first time, if Oliver might not have been right.

CHAPTER 12

FELLING DOWNS

THE PLUMES OF SMOKE rising from the chimneys of Felling Downs were in sight as the cyclopian force plodded along, traveling generally southeast now. They came to Felling Run, a small river, a swollen stream really, being no more than twenty feet across and averaging about waist deep. Running water was visible from the high banks, but most of the river remained frozen over, patches of gray ice lined by white snow.

Belsen'Krieg walked his sturdy ponypig right up to the bank, just south of the one bridge in sight, and considered the water and the town beyond. They could cross here and turn directly south for Montfort, crushing the village on their way, or they could turn south now and head into the foothills west of the city. The huge and ugly cyclopian leader still wanted to sack this town, still thought that the blood and the supplies would do his force good, but he was leery for some reason that he did not understand. Perhaps it was that the town was too tempting, too easy a kill. The people here knew that the cyclopians were on the way. Belsen'Krieg was certain of that, especially considering the peppering his force had taken all the way from Port Charley. Everyone in the south of Eriador knew about the march, and many obviously did not approve. So why would the folk of the village across the river remain in their homes, knowing that the cyclopians would be coming through? And why, Belsen'Krieg pondered, had the rebels in Montfort left this bridge, obviously the easiest route to the captured city, standing?

"A delay, my lord?" came a question from behind, startling the unusually introspective cyclopian. Belsen'Krieg looked over his shoulder to see four of his undercommanders astride their ponypigs, eyeing him curiously.

"The soldiers grow impatient," remarked the undercommander who had spoken before, a slender cyclopian with long and curly silver hair and great muttonchops sideburns, both attributes highly unusual for the race. The brute was called Longsleeves for his penchant for wearing fine shirts, buttoned high on the neck, with sleeves that ran all the way to the top of his thin hands.

Belsen'Krieg looked back across the Felling Run, to the plumes of smoke. The inviting plumes of smoke; the cyclopian knew that Longsleeves spoke truthfully, that his soldiers were verily drooling at the sight.

"We have to move them," another of the undercommanders put in.

"Across, or to the south?" Belsen'Krieg asked, more to himself than the others.

"To the south?" Longsleeves balked.

"We can go to the south, into the foothills, and approach Montfort from the western fields," answered a lesser cyclopian, just an aide to one of the mounted undercommanders. Longsleeves moved to strike the impertinent brute, but his master held the slender cyclopian back, explaining that this brute among the group was the most familiar with this region, having spent many years in the Montfort city garrison.

"Continue," Belsen'Krieg ordered the aide.

"Felling Run ain't much up that way," the brute went on, pointing to the south. "Just a few streams all runnin' together. We could go right up and walk across them, and still have two miles a'goin' before we got to Montfort."

The aide's excitement wasn't shared by the undercommanders, who understood the importance of sacking this town, giving their tired soldiers some play and some food. Belsen'Krieg recognized that fact and sympathized with his undercommanders and their fears of desertion. The town was just across the river, half a mile away perhaps, across rolling, easy fields. Quick and easy plunder.

But still that nagging sensation remained with the general. Belsen'Krieg had seen many, many battles, and like all of the finest warriors, he possessed a sixth sense concerning danger. Something here simply didn't smell right to him.

Before he could act upon those feelings, though, to explain them or simply to order the army to the south, his undercommanders hit him with every argument for crossing and sacking that they could find. They sensed the way their general was leaning and feared that they would lose this one easy battle before the pitched fight at Montfort's walls.

Belsen'Krieg listened to them carefully. He feared that he might be getting paranoid, upset about ghosts. Much of Eriador apparently sided with the rebels in Montfort—the bandits attacking his camps and the wagons of tainted supplies proved that—but by all appearances, most of the country remained quiet, not loyal to Greensparrow, perhaps, but certainly cowed.

The undercommanders continued to argue; they wanted a taste of blood and maybe some food. Belsen'Krieg doubted that they would find much of either in the inconsequential town across the river, but he relented anyway. He marched with a force of nearly fifteen thousand Praetorian Guards, after all, and the easier ground to Montfort was indeed on the other side of the river.

"We cross here," the general stated, and the faces of the four undercommanders brightened. "The town will be flattened," he further offered to their wicked smiles. "But," he said sternly, stealing the growing mirth, "we must be in sight of Montfort's walls before the day ends!"

The undercommanders each looked to Belsen'Krieg's aide, who bobbed his head eagerly. Montfort was no more than five miles of easy ground beyond the village of Felling Downs.

* * *

Not so far to the south, crouched behind hedgerows, crawling amidst tumbles of boulders, even in trenches dug along the back of a ridge, Luthien and his three hundred waited nervously. They had expected the cyclopians to swarm right across the bridge on the way to Felling Downs, but for some reason they did not understand, the army had paused.

"Damn," Luthien muttered as the moments passed uneventfully. They had gambled on the cyclopians crossing; if the brutes turned south before the river, then Luthien and his raiders would have to flee back to Caer MacDonald with all speed. Even if they got away without much fighting, as Luthien believed they could, nothing would be gained, only lost, for the few hundred here could have been better served by remaining in the city, in helping with the continuing defensive preparations.

"Damn," the young Bedwyr said again, and Siobhan, crouched beside him, had no words to comfort him this time. She, too, knew the gamble, and she sat quietly, chewing on her bottom lip.

Together they watched as several cyclopians ran ahead of the halted mass, running for the bridge. The brutes pulled up to a trot, then a walk as they neared the structure and began pointing out specific places to each other, making it quickly apparent that they had gone out to inspect the structure.

"Damn," came the predictable lament among the raiders, and this time it was Siobhan, not Luthien, who spoke the words.

The bridge across Felling Run was not a large structure. It was made completely of wood and stood no more than fifteen feet above the ice-covered stream. It was wide and solid, and had stood with only minor repairs for longer than anyone could remember. Ten horses, or seven wide ponypigs, could cross it abreast, and its gently arching roadway was grooved by the countless merchant wagons that had crossed it, making their way from Port Charley to Montfort.

The five cyclopians sent to inspect the structure were not tentative in the least as they came upon the solid wood. The fall to the river was only fifteen feet, after all, and the river was obviously shallow and not very swift running. The brutes fanned out, two to a side and one in the middle, directing the inspection. They went down to their knees, gripping the edges and bending over to take a look at what was underneath.

The great oak beams appeared to be solid, unbreakable. Even the cyclopians, never known for feats of engineering or construction of any kind, could appreciate the strength of the bridge. The call of "yok-ho," the cyclopian signal that all was well, came from one, then another, both on the right side of the bridge.

The brute peeking over the bridge's left-hand side, nearest to the eastern bank, noticed something strange. The wood under here was weathered and gray, except for two pegs the cyclopian spotted: new pegs, with sawdust still clinging to their visible edge.

"Yok-ho!" called the first brute on the left, who then joined the curious cyclopian near the eastern bank, the only one who had not given the signal.

"Yok-ho?" he asked, bending low to see what had so sparked his companion's interest.

The curious brute pointed out the new pegs.

"So?" his companion prompted. "It's been a tough winter blow. The bridge needed fixing."

The other cyclopian was not so certain. He had a nagging suspicion, and he wanted to crawl over the edge and snake in for a closer look. His companion wasn't thrilled with that idea, though.

"Call out yok-ho," the one-eye insisted.

"But the peg—"

"If you don't call it out, we'll be turning south," the other growled.

"If it falls—" the curious cyclopian tried to explain, but again he was cut short.

"Then those on it will tumble down," the other replied. "But those who get across, and we'll be in the front of that group, will get to the town and get to the food. My stomach's been growling all the day, and all of yesterday! So call it out, or I'll put my fist into your eye!"

"What do you see?" demanded the cyclopian standing in the middle of the bridge.

The curious one took a last look at the pegs, then at the scowl of his companion. "Yok-ho!" he cried out, and the brute in the middle, as eager as any to get to the town, didn't question the delay any further.

Word was relayed back to the waiting army, and they began to move immediately, tightening ranks so that they could get across the bridge as quickly as possible.

Under that bridge, tucked into cubbies between the great beams near to the center of the understructure, three dwarfs, who had heard the conversation at the lip of the bridge and now the thunder of marching footsteps and ponypig hooves on the planks above, breathed deep sighs of relief. Each dwarf carried a large mallet, ready to knock out designated pegs and drop the bridge when the signal came from the south.

Down to the south, Siobhan, Luthien, and all the others breathed relieved sighs, as well, as they watched the Avon army crossing over to the east. Luthien took out his folding bow and pinned it open; the others fitted long arrows to their bowstrings. Then they waited.

Half the force got across, including all of the cavalry, and still the raiders held their shots.

The lines of cyclopians stretched out across the way, nearing Felling Downs. The brutes would find the town deserted and all supplies gone, though the villagers had left more than a few traps, snares, and oil-soaked buildings, flint and steel attached to door jambs waiting for a cyclopian to walk in.

For the waiting marauders, the timing had to be perfect. They didn't want to trap too many cyclopians on this side of the bridge, but it would take them a couple of minutes to get down there to engage the brutes and they didn't want to wait so long as to allow all the cyclopians to run across. One elf was dug in less than two hundred feet from the bridge, in a deep hole beneath a lone tree. Her job was to count the remaining one-eyes and signal back, and so Luthien and the others waited for the flash of a mirror.

Most of the army was across, the trailing brutes growing more confident and less structured in their formations now. Siobhan nodded up and down the line and great bows bent back, anticipating the call.

The mirror flashed; the air hummed with the vibrations of bowstrings. The first volley went out to the bank just east of the bridge, a three-hundred arrow barrage to prevent any of the brutes who had already gone over from running back across before the bridge fell.

Confusion erupted from the cyclopians as the stinging, deadly darts whipped in. Howls and cries filtered up and down the ranks; to the south, a horn blew.

So much confusion hit those upon the bridge, scrambling brutes trying to decide which way to run, that the one-eyes never even heard the pounding as the dwarfs took up their mallets, slamming out the pegs.

The second barrage came flying from the south, this time plucking into the ranks of some three hundred brutes remaining on the western bank.

Commands rang out all along the cyclopian line, the army trying to turn about to meet the unexpected foe. Those cyclopians near the bridge scrambled to get into formation on both banks, lining up their great shields to deflect the next volley.

One group of cavalry, a dozen ponypig riders, including undercommander Longsleeves, came galloping onto the bridge from the west, trying to get back and take command of the force left behind.

Beams groaned and creaked; below came a tremendous cracking sound from the ice and splashes. The cavalry unit was more than halfway across, scattering cyclopian infantry, even knocking a few over the side.

The bridge collapsed beneath them.

Now all of the bowshots from the south were concentrated on those unfortunate cyclopians trapped on the west. Each barrage took less of a toll as more and more got into their tight defensive posture, great shields lined edge to edge.

With cries of "Free Eriador!" and "Caer MacDonald!" the raiders leaped up from their concealment, bows twanging as they charged. Within twenty feet of their opponents, the cyclopians came out of their metal shell and charged ahead, eager for close combat. But this tactic was known and had been anticipated, and almost as one, the rebels skidded down to one knee, pulling back for one more shot, point-blank, into their enemies.

That last volley decimated the cyclopian ranks, killed nearly a hundred of the brutes, and sent those remaining into a scramble of pure confusion.

Out came *Blind-Striker*, and Luthien Bedwyr, his crimson cape billowing in the morning breeze, led the charge.

Across the river, the cyclopian army hooted and cursed. Some threw their long spears, others fired crossbows, but cyclopians, having only one eye and no depth perception, were not adept at missile fire, and their barrage, however heavy, was ineffective.

Still, the enemy was in sight, and the cyclopians were hungry for blood. Many picked a careful course along the angled logs of the bridge which had not fallen, while others, on orders from their tyrant commander, swarmed down the banks, trying to cross on the ice.

Some got almost halfway before the ice broke apart, dropping them into the freezing waters.

On the western bank, the massacre was on in full. Outnumbered by more than two to one, the remaining cyclopians, Praetorian Guard all, put up a good fight initially. But as more died, and as it became apparent that little if any help would cross over from the eastern bank, groups of the brutes began to run off, back to the west, the way they had come, wishing they could run all the way to Carlisle in Avon!

They didn't get nearly that far. Barely a hundred yards from the bridge, they found more enemies, those independent rebel bands that had peppered the force since it had left Port Charley.

The rebels from Caer MacDonald saw the unexpected help as well, and their hearts soared and the cyclopians' heart for the battle fell apart.

Above it all was Luthien, running from fight to fight, slashing with *Blind-Striker* and calling out for Eriador, inspiring his warriors.

Those cyclopians across the river, particularly one huge and ugly brute atop a huge and ugly ponypig, also noticed the Crimson Shadow. Belsen'Krieg called for a crossbow.

Siobhan and the hundred elves who took part in the raid broke free of the melee as soon as it became apparent that the cyclopians would be easily slaughtered. Taking up their bows, the elves lined the western bank, more than willing to trade missile volleys with the one-eyes. Mostly, they concentrated their fire on those brutes splashing in the river, or crawling along the remains of the bridge. Half of the elves provided cover fire as the three courageous dwarfs crawled out of the bridge's wreckage and picked their way up the western bank.

In short order, the bridge was clear of one-eyes, and those still alive in the suddenly red-running river had turned about and were scrambling for their own ranks.

Luthien came up to the bank beside Siobhan, *Blind-Striker* in hand and dripping cyclopian blood. He looked to the half-elf—and then both fell away suddenly as a crossbow bolt cut the air between them. Turning to look across the bank, they recognized Belsen'Krieg and knew that this huge brute had been the one to shoot at them—to shoot at Luthien. It had been no random attempt.

The elves kept up their barrage, but the cyclopian army, willing to abandon comrades for the sake of their own hides, was fast pulling back, understanding that they could not trade volleys with the likes of elves.

Belsen'Krieg remained, statuesque atop his ponypig. The one-eyed general and Luthien stared at each other long and hard. The armies would meet in full very soon, of course, but suddenly it seemed to Luthien as if those forces, all of the men and dwarfs and elves, and all of the cyclopians, were no more than extensions of their two generals. Suddenly, the impending fight for Montfort, for Caer MacDonald, became a personal duel.

Before Luthien could stop her, Siobhan put up her bow and let fly, her arrow streaking across the river to strike Belsen'Krieg in the broad shoulder.

The cyclopian general hardly flinched. Without taking his unblinking stare from Luthien, the brute reached up and snapped off the arrow shaft. He nodded grimly, Luthien answered with a similar nod, and then Belsen'Krieg wheeled his ponypig and galloped away, riding through a hail of arrows, though if any hit him or his mount, it wasn't apparent.

Luthien stood silent on the bank, watching the monstrous brute depart. The enemy was real to him now, very real, and as awestricken and afraid as he had been when first he glimpsed the black and silver swarm that was the army of Avon, he was even more so having looked upon the powerful leader of that force.

On the western bank, it was over in a matter of minutes, with less than four-score casualties to the raiders, mostly wounds that would heal, and more than three hundred cyclopian dead littering the snowy and muddy field.

A complete victory for the rebels, but as the Avon army flowed away from the bridge, toward Felling Downs and Caer MacDonald beyond that, Luthien wondered how much this minor skirmish would ultimately affect the final outcome.

Later that morning, Oliver and Katerin and the force from Port Charley, still many miles to the west, saw the plumes of black smoke rising in the east, as Felling Downs was consumed by the fires, the rage, of the cyclopian army.

The sight was bittersweet, for the marching force had heard from the independent bands of the ambush set at Felling Downs that the fight went well. Still, those plumes of smoke reminded them all that the war would not be without cost, and on a more practical and immediate level, that they still had a long march ahead of them and a long fight after that.

As twilight settled in deep over Eriador, the folk from Port Charley set their last camp before the fight. Oliver rode out alone from their ranks, prodding Threadbare across the ghostly gray fields. He came up a hillock—a high ridge for this far north of the Iron Cross—and he saw the fires.

Hundreds of fires, thousands of fires, a vast sea of cyclopians. More enemies than boastful Oliver had ever seen gathered in one place, and the halfling was sorely afraid, more for Luthien and those in Montfort than for himself, for he understood that no matter how hard they marched and how early they left, the force from Port Charley would not come on the field until the end of the next day.

"Luthien will hold," came a voice that startled Oliver, nearly dropping him from his mount. Brind'Amour walked up beside him.

Oliver looked all about, but saw no mount nearby, and he understood that the old man had used a bit of wizardry to get out here.

"Luthien will hold for the first fight," Brind'Amour assured Oliver, as if he had read the halfling's every thought, every worry.

The words were of small comfort to Oliver as he continued to scan that vast encampment to the south and east.

*   *   *

Those cyclopian campfires were visible from the high towers of Caer MacDonald as well, and Luthien and Siobhan, atop the Ministry's highest platform, marked them well and watched them for a long time in silence.

They knew, too, that if those fires were visible to them, then Caer MacDonald's dark walls were visible to the hungry and angry cyclopians.

The city was quiet this night, deathly still.

CHAPTER 13

AGAINST THE WALL

THE NEXT WAS NOT A BRIGHT DAWN, the sky hazy gray with the first high clouds of yet another gathering storm. When shafts of sunlight did break through, the fields sparkled with wetness, as did the helms and shields and glistening speartips of the Avon army, forming into three huge squares, four to five thousand soldiers in each.

Luthien watched the spectacle from atop the low gatehouse of the city's inner wall. He and his group had crawled in just ahead of the Avon force, leaving the cyclopians to set their camp on the field, for the one-eyes had met up with more minor resistance in the foothills between Felling Downs and Montfort. No groups had actually engaged the vast army; they had just stung the one-eyes enough to keep them diverted, allowing Luthien's band to slip far to the south and cross the river, then dash back into the protection of the city as the night had deepened around them.

Before Luthien lay a hundred feet of empty ground, all structures and wagons having been removed by the dwarfs. The empty field ended at the lower outer wall, the base of which had been chopped and wedged, ready to drop outward, away from the city. Thick ropes pulled taut ran back into the courtyard, a third of the distance to the inner wall. These were pegged solidly into the ground, and beside each stood an ax-wielding dwarf.

Those dwarfs would have a long wait, Luthien hoped. The first defense would come from that outer wall; its low parapets were lined shoulder-to-shoulder by archers and pikemen. Luthien spotted Siobhan among that line, her long wheat-colored tresses hanging low out of a silvery winged helmet, her great longbow in hand.

The young Bedwyr next looked for Shuglin, but could not find the dwarf. In fact, Luthien saw none of the bearded folk, except for those twenty dwarfs ready to chop the lines and one or two in place along the outer wall. Luthien looked up and down his own line along the inner wall, but still, for some reason he did not understand, he found no dwarfs. He looked back to Siobhan instead, admiring her fierce beauty, her sheer strength of character. All those around looked to her for guidance as surely as they looked to the Crimson Shadow.

The whooshing sound of a catapult behind him, from the Ministry, brought the young man from his contemplations of the fair half-elf. He lifted his gaze beyond the outer wall and saw the three black and silver masses approaching, a row of solid metal, with shields butted together perhaps sixty-five fronting each of the squares. Oliver had warned Luthien that they would do this, calling the formations "testudos," but no words could have prepared Luthien for the splendor of this sight. One testudo was directly north of the city, a second northwest, and the third almost directly west, a three-pronged attack that would pressure the two main outer walls. At least they weren't surrounded, Luthien thought, but of course, Caer MacDonald could not easily be surrounded, since its southern and eastern sections flowed into the towering mountains, virtually impassable at this time of year.

Any relief that Luthien might have realized with that thought was lost as the Avon march progressed. The cyclopians came like a storm cloud, slowly, deliberately. Above the din of the march and the excitement along the wall, Luthien heard the cyclopian drummers striking a rhythmic, monotonous beat.

A heartbeat, continuous, inevitable.

A ball of flaming pitch hit the field in front of the brutes—some of those in the front rank were splattered. But their shields deflected the missiles and they never slowed.

A lump of panic welled in Luthien's throat, a sudden urge to run away, out of Caer MacDonald's back gate and into the mountains. He hadn't foreseen that it would be like this, so controlled and determined. He had expected the cyclopian leader to make some announcement, expected some horns to blow, followed by a roaring charge.

This was too calculated, too confident. The Praetorian Guard held tight ranks; their line hardly fluttered as the next catapult shot hit in their midst. A few were killed or wounded—some had to have been—but the mass didn't reveal any losses in the least, just rolled on to the cadence, continuous, inevitable. To Luthien, so, too, seemed the impending fall of Caer MacDonald.

Luthien glanced all around. All was suddenly quiet on his side of the wall, and he realized that the men and women around him were entertaining similar fears. A voice in Luthien's head told him that it was time for him to be the leader, the true leader. The rebels had hit a critical moment before the battle had even been joined.

Luthien climbed to the top of the battlement and drew *Blind-Striker* from its scabbard. "Caer MacDonald!" he cried. "Eriador free!"

Those waiting behind the outer wall glanced back, some confused, but some, like Siobhan, knew and appreciated what the young Bedwyr was up to.

Luthien ran along the wall to the gatehouse on the other side of Caer MacDonald's huge front gate. He continued his cry, and it became a chant, taken up by every soldier manning the city wall.

Those on the outer wall, with the enemy fast closing into range, did not cry out, but surely they were heartened by the cheering behind them. Up came the lines of bows, arrows fitted and ready.

The cyclopian army continued its slow and steady march. Fifty feet away. Forty.

Still Siobhan and her companions held their bows bent, seeing little to shoot at along the barricade of metal shields. Another catapult lob landed in the midst of the army, far back among the ranks, and then a ballista bolt, driving down from one of the Ministry's towers, slammed into the front line, and no shield could hold it back. It buckled the blocking metal in half and blasted through, skewering one cyclopian, and the force of the hit knocked those brutes flanking him from their feet, causing a temporary break in the line.

The archers were quick to let fly and the stinging arrows penetrated the mass, taking their toll.

Barely twenty feet away, the cyclopian square at the northwest bend in the outer wall broke ranks and charged, screaming wildly. The bow strings hummed; pikemen jabbed down from their higher perches, trying to keep the brutes from the eight-foot barrier.

Siobhan, farther to the north with her elves, called for a volley before the square facing them even broke ranks. It was a calculated gamble, and one that paid off, for at close range the powerful elfish longbows drove arrows right through the blocking shields, and the elves were quick enough to fit their next arrows so that they fired again almost immediately.

A third and fourth volley followed before the cyclopians could finish closing the twenty feet, but as devastating as the bow fire was, it hardly dented the great mass, five thousand Praetorian Guards to this square alone. The brutes did not panic, did not weep for their fallen. They swarmed the wall and clambered up it, often climbing over the backs of their own dead.

Siobhan's elves fought brilliantly—so did the folk, mostly humans, holding the northwestern corner and the western expanse—but their line was thin, far too thin, and in a matter of moments, the wall was breached in several places.

From the inner wall came three short blasts of a horn, and all on the outer wall who were able broke ranks and fled back for the city gate.

To their credit, those dwarfs ready with the axes waited until the very last moment, gave everyone fighting along the outer wall every possible second to get away. But then they could wait no more; cyclopians were inside the line and bearing down on them and if they did not put their axes to quick work on the ropes, they would find themselves engaged in close combat instead.

One by one, the ropes snapped, each with a huge popping sound, and the stones of the outer wall groaned.

Luthien held his breath; the wall seemed to hang in place for a long, long while, perhaps held up by the sheer bulk of the force on the other side. Finally, it tumbled, breaking from the west around to the north like a great wave upon a beach.

In truth, not too many cyclopians were killed by the falling wall. It didn't collapse, but rather fell like a tree, and many of the brutes were able to scramble back out of harm's way. But their formation was broken by the ensuing confusion, and when Luthien's line along the inner wall loosed their first barrage of arrows, more hit cyclopian flesh than blocking shields.

Luthien didn't witness that devastating barrage. He and fifty others were down in the courtyard behind the main gates, mounted on the finest steeds that could be found within the city. Caer MacDonald's inner doors were swung wide, and ropes and ladders were dropped over the wall to aid in the flight of those allies coming in from the outer wall. Archers picked their shots carefully, taking down the leading cyclopians so that as few as possible of the defenders would be caught in combat outside the city.

Out from the gates came the cavalry, led by Luthien, crimson cape and reddish hair flying wild behind him, *Blind-Striker* held high to the gray morning sky.

Beyond the rubble of the outer wall, Belsen'Krieg and his undercommanders regrouped quickly and sent on a new and furious charge. Luthien and his mounted allies prepared to meet it and slow it, so that those running from the outer wall could get to safety. The young Bedwyr regrouped the cavalry around him, set the line for the charge. The bulk of the cyclopians were sixty feet away, twenty feet inside the rubble of the outer wall.

Luthien's eyes widened in amazement as the ground erupted right at the feet of the enemy force, as Shuglin and his five hundred dwarfs crawled up from their concealment, hacking and chopping their hated, one-eyed enemies with abandon.

Another volley of arrows whipped down from the wall behind Luthien; the ballista atop the Ministry blasted a huge hole in one rank of the cyclopian line.

"Eriador free!" Luthien bellowed, and out he charged, fifty horsemen alongside him, running headlong into the writhing black-and-silver mass.

The most horrible and confusing minutes of Luthien Bedwyr's young life ensued, amidst a tangle of bodies, the whir of arrows, the screams of the dying. Every way he turned, Luthien found another cyclopian to slash; his horse was torn out from under him and he was caught by a dwarf whom he never got the chance to thank, for they were soon separated by a throng of slashing enemies.

Luthien got hit, several times, but he hardly noticed. He drove *Blind-Striker* halfway through one cyclopian, then yanked it free and slashed across, gouging the bulbous eye of another. The first one he had hit, though, was not quite dead, too enraged and confused and horrified all at once to lie down and die.

Luthien felt the warmth of his own blood rolling down the side of his leg. He spun back and moved to finish the grievously wounded brute, but never got the chance as another wave rolled in between them, pushing them far apart. Always before, even in the scrambles in and around the Ministry, Luthien's battles had been personal, had been face-to-face with an opponent, or side by side with a friend, until one could move along to the next fight. Not this time, though. Half the cyclopians Luthien engaged were already carrying wounds from previous encounters; most of the friends he spotted were carried away by the sheer press of that murderous frenzy before he could even acknowledge them.

With the archers who had fled the outer wall bolstering the line, the fire from the inner wall was devastating. And with Luthien's cavalry and the dwarfs scrambling amid the cyclopian ranks, the brutes could not form up into any defensive shell.

The momentum of the ambushing groups had played out, however, and though the cyclopian line had bent, it had not broken. The confusing battle turned into a frenzied retreat for Luthien's group and the dwarfs, what few could manage to get away from the roiling mass of Praetorian Guards.

They came out in bunches mostly, every one trailing blood, from weapon and from body, and not a single dwarf or rider would have made it back to the city had not the archers on the wall covered their retreat.

Luthien thought his life was surely at its end. He killed one cyclopian, but his sword got hooked on the creature's collarbone. Before he could extract the weapon and turn to defend himself, he got swatted on the ribs by a heavy club. Breathless and dizzy, the young Bedwyr spun and tumbled.

The next thing he knew, he was half-running, half-carried from the throng, heading for the wall. He heard the growls of cyclopians on his heels, heard the buzz of arrows above his head, but he was distant from it somehow.

Then he was dragged up a ladder, caught from above by several hands, and hauled over the wall. He looked back as he tumbled, and the last thing he saw before his consciousness left him was the face and blue-black beard of Shuglin as the dwarf, his dear friend, came over the wall behind him.

"You are needed up on the wall," came a call in Luthien's head, a distant plea, but a voice that he recognized. He opened bleary eyes to see Siobhan bending over him.

"Can you rise?" she asked.

Luthien didn't seem to understand, but he didn't resist as Siobhan lifted his head from the blanket and took up his arm.

"The wall?" Luthien asked, sitting up and shaking the daze from his mind. All the memories of earlier that morning, the horror of the pitched battle, the blood and the screams, flooded back to him then, like the images of a nightmare not yet forgotten in the light of dawn.

"We held," Siobhan informed him, prodding him on, forcing him to his feet. She took hold of him as he stood, steadying him. "We scattered them and stung them. Their dead litter the field."

Luthien liked the words, but there was something in Siobhan's words, an edge of anxiety, that told him she was trying to convince herself more than him. He wasn't surprised when she continued.

"But they have re-formed their lines and are advancing," the half-elf explained. "Your wounds are not so bad, and your presence is needed at the wall." Even as she spoke, she was dragging him along, and Luthien felt like an ornament, a figurehead, symbol of the revolution. At that moment, he didn't doubt that if he had died, Siobhan wouldn't tell anybody; she'd just prop him up against the wall, tie *Blind-Striker* to his upraised hand, and shove a dwarf under his cape to call out glorious cheers.

When Luthien got up to the wall, though, he began to appreciate the cold edge of Siobhan's actions. The field before Caer MacDonald, all the way to the rubble of the outer wall, was covered in bodies and red-soaked with blood, huge puddles of blood that couldn't find its way into the frozen ground. Every so often, someone from the wall would hurl something down to the field and the air would throb with beating wings as countless carrion birds lifted off into the gray sky—a sky that had grown darker as the day progressed.

It was such a surreal, unbelievable scene of carnage that Luthien could hardly sort it out. Most of the dead were cyclopians, all silver and black and red with blood, but among them were the corpses of many men and women, a few elves, and many, many of Shuglin's bearded folk.

That's what Luthien saw most of all: the dead dwarfs. The brave dwarfs who had sprung up in the midst of the marching army, causing chaos and destruction, though they knew they would pay dearly for their actions. It seemed to the young Bedwyr as if all of them were out there broken and torn, sacrificed not to save Caer MacDonald but only to ward off the first cyclopian charge.

His face ashen, breathing hard, Luthien looked at Siobhan. "How many?" he asked.

"More than three hundred," she replied grimly. "Two hundred of them dwarfs." Siobhan stood straighter suddenly, squared her shoulders and her delicate jaw. "But five times that number of cyclopians lay dead," she estimated, and it seemed to Luthien that there were at least that many bodies covering the field.

Luthien looked away, back to the field, then beyond the field and the rubble, to the swarming black-and-silver mass, the Avon army coming on once more. He took note of a lighter patch of gray in the sky and figured that it was not yet noon, yet here they came again, to repeat the scene of carnage, to cover the dead with a second layer.

"All in one morning," the young man whispered.

Luthien examined his line. There would be no falling outer wall this time, no ambush by Shuglin's people. This time, the cyclopians would march right to the inner wall, and if they overcame its defenders, if they got into the city, Caer MacDonald would be lost.

Would be lost, and the rebellion would be at its end, and Eriador would not be free. Luthien did not consider the personal implications of it all, did not even think that he might die in the next hours, or wonder about the consequences to himself if he did not die and the city was lost. Now, up on this wall, the situation was larger than that; there was too much more at stake.

Strength flowed through Luthien's battered limbs; he hoisted his sword high into the air, commanding the attention of all those nearby.

"Eriador free!" came the cheer. "Caer MacDonald!"

Next to Luthien, Siobhan nodded approvingly. She half-expected the young Bedwyr to pass out from his wounds and knew that he would find this next battle difficult indeed. But he had accomplished what she needed of him, and if he was among the dead after this attack, she would cultivate the legend; she would have every remaining soldier defending Caer MacDonald add the name of Luthien Bedwyr to the cheer.

Those thoughts were for another time, the half-elf told herself. The catapults fired, the ballistae twanged, and the squared cyclopian groups—two now, not three as in the first attack—plodded on. Upon the wall, a thousand bows bent back and fired, and then again, and again, and again, a thick hail of arrows whistling and thumping against shields, occasionally slipping through a crack in the cyclopian defensive formation.

Still they came on, the black-and-silver, undeniable flood. They crossed the rubble of the outer wall, stepped over or on top of the dead. An incessant popping noise, the rapid bursts of arrows slamming against metal, became one long drone, mixing with the hum of bowstrings, the very air vibrating.

The Praetorian Guard broke ranks less than fifty feet from the wall. Ladders appeared; dozens twirled ropes with heavy grapnels as they charged the wall. One large group supported a felled tree between their lines and charged the main gates.

Arrow volleys from the gatehouses decimated the group holding the battering ram, but many other cyclopians were nearby to take up the tree.

Now the ring of swords, steel on steel, was heard up and down the wall. Cries of rage mingled with cries of agony, snarls and wails, hoots of victory that became horrifying, agonizing shrieks a moment later as the next opponent struck hard.

At first, cyclopians died by the score, ten to one over the defenders. But as more grapnels came sailing over the wall, as more and more Praetorian Guards gained footing, stretching the line of the defenders, the ratio began to shift.

Soon it became five to one, then two to one.

Luthien seemed to be everywhere, running along the battlements, striking hard and fast before racing on to the next fight, chopping a taut cyclopian climbing rope on his way. He lost track of his kills and wasn't really certain how many brutes he actually finished anyway. He felt that the defenders would hold, though the price would be heavy indeed.

An explosion, a shudder along the wall near to the gatehouses, nearly knocked the young Bedwyr from his feet and did indeed tumble a couple of men and cyclopians nearby.

A second followed, then a third, accompanied by the sound of hammers working furiously.

"The door!" someone shouted, and Luthien understood. He glanced over the wall and saw the mass congregating, saw the end of the dropped tree, its mission completed.

Down from the wall leaped Luthien, into the courtyard, into the tangle. He believed that he was rushing to his death, but couldn't stop himself. The cyclopians were in the courtyard, pouring through the broken gates. This was where Caer MacDonald would fall or hold, and this was where Luthien Bedwyr had to be.

Soon, as it had been out in the courtyard for the first fight, there were no defined lines, just a mass of soldiers, killing and dying. Luthien tripped over one dying man, and the stumble saved his life, for as he lurched low, a cyclopian sword, still dripping with blood of the victim Luthien had tripped across, whipped high, just above the young Bedwyr's bent back. Luthien realized that if he stopped, he would be killed before he could turn and face this adversary, so he threw his weight ahead, plowing into another group.

Right into the midst of three cyclopians.

Up on the wall, Siobhan and her elves continued sending a stream of arrows into the mass outside of Caer MacDonald's wall, while the larger and stronger humans battled with those brutes stubbornly scrambling up the ropes and ladders.

"Find their leaders!" the half-elf commanded, and many of her archers were already doing just that. They scanned the mob, seeking out any one-eye giving orders, and whenever an elf spotted one, he called all those archers near to him to bear a concentrated barrage.

One by one, Belsen'Krieg's undercommanders went tumbling to the dirt.

*   *   *

Luthien went down to his knees in a spin, completing a semicircle and whipping his sword across, straight out, driving two of the cyclopians back. The young man brought his lead foot under him, coming about and up, batting the third brute's blade high and lunging forward, gutting the one-eye.

Luthien rushed forward, tearing free *Blind-Striker* as he passed, then cutting right around, using the falling brute as a shield from the other two, who were close on his heels. He came out behind the tumbling cyclopian, slashing and charging.

One of the cyclopians wielded a trident, the other a sword, and both weapons were knocked aside in that furious charge. The cyclopian with the trident jumped back, put one hand over the butt end of the weapon, and launched it straight for Luthien's head.

Luthien, quick as a cat, dropped down and parried, sword coming high and deflecting the angle of the deadly missile. He didn't let the trident fly past him, though, but caught it halfway along its shaft in his free hand as the sword defeated its momentum, then reversed its angle, bringing its butt to the ground just in front of him and angling it out to the side, setting it against the charge of the sword-wielder.

The cyclopian skidded to a stop, but got poked in the shoulder.

Luthien wasn't paying attention. He left the trident the moment it was set, rushing out the other way, toward the brute that had hurled the weapon. The cyclopian scrambled, trying to pull a short sword from its belt. It got the weapon out, but too late, while Luthien's sword slammed hard against its hilt, knocking it from the one-eye's grasp.

Straight up went *Blind-Striker*, cutting like a knife, slicing the brute's face from chin to forehead. The sword spun around and down in a diagonal swipe, tearing at the brute's collarbone, across its lower throat and down and under its right breast. Luthien managed yet another stab as the brute fell away, again in the belly.

The young Bedwyr whirled about, instinctively slashing his sword before him, just in time to pick off the sword of the remaining brute. Back came *Blind-Striker*, parrying the weapon again, and then a third time, and with each pass, Luthien gained ground, forced his opponent to backpedal. Pure rage drove the young man; this was his homeland; his Eriador. He stabbed and slashed, dropped and cut at the brute down low, then leaped up and poked at the cyclopian's eye.

"How many can you block?" he screamed into the brute's face, pushing it back, ever back, up on its heels until it stumbled.

A club knocked free from a nearby melee hit Luthien on the leg and he, too, stumbled, and the cyclopian tried to reverse the momentum, tried to go on the offensive. It jabbed with its short sword, but wasn't able to throw its weight into the thrust. Luthien fell back, then came forward in a rush, beyond the extended weapon, *Blind-Striker* driving straight into the brute's heart.

It had all happened in the span of a few moments; three kills before the blood had even dripped from the blade. Luthien tore his sword free and jumped about, expecting to be overwhelmed in the crush. He was surprised, for suddenly there seemed to be many fewer cyclopians in the courtyard. He looked at the doors and saw that Shuglin's tough three hundred had fought in a line to seal the courtyard, and now many dwarfs had their shoulders to the battered doors, holding them fast. Still, by Luthien's estimation, there should have been more cyclopians, more frenzied fighting, in the courtyard.

Luthien sprinted to a stack of crates piled nearby and leaped atop it, and from the better vantage point, he understood the cyclopian tactics. Instead of fighting a pitched battle just inside the gates, many of the one-eyes had broken away and were running and scattering along Caer MacDonald's streets.

A cry from the wall above Luthien declared that the cyclopians outside were in retreat. It was repeated all along the defensive line, accompanied by rousing cheers. With the slaughter becoming more and more one-sided inside the gates, the second assault, like the first, had been repelled.

Luthien didn't feel much like cheering. "Clever," he whispered, a private applause for his adversary, no doubt the huge and ugly cyclopian he had seen at Felling Run.

Siobhan was beside him a moment later, her shoulder wet with fresh blood. "They have broken away," the half-elf reported.

"And many have slipped into the city," Luthien replied grimly.

"We will hunt them down," Siobhan promised, a vow Luthien did not doubt. But Luthien knew, and Siobhan did, too, that hunting the brutes would be an expensive proposition. The fact that they would have to take the effort to search out these cyclopians was exactly the point of the maneuver, for it would take as many as ten defenders to search out each creature that had slipped into the many alleyways of Caer MacDonald.

Somewhere far away from the wall came the cry of "Fire!" and a plume of black smoke began a slow and steady ascent over the interior of the city. The cyclopians were already at work.

Luthien looked to the wall and thought again of his clever adversary, a tactician far better than he would expect from the crude one-eyed race.

There were, perhaps, twenty thousand enemies facing each other, another few thousand already lying dead, but suddenly it all seemed to be a personal struggle to Luthien, as it had out by Felling Run. The ugly cyclopian against him.

And if he lost, then all of Caer MacDonald would pay the dear price.

CHAPTER 14

TWILIGHT

$\mathcal{J}$T WILL SNOW TONIGHT," Siobhan remarked to Luthien and the others manning the wall around them. In the city behind them, several fires raged. Many cyclopians had been hunted down during the course of that afternoon, but others were still out there, prowling the shadows.

"He'll not wait," Luthien assured her.

The half-elf looked at the young man. The way he had spoken the words, and his referral to the enemy leader, and not to the Avon army, gave her insight into what the young Bedwyr might be thinking.

Siobhan looked over her shoulder, back toward the city, and saw another group of warriors, their faces covered in soot, emerging from one lane, heading for the wall. Below her, Shuglin's dwarfs worked hard at reinforcing the gate, but it had never been designed as a ward against so large a force. Up to now, battles for the city had usually been relatively small-scale, mostly against rogue cyclopian tribes. The main doors, though large, were not even bolstered by a portcullis, and though the plans had been drawn up to put one in place, the other defensive preparations, such as rigging the outer wall for collapse, had taken precedence.

"Replace them on the wall," Luthien instructed another man near to him, referring to the group coming out of the city. "And send a like number back into the city to hunt and join with the children and the elderly in battling the fires." The man, his face grim, nodded and left.

"March on," Luthien whispered into the biting wind as he looked back out over the fields, and Siobhan knew that he was calling to his enemy. This was a brutal battle, and only growing worse. All the able-bodied men and women had been fighting at the walls, but now even the children and the elderly, even those fighters who had been sorely wounded, had been forced to join in to fight cyclopians, or to fight flames. "Let us be with it."

"You are so certain that the one-eyes will come," Siobhan stated.

"The storm will be a big one," Luthien replied. "He knows. Their march to the city will be more difficult in the morning, if they can even come through the storm. Uphill and through blowing snow." Luthien shook his head. "No," he assured those around him. "Our enemy will not wait. The time to strike is now, with the sun still in the sky and the fires burning behind us, with our position weakened at the wall and the doors still hanging loose from the last assault."

"The dwarfs work well," one other man remarked, needing to report on some positive news.

Luthien didn't argue the point.

"They will come on," Siobhan agreed. "But can we hold?"

Luthien looked at her for just a moment, then glanced all around, at the faces of those nearby who had suddenly become quite interested in the conversation. "We will hold," Luthien said determinedly, teeth clenched. "We will drive them from our gates once more, kill them in the field, and then let the storm stop them and freeze what few are left alive. Eriador free!"

An impromptu cheer erupted from that section of the wall. Siobhan didn't join in. She stared long and hard at Luthien, though he, looking over the fields, didn't seem to notice her. She knew the truth of his little speech, knew that any apparent conviction in his words was for the sake of the others nearby. Luthien was no fool. Three, four, maybe even five thousand cyclopians were dead or wounded too badly to continue to fight, but between the defenders' dead and those who were within the city's interior, hunting cyclopians and battling flames, the force along the wall was at least as badly depleted, and every defender lost, every lost archer, who might fire a dozen arrows before the brutes even got near to the wall, was worth several cyclopians.

They had almost lost the wall in the last attack, and the odds then had been much more in their favor, the defenses more solid.

Luthien directed a sharp glance at the half-elf, as though he had some-how heard her silent reasoning. "Send the word throughout the city," he instructed. "Get everyone who is not at the wall or otherwise engaged, within the walls of the merchant section. Let most go into the Ministry."

Siobhan bit her lip. She was cold from loss of blood and the freezing wind, and from the confirmation that Luthien shared her doubts. These were plans of retreat, a contingency based on his belief that the outer wall, and thus, the outer city, would be lost before the nightfall.

"And give them all weapons," Luthien added as the half-elf started away. "Even the children. Even the very old."

Siobhan did not look back because she did not want Luthien to see her wince. The gravity of the potential defeat weighed heavily on her, as it did on Luthien. After the fighting, the victorious cyclopians would not show much mercy.

They were all seasoned to this type of battle now, after only a single day, and so there was no panic along the wall when the black-and-silver mass appeared again, in two huge squares, marching slowly toward them.

The heartbeat of the drums; the thunder of the footsteps. An occasional bow twanged, but at this distance, even arrows from the great elvish longbows had no chance of penetrating the blocking shield wall. Luthien wanted to pass the word along the line to hold all shots. The cyclopians would get closer, after all, much closer.

Luthien kept quiet, though, realizing that his desire to scold his own was wrought of his ultimate frustration and fear, and understanding that those same emotions guided the defenders who did fire their bows. The archers might not be doing any real damage to the cyclopian line, but they were bolstering their own courage.

It occurred to Luthien that courage and stupidity might not be so far apart.

The young Bedwyr shook that nonsense from his mind and from his heart. This was Caer MacDonald, his city, his Eriador, and there was nothing stupid about dying here for this concept called freedom, which Luthien had never truly known in the short two decades of his life.

The cyclopians reached the rubble of the outer wall and came over it, like an indomitable wave of black-and-silver death. Now the bows sang out, one after another, many at a time, and the catapults and ballistae fired off as fast as the crews manning them could reload baskets of stones or heavy spears. But how many could they kill? Luthien had to wonder as he, too, let fly with his bow. A hundred? Five hundred? Even if that were the case, the cyclopians could spare the losses. The air about Luthien hummed with the song of quivering bowstrings, but the cyclopian ranks did not falter. As the defenders on the wall had become quickly seasoned to the type of battle on this field, so had the Praetorian Guard, and the defenders of Caer MacDonald had nothing new or unexpected to throw at them.

The squares dissolved into a rushing mob. Out came the grapnels and hundreds of ropes, out came the ladders, dozens and dozens of stripped trees with branches pegged or tied on as cross-steps, for the cyclopians had not been idle during the hours of midday. Caer MacDonald's wall was not high enough to delay the charge; the defenders did not have the time to slaughter enough of the brutes, or cut enough of the ropes, or knock away enough of the ladders.

Luthien wondered if he should call the retreat immediately, run back to the inner wall by the Ministry with his soldiers, surrender the outer section of the city. In the few moments that he took to make up his mind, the decision was made for him. The battle was joined in full.

Shuglin's battered dwarfs, as solid a force as could be found, held the courtyard, ready for another breach along the main gates. Looking out from the gatehouse, Luthien realized that the dwarfs would not be enough. A swarm of Praetorian Guards battered at the barricaded doors. A line of cavalry waited behind them, the heavy ponypigs and the largest and strongest of the cyclopians. Luthien spotted the ugly general among those ranks. He wanted to call for a concentrated volley to that spot, but in looking around, he understood that it was too late; few on the wall still held their bows, and most of those who did were swinging the weapons like clubs, battering at the cyclopians as the brutes climbed up in stubborn, unending lines.

Luthien sprinted along the wall. He cut one rope, then a second, then heard a shout below and decided that the best place for him would be among the dwarfs. The breaches along the wall were dangerous, of course, but if the courtyard was lost, then so, too, would be the bulk of the city.

As he came down among Shuglin's throng, Luthien saw that the fighting had already begun at the gate. One of the doors was gone, buried under the weight of the press, and in the bottleneck at the gates, the dwarven and cyclopian dead began to pile up.

Luthien came across Shuglin and grabbed his friend by the shoulder, a farewell salute.

"We'll not hold them this time," the dwarf admitted, and Luthien could only nod as he had no words to reply to the grim, and apparently accurate, argument.

The cyclopians began to gain ground at the gate, the press of one-eyes forcing the dwarfs back. And each step back widened the area of battle, allowed room for more cyclopians to pour into the fight.

"Eriador free," Luthien said to Shuglin, and the two exchanged smiles, and together they rushed in to die.

* * *

Tears rimmed Siobhan's green eyes as she darted from position to position atop the wall, bolstering the defenses wherever a cyclopian had gained a foothold. Her sword carried dozens of nicks, from chopping through ropes and banging against the stone of the walltop, but the imperfections were hardly noticeable beneath the thick layer of blood and gore that stained the blade.

She ran on toward yet another break in the line, but skidded to a stop, nearly tumbling in a bloody slick, as she noticed a silver helmet coming up over the wall. Her sword crashed down, cleaving the helm, cleaving the cyclopian's skull.

Siobhan allowed herself a moment to catch her breath and survey the wall. Cyclopians were coming over in large numbers; soon they would be a virtual waterfall of bodies, leaping down into the city, Caer MacDonald, wiping out whatever gains the rebellion had made. Montfort's flag would fly again, it seemed, along with the pennant of Greensparrow, and under them, Siobhan's people, the Fairborn elves, would know slavery once more.

The half-elf shook her head and screamed at the top of her lungs. She would not play whore again for some merchant in Greensparrow's favor. No, she would die here, this day, and would kill as many Praetorian Guards as she could, in the hope—and it was fast becoming a fleeting hope—that her efforts would not be in vain, that those who came after her would be better off for her sacrifice.

Another silver helm appeared above the battlement; another cyclopian fell dead to the field below.

Luthien was fighting now, beside Shuglin, yet they were nowhere near the broken gate. The dwarven ranks could not hold tight enough to stem the cyclopian flow. It was like grabbing fine sand, too much fine sand to fit into your hand. And still the brutes were coming in an endless, incessant wave.

Luthien wondered when the enemy cavalry would burst through. He hoped that he would get a chance, just one chance, at the ugly cyclopian leader. He hoped that he might at least win a personal victory, though the war was surely lost.

Blind-Striker cut a circular parry, narrowly deflecting a cyclopian spear. Luthien realized the price of his distraction, feared for an instant that his fantasizing about the enemy leader had put him in a perilous position indeed, up on his heels with no room to retreat!

His one-eyed opponent noted the opening, too, and came on fiercely.

But suddenly the cyclopian lurched and fell away, and standing in its place was Shuglin, who offered a wink to his human friend.

"To the door?" the dwarf asked through the tangle of his blue-black beard.

"Is there any other place for us to be?" Luthien answered wistfully, and together they turned, looking for an opening that would lead them to the front lines of the fight.

They stopped suddenly as a sharp hissing sound erupted from the stone above the broken doors. Green sparks and green fire sputtered about the structure, and the fighting stopped as dwarfs, cyclopians, and men turned to watch.

There came a sparkling burst of bright fire, a puff of greenish-gray smoke, and then, as abruptly as it had appeared, it was extinguished, and where it had been, instead of smooth, unremarkable stone, loomed a portcullis—a huge portcullis!

"Where in the name of Bruce MacDonald . . ." Shuglin started to cry out, among the astonished cries of everyone else who witnessed the remarkable spectacle, particularly those unfortunate cyclopians directly below the massive, spiked creation.

Down came the portcullis, crushing the one-eyes below it, blocking the advance of those beyond the gate and preventing the retreat of the brutes inside.

The dwarfs didn't wait for an explanation, but fell into a battle frenzy, hoping to clear the courtyard quickly that they might bolster the defense of the wall.

Luthien spent a few moments marveling at the portcullis. He knew it was a creation of magic—he was one of the few in the battle who had ever personally witnessed such a feat before—but he wondered if someone in the fight had caused it, or if it was some unknown magic of Caer MacDonald, some magical ward built into the stones of the city to come forth when the rightful defenders were in dire need.

A horn from far across the field and cheers from those defenders on the wall who had a moment to consider the scene answered Luthien's questions. He broke free of the tangle in the courtyard, scrambled up to the parapet, and witnessed the charge of allies.

Luthien's gaze focused immediately on two mounts, a shining white stallion and an ugly yellow pony, and though they and their riders were but specks on the distant field, Luthien knew then that Oliver and Katerin had come.

Indeed they had, along with a force that had swelled to almost two thousand, the militia of Port Charley's ranks more than doubled by bands of rebels joining them along their march.

Arrows rained on the confused one-eyes outside of the wall. Here and there, bursts of flame erupted above the cyclopian heads, releasing shards of sharpened steel to drop among the brutes, stinging and blinding them.

Luthien knew magic when he saw it, and in considering the allies approaching, he knew who else had come to the call of Caer MacDonald. "Brind'Amour," he whispered, his voice filled with gratitude and sudden hope.

Siobhan was beside him then, wrapping him in a tight hug and kissing him on the cheek. Luthien wrapped one strong arm about her and did a complete pivot, a quick turn of pure joy.

"Katerin has come!" Siobhan cried. "And Oliver! And they've brought some friends!"

The moment of elation for the pair, and for all the other defenders, was quickly washed away by the reality of the continuing fight. Luthien surveyed the scene, trying to find some new plans. Even though the defenders were still outnumbered, he entertained the thought of destroying the entire cyclopian army on the field, there and then. If the confusion among the one-eyes could hold, if there was any desertion among their ranks . . .

But these were Praetorian Guards, and Luthien had not overestimated the cunning of their leader. Belsen'Krieg, too, paused and considered the battle, and then he turned his forces, all of them who were not trapped inside the city.

"No!" Luthien breathed, watching the thousands of black-and-silver clad Praetorian Guard forming into a new line as they ran straight toward the approaching reinforcements. Even from this distance, he could estimate the numbers of his allies, and he put them at no more than two thousand, less than one-fourth the number of enemies that would soon overwhelm them.

The young Bedwyr called for archers to fire into the ranks of the departing brutes; he wanted to organize a force that could rush out of the city to the aid of Katerin and Oliver. But the battle along the wall and in the courtyard was not yet won, and Luthien could only watch.

"Run," he whispered repeatedly, and his heart lifted a bit when the approaching force turned about in an organized retreat.

The Avon army gave chase, but Oliver and his companions had not been caught off guard by the cyclopians' turn. They had expected to be chased from the field, and were more than happy to oblige, running all the way back to Felling Run and across the river on makeshift bridges they had left behind, into defensible positions on the other bank.

Then the bridges were pulled down, and the cyclopians came upon a natural barrier they could not easily cross, especially with hundreds of archers peppering their ranks once more.

Frustration boiled in Belsen'Krieg, but he was no fool. He had lost the day, and probably near to two thousand soldiers, but now he was confident that the rebels had played out their last trick. Even with these unexpected reinforcements, the cyclopian leader did not fear ultimate defeat.

Tomorrow would be another day of war.

And so the cyclopian force moved north. The sun settled on the western horizon, somehow finding an opening among the thickening clouds to peek through and shine upon the walls of the city that was still known as Caer MacDonald.

At least for one more day.

CHAPTER 15

CHESS GAME

THE FIGHTING WITHIN THE CITY did not end at twilight. The wall and courtyard were cleared soon enough, but many cyclopians had slipped into the shadows of Caer MacDonald; several fights broke out in alleyways, and several buildings went up in flames.

Soon after sunset, too, the storm that Siobhan had predicted broke in full. It began as heavy sleet, drumming on the roofs of the houses within the city, drenching the fires of the encampments from Avon and Port Charley. As the night deepened and the temperature dipped, the sleet became a thick, wet snow.

Luthien watched it from the gatehouse, and later from the roof of the Dwelf. It seemed to him as if God, too, was sickened by the sight of the carnage, and so He was whitewashing the grisly scene. It would take more than snow, however deep it lay, to erase that image from Luthien Bedwyr's mind.

"Luthien?" came a call from the street below—Shuglin's throaty voice.

Luthien cautiously picked his way across the slippery roof and peered down at the dwarf.

"Emissary from Oliver's camp," Shuglin explained, pointing to the tavern door.

Luthien nodded and headed for the rain gutter that would allow him to climb down to the street. He had expected that their allies would send an emissary; he had wondered if perhaps the whole force might come into the city.

Apparently that was not the case, for the night grew long and the fires of the encampment still burned far in the west, beyond Felling Run. The emissary would explain the intentions of the force to him so that he could coordinate the movements of Caer MacDonald's defenses. Luthien found that his heart was racing as he slipped down the rain gutter, lighting gently on the street, which was already two inches deep with snow.

Perhaps it was Katerin who had come in, Luthien hoped. He hadn't realized until this very moment how badly he wanted to see the fiery, red-haired woman of Hale.

When he rushed into the Dwelf, he found that the emissary wasn't Katerin, or Oliver, or even Brind'Amour. It was a young woman, practically a girl, by the name of Jeanna D'elfinbrock, one of Port Charley's fisherfolk. Her light eyes sparkled when she looked upon Luthien, this legend known as the Crimson Shadow, and Luthien found himself embarrassed.

The meeting was quick and to the point—it had to be, for Jeanna had to get back to the encampment long before dawn, dodging cyclopian patrols all the way. Oliver deBurrows had wanted to bring Port Charley's force in, the young woman reported, but they could not safely cross Felling Run. The cyclopians were not so far to the north, and they were alert and would not allow such a move.

Luthien wasn't surprised. Many of Caer MacDonald's defenders were dead or wounded too badly to man the walls. If the two thousand or so reinforcements were allowed inside the city, the holes in the city's defenses would be plugged, and the cyclopians would have to resume their assault practically from the same place they had begun it the previous day.

"Our deepest thanks to you and all your force," Luthien said to Jeanna, and now it was her turn to blush. "Tell your leaders that their actions here will not be in vain, that Caer MacDonald will not fall. Tell Oliver, from me personally, that I know he will show up where most we need him. And tell Katerin O'Hale to take care of my horse!" Luthien couldn't help a sidelong glance at Siobhan as he spoke of Katerin, but the half-elf did not seem bothered in the least.

With that, Jeanna D'elfinbrock left the Dwelf and the city, picking her careful way across the snowy fields back through the raging storm the few miles to the Port Charley encampment.

Later that night, Luthien and Siobhan lay in bed, discussing the day past and the day yet to come. The wind had kicked up, shaking the small apartment in Tiny Alcove, humming down the chimney against the rising heat so that the air in the small room had a smoky taste.

Siobhan snuggled close to Luthien, propped herself up on one elbow, and considered the concentration on the young man's fair face. He lay flat on his back, staring up at the dark. But he was looking somewhere else, the perceptive half-elf knew.

"They are fine," Siobhan whispered. "They have campfires blazing and know how to shelter themselves from the weather. Besides, they have a wizard among them, and from what you've told me of Brind'Amour, he'll have a trick or two to defeat the storm."

Luthien didn't doubt that, and it was a comforting thought. "We could have swung them to the south and brought them into the city along the foothills," the young man reasoned.

"We did not even know the extent and location of their camp until well after sunset," Siobhan replied.

"It would only have taken a couple of hours," Luthien was quick to answer. "Even in the storm. Most of the lower trails are sheltered, and there was little snow on them to begin with." He breathed a deep, resigned sigh. "We could have gotten them in."

Siobhan didn't doubt what he was saying, but the last thing she wanted now for Luthien was added guilt. "Oliver knows the area as well as you," she reminded Luthien. "If the folk of Port Charley wanted to get into Caer MacDonald, they would have."

Luthien wasn't so certain of that, but the argument was moot now, for it was well past midnight and he couldn't do anything about the camp's location.

"Shuglin informs me that he and his kin have some new traps ready for the cyclopians," the half-elf said, trying to shift the subject to a more positive note. "When our enemies come on again, they'll find the wall harder to breach, and if they're caught out in the open for any length of time, Oliver and his force will squeeze them from behind."

"Oliver hasn't enough soldiers to do that."

Siobhan shook her head and chuckled. "Our allies will strike from a distance!" she insisted. "Hit with their bows at the back of the cyclopians, and run off across the fields."

Luthien wasn't so certain, but again he did not wish to press the argument. He continued to stare up at the ceiling, at the flickering shadows cast by the wind-dancing flames of the hearth. Soon he felt the rhythmic breathing of the sleeping Siobhan beside him, and then he, too, drifted off to sleep.

He dreamed of his adversary, the huge and ugly cyclopian. All the tactics of the day filtered through his thoughts, all the moves the brute had executed: the first powerful probe at the city; the second assault, the feint, where many cyclopian arsonists slipped in; and the tactic when the new army appeared on the field, the sudden and organized turn of the skilled Praetorian Guard. They would have been destroyed on the field then and there, would have been squeezed and in disarray, caught defenseless. But their leader had reacted quickly and decisively, had swung about and chased the folk from Port Charley all the way back across Felling Run.

Luthien's eyes popped open wide, though he had been asleep for only a little more than an hour. Beside him, Siobhan opened a sleepy eye, then buried her cheek against his muscular chest.

"He is not coming back," Luthien said, his voice sounding loud above the background murmur of the wind.

Siobhan lifted her head, her long hair cascading across Luthien's shoulder.

"The cyclopians," Luthien explained, and he slipped out from Siobhan's grasp and propped himself up on his elbows, staring at the red glow of the hearth. "They are not coming back!"

"What are you saying?" Siobhan asked, shaking her head and brushing her hair back from her face. She sat up, the blankets falling away.

"Their leader is too smart," Luthien went on, speaking as much to himself as to his companion. "He knows that the arrival of the new force will cost him dearly if he goes against our walls again."

"He has come to take back the city," Siobhan reminded.

Luthien pointed a finger up in the air, signaling a revelation. "But with everything that has happened, and with the storm, he knows that he may lose."

Siobhan's expression revealed her doubts more clearly than any question ever could. Cyclopians were a stubborn, single-minded race for the most part, and both she and Luthien had heard many tales of one-eye tribes charging in against overwhelming odds and fighting to the last living cyclopian.

Luthien shook his head against her obvious reasoning. "These are Praetorian Guards," he said. "And their leader is a cunning one. He will not come against the city tomorrow."

"Today," Siobhan corrected, for it was after midnight. "And how do you know?"

Luthien had an answer waiting for her. "Because I would not attack the city tomor—today," he replied.

Siobhan looked at him long and hard, but did not openly question his rationale. "What do you expect of him?" she asked.

Until that very moment, Luthien had no idea of what his adversary might be up to. It came to him suddenly, crystal clear. "He's going across the river," the young Bedwyr asserted, and by the end of this sentence, he was finding breath hard to come by.

Siobhan shook her head, doubting.

"He will go over the river and catch the folk of Port Charley out in the open," Luthien pressed, growing more anxious.

"His goal is the city," Siobhan insisted.

"No!" Luthien replied sharply, more forcefully than he had intended. "He will catch them in the open field, and when they are destroyed, he can come back at us."

"If he has enough of a force left to come back at us," Siobhan argued. "And by that time, we will have many more defenses in place." She shook her head again, doubting the reasoning, but could see by Luthien's stern visage that he was not convinced.

"Time works against our enemy," Siobhan reasoned. "By all accounts, they are practically without food, and they are far from home, weary and wounded."

Luthien wanted to remind her again that these were not ordinary cyclopians, were Praetorian Guard, but she kept going with her reasoning.

"And if you are right," she said, "then what are we to do? Oliver and the others are not fools. They will see the brutes coming, and then the way will be clear for them to get into Caer MacDonald."

"Our enemy will not leave an open path," Luthien said grimly.

"You have to trust in our allies," Siobhan said. "Our responsibilities are in defending Caer MacDonald." She paused and took note of Luthien's hard breathing. Clearly, the man was upset, confused, and worried.

"There is nothing for us to do," Siobhan said, and she bent low and kissed Luthien, then sat back up, making no move to cover her nakedness. "Trust in them," she said. Her hand moved along Luthien's cheek and down his neck, and his muscles relaxed under her gentle touch.

"But there is something," he said suddenly, sitting up and looking directly into Siobhan's eyes. "We can go out before dawn, along those trails in the north. If we circle . . ."

Luthien stopped, seeing the look of sheer incredulity on the half-elf's face.

"Go out from the city?" she asked, dumbfounded.

"Our enemy will catch them in the open," Luthien pleaded. "And then, if he decides that he hasn't enough of a force remaining to capture the city, he'll turn about and march for Port Charley, now wide open to him. The cyclopians will slaughter that town and dig in, and with the season moving toward spring, Greensparrow will have an open port in Eriador and will send a second, larger force across the mountains."

"How many are you thinking to send out?" the half-elf asked, concerned by Luthien's reasoning.

"Most," Luthien replied without hesitation.

Siobhan's expression turned grim. "If you send most out, and our enemy comes back against Caer MacDonald, he will be entrenched within the city before we can strike back at him. We will be defeated and without shelter, scattering across Eriador's fields."

Luthien expected that criticism, of course, and there was indeed much truth in what Siobhan was arguing. But he didn't think that his adversary would come back at the city right away. Luthien's gut told him that the cyclopians would cross the river.

"Is this because of her?" Siobhan asked suddenly, unexpectedly.

Luthien's jaw dropped open. The reference to Katerin in such a way pained him, even more because for just a moment, he wondered if it might be true.

Siobhan saw his wounded reaction. "I am sorry," she said sincerely. "That was a terrible thing to say." She leaned close and kissed Luthien again.

"I know that your heart is for Caer MacDonald," Siobhan whispered. "I know that your decisions are based on what is best for all. I never doubt that." She kissed him again, and again, deeply, and he put his arms about her and hugged her close, feeling her warmth, needing her warmth.

But then, in this night of revelations, Luthien pushed Siobhan out to arm's length, and his puzzled expression caught her off guard.

"This is not about me, is it?" he asked, accusingly.

Siobhan didn't seem to understand.

"All of this," Luthien said candidly. "The love we make. It is not me, Luthien Bedwyr, that you love. It is the Crimson Shadow, the leader of the rebellion."

"They are one and the same," Siobhan replied.

"No," Luthien said, shaking his head slowly. "No. Because the rebellion will end, one way or the other, and so might I. But then again, I might not die, and what will Siobhan think of Luthien Bedwyr then, when the Crimson Shadow is needed no more?"

Even in the quiet light, Luthien could see that Siobhan's shoulders, indeed her whole body, slumped. He knew that he had wounded her, but he realized, too, that he had made her think.

"Never doubt that I love you, Luthien Bedwyr," the half-elf whispered.

"But . . ." Luthien prompted.

Siobhan turned away, looked at the glowing embers in the hearth. "I never knew my father," she said, and the abrupt subject change caught Luthien by surprise. "He was an elf, my mother human."

"He died?"

Siobhan shook her head. "He left, before I was born."

Luthien heard the pain in her voice, and his heart was near to breaking. "There were problems," he reasoned. "The Fairborn—"

"Were free then," Siobhan interjected. "For that was before Greensparrow, nearly three decades before Greensparrow."

Luthien quieted, but then realized that Siobhan's tale made her nearly sixty years old! Much came into perspective for the young man then, things he hadn't even considered during the wild rush of the last few weeks.

"I am half-elven," Siobhan stated. "I will live through three centuries, perhaps four, unless the blade of an enemy cuts me down." She turned to face Luthien directly, and he could see her fair and angular features and intense green eyes clearly, despite the dim light. "My father left because he could not bear to watch his love and his child grow old and die," she explained. "That is why there are so few of my mixed heritage. The Fairborn can love humans, but they know that to do so will leave them forlorn through the centuries."

"I am a temporary companion," Luthien remarked, and there was no bitterness in his voice.

"Who knows what will happen with war thick about us?" Siobhan put in. "I love you, Luthien Bedwyr."

"But the rebellion is paramount," Luthien stated.

It was a truth that Siobhan could not deny. She did indeed love Luthien, love the Crimson Shadow, but not with the intensity that a human might love another human. Elves and half-elves, longer living by far, could not afford to do that. And Luthien deserved more, Siobhan understood then.

She slipped out of the bed and began pulling on her clothes.

A part of Luthien wanted to cry out for her to stay. He had desired her since the moment he had first seen her as a simple slave girl.

But Luthien stayed quiet, understanding what she was saying and silently agreeing. He loved Siobhan, and she loved him, but their union was never truly meant to be.

And there was another woman that Luthien loved, as well. He knew it, and so did Siobhan.

"The cyclopians will not come into the city tomorrow," Luthien repeated as Siobhan pulled her heavy cloak over her shoulders.

"Your reasoning calls for a tremendous gamble," the half-elf replied.

Luthien nodded. "Trust in me," was all that he said as she walked out the door.

CHAPTER 16

LUTHIEN'S GAMBLE

*L*UTHIEN BARELY SLEPT the rest of that night, just lay in his bed, staring at the shadows on the ceiling, thinking of Siobhan and Katerin, and the enemy. Mostly the enemy: *his* enemy, the hulking, ugly cyclopian, more cunning than any one-eye Luthien had ever known.

Siobhan returned to the apartment an hour before dawn to find Luthien fully awake, dressed, and sitting in a chair before the hearth, staring into the rekindled flames.

"He's not going to come," Luthien said to her, his voice even, certain. "He's going to take his army across the river and catch Oliver's force unawares."

After a few moments of silence, with Siobhan making no move to reply, Luthien glanced over his shoulder to regard the half-elf. She stood by the door, holding his cloak.

Luthien pulled on his boots and went to her, taking the garment and following her out of the apartment.

The city was already awake, full of activity, and most of the bustle was nearby. Siobhan had gathered practically all of the army, ready to follow

Luthien out of Caer MacDonald. The snow had turned into sleet and then to rain, but the wind had not abated. A thoroughly miserable morning, and yet, here they were, the thousands of Caer MacDonald's makeshift militia, ready to march hard and fast to the west, ready to brave the elements and the cyclopians. Luthien knew who had prompted them.

He looked at the half-elf then, standing calmly by his side, and his eyes were moist with tears of gratitude. He understood the depth of his gamble—if he was wrong and his adversary struck again against Caer MacDonald, the city would be overrun. Siobhan knew that, too, and so did every man and woman, every elf and dwarf, who had come out here this morning. They would take the gamble; they would trust in Luthien.

The young Bedwyr felt a huge weight of responsibility upon his shoulders, but he allowed himself only a moment of doubt. He had played this out in his mind over and over throughout the night and was confident that he understood his adversary, that he was correctly anticipating the enemy's move.

Siobhan and Shuglin pulled him to the side.

"I am not going with you," the dwarf informed him.

Luthien looked at Shuglin curiously, not knowing what to make of the unexpected declaration.

"The dwarfs will comprise most of the defenders left in Caer MacDonald," Siobhan explained. "They are best with the ballistae and catapults, and they have rigged traps that only they know how to spring."

"And we are not much good in the deep snow," Shuglin added with a chuckle. "Beards get all icy, you know."

Luthien realized then that Shuglin's hesitance to go out had nothing to do with any doubts the dwarf might harbor. Caer MacDonald had to remain at least moderately defended, for even if Luthien's assessment proved correct, the cyclopians might send a token force at the city to keep the defenders within the walls distracted.

"You have all the horses," Shuglin began, turning to the business at hand and unrolling a map of the region. "There are a few among you who know well the trails you'll need—we have even dispatched scouts to report back as you go along, in case the weather forces you to take an alternate route." As he spoke, the dwarf moved his stubby finger along the map, through the foothills beyond Caer MacDonald's southern gate, out to the west, around the Port Charley encampment, and then circling back to the north, back to the fields where they would meet the cyclopians.

They set out without delay, a long stream of six thousand desperate, determined warriors. All of the elves were among the ranks, and all of the cavalry group, though fewer than two hundred fit horses could be found in the entire city. Like ghosts in the predawn dark, they went without lights, without any bustle. Quietly.

Many carried longbows, each archer weighed down by several quivers of arrows. One group carried packs of bandages and salves, and the two dozen dwarfs that did go along were broken into groups of four, each group supporting a huge log across their shoulders. The going was slow on the slick trails—Luthien and the other horsemen had to walk their mounts all the way through the foothills—but the rain had cut hard into the snow. Every now and then they encountered a deep drift, and they bored right through it, using swords and axes as ice picks and shovels.

As the sky lightened with the approach of dawn, the Port Charley encampment came into sight in the fields to the north, just across Felling Run. Luthien found a high perch and stared long and hard in that direction, looking for some sign of the cyclopians.

Beyond the Port Charley encampment, the field was empty.

Doubts fluttered about the young Bedwyr. What if he was wrong? What if the cyclopians went to Caer MacDonald instead?

Luthien fought them away, concentrated on the chosen course. The ground leveled out just a few hundred yards to the north; a rider could get into the Port Charley encampment within twenty minutes. Luthien dispatched three, with information for Oliver. He told them to pick their way through the remaining rough terrain, then split up as they crossed the field in case cyclopian assassins were about.

Luthien saw those same three riders milling about the still-moving column a short while later. He went to them, confused as to why they were still there, and found that Siobhan had overruled him.

"My scouts near the base of the foothills have spotted cyclopian spies in the field," the half-elf explained.

Luthien looked again to the north, to the encampment. "Our friends should be informed of our position," he reasoned.

"We have little enough cover where we are," Siobhan replied. "If we are found out . . ." She let that notion hang heavily in the air, and Luthien didn't have to press the point. If his adversary found out about the move before the army of Avon marched, then their target would surely become Caer MacDonald.

Again doubts filled Luthien's mind. If cyclopian scouts were in the field between his column and the Port Charley encampment, might they already have learned of the march?

Siobhan saw a cloud cross the young man's face, and she put a comforting hand on Luthien's forearm.

The entire force took up a position northeast of the Port Charley camp, filtering down to the edge of the fields, out of sight, but ready to charge across and meet the foes. It was good ground, Luthien decided, for their rush, when it came, would be generally downhill into cyclopians marching across slippery, uneven ground.

When it came, Luthien wondered, or *if* it came? He continued to peer across the whitened fields, empty save the blowing rain.

A long hour passed. The day brightened and the rain turned into a cold drizzle. The folk of the Port Charley encampment were stirring, breaking down their tents, readying their gear.

Another hour, and still no sign.

Siobhan waited with Luthien. "Our allies do not cross the river," she kept saying, the implication being that Caer MacDonald was not under attack, that the cyclopians hadn't moved.

This did little to calm Luthien. He had thought that his adversary would attack at first light, hard and fast. He wondered if the cyclopians might be going the other way, around to the east, to come in against the city. If the cyclopians could manage the rough terrain, that would be a fine plan, for then the Avon army would not be caught in between the defenders and the Port Charley group—indeed, the reinforcements from Port Charley would have to swing all the way around the city, or cross through the city itself, just to get into the battle.

Near panic, Luthien looked around at his camp, at the cavalry rubbing down the dripping horses, at the dwarfs, oil-soaking their great logs, at the archers testing the pull of their bows. The young Bedwyr suddenly felt himself a fool, suddenly believed that he had set them all up for disaster. He wanted to break down the camp then, march back swiftly to Caer MacDonald, and he almost called out commands to do just that.

But he could not. They were too fully committed to change their minds. All they could do was sit and wait, and watch.

Another hour, and the rain picked up again, mixing with heavy sleet. Still no word from Caer MacDonald, though a plume of black smoke had risen into the gray sky above the city.

Another single arsonist, Luthien told himself. Not a full-scale battle—certainly not!

He was not comforted.

He looked at Siobhan, and she, too, seemed worried. Time worked against them and their hoped-for ambush, for if the cyclopians were not attacking, they were likely gathering information.

"We should try to get word to the Port Charley group," Luthien said to her.

"It is risky," she warned.

"They have to know," Luthien argued. "And if the cyclopians move against the city, we must be informed immediately to get in at their backs before they overrun the wall."

Siobhan considered the reasoning. She, like Luthien, knew that if the cyclopians did indeed throw their weight on the city, no amount of forewarning would matter, but she understood the young man's need to do something. She felt that same need as well.

She was just beginning to nod her agreement when the word came down the line, anxious whisper by anxious whisper.

"To the north!"

Luthien stood tall, as did all of those nearby, peering intently through the driving rain. There was the black-and-silver mass, finally making its way to the south, a course designed to encircle the Port Charley encampment and cut off any retreat to the west.

Luthien's heart skipped a beat.

Belsen'Krieg thought himself a clever brute. Unlike most of his one-eyed race, the burly cyclopian was able and bold enough to improvise. His goal was Montfort, and if he didn't get the city, he certainly would have some explaining to do to merciless Greensparrow.

But Belsen'Krieg knew that he could not take Montfort, not now, with this second force on the field, and likely with more rebels flocking in to join the cause. And so the cunning general had improvised. He split his remaining eleven thousand Praetorian Guards, sending three thousand straight south on the eastern side of Felling Run, to use the river as a defensive position as the Port Charley folk had used it against him. This group was not likely to see much fighting this day, but they would hold the encamped army to the western bank, where Belsen'Krieg and his remaining eight thousand would make short work of them.

The cyclopian main group had marched all morning, up to the north, then across Felling Run, and then back to the south, giving the enemy a wide berth so that they would not be discovered until it was too late. There was good ground west of the encampment, the cyclopian leader knew. He would squash this rebel rabble, and then, depending on his losses and the weather, he could make his decision: to go again against Montfort, or to turn back to the west and crush Port Charley.

Now the enemy was in sight; soon they would understand that they could not cross the river, and by the time they recognized the trap and were able to react to it, they would have no time to go in force into the mountains, either. Some might scatter and escape, but Belsen'Krieg had them.

Yes, the cyclopian leader thought himself quite clever that morning, and indeed he was, but unlike Luthien, Belsen'Krieg had not taken into account the cleverness of his adversary. As the cyclopian's force pivoted to the good ground in the west, another force had even better ground, up above them, in the foothills to the south.

"This is not so good," Oliver remarked to Katerin when word of the cyclopian move reached them. They stood together under a solitary tree, Threadbare and Riverdancer standing near to them, heads down against the driving sleet.

"Likely they've got the river blocked," Katerin reasoned, and she motioned that way—there was some movement on the fields to the east, across Felling Run. "We have to go into the mountains, and quickly."

"So smart," Oliver whispered, honestly surprised. The halfling didn't like the prospects. If the cyclopians chased them into the broken ground to the south, they could not hold their force together in any reasonable manner. Many would be slain, and many more would wander helplessly in the mountains to starve or freeze to death, or to be hunted down by cyclopian patrols.

But where else could they go? Certainly they couldn't fight the Avon army on even, open ground.

A pop and flash, and a smell of sulfur, came out of the tree above them, and they looked up just as Brind'Amour, materializing on a branch above and to the side, found his intended perch too slippery and tumbled to the ground.

The old wizard hopped up, slapping his hands together and straightening his robes as though he had intended the dive all along. "Well," he said cheerily, "are you ready for the day's fight?"

Katerin and Oliver stared at the happy wizard incredulously.

"Fear not!" Brind'Amour informed them. "Our enemies are not so many, and not so good. They are hungry and weary and a long, long way from home. Come along, then, to the horses and to the front ranks."

Oliver and Katerin couldn't understand the man's lightheartedness, for they did not know that the wizard had been watching through the night and the morning with far-seeing, magical eyes. Brind'Amour had known of the cyclopian pivot for some time, and he knew, too, about the secret friends perched in the south.

No need to tell Oliver and Katerin, Brind'Amour figured. Not yet.

Katerin brushed a lock of drenched hair back from her face and looked at Oliver. They exchanged helpless shrugs—Brind'Amour seemed to know what he was doing—retrieved their mounts, and followed the wizard. All the Port Charley camp came astir then, digging into defensible positions, preparing to meet the cyclopian charge.

"I do hope he has some big booms ready for them," Oliver said to Katerin after the wizard left them in the front ranks. The halfling stared across the open ground at the masses of black and silver.

"They are not so many," Katerin replied sarcastically, for the cyclopian force dwarfed them four to one, at least.

"Very big booms," Oliver remarked.

It seemed fitting to them both that the storm intensified with a burst of snow just as the cyclopians began their roaring charge.

To their credit, the hardy fisherfolk of Port Charley did not break ranks and flee. Word filtered down the line that a cyclopian group had indeed entrenched on the eastern riverbank, and it seemed as if the roaring mass of enemies would simply plow over them. But they did not flee. Their bowstrings took up a humming song, and the folk began to sing, too, thinking this to be their last stand.

Brind'Amour stood back from the front ranks, his skinny white arms uplifted to the sky, head tilted far back and eyes closed as he reached out with his magic toward the storm, to the energy of the thick clouds. Many of those simple fisherfolk about him were afraid, for they did not know of magic and had grown up all of their lives hearing that it was a devil-sent power. Still, none dared to try to interrupt the wizard's spell, and old Dozier, who remembered a time before Greensparrow, stayed close to the wizard, trying to comfort and reassure his frightened comrades.

Brind'Amour felt as if his entire body was elongating, stretching up to the sky. Of course it was not, but his spirit was indeed soaring high, reaching into those clouds and grasping and gathering the energy, focusing it, shaping it, and then hurling it down in the form of a lightning bolt into the front ranks of the charging cyclopians.

Black- and silver-clad bodies rebounded with the shock. One unfortunate brute took the blow full force, his metal armor crackling with blue sparks.

"Oh, that was very good!" Oliver congratulated. He looked up to his right, to Katerin on Riverdancer, sitting much higher than he. She wasn't watching the scene ahead, wasn't even looking back over her shoulder at the wizard. Rather, she was looking left, over Oliver, to the south.

"Not as good as that!" she replied.

Oliver spun about just as the horns sounded, just as Luthien's cavalry led the charge. The halfling spotted four plumes of black smoke as the dwarfs lit the logs, so soaked with oil that they defied the storm. Ropes had been strung around flat-headed pegs on each end of those logs, two dwarfs holding on to each end, running blindly, full out down the slope, rushing down with their rolling, burning rams.

"Luthien," Katerin whispered.

"I really do love the man," Oliver declared.

"So do I," Katerin said, under her breath, but Oliver caught every word, and he smiled, warmed by the thought (and more than a little jealous of his sandy-haired friend!).

The cyclopian formation became a mass of madness. The brutes fell all over each other trying to get out of the way; many hurled spears or even threw their swords in sheer desperation.

But the sturdy dwarfs held true to their course, came right up to the brutes before letting go of the logs, bowling down dozens of the one-eyes.

Right behind the dwarfs, firing bows as they came, charged Siobhan and her kin and the many men and women of Caer MacDonald. There was no way to stop on the slippery turf, but the force had no intention of stopping, or even slowing. They barreled on, their sheer momentum trampling down many enemies and sending many more running from the battle.

Tucked in the center of the line near the back of the cyclopian formation, Belsen'Krieg watched in pure frustration. The ugly general had never dreamed that the humans would be daring enough to come out of Montfort.

Another lightning bolt exploded among his troops. It killed only a few, but struck terror into the hearts of all those nearby. The battle had just begun, the folk of Port Charley hadn't even joined in yet, but Belsen'Krieg recognized the danger. His soldiers were exhausted and weak from hunger. He had lost some to desertion during the night, something practically unheard of in the Praetorian Guard. They needed a victory now, and Belsen'Krieg had thought he would gain one, an easy one, against the small encampment.

So he had thought.

Another bolt from the skies jolted the ground near the cyclopian leader, close enough so that he was splattered with the blood of a blasted brute.

The huge one-eye took up his sword. He focused on the battle that was drawing near; with typical cyclopian savagery, Belsen'Krieg decided to lead by example.

He encountered his first enemy a minute later. A quick pass with his ponypig, a quick swipe with his sword, and the brute moved on, his weapon dripping blood.

Luthien's group of a hundred and seventy cavalry were the first to hit the cyclopian line. Like those running behind them, the riders couldn't hope to slow down on the slick slope, and so they didn't try, using the sheer bulk of their strong mounts to run down the first ranks of one-eyes.

There were no targets to pick, only a mass to slash at, and Luthien did just that, connecting on every swing, cleaving helms and skulls, turning his horse this way and that, stabbing at anything that moved below him. He heard the shrieks of terror to the east, the rumble of the burning, rolling logs, and the screams as the bearded folk loosed their fury. He heard the hum of bowstrings and the clang of steel against steel and knew that all his forces had come crashing in.

A lightning bolt jolted the ground, another soon after, and Luthien, who had witnessed the fury of wizards, was glad that Brind'Amour was on his side.

Then, from up front came more screams, more ringing steel, and Luthien understood that the Port Charley folk had joined. He thought of Oliver and Katerin, on Threadbare and Riverdancer, and he hoped that his friends would survive.

But these were all fleeting, distant thoughts to the young Bedwyr, for the sea of black and silver churned below him. He took a hit on his thigh, a glancing blow that stung his horse more than it stung him. Luthien brought *Blind-Striker* whipping about, looking to pay the brute back. But the one-eye was already gone, had already moved along in the tangle. No problem for Luthien, though, for many other enemies were within striking distance. His great sword rushed down, smashing the side of a helmet with enough force to snap the neck of the creature wearing it.

And so it went for many minutes. A third of the horsemen had been pulled down, but many more cyclopians than that were dead around them, and many more scrambled to get away.

Luthien pressed on, followed the mass, hacking with abandon. Every so often he yelled out, "Eriador free!" and he sighed every time he was answered, every time he found confirmation that he had not been totally separated from his comrades.

*   *   *

It was not a long battle—not like the assault on Caer MacDonald's walls, or even like the swirling mass within the courtyard after the gates had been breached. The cyclopians, their morale low, seeing an easy victory become something terrible, broke apart wherever they were hit hard, scattering, trying to re-form into some defensive posture. But each time, they were hit again by the fierce Eriadorans; each time, their pocket formations were blasted apart.

By the time the cyclopians had come to fully understand the weight of the unexpected force from the south, several hundred were dead, and the presence of a wizard among the ranks of the fisherfolk, indeed a very powerful wizard, struck terror into their hearts. They had grown up under Greensparrow, the personal force of the wizard-king, and they knew.

They knew.

There was more organization and more determination wherever Belsen'Krieg and his mounted undercommanders made their appearance, but even the huge one-eyed general understood this disaster. He kept hoping that the three thousand across the river would join in, but that was not what he had instructed them to do. Belsen'Krieg recognized the limitations of his own race. The Praetotian Guard were fabulous soldiers, disciplined and brave (for cyclopians), but they did not improvise. They were led by a single figurehead, in this case Belsen'Krieg, and they moved as extensions of his will to direct and straightforward commands. Those brutes across the river had been told to dig in and hold the ground, and so they would, sitting there stupidly while the main force was massacred on the field.

The cyclopian general spotted Luthien and the Caer MacDonald cavalry, chopping his ranks apart directly south of his position. As soon as he recognized the young Bedwyr, the crimson-caped man from the river, Belsen'Krieg understood who had precipitated this ambush. As Luthien had recognized him as the cyclopian general, so he recognized Luthien's authority.

The cyclopian was too filled with rage to tip his shining helm at his cunning adversary. He wanted to pound his ponypig over to Luthien and chop the man down! But Belsen'Krieg was smarter than that. His formation, the classic military square at the start of the charge, was no more, and he could not reorganize any significant portion of his frightened and weary force. Not now. Not with the press from two sides and a wizard hurling lightning from the skies.

He thought of gathering as many as he could and charging straight to the east, toward the river, in an attempt to link up with his other force, but the scouts he sent out among the ranks came back shaking their ugly heads, for the main host from Caer MacDonald had come in at the southeastern corner and had already joined with the folk of Port Charley.

Belsen'Krieg looked again to the south, spotted Luthien for just a moment, crimson cape flying, sword swinging high. *That one again*, the cyclopian thought. *That miserable human has done this, all of this.*

The word came from Belsen'Krieg then, a command the Praetorian Guard were not used to following. "Run away!"

Luthien gradually came out of the mass of fighters, or rather, the mass gradually diminished about him. He had to work harder to search out targets then, and whenever he spotted a cyclopian, he kicked his horse into a short gallop and ran the brute down.

He was bearing down on one such enemy, the cyclopian's back to him, when the creature lurched over and groaned, apparently grabbing at its groin. Out from the side came a familiar, dashing halfling, the wide brim of his hat drooping low under the weight of snow.

Oliver ran about the brute, stabbing it repeatedly with his rapier.

Luthien was thrilled and surprised, so much so that he hardly noticed a second brute coming in at the halfling's back.

"Oliver!" he cried out, and he feared that he was too late.

But the ever-alert halfling was not caught unawares. He spun away from the brute he was fighting, down to one knee, and stabbed as the cyclopian whipped its sword high above his head. The rapier tip sank deep, into the one-eye's groin. Like its companion before it, the brute bent low and groaned, and Oliver's next thrust put a clean hole in its throat.

The halfling looked up then, as Luthien's horse pounded by, the young Bedwyr finishing off the first cyclopian Oliver had stung with one vicious swipe of *Blind-Striker*.

"I have lost my horse!" Oliver cried at his friend.

"Behind you!" came Luthien's reply as yet another Praetorian Guard, a huge cyclopian brandishing a spiked club, charged at Oliver's back.

Oliver whirled about and dropped; Luthien charged by, slicing his sword up at the brute. To its credit, the cyclopian got its club up to deflect *Blind-Striker*, though Luthien's momentum as his mount passed ripped the weapon from the one-eye's hand. The brute couldn't block Oliver's thrust, again low, aimed at that most sensitive of areas.

Luthien turned and finished the defenseless cyclopian as it doubled over.

"Why do you keep hitting them there?" demanded Luthien, a bit disgusted by Oliver's tendency for low blows.

"Oh," huffed the halfling as though he was wounded by the accusation. "If you were my size, you would swing for the eyeball?" Luthien's shoulders drooped and he sighed, and Oliver snapped his fingers in the young Bedwyr's direction.

"Besides," Oliver said coyly, "I thought you were fond of cabarachee shots." Luthien's eyes narrowed as he caught the reference to Katerin that night in the Dwelf. "This one-eye," Oliver pressed on, "perhaps he will fall in love with me." The snickering halfling glanced down at the brute, dead on the field. He shrugged and looked back at Luthien. "Well, perhaps he would have."

A rush of cavalry stormed past the friends then, one rider skidding his horse to a stop near Luthien. "The one-eye leaders," the man said breathlessly, "on ponypigs, getting away!"

Luthien turned his mount about and reached down to take Oliver's hand.

"But my pony!" the halfling protested as Luthien yanked him up behind the saddle. Oliver gave a shrill whistle and peered all about, but the snow was thicker now, blowing fiercely, and the yellow pony could not be seen.

The battle had stretched out along the fields far to the north, with the cyclopians in full flight. Luthien and his cavalry group, some twenty riders, ignored the running cyclopian infantry, concentrating instead on catching up to the ponypigs.

Ponypigs could move well, especially on the muddy fields, but not as well as horses, and soon Belsen'Krieg and his dozen remaining escorts were in sight.

On came the cavalry, crying for Eriador and Caer MacDonald. The cyclopian leaders knew that they were caught, knew that they could not outrun the horses, and so they turned, ready to meet the charge.

Luthien saw the huge one-eyed general, and Belsen'Krieg saw him. It seemed somehow as if they were removed from the field then, or that all of the others were, for the young Bedwyr put his mount in line, and so did the cyclopian leader, and no fighter on either side moved to intercept or interfere.

Luthien pulled up; so did Belsen'Krieg. They sat staring at each other, hating each other.

"Get off," Luthien said to Oliver.

The halfling considered the huge cyclopian, barely a dozen yards away. Oliver could see the hatred between these two, the rivalry, leader against leader. "Time to go," he agreed, and rolled off the rump of Luthien's mount, turning a complete somersault to land gingerly on his feet—well, almost, for he hit a particularly slick patch of ground and his feet flew out from under him, landing him unceremoniously on his backside. The embarrassed halfling glanced around, near to panic, but none of the others took any notice.

"Caer MacDonald!" Luthien growled at the cyclopian leader.

Belsen'Krieg tilted his huge head as he considered the words, then brightened with understanding. "Montfort," he corrected.

Luthien yelled out and charged; Belsen'Krieg pacing his every move. Their great swords rang loudly as they passed, with no substantial damage, though Luthien's arm tingled from the weight of the cyclopian's blow.

Oliver realized a problem then. He was standing alone in the middle of the field, and suddenly the huge brute was closer to him than was Luthien! The halfling whimpered and considered his rapier, seeming so puny against that mounted monstrosity, but to his ultimate relief, the brute did not even notice him, just wheeled the ponypig about and began the second pass.

Again their swords slashed across up high, connecting in the air between them. But Luthien had changed his grip this time, and *Blind-Striker* rotated down with the momentum of Belsen'Krieg's mighty swing, Luthien ducking and nearly getting his head shaved as the cyclopian's blade barreled through.

The agile Bedwyr had allowed his sword to roll right out of his hand, and he caught it almost immediately, his grip reversed. He thrust it straight out, aiming at Belsen'Krieg's thigh, but he wasn't quite quick enough and *Blind-Striker* drove deep into the ponypig's flank instead.

The powerful mount rambled past and Luthien had to let go of his reins and grab his sword hilt in both hands to avoid losing the weapon. He did hold on to the blade, and it did tear free of the passing ponypig, but Luthien got yanked from his horse in the process. He splashed down in the muddy field, struggling up in time to see Belsen'Krieg extracting himself from his downed mount.

"Now you die!" the cyclopian promised, stalking over without the slightest hesitation. The brutish general's great sword slashed, then came in a rapid backhand, and Luthien barely got his weapon up to parry.

Belsen'Krieg pressed the attack with an overhand chop and a straight thrust; Luthien blocked and hopped aside at the last moment.

The cyclopian came on savagely, but Luthien was up to the task, letting Belsen'Krieg play out his rage, deflecting or dodging every attack.

Every once in a while, the young Bedwyr found a slight opening and *Blind-Striker* penetrated Belsen'Krieg's defenses, but the young Bedwyr had to be quick and retract the blade immediately, ready to block the next vicious attack.

Though Luthien saw the thin lines of blood on his adversary, he understood that he was really doing very little damage. He felt like a buzzing wasp biting at a giant, an impossible match. Luthien pushed down any ensuing panic, telling himself that the wasp could win.

But only if it was perfect.

It went on for some time, Luthien dodging and stinging, but Belsen'Krieg seemed to feel nothing, and his attacks did not slow with exhaustion. This one was good, Luthien realized, far better than any cyclopian he had ever faced. And strong! Luthien knew that if he missed a single parry, if this brute connected even once, he would be cleaved in half.

And then it happened; Luthien, circling, stepped on a patch of uneven ice and skidded down to one knee. Belsen'Krieg was on him immediately, the great sword chopping down.

Up came *Blind-Striker*, horizontally above Luthien's head. Belsen'Krieg's sword hit it near the hilt and was stopped, but Luthien's arm buckled under the tremendous weight of the blow and he dropped his blade. He wasn't seriously wounded, he believed, but the pain was intense.

He grabbed up *Blind-Striker* in his left hand and thrust ahead, trying to force the one-eyed monster back. He got Belsen'Krieg in the belly, but not enough to stop the brute.

Luthien scrambled to get his blade up, but was knocked forward suddenly, as someone, something, ran up his back.

Springing from Luthien's shoulders, Oliver caught Belsen'Krieg by surprise. The cyclopian's eye widened, a wonderful target, but Oliver, off balance as Luthien slid to the side, missed it, his rapier stabbing Belsen'Krieg's cheek instead.

The cyclopian screamed and flailed his huge arms, falling back from the fight. He straightened out as Luthien and Oliver picked themselves up, standing side by side.

"You are a one-eyed, ugly thing," Oliver taunted. "You would not know the value of friends!"

As if to accentuate the halfling's point (and Oliver had timed things that way), a shining white stallion, long coat glistening with wetness, thundered right behind the cyclopian, slamming the huge brute across the shoulders and launching him headlong, face-first into the mud.

Belsen'Krieg came up sputtering to find himself surrounded by
Luthien and Oliver, and now Katerin O'Hale, magnificent atop Riverdancer, her red hair darkened with wetness and snow gathering on her
shoulders. Her smile was wide and bright, her green eyes sparkling more
than the ice crystals forming at the ends of her thick hair, as she considered the situation, the victory that was won this day.

Belsen'Krieg looked about for support. He saw his last undercommander lurch over and slide slowly off a ponypig, its falling bulk revealing the victorious horseman behind it, sword red with blood. More than
a dozen of Luthien's cavalry remained, along with the few Katerin had
brought with her, including one slight woman riding a yellow pony that
had little hair in its tail.

Oliver grinned at the sight of his beloved Threadbare, but turned serious at once when he faced the cyclopian leader.

"I think you should surrender," he remarked.

Belsen'Krieg looked around for a long while. Luthien could practically hear the creature's thoughts—the caged animal looking for an escape. There was none to be found. Luthien wasn't sure what Belsen'Krieg
would do, which way the brute would turn, but then, unexpectedly, the
one-eye threw his huge sword to the ground.

As one, the group relaxed, Luthien taking a stride toward the cyclopian leader. His sword arm still ached, but not so much that he could not
take up *Blind-Striker*, flexing his muscles and grimacing through the
pain.

Out came a knife, and daring, wild Belsen'Krieg charged ahead.

"Luthien!" Katerin and Oliver yelled together. Before the word had
even left their mouths, Luthien's free left hand whipped across, catching
the cyclopian by the wrist. Luthien could hardly move Belsen'Krieg's
massive arm, but he used the support to shift himself instead, inside the
angle of the rushing dagger. And as he moved, his own sword jabbed
ahead, creasing Belsen'Krieg's breastplate, cutting through the armor,
into the brute's lungs.

They held the macabre pose for a long moment, then Belsen'Krieg
growled—and the mouths of those witnessing the event dropped
open in disbelief—and began forcing his knife hand toward the
young Bedwyr.

Luthien tucked his shoulder down against his sword hand and jerked
at the blade, and Belsen'Krieg's movement came to an abrupt halt. Again
they held the pose, unblinking, their faces barely a few inches apart.

"One up," Luthien growled, and the dying Belsen'Krieg had no response, for indeed the young Bedwyr had been one step ahead of him throughout the battle.

Luthien jerked his blade again, then felt it sinking down as Belsen'Krieg's legs slowly buckled, bringing the brute to his knees. Luthien felt the strength go out of Belsen'Krieg's massive arm; the knife dropped to the ground.

Luthien pulled *Blind-Striker* free, but even without the support, Belsen'Krieg fell no farther. The dead cyclopian leader knelt on the field.

Already the snow began to gather about him.

CHAPTER 17

IMPLICATIONS

THE BATTLE—the rout—ended swiftly, with half of Belsen'Krieg's force killed and the other half running off blindly into the open fields. Losses to the Eriadorans were remarkably light; the folk of Port Charley could count their dead on the fingers of six hands, though Luthien's group, which had thrown itself into the cyclopian throng, was more battered.

Both Eriadoran armies gathered back together on the field near to where the Port Charley encampment had been. They tended their wounded, finished off any cyclopians who were sorely hurt, and put all the one-eye prisoners in line. Fortunately there weren't many prisoners, less than a hundred altogether, and these, having seen their proud Praetorian Guards routed so horribly, were little trouble.

The storm grew around them all, the day darkening, though it was near to noon. Brind'Amour organized the march with all of his archers in front. They fought a small skirmish as they crossed Felling Run, a couple of volleys of arrows mostly. The cyclopians responded by hurling heavy spears, but, with typical cyclopian accuracy, not a single Eriadoran was hit.

There wasn't much fight left in those entrenched Avon soldiers—they were beginning to break and flee before the Eriadorans ever got to the river. For the rest of that day, the biggest obstacle facing the army of Eriador was in getting back to the shelter of Caer MacDonald as the blizzard came on in full about them.

Back on Riverdancer, Luthien heard the cheers as he approached the walled city, for news of the rout had preceded the returning army. The young Bedwyr had lost a couple of friends this day, a woman and two men who frequented the Dwelf, but his sadness was tempered in the belief that his friends had not died in vain. They had won the day; Eriador had won the day! The victorious army along with their allies of Port Charley poured into the city, scattering among the streets, breaking up into small groups that they might recount the day's glorious events.

Luthien, Katerin, and Oliver went back to the apartment in Tiny Alcove to catch up on the events of the last few weeks. The young Bedwyr was thrilled to see his dearest friends again, particularly Katerin. He hadn't realized how much he had missed the woman. Of course he thought of Siobhan and their encounter the previous evening, but he hadn't really yet figured out what it all meant.

All that Luthien knew at the time was that he was glad, so glad, to see Katerin O'Hale once more.

Some time later, they were joined at the apartment by Brind'Amour, Siobhan, and Shuglin, who had also been quite busy that day.

"We killed every cyclopian running the streets of Caer MacDonald," the dwarf assured them. "No more fires."

Brind'Amour, reclining in the most comfortable of the three chairs in the small sitting room, hoisted a cup of wine in toast to that welcome news. Siobhan and Oliver, likewise seated and sipping wine, joined in, as did the other three, hoisting mugs of golden honey mead.

Seated on the stone hearth, Luthien looked across the open fireplace at Katerin, and they were warmed by more than the flames that burned between them.

"Well," Shuglin corrected himself, shifting closer to the hearth, "no more *unwanted* fires!"

That brought a slight chuckle from the group.

"We still have several thousand cyclopians running free across the countryside," Oliver remarked.

"Out in the blizzard," Katerin snorted.

"We will catch those who survive the storm," Siobhan said grimly.

Luthien nodded; on the way back into Caer MacDonald, pursuit groups had been arranged. The fleeing cyclopians would be hunted down.

"There are no towns nearby, except for Felling Downs," Siobhan went on. "And the brutes will find no shelter there, for the houses have all been razed. Likely, they will turn for Port Charley."

Luthien was hardly listening, more concerned with the half-elf's serious tone. The hard day's battle had been won, but Siobhan would not allow herself a break in the intensity. Yes, for Siobhan the rebellion was paramount, all-consuming. She would do whatever it took to free Eriador and free her people from Greensparrow.

Whatever it took, like bedding the Crimson Shadow? Luthien shook the notion away the moment he thought of it, scolding himself for thinking so little of Siobhan. There was something real between himself and the half-elf, something wonderful and warm, and though they both knew that it would never be more than it was now, Luthien vowed then and there that he would not look back on his lost relationship with Siobhan with doubt or remorse. He was a better man for knowing her; his life was happier because she remained a part of it. And in looking at her now, Luthien believed with all his heart that she felt the same way.

He turned his gaze from Siobhan, who continued talking of the duties still before them, across the hearth to Katerin. She had been staring at him, he realized, for she blushed (something rarely seen on Katerin's tanned cheeks) and turned her green eyes away.

Luthien gave a small smile to hide the pain and closed his eyes, holding fast his image of the woman from Hale as he rested his head back. He dozed then, as the conversation continued, even intensified, about him.

"Our fearless leader," Oliver remarked dryly, noticing Luthien's pose and rhythmic breathing.

All five had a laugh at Luthien's expense. Katerin reached across to shake him.

"Let him sleep," Siobhan bade her. Immediate tension filled the air between the two women as Katerin turned to regard the half-elf.

"He has labored day and night," Siobhan went on, ignoring the woman's visage, an expression that revealed the rivalry between the two.

Katerin straightened and dropped her arm to her side.

"Well, of course those cyclopians who fled this day will be of little consequence," Brind'Amour interjected, somewhat loudly and importantly, forcing all eyes to turn to him. "Many will die in the storm and those who do not will be in little condition to fight back when we catch up with them. They'll make to the west, of course, to their fleet, which is no longer their fleet!"

"Can Port Charley resist them?" Oliver asked in all seriousness, for most of that town's hardy souls were in Caer MacDonald.

"Few cyclopians will ever get there," Siobhan promised.

"And we'll get enough fighters there before the brutes arrive," Brind'Amour was quick to add. "They will be dogged every step, and we know the faster ways. No, they'll be little trouble. The army of Avon that came to our shores is defeated."

"But what does that mean?" Shuglin asked the question that was on everyone's mind.

Dead silence. In considering the long-term implications of this day's victory, each of them realized that it might, after all, be only a small thing, a flickering reprieve in the darkness that was Greensparrow.

"It means that we have won a battle," Brind'Amour said at length. "And now we have a fleet to hinder any further invasion through Port Charley.

"But Greensparrow will take us more seriously now," the wizard warned. "The snow is deep, and that favors us and awards us some time, but the days are warmer now and it will not last for long. We can expect an army marching out from Malpuissant's Wall soon after the melt, and likely another force coming through the passes of the Iron Cross, both of them greater than the force we just defeated on the field."

What had been a celebration quickly dissolved, stolen by the grim dwarf's necessary question and the obvious truth of the wizard's reminder.

Brind'Amour scrutinized each of his companions. These five, he knew, were representative of the Eriadorans. There was Katerin, proud Katerin, desperate for a return to the days of Eriador's freedom, Eriador's glory. Most of the islanders were like her—on Bedwydrin, Marvis, and Caryth—as were the folk of Port Charley and the tribes north of Eradoch, in the area of Bae Colthwyn.

There was Siobhan, angry Siobhan, stung by injustice and consumed by thoughts of revenge. So representative of the sophisticated people of Montfort—no, Caer MacDonald; it could be called that now—the wizard thought. She was the architect of it all, the cunning behind the rebellion, proud, but not too proud to allow the intrusions of a wizard when she understood that those intrusions would benefit her people.

There was Shuglin, whose people had suffered most of all. This one had moved past anger, Brind'Amour knew, and past resignation. Those dwarfs who had died in their suicidal ambush out by the fallen wall had been neither angry nor sad. They did as they believed they had to do, in the simple hope that Eriador, and their people, would have a better lot for their sacrifice. There he was, that blue-bearded dwarf, the purest of soldiers. Brind'Amour believed that if he had ten thousand like Shuglin, he could sweep Greensparrow and all of Avon from the face of the world.

There was Oliver, the epitome of Eriador's many foreign rogues. The rough land was a favored destination for those who could not fit in, either in Avon or Gascony, or even in lands farther removed. Oliver's value on the field could not be doubted, nor could his value as Luthien's trusted companion. But the true worth of Oliver, and of the many others who would no doubt surface as the rebellion spread, would be found in his knowledge of other places and other people. Should this rebellion, this war, reach a level where Gascony saw fit to become involved, Oliver's understanding of that place would prove invaluable. Oliver the diplomat? Brind'Amour considered that possibility for some time.

And there, last, was Luthien, still dozing with his back against the stone of the hearth. He was all of them, Brind'Amour realized. Proud as an islander, angry as one of Caer MacDonald, a pure, unselfish soldier, and the figurehead that Eriador desperately needed. After his exploits in the battle, Luthien had become undeniably the cornerstone on which Eriador would succeed or fail. Already the tale of "Luthien's Gamble" was spreading far from the city walls, mingling with the stories of the Crimson Shadow, the mysterious enemy to all that evil Greensparrow represented. Who would have guessed that the young man from Bedwydrin could rise so fast to such notoriety?

"I would have!" Brind'Amour answered his own question suddenly, and unintentionally, aloud. Embarrassed, the wizard cleared his throat many times and glanced about.

"What was that?" Luthien asked, stretching as he came awake.

"Nothing, nothing," the wizard apologized. "Just exercising my jaw at the mind's request, you know."

The others shrugged and let it go at that, except for shrewd Oliver, who kept his gaze on the wizard as though he was reading Brind'Amour's every thought.

"You know," the halfling began, drawing everyone's attention, "I was once in the wild land of Angarothe." Seeing that his proclamation apparently didn't impress anybody, the halfling quickly explained. "A hot and dusty land some distance to the south of Gascony."

"The War of Angar?" inquired Brind'Amour, more worldly than the others, despite the fact that he had spent most of the last few centuries asleep in a cave.

"War of anger?" Luthien snickered.

"Angar," Oliver corrected, appearing insulted. "Indeed," he answered the wizard. "I fought with deBoise himself, in the Fourth Regiment of Cabalaise."

The wizard cocked an eyebrow and nodded, seeming impressed, though the reference meant absolutely nothing to the others in the room. Oliver puffed with pride and looked about, but quickly deflated as he realized the ignorance of his audience.

"The Fourth of Cabalaise," he said with some importance. "We were in deepest Angarothe, behind the Red Lancers, the largest and most terrible of that country's armies."

Brind'Amour met the curious gaze of each of the others and nodded his understanding, lending gravity to Oliver's tale, though the wizard highly doubted that Oliver had ever been anywhere near to Angarothe. Few Gascons who had gone to that wild land had ever returned. But Brind'Amour did know the tale of deBoise and the Fourth, one of the classic victories in the history of warfare.

"We could not win," Oliver went on. "We were two hundred against several thousand, and not one of us thought that we would come out of there alive."

"And what did you do?" Luthien asked after a long and dramatic pause, giving the halfling the necessary prompt.

Oliver snapped his fingers in the air and blew a cocky whistle. "We attacked, of course."

"He speaks truly," Brind'Amour interjected before the expressions of profound doubt could grow on the faces of the other four. "DeBoise spread his line along the foliage marking the perimeter of the enemy encampment, each man with a drum. They used sticks to bang against trees, imitated the calls of huge elephants and other such warbeasts, all to make their enemy believe that they were many more, an entire army."

"The Red Lancers were weary of battle," Oliver added. "And they had no good ground to wage such a fight. And so they retreated to a mountain."

"DeBoise watched them and dogged them with empty threats, every step," Brind'Amour finished. "By the time the leaders of the Red Lancers came to understand the bluff, the Fourth had found the reinforcements it needed. The Red Lancers of Angarothe came off the mountain, thinking to overwhelm the small force, but were themselves overwhelmed. The only Gascon victory of the campaign."

Oliver turned a sour look on the old man at that last statement, but it melted away quickly, the halfling too eager to announce his own part in the strategic coup. "They wanted to call it Oliver's Bluff," he asserted.

Brind'Amour did well to hide his chuckle.

"A fine tale," Shuglin said, obviously not too impressed.

"But does it have a point?" Katerin wanted to know.

Oliver huffed and shook his head as though the question was ridiculous. "Are we not like the Fourth Regiment of Cabalaise?" he asked.

"Say it plainly," Shuglin demanded.

"We attack, of course," Oliver replied without hesitation. That widened more than a few eyes! Oliver paid no heed to their incredulity, but looked at the wizard, where he suspected he would find some support.

Brind'Amour nodded and smiled—he had been hoping all along that one of the others would make that very suggestion and save him the trouble. The wizard realized that he was more valuable agreeing with plans than in convincing the rebels to follow plans he had constructed.

Katerin rose from the hearth and slapped her hands against the back of her dusty breeches. "Attack where?" she demanded, obviously thinking the whole notion ridiculous.

"Attack the wall," Brind'Amour answered. "Malpuissant's Wall, before Greensparrow can run his army of Princetown north."

Suddenly the prospect didn't seem so absurd to Luthien. "Take Dun Caryth and cut the land in half," he put in. "With the mountains and the wall, and a fleet to guard our ports, we will force Greensparrow to attack us on ground of our choosing."

"And the daring conquest will make him think that we are stronger than we are," Oliver added slyly.

Siobhan's green eyes sparkled with hope. "And stronger we shall be," she asserted, "when the northern lands learn of our victory here, when all of Eriador realizes the truth of the rebellion." She looked around at the others, practically snarling with eagerness. "When all of Eriador comes to hope."

"Oliver's Bluff?" Brind'Amour offered.

No one disagreed and the halfling beamed—for just a moment. Suddenly it occurred to Oliver, who of course had not really been with de-Boise in Angarothe, that he had set them all on a most daring and dangerous course. He cleared his throat, and his expression revealed his anxiety. "I do fear," he admitted, and felt the weight of Luthien's gaze, and Siobhan's, Shuglin's, and Katerin's as well, upon his little round shoulders. "They have wizard types," the halfling went on, trying to justify his sudden turn. He felt that he had to show some doubt to avoid blame in the face of potential disaster. But if this did go off, and especially if it proved successful, the halfling dearly wanted it to be known as Oliver's Bluff. "I am not so keen on the idea of daring a group of wizard-types."

Brind'Amour waved the argument away. "Magic is not what it used to be, my dear Oliver," he assured the halfling, assured them all. "Else Morkney would have left Luthien in ashes atop the Ministry and left you frozen as a gargoyle on the side of the tower! And I would have been of more use on the field, I promise." There was conviction in the wizard's words. Ever since he had left the cave that had served for so long as his home, Brind'Amour had realized that the essence of magic had changed. It was still there, tingling in the air, though not nearly as strong as it had once been. The wizard understood the reason. Greensparrow's dealing with demons had perverted the art, had made it something dark and evil, and that, in turn, had weakened the very fabric of the universal tapestry, the source of magical power. Brind'Amour felt a deep lament at the loss, a nostalgia for the old days when a skilled wizard was so very powerful, when the finest of wizards could take on an entire army in the field and send them running. But Brind'Amour understood well enough that in this war with Greensparrow and the king's wizard-dukes, where he was the only wizard north of the mountains, an apparent lack of magical strength might be Eriador's only hope.

"To the wall, then," he said.

Luthien looked at Katerin, then to Shuglin, and finally, to Siobhan, but he needed no confirmation from his friends this time. Caer MacDonald was free, but it could not remain so if they waited for Greensparrow to make the next move. The war was a chess game and they were playing white.

It was time to move.

CHAPTER 18

WARM WELCOME

THE SNOW LET UP the next day, leaving a blanket twenty inches deep across the southern fields of Eriador, with drifts that could swallow a man and his horse whole, without a trace.

A huge force left Caer MacDonald anyway, mostly comprised of the folk from Port Charley, in pursuit of those seven thousand Praetorian Guards who had fled the battle. Wearing sheepskin mittens and thick woollen cloaks, with many layers of stockings under their treated doeskin boots and carrying sacks of dry kindling, the Eriadorans were well equipped for the wintry weather, but those cyclopians who had run off most certainly were not. Tired and hungry, many of them wounded and weak from loss of blood, that first frozen and snowy night took a horrible toll. Before they had gone two miles from Caer MacDonald's gates, the Eriadorans came upon lines of frozen bodies and shivering, blue-lipped cyclopians, their hands too numb and swollen for them even to hold a weapon.

And so it began, a trail of prisoners soon stretching several miles back to Caer MacDonald's gates. By midafternoon, more than a thousand had come in, and returning couriers estimated that two or three times that number were dead on the snowy fields. Still, a large force remained, making a direct line for Port Charley.

Brind'Amour used his magical sight to locate them, and with the wizard directing the pursuers, many cyclopians were caught and slaughtered.

Undercommander Longsleeves, still carrying wounds from the bridge collapse and with the head of an elvish arrow stuck deep in his shoulder, led the main host of some three thousand Praetorian Guards. They were dogged every step and had not the strength to respond to the attack in any way. Somehow they persevered and trudged on, cannibalizing their own dead and hunching their backs against the stinging, blowing snow.

Soon they were down to two thousand, their numbers barely larger than the force pursuing them, but the weather improved steadily and the snow diminished by the hour. Purely out of fear, Longsleeves kept them moving, kept them driving, until at last the tall masts of the Avon ships in the harbor of Port Charley came into view.

Among the cyclopian ranks there was much rejoicing, though every one of them understood that with the city in sight the force pursuing them would likely come on in full.

What the Avon soldiers didn't realize was that, while they were eyeing the masts for salvation, spotters among the folk within Port Charley were eyeing the cyclopians, locating shots for the crews, who had become quite proficient with the catapults on the captured ships.

One by one, the vessels loosed their flaming pitch and baskets of sharpened stones. Longsleeves would have called out a command to charge the city, but as fate would have it, the very first volley, a burning ball of sticky black tar, buried the undercommander where he stood, burned away his pretty hair, pretty sleeves, and his muttonchops.

Confused and frightened, the leaderless one-eyed brutes ran every which way, some charging Port Charley, others turning back east, only to meet old Dozier and his army. The slaughter was over within the hour, and it took only one of the captured ships to sail the remaining cyclopians to the north, where the Diamondgate would serve as their prison.

Back in Caer MacDonald, the preparations for the march to Malpuissant's Wall were well under way. A two-pronged movement was decided upon. Shuglin and his kin would go into the Iron Cross to guard the passes and hopefully to locate more of their own to bring into the rebellion. The main force, led by Brind'Amour himself, would strike out around the perimeter of the mountains.

The sheer daring of the move became apparent as those days of preparation slipped by. The force would not be so large, with the folk of Port Charley back in their city, and with so many dead and wounded. The Praetorian Guards, in such numbers, were simply too dangerous to be kept within the city, and so they, like their kin who had been caught on the field outside of Port Charley, would be carted west and then shipped north to the Diamondgate, from which there could be no escape.

That gave Luthien and Brind'Amour only a few thousand soldiers to work with, and it became quite apparent that Oliver's Bluff would depend upon how many reinforcements the Eriadorans might find as the days wore on. Word was spreading to the more northern towns, they knew, and cheers reverberated across the countryside for the freeing of Caer MacDonald. But they were asking much if they expected many farmers to come and join in the cause. The planting season was fast approaching, as was the prime fishing season for those Eriadorans who made their living at sea. And even with the stunning victories, both in taking the city, then in holding it against an army of Praetonian Guards, the Eriadorans had lived long enough under the evil Greensparrow's rule to understand that this fight was a long way from won.

"Oliver and I will go," Luthien announced to Brind'Amour one morning as the two walked the city wall, observing the preparations, overseeing the assembly of wagons and the mounds of supplies.

The wizard turned a curious eye on the young man. "Go?" he asked.

"Out before the army," Luthien explained. "On a more northerly arc."

"To roust up support," the wizard reasoned, then went very quiet, considering the notion.

"I will not be secretive about who I am," Luthien said. "I go openly as the Crimson Shadow, an enemy of the throne."

"There are many cyclopians scattered among those hamlets,"

Brind'Amour reminded. "And many merchants and knights sympathetic to Greensparrow."

"Only because they prosper under the evil king while the rest of Eriador suffers!" Luthien said, his jaw tight, his expression almost feral.

"Whatever the reason," Brind'Amour replied.

"I know the folk of Eriador," Luthien declared. "The true folk of Eriador. If they do not kill the cyclopians, or the merchants, it is only because they have no hope, because they believe that no matter how many they kill, many more will come to exact punishment upon them and their families."

"Not so unreasonable a fear," Brind'Amour said. The wizard was merely playing the role of nay-sayer now; he had already come to the conclusion that Luthien's little addition to the march was a fine move, a daring addendum to a daring plan. And they would likely need the help. Malpuissant's Wall had been built by the Gascons centuries before to guard against just such a rebellion, when the southern kingdom, after conquering Avon, had decided that it could not tame savage Eriador. The wall had been built for defense against the northern tribes, and would be no easy target!

"But now they will know hope," Luthien reasoned. "That is the measure of the Crimson Shadow, nothing more. What I do while wearing the cape long ago became unimportant. All that matters is that I wear the cape, that I let them think I am some hero of old returned to lead them to their freedom."

Brind'Amour stared long and hard at Luthien, and the young man became uncomfortable under that familiar scrutiny. Gradually the wizard's face brightened, and he seemed to Luthien then like a father, as Luthien hoped his father would be.

In all the excitement of the last few weeks, Luthien realized that he had hardly considered Gahris Bedwyr since Katerin's arrival with *Blind-Striker*, the Bedwyr family sword, bearing news that the rebellion was on in full on Isle Bedwydrin. How fared Gahris now? Luthien had to wonder. Homesickness tugged at him, but a mere thought of Ethan, his brother whom Gahris had sent away to die, and of Garth Rogar, Luthien's barbarian friend, ordered slain in the arena after Luthien had defeated him, stole that notion. Luthien had left Isle Bedwydrin, had left Gahris, for good reason, and now frantic events gave him little time to worry about the man he no longer considered to be his father.

He looked at Brind'Amour in a different light. Suddenly the young Bedwyr needed this wise old man's approval, needed to see him smile as Gahris had smiled whenever Luthien won in the arena.

And Brind'Amour did just that, and put his hand on Luthien's shoulder. "Ride out this day," he bade the young man.

"I will go to Bronegan, and all the way to the Fields of Eradoch," Luthien promised. "And when I return to you on the eastern edges of Glen Albyn, I will carry in my wake a force larger than the force which soon departs Caer MacDonald."

Brind'Amour nodded and clapped the younger Bedwyr on the back as Luthien sped off to find Oliver and their mounts that they might head out on the road.

The old wizard stood on the wall for some time watching Luthien, then watching nothing at all. He had set Luthien on this course long ago, the day in the dragon's cave when he had given the young man the crimson cape. He was responsible, in part at least, for the return of the Crimson Shadow, and when he considered Luthien now, so willing to take on the responsibility that had been thrust his way, Brind'Amour's old and wheezy chest swelled with pride.

The pride a father might have for his son.

CHAPTER 19

PASSAGE OF SPRING

*H*E DOES THE RIGHT THING," Siobhan remarked, coming up on the wall beside Katerin. Katerin didn't turn to regard the half-elf, though she was surprised that Siobhan had chosen this particular section of the wall, so near to her.

Below the pair, Oliver and Luthien rode out from the gates, Oliver on his yellow pony and Luthien tall and proud on the shining white Riverdancer. They had already said their farewells, all that they had cared to make, and so they did not look back. Side by side, they trotted their mounts across the courtyard to the fallen outer wall, the area still dotted with several cyclopian corpses that the burial details hadn't been able to clear away, black-and-silver lumps in the diminishing snow.

"They have a long ride ahead of them," Siobhan remarked.

"Who?" Katerin asked.

Siobhan glanced at her skeptically and took note that her gaze was away to the east, to the horizon still pink with the new dawn. Pointedly, the proud woman did not look at Luthien.

"Our friends," Siobhan answered, playing the foolish, adolescent game.

Now Katerin did look to Luthien and Oliver, just a casual glance. "Luthien is always on the road," she answered. "This way and that, wherever his horse takes him."

Siobhan continued to study the woman, trying to fathom her purpose.

"That is his way," Katerin stated firmly, turning to look at the half-elf directly. "He goes where he chooses, when he chooses, and let no woman be fool enough to think that he will remain for her, or by her." Katerin looked away quickly, and that revealed more than she intended. "Let no woman be fool enough to think that she can change the ways of Luthien Bedwyr."

The words were said with perfect calm and control, but Siobhan easily read the underlying bitterness there. Katerin was hurting, and her cool demeanor was a complete façade, while her words had been uttered in just the right tones to make them a barbed arrow, shooting straight for the half-elf's heart. Rationally, Siobhan understood and knew that Katerin had spoken out of pain. In truth, the half-elf was not insulted or wounded in any way by Luthien's departure, for in her mind, she and the young Bedwyr had come to terms with the realities of their relationship.

Siobhan remained silent for a long moment, considered her sympathy for Katerin and the words the woman had just thrown her way. The verbal volley had been strictly out of self-defense, Siobhan knew, but still she was surprised that Katerin would attack her so, would go to the trouble of trying to make her feel worse about Luthien's departure.

"They have a long ride ahead of them," Siobhan said once again. "But fear not," she added, with enough dramatic emphasis to grab Katerin's gaze. "I do know that Luthien does well on long rides."

Katerin's jaw slackened at the half-elf's uncharacteristic use of double entendre and Siobhan's sly, even lewd, tone.

Siobhan turned and slipped easily down the ladder, leaving Katerin, and the specter of Luthien and Oliver riding away to the north and east.

Katerin looked back to the now-distant riders, to Luthien, her companion all those years back in Bedwydrin, where they had lost their innocence together, in the ways of the world and in the ways of love. She had wanted to hurt Siobhan, verbally if not physically. She cared for the half-elf, deeply respected her and in many ways called Siobhan a friend. But she could not ignore her feelings of jealousy.

She had lost the verbal joust. She knew that, standing up on Caer MacDonald's wall in the chill of an early spring day, watching Luthien ride away, her face scrunched in a feeble attempt to hold back the tears that welled in her shining green eyes.

"You are so very good at running from problems," Oliver remarked to Luthien when the two were far from Caer MacDonald's wall.

Luthien eyed his diminutive companion curiously, not understanding the comment. "Likely, we're running into trouble," he replied. "Not away from it."

"A fight with cyclopians is never trouble," Oliver explained. "Not the kind that you fear, at least."

Luthien eyed him suspiciously, guessing what was to come.

"But you have done so very well in avoiding the other kind, the more subtle and painful kind," Oliver explained. "First you send Katerin running off to Port Charley—"

"She volunteered," Luthien protested. "She demanded to go!"

"And now, you have arranged to be away for perhaps two weeks," the halfling continued without hesitation, ignoring Luthien's protests.

Those protests did not continue, for Luthien realized that he was guilty as charged.

"Ah, yes," Oliver chided. "Quite the hero with the sword, but in love, alas."

Luthien started to ask what the halfling might be gibbering about and deflect Oliver's intrusions, but he was wise enough to know that it was already too late for that. "How dare you?" the young Bedwyr asked sharply, and Oliver recognized that he had opened a wound. "What do you know of it?" Luthien demanded. "What do you know of anything?"

"I am so skilled and practiced in the ways of *amour*," the halfling replied coolly.

Luthien eyed his three-foot-tall companion, the young Bedwyr's expression clearly relating his doubts.

Oliver snorted indignantly. "Foolish boy," he said, snapping his fingers in the air. "In Gascony, it is said, a merchant is only as good as his purse, a warrior is only as good as his weapon, and a lover is only as good as—"

"Oliver!" Luthien interrupted, blushing fiercely.

"His heart," the halfling finished, looking curiously at his shocked companion. "Oh, you have become such a gutter-crawler!" Oliver scolded.

"I just thought . . ." Luthien stammered, but he stopped and waved his hand hopelessly. With a shake of his head, he kicked Riverdancer into a faster canter, and the horse leaped ahead of Threadbare.

Oliver persisted and moved his pony to match the Morgan highlander's speed. "Your heart is not known to you, my friend," he said as he came up alongside Luthien. "So you run, but yet, you cannot!"

"Oliver the poet," Luthien said dryly.

"I have been called worse."

Luthien let it go at that, and so did Oliver, but though the conversation ended, Luthien's private thoughts on the matter most certainly did not. Truly the young man was torn, full of passion and full of guilt, loving Katerin and Siobhan, but in different ways. He did not regret his affair with the half-elf—how could he ever look upon those beautiful moments with sadness?—and yet, never had he wanted to hurt Katerin. Not in any way, not at any time. He had been swept up in the moment, the excitement of the road, of the city and the budding rebellion. Bedwydrin, and Katerin, too, had seemed a million miles and a million years removed.

But then she had come back to him, a wonderful friend of another time, his first love—and, he had come to realize, his only love.

How could he ever tell that to Katerin now, after what he had done? Would she even hear his words? Could he have heard hers, had the situation been reversed?

Luthien had no answers to the disturbing questions. He kept a swift pace toward the northernmost tip of the Iron Cross, trying to put Caer MacDonald far behind him.

The snow that had so hampered the cyclopians and left so many one-eyes dead on the field as they tried to flee became a distant memory, most traces of white swallowed by the softening ground of spring. Only two weeks had passed since the battle, and the snow, except in the mountains, where winter hung on stubbornly, was fast receding, and the trees were thickening with buds, their sharp gray lines growing red and brown and indistinct.

Luthien and Oliver had been out of Caer MacDonald for five days, and now, with several hundred soldiers filtering in from the west to join the campaign, Port Charley folk mostly, Brind'Amour began his march. Out they marched in long lines, many riding, but most walking, and all under the pennants of Eriador of old—the mountain cross on a green field.

At the same time, Shuglin and his remaining dwarfs, some two hundred of the bearded folk, left Caer MacDonald's southern gate, trudging into the mountains, their solid backs bent low by enormous packs.

"Luthien has passed through Bronegan," the wizard said to Katerin, who was riding at his side.

The young woman nodded, understanding that this was fact and not supposition, and not surprised that the wizard could know such things.

"How many soldiers has he added?" she asked.

"A promise of a hundred," the wizard replied. "But only to join with him if he returns through the town with many other volunteers in tow."

Katerin closed her eyes. She understood what was going on here, the most unpredictable and potentially dangerous part of the whole rebellion. They had won in Caer MacDonald and had raised the pennants of Eriador of old, which would give people some hope, but the farmers and the simple folk, living their quiet existence, hardly bothered by Greensparrow and matters politic, would only join in if they truly believed not only in the cause but in the very real prospect of victory.

"Of course they need to see the numbers," Brind'Amour said, as though that news should neither surprise nor dismay. "We expected that all along. I hate Greensparrow above all others," the old wizard said, chuckling. "And am more powerful than most, yet even I would not join an army of two, after all!"

Katerin managed a weak smile, but there remained a logical problem here that she could not easily dismiss. Not a single town north of Caer MacDonald, not another town in all of Eriador, except perhaps for Port Charley, could raise a significant force on its own. Yet the towns were independent of each other, under no single ruler. Each was its own little kingdom; they were not joined in any way, had not been even in the so-called "glorious" days of Bruce MacDonald. Eriador was a rugged land of individuals, and that is exactly what Greensparrow had exploited on his first conquest, and exactly what he would likely try to exploit again. The young woman tossed her shining red hair and looked around at the mass moving in fair harmony behind her. Here was a strong force— enough to take the wall, likely. But if Greensparrow struck back at them, even when they were secured behind the wall, even with the barrier of the mountains, even with the newly acquired fleet to hamper the king's efforts, they would need many more soldiers than this.

Many more.

"Where will Luthien turn?" Katerin asked, unintentionally voicing the question.

"To the Fields of Eradoch," Brind'Amour answered easily.

"And what will he find in that wild place?" Katerin dared to ask. "What have your eyes shown you of the highlanders?"

Brind'Amour shook his head, his shaggy white hair and beard flopping side to side. "I can send my eyes many places," he replied, "but only if I have some reference. I can send my eyes to Luthien at times, because I can locate his thoughts, and thus use his eyes as my guide. I can find Greensparrow, and several others of his court, because they are known to me. But as it was when I was trying to discern the fleet that sailed north from Avon, I am magically blind to matters wherein I have no reference."

"What have your eyes shown you of the highlanders?" Katerin pressed, knowing a half-truth when she heard it.

Brind'Amour snickered guiltily. "Luthien will not fail," was all that he would say.

CHAPTER 20

THE FIELDS OF ERADOCH

To THE CASUAL OBSERVER, the northwestern corner of Eriador was not so different in appearance from the rest of the country. Rolling fields of thick green grass—"heavy turf," the Eriadorans called it—stretched to the horizon in every direction, a soft green blanket, though on a clear day, the northern mountains could be seen back to the west, and even the tips of the Iron Cross, little white and gray dots, poked their heads above the green horizon far in the distance to the southwest.

There was something very different about the northeast, though, the Fields of Eradoch, the highlands. Here the wind was a bit more chill, the almost constant rain a bit more biting, and the men a bit more tough. The cattle that dotted the plain wore coats of shaggy, thick fur, and even the horses, Morgan Highlanders like Luthien's own Riverdancer, had been bred with longer hair as a ward against the elements.

The highlands had not seen as much snow this winter as normal, though still more fell here than in the southern reaches of Eriador, and the snow cover was neither complete nor very deep by the time Luthien and Oliver crossed through MacDonald's Swath and made their way into the region. Everything was gray and brown, with even a few splotches of green, as far as their eyes could see. Melancholy and dreary, winter's corpse, with still some time before the rebirth of spring.

The companions camped about a dozen miles east of Bronegan that night, on the very edge of the Fields of Eradoch. When they awakened the next morning, they were greeted by unusually warm temperatures and a thick fog, as the last of the snow dissipated into the air.

"It will be slow this day," Oliver remarked.

"Not so," Luthien replied without the slightest hesitation. "There are few obstacles," he explained.

"How far do you mean to go?" the halfling asked him. "They have left Caer MacDonald by now, you know."

Oliver spoke the truth, Luthien realized. Likely, Brind'Amour and Katerin, Siobhan and all the army had already marched out of the city's gates, flowing north and west, along the same course Luthien and Oliver had taken. Until they got to MacDonald's Swath. There, they would cross and go to the south, into Glen Albyn, while Luthien and Oliver had turned straight north, across the breadth of the swath, to Bronegan, and now, beyond that and into Eradoch.

"How far?" Oliver asked again.

"All the way to Bae Colthwyn, if we must," Luthien replied evenly.

Oliver knew the impracticality of that answer. They were fully three days of hard riding from the cold and dark waters of Bae Colthwyn. By the time they got there and back, Brind'Amour would be at the wall, and the battle would be over. But the halfling understood and sympathized with the emotions that had prompted that response from Luthien. They had been greeted warmly in Bronegan, with many pats on the back and many toasts of free ale. Yet the promises of alliance, from the folk of Bronegan and from several other nearby communities who sent emissaries to meet with Luthien, had been tentative at best. The only way that these folk of the middle lands would line up behind the Crimson Shadow, in open defiance of King Greensparrow, was if Luthien proved to them that the whole of Eriador would fight in this war. Luthien had to go back through Bronegan on his journey south, or at least send an emissary there, and if he and Oliver had not mustered any more support, then they would ride alone all the way back to Glen Albyn.

And so they were in the highlands, to face perhaps their most critical test of the unity of Eriador. The highlanders of Eradoch were an independent group, tough and hardy. Many would call them uncivilized. They lived in tribes, clans based on heritage, and often warred amongst themselves. They were hunters, not farmers, better with the sword than the plow, for strength was the byword of the Fields of Eradoch.

That fact was not lost on the young Bedwyr, the general who had engineered the defeat of Belsen'Krieg outside of Caer MacDonald. All the highlanders, even the children, could ride, and ride well, on their powerful and shaggy steeds, and if Luthien could enlist a fraction of the thousands who roamed these fields, he would have a cavalry to outmatch the finest of Greensparrow's Praetorian Guards. But the highlanders were a superstitious and unpredictable lot. Likely they had heard of Luthien as the Crimson Shadow, and so he and Oliver would not be riding into Eradoch unannounced. Their reception, good or bad, had probably already been decided.

The pair rode on through most of that day, Luthien trying to keep them headed northeast, toward Mennichen Dee, the one village in all the region. It was a trading town, a gathering point, and many of the highland clans would soon be making their way to the place, with excess horses and piles of furs to swap for salt and spices and glittering gemstones brought in by merchants of the other regions.

The fog didn't lift all that day, and though the pair tried to keep their spirits high, the soggy air and the unremarkable ground (what little of it they could see) made it a long and arduous day.

"We should camp soon," Luthien remarked, the first words either of them had spoken in some hours.

"Pity us in trying to build a fire this night," Oliver lamented, and Luthien had no words to counter that. It would indeed be a cold and uncomfortable night, for they'd not begin a fire with the meager and soaked twigs that they might find in the highlands.

"We'll make Mennichen Dee tomorrow," Luthien promised. "There is always shelter available there to any traveler who comes in peace."

"Ah, but there's the rub," the halfling said dramatically. "For do we come in peace?"

The ride seemed longer to Luthien, who again had no real answers for his unusually gloomy friend.

They traveled on as the sun, showing as just a lighter patch of gray, settled into the sky behind them, and very soon, Luthien felt that subtle tingle of alarm, that warrior instinct. Something just beyond his conscious senses told him to be on guard, and the adrenaline began to course through his veins.

He looked to Oliver and saw that his halfling companion, too, was riding a bit more tensely in the saddle, ready to spring away or draw his blade.

Riverdancer's ears flattened and then came back up several times; Threadbare snorted.

They came like ghosts through the fog, gliding over the soft grass with hardly a sound, their bodies so wrapped in layers of fur and hide, and with huge horned or winged helms upon their heads, that they seemed hardly human, seemed extensions of the shaggy horses they rode, seemed the stuff of nightmares.

Both companions pulled up short, neither going for his weapon, transfixed by the spectacle of this ghostly ambush. The highlanders, huge men, every one of them dwarfing even Luthien, came in from every angle, slowly tightening the ring about the pair.

"Tell me I am dreaming," Oliver whispered.

Luthien shook his head.

"Sometimes, perhaps, you should do only as you are told." Oliver scolded. "Even if it is a lie!"

The highlanders stopped just far enough from the pair so that they remained indistinguishable, seeming more like monsters than men. Oliver silently applauded their tactic—they knew the ground, they knew the fog, and they certainly knew how to make an appearance.

"They want us to move first," Luthien whispered out of the side of his mouth.

"I could fall on the ground and tremble," the halfling offered sarcastically.

"They kill cowards," Luthien said.

Oliver considered the honest emotions flitting through his mind at the ominous presence sitting barely a dozen yards away. "Then I am doomed," he admitted.

Luthien snickered despite the predicament. "We knew what we were riding into," he said at length, to remind himself and bolster his resolve.

"Greetings from Caer MacDonald," he called in as strong a voice as he could muster. "The city that was unrightfully placed under the name of Montfort by a man who would claim kingship of all Avon and all Eriador."

For a long while, there came no response. Then one rider moved up through the passive line, walking his black horse past the others and close enough for Luthien and Oliver to see him clearly.

The young Bedwyr's face screwed up with curiosity, for this one appeared to be no highlander. He was large, yet he wore no furs or hide, but rather a complete suit of black-plated armor, the likes of which Luthien Bedwyr had never before seen. It was creased and jointed, with metal gauntlets fastened securely into place. Even the man's feet were armored! His helm was flat-topped and cylindrical—Luthien noted that there were two eye slits and not one; this was no cyclopian—and he carried a huge shield, black like his armor and emblazoned with a crest that Luthien did not know: a death figure, skeletal arms spread wide, an upturned sword in one hand, a downward-pointing sword in the other. A pennant with a similar crest flew from the top of the long lance he held easily at his side. Even the man's horse was covered in armor—head and neck and chest and flanks.

"Montfort," the man declared in a deep voice. "Rightfully named by the rightful king."

"Uh-oh," Oliver moaned.

"You are not of the highlands," Luthien reasoned.

The armored man shifted on his horse, the beast prancing nervously. Luthien understood that his words had somewhat unnerved the man, for his guess had been on the mark. The man was not of Eradoch, and that meant whatever hold he had over the highlanders would be tenuous indeed. He had come to some measure of power and influence by sheer strength, probably defeating several of the greatest warriors of Eradoch. Anyone who could best him would likely inherit his position, and so Luthien already had his sights set on the man.

But with the man's imposing size and all that armor, the young Bedwyr was not so fond of that possibility.

"Who are you, then, you who tinkles in a hard spring rain?" Oliver asked.

"A hard spring rain?" Luthien whispered incredulously to the halfling.

"Tinkle, tinkle," Oliver whispered back.

The armored man squared his shoulders and brought himself up to his full height. "I am the Dark Knight!" he declared.

The companions thought on that one for a moment.

"But you would have to be," Oliver reasoned.

"You have heard of me?"

"No."

The Dark Knight grunted in confusion.

"You would have to be," Oliver reiterated. "Is that not why it is called night?"

"What?" the exasperated man asked.

"Unless there is a moon," Luthien offered.

Oliver smirked, pleasantly surprised. "You are getting very good at this," he offered to his friend.

"What?" the knight demanded.

Oliver sighed and shook his head. "So silly tinkler," he said. "If you were not dark, you would be the day."

They couldn't see the man's face under the metal helm, but they both imagined his jaw drooping open. "Huh?" he grunted.

The two friends looked to each and exchanged helpless shrugs. "Peasant," they said in unison.

"I am the Dark Knight!" the armored man declared.

"Charge straight in?" Luthien offered.

"Of course," Oliver replied, and they both whooped, Luthien

drawing *Blind-Striker* and kicking Riverdancer into a great leaping start. Threadbare didn't follow, though, Oliver sitting passively.

Luthien knew that he was in trouble as soon as the knight's lance dipped his way, as soon as he realized that the long weapon would slip past his guard, and probably through his chest, before he ever got close enough to nick his opponent's horse on the tip of its nose. He brought his sword arm down and grabbed up Riverdancer's bridle in both hands—only riding skills, not fighting skills, could save him now.

Luthien waited until the last possible second, then cut Riverdancer to the left, angling away from the knight, and the strong and agile steed responded, cutting hard, clumps of turf flying from its hooves. The knight apparently expected the move, though, for he, too, shifted, turning his lance enough to nick Luthien across the shoulder, a painful sting. The young Bedwyr grimaced and whipped his hands across the other way, yanking hard on Riverdancer's reins.

Again, the mighty horse responded, digging hooves deep into the sod. Luthien started to bring *Blind-Striker* up, but felt a twang in his right shoulder. Quick-thinking and quick-moving, the young Bedwyr caught up the sword in his left hand instead, and lashed out, striking hard along the center of the lance. Then he shifted his angle and swiped a vicious backhand that slammed the edge of the blade against the knight's breastplate.

The sword bounced harmlessly away.

The two riders pounded away from each other, the knight discarding his snapped lance and Luthien straightening in the saddle, taking up his sword in his right hand again and testing its grip. He noted the approving looks of the highlanders as he turned Riverdancer about, just short of their ranks. It was going well so far, the young Bedwyr realized, for they admired his courage, and probably they admired his horse. Riverdancer was much shorter than the Dark Knight's steed, but wider and stronger. And Riverdancer was a Highland Morgan, as fine a steed as had ever been bred on the Fields of Eradoch. Gahris Bedwyr had paid a small fortune for the shining white mount, and in studying the approving nods now coming his way, Luthien realized that the horse had been worth every gold coin.

The opponents squared off once more. The Dark Knight reached for his sword, and had it half out of its scabbard, but then a sour look crossed his face. He regarded the sword for a moment, then slid the weapon away, taking up a flail instead. He lifted it above his head, swinging it effortlessly, the spiked iron ball spinning lazily on its heavy black chain. Better than the lance, Luthien thought, for at least he would be close enough to strike before he got struck this time.

Luthien sighed and wondered what good that might do. He had hit his opponent hard the first time, a blow that should have felled the man. Yet the Dark Knight hadn't even grunted at the impact, and if he was feeling any pain now, he wasn't showing it.

On came the man, and Luthien shrugged and dug his heels into Riverdancer's powerful flanks. They passed close this time, close enough for Luthien to feel the puff of steam from the nostrils of the Dark Knight's towering steed.

Luthien snapped off a short backhand, catching the knight under the arm as he lifted his spinning flail for a swing. Up went *Blind-Striker* in a quick parry, just deflecting the iron ball before it crunched Luthien's skull.

This time, Luthien didn't allow the pass. He knew that he had the advantage in mounts here, and so he turned Riverdancer tightly, coming around behind the Dark Knight's steed. In a moment, he was pacing his opponent once more, and he got in three hard strikes with his sword before the armored man could turn about to retaliate. They ran the line together, side by side, hammering at each other. Luthien's hits were mostly clean, while *Blind-Striker* took the momentum from the flail each and every time. Still, the heavy ball battered the young Bedwyr, and Luthien's sword seemed to have little effect as it rebounded off the other's heavy plating.

Finally, each of them breathing heavily, the opponents broke apart, Luthien cutting Riverdancer fast to the side. He could not win this way, he knew, for the mounted battle was too frenzied for him to find a crease in the knight's armor. The Dark Knight apparently knew it, too, for he swung his mount about, aiming for Luthien.

"Pass!" he demanded, and on came the thundering charge once more.

Luthien bent low and whispered into Riverdancer's ear. "I need you now," he said to the horse. "Be strong and forgive me." Off they charged, kicking up the sod, angling for another close pass.

Luthien hunched his shoulders close to Riverdancer's strong neck and turned his mount right into the path of the charging opponent. The Dark Knight straightened in surprise, his horse breaking stride.

Exactly what Luthien had prayed for.

The young Bedwyr did not slow at all. Riverdancer plowed headlong into the Dark Knight's steed, bowling the horse over so that it practically sat on the ground before it was able to regain any semblance of balance.

The armored knight held on dearly, accepting the hit as Luthien thrust *Blind-Striker* around the tumbling horse's neck.

Luthien, knocked dizzy from the impact of the powerful steeds, held on dearly as well. He focused squarely on his target, had known what he needed to do before he had ever begun the charge. His one attack, the sword thrust, was not for the knight's breastplate—what would be the point?—or even for the slits in the man's helmet, which were out of reach as the knight leaned defensively backward. Luthien swung at the man's fingers, so that he dropped the reins. As the staggering Riverdancer shuffled to the side, Luthien looped those reins about his sword and tugged with all his strength, and the knight's horse lurched violently.

Luthien nearly overbalanced and tumbled off the other side of his horse, but held on stubbornly, looking back just in time to see the Dark Knight unceremoniously slide off the rear flank of his mount, thudding hard to the ground.

Luthien slipped off Riverdancer and nearly fell facedown as the world continued to spin about him. He staggered and stumbled his way to his supine opponent, the man trying futilely to rise in his heavy armor. The flail whipped across, catching the young Bedwyr off balance.

Luthien's eyes widened in surprise and he hurled himself backward, slipping in the mud to fall unceremoniously to the ground.

The knight rolled and managed to get up as Luthien rose, the two facing off.

"Your attack was immoral," the Dark Knight declared. "You struck my horse!"

"My horse struck your horse," Luthien corrected indignantly.

"There are rules of combat!"

"There are rules of survival!" Luthien countered. "How am I to fight one armored such as yourself? What risks do you take?"

"That is the advantage of station," the Dark Knight roared. "Come on, then, *sans equine*."

Sitting not far away, Oliver cocked his head curiously at the armored man's demeanor. That last statement was a Gascon saying, reserved for nobles mostly, meaning competition, not always combat, without horses. Who was this knight? Oliver wondered.

Luthien approached cautiously. He could hit the man a dozen times to little effect, but one swipe of the flail would cave in his skull, or reduce his ribs to little bits. And his right arm was hanging loose, still feeling the sting from the lance cut. The two circled and launched measured strikes for a few passes, then the Dark Knight roared and came in hard, whipping his flail across and back.

The man couldn't move so well in that encumbering armor, though, and Luthien easily danced aside, swatting the knight on the back of the shoulder. The knight turned and tried to follow, but the agile Luthien was always a step ahead of him, *tap-tapping* with *Blind-Striker*, as much to prod the man on as to inflict any real damage. Already the young Bedwyr could hear the man panting inside that heavy suit.

"An honorable man would stand and fight!" the Dark Knight proclaimed.

"A stupid man would stand and die," Luthien countered. "You speak of honor, yet you hide behind a wall of metal! You see my face, yet I see no more than dark orbs through the slits of a helm!"

That gave the man pause, for he stopped abruptly and lowered his flail. "A point well taken," he said, and to Luthien's amazement, he began to unstrap his heavy helmet. He pulled it off and Luthien grew even more amazed, for the man was much older than Luthien had expected, probably three times the young Bedwyr's age! His face was rugged and wide, skin leathery and creased by deep lines. His gray hair was cropped short, but he wore a huge mustache, also gray, a line of bushy hair from mid-cheek to mid-cheek. His eyes, dark brown, were large and wide-spaced, with a thick nose between, and only his chin was narrow, jutting forward proudly.

The Dark Knight tossed his helmet to the ground. "Now," he said, "fight me fairly, young upstart."

He charged once more, and this time, Luthien met the rush, *Blind-Striker* whipping across, its angle and timing perfect to intercept the flail across the chain, halfway between the ball and the handle. The ball wrapped tightly around Luthien's sword. He tugged hard, thinking to take the weapon from the man, but the Dark Knight proved incredibly strong, and though Luthien had the advantage of angle, the older man held on.

Luthien felt the throb in his shoulder, but forgot about it as the Dark Knight's armored left hand came across in a vicious hook, slamming Luthien right in the face. Warm blood rolled down from Luthien's nose and over his lip, tasting salty-sweet.

The young Bedwyr staggered back a step, then wisely threw himself forward before the man could land a second weighted punch. The Dark Knight did snap his knee up, and while Luthien was wise enough to turn one leg in to protect his groin, he took the hit on the thigh.

Luthien responded by jamming his open palm up under the Dark Knight's chin, breaking the clench. The young Bedwyr leaped back, tugging and scrambling frantically, pulling hard on the knot the flail's chain had become.

He got punched again, in the chest, then again, right on his wounded shoulder. He reacted in kind and grimaced at the sudden throbbing in his hand after banging it hard off the Dark Knight's unyielding breast-plate.

A left hook crashed in just under Luthien's ribs. He ran to the side, throwing his momentum into the tangle of weapons, trying to change the angle, or to push the flail handle back over the older man's hand, forcing him to let go.

Finally, *Blind-Striker* slid free of its tangle, so quickly that Luthien skidded right past his opponent and stumbled down to one knee. The Dark Knight turned to follow, whipped the flail in a circular motion over his head. His thought was to seize the moment and attack immedi-ately, but *Blind-Striker*'s blade was much finer and stronger than the Dark Knight had anticipated, and the flail was an old weapon, as old as its wielder. The iron chain, weakened by age and by the finest blade in all of Eriador, split at one link and the studded ball flew through the air.

Across the way, Threadbare hopped to Oliver's command, and the halfling deftly lifted his hands, protected by his fine green gauntlets, to basket-catch the object.

The Dark Knight, apparently oblivious to the loss of his weapon, roared and rushed ahead, waving the handle and half a chain. He slowed only upon noticing Luthien's suddenly amused expression.

"Excuse me, good sir knight," came the halfling's call from behind. The Dark Knight turned slowly, to see Oliver dangling the lost flail ball by the end of its broken chain. The knight looked from Oliver to his weapon, his face screwed up with disbelief. Then he saw the horizon sud-denly, and then the gray sky, as Luthien kicked his legs out from under him.

The young Bedwyr was atop him, straddling his breastplate, the tip of *Blind-Striker* at the man's throat.

"I beg of you," the Dark Knight began, and Luthien thought it out of character for this one to whine. "Please, good sir, allow me to offer a final prayer to God before you kill me," the Dark Knight explained. "You have won fairly—I offer no protests, but I ask that I might make my final peace."

Luthien didn't know how to react, so surprised to hear such talk from one of Greensparrow's professed followers. "Who are you?" he asked.

"Of course, of course, my name," the Dark Knight said. "And I, of course, must know yours before you kill . . ." The man sighed and let that thought go.

"I am Estabrooke of Newcastle," he declared. "Lord Protector, First of the Sixth Cavaliers."

Luthien looked over at Oliver, his lips silently mouthing, *"First of the Sixth?"* The young Bedwyr had heard of the group before, a band of knights dedicated as personal bodyguards of the king of Avon and of the governors of the six major cities in that southern kingdom. Luthien had thought the group disbanded with the arrival of Greensparrow, for the cyclopians now served as Praetorian Guard. Apparently, he thought wrong.

Luthien paused, understanding that he had to consider this matter very carefully. He lifted *Blind-Striker* away from the knight's throat and wiped the blood from his face, all the while staring at the curious old man lying supine below him.

"You are a long way from Newcastle," Luthien said.

The man straightened himself, seemed to regain a bit of his dignity despite his predicament. "I am on a mission," he declared. "The first for a cavalier since . . ." His face screwed up as he tried to remember. It had indeed been a long time.

"Well, no matter," Estabrooke said at length. "I have prayed. You may state your name and kill me now." He took a deep breath and locked his dark brown eyes on Luthien's cinnamon-colored orbs. "Have at it," he said matter-of-factly.

Luthien looked all around. Of course he would not kill this man, but he wanted to figure out how his action, or inaction, might be viewed by the rugged highlanders ringing him.

"I never heard the claim of a challenge to the death," Luthien said, stepping aside and extending his hand. The Dark Knight looked at him skeptically for a moment, then accepted the grasp, and Luthien helped him to his feet.

"I will see to our horses," Estabrooke offered, walking away as he noticed Oliver's approach.

Luthien saw the halfling, too, and with the blood still running from his bent nose, he wasn't very pleased. "You said that you would charge right in," the young Bedwyr scolded.

"I never said that," Oliver corrected.

"You *implied* it!" Luthien growled.

Oliver blew a deep breath and shrugged. "I changed my mind."

Their conversation came to an abrupt end a moment later when the ring of mounted highlanders suddenly converged, huge horsemen and wicked weapons, two-headed spears and axes with blades the size of a large man's chest, pinning the pair helplessly together.

Luthien cleared his throat. "Good sir Estabrooke," he began. "Might you talk to your . . . friends?"

CHAPTER 21

GLEN ALBYN

EXCITED WHISPERS CIRCULATED among the Eriadoran soldiers as they set their camp in the wide vale of Glen Albyn, northeast of the Iron Cross. They had nearly crossed the glen; Dun Caryth, the anchoring point of Malpuissant's Wall, was not yet in sight, but the mountain that harbored the fortress certainly was. The battle was no more than two days away, might even be fought on the next afternoon.

The Eriadorans believed that they could take Dun Caryth and all the wall with just the force from Caer MacDonald, the five thousand that had settled into Glen Albyn. Their hopes soared higher, for the whispers spoke of more allies. Luthien was on the way back to them, it was said, along with a thousand fierce riders of Eradoch and a like number of farmers-turned-warriors from the smaller hamlets of central Eriador. All the land had risen against Greensparrow, so it seemed to the soldiers as they set their camp that night.

Too many issues swarmed Katerin's thoughts and she could not sleep. Eriador had risen and would fight for freedom, or for death. It was something the proud woman of Hale had dreamed of since her youngest days, and yet, with the possibility of this fantasy looming right before her eyes, Katerin felt the joy tainted.

She had lost Luthien. She heard the whispers of friends talking behind her back, and though there was no malice, only sympathy in their quiet words, that stung Katerin all the more. She knew that Luthien and Siobhan were lovers, had known it for some time, but only now, with the rebellion nearing its end and the prospects of life after the war, did Katerin come to appreciate the weight of that truth.

She walked alone, quietly, past the guards and the groups huddled about campfires, many engaged in games of chance, or in soft songs from Eriador of old. Some took notice of her passing and waved, smiling broadly, but they understood from Katerin's expression that she meant to be alone this night, and so they granted her the desired solitude. Katerin walked right out of the northern perimeter of the encampment, out into the dark fields where the stars seemed closer suddenly, and there she stood alone with her thoughts.

The war was barely six months old, would likely not last another six months, and what, then, would be left for Katerin O'Hale? Win or lose against Avon, it seemed to Katerin that life without Luthien would not be complete. She had traveled nearly two hundred miles to be with him, and had gone nearly two hundred more on missions, including this march, for his army and his cause, and now it seemed to the young woman that all her efforts would be for naught.

Her sniffle was the only sound, and that was taken from her by the wind.

She was surprised, and yet, deep in her heart, she was not, when a slender form, much smaller than her own, walked quietly up beside her.

Katerin didn't know what to say. She had come out here to think of what could not be, to come to terms with the realities of her life, and here was Siobhan, apparently following her right out of the camp.

Siobhan!

Katerin didn't look at her, couldn't look at her. She sniffled again and cleared her throat, then turned abruptly back for the encampment.

"How very stubborn and very stupid you will be if you let the man who loves you, and the man whom you love, get away," Siobhan said suddenly, stopping Katerin dead in her tracks.

The red-haired woman wheeled about, eyeing her adversary skeptically. *How stupid will you be to let me have him?* she wondered, but she did not speak, too confused by what Siobhan might be hinting at.

Siobhan tossed her long and lustrous wheat-colored tresses over her shoulder, looked up at the stars, and then back at Katerin. "He is not the first man I have loved," she said.

Katerin could not hide the pain on her face at hearing the confirmation of their passion. She had known it was true, but in her heart had held out some last vestige of hope.

"And he will not be the last," Siobhan went on. Her gaze drifted back up to the stars, and Katerin didn't hate her quite so much in that moment, recognizing the sincere pain that had washed over her fair, angular features. "I will never forget Luthien Bedwyr," the half-elf said, her voice barely a whisper. "Nor you, Katerin O'Hale, and when you are both buried deep in the earth, I, young still by the measures of my race, will try to visit your graves, or at least to pause and remember."

She turned back to Katerin, who stood, mouth agape. Tears rimmed Siobhan's green eyes; Katerin could see the glistening lines that had crossed the half-elf's high cheekbones.

"Yes," Siobhan continued, and she closed her eyes and breathed deeply, feeling the warm breeze and tasting the first subtle scents of the coming spring. "I will mark this very night," she explained. "The smells and the sights, the warmth of the air, the world reawakening, and when in the centuries to come I feel a night such as this, it will remind me of Luthien and Katerin, the two lovers, the folk of legend."

Katerin stared at her, not knowing what to make of the unexpected speech and uncharacteristic openness.

Siobhan locked that stare with her own and firmed her jaw. "It should pain you that Luthien and I have loved," the half-elf said bluntly, catching Katerin off her guard, turning her emotions over once again. "And yet," Siobhan continued unabashedly, "I take some of the credit, much of the credit, for the person the young Luthien Bedwyr has become. This person can understand love now, and he can look at Katerin O'Hale through the eyes of a man, not the starry orbs of a lustful boy."

Katerin looked away, chewing on her bottom lip.

"Deny it if you will," Siobhan said, moving about so that the young woman had to look at her. "Let your foolish pride encase your heart in coldness if that is what you must do. But know that Luthien Bedwyr loves you, only you, and know that I am no threat."

Siobhan smiled warmly then, a necessary ending, and walked away, leaving Katerin alone with her thoughts, alone with the night.

Luthien and Oliver were camped on the fields south of Bronegan that night, part of a force nearly half the size of the army in Glen Albyn. After the victory over the Dark Knight, Estabrooke had indeed talked to his "friends" as Luthien had asked, giving Oliver and Luthien some breathing room and some time.

Noble to the core, Estabrooke promptly and openly ceded to Luthien his earned leadership position over the thousand assembled riders. Luthien eyed the man with concern as he did so, understanding that such a transition would not be easy.

Kayryn Kulthwain, a huge and fierce woman, the finest rider in all of Eradoch and the one Estabrooke had defeated in open challenge just a few days before, immediately reclaimed that position. By the ancient codes of the riders, the title could not be passed from outsider to outsider.

Luthien, son of an eorl and somewhat trained in the matters of eti-

quette, understood the basic traditions of Eradoch. Estabrooke had ascended to a position of leadership by defeating the leader of the gathered
rulers, but that position would have never been more than temporary.

Very temporary. Estabrooke was an outsider, and as soon as the highlanders could have determined a proper order of challenge, the Dark
Knight would have been forced to battle and win against every one of
the riders, one after another. And if any of them had defeated Estabrooke
on the field, there would have been no mercy.

"Is Kayryn Kulthwain the rightful leader?" Luthien had asked those
around him.

"By deed and by blood," one man answered, and others bobbed their
heads in agreement.

"I came not to Eradoch to lead you," Luthien assured them all, "but
to ask for your alliance. To ask that you join with me and my folk of
Caer MacDonald against Greensparrow, who is not our king."

The men and women of Eradoch were not a complicated folk. Their
lives were straightforward and honest, following a narrow set of precepts,
basic guidelines that ensured their survival and their honor. It was all
Luthien had to say. When he turned back for Bronegan, the riders of Eradoch were not behind him, they were beside him—and it seemed to
both Luthien and Oliver that the fiercely independent folk of Eradoch
had wanted to join all along, but had been bound otherwise by the Dark
Knight.

Now the two friends, the knight, and the riders were camped south
of Bronegan, along with hundreds of farmers who had taken up arms for
the cause, eager to join once they learned that Eradoch had come into
the alliance.

Luthien sat with Oliver long into the night, the halfling wrapped in
blankets and working furiously to clean his marvelous clothing, and to
polish his belt buckle and his rapier. Oliver had put his purple breeches
too close to the fire to dry, and Luthien watched in silent amusement as
the foppish trousers began to smolder.

The halfling shrieked when he noticed, yanking the breeches away
and putting a nasty stare on his content friend.

"I meant to tell you," Luthien offered innocently.

"But you did not!" Oliver stated.

Luthien shrugged, much as Oliver had shrugged earlier that same day,
after Luthien's painful encounter with the Dark Knight. "I changed my
mind," the young Bedwyr said, imitating his diminutive friend's Gascon
accent.

Oliver picked up a stick and heaved it at him, but Luthien got his arm up in time to deflect it—though the movement pained his injured shoulder. He laughed and groaned at the same time.

As if on cue, Estabrooke, seeming only half the size of the imposing Dark Knight without his full suit of armor, walked into the light of their fire, carrying a small bowl. "A salve," he explained, moving near to Luthien. "Should take the sting out of your wounds and clean them. Allow them to heal properly, you see." Like a protective mother, the older man bent over Luthien, scooping up a handful of the smelly gray salve.

Luthien tilted his head so that his thick hair shifted away from the shoulder, giving the older man the opportunity to apply the stuff. All the while Luthien and Oliver watched the man closely, still not quite understanding why Estabrooke, First of the Sixth Cavaliers, was even in Eriador at that time. Luthien hadn't broached the subject up to now, for the day had been one of rushed travel and impromptu alliances. The young man could not wait any longer.

"Why are you here?" he asked bluntly.

Estabrooke's look was incredulous. His lips pursed, sending his huge mustache out so far as to tickle the tip of his nose. "I am a Lord Protector," he answered, as though that should explain everything.

"But King Greensparrow, he is in Gascony," Oliver reasoned. "Why would he think to send you so far to the north?"

"Greensparrow?" Estabrooke echoed. "Oh, no, not that one! Duke Paragor, it was, Duke of Princetown and all that."

"When?" Luthien interrupted.

"I was visiting—fine city, that Princetown. The best of zoos, and the gardens!"

Oliver wanted to hear about the zoos, but Luthien kept his priorities. "The duke?" the young Bedwyr reminded.

Estabrooke looked at him curiously, seeming for a moment as though he did not understand. "Yes, of course, Paragor, skinny fellow," the Dark Knight said finally, recollecting his original train of thought. "Should get his face out of those books and into some pie, I say!

"Two weeks," he added quickly to defeat Luthien's mounting scowl. "Called me in for a grand banquet, then asked me to come north, to Era . . . Eradoy. I say, what was the name you gave to this place?"

"Eradoch," Oliver answered.

"Yes, Eradoch," Estabrooke continued. " 'Go to Eradoch,' so said Paragor. Put the ruffians in line. Long live the king, and all that, of course. It was necessary to oblige, being a Lord Protector of the First of the Sixth, of course, and Paragor being an emissary of the rightful king of Avon."

It made perfect sense to Luthien and Oliver. Duke Paragor saw the trouble brewing in Eriador and was close enough to the northern land to understand the value of the riders. The duke would not have impressed the fierce highlanders, and neither would his most usual cohorts, wizards and cyclopians. But then Estabrooke, a knight of the old school, a man of the sword and of indisputable honor, arrives in Princetown and the emissary is found.

"But why did you turn sides?" Oliver had to ask.

"I have not!" Estabrooke insisted as soon as be figured out what the halfling was implying. "Your friend beat me in fair challenge, and thus I am indebted to him for one hundred days." He looked to Luthien. "Of course you understand that you cannot use me as a weapon against my king. My sword is silent."

Luthien nodded and smiled, quite pleased. "In that time, good sir knight," he promised, "you will come to know the truth of your King Greensparrow and the truth of what we in Eriador have begun."

Now it was the half-elf's turn to mourn the loss of Luthien, though Siobhan had known since that windy and rainy night in Caer MacDonald that their love would not be. It was official now, final, as it had to be.

Still, it hurt, and so Siobhan decided that she, too, would find no sleep this night. She meandered for a while around the encampment, pausing long enough to join in the singing at one campfire, the gaming at another. Making her way toward the southeastern end, she came in sight of Brind'Amour's rather large tent. A lantern was burning inside, and the shadows showed the old wizard to be awake.

He was clapping his hands, a smile stretching from ear to ear, when Siobhan entered. She noted that he had just draped a cloth over a circular item atop a small pedestal—his crystal ball, she realized.

"You have seen Luthien," Siobhan reasoned. "And know now that the rumors of his force are true."

Brind'Amour looked at her curiously. "Oh, no, no," he replied. "Too much fog up there. Too much fog. I think I saw the boy earlier, but it might have been a highlander, or even a reindeer. Too much fog."

"Then we cannot confirm—" Siobhan began.

"Rumors usually hold some measure of truth," the wizard interjected.

Siobhan paused and sighed. "We will need to form two sets of tactics," she decided. "Two plans of battle. One without help from Luthien, and another should he ride in with his thousands."

"No need," Brind'Amour said cryptically.

Siobhan looked at him unblinkingly, in no mood for the wizard's games.

Brind'Amour recognized this and wondered for an instant what might be so troubling the half-elf. "Word of our victory in Caer MacDonald precedes us," he explained at once, anxious to bring a smile back to the fair Siobhan's face. "The pennant flying above Dun Caryth is the mountain cross on the green field!"

It hit Siobhan too unexpectedly and she screwed her face up, trying to decipher what Brind'Amour might be talking about. Gradually, it came clear to her. Brind'Amour had just claimed that the fortress anchoring Malpuissant's Wall was under the flag of Eriador of old! "The wall is taken?" the half-elf blurted.

"The wall is ours!" the wizard confirmed, lifting his voice.

Siobhan couldn't even speak. How could such a victory have been handed to them?

"The majority of those living at Dun Caryth and in the various gate towers all along the wall were not cyclopian, nor even Avon citizens, but Eriadorans," the old wizard explained. "They were servants to the soldiers, mostly, craftsmen and animal handlers, but with easy access to the armories."

"They heard of the Crimson Shadow," Siobhan reasoned.

Brind'Amour put his arms behind his head and leaned back comfortably against the center pole of his tent. "So it would seem."

CHAPTER 22

EYES FROM AFAR

HE WAS SO THIN as to appear sickly, skin hanging loosely over bones, eyes deep in dark circles. His once thick brown hair had thinned and grayed considerably, leaving a bald stripe over the top of his head. The rest he combed to the side and out, so that it appeared as if he had little wings behind his ears.

Frail appearances can be deceiving, though, as was the case with this man. Duke Paragor of Princetown was Greensparrow's second, the most powerful of the seven remaining dukes. Only Cresis, leader of the cyclopians, and the only duke who was not a wizard, was higher in line for the throne: a purely political decision, and one that Paragor was confident he could reverse should anything ill befall his king.

Paragor wasn't thinking much about ascension to the throne this day, however. Events in Eriador were growing increasingly disturbing. Princetown was the closest and the most closely allied of the Avon cities to that rugged northern land, and so Paragor had the highest stakes in the outcome of the budding rebellion in Eriador. Thus this wizard, proficient in the arts of divining, had watched with more than a passing interest. He knew of Belsen'Krieg's defeat on the fields outside of Montfort; he knew that the Avon fleet had been captured wholesale and sailed north. And he knew of his own failure, Estabrooke, who had been sent north with the intent of keeping the Riders of Eradoch out of the Crimson Shadow's fold.

That very morning, a surly Duke Paragor had watched a thousand riders follow the Crimson Shadow into the swelling rebel encampment in Glen Albyn.

"And all of this with Greensparrow away on holiday in Gascony!" the duke roared at Thowattle, a short and muscular cyclopian with bowed legs, bowed arms, and only one hand, having lost the other and half the forearm as well while feeding one of his own children to a lion in Princetown's famed zoo. The one-eyed brute had fashioned a metal cap and spike to fit over his limb, but the stump was too sensitive for such a device and so he could not wear it. Even with the loss, Thowattle was the toughest cyclopian in Princetown, unusually smart, and unusually cruel, even for one of his race.

"They are just Eriadorans," Thowattle replied, spitting the name derisively.

Paragor shook his head and ran the fingers of both hands through his wild hair, making it stick out all the farther. "Do not make the same mistake as our king," the duke cautioned. "He has underestimated our enemy to the north and the breadth of this uprising."

"We are the stronger," Thowattle insisted.

Paragor didn't disagree. Even if all of Eriador united against Greensparrow, the armies of Avon would be far superior, and even without the fleet that had been stolen, the Avon navy was larger, and manned with crews more acclimated to fighting from such large ships. But a war now, with many of Avon's soldiers away in southern Gascony, fighting with the Gascons in their war against the Kingdom of Duree, would be costly, and crossing the mountains or Malpuissant's Wall, fighting on the Eriadorans' home ground, would help to balance the scales.

"Fetch my basin," Paragor instructed.

"The one of red iron?" Thowattle asked.

"Of course," Paragor snapped, and he sneered openly when Thowattle's expression turned to doubt. The cyclopian left, though, and returned a moment later carrying the item.

"You've been using this too much," Thowattle dared to warn.

Paragor's eyes narrowed. Imagine a cyclopian scolding him concerning the use of magic!

"You told me yourself that divining is a dangerous and delicate act," the cyclopian protested.

Paragor's stare did not relent, and the cyclopian shrugged his broad shoulders and fell silent. Paragor would not discipline him for his insolence, and indeed the duke heard the truth in the cyclopian's words. Divining, sending his eyes and ears out across the miles, was a delicate process. Much could be seen and revealed, but often it was only half truths. Paragor could locate a specific familiar place, or a specific familiar person—in this case, as in the last few, it would be Estabrooke—but such magical spying had its limitations. A real spy or scout collected most of his information before he ever got to the target, and could then use whatever he learned from the target in true context. A wizard's eye, however, normally went right to the heart, blinded to all the subtle events, often the more important events, surrounding the targeted person or place.

Divining had its limitations, and its cost, and its trappings. Great magical energy was expended in such a process, and like a drug, the act could become addictive. Often during this process, more questions were formed than answers given, and so the wizard would go back to his crystal ball, or his enchanted basin, and send his eyes and ears out again, and again. Paragor had known of wizards found dead, drained of their very life force, slumped in their chairs before their divining devices.

But the duke had to go back again to Eriador. He had seen the defeat at Port Charley, the massacre on the fields of Montfort, and the ride of Eradoch, and all of it was inevitably leading his way, to Malpuissant's Wall, which was under his domain.

Thowattle placed the basin on a small round table in the duke's private study, a scarcely furnished and efficient room containing only the table, a large but rather plain desk and chair, a small cabinet, and a wall rack of several hundred compartments. The cyclopian then went to the cabinet and took out a jug of prepared water. He began to pour it into the basin, but it splashed a bit and an angry Paragor pulled the jug from his one hand, slapping him aside.

Thowattle just shook his ugly head skeptically; he had never seen the duke so flustered.

Paragor finished filling the basin, then produced a slender knife from under the voluminous folds of his brownish-yellow robes. He began to chant softly, waving one hand over the basin, then he stabbed his own palm and allowed his blood to drip into the water.

The chanting continued for many minutes, Paragor slowly lowering his face to within an inch of the bowl, peering deeply into the swirling red waters.

Peering deeply, watching the forming image . . .

"An easy victory," a young man—*the Crimson Shadow! Paragor realized by the cape he wore—was saying. He was in a large tent, surrounded by an odd crew: a foppish halfling, an old man that Paragor did not know, and three women, all very different in appearance. One was tall and strong, with hair the color of a rich sunset, another was much smaller of frame—perhaps with the blood of Fairborn—with angular features and long wheat-colored tresses, and the third was a rugged woman, dressed in the furs of a highlander. Paragor knew this one, Kayryn Kulthwain, the woman Estabrooke had beaten to take control of the folk of Eradoch.*

"But this army was up for a fight," the foppish halfling replied in a thick Gascon accent. *"And now we have no fight for them!"*

Paragor didn't quite understand, but he didn't let his mind wander at that time. He sent his gaze to the edges of the basin, seeking the object of his divining. There was Estabrooke, seated passively on a stool, resting against the side of the tent. What had happened to so quiet the commanding cavalier? the wizard-duke wondered. The resignation on Estabrooke's face might be the most unsettling thing of all!

Gradually Paragor realized that he was meandering from his course. Already he could feel the weight of the magic; his time was short. Near the center of the tent, of the basin, the Crimson Shadow was speaking once more.

"As the fingers of a hand have the folk of Eriador assembled," he said, *waxing poetic and holding his own hand up in the air.* "Come together into a fist."

"A fist that has punched King Greensparrow right in the nose," the old man said. *"A solid blow, but have we really hurt him?"*

"Eriador is ours," the red-haired woman declared.

"For how long?" the old man asked cynically.

That set them all back on their heels. "Greensparrow is in Gascony, that much we know," the old man continued. "And Greensparrow will return."

"The plan was yours, I remind you," the halfling protested.

"It did not go as planned."

"The objective was gained more easily," the halfling said.

"But not with the same effect as Oliver's Bluff," the old man snapped right back. *"We are not done, I fear. Not yet."*

"What is left?" the halfling asked.

"Forty-five miles is not so far a march in the spring," the old man said *slyly.*

The image in the divining basin faltered, Paragor's concentration destroyed by the sudden shock. Blanching white, the skinny wizard-duke fell back from the bowl. Princetown—the upstart fools were talking of marching to Princetown!

Paragor understood the peril. This was no small force, and Greensparrow had not acted quickly enough. The armies of Avon were not assembled for march and were nowhere near Princetown. And what other fight had the group declared already won?

Malpuissant's Wall?

The skinny duke ran his fingers through his hair again repeatedly. He had to think. He had to sit down in the dark and concentrate. He knew a little, but not enough, and he was tired.

Such were the limitations, and the cost, of divination.

"Princetown," Siobhan reasoned, following Brind'Amour's logic. "The Jewel of Avon."

"The stakes just rose for Oliver's Bluff," Brind'Amour confirmed.

"Greensparrow, he will never expect it, and never believe it," Oliver said. Then in quieter tones so that only Luthien could hear him clearly, he added, "Because I am standing right here and I do not believe it."

"Princetown is isolated," Brind'Amour explained. "Not another militia of any size within two hundred miles."

Siobhan wore a confused expression, half doubting the possibility, half intrigued by it. "They could send another fleet," she pointed out, "around the wall to cut us off from our home ground."

"They could," Brind'Amour conceded. "But do not underestimate the willingness of those Eriadorans who have not yet joined with us. The folk of Chalmbers, a fair-sized town, are not blind to the events along the mountains and along the wall. Besides," the old wizard added slyly, rubbing his wrinkled fingers together, "we will strike quickly, within the week."

Oliver understood that this might be his one chance to become a part of history, with his name attached to the daring assault. He also understood that the possibility existed that he, and all the rest of them, would be slaughtered on a field south of Eriador. Quite a risk, considering that the original objective of the rebellion (which, in fact, had only begun by accident!) had already been apparently attained. "Princetown?" he asked aloud, drawing attention. "To what point?"

"To force a truce," Brind'Amour replied without hesitation. The old wizard didn't miss the cloud that then crossed Luthien's face.

"Did you think to take it all the way?" Brind'Amour scoffed at the young Bedwyr. "Did you think to go all the way into Avon and conquer Carlisle? All of Eriador would have to march south, and we would still be outnumbered more than three to one!"

Luthien didn't know how to respond, didn't know what he was think-ing or feeling. The completion had come easily—the wall was theirs and, for all practical purposes, Eriador was out from under Greensparrow's shadow. Just like a snap of Oliver's green-gauntleted fingers. But for how long? Brind'Amour had asked. It seemed to Luthien then that the fight was far from over, that Greensparrow would come back after them again and again. Could they ever truly win? Perhaps they should take it all the way to Carlisle, Luthien thought, and end the dark shadow that was Greensparrow once and for all time.

"The common folk of Avon would join with us," he reasoned, a hint of desperation in his resonant voice. "As have the common folk of Eriador."

Brind'Amour began to argue, but Oliver interrupted with a raised hand. "I am schooled in this," the halfling explained, begging the wiz-ard's pardon.

"They would see us as invaders," Oliver said to Luthien. "And they would defend their homes against us."

"Then why is Princetown different?" Luthien asked sharply, not pleased at hearing the obvious truth.

"Because it is merely Oliver's Bluff," the halfling said, and then came the predictable snap of his fingers. "And I want to see the zoo."

"Only then do we offer a truce to Avon's king," Brind'Amour ex-plained. "With Princetown in our grasp, we'll have something to barter." Luthien's expression was doubtful, and Brind'Amour understood. The young man had grown up on an isolated island, far from the intrigue of the world's leaders. Luthien was thinking that, if Greensparrow was so powerful, the king could merely march northeast from Carlisle and take Princetown back by force, but what Luthien didn't understand was the embarrassment factor. The only chance Eriador had of breaking free of Avon was to become such a thorn in Greensparrow's side, such an embarrassment to him in his dealings with the southern kingdoms, particularly Gascony, that he simply didn't want to have to bother himself with Eriador anymore. Princetown conquered might just accomplish that; then again, the wizard had to admit, it might not.

"So there we have it," Brind'Amour said suddenly, loudly. "We take Princetown and then we offer it back."

"After we let the animals go," Oliver added, drawing amused smiles from all in the tent.

Simple and logical, it outwardly sounded. But not one of the planners, not Luthien nor Oliver, Katerin nor Siobhan, Kayryn Kulthwain nor even Brind'Amour believed it would be that simple.

The army came upon Malpuissant's Wall, among the most impressive structures in all of Avon, the next day. It stood fifty feet high and twenty feet wide, stretching nearly thirty miles from the eastern edge of the Iron Cross all the way to the Dorsal Sea. Gatehouses had been built every five hundred yards, the most impressive of these being the fortress of Dun Caryth. She reached out from the last sheer wall of the rugged mountains, blending the natural stone into the worked masonry of the wall. Half of Dun Caryth was aboveground, soaring towers and flat-topped walls brimming with catapults and ballistae, and half was below, in tunnels full of supplies and weapons.

In viewing the place, Luthien came to appreciate just how important this easily won victory had been. If his army had gone against the Praetorian Guards of Dun Caryth, they would have suffered terrible losses, and no siege could have lasted long enough to roust the brutes from the fortress. The uprising had come from within the fortress walls, though, and Dun Caryth, and all of Malpuissant's Wall, was theirs.

Their welcome was warm and full of celebration, the Eriadorans all feeling invulnerable, as if Greensparrow's name was no more than a curse to be hurled at enemies.

Brind'Amour knew better, but even the wizard could not help but be caught up in the frenzy when the victorious armies came together. And it was good for them, realized the wizard-turned-general: celebration further sealed their alliance and ensured that the less predictable folk, like the Riders of Eradoch, were fully in the fold.

So they enjoyed that day at the wall, swapped their stories of hard-won victory, and of friends who had given their lives. The army from Caer MacDonald, and from the northern fields, camped on the plain north of Dun Caryth that night.

Feeling invincible.

*   *   *

Back in his palace in Princetown, Duke Paragor paced the carpeted floor of his bedchamber. He was tired, his magic expended, but he wanted to call to Greensparrow.

Paragor shook his head, realizing what that distant communication would offer. Greensparrow would dismiss the whole affair, would insist that the upstarts in Eriador were a mob and nothing more.

Paragor considered his options. The nearest dukes, fellow wizards, were in Evenshorn, far to the south, and in Warchester, all the way around the southern spur of the Iron Cross, on the banks of glassy Speythenfergus. It would take them weeks to even muster their forces, and weeks more for their armies to trudge through the mud and melting snows to get to Princetown. The wizard-dukes could get to Paragor's side, of course, by using their magic—perhaps they could even bring along a fair contingent of Praetorian Guards. But would they really make a difference against the force he believed would be coming down from Eriador? And what of his own embarrassment if he called to them and begged them, and then the unpredictable Eriadorans did not come?

"But I have other allies!" Paragor snarled suddenly, startling Thowattle, who was sitting on the rug in a corner of the lavish room.

Thowattle studied his master carefully, recognizing the diabolical expression. Paragor meant to summon a demon, the cyclopian realized, or perhaps even more than one.

"Let us see if their will for war can be slowed," the wicked duke continued. "Perhaps if the Crimson Shadow is slain . . ."

"That would only heighten the legend," the wary cyclopian warned. "You will make a martyr of him, and then he will be more powerful, indeed!"

Paragor wanted to argue the point, but found that he could not; the unusually perceptive one-eye was right again. Paragor improvised—there were ways to kill a man's spirit without killing the man. "Let us suppose that I can break the will of the Crimson Shadow," Paragor offered, his voice barely above a whisper.

Perhaps he could break the man's heart.

CHAPTER 23

COLLECTING ALLIES

IT WAS A BARE ROOM, empty of all furnishings save a single brazier set upon a sturdy tripod near the southeastern corner. Each of the walls bore a single sconce holding a burning torch, but were otherwise plain and gray, as was the ceiling. The floor, though, was not so unremarkable. Intricate tiles formed a circular mosaic in the center of the room, its middle area decorated as a pentagram. The circle's outer perimeter was a double line, and within these arching borders were runes of power and protection.

Paragor stood within the circle now, with Thowattle by the brazier, the cyclopian carrying a small crate holding many compartments strapped about his burly neck. The duke himself had placed the tiles, every tiny piece, years before—a most painstaking process. More often than not, Paragor would have finished one section and upon inspection discover that it was not perfect. Then he would have to rip up all the tiles and start again, for the Circle of Sorcery, the protection offered the wizard against whatever evil demon he summoned, had to be perfect. The design had stood the test for several years, against many demons.

Paragor stood absolutely still, reciting the long and arduous chant, a call to hell itself interspersed with thousands of protection spells. Every so often, he lifted his left hand toward Thowattle and spoke a number, and the cyclopian reached into the appropriate compartment of his crate, took out the desired herb or powder, and plunked it into the burning brazier.

Sometimes the component created a heavily scented smoke, other times, a sudden burst of flame, a miniature fireball. Gradually, through the hours of the sorcerous process, the fires in the brazier began to mount. At first, there had been no more than a lick of flame; now a fair-sized fire raged in the middle of the brazier, the heat of it drawing sweat on the already smelly cyclopian.

Paragor seemed oblivious to it all, though in truth, he and his magic were the true source of the brazier's life. There were two types of sorcery: lending and true summoning. The first, lending, was by far the easier route, wherein the wizard allowed a demon to enter his body. The true summoning, which Paragor now attempted, was much more difficult and dangerous. Paragor meant to bring a demon in all its unholy majesty into this room, and then to loose it upon the world, following a strict set of instructions given it by the wizard.

Demons hated servitude and hated more those who forced it on them, but Paragor was confident in his sorcery. He would bring in Kosnekalen, a minor fiend, and one he had dealt with successfully on several occasions.

The flames in the brazier went from orange to yellow to bright white, their intensity and fury growing as Paragor shifted dancing. The wizard spun about his circle, never crossing the line, calling out emphatically, throwing all of his heart into the chant, an unholy tenor, his voice breaching the gates of hell.

He stopped suddenly, thrusting his left hand out toward Thowattle, calling for six, three times, and the cyclopian, no novice to this awful experience, reached into the sixth compartment of the sixth row, extracting a brown, gooey substance.

Into the brazier it went and the flames burned hotter still, so hot that the cyclopian had to back away several steps. Inside the circle, Paragor fell to his knees, his left hand extended, tears mixing with sweat on his sallow features.

"Kosnekalen!" he begged as black crackles of lightning encircled the white fires, as the flames reached a new level of life.

Thowattle fled to the northwestern corner and huddled, terrified, on the floor, covering his eyes.

A forked tongue flicked from the flames and behind it, a dark shadow appeared, a huge head capped by great curving horns. A monstrous, muscled arm reached out the side of the fires, followed by a leathery wing—a huge leathery wing!

Paragor's face went from pain to ecstasy to curiosity. Kosnekalen was a lithe demon, man-sized, with tiny tipped horns, but this fiend was much larger and, the wizard could already sense, much more powerful.

Clawed fingers raked the air as a second arm came forth, and then, in a burst of sheer power, the flames spewed forth the fiend, a gigantic, twelve-foot-tall monstrosity with smoking black flesh and scales. Its face was serpentine, long and wicked fangs jutting over its lower jaw, drool dripping beside them and hissing like acid as it hit the stone floor. Three-clawed feet scraped impatiently on the floor, drawing deep lines in the stone.

"Kosnekalen?" Paragor asked, his voice barely above a whisper.

"I called for Kosne—" the wizard began.

"I came in Kosnekalen's place!" the demon roared, its horrid voice, both grating and squealing, echoing off the bare walls.

Paragor tried hard to collect his wits. He had to appear in command here, else the demon would crash out of the room and go on a rampage, destroying everything in its path. "I require only a single service," the duke began. "One that should be pleasurable . . ."

"I know what you require, Paragor," the demon growled. "I know."

Paragor straightened. "Who are you?" he demanded, for he had to know the demon's name before he could demand a service of it. This could be a tricky and dangerous moment, the practiced sorcerer understood, but to his surprise, and his relief, the demon willingly replied.

"I am Praehotec," the beast said proudly. "Who was with Morkney when Morkney died."

Paragor nodded—he had heard a similar tale from Kosnekalen. Kosnekalen had been more than happy to tell the tale in great detail, and Paragor had sensed that there was a great rivalry between the fiends.

"I was denied a pleasure then," the evil Praehotec went on, barely sublimating its boiling rage. "I will not be denied that pleasure again."

"You hate the Crimson Shadow," Paragor reasoned.

"I will eat the heart of the Crimson Shadow," Praehotec replied.

Paragor smiled wickedly. He knew just how to open that heart to the fiend.

Paragor's vision had been narrowly focused on the events to the north of Princetown, in Glen Albyn and farther north, in Bronegan and the Fields of Eradoch, but that focus, those self-imposed blinders necessary for such divining, hadn't allowed him a view to the northwest, into the mountains of the Iron Cross.

Shuglin stood tall in those mountains, watching to the east, toward the wall and the city of Princetown. He and his remaining kin, less than three hundred of the bearded folk, had gone out from Caer MacDonald when the army had marched, but had traveled south into the heart of the towering mountains, where the snow still lay thick, where winter had not yet relinquished its icy grasp. Shuglin had gone to guard the mountain passes, though the dwarf and Brind'Amour, who had sent him, knew that those passes would be blocked for more than a month still, and maybe longer than that.

Brind'Amour was the only non-dwarf who knew the real mission behind Shuglin's dangerous march. That hope had been realized less than a week out from Caer MacDonald, in a deep, deep cavern high up from the city. For many years, the beleaguered dwarfs of Montfort, now Caer MacDonald, had heard rumors of their kin living free among the peaks of the Iron Cross. Most of the dwarfs were old enough to remember mountain dwarfs who had come into the city to trade in the days before Greensparrow, and one of the group, an old graybeard who had been enslaved in the mines since the earliest days of Greensparrow's reign, claimed to be from that tribe, the descendants of Burso Ironhammer. That old graybeard had survived twenty years of hard labor in the mines, then the fierce battles of Montfort. It was he, not Shuglin, who had led the troupe into the snow-packed passes, through secret tunnels, and ultimately into the deep cave, the realm of Burso's folk.

What Shuglin and the other city dwarfs found in that cavern made their hearts soar, made them know, for perhaps the first time, what it was to be a dwarf. Far below the snow-covered surface, in smoky tunnels filled more with shadow than light, the dwarfs had met their kin, their heritage. DunDarrow, the Ingot Shelf, the place was called, a complex of miles of tunnels and great underground caverns. Five thousand dwarfs lived and worked here, in perfect harmony with the stone that was the stuff of their very being. Shuglin looked upon treasures beyond anything he could imagine; piles of golden and silver artifacts, gleaming weapons, and suits of mail to rival those of the mightiest and wealthiest knights in all of the Avonsea Islands.

Though these were city dwarfs, they were welcomed with open arms by the king of the mines, Bellick dan Burso, and hundreds of the mountain folk gathered each night in several of the great halls to hear the tales of the battle, to hear of the Crimson Shadow and the victory in Montfort.

Now wrapped in thick furs, Shuglin stood on a high pass, waiting for King Bellick. The dwarf king, younger than Shuglin, with a fiery orange beard and eyebrows so bushy that they hung halfway over his blue eyes, was not tardy, and the eagerness of his step as he came onto the ledge gave Shuglin hope.

The city dwarf knew that he would be asking much of this king and his clan. Shuglin was glad that the king was a young dwarf, full of fire, and full of hatred for Greensparrow.

Bellick moved up to the ledge beside the blue-bearded dwarf and gave a nod of greeting. "We daresn't trade with Montfort since the wizard-king took the throne," Bellick said, something Shuglin had heard a hundred times in the two days he had been at DunDarrow.

Bellick gave a snort. "Many haven't seen the outside-the-mountains land in score of years," the dwarf king continued. "But we're loving the inside-the-mountain land, so we're contented."

Shuglin looked at him, not quite believing that claim.

"Contented," Bellick reiterated, and his voice didn't match the meaning of the word. "But we're not happy. Most have no desire to go out to the flatlands, but even they who are content are not liking the fact that we cannot go safely outside the mountains."

"Prisoners in your own home," Shuglin remarked.

Bellick nodded. "And we're not liking the treatment of our kin." He put his hand on Shuglin's strong shoulder as he spoke.

"You will come with me, then," the blue-bearded dwarf reasoned. "To the east."

Bellick nodded again. "Another storm gathers over the mountains," he said. "Winter will not let go. But we have ways of travel, underground ways, that will get us to the eastern edges of DunDarrow."

Shuglin smiled, but tried hard to keep his emotions hidden. So perhaps he was not out of the fighting yet, he mused. He would return to Luthien and Siobhan's side, with five thousand armed and armored dwarven warriors in his wake.

Luthien sat alone on the stump of a tree and let the melancholy afternoon seep into his mood. Oliver had been right, he knew. Over the last few weeks, Luthien had been running away from his emotions, first by sending Katerin to Port Charley, then by traipsing off with Oliver on the roundabout circuit to Glen Albyn. He could continue to justify his cowardice in the face of love by focusing on his bravery in the face of war.

But he did not. Not now. There was great excitement in the Eriadoran camp, with whispers that they would soon cross through Malpuissant's Wall and march south, but for Luthien, the battle suddenly seemed secondary. He believed that they could win, could take Princetown and force Greensparrow to grant them their independence, but what then? Would he become king of Eriador?"

And if he did, would Katerin be his queen?

It all came inescapably back to that. Sitting on that tree stump, looking up at the indomitable Dun Caryth, dark against a gray sky that was fast fading to black as the sun dipped low, Luthien found himself at odds, caught somewhere between responsibilities to the kingdom and to himself. He wanted to be the Crimson Shadow, the leader of the rebellion, but he also wanted to be Luthien Bedwyr, son of an eorl on an island far to the north, fighting only bloodless battles in the arena and romping through the woods with Katerin O'Hale.

He had come so far, so fast, but the journey would not be worth the cost if that price included the loss of his love.

"Coward," he berated himself, standing up and stretching. He turned about, facing the encampment, and started his march. He knew where Katerin would be, in a small tent across the way, on the northern edges of the wide camp, and he knew, too, that he had to face her now and put an end to his fear.

By the time he got to Katerin's tent, the sun was gone. A single lantern burned inside the tent, and Luthien could see Katerin's silhouette as she pulled off her leather jerkin. He watched that curvy shadow for a long while, full of admiration and passion. Siobhan was right, Luthien knew. He cared for the half-elf deeply, but this woman, Katerin, was his true love. When the wild rush of the rebellion was ended, even if they proved victorious, it would be a hollow win indeed for Luthien Bedwyr if Katerin would not stand with him.

He should go right into that tent and tell her that, he knew, but he could not. He walked off into the darkness, cursing himself, using every logical argument to try to overcome his fear.

It took him two hours to muster the courage to return, now carrying a lantern of his own, his clothing soaked by the mist that had come up and his bones chilled by the breeze.

"Straight in," he whispered determinedly, his stride quick and direct. "Katerin," he called softly when he got to the tent flap. He pushed it aside and stuck his head in, then brought the lantern around.

Then he froze with horror.

Katerin sprawled diagonally across her cot, her shoulders hanging over the edge, her head and one arm against the ground. It took Luthien several seconds to digest that sight, to shift his gaze even a bit.

To see the gigantic demon crouched in the shadows at the bottom of Katerin's cot, the beast's sheer bulk filling the corner of the tent.

"Do you remember, foolish man?" Praehotec snarled, and came forward a squatting step.

In one swift motion, Luthien set the lantern down and drew *Blind-Striker*, giving a yell and rushing forward wildly. His charge surprised the demon, who was more accustomed to watching men cower and run away.

Luthien smashed *Blind-Striker* across one of Praehotec's upraised arms, drawing a line of hissing, sputtering gray-green blood that smoked as it hit the ground.

Screaming and slashing, Luthien's fury would not relent. He didn't think of the creature he battled, didn't fear for his own death. All he knew was that Katerin, dear Katerin, was down, possibly dead, killed by this evil beast.

The flurry continued for many moments, a dozen strikes or more, before Praehotec loosed a ball of sparking lightning that launched Luthien backward, slamming him into a tent pole. He was up immediately, hair dancing on ends, cinnamon eyes narrowed as he fought against twitching muscles to tighten his grip on the sword.

"I will burn the skin from your bones," Praehotec wheezed, a grating, discordant voice. "I will—"

Luthien screamed at the top of his lungs and hurled himself forward. The demon whipped a huge wing out to intercept, taking a blow on its massive chest but buffeting and deflecting Luthien enough that the young man's weapon could not dig in.

Luthien tumbled to the side, gained control of the roll and spun about, slashing frantically, for he knew that the demon would be following.

Praehotec, out of range, sneered at him, but then the demon started suddenly, coming up a bit out of its crouch, its huge shoulders lifting the entire tent.

Luthien saw a glimmer, a rapier blade, sticking through the back of the tent, right over Katerin's cot, aimed precisely at Praehotec's rear end.

"Ahah!" came a triumphant cry from outside the tent.

Praehotec waved a clawed hand and a gout of flame disintegrated the material of the tent in that direction, revealing a very surprised Oliver deBurrows.

"I could be wrong," the halfling admitted as the demon turned.

An arrow whipped over Oliver's shoulder, thudding into the demon's ugly, snakelike face.

Praehotec roared, an unearthly, ghastly sound, and the hair on the nape of Luthien's neck tingled. The young Bedwyr rushed right in, his terror overcome by the thought of Katerin.

He scored a single hit with *Blind-Striker*, and then he was slapped away, tumbling, the whole world spinning. Lying flat against a corner, Luthien shook his head and forced himself to his knees, to see the demon approaching steadily, acidic drool dripping from its fanged maw.

Another arrow, and then another, zipped in to strike the fiend, but Praehotec seemed to take no notice of them. Oliver darted in, and then back out, stabbing with his blade, but Praehotec didn't care.

Paragor had instructed the beast not to kill Luthien, but mighty Praehotec took no commands from puny humans.

Luthien, believing that he was doomed, scrambled about, trying to find his dropped sword. He came up to his knees and balled his fists, determined to go out with sheer fury. Then he was blinded by a sudden brightness. Luthien fell back, thinking the demon had struck again with its magic.

He was wrong.

Brind'Amour followed his lightning bolt into the tent, and Praehotec, stung badly by the blast, and by the continuing stream of arrows from the other direction, knew that the game was at its end. The fiend leaped up and scooped the unconscious Katerin in one powerful arm.

"Think well the consequences of marching on Princetown!" the beast roared.

Brind'Amour stopped his next casting, for Katerin was in the way. Siobhan hit the fiend's back again with an arrow, but Praehotec straightened, lifting its free arm up high and thrashing the frail tent aside. Huge leathery wings beat furiously and the demon lifted away, climbing into the night sky.

"Katerin!" Luthien cried, trying to find his sword, trying to chase the beast down. He ran out unarmed and leaped high, catching one of Praehotec's clawed feet.

The other foot kicked him, sent him spinning away into unconsciousness.

A glowing spear appeared in Brind'Amour's hand and he hurled it up at the demon, scoring a sparking, explosive hit; two more arrows hummed from Siobhan's great bow, sticking painfully into the demon's legs.

But Praehotec was too strong to be brought down by the missiles. Away the beast flew, bearing Katerin, to the helpless cries of protest from the companions and from many others in the encampment who came to learn of the commotion.

Cries of protest and agony. Music to the fiend's ears.

CHAPTER 24

BECAUSE HE MUST

*H*E TOOK HER!" Luthien shouted, growing increasingly frustrated, even desperate, with the rambling conversation in Brind'Amour's tent some time later. They—the wizard, Oliver, Siobhan, and Kayryn—

were discussing the implications of the demon's raid. Now the focus was on whether or not they should still march to Princetown, or if the abduction of Katerin signaled a desire for a truce.

Estabrooke was in the tent, too, the knight sitting on a stool off to the side, thoroughly despondent.

"It is important to remember that the demon did not kill her," Brind'Amour replied to Luthien, the wizard trying to remain calm and comforting. "She is a prisoner, and will be more valuable to . . ."

"To whom?" Oliver wanted to know.

Brind'Amour wasn't sure. Perhaps King Greensparrow had discovered their progress and had reached out to them from Gascony. More likely, though, the wizard believed that the fiendish emissary had come from much closer, from Paragor, duke of Princetown.

"We cannot remain paralyzed on the field," Siobhan put in, and Kayryn added her support, going over to stand beside the half-elf. "This is no paid army, but men and women who have farms to tend. If we sit here waiting, we will lose many allies."

"Duke Paragor of Princetown took her," Brind'Amour decided. "He knows that we are coming, and knows that he cannot hold against us."

"We will have to alter some of the planning," Siobhan replied. "Perhaps we could send in spies, or offer a truce to the duke when we are right before his walls."

The calculating conversation began to make Luthien's blood boil. Paragor had stolen Katerin, but these friends spoke of larger plans and larger things. To Luthien Bedwyr, there was nothing more important in all the world, not even the freedom of Eriador, than Katerin's safe return. Brind'Amour and Siobhan would plan accordingly, doing whatever they could to help ensure the safety of the captured woman, but their primary concern was not for Katerin but for the rebellion.

As it should be, Luthien logically realized, but he could not follow such a course. Not now. He waved his arms in defeat, looked to the crestfallen Estabrooke, and stormed from the tent, leaving the others in a moment of blank and uncomfortable silence.

"Exactly what Duke Paragor was hoping for," Brind'Amour remarked. The wizard wasn't judging Luthien, merely making an observation.

"You know where he means to go?" Siobhan asked.

"He is already on his way," Oliver replied, understanding the young man too well. No one doubted the claim.

Brind'Amour wasn't sure how to respond. Should he try to dissuade Luthien? Or should he offer support, fall in with Luthien's obvious thinking that Katerin's safety should now be paramount? Brind'Amour was truly torn. He knew that he could not rush off in pursuit of the demon, for the sake of Katerin or anyone else. His responsibility was to no one person, but to Eriador as a whole.

"He should go," Siobhan said unexpectedly, drawing everyone's attention. She looked at the tent flap as she spoke, as though she was watching Luthien riding off even then. "That is his place."

When she looked back to the others, she noticed Oliver most of all, the halfling eyeing her suspiciously.

"More fuel for the legend of the Crimson Shadow," Siobhan insisted.

"Or does the woman scorned wish her lover dead?" Oliver asked bluntly.

Brind'Amour winced—the last thing they needed now was to be fighting amongst themselves!

"A fair question," Siobhan replied calmly, diffusing the tension. "But I am no woman, no human," she reminded the halfling. "Katerin is in peril, and so Luthien must go after her. If he does not, he will spend the rest of his days thinking himself a coward."

"True enough," Brind'Amour offered.

"We will not be led by a coward," Kayryn of Eradoch said coldly.

Oliver, as frustrated as Luthien had been, looked at them, one after the other. They spoke the truth, he knew; their reasoning was sound, but that did little to comfort the halfling. He had been beside Luthien from the beginning, before Brind'Amour had given the young Bedwyr the crimson cape, before whispers of the Crimson Shadow had ever passed down the back streets of Montfort. Now Luthien was doing as he must, was going after the woman he loved, and so Oliver, too, had to follow his heart and follow his friend.

He gave a curt bow to the others and walked from the tent.

Estabrooke, a noble man, a knight whose entire existence was founded on stringent principles, silently saluted the halfling and the brave man who had gone before Oliver.

Luthien paced Riverdancer easily along the edge of shadow cast by Malpuissant's Wall. The sun was low, breaking the horizon to the east, casting a slanted but narrow shadow into Eriador. Not as black as the shadow which had crossed the young Bedwyr's heart. It seemed to Luthien as if all the world had stopped the night before—as if everything, the rebellion, the coming invasion, had simply ceased, caught in a paralysis, a numbing of the spirit that would remain until Luthien reclaimed Katerin from the clutches of the demon and its evil master.

He wanted to hurry, to break Riverdancer into a powerful run, but he did not wish to attract too much attention, either from friends who might try to stop him, or from spying enemies who would warn the duke of Princetown.

He and his horse were by then a common sight to the guards at the gatetower closest to Dun Caryth, and so they let him cross through the wall into Avon without incident.

To Luthien's surprise a foppish halfling on a yellow pony was on the other side of the wall, sitting quietly, waiting for him.

"At least you waited until the morning," Oliver huffed and sniffled, looking thoroughly miserable, his little nose bright red. He sneezed, a tremendous sneeze for one so small, then brought a bright yellow-and-red checkerboard handkerchief up to wipe his nose and goatee.

"You have been out here all night?" Luthien asked.

"Since you left the meeting," Oliver replied. "I thought you would go straightaway."

Luthien didn't manage a smile, though he was touched by the halfling's loyalty. He didn't want Oliver along this time, however. He didn't want anyone along. "This is for me to do," he said firmly, and when Oliver didn't reply, Luthien made a ticking noise in Riverdancer's ear and gave a slight prod and the great shining stallion trotted off to the south.

Oliver and Threadbare paced him, the little pony scampering along to match Riverdancer's longer strides.

Luthien's scowl had no effect, and when he kicked Riverdancer to a faster trot, Threadbare, too, picked up speed. Finally, Luthien pulled his mount up short and sat staring at the halfling. Oliver looked at him curiously and sneezed again, showering the young man.

"This is for me to do" Luthien said again, more firmly.

"I do not argue," Oliver lisped.

"Me, alone," Luthien clarified.

"You could be wrong."

Luthien sighed and looked all about, as if trying to find some way out of this. He knew how stubborn Oliver could be, and he knew how fast that deceptive little beast Threadbare could run.

"Do you know anyone else so small enough to fit under the hem of your hiding cape?" Oliver asked logically.

Luthien stared at his friend for a long moment, then threw his hands up in defeat. In truth, the concession came as a huge relief to the young Bedwyr. He was determined to go after Katerin, and it frightened him to take another on the perilous, probably suicidal, journey, yet he realized that Oliver's place was indeed beside him, as his place would have been beside Oliver if the halfling's love had been whisked away in the night. So now he would have company for the long ride and the adventures to follow, a trusted friend who had gotten him out of many predicaments.

Before the pair began to move once more, they heard the sound of hooves behind them. They looked back toward the wall to see two riders, one large and wearing a horned highlander helm and the other small of frame.

"Siobhan," Oliver reasoned, and as the pair approached, Luthien saw that the halfling had guessed right. Now the young Bedwyr grew frustrated. He could rationalize having Oliver along, but this was getting out of hand!

Siobhan and the rider pulled up beside the companions.

"You are not going," Luthien offered, a preemptive strike against any argument to the contrary.

Siobhan looked at him curiously, as though she didn't understand. "Of course I am not," she said matter-of-factly. "My duty is to Eriador, and not to Luthien, or to Katerin."

For some reason that Luthien couldn't quite figure out, that statement hurt more than a little.

"But I condone your course," the half-elf went on. "And I wish you all speed and all victory. I expect to see you, and you," she said, looking at Oliver, "and Katerin, waiting for us when we breach Princetown's gate."

Luthien felt better.

"I have brought this," Siobhan went on, extending her hand to reveal an amber-colored stone the size of a chicken egg. "From Brind'Amour," she explained as Luthien took the stone. "When your task is complete, or when you are most in need, the wizard bids you to hurl it against a wall and speak his name three times."

Luthien felt the stone for some time, marveling at how light it was. He wasn't sure what the stone was all about, but he had seen enough of Brind'Amour's magic to understand that this was no small gift. "What of him?" the young Bedwyr asked, looking at the highlander.

"Do you mean to ride into Princetown?" the half-elf asked.

Luthien was beginning to catch on.

"Malamus will ride with you as far as the eastern end of Glen Durritch, almost in sight of Princetown," Siobhan continued. "And there he will wait with your mounts." Unexpectedly, the half-elf then slid down from her saddle, handing the reins to Malamus. "For Katerin," she said to Luthien. "My walk to the wall is not so far."

She nodded to Luthien, then to Oliver, and patted the rump of her horse as she started back for Malpuissant's Wall, back to the duties that would not allow her to accompany them.

Luthien watched her with sincere admiration. Siobhan wanted to go, he realized. Though she and Katerin were rivals in some respects, they also shared a deep regard for each other.

The young Bedwyr looked from Siobhan's back, to her gifts, to Brind'Amour's gift, and then to Oliver, sitting patiently, waiting for Luthien to lead on.

The night had been dark, but the day was dawning brighter.

Back atop the gatehouse at Malpuissant's Wall, Estabrooke, the First of the Sixth Cavalier, watched the small forms on the southern field, the Eriadorans in Avon, invading the proud knight's homeland. The image of the demon, of evil Praehotec, was still sharp in the old knight's mind. For twenty years Estabrooke had lived in the shadow of Greensparrow, hearing the tales of atrocities, of allegiances with demonkind. Some said that the horrible plague which had broken Eriador's will for war twenty years before had been brought on by the Avon king, but Estabrooke had dismissed such rumors as peasants' folly.

Some said that Greensparrow was a sorcerer of the darkest arts, a demon friend, a fiend himself.

But Estabrooke had dismissed such rumors, all the rumors.

Now the knight of the throne, the noble cavalier, had seen with his own eyes. The rumors had come true for poor, torn Estabrooke. They had materialized into a demonic, evil shape that the noble warrior could not shake.

He watched Luthien and Oliver ride off. Secretly, and though it were against everything the man had devoted his life to defending, Estabrooke hoped that they would succeed, would bring Katerin back safely and leave Duke Paragor, the same duke who had sent the cavalier to Eriador, dead in a pool of blood.

CHAPTER 25

GHOSTS

THE HIGHLANDER, Malamus, spoke not a word on the two days of riding it took the companions to get into Glen Durritch, the wide and shallow vale just southeast of Princetown. Here, there were no more trees for cover and only a single road, a brown snake winding through the thick green turf.

Luthien, playing the role of general again, studied the land, imagined a battle that could be fought and won here. The ground sloped up to the left and to the right, into rolling, tree-covered hills. Perfect cover and high ground. Elven archers could hit this road from those trees, he realized, and down here, there was no cover, no place to hide from the stinging, deadly bolts.

So intent was the young Bedwyr that he was caught fully by surprise when Oliver's rapier tapped him on the shoulder. Luthien pulled up on Riverdancer's reins and looked back to see the halfling dismounting.

"The western end of Glen Durritch," Malamus explained. Oliver motioned with his chin to the west and Luthien squinted against the low-riding sun. Mountains loomed dark and cold, not so far away, and before them . . .

What? Luthien wondered. A sparkle of white and pink.

Oliver walked by him. "Five miles," the halfling said. "And I do not like to walk in the dark!"

Luthien slipped down from Riverdancer and gave the reins over to Malamus. The highlander matched Luthien's gaze for a long moment. "The blessing of Sol-Yunda go with you, Crimson Shadow," he said suddenly and turned about, pulling hard with his massive, muscled arm to swing all three riderless mounts with him. "I await your return."

Luthien just grunted, having no reply in light of his surprise. Sol-Yunda was the god of the highlanders, a private god whom they said watched over their kin and held no regard for anyone else, friend or foe. The highlanders hoarded Sol-Yunda as a dragon hoarded gold, and for Malamus to make that statement, to utter those seven simple words, was perhaps the most heartening thing Luthien Bedwyr had ever heard.

He stood and watched Malamus for a few moments, then turned and sprinted to catch up with Oliver as the halfling plodded along, toward the spec of white and pink below the line of dark mountains.

Less than an hour later, the sun low in the sky but still visible above the

Iron Cross, the friends came close enough to witness the true splendor of Princetown and to understand why the place had earned the nickname as the Jewel of Avon.

It was about the same size as Caer MacDonald, but where Caer Mac-Donald had been built for defense, nestled in between towering walls of dark stone, Princetown had been built as a showcase. It sat on a gently rolling plain, just beyond the foothills, and was widespread and airy, not huddled like Caer MacDonald. A low wall, no more than eight feet high, of light-colored granite encompassed the whole of the place, with no discernable gatehouses or towers of any kind. Most of the houses within were quite large; those of wood had been white-washed, and the greater houses, those of the noblemen and the merchants, were of white marble tinged with soft lines of pink.

The largest and dominant structure was not the cathedral, as in most of the great cities of Avonsea. That building was impressive, probably as much as Caer MacDonald's Ministry, but even it paled beside the fabulous palace. It sat in the west of Princetown, on the highest ground closest to the mountains, four stories of shining marble and gold leaf, with decorated columns presented all along its front and with great wings northeast and southeast, like huge arms reaching out to embrace the city. A golden dome, shining so brightly that it stung Luthien's eyes to look upon it, stood in the center of the structure.

"This duke, he will be in there?" Oliver asked and Luthien didn't have to follow the halfling's gaze to know which building Oliver was talking about. "We should have kept our horses," the halfling remarked, "just to get from one end to the other."

Luthien snickered, but wasn't sure if Oliver was kidding or not. The young Bedwyr couldn't begin to guess how many rooms might be in that palace. A hundred? Three hundred? If he kicked Riverdancer into a full gallop, it should take him half an hour to circle the place but once!

Neither companion spoke, but they were both thinking the same thing: how so oppressive a kingdom could harbor such a place of beauty. This was grandeur and perfection; this was a place of soaring spirits and lifting hearts. Was there more to the Kingdom of Avon than Luthien, who had never been to the south before, understood? Somehow, the young Bedwyr simply could not associate this spectacle of Princetown with what he knew of the evil Greensparrow; this fabulous city spread wide before him seemed to mock his rebellion and, even more so, his anger. He knew that Princetown was older than Greensparrow's reign, of course, but still the city just didn't seem to fit the mental image Luthien had conjured of Avon.

"My people, they built this place," Oliver announced, drawing Luthien from his trance. He looked to the halfling, who was nodding as though he, too, was trying to figure out the origins of Princetown.

"There is a Gascon influence here," Oliver explained. "From the south and west of Gascony, where the wine is sweetest. There, too, are buildings such as this."

But not so grand, Luthien silently added. Perhaps the Gascons had built, or expanded, Princetown during their occupation of Avon, but even if Oliver spoke truthfully, and the architecture was similar to those structures in southwestern Gascony, Luthien could tell from Oliver's blank stare that Princetown was far grander.

Shaken by the unexpected splendor, but remembering Katerin in the clutch of the demon and focusing on that awful image, Luthien motioned to the north and started off at a swift pace; Oliver followed, the halfling's gaze lingering on the spectacle of Princetown. From somewhere within the city, near to the palace, it seemed, came a low and long roar, a bellow of pure and savage power. A lion's roar.

"You like cats?" Oliver asked, thinking of the zoo and wishing that he could have visited Princetown on another, more inviting, occasion.

The sky was dark and dotted with swift black clouds by the time the companions had circled Princetown, moving along the granite wall back to the south, toward the palace. They came around one sharp bend in the wall, and Luthien stopped, perplexed. Looking to the west, he discovered Princetown's dirty secret.

From the east, the place had looked so clean and inviting, truly a jewel, but here, in the west, the companions learned the truth. The ground sloped down behind the palace and the eight-foot wall that lined the city proper encircled into a bowl-shaped valley filled with ramshackle huts. Luthien and Oliver couldn't see much in the darkness, for there were not many fires burning down below, but they could hear the moans of the poor, the cries of the wretches who called a muddy lane their home.

Luthien found the sights and sounds heartening in a strange way, a confirmation that his conclusions of Greensparrow and the unlawful and ultimately evil kingdom were indeed correct. He sympathized with the folk who lived in that hidden bowl west of the city's splendor, but their existence gave him heart for the fight.

Oliver tugged on his cloak, stopping him.

"Close enough," the halfling whispered, pointing up to the side of the palace, looming dark and tall not so far away.

"Here now!" came a bellow from the wall, a guttural, cyclopian voice, and both friends dropped into a crouch, Luthien pulling the hood of his cape over his head and Oliver scampering under the folds of the magical crimson garment.

On the wall, several lanterns came up, hooded on three sides to focus the beam of light through the fourth. Luthien held his breath, reminding himself repeatedly that the cape would hide him as the beams crossed the field before him and over him.

"Get back to your holes!" the cyclopian roared and from the wall, several crossbows fired.

"I would like it better if the one-eyes could see us," Oliver remarked.

The barrage continued for several volleys and was then ended by a shared burst of grunting laughter from the wall. "Beggars!" one cyclopian snorted derisively, followed by more laughter.

Oliver came out from under the crimson garment and straightened his great, wide-brimmed hat and his own purple cape. He pointed to the south, toward the towering palace wall, and the pair moved on a few dozen yards.

Oliver went right up to the wall, listening intently, then nodding and smiling at the sound of snoring from above. He pushed his cape back from his shoulder and reached into the shoulder pouch of his "housebreaker," a harness of leather strapping that Brind'Amour had given him. Oliver wore the contraption all the time, though it was hardily noticeable against his puffy sleeves and layered, brightly colored clothing. It seemed to be no more than a simple, unremarkable harness, but like Brind'Amour himself, the looks were truly deceiving. This harness was enchanted, like many of the items it contained: tools of the burglary trade. From that seemingly tiny shoulder pouch, Oliver produced his enchanted grapnel, the puckered ball and fine cord. But before he could unwind and ready the thing, Luthien came over and scooped him up.

Oliver understood; the wall was only eight feet high, and Luthien could hoist him right to its lip. Quickly, the halfling looped the grapnel openly on his belt, within easy reach, and then he grabbed the lip of the wall, peering over.

A parapet ran the length of the wall on the other side, four feet down from the lip. Oliver looked back to Luthien, a wicked grin on his face. He put a finger over pursed lips, then held it up, indicating that Luthien should wait a moment. Then the halfling slipped over the wall, silent as a cat—a little cat, not the kind they had heard roaring earlier.

A moment later, while Luthien grew agitated and wanted to leap up and scramble over, Oliver came back to the wall and held out his hand to his friend. Luthien jumped and caught the lip of the wall with one hand, Oliver's hand with the other. He came over low, slithering like a snake, rolling silently to the parapet.

Luthien's eyes nearly fell from their sockets, for he and Oliver were right between two seated cyclopians! The startlement lasted only a moment, stolen by the simple logic that Oliver had been up here and knew the scene. On closer examination, Luthien realized that neither of these brutes was snoring any longer. Luthien looked to Oliver as the halfling wiped the blood from his slender rapier blade on the furred tunic of one dead brute.

Barely thirty feet away, the other group, the ones who had fired at the companions, continued a game of dice, oblivious to the invasion.

Oliver slipped under Luthien's cape and the two started off slowly, away from the dicing band, toward the looming wall of Princetown's palace.

They had to slip down from the wall and cross a small courtyard to get to the building, but it was lined with manicured hedgerows, and with Luthien's cape helping them, they had little trouble reaching the palace. Oliver looked up at the line of windows, four high. Light came from the first and second, but the third was much dimmer and the fourth was completely dark.

The halfling held up three fingers, and with a final glance around to make sure that no cyclopians were nearby, he twirled his grapnel and let fly, attaching it to the marble wall beside the third-story window.

The marble was as smooth as glass, but the puckered ball held fast, and after testing it, Oliver scampered up. Luthien watched from below as the halfling again went to his harness, producing a suction cup with a wide arm attached. Oliver listened at the window for a moment, then popped the cup onto it and slowly but firmly moved the compass arm in a circle, against the glass.

Oliver came back down a moment later, bearing the cut glass. "The room is emp—" he began, but he stopped and froze, hearing the approach of armored guards.

Luthien stepped up and swooped his cape over Oliver, then fell back against the wall, the halfling in tow.

Half a dozen cyclopians, wearing the black-and-silver uniforms of Praetorian Guards, came around the corner in tight formation, the one farthest from the wall carrying a blazing torch. Luthien ducked low under his hood, bending his head forward so that the cowl would completely block his face. He held his confidence in the enchanted cape, but could only hope now that the brutes wouldn't notice the fine cord

hanging down the side of the palace wall, and hope, too, that the cyclopians didn't accidentally walk right into him!

They passed less than four feet away, right by Oliver and Luthien as
though the two weren't even there. Indeed, to the cyclopians, they were
not, purely invisible under the folds of the crimson cape.

As soon as the brutes were out of sight, Luthien moved out of hiding
and Oliver jumped to the cord, climbing quickly, hand over hand.
Luthien braced the rope for a moment, allowing Oliver to get up to the
second story, then the young Bedwyr also took a tight hold and began
to climb, wanting to be off the ground as quickly as possible.

It seemed like many minutes drifted by, but in truth, the two friends
were inside the palace in the space of a few heartbeats. Oliver reached
out through the hole in the window and gave three sharp tugs on the
cord, freeing the puckered ball and pulling it in behind him. Gone without a trace—except for the circle of cut glass lying on the grass and the
image of a shadow, a crimson shadow, indelibly stained upon the white
wall of the palace.

Luthien settled himself and waited for his eyes to adjust to the shift
in the level of darkness. They were in the palace, but where to go? How
many scores of rooms could they possibly search?

"He will be near the middle," reasoned Oliver, who knew his way
around nobility fairly well. "In the rooms to one or the other side of the
dome. That dome signals the chapel; the duke will not be far from it."

"I thought the cathedral was the chapel," Luthien said.

"Duke-types and prince-types are lazy," Oliver replied. "They keep a
chapel in their palace home."

Luthien nodded, accepting the reasoning.

"But the dungeons will be below," Oliver went on. He saw the horrified look crossing his friend's face and quickly added, "I do not think
this Duke Paragor would put so valuable a prisoner as Katerin in the
dungeons. She is with him, I think, or near to him."

Luthien did not reply, just tried hard to keep his breathing steady.
Oliver took that as acceptance of his reasoning.

"To the duke, then," Oliver said, and started off, but Luthien put a
hand on his shoulder to stop him.

"Greensparrow's dukes follow no law of God," the young Bedwyr reminded him, suddenly wondering if the halfling's reasoning was sound.
"They care not for any chapel."

"Ah, but the palace was built before Greensparrow," the halfling
replied without the slightest hesitation. "And the old princes, they did
care. And so the finest rooms are near to the dome. Now, do you wish

to sit here in the dark and discuss the design of the palace, or do you wish to be off, that we might see the truth of the place?"

Luthien was out of answers and out of questions, so he shrugged and followed Oliver to the room's closed door, distinguishable only because they saw the light from the corridor coming through the keyhole.

That hole was about eye-level with the halfling, and he paused and peeked through, then boldly opened the door.

In the light, Luthien came to see that Princetown's palace was as fabulous on the inside as on the outside. Huge tapestries, intricately woven and some with golden thread interlaced with their designs, covered the walls, and carved wooden pedestals lined the length of the corridor, each bearing artwork: busts of previous kings or heroes, or simple sculptures, or even gems and jewels encased in glass.

More than once, Luthien had to pull Oliver along forcibly, the halfling mesmerized by the sight of such treasures within easy grasp.

There was only one treasure that Luthien Bedwyr wanted to take from this palace.

Gradually, the companions neared the center of the palace. The hallways became more ornate, more decorated, the treasures greater and more closely packed together, giving credence to Oliver's reasoning concerning the likely location of the duke. But so, too, did the light grow, with crystal chandeliers, a hundred candles burning in each, hanging from the ceiling every twenty paces along the corridor. Many doors were thrown wide, and all the side rooms lit; though it was very late by then, near to midnight, the palace was far from asleep. A commotion caught the pair, particularly Luthien, off guard; the young Bedwyr even considered turning around and hiding until later. But Oliver would hear none of that. They were inside now, and any delay could be dangerous for them and for Katerin.

"Besides," Oliver added quietly, "we do not even know if the party will end. In Gascony, the lords and ladies are known to stay up all the night, every night."

Luthien didn't argue, just followed his diminutive companion into the party. Merchants and their prettily dressed ladies danced in the side rooms, often sweeping out into the hall to twirl through the next open door, joining yet another of the many parties. Even worse for Luthien and Oliver, Praetorian Guards seemed to be around every corner.

The halfling thought that they should walk openly, then, and pretend to be a part of it all; Luthien, realizing that even the magical crimson cape could not fully shield them from this growing mob, reluctantly agreed. He was well dressed, after all, especially with the fabulous cape shimmering over his shoulders, and Oliver always seemed to fit in. And so they half walked, half danced their way along the corridors. Oliver scooped two goblets of wine from the first cyclopian servant they passed who was bearing a full tray.

The atmosphere was more intoxicating than the wine, with music and excited chatter, promises of love from lecherous merchants to the many fawning ladies. Oliver seemed right at home, and that bothered Luthien, who preferred the open road. Still, as he became confident that their disguise, or lack of one, was acceptable in this company, particularly with Oliver's foppish clothing and his own magnificent cape, Luthien grew more at ease, even managed a smile as he caught in his arms one young lady who stumbled drunkenly out of a room.

Luthien's smile quickly disintegrated; the painted and perfumed woman reminded him much of Lady Elenia, one of Viscount Aubrey's entourage who had come to Dun Varna, his home on faraway Isle Bedwydrin. Those two ladies who had accompanied Aubrey, Elenia and Avonese, had started it all; their bickering had precipitated the death of Garth Rogar, Luthien's boyhood friend.

Luthien stood the woman up and firmly straightened her, though she immediately slumped once more.

"Ooh, so strong," she slurred. She ran her fingers down one of Luthien's muscled arms, her eyes filled with lust.

"Strong and available," Oliver promised, figuring out the potential trouble here. He stepped in between the two. "But first, my strong friend and I must speak with the duke." The halfling looked around helplessly. "But we cannot find the man!"

The woman seemed not to notice Oliver as he rambled along. She reached right over his head to again stroke Luthien's arm, not fathoming the dangerous glare the young Bedwyr was now giving her.

"Yes, yes," Oliver said, pulling her arm away, pulling it hard to bend her over so that she had to look at him. "You might rub all of his strong body, but only after we have met with the duke. Do you know where he is?"

"Oh, Parry went away a long time ago," she said, drawing frowns from the companions. A million questions raced through Luthien's mind. Where might Paragor have gone? And where, then, was Katerin?

"To his bedchamber," the lady added, and Luthien nearly sighed aloud with relief. Paragor was indeed in the palace!

The lady bent low to whisper, "They say he has a lady there."

Oliver considered her jealous tones and, understanding the protective, even incestuous, ways of a noble's court, the halfling was not surprised by what was forthcoming.

"A foreigner," the lady added with utter contempt.

"We must find him then, before . . . before . . ." The halfling searched for a delicate way to phrase things. "Before," he said simply, with finality, adding a wink to show what he meant.

"Somewhere that way," the lady replied, waggling a finger along the corridor, in the same direction the companions had already been traveling.

Oliver smiled and tipped his hat, then turned the woman about and shoved her back into the room from whence she came.

"These people disgust me," Luthien remarked as the pair started off once more.

"Of course," Oliver outwardly agreed, but the halfling remembered a time not so long ago when he, too, had played these noble party games, usually lending a sympathetic shoulder for those ladies who had not snared the richest or the most powerful or the most dashing (though Oliver always considered himself the most dashing). Of course they were disgusting, as Luthien had said, their passions misplaced and shallow. Few of the nobles of Gascony, and of Avon, too, from what the halfling was now seeing, did anything more substantial than organize their drunken parties, with the richest foods and dozens of young painted ladies. These frequent occasions were orgies of lust and greed and gluttony.

But, in Oliver's thinking, that could be fun.

The pair grew more cautious as they continued toward the center of the palace, for they found fewer partygoers and more cyclopians, particularly Praetorian Guards. The music dimmed, as did the lighting, and finally, Luthien decided that they should drop the façade and hide under the protection of the magic cape.

"But how are we to find information to lead us to the man?" Oliver protested.

It was a good point, for they still had no idea of which room might be Duke Paragor's, and no idea if this "foreigner" the lady had spoken of was even Katerin. But Luthien did not change his mind. "Too many cyclopians," he said. "And we are increasingly out of place, even if we were invited guests to the palace."

Oliver shrugged and hid under the cape; Luthien moved to the side of the corridor, inching from shadow to shadow. A short while later, they came to a stairwell, winding both up and down. Now they had a true dilemma, for they had no idea of which way to go. The fourth floor, or the second? Or should they remain on this level, for the corridor continued across the way?

The companions needed a measure of luck then, and they found it, for a pair of servants, human women and not cyclopian, came bustling up the stairs, grumbling about the duke. They wore plain white garb—Oliver recognized them as cooks, or as maids.

"E's got 'imself a pretty one this night," said an old woman, a single tooth remaining in her mouth, and that bent and yellow, sticking out over her bottom lip at a weird angle. "All that red hair! What a firebrand, she be!"

"The old wretch!" the other, not much younger and not much more attractive, declared. "She's just a girl, she is, and not 'alf 'is age!"

"Shhh!" the one-tooth hissed. "Yer shouldn't be spaking so o' the duke!"

"Bah!" snorted the other. "Yer knows what he's doin'. He sends us away fer a reason, don't yer doubt!"

"Glad I am then, that we is done fer the night!" said one-tooth. "Up to bed wit me!"

"And down to bed with the duke an' the girl!" the other shrieked, and the two burst out in a fit of cackling laughter. They walked right beside the companions, never noticing them.

It took all the control Luthien could muster for him to wait until the pair had passed before running down the stairs. Even then, Oliver tried to hold him back, but Luthien was gone, taking three steps at a time.

Oliver sighed and moved to follow, but paused long enough to see that the cape had left another of its "crimson shadows" on the wall beside the stairwell.

Their options were fewer when they came down to the next level. Three doors faced the stairwell, each about a dozen feet away. The two to the sides were unremarkable—Luthien could guess that they opened into corridors. He went to the third, curbed his urge to charge right through, and tried to gently turn the handle instead.

It was locked.

Luthien backed up and snarled, meaning to burst right through, but Oliver was beside him, calming him. From yet another pouch of his remarkable housebreaker, the halfling produced a slender, silver pick. A moment later, he looked back from the door at Luthien and smiled mischievously, the lock defeated. Luthien pushed right past him and went through the door, coming into yet another corridor, this one shorter, incredibly decorated in tiled mosaics, and with three doors lining each side.

One of those, the middle door to Luthien's left, had a pair of burly Praetorian Guards in front of it.

"Hey, you cannot come in here!" one of the brutes growled, approaching as it spoke and moving its hand to the heavy cudgel strapped to its belt.

"My friend here, he needs a place to throw up," Oliver improvised, jabbing Luthien as he spoke.

Luthien lurched forward, as though staggering and about to vomit, and the horrified cyclopian dodged aside, letting him stumble past. The brute turned back to complain to Oliver, but found a rapier blade suddenly piercing its throat.

The other Praetorian, not seeing the events behind Luthien, moved to slap the apparently drunken man aside. Luthien caught the hand and moved in close, then the guard went up on its toes, its expression incredulous as *Blind-Striker* sunk into its belly, angled upward, reaching for its lungs and heart.

Oliver shut the door to the stairwell. "We must hope that we are in the right place," he whispered, but Luthien wasn't even listening and wasn't waiting for any lockpicking this time. The young Bedwyr roared down the corridor, cutting to the right, then back sharply to the left, slamming through the door into Duke Paragor's private bedchamber.

Paragor was inside, sitting with his back to his desk in the right corner of the room, facing the bed, where Katerin sat, ankles and wrists tightly bound, a Praetorian flanking her on either side.

Something else, something bigger and darker, with leathery wings and red fires blazing in its dark eyes, was in the room as well.

CHAPTER 26

THE DEMON AND THE PALADIN

*L*UTHIEN'S FIRST INSTINCTS were to go to Katerin, but he kept his wits about him enough to realize that the only chance he and Katerin had was to be rid of the wizard quickly, and hopefully the wizard's demon along with the man. The young Bedwyr took one running step toward the bed, then cut sharply to the right, cocking back *Blind-Striker* with both hands.

The wizard jumped up and shrieked, throwing his skinny arms in front of him in a feeble attempt at defense. Luthien cried out for victory and brought the sword in a vicious arc, just under the flailing arms, and the young man snarled grimly as the sword struck against the wizard's side, boring right across. He saw the wizard's robes, brownish-yellow in hue, fitting for the sickly looking man, fold under the weight of the blow, saw them follow the blade's path.

Blind-Striker had moved all the way around, left to right, and the robes with it, before Luthien realized that Paragor was not there, that the wizard somehow was no longer in these robes. The young Bedwyr stumbled forward a step, overbalancing as his sword found nothing substantial to hit. He caught himself and wheeled about, the brownish-yellow robes folded over his blade.

He saw a shimmer across the room against the wall beyond the foot of the bed, as Paragor came back to corporeal form, wearing robes identical to the ones wrapped over Luthien's sword. He saw Praehotec, eyes blazing, rage focused squarely on Luthien, coming over the bed, rushing right past Katerin and barreling over one of the cyclopians as he went, the fiend's great wings buffeting both Katerin and the other one-eyed guard.

Luthien knew that he was dead.

Like his companion, Oliver thought the key to this fight would be in slaying the wizard. And like his companion, Oliver came to understand that getting to Paragor would not be easy. At first, the halfling started right, following Luthien. Then, seeing that Luthien would get the attack in, Oliver had cut back toward the middle of the room, toward Katerin. The halfling's eyes bulged when he realized Paragor's magical escape, and how they bulged more when Oliver saw Praehotec, gigantic and horrid Praehotec, coming over the bed!

With a squeak, Oliver dove down, crossing under the tumbling cyclopian and slipping under the bed as the demon charged out. The agile halfling recovered quickly, in a roll that turned his prone body about, and he scrambled right back out the way he had come in so that he could stab at the downed one-eye with his rapier. He scored a hit, then a second and a third, but the stubborn brute was up to its knees, bellowing like an animal, turning around to face the halfling.

Oliver stuck it once again as it turned, and then the halfling let out a second squeak and faded back under the bed, the enraged cyclopian in close pursuit.

From the very beginning, Katerin had not been a model prisoner, and she kept up her reputation now. She accepted the hit as Praehotec passed, the demon's wing knocking her flat to the bed and blasting her breath away. Her instincts yelled for her to go to Luthien, to die beside him, for she knew that he could not defeat this monstrous beast. But her wits told her to inflict as much pain on wretched Paragor as she could, and so as she went flying downward, she tensed her muscles and threw herself into the fall, hitting the cushioned bed with enough force to bounce right back to a sitting position. The second cyclopian, half on the bed and half off, dazed by the weight of Praehotec's wing, was more concerned with its companion, who was scrambling under the bed, than with Katerin.

The brute felt her arms come across its broad shoulders, the chain binding her wrists scraping its face as her wrists came down in front of its burly neck. In a split second, the cyclopian felt Katerin's feet against its upper back, and she was pushing and tugging with all of her strength, her chained wrists tight across the one-eye's throat.

The dominant thought in Paragor's mind as he easily vanished from in front of Luthien's mighty swing was that he had erred in keeping Praehotec so long. Before he ever came back to his corporeal form, the wizard knew that the demon would be going after Luthien, meaning to kill the young man and tear him apart, to punish the young Bedwyr, this legendary Crimson Shadow, for its defeat on the high tower of the Ministry.

Thowattle's warnings of turning the young man into a martyr echoed in Paragor's mind, and so his first attack, a beam of searing, crackling, white energy, was aimed not at Luthien, nor any of his companions, but at Praehotec.

The demon was close enough to Luthien by then that the wizard's attack appeared to be an errant casting. The white bolt slammed Praehotec's leathery wing, doing no real damage to the beast, but stopping its charge, slamming the monster against the far wall.

Luthien, fighting hard to curb his terror, lunged forward, thrusting *Blind-Striker* with all his strength. The mighty sword had been forged by the dwarves of the Iron Cross in ages past, its blade of beaten metal folded a thousand times. Now, after centuries of use, it was better than when it was forged, for as the blade wore down, each layer was harder than the previous. It sank deep into demon flesh. Luthien ignored the hot, greenish gore that erupted from Praehotec's torn torso and pushed on, throwing all his weight behind the attack. *Blind-Striker* went in right up to its jewelled and golden hilt—the sculpted dragon rampant. The sharpened points of the sculpture's upraised wings, the formidable crosspiece of the weapon, gouged small holes in the demon's flesh.

Luthien, snarling and screaming, looked up into the demon's fiery eyes, thinking he had won, thinking that no beast, not even a monster of the Abyss, could withstand such a strike.

Praehotec seemed in agony, green gore oozing from the wound, but gradually a wicked grin widened across the monster's serpentine face. A trembling, clawed hand reached out to Luthien, who backed off to arm's length only, not daring to withdraw the blade. A long, low growl came from the pained demon's maw; Praehotec's trembling, weakened hand caught Luthien by the front of his tunic and pushed him, the twelve-foot giant extending its long arm, driving Luthien back step by step, and since the young Bedwyr didn't dare let go of *Blind-Striker*, the sword followed, sliding from the wound.

When Praehotec's arm was fully extended, *Blind-Striker* was only a few inches deep in the monster's chest. Luthien yanked it all the way out and snapped it straight up, nicking the bottom of Praehotec's jaw. Before he could do any more harm, though, the demon clenched its hand tighter and yanked its arm out to the side, hurling Luthien back by the door.

The young Bedwyr came up in a roll to see Paragor casting straight at him. Through the open door Luthien dove, pulling it closed behind him.

The door slammed all the faster when Paragor's blast of lightning hit it, splitting the wood right down the middle so that splinters followed Luthien out into the hall. Luthien was up again in an instant, meaning to charge right back in, but he had to dive aside as the door exploded and Praehotec burst through.

Luthien skittered behind the beast, back in front of the door. He saw Katerin on the bed, tugging for all her life, the cyclopian gasping and clawing at her hands and wrists. He saw the second brute, dodging futilely side to side as it tried to squirm under the bed, as Oliver's darting rapier poked it again and again.

"Get out!" Luthien cried to Oliver and he pulled the amber gemstone from his pouch and sent it skidding under the bed, hoping the halfling would see it and find the chance to take Katerin along with him if that stone was indeed an escape.

Paragor was approaching, dark eyes focused right on Luthien, as though nothing or no one else mattered in all the world. The duke's hair flared in wild wings behind his ears, and he seemed inhuman, as monstrous as the beast Praehotec.

Luthien accepted that he was overmatched, but he didn't care. All that mattered was that Katerin and Oliver might escape, and so the young Bedwyr spun about, snarling with fury and slashed *Blind-Striker* across Praehotec's back, right between the wings.

The demon howled and whipped around, clawed hand raking. But Luthien was already gone, rolling to the side, and Praehotec's great hand caught nothing but the door jamb and remaining pieces of the door, launching a volley of splinters right into Paragor's face.

"Fool!" the duke yelled, hands going to his bloody face. "Do not kill him!"

Even as Paragor yelled his instructions, *Blind-Striker* came in again, a crushing blow to the side of the crouching demon's head. Praehotec let out a wail, and no commands the wizard-duke could utter then, no reasoning, would have contained the fiend's fury. Praehotec wheeled wildly, filling the corridor with its huge form, preventing Luthien from skipping behind this time.

They faced off, the demon still in a crouch, its wings tight to its back so they would not scrape against the walls. The corridor was small and rather narrow, had been built for defense, and its ceiling was not high enough to accommodate the tall fiend. Praehotec was at no disadvantage, though; it could fight this way easily enough.

Luthien, too, went into a crouch, backing down the hall as the demon stalked him. Clawed hands came at him, and all the young Bedwyr could do was whip his sword back and forth, parrying. Luthien nearly tripped over one of the dead cyclopians, and knew that if he had, his life would have come to a sudden and violent end.

Regaining his footing and looking up at his foe, Luthien watched in blank amazement as two dagger-length beams of red light emanated from Praehotec's blazing eyes. The serpentine maw turned up into another of those awful grins as the demon crossed its eyes to angle the beams. As soon as the light beams touched, a third beam burst forth, a red line that hit Luthien square in the chest, hurling him backward.

He fought for his breath, felt the burn, the spot of sheer agony, and saw the grinning beast still approaching. He tried to backpedal, all his sensibilities told him to flee, but the door held firm behind him, and it could only open one way, into the corridor.

Had Luthien been thinking clearly, he might have stepped aside and thrown it wide, then run out into the palace proper. But he could not stop and reason, not with the pain and with Praehotec so close, great arms reaching for him. And then his chance was lost altogether as Praehotec worked more magic, swelling and twisting the door in its jamb so that it would not open at all.

"Will you fall down and die, you ugly offspring of a flounder and a pig?" Oliver shouted, poking the cyclopian yet again. He had pierced the creature twenty times, at least. Its face, its chest, and both its reaching hands spotted bright lines of blood. But the brute didn't cry out, didn't complain at all, and didn't retreat.

Something skittered beside Oliver and he heard Luthien call out for him to escape. Without even knowing what it might be, the halfling instinctively scooped up the bauble. Then he changed tactics. He poked at the cyclopian again, but fell back as he did so, allowing the brute to get further under the bed. When it had squeezed in all the way, Oliver, much smaller and more maneuverable in the tight quarters, poked it hard in the forehead, then scampered out the other side, coming to his feet to find Katerin still tugging with all her strength, though the strangled brute was no longer fighting back.

"I think you can stop now," the halfling remarked dryly, bringing Katerin from her apparent trance. "But if you really want to fight," Oliver continued, dancing away from the bed as the crawling cyclopian swiped at him, "just wait a moment."

Oliver danced away; Katerin stood up. She looked at the door, and so did the halfling, watching Paragor's back, the wizard apparently picking at his face, as he exited the room.

Then Katerin's attention was back to the immediate problem: the cyclopian reemerging from under the bed. She crouched and waited, and as the brute stood up, she called to it. As soon as it turned, Katerin leaped and tumbled, hooking her chained wrists under the one-eye's chin and rolling right over the brute's shoulder.

She came around and down hard to her knees on the floor, tugging the cyclopian viciously behind her, bending back its back and neck. She hadn't planned the move, but thought it incredibly clever and deadly indeed, but the cyclopian was stronger than she realized, and she was not heavy. The brute's bloody hands reached back over its shoulders and clasped Katerin by the elbows, then tugged so hard that the sturdy woman gave out a scream.

Oliver, busy examining the amber gem, casually strolled right in front of the engaged one-eye. The brute, straining to look back at Katerin, didn't even notice him.

"Ahem," the halfling offered, tapping his rapier on top of the brute's head.

The cyclopian visibly relaxed its hold on Katerin and slowly turned to face front, to stare into the tip of Oliver's rapier.

"This is going to hurt," Oliver promised, and his blade darted forward.

The brute let go and grabbed wildly, trying to intercept, but the halfling was too quick and the rapier tip drove into the cyclopian's eye.

Oliver walked away, examining the stone once more, trying to recall all that Siobhan had said when she had given it to Luthien. Katerin, her arms free once more, for the blinded brute was wailing and thrashing aimlessly, turned herself over to face the creature's back, twisting the chains tight about its neck.

Had the powerful cyclopian grabbed her again, it might have been strong enough to break the strangling hold, but the one-eye was beyond reason, insane with pain. It thrashed and jerked, rolled to one side and then the other. Katerin paced it, her bindings doing their deadly work.

Oliver wasn't watching. He moved to the bottom of the bed and hurled the amber gemstone at the wall, calling three times for Brind'Amour. It shattered when it hit, but before a single piece of it could fall to the floor, it became something insubstantial, began to swirl as a fog, becoming part of the wall, transforming the wall.

Oliver recognized the magical tunnel and understood that he and Katerin could get away. "Ah, my Brind'Amour," the halfling lamented, and then he looked from the potential escape route to the shattered door. None of the three, not Luthien, the demon, or the wizard, was in sight.

"I hate being a friend," the halfling whispered, and started toward the door.

Before he had gone three steps, though, two forms came rushing through the amber fog into the room. Oliver's jaw drooped open; Katerin, finishing her latest foe, dared to hope.

Brind'Amour and Estabrooke.

The parries came furiously and in rapid succession, *Blind-Striker* whipping back and forth, left and right, always intercepting a hand just before it raked at Luthien—or just after, before the demon could gain a firm hold or sink its terrible claws in too deep. Luthien couldn't keep it up; he knew that, and knew, too, there was no way for him to launch any effective counter measures.

Beams of red light began to extend from Praehotec's blazing eyes.

Luthien screamed, put one leg against the door and hurled himself at the beast, rushing in between the extended, grasping arms. He came in high, but dropped low as Praehotec crossed its eyes, the beams joining and sending forth another jarring bolt that flashed over Luthien's head and slammed into the door, blasting a fair-sized crack.

Luthien stabbed straight out, scoring a hit on Praehotec's belly. Then he slashed to his right, gouging the demon's great wing, and followed the blade, rolling around the beast, trying to go between Praehotec and the wall and get into the larger area of the corridor.

Praehotec turned, and though the giant couldn't keep up with Luthien's scrambling, the beast did swing a leg fast enough, lifting a knee into Luthien's side and slamming him painfully against the corridor wall.

Luthien bounced out the other side, still scrambling on all fours, scraping his knuckles and gasping for breath, trying to make it back to the door of the wizard's room, though he didn't even have his head up, so bad was the pain.

He saw the hem of the wizard's brownish-yellow robes, a sickly color for a sickly man.

Luthien forced himself to his knees, threw his back against the wall, and squirmed his way up to a standing position. Before he ever fully straightened, before he ever truly looked Paragor in the eye, he heard the crackle of energy.

Blue lines of power arced between Paragor's fingers, and when he thrust his hands toward Luthien, those lines extended, engulfing the man in a jolting, crackling shroud.

Luthien jerked spasmodically. He felt his hair standing on end, and his jaw chattered and convulsed so violently that he bit his tongue repeatedly, filling his mouth with blood. He tried to look at his adversary, tried to will himself toward the wizard, but his muscles would not react to his call. The spasms continued; Luthien slammed the back of his head against the wall so violently that he had to struggle to remain conscious.

He hardly registered the movement as Praehotec finally turned and advanced, a clawed hand reaching for his head.

With a roar of victory, the beast grabbed for its prey, meaning to squash Luthien's skull. But the energy encircling the young Bedwyr sparked on contact and blew the demon's hand aside. Praehotec looked at Paragor, serpentine face twisted with rage.

"You cannot kill this one!" the duke insisted. "He is mine. Go to his lover instead and take her as you will!"

Luthien heard. Above all the crackling and the pain, the sound of his own bones and ligaments popping as he jerked about, he heard. Paragor had sent Praehotec to Katerin. He had given the demon permission to kill Katerin . . . or worse.

"No," Luthien growled, forcing the word from his mouth. He straightened, using the wall for support, and somehow, through sheer willpower, he managed to steady himself enough to look the evil duke in the eye.

Both Paragor and Praehotec stared at the young Bedwyr with a fair amount of respect, and so it was Luthien, gazing over the duke's shoulder, who noticed the blue-robed wizard at the open doorway to the duke's bedchamber.

Brind'Amour's hands moved in circles as he uttered a chant. He took a deep, deep breath and brought his hands back behind his ears, then threw them forward, at the same time blowing with all his might.

Luthien got the strange image of the wizard as a boy, blowing out the candles upon his birthday cake.

There came an explosion of light, and a great and sudden burst of wind that flattened Luthien against the wall at the same time as it blew out the arcing energy emanating from Paragor's hands, freeing the trapped young Bedwyr.

Paragor stumbled, then turned about, glaring at this new adversary, recognizing him as the old man he had seen in the divining basin. Now, with the display of power from the man, Paragor pieced things together.

"You," he snarled accusingly, and Brind'Amour knew that the wizard-duke, who knew the stories of the ancient brotherhood and had no doubt been warned of Brind'Amour by Greensparrow, at last saw him for who he really was. With a primal scream, Paragor lifted his hands, and they glowed that sickly brownish-yellow color. The wizard-duke charged, his hands going for the old man's throat.

By the time Luthien gained enough of his senses to look up, he was lying on the floor, a sheet of golden light suspended in the air above him. He saw the giant, shadowy form of Praehotec through that veil, saw the demon's huge foot rise up above him.

Luthien closed his eyes, tried to grab his sword, but could not reach it in time, and screamed out, thinking he was about to be crushed.

But then it was Praehotec who was screaming, terrible, awful wails of agony, for as the demon's foot entered the sheet of golden light, it was consumed, torn and ripped away.

Brind'Amour's hands, glowing a fierce blue to match his own robes, came up to meet the duke's charge. He caught Paragor's hands in his own and could feel the disease emanating from them, a withering, rotting touch. Brind'Amour countered the only way he knew how, by reciting chants of healing, chants of ice that would paralyze Paragor's invisible flies of sickness.

Paragor twisted and growled, pressing on with all his might. And Brind'Amour matched him, twisted and turned in accord with each of the duke's movements. Then Paragor yanked one hand away suddenly, breaking the hold, and slapped at Brind'Amour's face.

The old wizard intercepted with a blocking arm, accepting the slap, and his forearm, where his unprotected skin was touched by the evil duke, wrinkled and withered, pulling apart into an open sore.

Brind'Amour responded by slamming his own palm into Paragor's nose, and where the blue touched Paragor's skin, it left an icy, crystalline whiteness, the duke's nose and one cheek freezing solid.

Gulping for breath, the evil duke grabbed Brind'Amour's hand with his own and the struggle continued. Paragor tried to pull Brind'Amour to the side, but to the duke's surprise, the old wizard accepted the tug, even threw his own weight behind it, sending both of them tumbling down the hall, away from Luthien and Praehotec.

Luthien gawked at the spectacle, as Praehotec, unable to stop the momentum, sank more and more of its foot, then its ankle, into the light.

No, Luthien realized then, not light. Not a sheet of singular light, as he had first thought, but a swirling mass of tiny lights, like little sharp-edged diamonds, spinning about so fast as to appear to be a single field of light.

How they ate at the demon flesh, cutting and gobbling it into nothingness!

Everything turned red then, suddenly, as Praehotec loosed another of its powerful eye bolts, and an instant later, Luthien felt the demon's blood and gore washing over him. He twisted and squirmed and looked up to find Brind'Amour's protective barrier gone, along with half of Praehotec's leg. The demon's acidic lifeblood gushed forth, splattering the wall and floor and Luthien.

He took up his sword and rolled out from under the wounded demon, came up to his knees just as Oliver, rapier held before him, came gliding past with Estabrooke, the Dark Knight's great sword glowing a fierce and flaming white.

Luthien tried to rise and join them, but found that he hadn't the strength, and then Katerin was beside him, bracing his shoulders, hugging him close. She kissed him on the cheek—and he saw that she had taken a cudgel from one of the dead guards.

"I must go," she whispered, and she scrambled up and ran off, not toward Oliver, Estabrooke, and the demon, but the other way.

Luthien looked back to see Brind'Amour and Paragor rolling and thrashing, alternately crying out. The sight brought the young Bedwyr further out of his stupor; he could control his muscles once more, but how they ached! Still, Luthien knew that he could not sit there, knew that the fight was not yet won.

"Ick!" Oliver said, skidding to a stop before he hit the puddle of demon gore.

Praehotec, leaning against the wall, didn't seem to notice the halfling. It looked right over Oliver's head to the shining sword and the armored man, this cavalier, this noble warrior, a relic of a past and more holy age. The demon recognized what this man was, the most hated of all humankind.

"Paladin," Praehotec snarled, drool falling freely to the floor. Out came the great leathery wings as the beast huffed itself up to its most impressive stance, straight and as tall as the corridor would allow, despite its half-devoured leg.

Oliver was impressed by the fiend's display, but Estabrooke, crying to God and singing joyfully, charged right in and brought his sword down in a great sweeping strike. The halfling watched his courage, knew the demon's word, and understood what this man they had met on the fields of Eradoch truly was. "*Douzeper*," the halfling muttered.

Estabrooke sheared off Praehotec's raised arm.

The demon's other arm came around, battering the man; twin beams became one before Praehotec's eyes, flashing out, searing through the knight's armor, aimed at his heart. The stump of the demon's other arm became a weapon as Praehotec whipped it back and forth, sending a spray of acidic blood into the slits of Estabrooke's helm.

Still Estabrooke sang, through the blindness and the pain, and he slashed again, gouging a wing, digging into the side of the demon's chest with tremendous force.

Praehotec, balanced on just one foot, rocked to the side and nearly tumbled. But the beast came back furiously, with a tremendous, hooking blow that rang like a gong when it connected with the side of Estabrooke's helm and sent the cavalier flying away, to crumple in the corner near to the battered door.

Finally, the wizards broke their entanglement, each scrambling to his feet, dazed and sorely stung. Several lesions showed on Brind'Amour's skin and the sleeves of his beautiful robes were in tatters. Paragor looked no better, one leg stiff and frozen, icy blotches on his face and arms. The duke shivered and shuddered, but whether it was from the cold or simple rage, Brind'Amour could not tell.

Both were chanting, gathering their energies. Brind'Amour let Paragor lead, and when the duke loosed his power in the form of a bright yellow bolt, Brind'Amour countered with a stroke of the richest blue.

Neither bolt stopped, or even slowed, the other, and both wizards accepted the brutal hits, energy that struck about their heads and shoulders and cascaded down, grounding out at their feet, jolting them both.

"Damn you!" Paragor snarled. He seemed as if he would fall; so did

Brind'Amour, the older wizard amazed at how strong this duke truly was.

But Paragor was nearing the end of his powers by then, and so was Brind'Amour, and it was not magic, not even a magical weapon, that ended the battle.

Katerin O'Hale crept up behind the wizard-duke and slammed the cyclopian cudgel down onto the center of his head, right between the hair "wings." Paragor's neck contracted and his skull caved in. He gave a short hop, but this time he held his footing only for a split second before falling dead to the floor.

There was no rest, no reprieve, for Praehotec. Before the demon could turn around, Oliver's rapier dug a neat hole between the ribs of its uninjured side, and more devastating still was the fury of Luthien Bedwyr.

Luthien did not know that word Praehotec had uttered—"paladin"—but he knew the truth of Estabrooke, knew that the man was not just any warrior, but a holy warrior, grounded in principles and in his belief in God. To see him fall wounded Luthien profoundly, reminded him of the evil that had spread over all the land, of the sacrilege in the great cathedrals, where tax rolls were called, of the enslavement of the dwarfs and the elves. Now that fury was loosed in full, defeating any thoughts of fear. Luthien slashed away relentlessly with *Blind-Striker*, battering the demon about the shoulders and neck, pounding Praehotec down onto the sheared leg, which would not support the beast's great weight.

Praehotec tumbled to the ground, but Luthien did not relent, striking with all his strength and all his heart. And then, amazingly, Estabrooke was beside him, that shining sword tearing horrible wounds in the demon.

Again Praehotec's rage was aimed at the cavalier. The demon kicked out with its good foot and at the same time opened wide its maw and vomited, engulfing Estabrooke with a torrent of fire.

The knight fell away, and this time did not rise.

Luthien's next strike, as soon as the fires dissipated, went into the demon's open maw, drove through the back of Praehotec's serpent mouth, and into the beast's brain. Praehotec convulsed violently, sending Luthien scrambling away, and then the battered beast melted away and dissolved into the floor, leaving a mass of gooey green ichor.

Luthien rushed to Estabrooke and gently turned up the faceplate of the fallen knight's helm.

Estabrooke's eyes stared straight up, unseeing, surrounded by cracked skin, burned by demon acid. Luthien heard banging on the door, cyclopian calls for Duke Paragor, but he could not tear himself away from the grievously wounded man.

Somehow Estabrooke smiled. "I pray you," the knight gasped, blood pouring from his mouth. "Bury me in Caer MacDonald."

Luthien realized how great a request that was. Estabrooke, this noble warrior, had just validated the revolution in full, had asked to be buried away from his homeland, in the land that he knew to be just and closer to God.

Luthien nodded, could not speak past the lump in his throat. He wanted to say something comforting, to insist that Estabrooke would not die, but he saw the grievous wounds and knew that anything he might say would be a lie.

"Eriador free!" Estabrooke said loudly, smiling still, and then he died.

"*Douzeper*," Oliver whispered as he crouched beside Luthien. "Paladin. A goodly man."

The banging on the door to the outer corridor increased.

"Come, my friend," Oliver said quietly. "We can do no more here. Let us be gone."

"Lie down and pretend that you are dead," Brind'Amour said suddenly, drawing both friends from the dead cavalier. They looked at each other, and then at the wizard, curiously.

"Do it!" Brind'Amour whispered harshly. "And you, too," he said, turning to Katerin, who seemed as confused as Luthien and Oliver.

The three did as the wizard bade them, and none of them were comfortable when their skin paled, when more blood suddenly covered Katerin and Oliver, who had not been splattered and beaten, as had Luthien.

Their startlement turned to blank amazement when they regarded the wizard, his familiar form melting away, his white hair turning gray and thinning to wild wings over his ears and his head disappearing altogether. As soon as his blue robes turned brownish-yellow, the three understood, and as one, they looked down the hallway to see the dead duke now wearing the form of Brind'Amour.

The wizard clapped his hands together and the door, swollen by Praehotec's magic, shrunk and fell open before the blows of the cyclopians, led by Paragor's lacky, Thowattle. The brutes skidded to a stop, overwhelmed by the grisly scene, two dead cyclopians, three mutilated humans and one halfling, and a mess of bubbling green and gray slime.

"Master?" Thowattle asked, regarding Brind'Amour.

"It is over," Brind'Amour replied, his voice sounding like Paragor's.

"I will clean it at once, my master!" Thowattle promised, turning to leave.

"No time!" Brind'Amour snapped, stopping the one-armed brute in its tracks. "Assemble the militia! At once! These spies wagged their tongues before I finished with them and told me that a force has indeed gathered at Malpuissant's Wall."

The three friends, lying still on the floor, had no idea of what the old wizard was doing.

"At once!" Thowattle agreed. "I will have servants come in to clean . . ."

"They stay with me!" Brind'Amour roared, and he waggled his fingers at the three prone friends and began a soft chant. Luthien, Oliver, and Katerin soon felt a compulsion in their muscles, and heard a telepathic plea from their wizard friend asking them to follow along and trust. Up they stood, one by one, appearing as zombies.

"What better torment for the doomed fools of Eriador than to see their heroes as undead slaves of their enemy?" the fake duke asked, and Thowattle, always a lover of the macabre, smiled wickedly. The brute gave a curt bow and its cyclopian companions followed suit. Then they were gone, and Brind'Amour, with a wave of his hand, closed the door behind them and swelled it shut once more.

"What was that about?" Oliver asked incredulously, for a moment, even wondering if this was really Brind'Amour, and not Paragor, standing in the hall.

"Glen Durritch," Brind'Amour explained. "Even as we sit here and banter, our army, under Siobhan's direction, has taken the high ground all about Glen Durritch. My excited cyclopian fool will give orders to double-time to Malpuissant's Wall, to meet with the Eriadorans there."

"And the Princetown garrison will be slaughtered in the glen," Luthien reasoned.

"Better than fighting them when they're behind city walls," the devious wizard added. Brind'Amour looked back at Oliver. "You and I once spoke of your value to Eriador beyond the battles," he said, and Oliver nodded, though Luthien and Katerin had no idea of what the two were talking about.

"The time has come," Brind'Amour insisted, "though I will need the rest of the night to recuperate and regain any measure of my magical powers."

Brind'Amour looked closely at Estabrooke then, and sighed deeply, truly pained by the sight. He had spoken with the cavalier at length over the last couple of days, and was not surprised when Estabrooke had insisted on sitting beside him, waiting in case the magical tunnel should open. Brind'Amour hadn't hesitated in the least about letting the knight accompany him, fully trusting the man, realizing the goodness that guided the knight's every action. Estabrooke's death was a huge loss to Eriador and to all the world, but Brind'Amour took heart that the man had redeemed his actions on behalf of the evil Paragor, had seen the truth and acted accordingly.

"Come," Brind'Amour said at length, "let us see what niceties Paragor's palace has to offer to four weary travelers."

CHAPTER 27

DIPLOMACY

*L*UTHIEN DIDN'T KNOW how to approach her. She sat quiet and very still on the bed in the room she had commandeered, across the hall and down one door from Duke Paragor's bedchamber. She had let him in without argument, but also without enthusiasm.

So now the young Bedwyr stood by the closed door, studying Katerin O'Hale, this woman he had known since he was a boy, and yet whom he had never really seen before. She had cleaned up from the fight and wore only a light satin shift now, black and lacy, that she had found in a wardrobe. It was low cut, and really too small for her, riding high on her smooth legs.

An altogether alluring outfit on one as beautiful as Katerin, but there was nothing inviting about the way the woman sat now, back straight, hands resting in her lap, impassive, indifferent.

She had not been wounded badly in the fight and had not suffered at the hands of Duke Paragor. No doubt the abduction had been traumatic, but certainly Katerin had been through worse. Since the fight, though, after those first few moments of elation, the woman had become quiet and distant. She had reacted to Luthien as her savior for just a moment, then moved away from him and kept away from him.

She was afraid, Luthien knew, and probably just as afraid that he would come to her this night as that he would not. Until this moment, Luthien had not truly considered the implications of his relationship with Siobhan. Katerin's jealousy, her sudden outburst that night at the

Dwelf, had been an exciting thing for Luthien, a flattering thing. But those outbursts were gone now, replaced by a resignation in the woman, a stealing of her spirit, that Luthien could not stand to see.

"I care for Siobhan," he began, searching for some starting point. Katerin looked away.

"But not as I love you," the young man quickly added, taking a hopeful stride forward.

Katerin did not turn back to him.

"Do you understand?" Luthien asked.

No response.

"I have to make you understand," he said emphatically. "When I was in Montfort . . . I needed . . ."

He paused as Katerin did turn back, her green eyes rimmed with tears; her jaw tightened.

"Siobhan is my friend and nothing more," Luthien said.

Katerin's expression turned sour.

"She was more than my friend," Luthien admitted. "And I do not regret . . ." Again he paused, seeing that he was going in the wrong direction. "I do regret hurting you," he said softly. "And if I have done irreparable harm to our love, then I shall forever grieve, and then all of this, the victories and the glory, shall be a hollow thing."

"You are the Crimson Shadow," Katerin said evenly.

"I am Luthien Bedwyr," the young man corrected. "Who loves Katerin O'Hale, only Katerin O'Hale."

Katerin did not blink, did not offer any response, verbal or otherwise. A long, uncomfortable moment passed, and then Luthien, defeated, turned toward the door.

"I am sorry," he whispered, and went out into the hall.

He was down at the other end, nearing his door, when Katerin called out his name behind him. He turned and saw her standing there, just outside of her door, tall and beautiful and with a hint of a smile on her fairest of faces.

He moved back to her slowly, guardedly, not wanting to push her too far, not wanting to scare her away from whatever course she had chosen.

"Don't go," she said to him, and she took his hand and pulled him close. "Don't ever go."

From a door across the hall, barely cracked open, a teary-eyed Oliver watched the scene. "Ah, to be young and in Princetown in the spring," the sentimental halfling said as he closed his door after Luthien and Katerin had disappeared.

The halfling waited a moment, then opened the door again and exited his room, dressed in his finest traveling clothes and with a full pack over his shoulder, for though it was night, Oliver had a meeting with Brind'Amour, and then a long, but impossibly quick, road ahead.

The next morning, the proud Princetown garrison marched out of the city to much fanfare. The long line moved swiftly, out to the east and south, meaning to swing through the easy trails of Glen Durritch and then turn north to Malpuissant's Wall, where they would put down the rebels.

But the rebels were not at the wall. They were waiting, entrenched in the higher ground of the glen, and the Princetown garrison never made it out the other side.

The length of the cyclopian line was barraged with missile fire, elvish bowstrings humming, each archer putting three arrows in the air before the first had ever hit its mark. After the first few terrible moments, the cyclopians tried to form up into defensive position, and the Riders of Eradoch came rushing down upon them, cutting great swaths through their lines, heightening the confusion.

Then there was no defense, no organized counterattack, and the slaughter became wholesale. Some cyclopians tried to run out the eastern end of the glen, but the jaws of the fierce Eriadoran army closed over them. Others, near the back of the long line, had an easier time getting out of the glen's western end, but they found yet another unpleasant surprise awaiting them, for in the mere hour they had been out of the city, an army of dwarfs had encircled Princetown.

Not a single cyclopian got back to the city's gates that fateful morning.

Greensparrow shifted in his seat, a smile painted on his face, trying to appear at ease and comfortable, though the high-backed and stiff, stylish Gascon chair was anything but comfortable. The Avon king had to keep up appearances, though. He was in Caspriole, in southwestern Gascony, meeting with Albert deBec Fidel, an important dignitary, one of the major feudal lords in all of Gascony.

For some reason that Greensparrow could not understand, deBec Fidel had turned the conversation to events in Eriador, which Greensparrow truly knew little about. As far as the vacationing king of Avon was aware, Belsen'Krieg was in Montfort, though the last message from one of his underling wizards, Duchess Deanna Wellworth of Mannington, had hinted at some further trouble.

"What do you mean to do?" deBec Fidel asked in his thick accent, his blunt question catching Greensparrow off his guard. Normally deBec Fidel was a subtle man, a true Gascon dignitary.

"About the rebels?" the Avon king replied incredulously, as though the question hardly seemed worth the bother of answering.

"About Eriador," deBec Fidel clarified.

"Eriador is a duchy of Avon," Greensparrow insisted.

"A duchy without a duke."

Greensparrow controlled himself enough not to flinch. How had deBec Fidel learned of that? he wondered. "Duke Morkney failed me," he admitted. "And so he will be replaced soon enough."

"After you replace the duke of Princetown?" deBec Fidel asked slyly.

Greensparrow gave no open response, except that his features revealed clearly that he had no idea what the lord might be speaking about.

"Duke Paragor is dead," deBec Fidel explained. "And Princetown— ah, a favorite city of mine, so beautiful in the spring—is in the hands of the northern army."

Greensparrow wanted to ask what the man was talking about, but he realized that deBec Fidel would not have offered that information if he had not gotten it from reliable sources. Greensparrow's own position would seem weaker indeed if he pretended that he did not also know of these startling events.

"The entire Princetown garrison was slaughtered on the field, so it is said," deBec Fidel went on. "A complete victory, as one-sided as any I have ever heard tell of."

Greensparrow didn't miss the thrill, and thus, the threat, in deBec Fidel's voice, as though the man was enjoying this supremely. An emissary from Eriador had gotten to the man, the wizard-king realized, probably promising him trade agreements and free port rights for Caspriole's considerable fishing fleet. The alliance between Avon and Gascony was a tentative thing, a temporary truce after centuries of countless squabbles and even wars. Even now, much of Greensparrow's army was away in lands south of Gascony, fighting beside the Gascons, but the king did not doubt that if Eriador offered a better deal concerning the rich fishing waters of the Dorsal Sea, the double-dealing Gascons would side with them.

What had started as a riot in Montfort was quickly becoming a major political problem.

Behind one of the doors of that very room, his ear pressed against the keyhole, Oliver deBurrows listened happily as deBec Fidel went on, speaking to Greensparrow of the benefits of making a truce with the rebels, of giving Eriador back to Eriador.

"They are too much trouble," the feudal lord insisted. "So it was when Gascony ruled Avon. That is why we built the wall, to keep the savages in the savage north! It is better for all that way," deBec Fidel finished.

Oliver's smile nearly took in his ears. As an ambassador, a Gascon who knew the ways of the southern kingdom's nobles, the halfling had done his job perfectly. The taking of Princetown might nudge Greensparrow in the direction of a truce, but the not-so-subtle hint that mighty Gascony might favor the rebels in this matter, indeed that the Gascons might even send aid, would surely give the wizard-king much to consider.

"Shall I have your room prepared?" Oliver heard deBec Fidel ask after a long moment of uncomfortable silence.

"No," Greensparrow replied sharply. "I must be on my way this very day."

"All the way back to Carlisle," Oliver snickered under his breath. The halfling flipped an amber gemstone in his hand, agreeing with Greensparrow's sentiments, thinking that it might be time for him, too, to be on his way.

CHAPTER 28

THE WORD

*L*UTHIEN AND KATERIN sat astride their mounts on a hill overlooking the shining white-and-pink marble of Princetown. The sun was low in the eastern sky, beaming past them, igniting the reflected fires along the polished walls of the marvelous city. In the famed Princetown zoo, the exotic animals were awakening to the new day, issuing their roars and growls, heralding the sunrise.

Other than those bellowing sounds, the city was quiet and calm, and the panic that had begun after the news that Duke Paragor was slain and the garrison slaughtered had settled.

"Brind'Amour told the Princetowners that neither the Eriadoran nor the dwarfish army would enter the city," Luthien remarked. "They trust in the old mage."

"They have no choice but to trust in him," Katerin answered. "We could march into the city and kill them all in a single day."

"But they know we will not," Luthien said firmly. "They know why we have come."

"They are not allies," Katerin reminded him. "And if they had the strength to chase us away, they would do so, do not doubt."

Luthien had no reply; he knew that she was right. Even though he knew of Brind'Amour's intention of retreating back to Eriador, Luthien had hoped that, after the massacre in Glen Durritch and if the folk of Princetown embraced the Eriadoran cause, they might continue this war, indeed might take it all the way to Carlisle. It had been as Oliver had predicted on that day of planning the attack. The Princetowners were calm now, trusting, praying that the threat to their personal safety was ended, but they made no pledges of allegiance to the Eriadoran flag.

"And know, too," Katerin said grimly, pounding home her point, "that our army will indeed enter the city and lay waste to any who oppose us if we find another of Greensparrow's armies marching north to do battle."

Luthien hardly heard the words, because he had not wanted to hear them, and also because he noticed Oliver upon Threadbare, riding up the hill to join them. Also, to the left, the south, and still very far away, Luthien noticed the expected entourage approaching the captured city. Several coaches moved in a line, all streaming pennants, fronted and flanked by cyclopians upon ponypigs, the one-eyes smartly dressed in the finest regalia of the Praetorian Guard. Luthien did not recognize all of the pennants, but he picked out the banner of Avon and figured that the rest were the crests of the southern kingdom's most important families, and probably the banners of the six major cities, as well. Most prominent among the line, along with the banner of Avon, was a blue pennant showing huge hands reaching out to each other across a gulf of water.

"Mannington, I think," Katerin remarked, watching the same show and picking out the same, prominent banner.

"Another duke?" Luthien asked. "Come to parley or work foul magic?"

"Duchess," came a correction from below as Oliver hustled his pony toward the pair. "Duchess Wellworth of Mannington. She will speak for Greensparrow, who is still in Gascony."

"Where have you been?" Luthien and Katerin asked together, for neither had seen the halfling in the five days since Duke Paragor was dispatched.

Oliver chuckled quietly, wondering if they would even believe him. He had used Brind'Amour's magical tunnel to cross a thousand miles, and then a thousand miles back again. He had met with dignitaries, some of the most important men in Gascony, and had even, on the occasion of passing the man in the hall, tipped his great hat to King Greensparrow himself! "It was time for me to go home!" the foppish halfling roared cryptically, and he would say no more, and Luthien and Katerin, too involved in speculating about the meeting that would soon take place, did not press the point.

Luthien had wanted to attend that parley, but Brind'Amour had frowned upon the notion, reminding the young Bedwyr that the coming negotiator was probably a wizard and would be able to recognize the young man, perhaps, or at least to relay information about Luthien to the king in the south. As far as Greensparrow and his cronies were concerned, Brind'Amour realized that Eriador would be better served if the Crimson Shadow remained a figure of mystery and intrigue.

So Luthien had agreed to stay out of the city and out of the meeting. But now, watching the line of coaches disappearing behind the gray granite wall, the young Bedwyr wished he had argued against Brind'Amour more strongly.

By all measure, Duchess Deanna Wellworth was a beautiful woman, golden hair cut to shoulder length and coiffed neatly, flipped to one side and held in place by a diamond-studded pin. Though she was young— certainly she had not seen thirty winters—her dress and manner were most elegant, sophisticated, but Brind'Amour sensed the power and the untamed, wild streak within this woman. She was an enchantress, he knew, and a powerful one, and she probably used more than her magic to get men into difficult situations.

"The fleet?" she asked abruptly, for from the moment she had sat down at the long, oak table, she had made it clear that she wanted this parley concluded as quickly as possible.

"Scuttled," Brind'Amour answered without blinking.

Deanna Wellworth's fair features, highlighted by the most expensive makeup, but not heavily painted in typical Avon fashion, turned into a skeptical frown. "You said we would deal honestly," she remarked evenly.

"The fleet is anchored near to the Diamondgate," Brind'Amour admitted. The old wizard drew himself up to his full height, shoulders back and jaw firm. "Under the flag of Eriador free."

His tone told Wellworth beyond any doubt that Greensparrow would not get his ships back. She hadn't really expected Eriador to turn them over, anyway. "The Praetorian Guards held captive on that rock of an island?" she asked.

"No," Brind'Amour answered simply.

"You hold near to three thousand prisoners," Wellworth protested.

"They are our problem," Brind'Amour replied.

Deanna Wellworth slapped her hands on the polished wood of the table and rose to leave, signaling to the Praetorian Guards flanking her. But then the other negotiator across the table from her, a blue-bearded dwarf, cleared his throat loudly, a not-so-subtle reminder of the additional force camped in the mountains, not far away. Princetown was lost, and the enemy was entrenched in force, and if an agreement could not be reached here, as Greensparrow had instructed, Avon would find itself in a costly war.

Deanna Wellworth sat back down.

"What of the cyclopian prisoners taken in Glen Durritch?" she asked, her voice edged in desperation. "I must bring some concession back to my king!"

"You are getting back the city," Brind'Amour said.

"That was known before I was sent north," Deanna protested. "The prisoners?"

Brind'Amour looked at Shuglin and gave a slight chuckle, an indication of agreement, and he explained with a wide and sincere smile, "We have no desire to march a thousand one-eyes back into Eriador!"

Deanna Wellworth nearly laughed aloud at that, and her expression caught Brind'Amour somewhat off his guard. It was not relief that fostered her mirth, the wizard suddenly realized, but agreement. Only then did the old wizard begin to make the connection. Mannington had always been Avon's second city, behind Carlisle, and a seat of royalty-in-waiting.

"Wellworth?" Brind'Amour asked. "Was it not a Wellworth who sat upon Avon's throne, before Greensparrow, of course?"

All hint of a smile vanished from Deanna's fair face. "An uncle," she offered. "A distant uncle."

Her tone told the keen-minded wizard that there was much more to this one's tale. Deanna had been in line for the throne, no doubt, before Greensparrow had taken it. How might she feel about this rogue wizard who was now her king? Brind'Amour dismissed the thoughts; he had other business now, more pressing and more important for his Eriador.

"You have your gift for your king," he said, thus bringing the meeting to conclusion.

"Indeed," Deanna replied, still tight-lipped after the inquiry about her royal lineage.

Luthien and Katerin watched, Oliver and Siobhan watched, and all the army of Eriador and all the dwarfs of the Iron Cross watched, as Brind'Amour, Shuglin beside him, and Duchess Deanna Wellworth close behind, ascended the tallest tower in Princetown, the great spire of the cathedral. When he was in place, his voluminous blue robes whipping about him in the stiff breeze, the wizard spoke out, spoke to all the folk of the land, Eriadoran and Avonite alike, in a voice enhanced by magic so that it echoed to every corner of Princetown.

"The time has come for the folk of Eriador to turn north," the old wizard declared. "And for the dwarfs of the Iron Cross to go home."

And then he said it, the words that Luthien Bedwyr and Katerin O'Hale had waited so very long to hear.

"Eriador is free!"

EPILOGUE

A KINGDOM? A DEMOCRACY?" Oliver spat derisively. "Government, *ptooey!*" They had been on the road for a full week, and though spring was on in full, the weather had been somewhat foul—not the expected weather considering the glorious return to Caer MacDonald. Now, with the walls of the mountain city finally in sight, the Ministry sitting huge and imposing up on the hill, their conversation had turned to the coronation of free Eriador's king.

There had never been a doubt in Luthien's mind about who that should be. Several of the folk had called for the Crimson Shadow to take up the reins as their leader, but Luthien knew his talents and his limitations. Brind'Amour would be king, and Eriador would be better off for it!

"Ptooey?" Katerin echoed.

"Government," Oliver said again. "Do you know the difference between a kingdom and a democracy?"

Katerin shrugged—she wasn't even certain what this concept of democracy, which Brind'Amour had raised soon after they had all crossed back in to Eriador, exactly was.

"In a kingdom," the halfling explained, "a man uses power to exploit man. In a democracy, is the other way around."

It took Luthien and Katerin a long moment to catch on to that remark.

"So, by your reasoning, Eriador would be better off without a king?" Luthien asked. "We can just let the towns run themselves . . ."

"They will anyway," Oliver put in, and Katerin had to agree. Few of Eriador's proud folk would bend to the will of anyone who was not of their particular village.

"Still, we need a king," Luthien went on determinedly. "We need someone to speak for the country in our dealings with other lands. It has always been that way, long before anyone ever heard of Greensparrow."

"And Brind'Amour will keep the people of Eriador together," Oliver agreed. "And he will deal fairly with the dwarfs and the elfish-types, of that I do not doubt. But still, government . . ."

"*Ptooey!*" Luthien and Katerin spat together, and the three enjoyed a hearty laugh.

The coronation of King Brind'Amour went off perfectly, on a bright and sunny day less than a week after the army had rolled back into Caer MacDonald. If there were any who disagreed with the choice, they were silent, and even the rugged highlanders seemed pleased by the pomp and the celebration.

Brind'Amour had ascended to the role of leader now, with the battles of swords apparently ended and the diplomatic duels about to begin, and Luthien was glad for the reprieve, glad that the weight and responsibility had been lifted from his shoulders.

Temporarily, Luthien held no illusions that his duties had ended, or that the war had ended. He had discussed the matter at length with Brind'Amour, and both of them were of the mind that Greensparrow had so readily agreed merely to buy himself some needed time. Both of them knew that there might remain yet a larger battle still to be fought.

Luthien thought of Estabrooke then, who had given so many years in service to the Kingdom of Avon. He thought of Estabrooke, who would be buried in Caer MacDonald. A lifelong service to Avon, and the noble knight had asked to be buried in Eriador. Luthien would have to think long and hard on that irony.

But all such dark thoughts were for another day, Luthien told himself as the decorated coach approached the platform that had been constructed in the wide plaza near to the Ministry. Brind'Amour, looking regal indeed in huge purple robes, with his shaggy hair and beard neatly trimmed and brushed, stepped out of that coach and ascended the stairs to the joyful cries of the thousands gathered.

Gathered to mark this day, Luthien reminded himself, forcing all thoughts of Greensparrow far from his consciousness.

This day. Eriador free.

THE
DRAGON
KING

To Diane, and to Bryan, Geno, and Caitlin

PROLOGUE

THE AVONSEA ISLANDS knew peace, but it was a tentative thing, founded on a truce that neither kingdom, Avon or Eriador, truly desired, a truce signed only because continuing the war would have been too costly for the outlaw king of Avon and too desperate for the ill-equipped and outmanned fledgling kingdom of Eriador.

In that northern land, the wizard Brind'Amour was crowned, and the excitement of the common people, an independent and rugged breed, was rightly high. But King Brind'Amour, grown wise by the passage of centuries, tempered his own hopes in the sobering understanding that, in mighty Avon, evil Greensparrow remained as king. For twenty years Greensparrow had held Eriador in his hand, giving him dominance of all the islands, and Brind'Amour understood that he would not so easily let go, whatever the truce might say. And Greensparrow, too, was a wizard, with powerful demonic allies, and a court that included four wizard-dukes and a duchess of considerable sorcerous power.

But though he was the only wizard in all of Eriador, alone in magical power against Greensparrow's court, Brind'Amour took comfort that he, too, had powerful allies. Most prominent among them was Luthien Bedwyr, the Crimson Shadow, who had become the hero of the nation and the symbol of Eriador free. It was Luthien who slew Duke Morkney, Luthien who led the revolt in Montfort, taking back the city and restoring its true Eriadoran name of Caer MacDonald.

For now at least, Eriador was free, and all the people of the land—the sailors of Port Charley and the three northern islands, the fierce Riders of Eradoch, the sturdy dwarfs of the Iron Cross, the Fairborn elves, and all the farmers and fishermen—were solidly aligned behind their king and their land.

If Greensparrow wanted Eriador back in his unlawful grasp, he would have to fight them, all of them, for every inch of ground.

CHAPTER 1

ENEMY OLD, ENEMY NEW

A SIMPLE SPELL BROUGHT him unnoticed past the guards, out from the main gates of the greatest city in all of Avonsea, mighty Carlisle on Stratton. Under cover of a moonless night, the man rushed along, fighting the rebellion, the inner turmoil, of his other self, the impatience of a being too long imprisoned.

"Now!" implored a silent call within him, the willpower of Dansallignatious. "Now."

Greensparrow growled. "Not yet, you fool," he warned, for he knew the risks of this journey, knew that to reveal himself to the Avonese populace, to show his subjects who and what he truly was, would surely overwhelm them. Dansallignatious, the other half of this man who was king, didn't agree, had never agreed, through all the years of Greensparrow's reign, through all the centuries before that since the time when the two, wizard and familiar being, had become one. To Dansallignatious, the revelation would only make them grovel all the more, would make Greensparrow greater in their eyes, would even cow the kings of neighboring countries into paying homage to the ultimate power that was Avon.

But then, Greensparrow reasoned, Dansallignatious would think that way; it was the way of his kind!

Through the fields the king ran, his feet hastened by a simple enchantment. Past the outlying farms, past the small huts where single candles behind windows showed that the folk were still awake. He felt a tug on his spine, an itch across his powdered skin.

"Not yet," Greensparrow implored Dansallignatious, but it was too late. The beast could no longer be contained. Greensparrow tried to run on, but a painful crack in his leg sent him sprawling in the thick grass. Then he was crawling, inching his way over a ridge, to roll down into the shelter of a grassy hollow.

His screams brought the farmers of three nearby cottages to their windows, peering out cautiously into the dark night. One man took up his ancient family sword, a rusted old thing, and dared to go out, moving slowly toward the continuing sound.

He had never heard such torment, such agony! It came from ahead, on the other side of a grassy bluff.

But then it quieted, suddenly, and the farmer thought that the man must have been killed.

Only then did he realize his own foolishness. Something behind that hill had apparently just murdered a man. What made him, a simple farmer with no experience or training with the sword, think that he would fare any better? Slowly, he began to back away.

Then he stopped, stricken.

A huge horned head lifted out of the shallow, rising, rising, ten feet, twenty feet above him. Lamplight orbs, yellow-green in color, reptilian in appearance, locked on to the man, showed him his doom.

The farmer's breath came in labored gasps. He wanted desperately to turn and run, but the sheer magnificence of the beast held him fast. Up came the dragon to the top of the bluff, great claws rending the earth as it moved, its wide-spread wings and tremendous bulk, eighty feet from horned head to swishing tail, blotting out the night sky.

"It feels good, Greensparrow," the beast said suddenly.

"Do not speak that name!" the beast then said, in the same thunderous voice, but with a different tone altogether.

"Greensparrow?" the farmer managed to whisper, confused, overwhelmed.

"Greensparrow!" insisted the dragon. "Do you not know your king? On your knees!"

The sheer power of the voice knocked the trembling farmer over. He scrambled to his knees, bowing his head before this most awful of creatures.

"You see?" asked the part that was Dansallignatious. "They fear me, worship me!"

The words were barely out before the dragon's face twisted weirdly. The voice that signified Dansallignatious started to protest, but the words were blasted away as a huge gout of fire burst forth from the dragon's mouth.

The blackened corpse beside the melted sword was not recognizable.

Dansallignatious shrieked, outraged that his fun with the peasant had been cut short, but Greensparrow willed himself into flight then and the sheer freedom of the cool night air flowing over leathery wings brought such joy and exhilaration to the dragon king that all arguments seemed petty.

A crowd of farmers gathered about the side of the bluff the next day, staring at the scorched grass and the blackened corpse. The Praetorian Guards were called in, but, as was usually the case where the brutish, unsympathetic cyclopians were involved, they were of little help. Reports of the incident would go back to Carlisle, they promised, snickering as they watched the dead man's grieving family.

More than one of the folk gathered claimed to have seen a great winged beast flying about on the previous night; that, too, would be told in Carlisle.

Greensparrow, comfortably back in the slender, almost effeminate form that his subjects had come to know so well, the dark side of him that was Dansallignatious appeased by the night of freedom, dismissed the reports as the overactive imaginations of simple peasants.

"To be sure, even the fishing is better these days!" howled an exuberant Shamus McConroy, first hand on *The Skipper*, a fishing boat out of the village of Gybi, the north port of Bae Colthwyn on Eriador's windswept northeastern shore. So named for its tendency to leap headlong through the high breakers, half-clear of the water, *The Skipper* was among the most highly regarded vessels of Bae Colthwyn's considerable fishing fleet. She was a thirty-footer, wide and with one square sail, and a crew of eight, salty old seadogs all, with not a hair among them that wasn't turning to gray.

Old Captain Aran Toomes liked it that way, and steadfastly refused to train a younger replacement crew. "Got no time for puppies," the crusty captain grumbled whenever someone remarked that his boat was a doomed thing—"mortal as a man" was the saying. Toomes always accepted the ribbing with a knowing snarl. In Bae Colthwyn, on the Dorsal Sea, where the great killer whales roamed in huge packs and the weather turned ugly without warning, fishermen left widows behind, and more "puppies" drowned than reached manhood. Thus, the crew of *The Skipper* was a reckless bunch of bachelors, hard drinkers and hard riders, challenging the mighty Dorsal Sea as though God above had put the waves in their path as a personal challenge. Day after day, she went out farther and faster than any other boat in the fishing fleet.

So it was this midsummer day, *The Skipper* running the breakers, sails full and straining. The weather seemed to shift every hour, from sunny bright to overcast, that curious mixture on the open water where a body was never quite comfortable, was always too hot or too cold. Younger, less experienced sailors would have spent a fair amount of time at the rail, bidding farewell to their morning meal, but *The Skipper*'s crew, more at home on the water than on land, took the dramatic changes in bowlegged stride.

And their spirits were higher than normal this fine day, for their land, beloved Eriador, was free once more. Prodded by a rebel army that had pushed all the way to the Avon city of Princetown, King Greensparrow of Avon had let Eriador out of his grasp, relinquishing the land to the people of Eriador. The old wizard Brind'Amour, a man of Eriadoran stock, had been crowned king in Caer MacDonald as the season had turned to summer. Not that life would be much different for the fisher-folk of Bae Colthwyn—except of course that they would no longer have to deal with cyclopian tax bands. King Greensparrow's influence had never really carried that much weight in the rugged land of northeastern Eriador, and not one in fifty of the people along the bay had ever gone further south than Mennichen Dee on the northern edges of the Fields of Eradoch.

Only the folk of southern Eriador, along the foothills of the Iron Cross mountain range, where Greensparrow's tyranny was felt in force, would likely see any dramatic difference in their day-to-day existence, but that wasn't the point of it all. Eriador was free, and that cry of inde-pendence echoed throughout the land, from the Iron Cross to Glen Albyn, to the pinelands of the northeast and the splashing, rocky shore-line of Bae Colthwyn, to the three northern isles, Marvis, Caryth, and giant Bedwydrin. Simple hope, that most necessary ingredient of happi-ness, had come to the wild land, personified by a king that few north of MacDonald's Swath would ever glimpse, and by a legend come to life called the Crimson Shadow.

When the news of their freedom had come to the bay, the fleet had put out, the fishermen singing and dancing on the decks as though they honestly expected the waters to be fuller with fish, as though they ex-pected the dorsal whales to turn and flee at the mere sight of a boat fly-ing under the flag of Eriador old, as though they expected the storms to blow less fierce, as though Nature herself should bow down to the new king of Eriador.

What a wonderful thing is hope, and to all who saw her this season, and especially to the men who crewed her, it seemed as if *The Skipper* leaped a little higher and ran the dark waters a little faster.

Early that morning, Shamus McConroy spotted the first whale, its black dorsal fin standing higher than a tall man, cutting the water barely fifty feet off their starboard bow. With typical abandon, the eight seadogs hurled taunts and whisky bottles the great whale's way, challeng-ing and cursing, and when that fin slipped under the dark water, mov-

ing away from the boat, they gave a hearty cheer and paid it no more
heed. The least experienced of them had spent thirty years on the water,
and their fear of the whales was long since gone. They could read the
dangerous animals, knew when to taunt and when to turn, when to
dump a haul of fish into the water as a diversion, and when, as a final
stance, to take up their long, pointed gaff hooks.

Soon after, all signs of land long gone, Aran Toomes put the morning
sun over his right shoulder, running *The Skipper* southeast toward the
mouth of the straits between Eriador and the Five Sentinels, a line of
brooding islands, more stone than turf. Toomes meant to keep his boat
out for the better part of a week, putting a hundred miles a day behind
him. His course would take him out to the north of Colonsey, the largest
and northernmost of the Five Sentinels, and then back again to the bay.
The water was colder out there, the old captain knew, just the way the
cod and mackerel liked it. The other boats of Bae Colthwyn's fleet knew
it, too, but few had the daring of *The Skipper*, or the confidence and sea
know-how of Aran Toomes.

Toomes kept his course true for three days, until the tips of Colonsey's steep mountains were in sight. Then he began his long, slow turn,
a hundred-and-eighty-degree arc, bringing her around to the northwest.
Behind him, working furiously, drinking furiously, and howling with
glee, his seven crewmen hauled in side-nets and long lines loaded with
fish: beautiful, shiny, smelly, flopping cod and mack, and even blues,
nasty little predators who did nothing more than swim and bite, swim
and bite, never stopping long enough to finish devouring whatever unfortunate fish had given them the mouthful. Shamus McConroy worked
a belaying pin wildly, thunking blues on the head until those tooth-filled
mouths stopped their incessant snapping. He got a nasty bite on the
ankle, cutting him right through his hard boots, and responded by hoisting the ten-pound blue by the tail and whacking it repeatedly against the
rail, to the hoots and cheers of the others.

For the seadogs, this was heaven.

The Skipper was lower in the water halfway through the turn, her hold
nearly full. The crew went down to one line, two men working it, while
the other five sorted through the load, pulling out smaller fish that were
still alive and tossing them over, wanting to replace them with bigger
specimens. It was all a game at this point, a challenge for fun, for a dozen
smaller fish were just as valuable as the eight bigger ones that would fill
their space in the hold, but the old sailors knew that the long days went
faster when the hands were moving. Here they were, full of fish three

hundred miles from port, with little to do but keep the sail in shape and steer the damned boat.

"Ah, so we're not the only boat with the gumption and heads to come out for a full hold," Shamus remarked to Aran. Grinning at old Aran's skeptical look, Shamus pointed to the northern horizon, where a darker speck had become evident within the line of bluish-gray.

"A pity we've not a bigger hold," Aran replied lightheartedly. "We could have fished the waters clean before ever they arrived!" The crusty captain finished the statement by clapping the crewman hard on the back.

That brought a chuckle from Shamus.

The Skipper continued along its merry way, the weather crisp and clear, the sea high, but not choppy, and the fishing more for sport now than for business. It wasn't until later that afternoon that Aran Toomes began to grow concerned. That speck on the horizon was much larger now, and, to the captain's surprise, it showed no sail on its single, square-rigged mast; thus it was no fishing boat from Bae Colthwyn. It was moving, though, and swiftly, and it seemed to be angling to intercept *The Skipper*.

Toomes brought the fishing boat harder to port, turning more westerly.

A few moments later, the other boat corrected its course accordingly.

"What do you know?" Shamus asked as he came forward to join Toomes at the wheel.

"I don't know," Aran Toomes replied grimly. "That's what's got me to thinking."

By now, the crew of *The Skipper* could see the froth at the side of the approaching vessel, a turbulence that could only mean a bank of great oars, pulling hard. In all the Dorsal Sea, only one race normally used boats that could be so oared, as well as sailed.

"Huegoths?" Shamus asked.

Aran Toomes couldn't find the will to answer.

"What are they doing so far to the south and east?" Shamus asked rhetorically.

"We don't know that they're Huegoths!" Aran Toomes yelled at him.

Shamus went numb and silent, staring at Toomes. The captain, who could laugh at a dorsal whale, seemed truly unnerved by the thought that this approaching vessel might be a Huegoth longship.

"Huegoths be the only ones who run so swift with oars," remarked another of the crew. The long line was forgotten now.

Aran Toomes chewed at his bottom lip, trying to find some answer.

"She runs with beauty," Shamus remarked, his gaze fixed on the longship. It was true enough; the design of the ships of Huegoth barbarians was nothing short of beautiful, finer than anything else on the northern seas. The graceful longships, seventy feet in length, were both solid and swift and cut the swells with hardly a ripple.

"Empty the hold," Aran Toomes decided.

The expressions of the other seven ranged from eager to incredulous. For several of the crewmen, this command seemed impossible, ridiculous. They had risked much in coming out this far to the southwest, so long from port, and those risks had been accepted precisely for the prize of fish in the hold. Now the captain wanted to throw away their catch?

But the other four men, including Shamus McConroy, who had dealt with savage Huegoths before, agreed wholeheartedly with the call. Laden with several tons of fish, *The Skipper* could not outrun the longship; even empty, they could only hope to keep ahead of the Huegoths long enough for the oarsmen to tire. Even then, the Huegoths could put up a sail.

"Empty it clear!" roared Aran, and the crew went to work.

Toomes studied the wind more carefully. It was generally from the south, not a good thing considering that the Huegoths, who did not depend on the wind, were coming down from the north. If he tried to turn *The Skipper* about, he'd be running into headwinds, practically standing still on the water.

"Let's see how good you can turn," the captain muttered, and he angled back to the north. He'd go in close, cut right by the Huegoths. If *The Skipper* could survive that single pass, and avoid the underwater ram that no doubt stuck out from the front of the barbarian ship, Toomes would have the wind at his back while the longship turned about.

A few hundred yards separated the vessels. Toomes could see the activity on the barbarians' top deck, huge men running to and fro. He could see the tall, curving forecastle, carved into the likeness of a wolf.

Then he saw the smoke, rising up suddenly from the longship's center. For an instant, the captain thought the longship had somehow caught fire, thought that perhaps one of the galley slaves had sabotaged the Huegoth raiders. But Toomes quickly realized the truth, and knew that his dear ship was in worse trouble still.

"Get you behind a wall!" the captain yelled to his crew when the ships were less than a hundred yards apart, when he could make out individual Huegoths leaning over the rail, their expressions bloodthirsty.

Shamus ran forward with a huge shield that he kept in the hold. He placed it to cover as much of the captain at the wheel as possible, then crouched low beside Toomes.

Toomes had meant to go much closer, to practically dance with the Hue-goth boat before executing his sharp turn, to port or to starboard, whichever way seemed to give the most light between the jockeying vessels. He had to commit sooner, though. He knew that now, with the black smoke billowing high.

He turned right, starboard, and when the longship's left bank began to drag in the water, pulling her to port, Toomes cut back to port harder than he had ever tried to turn *The Skipper*. The good ship seemed to hesitate, seemed to stand right up in the water, beams creaking, mast groaning. But turn she did, and her sails dipped for just an instant, then swelled with wind, racing her off in the new direction, which by comforting coincidence put *The Skipper* straight in line with Bae Colthwyn.

A barrage of flaming arrows soared out from the longship, a score of fiery bolts trailing black lines of smoke. Many fell short, most missed widely, but one did catch on the prow of *The Skipper*, and another found the starboard edge of the mast and sail.

Shamus McConroy was there in an instant, batting at the flames. Two other crewmen came right in with buckets, dousing the fires before they could do any real damage.

At the wheel, eyes locked on his adversary, Aran Toomes wasn't comforted. Now the longship's left bank pulled hard, while the right bank hit the water in reverse, pivoting the seventy-foot vessel like a giant capstan.

"Too fast," old Aran muttered when he saw the incredible turn, when he realized that *The Skipper* would have a difficult time getting past that devastating ram. Still, Aran was committed to his course now; he could not cut any harder, or try to pull back to starboard.

It was a straight run, wind in the sails of *The Skipper*, oars pounding the waters to either side of the longship. The little fishing boat got past the longship's prow and started to distance herself from the still-turning Huegoths. For an instant, it seemed as though the daring move might actually succeed.

But then came the second volley of flaming arrows, crossing barely thirty feet of water, more than half of them diving into the vulnerable sails. Shamus, still working to repair the minor damage from the first volley, took one right in the back, just under his shoulder blade. He stumbled forward while another man swatted his back furiously, trying to douse the stubborn flames.

That fire was the least of Shamus McConroy's problems. He reached the wheel, verily fell over it, leaning heavily and looking close into Aran Toomes's grim face.

"I think it got me in the heart," Shamus said with obvious surprise, and then he died.

Aran cradled the man down to the deck. He looked back just once, to see *The Skipper's* sails consumed by the flames, to see the longship, straightened now and in full row, banks churning the water on both sides, closing in fast.

He looked back to Shamus, poor Shamus, and then he was lurching wildly, flying out of control, as the devastating ram splintered *The Skipper's* rudder and smashed hard against her hull.

Sometime later—it seemed like only seconds—a barely conscious Aran Toomes felt himself dragged across the deck and hauled over to the Huegoth ship. He managed to open his eyes, looking out just as *The Skipper*, prow high in the air, stern already beneath the dark canopy, slipped silently under the waves, taking with it the bodies of Shamus and Greasy Solarny, an old seadog who had sailed with Aran for twenty years.

As he let go of that terrible sight, focused again on the situation at hand, Aran heard the cries for his death, and for the death of the five other remaining crewmen.

But then another voice, not as gruff and deep, overrode the excited Huegoths, calming them little by little.

"These men are not of Avon," said the man, "but of Eriador. Good and strong stock, and too valuable to kill."

"To the galley!" roared one Huegoth, a cry quickly taken up by all the others.

As he was lifted from the deck, Aran got a look at the man who had saved him. He wasn't a small man, but certainly not of giant Huegoth stock, well-toned and strong, with striking cinnamon-colored eyes.

The man was Eriadoran!

Aran wanted to say something, but hadn't the breath or the chance.

Or the clarity. His life and the lives of his remaining crewmen had been spared, but Aran Toomes had lived a long, long time and had heard tales of the horrors of life as a Huegoth galley slave. He didn't know whether to thank this fellow Eriadoran, or to spit in the man's face.

CHAPTER 2

DIPLOMACY

ET OUT OF THAT BED, OLIVER!" came the yell, followed by a resounding pound. "Awaken, you half-sized mischief-maker!"

Siobhan slammed her open palm against the closed door again, then clenched her fists in frustration and half-growled, half-screamed as loudly as she could. "Why didn't you just go with Luthien?" she demanded, and pounded the door again. Then the energy seemed to drain from the slender and beautiful half-elf. She turned about and fell back against the door, brushed her long wheat-colored hair from her face, and took a deep breath to calm herself. It was mid-morning already; Siobhan had been up for several hours, had bathed and eaten breakfast, had seen to the arrangements in the audience hall, had discussed their strategy with King Brind'Amour, had even met secretly with Shuglin the dwarf to see what unexpected obstacles might be thrown in their path.

And Oliver, who had remained in Caer MacDonald to help Siobhan with all of these preparations, hadn't even crawled out of his fluffy bed yet!

"I really hate to do this," Siobhan remarked, and then she shook her head as she realized that a few short days with Oliver already had her talking to herself on a fairly regular basis. She rolled about to face the door and slipped down to one knee, drawing out a slender pick and a flat piece of metal. Siobhan was a member of the Cutters, a band of thieving elves and half-elves who had terrorized the merchants of Caer MacDonald when the city had been under the control of Greensparrow's lackey, Duke Morkney. Siobhan often boasted that no lock could defeat her, and so she proved it again now, deftly working the pick until her keen elven ears heard the tumblers of Oliver's door click open.

Now came the dangerous part, the half-elf realized. Oliver, too, had no small reputation as a thief, and the foppish halfling often warned people about uninvited entry to his private room. Slowly and gently, Siobhan cracked the door, barely an inch, then began sliding the metal tab about its edge. She closed her green eyes and let her sensitive fingers relay all the information she needed, and sure enough, halfway across the top of the door, she found something unusual.

The half-elf rose to her tiptoes, smiling as she came to understand the nature of the trap. It was a simple tab, wedged between door and jamb and no doubt supporting a pole or other item that was propping the edge of a hung bucket—probably filled with water.

Cold water—that was Oliver's style.

Carefully the graceful half-elf pushed the door a bit further, and then some more, until she exposed one edge of the supporting tab. Then she used her piece of flattened metal to extend the tab, and gently, so gently, she pushed the door a bit more. Now came the tricky part, as Siobhan had to slip into the room, contorting and sucking in her breath to avoid the doorknob. She barely fit, and had to push the door still more, nearly dislodging both tabs and sending the bucket—for she could now see that it was indeed a large bucket, suspended from the ceiling—into a spin that would soak her fine dress.

She paused for a moment and considered her predicament, resolving that if Oliver's little game ruined her outfit, the finest clothes she possessed, she would steal his treasured rapier blade, take it to a smithy friend, and have it tied into a knot!

The door creaked; Siobhan held her breath and slowly swiveled her hips into the room.

Her dress caught on the doorknob.

With a profound sigh, and a lament at how impractical this fashion statement truly was, Siobhan simply unstrapped the bulky garment and slid right out of it, leaving it on the knob as she wriggled around the door. She pulled the dress in behind her and gently closed the door, then turned about to a sight that opened wide her shining green eyes.

The door made a tinkling sound as it closed, drawing her attention. There, on the inside knob, hung Oliver's golden-brocade shoulder belt and baldric, lined with tiny bells. On the floor directly before the entrance was a green stocking, topped in silk. Further in lay a pair of green gauntlets, one on top of the halfling's signature purple velvet cape. Beyond the cape were a pair of shiny black shoes, impeccably polished. The line of strewn clothing continued with a sleeveless blue doublet, the second stocking, and a white silken undertunic, crumpled against the foot of a huge, four-posted bed. Oliver's wide-brimmed hat, one side pinned up tight and plumed with a huge orange feather, hung atop one of the corner posts—how the diminutive halfling ever got the thing up the seven feet to the top of it, Siobhan could only guess.

Siobhan let her eyes linger on the hat a moment, considering the feather, drooping as though it, too, had spent too many hours of the previous night in high partying.

With a sigh of resignation, Siobhan folded her dress carefully over her arm and crept closer. She covered her eyes and snickered when she spotted the halfling, facedown atop the oversized down comforter, arms and legs out wide to the sides and straddling a pillow that was larger than he. He was wearing his breeches (purple velvet, to match the cape), at least, but they were wrapped about his head and not where they belonged. The half-elf moved around the mounting stairs, a set of five for the little halfling, and right up to the side of the bed.

How might she wake the little one? she mused, and snickered again when Oliver let out a great snore.

Siobhan reached over and flicked a finger against Oliver's shining, naked buttock.

Oliver snored again.

Siobhan tickled him under the arm. The halfling started to roll over, but Siobhan, with a frightened squeal, put a hand on his shoulder and held him in place.

"Ah, my little buttercup," Oliver said, startling the half-elf. "Your bosom does so warm my body."

Siobhan couldn't tell for certain, but it sounded as if Oliver was kissing the pillow under the breeches-wrap.

Enough of that, Siobhan decided, and this time she reached over and gave the halfling a stinging slap.

Up popped his head, one pant leg flopping over his face. Oliver blew a couple of times, but the material was too heavy to be moved that way. Finally the halfling reached up and slowly pushed the obstacle out of his eyes.

How those brown and severely bloodshot eyes widened when he saw Siobhan standing beside his bed in her petticoats, her dress over her arm! Oliver slowly shifted his gaze, to consider his own naked form, then snapped his gaze back to Siobhan.

"Buttercup?" the dazed halfling asked, and a smile widened over his face, his dimples shining through.

"Do not even think it," Siobhan replied evenly.

Oliver ran a hand over his neatly trimmed goatee, then through his long and curly brown locks, taking the pants off as he went, as he tried to piece together the events of the previous night. Most of it was a blur, but he remembered a certain maid-servant . . .

The halfling's eyes nearly fell from their sockets when he realized then that Siobhan wasn't in his room for any amorous reason, that she had come in to wake him and nothing more, and that he was . . .

"Oh!" Oliver wailed, spinning about to a sitting position. "Oh, you unabashed . . ." He stammered, choking with embarrassment. "Oh, where is my sword?" he howled.

Siobhan's eyes roamed down the halfling's chest and lower, and she gave a mischievous smile and a slight shrug of her shoulders.

"My rapier blade!" the flustered halfling corrected. "Oh, you . . ." Oliver fumed and leaped from the bed, fumbling with his breeches and nearly tripping over them as he struggled to put them over his moving feet. "In Gascony, we have a name for a woman such as you!" he said, spinning to face the half-elf.

Siobhan's fair features tightened into a threatening scowl.

"Dangerous," she said, a pointed reminder to the halfling.

Oliver froze, considering the word and considering this most beautiful of females. Finally, he gave up and shrugged. Dangerous was a good word for her, Oliver decided, in more ways than one.

"You could have knocked before entering my private room," said the halfling, in controlled tones once more.

"I nearly beat your door down," Siobhan retorted. "You have, perhaps, forgotten our meeting with King Bellick dan Burso of Dun-Darrow?"

"Forgotten it?" Oliver balked. He scooped up his silken undertunic and pulled it over his shoulders. "Why, I have spent all the night in preparation. Why do you think you have found me so weary?"

"The pillow was demanding?" Siobhan replied, looking to the disheveled bed.

Oliver growled and let it pass. He dropped suddenly to one knee, slapped aside the edge of the comforter to reveal the hilt of his rapier, then drew the blade out from between the mattresses. "I do not take lightly my so important position," he said. "Halflings are more attuned . . ."

"A-too-ned?" Siobhan interrupted, mocking Oliver's Gascon accent, which seemed to extend every syllable of every word.

"Attu-ned!" Oliver gruffly answered. "Halflings are more attu-ned to the ways and likes of dwarfs than are peoples, and elfy-types!"

"Elfy-types?" Siobhan whispered under her breath, but she didn't bother to interrupt openly, for Oliver had hit his verbal stride. On he rambled about the value of halfling diplomats, of how they had stopped this war or that, of how they had talked "stupid human king-types" right out of their "jew-wels," family and otherwise. As he spoke, the halfling looked all around, then finally up, to see his hat atop the post. Not missing a syllable, Oliver flipped the rapier to catch it by the blade and threw it straight up, hilt first. It clipped the hat, lifting it from the post, and down both came.

Oliver caught the blade by the hilt above his head and moved it incredibly smoothly to poke the floor beside his bare, hair-topped foot, striking a gallant pose.

"So there," finished the halfling, who had regained his dignity, and on cue his hat fell perfectly atop his head.

"You have style," Siobhan had to admit. Then she added with a snicker, "And you are cute without your clothes."

Oliver's heroic pose disintegrated. "Oh!" he wailed, lifting the rapier and poking it down harder—and this time nicking the side of his foot.

Trying to hold to his fast-falling dignity, the halfling spun and ambled away, scooping his doublet, stockings, shoes, and gauntlets as he went. "I will find my revenge for this!" Oliver promised.

"I, too, sleep without any clothes," Siobhan said teasingly.

Oliver stopped dead in his tracks and nearly fell over. He knew that Siobhan was toying with him, hitting his amorous spirit where it could not defend itself, but the conjured image evoked by those six little words overwhelmed him, sent him into a trembling fit from head to hairy toe. He turned about, stammering for some retort, then just squealed in defeat and stormed to the door, grabbing his baldric as he passed.

Forgetting his own trap.

Down fell the supporting tab and over went the suspended bucket, dropping cold water all over the halfling, sending the brim of his great hat drooping low.

Oliver, cooled, turned back to Siobhan. "I meant to do that," he insisted, and then he was gone.

Siobhan stood in the room for a long while, shaking her head and laughing. Despite all the trouble this one caused, there was indeed something charming about Oliver deBurrows.

Oliver was back in form in time for the all-important meeting at the assigned house, a commandeered piece of real estate that had formerly belonged to a nobleman loyal to Greensparrow. The man had fled Eriador, and Brind'Amour had taken his house to use as the palace of Caer MacDonald, though most business was conducted at the Ministry, the huge cathedral that dominated the city. Oliver had dried off and somehow managed to get his wide-brimmed hat to stand out stiffly again—even the feather was properly rigid. Siobhan stared at that transformation incredulously, wondering if the halfling possessed more than one of the outrageous, plumed "chapeaus," as he called them.

Oliver sat on a higher stool on one side of a huge oaken table, flanking King Brind'Amour on the left, while Siobhan sat on the old wizard's right.

Across from them sat a quartet of grim-faced dwarfs. King Bellick dan Burso was directly across from Brind'Amour, his blue eyes locking intently with the wizard's—though Brind'Amour could hardly see them under the dwarf's tremendous eyebrows, fiery orange in hue, like his remarkable beard. So bright and bushy was that beard, and long enough for Bellick to tuck it into his belt, that it was often whispered that the dwarf king wore a suit of living flames. Shuglin, friend to the rebels who had conquered Caer MacDonald, sat beside Bellick, calm and confident. It had been Shuglin, a dwarf of Caer MacDonald and not of the Iron Cross, who had initiated this meeting and all the discussions between his mountain brethren and the new leaders of Eriador. Any alliance between the groups would benefit both, Shuglin realized, for these two kings, Bellick and Brind'Amour, were of like mind and goodly ilk.

Two other dwarfs, broad-shouldered generals, flanked King Bellick and Shuglin.

The formal greetings went off well, with Oliver doing most of the talking, as Brind'Amour had planned. This was their party, after all; through the emissary Shuglin, it had been Brind'Amour, and not Bellick, who had requested the summit.

"You know our gratitude for your help in overcoming Princetown," Brind'Amour began quietly. Indeed the dwarfs did know, for Brind'Amour had sent many, many messengers, all of them bearing gifts, to the stronghold of DunDarrow, the dwarfish underground complex nestled deep in the Iron Cross mountain range. Bellick's folk had arrived on the field outside of Princetown, Avon's northernmost city, just in time to cut off the retreat of the Avon garrison, which had been routed in Glen Durritch by the Eriadorans. With Bellick's sturdy force blocking the way, the victory had been complete. "Eriador owes much to King Bellick dan Burso and his warriors," Brind'Amour reaffirmed.

Bellick gave an accepting nod. "Princetown would have fallen in any event, even without our help," the dwarf replied graciously.

"Ah, but if the soldiers of Princetown had gotten back behind their so high walls . . ." Oliver put in, though it was certainly not his place to interrupt.

Brind'Amour only chuckled, more than used to the halfling's often irreverent ways.

Bellick did not seem so pleased, a fact that made Brind'Amour eye him curiously. At first, the wizard thought that the dwarf had taken insult at Oliver's interruption, but then he realized that something else was bothering Bellick.

The dwarf king looked to Shuglin and nodded, and Shuglin stood solemnly and cleared his throat.

"Twenty Fairborn were slain yestereve in the foothills of the Iron Cross," he reported. "Not twenty miles from here."

Brind'Amour sank back in his high-backed chair and looked to Siobhan, who bit her lip and nodded her head in frustration. The half-elf had heard rumors of the battle, for her people, the Fairborn, were not numerous throughout Avonsea, and kept general tabs on each other. Now it seemed the number of Fairborn had diminished once again.

"Cyclopian raiders," Shuglin continued. "A group of at least a hundred."

"Never before have the one-eyes been so organized," Bellick added. "It would seem that your little war has riled the beasts from the deep mountain holes."

Brind'Amour understood the dwarf's frustration and the accusation, if that was what Bellick had just offered. The cyclopian activity along the northern foothills of the Iron Cross had indeed heightened tremendously since the signing of the truce with Greensparrow of Avon. Brind'Amour kept his gaze on Siobhan for a long moment, wondering how she would react. Then he looked to Oliver, and realized that his companions also understood that the cyclopian activity so soon after the truce was not a coincidence.

Shuglin waited for Brind'Amour to turn back to him before he resumed his seat. The wizard noted a slight nod from the black-bearded dwarf, an encouragement the beleaguered king of Eriador sorely needed at that time.

"The one-eyes have struck at several villages," Brind'Amour explained to Bellick.

"Perhaps they believe that with King Greensparrow no longer concerned with Eriador, the land is free for their pillaging," Bellick replied, and from his tone it seemed that he didn't believe that statement any more than did Brind'Amour. Both kings knew who was behind the cyclopian raids, but neither would speak it openly, especially since they hadn't yet reached any formal agreement with each other.

"Perhaps," Brind'Amour said. "But whatever the cause of the cyclopian raids, it only stands to reason that both your dwarfs and the folk of Eriador would profit from an alliance."

Bellick nodded. "I know what you're wanting from me and my kin, King Brind'Amour," he said. "You need a mountain army, protection from the one-eyes, and security against Greensparrow, should the Avon king decide to come calling once more. What I want to know is what you've to offer to my folk."

Brind'Amour was a bit surprised by the dwarf's straightforwardness. A diplomatic summit such as this could roll on for days before the obvious questions were so plainly asked. Shuglin had warned the wizard about the dwarf king's blunt style, and now, with so much trouble brewing and reports arriving daily about cyclopian raids, Brind'Amour found that he liked straightforward Bellick all the more.

"Markets," Brind'Amour replied. "I offer you markets. Both Caer MacDonald and Dun Caryth will be open for you, and with Eriador trying to establish her true independence, we shall be drilling a formal militia, and shall require many weapons."

"And none forge better weapons than your dwarfs," Siobhan quickly added.

Bellick put his elbows up on the oaken table and crossed his fingers in front of his hairy face. "You wish DunDarrow to become a city of Eriador," he said bluntly, and somewhat sourly.

"We considered an alliance of separate kingdoms," Brind'Amour replied without hesitation, "but I truly believe that—"

"That with DunDarrow under your control, you will get the supplies you so desperately need much more cheaply," interrupted Bellick.

Brind'Amour sat back once more, staring intently at the dwarf king. After a short pause, he started to respond, but Bellick cut him short with an upraised hand.

"It's true enough," the dwarf said, "and I admit that I would be doing much the same if I found myself in your tentative position. The king of Avon wants Eriador, not DunDarrow—by the stones, he'd not find us anyway, and not take us if he did!" The orange-bearded dwarf's voice rose excitedly, and his three brethren were quick to take up the cheer.

Oliver, wanting the floor, tapped Brind'Amour on the arm, but Bellick began again before the wizard could acknowledge the halfling.

"So I am not blaming you," Bellick said. "We came out of the mountains to Princetown because of what you and yours have done for our kin, those enslaved in the city and the mines, and in all of Eriador. We know you as dwarf-friend, no small title. And, to be truthful, DunDarrow, too, would profit by securing as tight an alliance with Eriador as you desire."

"None but the king of DunDarrow may rule in DunDarrow," said the dwarf warrior seated beside Shuglin.

"And he who rules in DunDarrow must be of Clan Burso," the other general added. "Of dwarven blood, and only dwarven blood."

Brind'Amour, Siobhan, and Oliver all understood that the interruptions had been planned, the words carefully rehearsed. Bellick wanted Brind'Amour to see his predicament clearly, even if the dwarf decided to join in with Eriador.

Brind'Amour began to respond, to offer the dwarfs all respect, but this time Oliver leaped from his chair and scrambled atop the table.

"My good fellow furry folk," the halfling began.

Shuglin groaned; so did Siobhan.

"I, too, am a citizen of Eriador," Oliver continued, ignoring the audible doubts. "In service to King Brind'Amour!" He said it dramatically, as if expecting some applause, and when none came, he seemed caught off guard, stumbling verbally for just a moment.

"But not a one rules Oliver deBurrows except for Oliver deBurrows!" With that, the halfling drew his rapier and struck a dramatic pose.

"Your point?" Bellick asked dryly.

"A duocracy," the halfling explained.

There came a round of murmurs and questions, no one having any idea of what a "duocracy" might be.

"Eriador is Brind'Amour's," Oliver went on. "In Eriador, he rules. And yet, he would not tell the Riders of Eradoch what to do in Mennichen Dee. Nor would he tell Gahris, who rules on Isle Bedwydrin, how to handle his affairs of state."

"Not unless he had to," Siobhan put in, drawing a sour look from the halfling.

"Please, I am speaking," Oliver huffed at her.

Siobhan winked at him, further throwing him off, but other than that, the half-elf let him go on.

"So it shall be with the dwarfs, but even more so," Oliver explained. He had to pause then, for a moment, as he considered the signals Siobhan was throwing his way. Was she merely teasing? As he considered the possibilities, the sheer beauty and intelligence of this most wonderful half-elf, Oliver hoped that she was not!

"You were saying," Brind'Amour prompted.

"I was?"

"So it shall be with the dwarfs, but even more so," Siobhan put in.

"Ah, yes!" beamed the halfling, and he brightened all the more when Siobhan offered yet another wink. "A duocracy. DunDarrow will become a city of Eriador, but the king of Eriador will have no say over matters of state within DunDarrow."

Both Bellick and Brind'Amour seemed somewhat intrigued, and also a bit confused.

"I have never heard of such a government," Brind'Amour put in.

"Nor have I," agreed Bellick.

"Nor have I!" Oliver admitted. "And since it hasn't been done before, it should work all the better!"

"Oliver is no supporter of government," Brind'Amour explained, noticing Bellick's confused expression.

"Ah," replied the dwarf, then to Oliver, "In this duocracy, what am I? Servant of Brind'Amour or king of DunDarrow?"

"Both," said the halfling. "Though never would I call one in the line of Burso Ironhammer a 'servant.' No, not that. Ally to Eriador, allowing Brind'Amour to determine all our course through the greater . . . er, larger, though certainly more boring, issues outside of Eriador."

"Sounds like a servant," one of the dwarven generals said distastefully.

"Ah, but it all depends upon how you look at it," Oliver replied. "King Bellick does not want to deal with such diplomatic matters as fishing rights or emissaries from Gascony. No, no, King Bellick would rather spend his days at the forge, I am sure, where any good dwarf belongs."

"True enough," admitted the orange-bearded king.

"In that light, it seems to me as if Brind'Amour was King Bellick's servant, handling all the troublesome pettiness of government while King Bellick beats his hammer, or whatever it is you dwarfs beat."

"And of course, in any matters that concern DunDarrow directly or indirectly, I would first inform you and seek your counsel and your decision," Brind'Amour cut in, wanting to keep Oliver's surprising momentum flowing.

The four dwarfs called for a break, then huddled in the corner, talking excitedly. They came back to the table almost immediately.

"There are details to be defined," Bellick said. "I would protect the integrity of DunDarrow's sovereignty."

Brind'Amour sagged in his chair.

"But," Bellick added, "I would be loving the expression on ugly Greensparrow's face when he hears that DunDarrow and Eriador are one!"

"Duocracy!" shouted Oliver.

They adjourned then, with more progress made than Brind'Amour had dared hope for. He left with Oliver and Siobhan, all three in fine spirits, and of course, with Oliver retelling, and embellishing, his inspirational interruption.

"I did notice, though," Brind'Amour remarked when the breathless halfling paused long enough for him to get a word in, "that in your lit-

tle speech, you referred to my counterpart as *King Bellick,* while I was
referred to as merely *Brind'Amour.*"

Oliver started to laugh, but stopped short, seeing the wizard's serious
expression. There were many people in the world whom Oliver did not
want for enemies, and mighty Brind'Amour was at the very top of that
list.

"It was not a speech," Oliver stammered, "but a performance: Yes, a
performance for our hairy dwarf-type friends. You noticed my subtle
error, and so did Bellick . . ."

"King Bellick," Brind'Amour corrected. "And I noticed that it was
but one of your errors."

Oliver fumbled about for a moment. "Ah, but I knew you before you
ever were king," he reminded the wizard.

Brind'Amour could have kept up the feigned anger all the day, taking
pleasure in Oliver's sweat, but Siobhan's chuckling soon became infectious, and Oliver howled loudest of all when he realized that the wizard
was playing games with him. He had done well, after all, with his im-
provisation of "duocracy," and it seemed as if the vital agreement between Bellick and Brind'Amour was all but signed.

Oliver noticed, too, the strange way Siobhan was looking at him.

Respect?

Menster, in the southwestern corner of Glen Albyn, was much like
any other tiny Eriadoran community. It had no militia, was in fact little
more than a collection of a few houses connected by a defensive wall of
piled logs. The people, single men mostly, farmed a little, hunted a lot,
and fished the waters of a clear, babbling stream that danced down from
the higher reaches of the Iron Cross. Menster's folk had little contact
with the outside world, though two of the hamlet's younger men had
joined the Eriadoran army when that force had marched through Glen
Albyn on their way to Princetown. Both those young men had returned
with tales of victory when the army came through again, heading west
this time, back to Caer MacDonald.

And so there had been much rejoicing in Menster since the war. In
years past, the village had been visited often by Greensparrow's tax collectors, and like most independent-minded Eriadorans, the folk of Menster were never fond of being under the shadow of a foreign king.

With the change in government, with Eriador in the hands of an Eriadoran, their lives could only get better, or so they believed. Perhaps they
might even remain invisible to the new king of Eriador, an unnoticed little hamlet, untaxed and unbothered. Just the way they wanted it.

But Menster was not invisible to the growing cyclopian horde, and though the people of Menster were a sturdy folk, surviving in near isolation on the rugged slopes of the Iron Cross, they were not prepared, could not have been prepared, for the events of one fateful midsummer's night.

Tonky Macomere and Meegin Comber, the two veterans of the Princetown campaign, walked the wall that night, as they did most nights, keeping watch over their beloved village. Meegin was the first to spot a cyclopian, ambling through the underbrush some forty yards from the wall.

"Graceful as a one-legged drunken bear," he whispered to Tonky, when the lanky man noted Comber's hand motion and moved over to his fellow guard.

Neither was overly concerned; cyclopians often came near to Menster, usually scavenging discarded animal carcasses, though sometimes, rarely, testing the readiness of the townsfolk. The village sat on a flat expanse of ground, cleared all about the irregular-shaped wall for more than a hundred feet. Given that cyclopians were terrible with missile weapons (having only one eye and little depth perception) and that the thirty or so hunter-folk of Menster were all expert archers, the defenders of the city could decimate a hundred one-eyes before the brutes could cross the fields. And cyclopians, so surly and chaotic, hating everything, even each other, rarely ever banded in groups approaching a hundred.

"Oops, there's another one," said Tonky, motioning to the right.

"And another behind it," added Comber. "Best that we rouse the folk."

"Most're up already," Tonky put in. Both men turned about to regard the central building of the hamlet, the town meetinghouse and tavern, a long and low structure well-lit and more than a little noisy.

"Let's hope they're not too drunk to shoot straight," Comber remarked, but again the conversation was lighthearted, and without much concern.

Comber set off then, meaning to run a quick circuit of the wall, checking the perimeter, then dart down and inform the village of potential danger. Menster had drilled for scenarios exactly such as this a thousand times and all thirty archers (excepting a few who indeed were too drunk), would be in place in mere seconds, raining death on any cyclopians that ventured too near. Halfway around his intended circuit, though, Comber skidded to a stop in his tracks and stood staring out over the wall.

"What do you see?" Tonky called as quietly as possible from across the way.

Comber let out a shriek.

Instantly the bustle halted in the central structure, and men and women began pouring forth from its doors, bearing longbows, heading for the wall.

Comber was shooting his bow by then, repeatedly, and so was Tonky, letting arrows fly and hardly aiming, for so great was the throng charging from the brush and across the clearing that it was almost impossible to miss.

More villagers scrambled up the wall and took up their bows, and cyclopians fell dead by the dozens.

But the one-eyes, nearly a thousand strong, could afford the losses.

All the wall seemed to groan and creak when the brutish masses slammed against it, setting ladders and chopping at the logs with great axes.

The folk of Menster remained controlled, emptied their quivers and called for more arrows, shooting point-blank at the brutes. But the wall was soon breached, cyclopians scrambling over the top and boring right through, and most of the folk had to drop their bows and take up sword or spear, or whatever was handy that might serve as a club.

In close, though, the defenders' advantage was lost, and so, both sides knew, was Menster.

It was over in a few minutes.

Suddenly Menster, or the utter carnage that had been Menster, was no longer an unnoticed and unremarkable little village to King Brind'Amour, or to anyone living along Eriador's southern border.

CHAPTER 3

BITTERSWEET

THE FIRST SLANTED RAYS of the morning sun roused Katerin O'Hale. She looked about her camp, to the gray ashes of the previous night's fire, to the two horses tethered under a wide elm, and to the other bedroll, already tied up and ready to pack away. That didn't surprise Katerin; she suspected that her traveling companion had found little sleep.

The weary woman dragged herself out from under the blankets, stood tall, and stretched away the pains of sleeping on hard ground. Her legs were sore, and so were her buttocks. For five days, she and Luthien had ridden hard to the north, across the breadth of Eriador, to the mainland's north-western tip. Now, turning her back to the morning sun, Katerin could see the haze from the straits where the Avon Sea met the Dorsal, and through that haze, not so far away, loomed the ghostly gray forms of Isle Bedwydrin's rolling, melancholy hills.

Home. Both Katerin and Luthien had been raised on the island, the largest in Avonsea, save the mainland and giant Baranduine to the south and west. The two companions had spent nearly all of their lives on Bed-wydrin, Luthien in Dun Varna, the largest city and seat of power, and Ka-terin across the way, on the western shores, in the hardy village of Hale. When she had hit her mid-teens, Katerin had gone to Dun Varna to train as a warrior in the arena, and there she had met Luthien.

She had fallen in love with the son of Eorl Gahris Bedwyr, and had fol-lowed him across the country, all the way into Avon at the head of an army.

The war was over now, at least for a while, and the two were going home. Not for a vacation, but to see Gahris, who, by all reports, lay near death.

Looking at the island, so near, and thinking of their purpose, Katerin understood that Luthien hadn't slept well the previous night. Likely he hadn't slept at all for several days. The woman looked all around, then crossed the small camp and climbed a rise, crouching low as she neared the top.

In a clearing beyond stood Luthien, stripped to the waist and holding *Blind-Striker*, the Bedwyr family sword.

What a marvelous weapon was that sword, its perfect blade of tightly wrapped metal gleaming in the morning sun, outshone only by its golden, bejeweled hilt, sculpted into the shape of a dragon rampant, the out-stretched wings serving as a formidable cross-piece.

Katerin's shining green eyes did not linger long on the weapon, for more marvelous still was the specter of Luthien. He stood two inches above six feet, with wide shoulders and a broad chest, golden-tanned, and arms lined by strong and sinewy muscles that flexed and corded as he moved through his morning practice regimen. He was thicker, stronger, than he had been when they had fought in the arena in Dun Varna, Ka-terin decided. No more a boy, but a man. His eyes, striking cinnamon-colored orbs, the trademark of family Bedwyr, showed that change as well. They still held their youthful luster, but now that gleam was tem-pered by the intensity of wisdom.

Blind-Striker seemed to weave invisible strands into the air as it moved about Luthien, sometimes guided by one hand, sometimes by two. Luthien turned and dipped, came up high and arched gracefully downward, but though he was often facing her, Katerin did not fear that he would take any notice. He was a complete fighter, full of concentration despite his weariness, and his trance during his practice routine was complete. Up went *Blind-Striker*, straight over Luthien's head, held in both hands, the young man's arms and body perfectly squared. Slowly Luthien shifted to the side, letting go of the heavy sword with his right hand and bringing the weapon down inch by inch with his left. His right hand dragged along his left forearm during the descent, across the elbow, and over his biceps. Everything stopped together, left arm straight out, on the exact plane with his shoulders, while his right arm remained bent over his head, the tips of his fingers barely touching the left shoulder.

Katerin studied him for the long seconds as he held the pose. The sword was heavy, especially held horizontally, so far from his body, but Luthien's strong arm did not quiver. Katerin's eyes roved to the smaller details, to the intense eyes and Luthien's hair, long and wavy and a dark, rich shade of blond, showing highlights of red in the sun.

Katerin instinctively brought her hand to her own hair, a thick red mane, and she pulled it back from her face. How she loved Luthien Bedwyr! He was in her thoughts all the time, in her dreams—which were always pleasant when he was in her arms. He had left her, had left Bedwydrin, shortly after a tragic incident in which his best friend had been killed. Luthien had exacted revenge on the murderer and then had taken to the road, a road that had joined him up with Oliver deBurrows, highwayhalfling; a road that had led him to Brind'Amour, who was at that time a recluse living in a cave. It was Brind'Amour who had given to Luthien the crimson cape, thus resurrecting the legendary Crimson Shadow.

And that road, too, had led Luthien to Siobhan, beautiful Siobhan, who had become his lover.

That fact still pained Katerin greatly, though she and Siobhan had become friends, and the half-elf had confided that Luthien loved only Katerin. In reality, Siobhan was no longer a threat to Katerin's relationship with Luthien, but the proud woman could not easily shake the lingering image of the two together.

She would get over it, though. Katerin resolved to do that, and Katerin was not one to fail at anything she determined to do. Siobhan was a friend, and Luthien was Katerin's lover once more.

Once more and forever, he had promised, and Katerin trusted in that oath. She knew that Luthien loved her as much as she loved him. That love brought concern now, for, despite the strong pose, Luthien was plainly exhausted. They would cross Diamondgate this day, onto the shores of Isle Bedwydrin, and would make Dun Varna three or four days after.

Luthien would face Gahris once more. The father he had dearly loved, but the man, too, who had so disappointed the young Bedwyr. When his friend had been murdered, Luthien had learned the truth of the world under King Greensparrow. The young man had learned as well that his father lacked the courage and conviction he expected, for Gahris had sent Luthien's older brother away to die for fear of the evil, unlawful king. It had been a blow from which Luthien had never recovered, not even when Katerin had arrived in Caer MacDonald bearing the family sword and news that Gahris had taken up the revolt.

"We must be on the road at once if we are to catch the first ferry," Katerin called, breaking Luthien's trance. He turned to regard her, relaxing his taut muscles and letting *Blind-Striker*'s tip slip low. Not surprised by the interruption or the command, Luthien answered with a simple nod.

Ever since word had come to Caer MacDonald that Gahris, eorl of Bedwydrin, had taken ill, Katerin had hurried Luthien along. She understood that Luthien had to get to his father before the man died, to make peace with him else he might never find peace with himself.

Determined to make the ferry—for if they missed it, they would have to wait hours for the next—Katerin rushed off to pack her bedroll, while Luthien went to see to the horses. They were away in mere minutes, riding hard to the west.

Diamondgate was quite different from how Luthien remembered it. The place was so named because of the flat, diamond-shaped island, a black lump of stone, a hundred yards out from shore, halfway across the channel to Isle Bedwydrin. Here ran the ferries between Bedwydrin and the mainland, two dwarven-crafted barges, inching their way through the white-capped, dark water along thick guide ropes. These were marvelous constructions, flat and open and huge, but so perfectly geared that a single man could turn the crank to pull them, no matter how laden. One was always in operation, unless the weather was too foul, or great dorsal whales had been spotted in the channel, while the other was always down for maintenance. The folk could not be too careful when traversing the dark waters around Isle Bedwydrin!

All the main features of the place were the same: the ferries, the abundant stones, the giant wharves, and the old wharves, ghosts of another day, testament to the power of the sea. Even the weather was the same, dull and gray, the water dark and ominous, whipping into little whitecaps as it danced about the channel. Now, though, there were many great warships moored in the area, nearly half of the fleet Eriador had captured from Avon when the southern kingdom's invading army had landed in Port Charley. Also, several huge structures had been built on Diamondgate Island, barracks to house the three thousand cyclopians taken prisoner in that war. Most of those brutes were gone now—there had been an open revolt on Diamondgate in which many cyclopians had been killed, and Gahris Bedwyr had ordered the remaining groups to be split up, with most taken from the island to smaller, more manageable prison camps.

The structures on Diamondgate remained intact and in repair though, by order of King Brind'Amour, just in case a new group of prisoners was taken.

The companions rode down to the wharves and right onto the barge with their mounts, Katerin on a sturdy Speythenfergus gray and Luthien on Riverdancer, his prized Highland Morgan. The powerful Riverdancer was a remarkable stallion, shining white and well-muscled, with the longer hair that distinguished the short but powerful Highland Morgan breed. Few in all of Eriador, and none on Bedwydrin, possessed a finer or more distinctive steed, and Riverdancer, more than anything else, drew attention to Luthien.

He heard the whispers before the barge even left the shore, heard men talking about the "son of Gahris" and "the Crimson Shadow."

"You should not have worn the cape," Katerin remarked, seeing his uneasiness.

Luthien only shrugged. Too late now. His notoriety had preceded him. He was the Crimson Shadow, the legend walking, and, though Luthien was sure he hadn't truly earned it, the common folk showed him great respect, even awe.

The whispers continued throughout the long and slow journey across the channel; as the ferry passed near to Diamondgate, scores of cyclopians lined the rocks, staring at Luthien, some hurling insults and threats. He simply ignored them; in truth, taking their outrage as confirmation of his heroics. He couldn't be comfortable with the pats on the back from his comrades, but he could accept cyclopian insults with a wide smirk.

The ferry was met on Bedwydrin's shore by all the dock hands, actually applauding as Luthien rode forth onto the wharf. Luthien's previous crossing, a daring escape from ambushing cyclopians, and, as it turned out, from a giant dorsal whale, had become legend here, and the companions heard many conversations—exaggerations, Luthien knew—referring to that event. Soon enough, Luthien and Katerin managed to slip away and were clear of the landing, riding free and easy along the soft turf of Isle Bedwydrin, their home. Luthien remained obviously uncomfortable, however.

"Is everything I do to be chronicled for all to read?" he remarked a short time later.

"I hope not everything," Katerin replied slyly, batting her eyes at Luthien when he turned to regard her. The woman of Hale had a good laugh then, thrilled that she could so easily draw a blush from Luthien.

The three subsequent days of riding passed swiftly and uneventfully. Both Luthien and Katerin knew the trails of Bedwydrin well enough to avoid any settlements, preferring the time alone with each other and with their thoughts. For the young Bedwyr, those thoughts were a tumult of stormy emotions.

"I have been to Caer MacDonald," he told Katerin solemnly when at last Dun Varna, and the large white estate that was his family home, came into view. "To Eradoch, as well, and I have ridden beside our king all the way to Princetown in Avon. But suddenly that world seems so far away, so removed from the reality of Dun Varna."

"It feels as though we never left the place," Katerin agreed. She turned to Luthien and they locked stares, sharing emotions. For both of them, the trip across the isle had been like a trot through memory, bringing them back to simpler and, in many ways, happier days.

Eriador was better off now, was free of Greensparrow, and no longer did the people of Bedwydrin, or of all the land, have to tolerate the brutal cyclopians. But for many years Greensparrow had been a name empty of meaning, a distant king who had no effect on the day-to-day lives of Luthien Bedwyr and Katerin O'Hale. Not until two dignitaries, Viscount Aubrey and Baron Wilmon, had arrived in Dun Varna, bringing with them the truth of the oppressive king, had Luthien understood the plight of his land.

There was peace in ignorance, Luthien realized, looking at that shining white estate nestled on the side of the hill facing the sea. It had been only a year and a half since he had learned the truth of his world, and had gone out on the road. Only a year and a half, and yet all of reality had turned upside down for young Luthien. He remembered his last full summer in Dun Varna, two years previous, when he spent his days training for the arena, or fishing in one of the many sheltered bays near to the town, or off alone with Riverdancer. Or fumbling with Katerin O'Hale, the two of them trying to make some sense of love, learning together and laughing together.

Even that had changed, Luthien realized in looking at the beautiful woman. His love for Katerin had deepened because he had learned to honestly admit to himself that he did indeed love her, that she was to be his companion for all his life.

Still, there was something more exciting about those days past, about the unsure fumbling, the first kiss, the first touch, the first morning when they awoke in each other's arms, giggling and trying to concoct some story so that Gahris, Luthien's father and Katerin's formal guardian, wouldn't punish them or send Katerin back across the isle to the village of Hale.

Those had been good times in Dun Varna.

But then Aubrey had come, along with Avonese, the perfumed whore who had ordered the death of Garth Rogar, Luthien's dear friend. The two had opened Luthien's eyes to Eriador's subjugation, to the truth of the supposed Avonese nobility. Those pretentious fops had forced Luthien to spill his first blood—that of a cyclopian guard—and to take to the road as a fugitive.

"I wonder if Avonese remains in chains," Luthien remarked, though he had meant to keep the thought private.

"Eorl Gahris sent her south," Katerin replied. "At least, that is what one of the deckhands on the ferry told me."

Luthien's eyes widened with shock. Had his father freed the woman, the wretch who had caused the death of his dear friend? For an instant, the young Bedwyr despised Gahris again, as vividly as he had when he learned that Gahris, in an act of pure cowardice, had sent his older brother, Ethan, off to war to die because he feared that Ethan would cause trouble with Greensparrow's henchmen.

"In chains?" Luthien dared to ask, and he prayed that this was the case.

Katerin sensed his sudden anxiety. "In a box," she replied. "It seems that Lady Avonese did not fare well in the dungeon of Dun Varna."

"There are no dungeons in Dun Varna," Luthien protested.

"Your father made one especially for her," Katerin said.

Luthien was satisfied with that answer, and yet it was with mixed emotions that he entered Dun Varna and rode the red limestone and cobblestone streets to the grand entrance of House Bedwyr.

He and Katerin were met at the door by other reminders of their past, men and women they had not seen in more than a year, men and women both smiling and grim, glad for the young Bedwyr's return, and yet saddened that it should be on such an occasion as this.

Gahris's condition had worsened, Luthien was informed, and when the young Bedwyr went up to the room, he found his father sunk deep into the cushions of a large and soft bed.

The man's cinnamon eyes had lost their luster, Luthien realized as soon as he moved near to Gahris. His thick shock of silvery-white hair had yellowed, as had his wind-creased face, a face that had weathered countless hours under the Bedwydrin sun. The once-corded muscles on Gahris Bedwyr's arms had slackened, and his chest had sunk, making his shoulders seem even broader, though not so strong. Gahris was a tall man, three inches above Luthien and as tall as Luthien's older brother, Ethan.

"My son," Gahris whispered, and his face brightened for just a moment.

"What are you doing in bed?" Luthien asked. "There is so much to be done. A new kingdom to raise."

"One that will be better than the time of Greensparrow," Gahris replied, his voice barely a whisper. "And better than what was before Greensparrow. I know it will be so, because my son will play a hand in its formation." As he spoke, he lifted his arm and took Luthien by the hand. The old man's grip remained surprisingly strong, lending Luthien some hope.

"Katerin is with me," Luthien said, and turned to motion Katerin to the bedside. She drifted over, and the eorl's face brightened again, verily beamed.

"I had hoped to live to see my grandchildren," Gahris said, bringing more of a blush from Luthien than from Katerin. "But you will tell them about me."

Luthien started to protest that admission that Gahris was dying, but Katerin spoke first. "I will tell them," she promised firmly. "I will tell them of the eorl of Bedwydrin, whose people loved him, and who rid the isle of wretched cyclopians!"

Luthien looked back and forth between the two as Katerin spoke, and realized that any protests he might make would be obviously false and discomforting. At that moment, the young man had to admit the truth to himself: his father was dying.

"Will you tell them of Gahris the Coward?" the old man asked. He managed a small chortle. "How I bent to the will of Greensparrow," he scolded. "And Ethan . . . ah, my dear Ethan. Have you heard anything . . . ?"

The question fell away as Gahris looked upon Luthien's grim expression, learning from that face that Ethan was truly gone to him, that Luthien had not found his brother.

"If ever you see him," Gahris went on, his voice even softer, "will you tell him of the end of my life? Will you tell him that, in the end, I stood tall for what was right, for Eriador free?"

Katerin eyed Luthien intently as the moments slipped past, realizing that her love was in a terrible dilemma at that moment, a crossroad that might well determine the path of his life. Here he was, facing Gahris once more, with one, and only one, chance to forgive his father. Gahris needed that forgiveness, Katerin knew, but Luthien needed it more.

Without saying a word, Luthien drew out *Blind-Striker* and lay it on the bed, across Gahris's legs.

"My son," Gahris said again, staring at the family sword, his eyes filling with tears.

"It is the sword of family Bedwyr," Luthien said. "The sword of the rightful eorl, Gahris Bedwyr. The sword of my father."

Katerin turned away and wiped her eyes; Luthien had passed perhaps his greatest test.

"You will take my place when I am gone?" Gahris asked hopefully.

As much as he wanted to comfort his father, Luthien couldn't commit to that. "I must return to Caer MacDonald," he said. "My place now is beside King Brind'Amour."

Gahris seemed disappointed for just a moment, but then he nodded his acceptance. "Then you take the sword," he said, his voice stronger than it had been since Luthien had entered the room, stronger than it had been in many days.

"It is your—" Luthien began to protest.

"It is mine to give," Gahris interrupted. "To you, my chosen heir. Your gift of forgiveness has been given and accepted, and now you accept from me the family sword, now and forever. This business with Greensparrow is not finished, and you will find more use for *Blind-Striker* than I, and better use. Strike hard for family Bedwyr, my son. Strike hard for Eriador!"

Luthien reverently lifted the sword from the bed and replaced it in its scabbard. The verbal outburst had cost Gahris much energy, and so Luthien bade his father rest and took his leave, promising to return after he had cleaned up from the road and taken a meal.

He kept his promise and spent the bulk of the night with his father, talking of the good times, not the bad, and of the past, not the future.

Gahris Bedwyr, eorl of Bedwydrin, died peacefully, just before the dawn. Arrangements had already been made, and the very next night the proud man was set adrift in a small boat, into the Dorsal Sea that was so important to the lives of all in Dun Varna. No successor was immediately named; rather, Luthien appointed a steward, a trusted family friend, for as he had explained to his father, Luthien could not remain in Dun Varna. Bigger issues called out to him from Caer MacDonald; his place was with Brind'Amour, his friend, his king.

Luthien and Katerin left Dun Varna the very next day, both of them wondering if they would ever again look upon the place.

Katerin noticed the change in Luthien immediately. He slept well and rode alert and straight as they made their way back to the south, to Diamondgate and then to the mainland.

Katerin worried about him for a long while, seeing that he was not grieving for his loss. She couldn't understand this at first—when she had lost her own father, to a storm on the Avon, she had cried for a fortnight. Luthien, though, had shed few tears, had stoically placed his hand on his father's chest as Gahris lay in the small boat and had pushed it away, as if he had pushed Gahris from his mind.

Gradually, Katerin came to realize the truth, and she was glad. Luthien wasn't grieving now because he had already grieved for Gahris, on that occasion when the young man had been forced to flee the law of Bedwydrin. To Luthien, Gahris, or the man he had thought Gahris to be, had died on the day the young Bedwyr learned the truth about his brother Ethan and about his father's cowardice. Then, when Katerin had arrived in Caer MacDonald, bearing *Blind-Striker* and news that Bedwydrin was in open revolt against Greensparrow, Luthien's father had come alive once more.

Luthien, Katerin now realized, had viewed it all as a second chance, borrowed time, a proper way to bid farewell to the redeemed Gahris. Luthien's grieving had been long finished by the time he knelt by his dying father's bed. Now his cinnamon eyes no longer seemed full of pain. Gahris had made his peace, and so had his son.

CHAPTER 4

GYBI

PROCTOR BYLLEWYN STOOD solemnly on the sloping parapet of the Gybi monastery, staring out from his rocky perch to the foggy waters of Bae Colthwyn. More than a hundred gray ghosts slipped through that mist, Colthwyn fishing boats mostly, tacking and turning frantically, all semblance of formation long gone. The sight played heavy on the shoulders of the old proctor. These were his people out there, men and women who looked to him for guidance, who would give their lives at his mere word. And indeed, it had been Proctor Byllewyn's decision that the fishing boats should go to meet the invaders, to keep the fierce Huegoths busy out on the dark and cold waters and, thus, away from the village.

Now Byllewyn could only stand and watch.

The captains tried to stay close enough for their crews to shoot their bows at the larger vessels of the Huegoths, but they had to be perfect and swift to keep away from the underwater rams spearheading those terrible Huegoth longships. Every so often, one of the fishing boats didn't turn swiftly enough, or got held up by a sudden swirl of the wind, and the horrible cracking sound of splintering wood echoed above the waters, above the shouted commands and the terrified screams of the combatants.

"Twenty-five Huegoth longships have entered the bay, by last accounting," said Brother Jamesis, standing at Byllewyn's side.

"It is only an estimate," Jamesis added when the proctor made no move to reply.

Still the old man stood perfectly still and unblinking, only his thick shock of gray hair moving in the wind. Byllewyn had seen the Huegoths before, when he was but a boy, and he remembered well the merciless and savage raiders. In addition to the rowing slaves, twenty on a side, the seventy-foot longships likely carried as many as fifty Huegoth warriors, their shining shields overlapped and lining the upper decks. That put the number in the bay at more than twelve hundred fierce Huegoths. Colthwyn's simple fishing boats were no match for the deadly longships, and the men on the shore could only hope that the brave fishermen would inflict enough damage with their bows to dissuade the Huegoths from landing.

"One of the raiders flies the pennant of *The Skipper*, upside down, on its forward guide rope," the somber Jamesis further reported, and now Byllewyn did flinch. Aran Toomes and all the crewmen of *The Skipper* had been dear, long-standing friends.

Byllewyn looked down the sloping trail to the south, to the village of Gybi. Already many of the townsfolk, the oldest and the youngest, were making their way along the red-limestone mile-long walk that climbed the side of the knoll to the fortress monastery. The more able-bodied were down by the wharves, waiting to support the crews when the fishing boats came rushing in. Of course, the small fleet had not put out with any intentions of defeating the Huegoths at sea, only to buy the town time for the people to get behind the monastery's solid walls.

"How many boats have we lost?" Byllewyn asked. With the refugees now in sight, the proctor was considering ringing the great bell of Gybi, calling in the boats.

Jamesis shrugged, having no definite answer. "There are Colthwyn men in the water," he said grimly.

Byllewyn turned his gaze back to the mist-shrouded bay. He wished that the skies would clear, just for a moment, so that he could get a better feel for the battle, but he realized that the shroud was in truth a blessing for the fishermen. The Colthwyn fisherfolk knew every inch of these waters, could sail blindly through them without ever getting near the shallows or the one reef in the area, a long line of jagged rocks running straight out into the bay just north of the monastery. The Huegoth mariners also understood the ways of the sea, but these were foreign waters to them.

Byllewyn did not ring the bell; he had to trust in the fisherfolk, the true masters of the bay, and so it went on, and on.

The cries only intensified.

Stubbornly, the proud fisherfolk kept up the seaborne resistance, darting all around the larger Huegoth vessels, boats working in pairs so that if the Huegoth made a sudden turn to intercept one of them, the archers on the second would find their line of sight opened for a stern rake on the longship. Still, the fisherfolk had to admit that they were doing little real damage to the Huegoths. A dozen Colthwyn boats had been sent under the dark waters, but not a single Huegoth had gone down.

Captain Leary of the good boat *Finwalker* noted this fact with great concern. They were making the Huegoths work hard, peppering them with arrows and probably wounding or killing a few, but the outcome seemed assured. The more boats the Colthwyn defenders lost, the more quickly they would lose more. When a dozen additional Colthwyn ships were caught and sunk, the support for the remaining boats would be lessened, and all too soon it would reach the point where the defenders had to flee back to port, scramble out of their boats helter-skelter, and run the path to the monastery.

The defenders needed a dramatic victory, needed to send one of those seemingly impregnable longships to its watery death. But how? Arrows certainly wouldn't bring one down and any attempt at ramming would only send the Colthwyn boat to the bottom.

As he stood in thought, *Finwalker* rushed past the wolf's-head forecastle of a longship, close enough so that the captain could see the Huegoth's ram under the water. The Huegoth was in the midst of a turn, though, with little forward momentum, and *Finwalker*'s crew got off a volley of arrows, taking only a few in return as the boat glided past.

Leary looked to the woman at the wheel. "North," he instructed.

The woman, Jeannie Beens, glanced over her shoulder, to the longship and the two Colthwyn boats that had been working in conjunction with *Finwalker*. If she turned north, she would leave the Colthwyn boats behind, for one of them was sailing southeast, the other due west. The Huegoth, though, was facing north, and with those forty oars would soon leap in pursuit.

"North," Leary said again, determinedly, and the steers-woman obeyed.

Predictably, the Huegoth came on, and though the wind was from the southeast, filling *Finwalker*'s sails, the longship was swift in the pursuit. Even worse, as soon as the general battle, and the other two Colthwyn boats, were left behind, the Huegoths put up their own single square sail, determined to catch this one boat out from the pack and put it under.

Leary didn't blink. He told his archers to keep up the line of arrows, and instructed the steerswoman on the course he wanted.

Jeannie Beens stared at him blankly when she deciphered the directions. Leary wanted her to swing about, nearly out of the bay, and come back heading south much closer to the shore.

Leary wanted her to skim the reef!

The tide was high, and the rocks would be all but invisible. There was a break along the reef—Nicker's Slip, the narrow pass was called—that a boat could get through when the water was this high, but finding that small break when the rocks were mostly submerged was no easy task.

"You've sailed these waters for ten years," Captain Leary said to the woman, seeing her uncertainty. "You'll find the Slip, but the longship, turning inside our angle and flanking us as they pursue, will only get their starboard side through." Leary gave a mischievous wink. "Let's see how well half a longship sails," he said.

Jeannie Beens set her feet wide apart and took up the wheel more tightly, her sun-and-wind-weathered features grim and determined. She had been through Nicker's Slip on two occasions: once when Leary wanted to show her the place for no better reason than to prove to her that she was a fine pilot, and a second time on a dare, during a particularly rowdy party when a dorsal whale had been taken in the bay. On both of those occasions, though, the tide had been lower, with the rocks more visible, and the boats had been lighter, flat-bottomed shore-huggers that drew only a couple of feet. *Finwalker*, one of the largest fishing boats this far north in the bay, drew nine feet and would scrape and splinter if Leary tried to put her through when the tide was low, might even rub a bit now, with the water at its highest. Even worse for Jeannie was the damned fog, which periodically thickened to obscure her reference points.

When the high dark outline of the monastery dipped behind her left shoulder, Jeannie Beens began her wide one-hundred-eighty-degree turn back to the south. As Leary had predicted, the Huegoth turned inside *Finwalker*, closing some ground and giving chase off the fishing boat's port stern. Now the Huegoth archers had a better angle and their bows twanged mercilessly, a rain of arrows, broadheads, and flaming bolts falling over *Finwalker*.

Two crewmen fell dead; a third, trying to put out a fire far out on the mast's crossbeam, slipped overboard and was gone without a cry. Leary himself took an arrow in the arm.

"Keep to it!" the captain yelled to Jeannie.

The woman refused to look back at their pursuers, and blocked out the growing shouts of the Huegoths as the longship rapidly gained. The wind did not favor *Finwalker* any longer; her turn had put the stiff breeze straight in off her starboard bow. Her sails had been appropriately angled as far as possible, and she made some headway, but the Huegoths dropped their sail altogether, and the pounding oars drove the longship on.

More arrows sliced in; more of *Finwalker*'s crew fell. Jeannie heard the roars, heard even the rhythmic beating of the drum belowdecks on the longship, prodding the rowing slaves on.

Huegoths called out taunts and threats, thinking they had the boat in their grasp.

Jeannie blocked it all out, focused on the shoreline, its features barely distinguishable through the heavy mist. There was a particular jag signaling the reef line, she knew, and she pictured it in her mind, trying hard to remember it exactly as it had appeared on those two occasions when she had gone through Nicker's Slip. She focused, too, on the bell tower of Gybi monastery and on the steeple of the meetinghall in the town, further ahead to the south, recalling the angle. She had to calculate their angle so that the two towers would line up, three fingers between them, at the moment *Finwalker* passed the jag and entered the reef line.

Leary gave a shout and fell to his knees beside her, holding his now bleeding forehead. Beyond him, Jeannie noted the bloody arrow that had just grazed him, embedded deep into *Finwalker*'s rail, its shaft shivering.

"Hold steady," Leary implored her. "Hold . . ." The captain slumped to the deck.

Jeannie could hear the oars pounding the water; smoke began to drift about her as more of the flaming arrows found their deadly hold. She heard a Huegoth call out—to her!—the barbarian apparently excited to find that a woman was on board.

Jeannie couldn't help but glance back, and saw that a pair of massive Huegoths were standing along the forward edge of the longship, preparing to leap aboard *Finwalker*. The longship could not come up beside *Finwalker*, Jeannie realized, because its oars would keep it too far away for the Huegoths to board. But positioned just to the side and behind, the prow of the longship could get within a few feet of the fishing boat.

They weren't much farther away than that right now, and Jeannie wondered why her fellows weren't shooting the brazen Huegoths dead. Then she realized, to her horror, that none of *Finwalker*'s crew could take to their bows. Most of the crew lay dead or wounded on the deck, and those who could still function were too busy battling fires to battle the fierce men of Isenland!

Jeannie turned her eyes back to the reef and the shore, quickly determined her angle and made a slight adjustment, putting a few extra feet between *Finwalker* and the longship.

She saw the jag, instinctively lifted her hand up between the images of the bell tower and the steeple, thumb and little finger tucked back tight.

Three fingers—almost.

Finwalker groaned and shook, her starboard side scraping hard. She leaned hard, but came through, and though her seaworthiness had surely been compromised, the reef was behind her.

The longship did not fare so well. Her prow hit the rocks, bouncing her to the right, and she plowed on, her left bank of oars splintering and catching, swinging her about. Nicker's Slip was a narrow pass, and as the seventy-foot craft hooked and turned, her stern crunched sidelong across the gap, into the reef. Huegoths tumbled out by the dozen, and those poor slaves at the oars fared little better as the great ship split in half, to be battered and swallowed by the dark waters.

Jeannie Beens saw none of it, but heard the cheers from those crewmen still standing. She pulled *Finwalker* hard to starboard, angling for shore, for she knew that the boat was taking water and was out of the fight.

The little boat had scored even, one-to-one, but more important, the daring heroics of *Finwalker* did not go unnoticed, not by the Bae Colthwyn fisherfolk nor by the Huegoth raiders. Leary's decision had been based on the captain's belief and hope that this was not a full-scale invasion force, but a powerful probe into Gybi's defenses. No doubt the Huegoths meant to go into the town, but Leary didn't think they had the manpower to lay siege to the monastery, and didn't think they meant to stay for long.

As it turned out, he was right. The Huegoths had not expected to suffer any considerable losses on the water, certainly hadn't believed they would lose a longship, and soon after the incident, the raiders turned their prows back out to the open sea and sped off into the veil of fog.

The fisherfolk of Gybi could not claim victory, though. They had lost almost twenty boats, with twenty others damaged, and more than a hundred folk lost to the cold waters of the bay. In a town of three thousand, that meant that almost every family would grieve that night.

But Leary's daring and Jeannie Beens's grit and skill had bought them time, to plan or to flee.

"The Huegoths will be back in force," Brother Jamesis said at the all-important meeting that night in the monastery.

"They have a base somewhere near here," Leary reasoned, his voice shaky, for the wounded man had lost a lot of blood. "They could not have sailed all the way from Isenland, only to turn about to sail all the way back, and that before they even resupplied in the town!"

"Agreed," said Proctor Byllewyn. "And if their base is near Colthwyn, then it is likely they will return, in greater numbers."

"We must assume the worst," added another of the brothers.

Proctor Byllewyn leaned back in his seat, letting the conversation continue without him while he tried to sort things through. Huegoths hadn't been seen so close to Eriador's shores in such numbers in many, many years. Yet now, just a few months after the signing of the truce with King Greensparrow, the barbarian threat had returned. Was it coincidence, or were those events linked? Unpleasant thoughts flitted through Byllewyn's mind. He wondered if the Huegoths were working secretly with Greensparrow. Perhaps it was less contrived than that, though certainly as ominous: that the Isenlanders had merely come to the conclusion that with the two nations of Avonsea separated, with Eriador no longer afforded the protection of the mighty Avon navy or the promise of severe retribution from the powerful King Greensparrow and his wizard-duke allies, the plunder would be easily gotten. Proctor Byllewyn recalled an incident a few years before, when he was returning from a pilgrimage to Chalmbers. He had witnessed a Huegoth raiding ship overtaken by an Avon warship. The longship had been utterly destroyed and most of the floundering Huegoths left in the water to drown or to feed the dorsal whales. And those few Huegoths who had been plucked from the sea found their fate more grim: keel-hauling. Only one Isenlander had been left alive, and he had been set adrift in a small boat, that he might find his way back to his king and tell of the foolishness of raiding the civilized coast. That vivid memory made Byllewyn think even less of the possibility that the Huegoth king would have allied with Greensparrow.

"As far as the Huegoths know, Eriador has little in the way of warships," Brother Jamesis was saying, a related line of thought that brought the proctor back into the conversation.

Byllewyn looked around at the faces of those gathered, and he began to see a dangerous seed germinating there. The people were wondering if the break from Avon and the protective power of Greensparrow was a good thing. Most of the men and women in the room, besides Byllewyn and Captain Leary, were young, and did not remember, or at least did not appreciate, Eriador before Greensparrow. In the face of such a disaster as the Huegoths, it was easy to judge the years under Greensparrow in a softer light. Perhaps the unfair taxes and the presence of brutish cyclopians was not such a bad thing when viewed as protection from greater evils . . .

Byllewyn, fiercely independent, knew that this was simply not true, knew that Eriador had always been self-sufficient and in no need of protection from Avon. But those determined notions did little to dispel the very real threat that had come so suddenly to Gybi's dark shores.

"We must dispatch an emissary to Mennichen Dee in Eradoch," he said, "to enlist the riders in our defense."

"If they are not dancing about the Iron Cross with the good King Brind'Amour," another man remarked sarcastically.

"If that is the case," Byllewyn interrupted, defeating the rising murmurs of discontent before they could find any footing, "then our emissary must be prepared to ride all the way to Caer MacDonald."

"Yes," said the same sarcastic fisherman, "to the throne seat, to beg that our needs not be ignored."

The proctor of Gybi did not miss the vicious tone of the voice. Many of the locals had voiced their opposition to the anointment of the mysterious Brind'Amour as king of Eriador, declaring that Byllewyn, the long-standing proctor of Gybi, would be the better choice. That sentiment had been echoed across much of northeastern Eriador, but the movement had never gained much momentum since Byllewyn himself had put an end to the talk. He wondered now, given the grim mood, how long it would be before he would be dissuading similar opinions once more.

"Caer MacDonald, then!" another man growled. "Let us see if our newly proclaimed king has any bite in him."

"Here, here!" came the agreeing chorus, and Byllewyn sat back thoughtfully in his chair, his fingertips tapping together before his eyes. He didn't doubt that Brind'Amour—that anyone who could wrest control from Greensparrow—had bite, but he was also pragmatic enough to realize that, with the kingdoms separate once more, many ancient enemies, Huegoth and cyclopian, might indeed see Eriador as vulnerable.

The arrival of Huegoths would be a major test for Brind'Amour, one that the new king could not afford to fail.

The proctor of Gybi, a man of small ambition and generous heart, would pray for him.

CHAPTER 5

SOUGLES'S GLEN

AH, WE'LL BE EATING WELL when the money starts a'flowing outa Caer MacDonald!" exclaimed Sougles Bellbanger, a rugged dwarf with hair and beard the color of rich tea. He hoisted his flagon high into the crisp night air.

Ten of his fellows, sitting about a huge bonfire, did likewise, all looking to the stars shining brightly and clearly visible through the break in the forest above this small glen.

"Keep it quiet!" yelled yet another of the bearded folk, who was curled up on a bedroll not so far away. Beside him, a dwarf snored loudly, and so when his call to the partying group at the fire went unnoticed, he slapped the snoring dwarf instead, just for the satisfaction.

"Sleeping on this night!" Sougles howled derisively. "Plenty of time for that after we've sold our goods."

"After we've spent the gold we've got for selling our goods!" corrected one of the others, and again, the mugs came up high into the air.

"And after we get the gold, you'll all be too weary to spend it properly," grumbled the dwarf from the bedroll. "And I'll be helping meself, thank you."

That brought still more wild cheering from the gathering at the fire, along with many snorts. They were tough and ready dwarfs of DunDarrow; they could party all this night, go into the little settlement—Menster, it was called—in the morning, then spend the rest of the day selling their goods and quickly giving back most of the gold to the folk of Menster in exchange for ale and good food, and then comfortable lodgings before they made their trek back into the mountains to the nearest entrances of DunDarrow. That was the way it would work, now that Brind'Amour was king, now that Bellick dan Burso was in Caer MacDonald signing a pact to make Eriador and DunDarrow as one.

And so they partied, howled and drank, tore off huge chunks of venison and threw the bones at the complainer in the bedroll. It went on most of the night, ending only in surprise as a ragged human, bleeding from the forehead, stumbled into camp.

Up came the dwarfs and out came their weapons, huge axes, short, thick swords, and heavy hammers that could spin through the air and take down a target at thirty paces.

The man, seemingly oblivious to his surroundings, stumbled further, nearly tripping headlong into the fire. Two dwarfs had him in an instant, propping him by the arms.

"What're you about?" demanded Sougles.

The man whispered something too low for the dwarf to hear, considering the grumbling conversations erupting all about. Sougles called for quiet and moved closer, cocking his head to put his ear in line with the man's lips.

"Menster," the man repeated.

"Menster?" Sougles asked loudly, and the word hushed his fellows. "What about Menster?"

"Them," whispered the man, and he slumped.

"Them?" Sougles asked loudly, turning to his companions.

"Them!" one of the dwarfs yelled in response, pointing to the dark line of trees, to the bulky shapes moving within those shadows.

In all of Avonsea, in all the world, no two races hated each other more profoundly than did cyclopians and dwarfs, and when the one-eyes came howling out of the brush, thinking to overwhelm the dwarvish encampment, they found themselves running headlong into a wall of determination. Outnumbered nearly ten to one as the horde poured in, the dwarfs locked in a ring about their fire, fighting side to side, hacking and slashing with abandon, and singing as though they were glad for the fight. Every so often, one of the dwarfs would manage to reach back to retrieve a flaming brand, for dwarfs enjoyed nothing more than putting the hot end of a burning stick into the bulbous eye of a cyclopian.

A sword in each hand, Sougles Bellbanger slashed out the knees of any cyclopian that ventured near, and more often than not, the cunning dwarf managed to thrust his second sword into the wounded brute's torso before it ever hit the ground.

"Oh, good sport!" Sougles yelled often, and though they were taking some hits, and a couple had gone down, the dwarfs heartily agreed. In only a few moments, a score of cyclopians lay dead or dying, though still more poured from the trees to take up the fight.

It went on and on; those dwarfs who had been caught without their boots on felt the puddles of blood rising up to mid-ankle. Half an hour later, they were still fighting, and still singing, all traces of drink pushed from their blood by fiery adrenaline. Every time a dwarf fell, he was pushed back, and the ring tightened defensively. They were running out of room, Sougles knew, for he could feel the heat of the fire licking at his backside, but by this time the cyclopians had to clamber over their own dead to get near the fighting. And the ranks of one-eyes were indeed thinning, with many others running off into the woods, wanting no part of this deadly dwarven brigade.

Sougles believed that they would win—all the dwarfs held faith in their battle prowess. The fire, untended for so long, was burning low by this time and had become a heap of charred logs and glowing ashes, bluish flames rising to lick the cold air every so often. Sougles worked hard to devise a plan where he and his fellows might make use of that; perhaps they could retreat part of the line over the dying fire, using it as a weapon, kicking embers up at the one-eyes. Yes, he decided, they could launch a fiery barrage at the cyclopian line and then come roaring back across the embers, charging hard into the confused brutes.

Before Sougles could begin to pass word of the move, though, the fire seemed to execute a plan of its own. Blue flames exploded high into the air, changing hue to bright white, and all the embers flew out onto the backs of the dwarfs, nipping at them, stinging them and singeing their hair. Even worse, the mere surprise of the explosion destroyed the integrity of the dwarvish defensive ring. Dwarfs jumped, not in unison, and the cyclopians, who did not seem so startled, were quick to wedge in between their bearded adversaries, to separate the dwarfs. Soon Sougles, like many of his fellows, found himself battling cyclopians frantically on all sides, slashing and dodging, ducking low and running about. He did well, killed another one-eye and cut yet another's legs out from under it. But the experienced dwarf knew that he could not keep up the pace, and understood that one hit—

Sougles felt the crude spear burrow deep into the back of his shoulder. Strangely, he had no sensation of burning pain, just a dull thud, as though he had been punched. He moved to respond, but alas, his arm would not lift to his mind's call. Seeing the opening, a second one-eye howled and charged straight in.

Across came Sougles's other blade, somehow parrying the thrust of the charging brute and turning the one-eye aside.

But then Sougles was hit in the other side, and behind him the spearwielder prodded wildly, bending the dwarf forward, and then to the ground, where the one-eyes fell over him with abandon.

Some distance from the action and the fire, the cyclopian leader looked down at the person standing next to him, his one eye scrunched up with anger. "Yer should'a done that afore," the brute scolded.

The young woman gave a shake of her head, though her neatly coiffed blond hair hardly moved. "Magic cannot be rushed," she declared, and turned away.

The cyclopian watched her go, not so certain of her motives. It never seemed to bother the duchess much when one-eyes died.

Upon his return to Caer MacDonald, Luthien reported immediately to Brind'Amour the news that Eorl Gahris of Bedwydrin was dead. The old wizard was truly saddened and offered his condolences to Luthien, but the young man merely nodded his acceptance and begged his leave, which the king readily granted.

Coming out of the Ministry, the sun gone in the west and the stars beginning to twinkle above, Luthien knew where to go to find Oliver. The Dwelf, a tavern in the rougher section of the city with a reputation for catering to nonhumans even in Duke Morkney's time, had become the most popular sitting room in the city. "Here the Crimson Shadow laid plans for the conquest of Caer MacDonald," claimed the fairly accurate rumors, and so the small tavern had gained a huge celebrity. Now sturdy dwarvish guards lined the entryway, while a discriminating elf walked the line, determining which would-be patrons might enter.

Luthien, of course, was allowed entry without question, both dwarfs and the elf going to proper military posture as he passed. So used was he to the behavior, the young Bedwyr hardly gave it a thought as he swept into the crowded room.

He found Oliver and Shuglin sitting together on high stools at the bar, the dwarf huddled over a mug of thick, foaming ale and Oliver leaning back, holding a glass of wine up before the nearest light source that he might properly inspect its coloring. Tasman, the bartender, noted Luthien's approach and nodded grimly at the young man, then motioned toward Luthien's two friends.

Luthien came up between them, putting his hands on their backs. "My greetings," he said quietly.

Oliver looked into the young man's cinnamon eyes and knew immediately what had happened. "How fares your father?" he asked anyway, thinking that Luthien would need to talk about it.

"Gahris has passed," Luthien replied evenly, stoically.

Oliver started to offer his condolences, but saw by the look on Luthien's face that the young man was dreading that. Instead the halfling lifted his glass once more and called out loudly, "To Gahris Bedwyr, eorl of Bedwydrin, friend of Caer MacDonald, thorn in the buttocks to Greensparrow. May he find just rewards in the world that is after our own!"

Many others in the Dwelf hoisted their mugs and called out, "Hear, hear!" or "Gahris!"

Luthien stared long and hard at his diminutive friend, the halfling who always seemed to know how to make things better. "Has the alliance been signed?" the young Bedwyr asked, wanting—needing—to change the subject.

Oliver's bright face went grim. "We were that close," he said, holding thumb and index finger a fraction of an inch apart. "But then the stupid one-eyes . . ."

"Fifteen dwarfs," Shuglin added. "Slaughtered near the village that used to be called Menster."

"Used to be called?" Luthien's voice was weak.

" 'Kindling' would be a better name now," explained Oliver.

"The agreement was in hand," Shuglin went on. "A duocracy, Oliver called it, and both kings, Brind'Amour and Bellick dan Burso, thought it a most splendid arrangement."

"Greensparrow, he would not have liked it," Oliver remarked. "For he would have found the mountains blocked by an army of dwarfs loyal to Eriador."

"But after the slaughter in Sougles's Glen—that's what we've named the place—King Bellick has decided to take matters under advisement," Shuglin said and drowned the bitterness with a great draining gulp of his ale.

"But that makes no sense," Oliver protested. "Such a fight should show clearly the need for alliance!"

"Such a fight shows clearly that we might not want to be involved," Shuglin grumbled. "King Bellick is considering a retreat to our own mines and our own business."

"That would be so very stupid . . ." Oliver started to say, but a threatening look from Shuglin told him that the matter was not up for debate.

"Where is Bellick?" Luthien asked. Unlike Oliver, whose view was apparently clouded by hope, and by his own prideful desire that his suggestion of duocracy be the determination of history's course, the young Bedwyr understood Bellick's hesitance. It was likely that the dwarf king was not even secure in his trust of the Eriadorans, perhaps even wondering whether Brind'Amour, and not Greensparrow, was behind the raids, using them for political gain.

"In Brind'Amour's house still," replied Oliver. "He will go to the mines on the morrow, and then return in a ten-day."

Luthien was not really surprised at the news. The cyclopian raids had become so frequent that many sourly called this the Summer of the Bleeding Hamlet. But that fact only made it even more clear to Luthien that the dwarfs should join with the folk of Eriador. What they needed now was to erase all suspicions between the sides, to put the blame for the raids squarely where it belonged: with the cyclopians, and with the one who was spurring them on.

"Would King Bellick desire revenge for Sougles's Glen?" Luthien asked Shuglin, and the dwarf's face brightened immediately, shining wherever it showed around his tremendous bluish-black beard.

"Then arrange for a dwarvish force to accompany me into the mountains," Luthien went on.

"You have spoken to Brind'Amour about this?" Oliver put in.

"He will not oppose it," Luthien assured the halfling.

Oliver shrugged and went back to his wine, obviously not convinced.

Neither was Luthien, actually, but the young Bedwyr would take his problems one at a time.

And he found another one waiting for him when he caught up to Brind'Amour later that same evening, the wizard standing atop the highest tower of the Ministry, alone with the stars. Brind'Amour politely listened to all of Luthien's plans and arguments, nodding his head to keep the young man talking, and it took some time before Luthien even began to understand that something was deeply troubling his friend.

"All in good order," Brind'Amour said when Luthien decided that he had babbled enough. "Fine idea including the dwarfs; they're the best in the mountains, after all, and eager to spill cyclopian blood. And if Greensparrow is behind the raids—and we both know that he is—let Bellick's folk see the proof, if there is any proof, firsthand."

Luthien's smile was blown away a moment later.

"You cannot go."

Luthien's jaw dropped open. "But . . ."

"I need you," Brind'Amour said plainly. "We have more trouble, worse trouble, brewing in the east."

"What could be worse than cyclopians?"

"Huegoths."

Luthien started to protest, until the response truly sank in. Huegoths! Among Eriador's, among all of Avonsea's, oldest enemies and worst nightmares.

"When?" Luthien stammered. "A rogue vessel or coordinated raid? Where? How many ships . . . ?"

Brind'Amour's steady hand, patting the air gently before the young Bedwyr, finally calmed him to silence. "I have spoken with an emissary from the village of Gybi on Bae Colthwyn," the king explained. "It was a substantial attack, more than a score of longships. They did not come ashore, but they would have, except for the courage of Gybi's folk."

Luthien did not immediately reply, trying to collect his wits in the face of such disturbing news.

"We know in our hearts that Greensparrow uses the cyclopians to daunt the solidarity of our kingdom," Brind'Amour went on, "and to destroy any potential alliance between Eriador and DunDarrow. I suspect that the king of Avon has not in any way surrendered Eriador to the Eriadorans, as the truce would indicate."

"And thus you believe that Greensparrow might also be in league with the Huegoths," Luthien reasoned.

Brind'Amour shook his head halfheartedly. He did indeed fear that to be the case, but he honestly couldn't see how the wizard-king of Avon could have forged such an alliance. Huegoths respected physical might. They had little use for the "civilized" folk of Avon, and open hatred for wizardry. Brind'Amour, a sturdy northman himself, might be able to deal with them, but by all appearances Greensparrow was a fop, a physical weakling, who made no secret of his magical powers. Furthermore, even though an alliance with the Huegoths would strengthen Avon's position, Brind'Amour didn't believe that Greensparrow would want to deal with the barbarian Isenlanders.

"The man will gladly deal with cyclopians," Luthien reminded him when he spoke that thought aloud.

"He will gladly dominate stupid one-eyes," Brind'Amour corrected. "But no king who is not Huegoth will bend the will of the fierce Isenlanders."

"Even with wizardry?"

Brind'Amour sighed, having no answer. "Go to Gybi," he bade Luthien. "Take Oliver and Katerin with you."

The request disappointed the young Bedwyr, who sorely wanted to go into the mountains in search of the raiding cyclopian forces, but he did not complain. Luthien understood the importance of handling the Huegoths, though he wanted badly to believe that the raid on Gybi might be a coincidence, and not a long-term threat.

"I have already sent word to the Riders of Eradoch," Brind'Amour explained. "A fair-sized force is nearing Gybi now, to bolster their defenses, and watches have been ordered along all the eastern coast as far south as Chalmbers."

Luthien saw then how important Brind'Amour considered the appearance of the Huegoths, and so the young Bedwyr did not argue the command. "I will make my preparations," he said and bowed, then turned to leave.

"Siobhan and the Cutters will accompany Shuglin into the mountains," Brind'Amour said to him, "to gather as much information as possible on the cyclopians. They will be waiting for you when you return." Brind'Amour gave a wink. "I will use some magic to facilitate your journey, that you might get your chance to put *Blind-Striker* to good use on the bloodshot eyes of cyclopians."

Luthien looked back to the old king and smiled, genuinely grateful.

Brind'Amour's return smile disappeared the moment Luthien was out of sight. Even if Greensparrow wasn't behind the Huegoth raid, the fledgling kingdom of Eriador was in serious trouble. Brind'Amour had brought about his victory over Avon in large part through hints to Greensparrow from the Gascons that they favored a free Eriador, that they might even enter the war on Eriador's side. But Brind'Amour had received such subtle aid from the vast southern kingdom of Gascony only by promising some very favorable port deals. Now, with the presence of the Huegoths, the new king had been forced to send word south to Gascony that the eastern stretches of Eriador, including the important port of Chalmbers, were not to be approached without heavy warship escort.

The Gascons would not be pleased, Brind'Amour knew; they might even come to the conclusion that Eriador was a safer place for their merchant ships under the protective rule of Greensparrow. One word to that effect from Gascony to the Avon king might launch Eriador back into an open war with Avon, a war that Brind'Amour feared they could not win. Avon had many more people, with a better trained and better equipped army and vicious cyclopian allies. And though Brind'Amour believed himself a wizardous match for Greensparrow, he couldn't ignore the fact that, as far as he could tell, he was Eriador's sole magical strength, while Greensparrow had at least four wizard-dukes and the duchess of Mannington in his court.

And if the mighty Huegoths, too, were in Greensparrow's hand . . .

The situation in Gybi had to be dealt with at once and with all attention, Brind'Amour knew. Luthien, Katerin, and Oliver were his best emissaries for such a mission, and the king had already dispatched nearly two-score of his own warships, almost half of his fleet, from Diamondgate, to sail around the northern reaches of Eriador and meet up with Luthien in Gybi.

The king of fledgling Eriador spent all that night atop the Ministry, thinking and worrying, looking for his answers in the stars, but finding nothing save potential disaster.

CHAPTER 6

THE DUCHESS OF MANNINGTON

SHE WAS A SMALL WOMAN, slender and with her golden hair neatly cropped. She wore many valuable jewels, including a diamond hairpin and a brooch that glittered in the softest of lights. By all measures, Deanna Wellworth, the duchess of Mannington, was most elegant and sophisticated, undeniably beautiful, and so she seemed out of place indeed in the cold and rugged Iron Cross, surrounded by smelly, burly cyclopians.

The one-eyed leader, a three-hundred-pounder that stood halfway between six and seven feet, towered over Deanna. The brute could reach out with one hand and squash her flat, so it seemed, and, considering the tongue-lashing Deanna was now giving, the cyclopian appeared as though it wanted to do just that.

But Deanna Wellworth was hardly concerned. She was a duchess of Avon, one of Greensparrow's court, and with Duke Paragor of Princetown killed by Brind'Amour of Eriador, she was perhaps the strongest magician in all of Avon except for the king himself. She had a protection spell ready now, and if Muckles, the cyclopian leader, swung a hand out at her, it would burst into flames that the one-eye could not extinguish in any way short of leaping into the Avon Sea.

"Your murderers are out of control," Deanna ranted, her blue eyes, soft in hue to appear almost gray, locked on the face of ugly Muckles.

"We kill," the cyclopian responded simply, which was about the only way Muckles could respond. What flustered Deanna most about this assignment in the God-forsaken mountains was the fact that stupid Muckles was probably the smartest of the cyclopian group!

"Indiscriminately," Deanna promptly added, but she shook her head, seeing that the one-eye had no idea of what that word might mean. "You must choose your kills more carefully," she explained.

"We kill!" Muckles insisted.

Deanna entertained the thought of calling in Taknapotin, her familiar demon, and watching the otherworldly beast eat Muckles a little bit at a time. Alas, that she could not do. "You killed the dwarfs," she said.

That brought howls of glee from all the cyclopians nearby, brutes who hated dwarfs above anything. This tribe had lived in the Iron Cross for many generations and had occasionally run into trouble with the bearded folk of secret DunDarrow. The cyclopians thought that the woman's statement was the highest compliment anyone could pay them.

Deanna hardly meant it that way. The last thing Greensparrow wanted was an alliance between Eriador and DunDarrow. By her reasoning, any threat to DunDarrow would only strengthen the dwarfs' resolve to ally with Brind'Amour.

"If the result of your killing the dwarfs . . ."

"Yerself helped!" Muckles argued, beginning to catch on that Deanna was truly angered about the massacre.

"I had to finish what you stupidly started," Deanna retorted. Muckles began to counter, but Deanna snapped her fingers and the brute staggered backward as though it had been punched in the mouth. Indeed, a small line of blood now trickled from the side of Muckles's lip.

"If your stupidity has brought the dwarfs together with our enemies in Eriador," Deanna said evenly, "then know that you will face the wrath of King Greensparrow. I have heard that he is particularly fond of cyclopian skin rugs."

Muckles blanched and looked around at his grumbling soldiers. Such rumors about fierce Greensparrow were common among the cyclopians.

Deanna looked across the encampment, to where the dozen dwarf heads were drying out over a smoky firepit. Disgusted, she stormed away, leaving Muckles with her threats and a score of nervous subordinates. She didn't bother to look back as she passed from the small clearing into a wider meadow, where she was expected.

"Do you truly believe that the killings will ally DunDarrow with Brind'Amour?" asked Selna, Deanna's handmaid, and the only human out here in the wretched mountains with her.

Deanna, thoroughly flustered, only shrugged as she walked by.

"Do you really care?" Selna asked.

Deanna stopped dead in her tracks and spun about, curiously regarding this woman, who had been her nanny since childhood. Did Selna know her so very well?

"What do you imply by such a question?" Deanna asked, her tone openly accusing.

"I do not imply anything, my Lady," Selna replied, lowering her eyes. "Your bath is drawn, in the cover of the pine grove, as you commanded."

Selna's submissive tone made Deanna regret speaking so harshly to this woman who had been with her through so very much. "You have my gratitude," the duchess said, and she paused long enough for Selna to look up, to offer a smile of conciliation.

Deanna was very conscious of the shadows about her as she undressed beside the steaming porcelain tub. The thought of cyclopians lewdly watching made her stomach turn. Deanna hated cyclopians with all her heart. She thought them brutish, uncivilized pigs, as accurate a description as could be found, and these weeks in the mountains among them had been nothing short of torture for the cultured woman.

What had happened to her proud Avon? she wondered as she slipped into the water, shuddering at the intensity of the heat. She had given Selna a potion to heat the bath, and feared that the handmaid had used too much, that the water would burn the skin from her bones. She quickly grew accustomed to it, though, and then poured in a second potion. Immediately the water began to churn and bubble, and Deanna put her weary head back on the rim and looked up through the pine boughs to the shining half-moon.

The image brought her back through a score and two years, to when she was only a child of seven, a princess living in Carlisle in the court of her father the king. She was the youngest of seven, with five boys and a girl ahead of her, and thus far removed from the throne, but she was of that family nonetheless, and now remained as the only surviving member. She had never been close to her siblings, or to her parents. "Deanna Hideaway," they called her, for she was ever running off on her own, finding dark places where she could be alone with her thoughts and with the mysteries that filtered through her active imagination.

Even way back then, Deanna loved the thought of magic. She had learned to read at the age of four, and had spent the next three years of her life immersed in all the tomes detailing the ancient brotherhood of wizards. As a child, she had learned of Brind'Amour, who was now her enemy, though he was thought long-buried, and of Greensparrow, and how thrilled the young girl had been when that same Greensparrow, her father's court mystic, had come to her on a night such as this and offered to tutor her privately in the art of magic. What a wonderful moment that had been for young Deanna! What a thrill, that the lone surviving member of the ancient brotherhood would choose her as his protégée!

How then had Deanna Wellworth, once in line for the throne of Avon, wound up in the Iron Cross, serving as counsel to a rogue band of bloodthirsty cyclopians? And what of the folk of the Eriadoran villages they had routed, and of the dwarfs, massacred for reasons purely political?

Deanna closed her eyes, but couldn't block out the terrible images of slaughter; she covered her ears, but couldn't stop the echoing screams. And she couldn't stop the tears from flowing.

"Are you all right, my Lady?" came the stark question, shattering Deanna's visions. Her eyes popped open wide to see Selna standing over her churning tub, the woman's expression concerned, but in a way that seemed strange and unsettling to Deanna.

"Are you spying on me?" the duchess demanded, more sharply than she had intended. She realized her error as soon as she snapped out the words, for she knew that her tone made her appear guilty.

"Never that, my Lady," Selna replied unconvincingly. "I only returned with your blanket, and saw the glisten of tears in the moonlight."

Deanna rubbed her hand across her face. "A splash from the tub, and nothing more," she insisted.

"Do you long for Mannington?" Selna asked.

Deanna stared incredulously at the woman, then looked all around, as though the answer should be obvious.

"As do I," Selna admitted. "I am glad that is all that is troubling you. I had feared—"

"What?" Deanna insisted, her tone razor sharp, her soft eyes flashing dangerously.

Selna gave a great sigh. Deanna had never seen her act this cryptic before, and didn't like it at all. "I only feared," the handmaid began again, but stopped short, as if searching for the words.

Deanna sat forward in the tub. "What?" she demanded again.

Selna shrugged.

"Say it!"

"Sympathy for Eriador," the handmaid admitted.

Deanna slumped back in the hot water, staring blankly at Selna.

"Have you sympathy for Eriador?" Selna dared to ask. "Or, the God above forbid, for the dwarfs?"

Deanna paused for a long while, trying to gauge this surprising woman she had thought she knew so well. "Would that be so bad?" she asked plainly.

"They are our enemies," Selna insisted. "Sympathy for Eriador . . ."

"Decency for fellow humans," Deanna corrected.

"Some might see it as weakness, however you describe it," the hand-maid answered without hesitation.

Again Deanna was at a loss for a reply. What was Selna implying here? The older woman had often served as Deanna's confidante, but this time Selna seemed removed from the conversation, as though she knew something Deanna did not. Suddenly, Deanna found that she didn't trust the woman, and feared that she had already revealed too much.

The water was cooling by this time, so Deanna rose up and allowed Selna to wrap her in the thick blanket. She dressed under cover of the pine grove and went to her tent, Selna following close behind.

The duchess's sleep was fitful, full of images that she could not block out or explain away. She felt a coldness creeping over her, a darkness deeper than the night.

She awoke in a cold sweat, to see a pair of red-glowing eyes staring down at her.

"Mistress," came a rasping, familiar voice, the voice of Taknapotin, Deanna's familiar demon.

The groggy duchess relaxed at once, but her relief lasted only as long as the second it took her to realize that she had not summoned the demon. Apparently, the beast had come from the fires of Hell of its own accord!

She saw Taknapotin's considerable array of gleaming teeth as the demon, apparently recognizing her concern, smiled widely.

No, not of its own accord, Deanna realized, for that simply could not be. Demons were creatures brought to the world by human desires, but who, other than Deanna Wellworth, could so summon Taknapotin? For a moment, Deanna wondered if she had somehow called to the fiend in her sleep, but she quickly dismissed that possibility. Bringing a demon to the material world was never that easy.

There could be only one answer then, and it was confirmed when next Taknapotin spoke.

"You are relieved of your duties here," the beast explained. "Go back to your place in Mannington."

Greensparrow. Only Greensparrow was powerful enough to summon Deanna's familiar demon without the duchess knowing about it.

"Duke Resmore of Newcastle will guide the cyclopian raiders," Taknapotin went on.

"By whose command?" Deanna asked, just because she needed to hear the name out loud.

Taknapotin laughed at her. "Greensparrow knows that you have little heart for this," the fiend said.

Selna, Deanna realized. Her handmaid, among her most trusted confidantes for the last twenty years, had wasted no time in reporting her sympathies to Greensparrow. The notion unsettled Deanna, but she was pragmatic enough to set her emotions aside and realize that her knowledge of the informant might be put to profitable use.

"When may I leave this wretched place?" Deanna asked firmly. She worked hard to compose herself, not wanting to appear as though she had been caught at anything treasonous. Of course it was perfectly logical that she would not want to be here with the one-eyes—she had protested the assignment vehemently when Greensparrow had given it to her.

"Resmore is outside, talking with Muckles," the fiend answered with a snicker.

"If you are finished with the task for which you were summoned, then be gone," Deanna growled.

"I would help you dress," Taknapotin replied, grinning evilly.

"Be gone!"

Instantly the beast vanished, in a crackling flash that stole Deanna's eyesight and filled her nostrils with the thick scent of sulfur.

When the smoke, and Deanna's vision, cleared, she found Selna at the tent flap, holding Deanna's clothing over her arm. How much this one already knew, the duchess mused.

Within the hour, Deanna had wished Resmore well and had departed the mountains, via a magical tunnel the duke of Newcastle had conveniently created for her. Trying to act as if nothing out of place had happened, indeed, trying to seem as though the world was better now that she was in her proper quarters in Mannington's palace, she dismissed Selna and sat alone on the great canopy bed in her private room.

Her gaze drifted to the bureau, where sat her bejeweled crown, her trace to the old royal family. She thought back again to that day so long ago, when drunk with the promise of magical power she had made her fateful choice.

Her thoughts wound their way quickly through the years, to this point. A logical procession, Deanna realized, leading even to the potential trouble that lay ahead for her. The cyclopians were not happy with her performance in the mountains, and rightly so. Likely, Muckles had complained behind her back to every emissary that came out of Avon. When Cresis, the cyclopian duke of Carlisle, heard the grumbles, he had probably appealed to Greensparrow, who had little trouble getting to Selna and confirming the problem.

"As it is," Deanna said aloud, her voice full of grim resignation, "let Resmore have the one-eyes and all their wretchedness." She knew that she would be disciplined by Greensparrow, perhaps even forced to surrender her body to Taknapotin for a time, always a painful and exhausting possession.

Deanna only shrugged. For the time being, there was little she could do except shrug and accept the judgments of Greensparrow, her king and master. But this was not the life Deanna Wellworth had envisioned. For those first years after her family's demise, she had been left alone by Greensparrow, visited rarely, and asked to perform no duties beyond the mostly boring day-to-day routines of serving the primarily figurehead position as duchess of Mannington. She had been thrilled indeed when Greensparrow had called her to a greater service, to serve in his stead and sign the peace accord with Brind'Amour in Princetown. Now her life would change, she had told herself after delivering the agreement to her king. And so it had, for soon after Greensparrow had sent her to the mountains, to the cyclopians, staining her hands with blood and shadowing her heart in treachery.

She focused again on the crown, its glistening gemstones, its unkept promises.

The dwarf howled in pain and tried to scamper, but the hole he was in was not wide and the dozen cyclopians prodding down at him with long spears scored hit after stinging hit.

Soon the dwarf was on the ground. He tried to struggle to his knees, but a spear jabbed him in the face and laid him out straight. The cyclopians took their time in finishing the task.

"Ah, my devious Muckles!" roared Duke Resmore, a broad-shouldered, rotund man, with thick gray hair and a deceivingly cheery face. "You do so know how to have fun!"

Muckles returned the laugh and clapped the huge man on the back. For the brutal cyclopian, life had just gotten a little better.

CHAPTER 7

MASTERS OF THE DORSAL SEA

*R*UEGOTH!" cried one of the crewmen, a call seconded by another man who was standing on the crosspiece of the warship's mainmast.

"She's got up half a sail, and both banks pulling hard!" the man on the crosspiece added.

Luthien leaned over the forward rail, peering out to sea, amazed at how good these full-time seagoers were at discerning the smallest details in what remained no more than a gray haze to his own eyes.

"I do not see," remarked Oliver, standing beside Luthien.

"It can take years to train your eyes for the sea," Luthien tried to explain. (And your stomach, he wanted to add, for Oliver had spent the better part of the week and a half out of Gybi at the rail.) They were aboard *The Stratton Weaver*, one of the great war galleons captured from the Avon fleet in Port Charley now flying under Eriador's flag. In favorable winds, the three-masted *Weaver* could outrun any Huegoth longship, and in any condition could outfight three of the Huegoth vessels combined. With a keel length of nearly a hundred feet and a seasoned crew of more than two hundred, the galleon carried large weaponry that could take out a longship at three hundred yards. Already the crew at the heavy catapult located on the *Weaver*'s higher stern deck were loading balls of pitch into the basket, while those men working the large swiveling ballistae on the rail behind the foremast checked their sights and the straightness of the huge spears they would soon launch the barbarians' way.

"I do not see," Oliver said again.

"Fear not, Oliver, for Luthien is right," agreed Katerin, whose eyes were more accustomed to the open waters. "It can take years to season one's eyes to the sea. It is a Huegoth, though—that is evident even to me, though I have not been on the open sea in many months."

"Trust in the eyes of our guides," Luthien said to the halfling, who appeared thoroughly flustered by this point, tap-tapping his polished black shoe on the deck. "If they call the approaching vessel as a Huegoth, then a Huegoth it is!"

"I do not see," Oliver said for the third time, "because I have two so very big monkey-types blocking the rail in front of me!"

Luthien and Katerin looked to each other and snorted, glad for the relief that was Oliver deBurrows when battle appeared so imminent. Then, with great ceremony, they parted for the halfling.

Oliver immediately scrambled up to the rail, standing atop it with one hand grasping a guide rope, the other cupped over his eyes—which seemed pointless, since the brim of his huge hat shaded his face well enough.

"Ah yes," the halfling began. "So that is a Huegoth. Curious ship.

One, two, three . . . eighteen, nineteen, twenty oars on each side, moving in harmony. Dip and up, dip and up."

Luthien and Katerin stared open-mouthed at each other, then at the tiny spot on the horizon.

"Oh, and who is that big fellow standing tall on the prow?" Oliver asked, and shuddered visibly. The exaggerated movement tipped Luthien off, and he sighed and turned a doubting expression upon Katerin.

"I would not want to fight with that one," the halfling went on. "His yellow beard alone seems as if it might scrape the tender skin from my halfling bones!"

"Indeed," Luthien agreed. "But it is the ring upon his finger that I most fear. See how it resembles the lion's paw?" Now it was Luthien's turn to feign a shudder. "Knowing Huegoth savagery and cunning, it is likely that the claws can be extended to tear the face from an adversary." He shuddered again, and with a grinning Katerin beside him, began to walk away.

Katerin gave him a congratulatory wink, thinking that he had properly called Oliver's bluff.

"Silly boy," the irrepressible halfling shouted after them. "Can you not see that the ring has no more than jew-wels where the retracted claws should be? Ah, but the earring . . ." he said, holding a finger up in the air.

Luthien turned, meaning to respond, but saw Katerin shaking her head and realized that he could not win.

"Fine eyes," remarked Wallach, the captain of *The Stratton Weaver*. He aimed his sarcasm squarely at Oliver as he and Brother Jamesis of Gybi walked over to join Luthien and Katerin.

"Fine wit," Katerin corrected.

"How long until we close?" Luthien asked.

Wallach looked out to the horizon, then shrugged noncommittally. "Could be half an hour, could be the rest of the day," he said. "Our friends in the longship are not running straight for us. They travel to the southeast."

"Do they fear us?" Luthien asked.

"We would overmatch them," replied Wallach confidently. "But I've never known Huegoths to run from any fight. More likely, they're wanting to take us near to Colonsey, into shallower waters where they might beach us, or at least outmaneuver us."

Luthien smiled knowingly at Wallach. This captain had been chosen to lead *The Stratton Weaver* out of Gybi because he, more than any other commanding one of the warships, was familiar with these waters. Wallach had lived in the settlement of Land's End on Colonsey for more than a dozen of his fifty years, and had spent nearly every day of that decade-and-two upon the waters of the Dorsal.

"They will think they have the advantage as we near the island," Katerin remarked slyly.

Wallach chuckled.

"We do not wish to fight them," Luthien reminded them both. "We have come out alone to parley, if that is possible." That was indeed the plan, for *The Stratton Weaver* had left her support fleet of thirty galleons in Bae Colthwyn.

"Huegoths aren't much for talking," Katerin remarked.

"And they respect only force," added Wallach.

"If we have to cripple the longship, then so be it," said Luthien. "We'll take them as bloodlessly as possible, but on no account will we let them slip from our grasp."

"Never that," said Jamesis, whose face had become perpetually grim since the arrival of the fierce Huegoths in the bay, since his peaceful existence in the quiet monastery had been turned upside down.

Luthien carefully studied the monk. He thought the folk of Gybi quite impressive for allowing him to execute his plan of parley. With thirty galleons at their disposal, the folk wanted nothing more than to exact revenge on the Huegoths for the loss of so many good men in Bae Colthwyn. But whatever their desires, the bell tower in Gybi had tolled wildly when Luthien and his companions had arrived, answering the call from Gybi to the new king. And the celebration had exploded yet again when the Eriadoran fleet had come into view north of the bay, rushing hard under full sail. Thus, Proctor Byllewyn had gone along with Luthien's desires and *The Stratton Weaver* had put out to sea, an armed and capable emissary, a diplomat first, a warship second.

"Run up the flag of parley," Luthien instructed Wallach. The young Bedwyr's gaze never left Jamesis as he spoke, searching for the monk's approval. Jamesis had argued against Luthien coming out here, and had found much support in the debate, even from Katerin and Oliver.

"The white flag edged in blue is known even to the Huegoths," Jamesis said grimly. "An international signal of parley, though Huegoths have been known to use it to get advantageously near to their opponent."

"The man's eyes, they are so blue!" exclaimed Oliver from the rail, the perfect timing to break the tension. Jamesis and Wallach cast the halfling a sidelong glance, but Luthien and Katerin only chuckled knowingly. Oliver couldn't see the Huegoth's eyes, they knew, couldn't see the oars of the longship, could hardly make out the vessel at all within the gray haze. But how wonderfully the halfling could play the game! Luthien had come to calling Oliver "the perfection of bluff" for good reason indeed.

A few minutes later, the flag of parley went up high on the mainmast of *The Stratton Weaver*. Wallach and the others watched carefully as more minutes slipped by, but, though the lookouts assured the captain that the Huegoths were close enough to discern the flag, the longship didn't alter her course or slow in the least.

"Running for Colonsey," Wallach repeated.

"Follow her in, then," Luthien instructed.

The captain cocked an eyebrow the young Bedwyr's way.

"You fear to give chase?" Luthien asked him.

"I would feel better about it if my king's second wasn't aboard," Wallach replied.

Luthien glanced nervously about.

Wallach knew that his simple logic had stung the young man, but that didn't stop him from ramming home his point. "If the Huegoths are in league with Greensparrow, as we fear, then wouldn't Luthien Bedwyr be a prize to give to the man? I'll not want to see Greensparrow's expression when the Crimson Shadow is handed over to him."

The argument was growing tedious to Luthien, one he had been waging since the meeting at Gybi when it was decided that the first course would be an attempt of parley with the Huegoths. Luthien had insisted that he be on the lone ship running out of the harbor. Even Katerin, so loyal to the young Bedwyr, had argued against that course, insisting that Luthien was too valuable to the kingdom to take such risks.

"The Crimson Shadow was a prize that Morkney of Montfort wanted to give to Greensparrow," Luthien replied. "The Crimson Shadow was a prize that General Belsen'Krieg promised to the evil king of Avon. The Crimson Shadow was a prize that Duke Paragor of Princetown coveted above all else."

"And they are all dead for their efforts," Brother Jamesis finished for him. "And thus you feel that you are immortal."

Luthien started to protest, but Oliver beat him to it.

"Can you not see?" the halfling asked, scrambling down to Luthien's side. "You say that my sometimes so unwise friend here is too valuable, but his value is exactly that which you wish to protect him from!"

"Oliver is right," added Katerin, another unexpected ally. "If Luthien hides behind the robes of Brind'Amour, if the cape is not seen where it is needed most, then the value of the Crimson Shadow is no more."

Wallach looked to Jamesis and threw up his hands in defeat. "Your fate is not ours to decide," the monk admitted.

"To Colonsey, then," said Wallach and he turned for the helm.

"Only if you think that the wisest course for your ship," Luthien said abruptly, turning the captain about. "I would not have you sailing into danger by my words. *The Stratton Weaver* is yours, and yours alone, to command."

Wallach nodded his appreciation of the sentiment. "We knew the danger when we came out," he reminded Luthien. "And every person aboard volunteered, myself chief among them. To a man and woman, we understand the perils facing our Eriador, and are willing to die in defense of our freedom. If you were not aboard, my friend, I would not hesitate to give chase to the longship, to force the parley, even if all the Huegoth fleet lay in wait!"

"Then sail on," Luthien bade him. With nods, both Wallach and Jamesis took their leave.

The Stratton Weaver angled inside the longship, turning to the east, but the Huegoths rowed fiercely and the galleon could not cut her off. Still, they got close enough for the barbarians to get a clear glimpse of the flag of parley, and the Huegoth reaction proved telling.

The longship never slowed, continuing on her way to the southeast. The great galleon took up the chase, and soon the gray tips of Colonsey's mountainous skyline were in plain sight.

"You still believe they are trying to beach us?" Luthien asked Wallach sometime later.

"I believe they were running for aid," Wallach explained, pointing out to starboard, where yet another longship was coming into sight, sailing around the island.

"Convenient that another was out and about and apparently expecting us," Luthien remarked. "Convenient."

"Ambushes usually are," Wallach replied.

A third Huegoth ship was soon spotted rowing in hard from port, and a fourth behind it, and the first vessel put up one bank of oars and turned about hard.

"We do not know how they will play it," Luthien was quick to say. "Perhaps now that the longship has its allies nearby, the Huegoths will agree to the parley."

"I'll allow no more than one of them to get close," Wallach insisted. "And that only under a similar flag of truce." He called up to his catapult crew then, ordering them to measure their aim on the lone ship to starboard. If a fight came, Wallach meant to sink that one first, giving *The Stratton Weaver* an open route out to deeper waters.

Luthien couldn't disagree, despite his desire to end these raids peacefully. He remembered Garth Rogar, his dearest of friends, a Huegoth who had been shipwrecked at a young age and washed up on the shores of Isle Bedwydrin. Luthien had unintentionally played a hand in Garth's death by defeating the huge man in the arena. If it had been Luthien who had gone down, Gahris would never have allowed the down-pointing-thumb signal that the defeated be vanquished.

Logically, Luthien Bedwyr held no fault in Garth Rogar's death, but guilt was never a slave to logic.

And so Luthien had determined to honor Garth Rogar's memory in this trip to Gybi and out onto the waters of the Dorsal Sea by resolving the conflict with the Huegoths as peacefully as possible. Despite those desires, Luthien could not expect the men and women who crewed *The Stratton Weaver* to leave themselves defenseless in the face of four longships. Wallach and his crew had been brave beyond the call of duty in merely agreeing to come out here alone.

"We could be in for a fight," Luthien said to Katerin and Oliver when he returned to their side at the forward rail.

Oliver looked out at the longships, white froth at their sides from the hard pull of oars. Then he looked about the galleon, particularly at the catapult crew astern. "I do so hope they are good shots," the halfling remarked.

With the odds suddenly turning against them, both Luthien and Katerin hoped so as well.

A call from above told them that a fifth longship had been spotted, and then a sixth, both following in the wake of the ship to starboard.

"Perhaps it was not so good an idea for the king's closest advisor to personally come out this far," Oliver remarked.

"I had to come out," replied Luthien.

"I was talking about myself," Oliver explained dryly.

"We've never run from a fight," Katerin said with as much resolve as she could muster.

Luthien looked into her green eyes and saw trepidation there. The young man understood completely. Katerin was not afraid of battle, never that, but this time, unlike all of the battles of Eriador's revolution, unlike all of the real battles that either she, or he, had ever fought, the enemy would not be cyclopian, but human. Katerin was as worried about killing as she was about being killed.

Captain Wallach verily raced the length of the deck, readying his crew. "Point her to the forward ship," he instructed the catapult gunners, for the longship coming straight at the galleon was the closest, and the fastest closing.

"Damn you, put up your flag of parley," the captain muttered, finally coming to the forward rail alongside the three companions.

As if on cue, the approaching longship's banks of oars lifted out of the water, the long and slender craft quickly losing momentum in the rough seas. Then a horn blew, a note clear and loud, careening across the water to the ears of *The Stratton Weaver*'s anxious crew.

"War horn," Katerin said to Wallach. "They're not up for parley."

Horns rang out from the other five longships, followed soon after by howls and yells. On came the vessels, save the first, which sat in the water, as if waiting for the galleon to make the first move.

"We cannot wait," Wallach said to an obviously disappointed Luthien.

"Three more to port!" came a cry from above.

"We'll not run out of here," remarked Katerin, studying the situation, seeing the noose of the trap drawing tight about the galleon.

Wallach turned back to the main deck, ordering the sails dropped to battle-sail, tying them down so that the ship could still maneuver without presenting too large a target for the Huegoth archers and their flaming arrows.

Luthien turned with him, and noticed Brother Jamesis approaching, his expression as grim as ever. Luthien matched the man's stare for a short while, but in truth it had been Luthien's decision to parley, it had been Luthien's doing that had put the crew in jeopardy. The young Bedwyr turned back to the water, then felt Jamesis's hand on his shoulder.

"We tried as we had to try," the monk said unexpectedly, "else we would have been no better than those we now, it would seem, must fight. But fear not, my Lord Bedwyr, and know that every longship we sink this day . . ."

"And there will be many," Wallach put in determinedly.

". . . will be one less to terrorize the coast of Bae Colthwyn," Jamesis finished.

Wallach looked to Luthien then, and motioned to the nearest longship, as if seeking the young man's approval.

It was not an easy choice for a man of conscience such as Luthien Bedwyr, but the Huegoths had made it clear that they were up for a battle. On the waters all about *The Stratton Weaver* horns were blowing wildly and calls to the Huegoth god of war drifted across the waves.

"They view battle as an honorable thing," Katerin remarked.

"And that is what damns them," said Luthien.

The ball of flaming pitch soared majestically through the afternoon sky, arcing delicately and then diving like a hunting bird that has spotted its quarry. The longship tried to respond—one bank of oars fell into the water and began to churn the ship about.

Too late. The gunners aboard the galleon had taken a full ten minutes to align the not-so-difficult shot. The longship did a quarter-turn before the missile slammed in, catching it square amidships, nearly knocking it right over.

Luthien saw several Huegoths, their furred clothing ablaze, leap overboard. He heard the screams of those others who could not get away. But the longship, though damaged, was not finished, and the oars fell back into the water and on it came.

Shortly thereafter, the Huegoth leader showed himself, rushing up to the prow of his smoking vessel, raising his sword in defiance and shouting curses the galleon's way.

To Luthien, the man's pride was as evident as his stupidity, for the ten other longships (for two more had joined in) were still too far away to offer support. Perhaps the Huegoth didn't understand the power of a war galleon; more likely, the battle-lusting man didn't care.

Wallach turned the galleon broadside to the longship. Another ball of pitch went out, hissing in protest as it crunched through several oars to fall into the water. On the longship came; the barbarian leader climbed right atop the sculpted forecastle, lifting his arms high to the sky.

He was in that very position, crying out to his battle-god, when the ballista-fired spear drove through his chest, hurling his broken body half the length of the longship's deck.

Still the vessel came on, too close now for the catapult, which Wallach ordered to move on to another target. Both ballistae opened up, though, as did a hundred archers, bending back great longbows, sweeping clear the deck of the Huegoth ship.

But still it came on.

The ballistae concentrated on the waterline near to the oars, their spearlike missiles cracking hard into the Huegoth hull.

"Move us!" Captain Wallach cried to his helmsman, and the man, and all those helping with the rigging, were trying to do just that. The Eriadoran crew couldn't believe the determination of the Huegoths. Most of the barbarian crew was certainly dead; the Eriadorans could see the bodies lying thick about the longship's deck. But they could hear the drumming of the slave drivers, the rhythmic beat, and though the slaves now surely outnumbered the captors many times over, the slaves didn't know it!

The Stratton Weaver slipped ahead a few dozen yards, and the longship, with no one abovedecks to steer her, did not compensate. The vessel crossed close in the galleon's wake, though, close enough so that her right bank of oars splintered on the great warship's stern, close enough so that three crewmen aboard the galleon were able to drop a barrel of flaming oil onto her deck.

That threat was ended, but the other Huegoths came on side by side, ten longships working in perfect concert. The catapult crew worked furiously, the ballistae fired one great spear after another, and another Huegoth vessel was sent to the bottom, a third damaged so badly that it could not keep up with its brethren.

Archers lined the rails, and their volleys were returned by Huegoth arrows and spears, many tipped with flame. Luthien had his bow out, too, and he took down one Huegoth right before the man could heave a huge spear the galleon's way. Oliver and Katerin and many others, meanwhile, worked at tending to the increasing number of wounded, and at putting out the stubborn fires before they could cause real damage.

Captain Wallach seemed to be everywhere, encouraging his warriors, calling out orders to his helmsman. But all too soon, the great galleon shuddered under the force of a ram, and the awful sound of cracking wood came up through the open hatches of *The Stratton Weaver*'s deck.

Grappling hooks soared over the rail by the dozen. Luthien drew out *Blind-Striker* and ran along, cutting ropes as fast as he could, while archers bent back their bows and let fly repeatedly, hardly taking the moment to aim.

The young Bedwyr could not believe the courage and sheer ferocity of the Huegoths. They came on without regard for their safety, came on with the conviction that to die in battle was a holy thing, a death to be envied.

There came a second shudder as a longship rammed them to port, then a third as another charged head-on into the *Weaver*'s prow, nearly destroying itself in the process. Soon there seemed to be as many Huegoths aboard the galleon as Eriadorans, and even more continued to pour over the rail.

Luthien tried to get to Wallach, who was fighting fiercely near to the prow. "No!" the young Bedwyr cried, and pulled up, staring in horror, as one Huegoth impaled the captain with the sharp prong of a grapnel. The rope went taut immediately, hurling the screaming Wallach over the rail.

Luthien jumped, startled, as a Huegoth bore down on him from the side. He knew the barbarian had him, that his hesitation in the face of such brutality had cost him his life.

But then the barbarian stopped short and turned to look curiously at a foppishly dressed halfling balancing along the rail, or more particularly, at the halfling's rapier, its slender blade piercing the man's ribs.

The Huegoth howled and leaped up, meaning to catch hold of Oliver and take the halfling over with him, but even as he found his footing, it was knocked away by the sure swipe of a belaying pin, cracking hard against the side of the man's knee. Over the rail he tumbled, and Katerin managed to pop him again, right in the head, before he disappeared from sight.

"I do so like fighting better atop my dear Threadbare," Oliver remarked.

"Think of the battle in the Ministry," Luthien said to them both. "Our only chance is to get as many together in a defensive group as possible."

Katerin nodded, but Oliver shook his head. "My friend," he said evenly, "in the Ministry, we survived because we ran away." Oliver looked around, and the others didn't have to follow his gaze to understand that this time, out on the open sea, there could be no retreat.

The valiant crew of *The Stratton Weaver* fought on for more than an hour, finding their first break when they came to a stand-off. Luthien, Katerin, Oliver, and fifty men and women held the high stern deck, while a hundred Huegoths on the main deck below pulled prisoners and cargo off the badly listing galleon. The prospects for the Huegoths fighting their way up the two small ladders to the higher deck were not good, but then, with their ships fast filling with captured booty and prisoners and *The Stratton Weaver* fast filling with water, they really didn't have to.

Luthien saw this, as did the others, and so they had to come up with the strength for a last desperate charge. There was no hope of winning, they all knew, and no chance of escape.

Then a brown-robed figure was brought forward and thrown to the deck by a huge Huegoth.

"Brother Jamesis!" Luthien cried.

The monk pulled himself up to his knees. "Surrender your sword, my friend," he said to Luthien. "Rennir of Isenland has assured me that he will accept it."

Luthien looked around doubtfully to his fellows.

"Better the life of a galley slave than the watery death!" peaceable Jamesis pleaded.

"Not so!" cried one Eriadoran, and the woman untied a guide rope, took it under her arm and leaped out, soaring heroically into the Hue-goth throng. Before her companions could move to follow or to stop her, though, a long spear came up and stabbed her hard, dropping her to the deck. Huegoths fell over her like wolves. Finally she came out of the tangle, in the grasp of one huge barbarian who ran her to the rail and slammed her face hard upon it.

He let go then, and somehow the woman managed to hold her footing, but just long enough for another barbarian to skewer her through the belly with a long trident. The muscled man lifted her trembling form high off the deck and held the macabre pose for a long moment before tossing her overboard.

"Damn you!" Luthien cried, starting down the ladder, his knuckles white with rage as he clutched his mighty sword.

"No more!" wailed Jamesis, the monk's desperation bringing Luthien from his outrage. "I beseech you, son of Bedwyr, for the lives of those who follow you!"

"Bedwyr?" mumbled a curious Rennin, too low for anyone to hear.

Looking back at the fifty men and women in his wake, Luthien ran out of arguments. He was partly responsible for this disaster, he believed, since he had been one of the chief proponents of sending a lone ship out to parley. The entirety of Luthien's previous experience with Huegoths had been beside his friend Garth Rogar in Dun Varna, and that man was among the most honorable and reasonable warriors the young Bedwyr had ever known.

Perhaps due to that friendship, Luthien hadn't been prepared for the savage men of Isenland. Now a hundred Eriadorans, or even more, were dead, and half that number had already been hauled aboard the long-ships as prisoners. His cinnamon eyes moist with frustration, Luthien tossed *Blind-Striker* down to the main deck.

Sometime later, he and his companions watched from the deck of a Huegoth longship as *The Stratton Weaver* slipped quietly under the waves.

CHAPTER 8

PROSPECTS

*L*UTHIEN HEARD THE WHIPS cracking on the decks of other Huegoth vessels, heard the cries of the unfortunate Eriadoran sailors as they were shuffled belowdecks and chained to benches. Some of the prisoners on his own longship were treated similarly, and it seemed as if Luthien and his friends would find no escape. The grim prospects of a life as a galley slave loomed large before the young Bedwyr, but he was more afraid for his closest companions than for himself. What would the Huegoths make of Oliver, who was obviously too small to row? Would the foppish halfling become a source of entertainment, a longship jester subject to the whims of the brutal barbarians? Or would the fierce men of Isenland simply jettison him overboard like so much useless cargo?

And what of Katerin? For Katerin, and the half dozen other women captured in the battle, Luthien feared even more. Huegoth raiders were away from home for long, long stretches, time counted in months more than in weeks. What pleasures might the merciless barbarians make of such a delicacy as Katerin O'Hale?

A violent shudder brought the young Bedwyr from the dark thoughts, forced him to focus on the reality instead of the prospects. Fortunately, Katerin and Oliver were on the same longship as he, and they, along with Luthien and Brother Jamesis, had thus far not been so much as scratched. It would stay that way, Luthien told himself determinedly. He resolved that if the barbarians meant to kill Oliver, or if they tried to harm Katerin in any way, he would fight them again, this time to the most bitter end. He had no weapons save his bare hands, but in defense of Oliver and especially Katerin, he held faith that those hands would be deadly.

The Huegoths were quite proficient in the role of captors, Luthien soon realized, for he and all the others were properly secured with thick ropes and guarded closely by a score of huge warriors. When that was finished, a selection process began on the longship, a magnificent vessel that Luthien figured to be the flagship of the fleet. Old and used-up galley slaves, men too weak and malnourished to continue to pull to the demands of the barbarians, were dragged onto the deck, while newer prisoners were ushered below and chained in their place. Luthien knew logically what the Huegoths meant to do, and his conscience screamed out at him to take action, any action. Still, the barbarians kept their intentions just mysterious enough for the young Bedwyr and the others, particularly those slaves who looked upon the sun for the first time in weeks, to hold out some hope. That hope, that thought that they all might indeed have something to gain through obedience and something to lose by causing trouble, proved paralyzing.

Thus, Luthien could only close his eyes as the replaced galley slaves, withered and beyond usefulness in the cold eyes of the Huegoths, were pushed overboard.

"I, too, will find such a fate," Oliver said matter-of-factly. "And I do so hate the water!"

"We do not know that," whispered Brother Jamesis, his voice trembling. Jamesis had facilitated the surrender, after all, and now he was watching the fruits of his action. Perhaps it would have been better for them all if they had battled to the last on the sinking *Weaver.*

"I am too small to row," Oliver replied. He was surprised to find that his greatest lament at that moment was that he had not found time to explore the intriguing possibilities with Siobhan.

"Quiet," Luthien sharply bade them both. "There is no gain in giving the Huegoths ideas."

"As if they do not already know!" said Oliver.

"They may think you a child," Katerin put in. "Huegoths have been known to take in orphaned children and raise them as Isenlanders."

"Such a comforting thought," Oliver said sarcastically. "And tell me, what will become of me when I do not grow?"

"Enough!" Luthien commanded, sheer anger causing his voice to rise enough to get the attention of the nearest Huegoth guard. The huge man looked Luthien's way and issued a low growl, and the young Bedwyr smiled meekly in reply.

"We should not have let them bind us," Luthien lamented out of the side of his mouth.

"We could have stopped them?" Oliver asked.

The group quieted as a band of barbarians came toward them, led by Rennir, the Huegoth leader.

"I must protest!" Brother Jamesis called immediately to the large man.

Rennir's white teeth showed clearly within the bushy blond hair that covered his face. His teasing expression revealed that he had heard similar words before, that he had watched "civilized" folk witness Huegoth justice on previous occasions. He stalked toward Jamesis so boldly that the monk shrank back against the rail and Luthien and the others thought for a moment that Rennir would simply heave Jamesis into the sea with the floundering slaves.

"We had an arrangement," Jamesis said, much more humbly, when the Huegoth leader stopped right before him. "You guaranteed the safety . . ."

"Of your men," Rennir was glad to finish. "I said nothing about the slaves already within my longships. Where would I put you all?" The Huegoth turned a wry smile over his shoulder, back to the chuckling group of his kinsmen standing near.

Brother Jamesis searched hard for some rational argument. Indeed, the Huegoth was holding true to the wording of their agreement, if not the spirit. "You do not have to execute those who have served you," Jamesis stuttered. "The island of Colonsey is not so far away. You could drop them there . . ."

"Leave enemies in our wake?" Rennir thundered. "That they might wage war with us once more?"

"You would find fewer enemies if you possessed the soul of a human," Luthien offered, drawing Rennir's scowl his way. Rennir began a slow and ominous walk toward the young Bedwyr, but Luthien, unlike Jamesis, did not shrink back. Indeed Luthien stood tall, jaw firm and shoulders squared, and his cinnamon-colored eyes locked on the gray orbs of the giant Huegoth. Rennir came right up to him, but though he was taller by several inches, he did not seem to tower over Luthien.

The dangerous stares lasted for a long while, neither man speaking or even blinking. Then Rennir seemed to notice something—something about Luthien's appearance—and the Huegoth leader visibly relaxed.

"You are not of Gybi," Rennir stated.

"I ask you to retrieve those men in the sea," Luthien replied.

Several barbarians began to chuckle, but Rennir held up his hand, no mirth crossing his deadly serious features. "You would show mercy if those in the sea were of Isenland blood?"

"I would."

"Have you?"

The surprising question nearly knocked Luthien over. What in the world was Rennir talking about? Luthien searched frantically for some response, realizing that his answer now might save the lives of the poor slaves. In the end, he could only shake his head, though, not understanding the Huegoth's intent.

"What is your name?" Rennir asked.

"Luthien Bedwyr."

"Of Isle Bedwydrin?"

Luthien nodded and glanced over at Oliver and Katerin, who could only shrug in reply, as confused as he.

"Have you?" Rennir asked again.

It clicked in Luthien's head. Garth Rogar! The man was referring to Garth Rogar, Luthien's dearest friend, who had been pulled from the sea by Luthien and raised in the House of Bedwyr as a brother! But how could Rennir possibly know? Luthien wondered.

At that critical moment, it didn't matter, and Luthien didn't have the time to debate it. He squared his shoulders once more, looked sternly into Rennir's gray eyes, and said with all conviction, "I have."

Rennir turned to his fellows. "Drag the slaves from the water," he commanded, "and pass word to the other boats that none are to be drowned."

Rennir turned back to Luthien, the Huegoth's face wild, frightening. "That is all I owe to you," he stated and walked away. As he did, he put a lewd stare over Katerin, then chuckled.

"You owe me a place beside my men," Luthien stated, stopping Rennir short. "If they are to row, then so am I!"

The Huegoth thought on that for a moment, then threw his head back and roared heartily. He didn't bother to look back again as he joined his fellows.

The longships moved in a wide formation around the western shore of Colonsey. This somewhat surprised Luthien and his companions, who thought the barbarians would put out to the open sea. They learned the truth when they came into a sheltered bay, passing through a narrow opening, practically invisible from the sea, into a wide and calm lagoon.

A hundred longships were tied up along the rocky beach. Further inland, up the rocky incline, dozens of stone and wood huts dotted the stark landscape, and smoke wafted out of many cave openings.

"When did this happen?" a stunned Brother Jamesis muttered.

"And what of Land's End?" Luthien asked, referring to the small Eriadoran settlement around to the eastern side of the island. If this many Huegoths had formed a base on Colonsey, it did not bode well for the hundred or so people in the rugged, windswept settlement. Luthien understood the trouble the barbarians had gone to, and realized then beyond any doubt that their attacks on Bae Colthwyn were not intended as minor raids. They had wood here, in large supply, though there was little on rocky Colonsey, and Luthien took note that there were many Huegoth women among those gathering at the shore to greet the returning longships. This was a full-scale invasion, and Luthien grimaced as he thought of the misery that would soon befall his dear Eriador.

Slaves were not normally taken off the longships when they were in harbor, and as the other boats put in, most of the Huegoths clambered over the side, splashing into shore, leaving just a few guards behind. Luthien's thoughts immediately turned to the potential for escape, but he was surprised when Rennir's boat put in and a group of Huegoths came and gathered him up with his three companions, ushering them roughly ashore.

Luthien never got the obvious questions out of his mouth when he stumbled onto the rocky beach, Rennir taking him by the collar and dragging him along to the largest hut of the settlement.

"Beg before Asmund, who is king!" was all the Huegoth said as he pulled Luthien past the guards and into the open single-roomed structure.

His hands still bound behind his back, Luthien stumbled down to one knee. He recovered quickly, forced himself not to look back as he heard Katerin, or Jamesis, perhaps, go down behind him. As calmly as he could manage, Luthien straightened himself on his knees, regaining a measure of dignity before he looked upon the Huegoth king.

Asmund was an impressive figure indeed, barrel-chested, with a huge gray beard, brown, weathered skin, and light blue eyes so intense that they seemed as if they could bore holes through hard wood.

But Luthien hardly noticed the king. He was more stricken by the sight of the man standing casually beside the great Asmund.

A man with cinnamon-colored eyes.

CHAPTER 9

THE ERIADORAN TIE

"ETHAN," Katerin muttered in disbelief.

Gasping for breath, Luthien started to rise and was promptly grabbed by Rennir. Luthien growled and pulled away from the huge man, determined to stand before Asmund, and especially before Asmund's escort. It was Ethan, obviously, but how his brother had changed! A stubbly beard graced his fine Bedwydrin features and his hair had grown much longer. The most profound change, though, was the man's eyes, intense and wild, perfectly dangerous.

"You know him?" Oliver whispered to Katerin.

"Ethan Bedwyr," Katerin said loudly. "Luthien's brother."

"Ah, so I see," said Oliver, taking note of the distinct resemblance between the men, particularly in the rare cinnamon coloring of their eyes. Then, as he realized the truth of this impossible situation, the halfling's jaw dropped in speechless astonishment.

Asmund, seeming quite amused, turned Ethan's way, giving the floor to the Eriadoran.

Luthien's heart and hopes soared. "My brother," he said breathlessly as Ethan walked over to him.

The older Bedwyr pushed Luthien down to the floor. "No more," he said.

"What are you doing?" Katerin cried out, rushing to intervene.

"A woman of spirit!" howled huge Asmund as Rennir grabbed the thrashing Katerin in his massive arms.

"What is wrong with you?" Luthien demanded of Ethan, rolling up to one knee and staring hard at his brother. He looked to Rennir, then back to Ethan, pleading, "Stop him!"

Ethan shook his head slowly. "No more," he said again to Luthien, but he did indeed turn to Rennir and bade the man to let go of Katerin O'Hale.

"If you're thinking that I'm to be grateful, then you're thinking wrong!" Katerin roared at him, moving up to face him squarely. "You are on the wrong side of the ropes, son of Gahris!"

Ethan tilted his head back, his features taking on a look that seemed both distant and superior. He never blinked, but neither did he lash out at Katerin.

"You are with them," Luthien stated.

Ethan looked at him incredulously, as though that much should have been obvious.

"Traitor!" Katerin growled.

Ethan's hand came up and Katerin turned away, fully expecting that she would be slapped.

The blow never came, though, as Ethan quickly regained his composure. "Traitor to whom?" he asked. "To Gahris, who banished me, who sent me away to die?"

"I searched for you," Luthien put in.

"You found me," Ethan said grimly.

"With Huegoths," Luthien added, his tone derisive. More than a few barbarians around him growled.

"With brave men," Ethan retorted. "With men who would not be ruled by an unlawful king from another land!"

That gave Luthien some hope concerning the greater situation at least. Perhaps this Huegoth invasion wasn't in any way connected to Greensparrow.

"You are Eriadoran!" Katerin yelled.

"I am not!" Ethan screamed back at her. "Count me not among the cowards who cringe in fear of Greensparrow. Count me not among those who have accepted the death of Garth Rogar!" He looked Luthien right in the eye as he finished the thought. "Count me not among those who would wear the colors of Lady Avonese, the painted whore!"

Luthien breathed hard, trying to sort out his thoughts. Ethan here! It was too crazy, too unexpected. But Ethan did not know of all that had transpired, Luthien reminded himself. Ethan likely thought that things were as he had left them in Eriador, with Greensparrow as king and Gahris as one of his many pawns. But where did that leave Luthien? Even if he convinced Ethan of the truth, could he forgive his brother for allying with savage Huegoths against Eriador?

"How dare you?" Luthien roared, struggling to his feet.

"Greensparrow—" Ethan began to counter.

"Damn Greensparrow!" Luthien interrupted. "Those ships that your newfound friends attacked were Eriadoran, not Avonese. The blood of fellow Eriadorans is on your hands!"

"Damn you!" Ethan yelled back, slamming into Luthien so forcefully that he nearly knocked his younger brother over once more. "I am Huegoth now, and not Eriadoran. And all ships of Avonsea serve Greensparrow."

"You murdered—"

"We wage war!" Ethan snapped ferociously. "Let Greensparrow come north with his fleet, that we might sink them, and if Eriadorans also die in the battle, then so be it!"

Luthien looked from Ethan to Asmund, the Huegoth king smiling widely, and smugly, as though he was thoroughly enjoying this little play. It struck Luthien that his brother might be more of a pawn than an advisor, and he found at that moment that he wanted nothing more than to rush over and throttle Asmund.

But in looking back to Ethan, Luthien had to admit that his brother didn't seem to need any champion. Ethan's demeanor had changed dramatically, had become wild to match the raging fires in his eyes. Gahris's actions in banishing Ethan had come near to breaking the man, Luthien realized, and in that despair, Ethan had found a new strength: the strength of purest anger. Ethan seemed at home with the Huegoths, so much so that the realization sent a shudder coursing through Luthien's spine. He had to wonder if this really was his brother, or if the brother he had known in Dun Varna was truly dead.

"Greensparrow will not come north," Luthien said quietly, trying to restore some sense of calm to the increasingly explosive discussion.

"But he will," Ethan insisted. "He will send his warships north, one by one or in a pack. Either way, we will destroy them, send them to the bottom, and then let the weakling wizard who claims an unlawful throne be damned!"

He would have gone on, but Luthien's sudden burst of hysterical laughter gave him pause. Ethan tilted his head, tried to get some sense of why his brother was laughing so, but Luthien threw his head back, roaring wildly, and would not look him in the eye. Ethan turned to Katerin instead, and to Luthien's other companions, but they offered no explanation.

"Are you mad, then?" Ethan said calmly, but Luthien seemed not to hear.

"Enough!" roared Asmund, and Luthien stopped abruptly and stared hard at his brother and the Huegoth king.

"You do not know," the younger Bedwyr brother stated more than asked.

Ethan's wild eyes calmed with curiosity and he cocked his head, his unkempt hair, even lighter now than Luthien remembered it, hanging to his shoulder.

"Greensparrow no longer rules in Eriador," Luthien said bluntly. "And his lackeys have been dispatched. Montfort is no more, for the name of Caer MacDonald has been restored."

Ethan tried to seem unimpressed, but how his cinnamon-colored eyes widened!

" 'Twas Luthien who killed Duke Morkney," Katerin put in.

"With help from my friends," Luthien was quick to add.

"You?" Ethan stammered.

"So silly barbarian pretender-type," Oliver piped in with a snap of his green-gauntleted fingers, "have you never heard of the Crimson Shadow?"

That name brought a flicker of recognition to Ethan; it seemed as if the legend had spread wider than the general political news. "You?" Ethan said again, pointing and advancing a step toward Luthien.

"It was a title earned by accident," Luthien insisted.

"But of course you have heard of Oliver's Bluff," the halfling interrupted, skipping forward and stepping in front of Luthien, so that his head was practically in Ethan's belly, and puffing his little chest with pride.

Ethan looked down at Oliver and shook his head.

"It was designed for Malpuissant's Wall," the halfling began; "but since the wall was taken before we ever arrived, we executed this most magnificent of strategies on Princetown itself. That is right!" Oliver brought his hand up right in Ethan's face and snapped his fingers again. "The very jew-wel of Avon taken by the forces of cunning Oliver deBurrows!"

"And you are Oliver deBurrows?" Ethan surmised dryly.

"If I had my so fine rapier blade, I would show you!"

A dangerous scowl crossed Ethan's features, one that Asmund did not miss. "That can be arranged, and quickly!" the Huegoth king said with a snort, and all the barbarians in the tent began to laugh and murmur, apparently pleased at the prospect of a duel.

Luthien's arm swept around the dramatically posing Oliver and pushed the halfling back. Luthien knew well his brother's battle prowess and he wasn't keen on the idea of losing his little halfling friend, however annoying Oliver might sometimes be.

"It is all true," Luthien insisted to Ethan. "Eriador is free, under King Brind'Amour."

Ethan turned back to find Asmund staring hard at him, searching for some confirmation or explanation of the unknown name. Ethan could only shrug, for he had never heard of this man Luthien claimed was now ruling the northern kingdom of Avonsea.

"He was of the ancient brotherhood," Luthien explained, seeing their skepticism. "A very mighty . . ." Luthien paused, realizing that it might not be a good thing to reveal Brind'Amour's true profession to the Huegoths, who distrusted magic. "A very mighty and wise man," Luthien finished, but he had already said too much.

"The ancient brotherhood," Ethan said to Asmund, "thus, the king of Eriador, too, is a wizard."

Asmund snorted derisively.

The fact that Ethan betrayed that secret so matter-of-factly gave Luthien some idea of how far lost his brother truly was. Luthien needed something to divert the conversation, he realized, and he only had one card to play. "Gahris is dead," he said calmly.

Ethan winced, but then nodded his acceptance of the news.

"He died peacefully," Luthien said, but again, Ethan didn't seem very concerned.

"Gahris died many years ago," Ethan remarked. "He died when our mother died, when the plague that was Greensparrow swept across Eriador."

"You are wrong!" Katerin O'Hale said boldly. "Gahris made certain that no cyclopians remain alive on Bedwydrin, and Lady Avonese—"

"The whore," Ethan sneered.

Katerin snorted, not disagreeing in the least. "She died in the dungeon of House Bedwyr."

"There are no dungeons in House Bedwyr," Ethan said doubtfully.

"Eorl Gahris built one just for her," Katerin replied.

"What is this all about, Vinndalf?" Asmund asked.

Ethan turned to his king and shrugged once again, in truth, too surprised to sort through it all.

"Vinndalf?" Luthien echoed.

Ethan squared his shoulders. "My proper name," he insisted.

Now Luthien could no longer contain his mounting anger. "You are Ethan Bedwyr, son of Gahris, who was eorl of Bedwydrin," the younger brother insisted.

"I am Vinndalf, brother of Torin Rogar," Ethan retorted.

Luthien moved to respond, but that last name caught him off his guard. "Rogar?" he asked.

"Torin Rogar," Ethan explained, "brother of Garth."

That took the wind from Luthien. He wanted to meet the brother of Garth Rogar—that thought reverberated in his mind. He sublimated it, though, realizing that such a meeting was for another time. For now, Luthien's duty was clear and straightforward. Fifty lives depended on him, and the ante would be even greater if the Huegoths continued their raids along Eriador's coast. All that Luthien had discovered in this meeting, particularly the fact that the Huegoths did not know of recent events in Eriador, and thus could not be in any alliance with Avon, had given him hope. That hope, though, was tempered by the specter of this man standing before him, by Ethan, who was not Ethan.

"Then my greetings to Vinndalf," Luthien said, surprising Katerin, who stood scowling at his side. "I come as emissary of King Brind'Amour of Eriador."

"We asked for no parley," Asmund said.

"But you know now that your attacks on Eriadoran ships and coast do no harm to Greensparrow," Luthien said. "We are not your enemies."

That brought more than a few laughs from the many Huegoths in the hut, and laughter from outside as well, confirming to Luthien that this meeting of the lost brothers had become a public spectacle.

"Ethan," Luthien said solemnly. "Vinndalf, I am, or was, your brother."

"In a world from which I was banished," Ethan interrupted.

"I looked for you," Luthien said. "I killed the cyclopian who murdered Garth Rogar, and then I looked for you, to the south, where you were supposedly heading."

"I took him there," Oliver had to say, if for no other reason than the fact that the halfling couldn't stand being on the sidelines of any conversation for so long.

"I, too, considered our father dead," Luthien went on, "though I assure you that in the end the man redeemed himself."

"He thought of you on the night he died," Katerin put in. "His guilt weighed heavily on him."

"As it should have," said Ethan.

"Agreed," Luthien replied. "And I make no excuses for the world from which you fled. But that world is no more, I promise. Eriador is free now."

"What concern have we of your petty squabbles?" Asmund asked incredulously. As soon as he regarded the man, Luthien realized that the Huegoth feared that Luthien might be stealing some fun here. "You speak of Greensparrow and Eriador as though they are not the same. To us, you are *degjern-alfar,* and nothing more!"

Degjern-alfar. Luthien knew the word, an Isenland term for any who was not Huegoth.

"And I am Huegoth," Ethan insisted before Luthien could make any points about his Eriadoran blood. Ethan looked to a nodding Asmund. "Huegoth by deed."

"You are a Huegoth who understands the importance of what I say," Luthien added quickly. "Eriador is free, but if you continue your raids, you are aiding Greensparrow in his desires to take us back under his evil wing." For the first time, it seemed to Luthien as if he had gotten through to his stubborn brother. He knew that Ethan, whatever his claim of loyalty, was thrilled at the idea that Eriador had broken free of Avon, and Luthien knew, too, that the thought that the Huegoth actions, that Ethan's own actions, might be aiding the man who had, by sending the plague, murdered their mother and broken their father, was truly agonizing to Ethan.

"And what would you ask of me?" the older Bedwyr brother asked after a short pause.

"Desist," said Oliver, stepping in front. Luthien wanted to slap the halfling for taking center stage at that critical point. "Take your silly boat and go back to where you belong. We have four-score warships—"

Luthien pushed Oliver aside, and when the halfling tried to resist, Katerin grabbed him by the collar, spun him about and scowled in his face, a look that conjured images in Oliver of being thrown to the floor and sat upon by the woman.

"Join with us," Luthien said on a sudden impulse. He realized how stupid that sounded even as the words left his mouth, but he knew that the last thing one should do to a Huegoth (as Oliver had just done) was issue a challenge of honor. Threatening King Asmund with eighty galleons would force the fierce man to accept the war. "With nearly four-score warships and your fleet, we might—"

"You ask this of me?" Ethan said, slapping himself on the chest.

Luthien straightened. "You are my brother," he said firmly. "And were of Eriador, whatever your claim may now be. I demand that you ask of your king to halt the raids on Eriador's coast. For all that has happened, we are not your enemies."

Ethan snorted and didn't even bother to look over his shoulder at Asmund. "Do not put too much weight on my ability to influence my Huegoth brothers," Ethan said. "King Asmund, and not I, decides the Huegoth course."

"But you were willing to go along," Luthien accused, his face twisting in sudden rage. "While Eriadorans died, Ethan Bedwyr did nothing!"

"Ethan Bedwyr is dead," the man called Vinndalf replied.

"And does Vinndalf not remember all the good that Luthien Bedwyr brought to his younger life?" Katerin asked.

Ethan's broad shoulders slumped for just an instant, a subtle indication that Katerin had hit a chord. Ethan straightened quickly, though, and stared hard at Luthien.

"I will beg of my king to give you this much," Ethan said evenly. "On mighty Asmund's word, we will let you leave, will deliver you and Katerin and your puffy and puny friend back to the coast of Bae Colthwyn, south of Gybi."

"And the others?" Luthien asked grimly.

"Fairly taken," Ethan replied.

Luthien squared up and shook his head. "All of them," he insisted. "Every man and woman returned to Eriador, their home."

For a long moment, it seemed a stand-off. Then Rennir, who was enjoying it all, crossed the room to Ethan and handed the man *Blind-Striker.* Ethan looked long and hard at the sword, the most important relic of his former family. After a moment, he chuckled, and then, eyeing Luthien in an act of open defiance, he strapped the magnificent weapon about his waist.

"You said you were no longer of family Bedwyr," remarked Luthien, looking for some advantage, and trying to take the edge from his own rising anger. Seeing Ethan—no, Vinndalf—wearing that sword was nearly more than Luthien could take.

"True enough," Ethan replied casually, as though that fact was of no importance.

"Yet you wear the Bedwyr sword."

Now it was Ethan's turn to laugh, and Rennir and Asmund, and all the other Huegoths joined in. "I wear a weapon plundered from a vanquished enemy," Ethan corrected. "Fairly won, like the men who will serve as slaves. Take my offer, former brother. Go, and with Katerin. I cannot guarantee her safety here, and as for your little friend, I can assure you that he will find a most horrible fate at the hands of the men of Isenland, who do not accept such weakness."

"Weakness?" Oliver stammered, but Katerin slapped her hand over his mouth to shut him up before he got them all killed.

"All of them," Luthien said firmly. "And I'll have the sword as well."

"Why should I give to you anything?" Ethan asked.

"Do not!" roared Luthien as the laughter began to mount around him once more. "I ask for nothing from one so cowardly as to disclaim his heritage. But I'll have what I desire, by spilled blood if not by family blood!"

Ethan's head tilted back at that open challenge. "We have fought before," he said.

Luthien didn't answer.

"I was victorious," Ethan reminded.

"I was younger."

Ethan looked to Asmund, who made no move.

"The slaves are not yours to give," said Rennir. "The capture was mine."

Ethan nodded his agreement.

"Fight for the sword, then," offered Asmund.

"All of them," Luthien said firmly.

"For the sword," Ethan corrected. "And for your freedom, and the freedom of Katerin and the little one. Nothing more."

"That much, save the sword, was already offered," Luthien argued.

"An offer rescinded," said Ethan. "You challenged me openly. Now you will see it through, though the gain is little more than what you would have found without challenge, and the loss—and you will lose— is surely greater!"

Luthien looked to Asmund and saw that he would find no sympathy there, and no better offers. He had stepped into dynamics that he did not fully understand, he realized. It seemed to Luthien as though Asmund had desired this combat from the moment the king learned that Luthien and Ethan were brothers. Perhaps it was a test of Ethan's loyalty, or more likely, brutal Asmund just thought it would be fine sport.

Behind Luthien, Katerin O'Hale's voice was as grim as anything the young Bedwyr had ever heard. "Kill him."

The words, and the image they conjured, nearly knocked Luthien over. He was hardly conscious, his breath labored, as his companions were pushed away, as Rennir handed him a sword, as Ethan drew out *Blind-Striker* and began a determined and deadly approach.

CHAPTER 10

SIBLING RIVALRY

ETHAN'S INITIAL SWING BROUGHT Luthien's swirling thoughts back to crystal clarity, his survival instincts overruling all the craziness and potential for disaster. The weapon Rennir had given him was not very balanced, and was even heavier than the six-pound, one-and-a-half-handed *Blind-Striker*. He took it up in both hands and twisted hard, dipping his right shoulder and laying the blade angled down.

Blind-Striker hit the blocking blade hard enough for Luthien to realize that if he hadn't thrown up the last-second parry, he would have been cut in half.

"Ethan!" he yelled instinctively as a rush of memories—of fighting in the arena, of training as a young boy under his older brother's tutelage, of sharing quiet moments beside Ethan in the hills outside of Dun Varna—assaulted him.

The man who was known as Vinndalf didn't respond to the call in the least. He backed up one step and sent *Blind-Striker* around the other way, coming straight in at Luthien's side.

Luthien reversed his pivot, and his grip, dropping his left shoulder this time, launching the heavy weapon the other way and cleanly picking off the attack. Ahead came Luthien's left foot; the logical counter was a straightforward thrust.

Ethan was already moving, directly back, out of harm's way and not even needing to parry the short attack. That done, he took up his sword, the magnificent Bedwyr sword, in both hands and began to circle to his right.

Luthien turned with him. He could hardly believe that he had so thrust at his own brother, that if Ethan had not been so quick, he would be lying on the floor, his guts spilling. Luthien dismissed such images. This was for real, he told himself; this was for his very life and the lives of his dearest friends, as well. He could not be distracted by contrary feelings, could not think of his opponent as his brother. Now he tried to remember again the arena in Dun Varna, tried to remember the style of Ethan's moves.

Ethan dropped his shoulder and came ahead in a quick-step, lunging for Luthien's lead knee. The attack stopped short, though, before *Blind-Striker* even tapped Luthien's parrying blade, and Ethan threw himself to the side, his other foot rushing right beside his leading leg, turning him in a complete circuit. Down to one knee he went, both hands on his sword as it came across in a devious cut.

Luthien had seen the trick before and was long out of danger before Ethan even finished.

Ethan had been a mature fighter when last they had battled, and so Luthien thought it unlikely that his tactics would have changed much. But Luthien had been young on that occasion, a novice fighter just learning the measure of single combat.

That was his advantage.

Ethan was up to his feet, dropping one hand for balance and charging hard in the blink of an eye, *Blind-Striker* going left, right, straight ahead, then right again. Steel rang against steel, Luthien working furiously to keep the deadly blade at bay. Those attacks defeated, Ethan took up the weapon in both hands and chopped hard at Luthien's head, once, twice, and then again.

Luthien beat them all, but stumbled backward under the sheer weight of the furious blows. He wanted to offer a fast counter, but this sword, half-again as heavy as the weapon he was used to carrying, would not allow for any quick response. And so he backed away as wild-eyed Ethan forged onward, slamming with abandon.

Now Luthien concentrated on conserving his strength, on picking off the attacks with as little motion as possible. He willingly gave ground, came near to the hut wall and shifted his angle so that, propelled by yet another brutal blow, he went right out the door into the dazzling daylight.

A throng of Huegoths swarmed about the battling brothers; Luthien saw Katerin and Oliver come to the door, Rennir roughly pushing them aside to make way for grinning Asmund.

Oh, this was great play for the fierce Isenlanders, Luthien realized.

The uneven and stony ground somewhat took away Ethan's advantage of wielding the lighter and quicker weapon. Suddenly footwork was of the utmost importance, and no warrior Luthien had ever met, with the possible exception of fleet-footed Oliver deBurrows, was better at footwork than he. Luthien skittered right along the uneven ground, deftly trailing his heavy sword to pick off any of pursuing Ethan's attacks. He came to a spot where the ground sloped steeply and saw his chance. Up Luthien went, beyond *Blind-Striker*'s reach as Ethan came by below him, and then down Luthien charged in a fury, suddenly pressing his brother with a series of momentum-backed chops.

Perfectly balanced, Ethan was up to the defense, picking off or dodging each blow. It occurred to Luthien then, when he thought he had gained an advantage, that the endgame of this combat would not go well. Win or lose, the young Bedwyr would find himself in a bind. Would it be to the death? And if so, how could Luthien possibly kill his own brother? And even if it wasn't to the death, Luthien understood that he had much to lose, and so did Ethan, for Ethan had likely only gained acceptance among the fierce barbarians through skill in battle. Now, in this encounter, if Ethan lost their respect . . .

Luthien didn't like the prospects, but he had no time to pause and try and discern another way out. Ethan went up high on the sloping stone, trying to get the angle above him, and he had to work furiously to keep up.

Out came *Blind-Striker* in a wicked thrust, suddenly, as the brothers picked their way up the stone. Luthien couldn't possibly get his heavier blade in line in time, nor could he dodge in the difficult position, so he rolled instead, out from Ethan and then down the slope, coming lightly to his feet some twenty feet below his brother.

He heard Katerin cry out for him, and Oliver's groan in the midst of the cheers of a hundred bloodthirsty Huegoths.

Down came Ethan, spurred on by his comrades, but Luthien was not going to grant him the higher ground. Off sped the younger Bedwyr, running away from the slope. Ethan yelled out as he pursued, even going so far as to call his brother a coward.

Luthien was no coward, but he had learned the advantage of choosing his ground. So it was now, with Ethan fast closing. Luthien turned along the beach to a small jetty, skipping gingerly atop its stones. Now he had the high ground, but Ethan, so enraged, so full of adrenaline, did not slow, came in hacking wildly, thrusting *Blind-Striker* this way and that, searching for a hole in Luthien's defenses.

There was no such hole to be found; Luthien's blocks were perfect, but Ethan did manage to sidle up the rocks as he attacked, gradually coming near to Luthien's level. Luthien saw the tactic, of course, and could have stopped it by shifting to directly block his brother, but he had something else in mind.

Up came Ethan. Luthien's sword started for the man's knees and Ethan jumped back, launching a vicious downward cut.

Luthien's thrust had been a feint; before he ever got close, and as Ethan started the obvious counter, the young Bedwyr moved back a step, reversed his grip on his heavy sword, and shifted it, not to block *Blind-Striker*, but to deflect the sword. As Ethan's weapon scraped by, Luthien turned his blade over it and shoved it down for the rocks, and off-balance Ethan could not resist. Sparks flew from *Blind-Striker*'s fine tip as the gleaming blade dove into a crevice between the stones.

From his lower angle, Ethan could not immediately pull it out. One step up would allow him to extract the blade, yet he could not make that step. He had lost a split second, and against cunning Luthien, a split second was too long.

Endgame.

Luthien knew it, but had no idea of what to make of it. Images of Katerin and Oliver as Huegoth prisoners flashed in his mind, yet this fledgling Eriador would not likely survive his victory. His foot slipped out from under him suddenly, and down he went to the stone, his sword bouncing away. He rolled up to a sitting position, holding his bruised and bleeding hand.

Ethan stood over him, *Blind-Striker* in hand. In looking into his eyes, those trademark Bedwyr eyes, Luthien thought for a moment that his brother would surely kill him.

Then Ethan paused, seeming unsure of himself, a mixture of frustration and rage. He couldn't do it, could not kill his brother, and that fact seemed to bother the man who called himself Vinndalf more than a little.

Blind-Striker came in to rest at the side of Luthien's neck.

"I claim victory!" Ethan bellowed.

"Enough!" roared Asmund before Ethan had even finished. The Huegoth king said something to the man standing beside him, and a host of Huegoths moved to join the brothers.

"Into the King's Hall!" one of them commanded Ethan, while two others roughly hoisted Luthien to his feet and half-carried him across the beach, past the hundred sets of curious eyes, Oliver's and Katerin's among them, and into King Asmund's quarters. There, Luthien was thrown to the floor, right beside his standing brother, and then all the Huegoths, save Asmund himself, quickly departed.

Luthien spent a moment looking from the seated king to his brother, then slowly rose. Ethan would not look at him.

"Clever boy," Asmund congratulated.

Luthien eyed him skeptically, not knowing what he was driving at.

"You had him beaten," Asmund said bluntly.

"I thought so, but—" Luthien tried to reply.

Asmund's laughter stopped him short.

"I claim victory!" Ethan growled.

Asmund abruptly stopped his laughing and stared hard at Ethan. "There is no dishonor in defeat at the hands of a skilled warrior," the Huegoth insisted. "And by my eyes, your brother is as skilled as you!"

Ethan lowered his gaze, then sighed deeply and turned to Luthien. "You tricked me twice," he said. "First in putting my blade between the rocks, and then by pretending to stumble."

"The stones were wet," Luthien protested. "Slick with weeds."

"You did not trip," Ethan said.

"No," Asmund agreed. "He fell because he thought it better to fall." The king laughed again at the incredulous expression that came over Luthien. "You would not kill Ethan," the keen leader explained. "And you held faith that he would not kill you. Yet if you defeated him, you feared that, though our agreement would be honored concerning the sword and the release of you and your friends, any chance of the greater good, of ending our raids along your coast, would be destroyed."

Luthien was truly at a loss. Asmund had seen through his ploy so easily and so completely! He had no answer and so he stood as calmly as he could manage and waited for the fierce king's judgment.

Ethan seemed more upset by it all than did Asmund. He, too, could not deny the truth of Asmund's perception. When *Blind-Striker* had gone into that crevice, Luthien had gained a seemingly insurmountable advantage, and then Luthien had fallen. In retrospect, Ethan had to admit that his brother, so balanced and so in command of his movements, could not have slipped at that critical moment.

Asmund spent a long while studying the pair. "You are the only Eriadorans I have come to know in heart," he said finally. "Brothers of a fine stock, I admit."

"Despite my intended slip?" Luthien dared to ask, and he relaxed more than a little when Asmund laughed again.

"Well done!" the king roared. "Had you beaten Ethan, your gain would have been your life and the lives of your two closest companions. And the sword, no small thing."

"But the price would have been too high," Luthien insisted. "For then our parley would have been ended, and Ethan's standing in your eyes might have been lessened."

"Would you die for Eriador?" Asmund asked.

"Of course."

"For Ethan, who we now name Vinndalf?"

"Of course."

The simple way Luthien answered struck Ethan profoundly, forced him to think back on his days in Dun Varna with his younger brother, a boy, then a man, he had always loved. Now Ethan was truly wounded, by his own actions, by the notion that he might have killed Luthien in their duel. How could he have ever let his rage get so much control over him?

"Would Ethan die for you?" Asmund asked.

"Yes, he would," Luthien replied, not even bothering to look to his brother for confirmation.

Asmund roared with laughter again. "I like you, Luthien Bedwyr, and I respect you, as I respect your brother."

"No more his brother," Ethan remarked before he could consider the words.

"Always," Asmund corrected. "If you were not his brother still, you would have claimed victory with your sword and not your mouth."

Ethan lowered his gaze.

"And I would have struck you dead!" Asmund yelled, coming forward, startling both Ethan and Luthien. The king calmed quickly and moved back into his chair. "When we earlier spoke, you claimed that we were not enemies," he prompted to Luthien.

"We are not," Luthien insisted. "Eriadorans fight Huegoths only when Huegoths attack Eriador. But there is a greater evil than any enmity between our peoples, I say, a stain upon the land—"

Asmund patted his hand in the empty air to stop the speech before

Luthien could get into the flow. "You need not convince me of the foulness of Avon's king," the Huegoth explained. "Your brother has told me of Greensparrow and I have witnessed his wickedness. The plague that swept Eriador was not confined to your borders."

"Isenland?" Luthien asked breathlessly.

Asmund shook his head. "It never reached our shores because those afflicted at sea daren't ever return," he explained. "Our priests discovered the source of the plague, and ever since, the name of Greensparrow has been a cursed thing.

"You were the best friend of Garth Rogar," the king said suddenly, changing the subject and catching Luthien off guard. "And Torin Rogar is among my closest of friends."

This was going quite well, Luthien dared to hope. He was certain that he, Oliver, and Katerin would be granted their freedom; now he wanted to take things to the next level.

"Garth Rogar was the only Huegoth I came to know in heart," he said. "Representative of a fine stock, I say!"

Again Asmund bellowed with laughter.

"We are not your enemy," Luthien said determinedly, drawing the king into a more serious mode.

"So you say," he remarked, leaning forward in his chair. "And is Greensparrow your enemy?"

Luthien realized that he was moving into uncharted ground here. His gut instinct told him to yell out "Yes," but formally, such a proclamation to a foreign king could turn into serious trouble.

"You hinted at an alliance between our peoples to wage war on Greensparrow," Asmund went on. "Such a treaty might be welcomed."

Luthien was at once hopeful and tentative. He wanted to respond, to promise, but he could not. Not yet.

Asmund watched his every movement: the way his hands clenched at his side, the way he started to say something, then bit back the words. "Go to your King Brind'Amour, Luthien Bedwyr," the Huegoth leader said. "Deliver to me within the month a formal treaty naming Greensparrow as our common enemy." Asmund sat back, smiling wryly. "We have come for war, in the name of our God and by his will," he proclaimed, a not-so-subtle reminder to Luthien that he was dealing with a fierce people here. "And so we shall fight. Deliver your treaty or our longships will lay waste to your eastern coast, as we had planned."

Luthien wanted to respond to that challenge as well, to counter the threat with the promise of many Eriadoran warships to defend against the Huegoths. Wisely, he let it pass. "A month?" he asked skeptically. "I can hardly get to Caer MacDonald and back within the month. A week to Gybi—"

"Three days in a longship," Asmund corrected.

"And ten days of hard riding," Luthien added, trying not to think of the suffering the galley slaves would surely know in delivering him so far, so fast.

"I will send your brother to Gybi to serve as emissary," Asmund conceded.

"Send him to Chalmbers, directly west of here," Luthien asked. "A shorter ride on my return from Caer MacDonald."

Asmund nodded. "A month, Luthien Bedwyr, and not a day more!"

Luthien was out of arguments.

With that, Asmund dismissed him and Ethan, who was charged with making the arrangements to deliver Luthien, Katerin, Oliver, and Brother Jamesis back to the Eriadoran mainland. The other fifty Eriadorans were to remain as prisoners, but Luthien did manage to get a promise that they would not be mistreated and would be released if and when the treaty was delivered.

Within the hour, the ship was ready to depart. Luthien's three companions were on board, but the young Bedwyr lingered behind, needing a private moment with his brother.

Ethan seemed truly uncomfortable, embarrassed by the entire situation, of his choices and of his role in the Huegoth raids.

"I did not know," he admitted. "I thought that all was as it had been, that Greensparrow still ruled in Eriador."

"An apology?" Luthien asked.

"An explanation," Ethan replied. "And nothing more. I do not control the actions of my Huegoth brothers. Far from it. They only tolerate me because I have shown skill and courage, and because of the tale of Garth Rogar."

"I did go south to find you," Luthien said.

Ethan nodded, and seemed appreciative of that fact. "But I never went to the south," he replied. "Gahris commanded me to go to Port Charley, then to sail to Carlisle, where I would be given a rank of minor importance in the Avon army and sent to the Kingdom of Duree."

"To battle beside the Gascon army in their war," Luthien put in, for he knew well the tale.

Ethan nodded. "To battle, and likely to die, in that distant kingdom. But I would not accept that banishment and so chose one of my own instead."

"With the Huegoths?" Luthien was incredulous.

Ethan shook his head and smiled. "Land's End," he corrected. "I went south from Bedwydrin for a while, then turned east, through MacDonald's Swath. My destination became Gybi, where I paid handsomely for transport, in secret, to the Isle of Colonsey. I believed that I could live out my life quietly in Land's End. They ask few questions there."

"But the Huegoths came and crushed the settlement," Luthien accused, and his voice turned grim as he spoke of the probable deaths of many Eriadorans.

Ethan shook his head and stopped his brother's errant reasoning. "Land's End remains intact to this day," Ethan replied. "Not a single man or woman of that settlement has been injured or captured."

"Then how?"

"My boat never got there, for it was swamped in a storm," Ethan explained. "The Huegoths pulled me from the sea; chance alone put them in my path, and it was simple chance, simple good fortune, that the captain of the longship was Torin Rogar."

Luthien rested back on his heels and spent a long moment digesting the story. "Good fortune for you," he said. "And for Eriador, it would seem."

"I am pleased by what you have told me of our Eriador," Ethan said, unstrapping *Blind-Striker* and handing it back to Luthien. "And I am proud of you, Luthien Bedwyr. It is right that you should wear the sword of family Bedwyr." Ethan's face grew grim and uncompromising. "But understand that I am Huegoth now," he said, "and not of your family. Deliver your treaty to my king or we—and I—will fight you."

Luthien knew that the words were a promise, not a threat, and he believed that promise.

CHAPTER 11

POLITICS

INCREDIBLY, LESS THAN TWO WEEKS after leaving the Huegoth encampment in Colonsey, Luthien and Oliver had the great Ministry of Caer MacDonald in sight. They had covered hundreds of miles, by sea and by land, and Riverdancer and Threadbare were haggard. Katerin had not returned with them; rather, she had gone south from Gybi by longship, with Ethan and Brother Jamesis, headed for the Eriadoran port city of Chalmbers.

"The journey back should be easier," Luthien remarked to his exhausted companion. "We shall use Brind'Amour's magics to cross the land. Perhaps our king will accompany us, wishing to sign the treaty personally with Asmund of Isenland."

Oliver grimaced at the young Bedwyr's continued optimism. All along the journey, the halfling had tried to calm Luthien down, had tried to temper that bubbly optimism with some very real obstacles that Luthien apparently was not counting on. So far, Oliver had tried to be subtle, and apparently it wasn't working.

He pulled Threadbare up short, and Luthien did likewise with Riverdancer, sidling up to the halfling, following Oliver's gaze to the great cathedral. He figured that Oliver just wanted a moment with the spectacular view of this city that had become their home.

"Brind'Amour will not agree," Oliver said bluntly.

Luthien nearly toppled from his mount, sat staring open-mouthed at his diminutive companion.

"My bumpkin-type friend," the halfling explained, "there is a little matter of a treaty."

Luthien thought Oliver was referring to the pending treaty with Asmund. Was the halfling saying that Brind'Amour would never agree to terms with the Huegoths? The young Bedwyr moved to argue the logic, but Oliver merely rolled his eyes and gave Threadbare a kick, and the skinny yellow pony trotted on.

The two friends stood before Brind'Amour in the audience room at the Ministry within the hour, with Luthien happily spilling the details of the Huegoth advance, and the potential for a truce. The old wizard who was Eriador's king beamed at the news that the Huegoths were not in league with Greensparrow, but that wide smile gradually diminished, and Brind'Amour spent more time looking at worldly Oliver than at Luthien, as the young Bedwyr's full tale began to unfold.

"And all we need do is deliver the treaty within the month to King Asmund," Luthien finished, oblivious to the grim mood about him. "And Greensparrow be damned!"

If the young Bedwyr expected Brind'Amour to turn cartwheels in joy, he was sorely disappointed. The king of Eriador eased back in his great chair, rubbing his white beard, his eyes staring into empty air.

"Should I pen a draft for you?" Luthien asked hopefully, though he was beginning to catch on that something was surely amiss here.

Brind'Amour looked at him directly. "If you do, you must also pen a fitting explanation to our Gascon allies," he replied.

Luthien didn't seem to understand. He looked to Oliver, who only shrugged and reminded him again that there was a treaty that might get in the way.

Suddenly Luthien understood that Oliver hadn't been doubting the potential treaty between Brind'Amour and Asmund, but about a treaty that had already been signed.

"Nothing is ever as easy as a bumpkin-type would think," the halfling said dryly.

Luthien decided that he would have to speak to Oliver about that bumpkin reference, but this was neither the time nor the place.

"There is a matter of a treaty signed by myself and the duchess of Mannington, acting on King Greensparrow's behalf," Brind'Amour clarified, taking up the halfling's argument. "We are not at war with Avon, and our truce does not include a provision for acceptable invasions."

The sarcasm stung Luthien profoundly. He understood the pragmatism of it all, of course, but in his mind Greensparrow had already broken the treaty many times over. "Sougles's Glen," he said grimly. "And Menster. Have you forgotten?"

Brind'Amour came forward at once, eyes gleaming. "I have not!" he yelled, the sheer strength of his voice forcing Luthien back a step. The old wizard calmed at once and eased himself to a straight posture. "Cyclopian raids, both," Brind'Amour said.

"But we know that Greensparrow was behind them," Luthien replied, full of determination, full of frustrated rage.

"What is known and what can be proven are oft two very different things," Oliver remarked.

"True enough," agreed the king. "And on strictly moral grounds, I agree with you," he said to Luthien. "I have no discomfort with the morality of launching a war, with Huegoth allies, against the king of Avon. Politically, though, we would be inviting complete disaster. Any attack on Avon would not rest well with the lords of Gascony, for it would disrupt their trade with both our kingdoms and make a mockery of their aid to us, playing the role of victims, in the previous war. They would not help us this time, I fear. They might even offer some warships to Greensparrow, that the war, and particularly the Huegoth threat, be quickly ended."

Luthien clenched his fists at his sides. He looked to Oliver, who only shrugged, and then back to Brind'Amour, though he was so angry that he was viewing a wall of red more than any distinct forms. "If we do not ally with Asmund," he said slowly, emphasizing each word, "then we will be forced into a war with the Huegoths."

Brind'Amour agreed with the assessment, nodding and then giving a small chuckle. "The ultimate irony," he replied. "Might it be that Eriador will join in common cause with Avon against the Huegoths?"

Luthien rocked back on his heels.

"Oh, yes," Brind'Amour assured him. "While you were on the road, King Greensparrow's emissary reached out to me, begging alliance against the troublesome barbarians of Isenland."

"But what of Menster?" Luthien protested. "And what of Sougles's Glen, and all the other massacres perpetrated by—"

"By the one-eyes," Oliver interrupted. "My pardon," he quickly added, seeing Luthien's dangerous glower, "I am but playing the role of the Gascon ambassador."

"Cyclopians prompted by Greensparrow!" Luthien growled back at him.

"You know that and I know that," Oliver replied, "but the Gascons, they are another matter."

"Oliver plays the role well," Brind'Amour remarked.

Luthien sighed deeply, trying to calm his rising ire.

"Greensparrow has prompted the raids," the Eriadoran king said to soothe him.

"Greensparrow will never accept Eriador free," Luthien replied.

"So be it," said Brind'Amour. "We will deal with him as we can. While you were gone, our forces were not idle. Siobhan and the Cutters have been working with King Bellick dan Burso's dwarfs, and have discovered the whereabouts of a large cyclopian encampment."

"So we ally with Greensparrow against the Huegoths at sea, while we fight against his allies in the mountains," Luthien said distastefully.

"I told you that you would not so much enjoy politics," Oliver remarked.

"As of now, I don't know what we shall do," Brind'Amour answered. "But there are many considerations to every action when one speaks for an entire kingdom."

"Surely we will attack the cyclopians," Luthien said.

"That we shall," Brind'Amour was glad to assure him. "I do not believe that our Gascon allies would protest any war between Eriador and the cyclopians."

"One-eyes, ptooey!" spat Oliver. "In Gascony, we consider a cyclopian eye an archery target."

Luthien was far from satisfied, but he realized that he was involved in something much bigger than his personal desires. He would have to be satisfied; at least he might soon get the chance to exact revenge for the folk of Menster.

But there was something deeper tugging at his sensibilities as he and Oliver exited the audience room in search of Siobhan. He had just over two weeks remaining to deliver the treaty or Eriador would be at war once more with the Huegoths—and Luthien would be at war with his own brother.

Oliver kept beside his sullen friend for the rest of the day, from a long quiet stay at the Dwelf to a walk along the city's outer wall. Luthien wasn't speaking much and Oliver didn't press him, figuring that the young man had to get through all the shocks—Ethan siding with the Huegoths and the reality of political intrigue—on his own.

Shortly before sunset, with news that Siobhan would be back in the city that night, Luthien's face brightened suddenly. In looking at him, Oliver understood that the young man had come up with yet another plan. Hopefully a better-informed course of action than his previous ideas, Oliver prayed.

"Do you think that Brind'Amour would ally with the Huegoths if Greensparrow was first to break the treaty?" Luthien asked.

Oliver shrugged noncommittaly. "I can think of better allies than slavers," he said. "But if the gain was the potential downfall of King Greensparrow, then I think he might be convinced." Oliver eyed Luthien, and particularly, Luthien's wry smile, suspiciously for a short while. "You have an idea to entice Greensparrow into action against Eriador?" the halfling asked. "You think you can get him to break the treaty?"

Luthien shook his head. "Greensparrow already has broken the treaty," he insisted, "merely by inciting the cyclopians against us. All we need to do is get proof of that conspiracy—and quickly."

"And how do you mean to accomplish such a task?" Oliver wanted to know.

"We will go to the source," Luthien explained. "Siobhan will return this night with information about the cyclopian encampment. No doubt Brind'Amour will order action against that band immediately. All we have to do is get there first and get our proof."

Oliver was too surprised to find any immediate response. Vividly, though, the halfling didn't miss Luthien's reference to "we."

CHAPTER 12

LIVING PROOF

*L*UTHIEN AND OLIVER eased up side by side toward the top of the boulder. They could hear the bustle of the cyclopian encampment below, in a stony clearing surrounded by pines, boulders, and cliff walls. Luthien glanced to the side as he neared the rim, then moved quickly to pull the wide-brimmed hat from Oliver's head.

Oliver started to cry out in protest, but Luthien anticipated such a reaction and put his hand over the halfling's mouth, motioning with the other hand for Oliver to remain quiet.

"I tell you once to give me back my hat," the halfling whispered.

Luthien handed it over.

"And for you," the halfling went on, "and your woman friend," he added quickly, recalling all the times Katerin had also so bullied him, "if you ever put your dirty hand over my mouth again, I will bite you hard."

Luthien put his finger to pursed lips, then pointed in the direction of the cyclopian encampment.

Up rose the pair, Luthien merely extending to his full height, Oliver having to find one more foothold. They eased over the boulder's rim together, looking down on their adversaries. From this angle, the camp seemed almost surreal, too vivid with its brightness against the backdrop of the dark night. The companions spotted several small campfires, but these could not account for the almost daylight brilliance within the encampment, or for the fact that the light had not been so visible from any other vantage point, as though it was somehow contained within the perimeter of the camp.

Luthien immediately understood that magic had to be its source, but he knew that cyclopians did not use magic. The one-eyed brutes certainly were not smart enough to unravel the mysteries of the magical arts.

But Luthien could not deny what he saw. Everything in the clearing, the scores of cyclopians milling about, the uneven shapes of the many stones, the rack of weapons against the cliff wall opposite his perch, was vividly clear, stark in outline.

Luthien looked to Oliver, who only shrugged, similarly mystified. "Cyclopian wizard?" the halfling mouthed.

Both turned back to the encampment and found their answer as a broad-shouldered, large-bellied man walked into view, laughing cheerily

as he talked with a large cyclopian. He wore a dark-colored tabard, richly
embroidered, that hung to his knees. Even from this distance, Luthien
could see the sheen on his hose, indicating that they were silk, or some
other exotic and expensive material, and the buckles of his shoes
gleamed as only the purest silver could.

"I count two eyes on that one," Oliver whispered.

Luthien was nodding. He didn't recognize the man, but the presence
of magic and the rich, regal dressings led him to believe that he could
guess the man's title. This was one of Greensparrow's dukes; this was all
the proof that Brind'Amour would need.

The man, laughing still, clapped his cyclopian companion hard on
the back, then reached up and put a fur-trimmed cap with a golden insignia sewn into its front atop his thick gray hair. Another cyclopian
came by and handed him a huge mug, which he lifted to his beardless
face and nearly drained in one gulp.

Some of the contents spilled out, running down the man's considerable jowls, and the cyclopian burst out in laughter. The man followed
suit, roaring wildly.

"Brind'Amour will laugh louder than he when we deliver this one to
Caer MacDonald," Luthien whispered.

"How are we to get to him?" Oliver asked the obvious question. If this
was indeed a wizard, then capturing him in the impending battle would
be near to impossible.

Luthien smiled wryly and held out the edge of his marvelous crimson
cape. The Crimson Shadow could get into that encampment unde-
tected, no matter how bright the light!

"You mean to sneak in and steal him away?" Oliver asked incredulously.

"We can do it," Luthien replied.

Oliver groaned softly, rolled over to put his back against the boulder,
and slumped down from the rim. "Why is it always 'we'?" he asked. "Perhaps you should find another to go with you."

"But Oliver," Luthien protested, coming down beside his friend, his
smile still wide, "you are the only one who will fit under the cape."

"Oh, lucky Oliver," grumbled the halfling.

They moved away from the camp, to inform the nearest elves of their
plan. More than two hundred dwarfs were in the area, along with the
forty elves and half-elves, including Siobhan, that now comprised the
spying band known as the Cutters. The original plan was to go in hard
and fast under the cries of "Sougles's Glen!" and slaughter every cyclopian. Luthien, with help from Siobhan, had convinced the fierce dwarfs

otherwise, had shown them the potential for greater good by exercising restraint until the proof they needed could be found.

Luthien and Oliver were back at their high perch soon after, waiting for the majority of one-eyes to drift off to sleep, or at least for the light to go down somewhat. An hour passed, then another. The sliver of the waning moon moved low in the western sky, and was soon swallowed up by turbulent black clouds. The rumble of distant thunder tingled under their feet.

The man Luthien had targeted as a duke continued to laugh and to drink, sitting about a fire, throwing bones with a handful of brutish cyclopians. Even with the magical cape, there was no way that Luthien could get near to him without a fight.

But then came a break. The man belched loudly and stood up, brushing the dust and twigs from his tabard. He drained the rest of his mug, belched again, and walked away, toward the perimeter of the encampment, just to the right and below the watching companions.

"Whatever goes in . . ." Oliver whispered.

He and Luthien slipped down the back side of the boulder and crept along in the darkness, inching their way in the general direction to intercept the man. Soon they were following a steady stream of sound, and spotted the man standing beside a tree, supporting himself with one hand, while the other held up the front of his tabard. He was fully twenty yards from the encampment, with most of that distance blocked by tangled trees and shrubs.

"Do not get too close," Oliver warned. "It seems that he has a missile weapon."

Luthien stifled a nervous chuckle and inched his way in. He froze as he stepped on one stick, which cracked apart loudly. Oliver froze in place, too, a horrified expression on his face.

The companions soon realized that they had nothing to worry about. The drunken man was oblivious to them, though he was barely ten feet away. Luthien considered his options. If he rushed up and punched hard but did not lay the man low, his cry would surely alert the cyclopians. Certainly Luthien couldn't strike with his sword, for he wanted the man alive.

The threat should suffice, Luthien decided, and with a look about for Oliver, who was suddenly not to be seen, the young Bedwyr drew out *Blind-Striker*. Luthien couldn't dare call out for his missing halfling friend, so he took a deep and steadying breath, rushed the last few feet, and lifted his blade up before the man's face.

"Silence!" Luthien instructed in a harsh whisper, bringing the finger of his free hand to pursed lips.

The man looked at him curiously and continued his business, as though the possibility of capture hadn't yet occurred to him.

Luthien wagged the blade in the air. The man, startled from his stupor, widened his eyes suddenly and straightened. Thinking that he was about to cry out, Luthien lunged forward, meaning to put his swordtip right to the man's throat.

But the man was faster, his motion simpler. His hand moved from the tree and in a single arc, yanked a talisman from his tabard and swished in a downward swipe. A field of shimmering blue came up before him.

Luthien's momentum was too great for him to react. *Blind-Striker's* tip hit the field and threw sparks, and the sword was violently repelled, flying back over Luthien's head, yanking his arm painfully. Luthien, though, was still moving forward, and he, too, couldn't avoid the shield. He yelped and rolled his shoulder defensively, barely brushing the bluish light. But that was all the repelling magic needed, and the young Bedwyr found himself flying backward, off his feet, to crash into the trees.

The jolly wizard's laugh was stifled before it ever began, as he felt a sting in his belly. He looked down to see Oliver, standing on his side of the repelling field, rapier drawn and poking.

"Aha!" said the halfling. "I have gone around your silly magics and am inside your so clever barrier." Oliver's beaming expression suddenly turned sour and he looked down. "And my so fine shoes are wet!" he wailed.

The man moved fast; so did Oliver, meaning to stick him more forcefully. But to the halfling's horror, a single word from the wizard transformed his rapier blade into a living serpent, and it immediately turned back on him!

And the wizard's huge and strong hands were coming for him as well! Right for his throat.

Oliver cried out and threw his rapier over his head, then moved to dodge. The attack never came, though, for the blade-turned-serpent struck the repelling shield and rebounded straight out, hitting the wizard square in the face. Now it was Duke Resmore's turn to cry out, reaching frantically for the writhing snake.

Oliver darted between the man's legs, turned about and grabbed the edges of his tabard. Up the halfling scrambled, taking the serpent's place as the man threw it to the ground. Oliver grabbed on to one ear for support, and the man's head jerked backward, his mouth opening to cry out. Oliver promptly stuffed his free hand into that mouth.

Luthien came around the edge of the shield, *Blind-Striker* in hand. Some of the cyclopians the duke had left behind were heading in their direction and calling out the name of "Resmore." They had to go, and quickly, Luthien knew, and if this wizard, Resmore, would not cooperate, Luthien meant to strike him dead.

"My gauntlets, they are leather, yes?" Oliver asked.

"Yes."

"But he is biting right through them!" Oliver squealed. Out came the hand, and the wizard-duke wasted no time.

"A'ta'arrefi!" he cried.

Barely twenty yards away, a host of cyclopians cried out.

Two running strides brought Luthien up to the man, and a solid right cross to the jaw dropped him where he stood, forcing Oliver to leap away, rolling in the twigs.

"One-eyes!" the halfling groaned as he came up, but he found some hope when he spotted his rapier, the blade whole again. "Take his silly cap, and let us go!"

Luthien shook the pains out of his bruised hand and moved to comply, realizing that the insignia on that cap might suffice. He stopped, though, as Oliver spoke again.

"Do you smell what I smell?" the halfling asked.

Luthien paused, and indeed he did, an all-too-familiar odor. Sulfurous, noxious. The young Bedwyr looked to Oliver, then turned to follow Oliver's gaze, back over his shoulder, to a spinning ball of orange flames, quickly taking the shape of a bipedal canine with goatlike horns atop its head and eyes that blazed with the red hue of demonic fires.

"Oh, not again," the beleaguered halfling moaned.

The monster's howl split the night.

"Let me guess," Oliver said dryly. "You are A'ta'arrefi?"

The creature was not large, no more than four feet from head to tail, but its aura, that sensation of might that surrounded every demon, was nearly overwhelming. Luthien and Oliver had battled enough of the fiends to know that they were in serious trouble, a fact made all the more obvious when A'ta'arrefi opened wide its fanged maw, wide enough, it seemed, to swallow Oliver whole!

Above them all, a bolt of lightning crackled through the rushing black clouds, a fitting touch, it seemed, to this hellish scenario. The sudden light showed the companions that cyclopians were all about them now, fanning out in the woods and keeping a respectable distance, whispering that this was the Crimson Shadow.

Luthien hardly gave the brutes a thought, focusing, as he had to, on the caninelike demon.

Out of that huge maw came a forked tongue, a hissing bark, and A'ta'arrefi, with speed that stunned the companions, leaped forward, dancing in the unholy symphony of the angry storm.

Oliver screamed. Luthien did, too, and raised *Blind-Striker,* though he knew that he could not be quick enough to intercept the charge.

And then he was blinded, and so was Oliver, and so were the cyclopians, as a lightning stroke came down right in front of him. Luthien felt his muscles jerking wildly, felt his hair dancing, and realized that he had been lifted right off the ground by the terrific impact. Somehow he came back down on his feet and held his tentative balance, though he soon enough realized that, with the demon charging, he might have been wiser to fall to the side.

But the expected attack never came, and Luthien heard before he saw, that battle had been joined in the woods about him. He heard the twang of elvish bows, the thunder of a dwarven charge, the cries of surprised and quickly dying cyclopians.

Finally, Luthien's vision cleared, and he saw that A'ta'arrefi was no more—no more than a blackened forked tongue lying on the ground at Luthien's feet.

As abrupt as the lightning bolt came the downpour, a torrent of rain hissing through the trees. Luthien pulled the hood of his crimson cape over his head, purely an instinctual movement, made with hardly a thought, for the young man was surely dazed.

Resmore's groan brought Luthien back to the situation at hand. He shook the dizziness from his head and turned to the prone duke. He couldn't stifle a burst of laughter as he spotted Oliver, sitting beside the man, the halfling's usually curly hair straightened and standing on end.

"Boom," the foppish halfling muttered and toppled to lie across the duke. The jarring woke the man.

Luthien skidded down atop him to hold him in place.

"I will deliver you personally to King Greensparrow," the dazed and drunken Resmore slurred.

Luthien slugged him again to silence him, and when the man went still, Luthien lay atop the pile, spreading his shielding crimson cape to hide them all. He wanted to get up and join in the fight, but he understood the importance of his inaction, both to safeguard his all-valuable prisoner and to ensure that the magic-wielder could not wake up again and get into the fray.

Besides, Luthien soon realized, it was all going the way of the dwarfs and elves. Vengeance fueled the chopping axes and pounding hammers, and none could fight better in the darkness than elves, and none were better with deadly bows. The cyclopians had been caught by surprise, and even worse for them, they had been sitting within a brightly lit encampment and were now perfectly blind to the night. •

Luthien thought he would have to fight, though, when he heard one terrified one-eye come rushing out of the brush, sloshing through the growing mud puddles, running straight for the unseen pile of bodies. The young Bedwyr turned slowly, so as not to give up the camouflage, and he spotted the cyclopian, looking back desperately over its shoulder, at about the same instant it ran smack into Resmore's repelling shield.

Back the one-eye flew, meeting up with a pair of dwarfs as they burst out of the brush.

"I didn't think he'd have the guts to charge!" one of the dwarfs roared, coming to his feet and promptly bringing his axe into the stunned cyclopian's backbone.

"Nor did myself!" howled the other, caving in the one-eye's skull with his heavy hammer.

"His children should be proud!" the first dwarf proclaimed.

"His children should be orphans!" cried the second, and off they ran, happily, looking for more one-eyes to smack.

Luthien eased his head back down, shifted himself more completely under the cape. It was better to stay out of this one, he decided.

CHAPTER 13

EVIDENCE AND ERROR PAST

THE RETURN TO CAER MACDONALD was heralded by cries of vengeance sated and by trumpets blowing triumphantly along the city's walls. Word of their victory had preceded Luthien and his forces, as well as the whispers that a wizard, one of Avon's dukes, had been captured in the battle.

Luthien and Oliver flanked Resmore every step of the way, with weapons drawn and ready. The duke hadn't said much; not a word, in fact, other than a stream of threats, invoking the name of Greensparrow often, as though that alone should send his captors into a fit of trembling. He was tightly bound, and often gagged, but even with that, Luthien held *Blind-Striker* dangerously near to the man's throat, for the young Bedwyr, more experienced than he wanted to be with the likes of wizard-dukes, would take no chances with this man. Luthien had no desire to face A'ta'arrefi, or any other demon again, nor would he let Resmore, his proof that Greensparrow was not honoring the truce, get away.

Men, women, and many, many children lined the avenues as the victorious procession entered Caer MacDonald. Siobhan and Shuglin led the way, with the elvish Cutters in a line behind their leader, and twenty dwarfs following Shuglin. In the middle of this powerful force walked Luthien, Oliver, and their most valuable prisoner. Another score of dwarfs took up the rear, closely guarding the dozen ragged cyclopian prisoners. If the bearded folk had been given their way, all the cyclopians would have been slaughtered in the mountains, but Luthien and Siobhan had convinced them that prisoners might prove crucial now, for all the politics of the land. Aside from these forty soldiers returning to Caer MacDonald, the rest of the bearded folk, along with another dozen cyclopian prisoners, had remained in the Iron Cross, making their way to DunDarrow to bring word of the victory to King Bellick dan Burso.

Cheers accompanied the procession every step along the main way of Caer MacDonald; many tossed silver coins or offered fine wine or ale, or plates heaped with food.

Oliver basked in the moment, even standing atop his pony's back at one point, dipping a low bow, his great hat sweeping. Luthien tried to remain vigilant and stoic, but couldn't contain his smile. At the front of the column, though, Siobhan and Shuglin paid the crowd little heed. These two exemplified the suffering of their respective races at the hands of Greensparrow. Shuglin's folk, those who had been caught, had long been enslaved, working as craftsmen for the elite ruling and merchant classes until they outlived their usefulness, or gave their masters some excuse to send them to torturous labor in the mines. Siobhan's folk had fared no better in the last two decades. Elves were not numerous in Avonsea—most had fled the isles for parts unknown many years before Greensparrow's rise—but those who were caught during the reign of the evil king were given to wealthy homes as servants and concubines. Siobhan, with blood that was neither purely elven nor purely human, was on the lowest rung of all in Greensparrow's racial hierarchy, and had spent many years in the service of a merchant tyrant who had beaten and raped her at will.

So these two were not smiling, and would not rejoice. For Luthien, victory had come when Eriador was declared free; for Shuglin and Siobhan, victory meant the head of Greensparrow, staked up high on a pole.

Nothing less.

King Brind'Amour met them in the plaza surrounding the Ministry. Purposefully, the king made his way past Siobhan and Shuglin, holding up his hand to indicate that they should wait to tell their tale. Down the line he went, his eyes locked on one man in particular, and he stopped when he came face-to-face with the prisoner.

Brind'Amour reached up and pulled the gag from the man's mouth.

"He is a wizard," Luthien warned.

"His name is Resmore," Oliver added.

"One of Greensparrow's dukes?" Brind'Amour asked the man, but Resmore merely "harrumphed" indignantly and lifted his fat face in defiance.

"He wore this," Oliver explained, handing the expensive cap over to his king. "It was not so much a trick for me to take it from him."

Luthien's sour expression was not unexpected, and Oliver purposefully kept his gaze fixed on his king.

Brind'Amour took the hat and turned it in his hands, studying the emblem: a ship's prow carved into the likeness of a rearing stallion, nostrils flared, eyes wild. "Newcastle," the Eriadoran king said calmly. "You are Duke Resmore of Newcastle."

"Friend of Greensparrow, who is king of all Avonsea!" a flustered Resmore replied.

"And king of Gascony, I am so sure," Oliver added sarcastically.

"Not by treaty," Brind'Amour reminded Resmore calmly, the old wizard smiling at the duke's slip. "Our agreement proclaims Greensparrow as king of Avon and Brind'Amour as king of Eriador. Or is it that you deem the treaty immaterial?"

Resmore was sweating visibly now, realizing his error. "I only meant . . ." he stammered, and then he stopped. He took a deep breath to steady himself and lifted his chin proudly once more. "You have no right to hold me," he declared.

"You were captured fairly," Oliver remarked. "By me."

"Unlawfully!" Resmore protested. "I was in the mountains, by all rights, in land neutral to our respective kingdoms!"

"You were on the Eriadoran side of the Iron Cross," Brind'Amour reminded him. "Not twenty miles from Caer MacDonald."

"I know of no provisions in our treaty that would prevent—" Resmore began.

"You were with the cyclopians," Luthien promptly interrupted.

"Again, by word of the treaty—"

"Damn your treaty!" Luthien shouted, though Brind'Amour tried to calm him. "The one-eyes have been raiding our villages, murdering innocents, even children. At the prompting of your wretched king, I say!"

A hundred voices lifted in accord with the young Bedwyr's proclamation, but Brind'Amour's was not among them. Again the king of Eriador, skilled in matters politic, worked hard to quiet them all, fearing that a mob would form and his prisoners would be hanged before he could gather his evidence.

"Since when do one-eyes need the prompting of a human king to raid and pillage?" Resmore sarcastically asked.

"We can prove that this very band you were captured beside was among those participating in raids," Brind'Amour said.

"Of which I know nothing," Resmore replied coolly. "I have only been with them a few days, and they have not left the mountains in that time—until you illegally descended upon them. Who is the raider now?"

Brind'Amour's blue eyes flared dangerously at that last remark. "Pretty words, Duke Resmore," he said grimly. "But worthless, I assure you. Magic was used in the massacre known as Sougles's Glen; its tracings can still be felt by those attuned to such powers."

Brind'Amour's not-so-subtle proclamation that he, too, was a wizard seemed to unnerve the man more than a little.

"Your role in the attacks can be proven," Brind'Amour went on, "and a wizard's neck is no more resistant to the rope than is a peasant's."

The mob exploded with screams for the man's death, by hanging or burning, or whatever method could be quickly expedited. Many seemed ready to break ranks and beat the man. Brind'Amour would hear none of it, though. He motioned for Luthien and the others to take Resmore and the cyclopians into the Ministry, where they were put into separate dungeons. Resmore was assigned two personal guards, elves, who were quite sensitive to magic, who stood over the man continually, swords drawn and ready.

"We should thank you for your role in the capture," Luthien remarked to Brind'Amour, walking the passageways along the smaller side rooms in the great structure beside Oliver and their king.

"Oh yes," Oliver piped in. "A so-very-fine shot!"

Brind'Amour slowed enough to stare at his companions, his expression showing that he did not understand.

"In the mountains," Luthien clarified. "When Resmore called in his demon."

"You faced yet another hellish fiend?" Brind'Amour asked.

"Until your so booming bolt of lightning," Oliver replied. "On came the beast for Luthien—he would not approach my rapier blade, you see."

"A'ta'arrefi, the demon was called," Luthien interrupted, not willing to hear Oliver's always-skewed perspective.

Still Brind'Amour seemed not to understand.

"He resembled a dog," Luthien added, "though he walked upright, as a man."

"And his tongue was forked," Oliver added, and it took the halfling's two companions a moment to decipher that last word, which Oliver's thick Gascon accent made sound as though it were two separate words, "for-ked." The halfling's gesture helped in the translation, for he put two wiggling fingers up in front of his mouth.

Brind'Amour shrugged.

"Your lightning bolt," Luthien insisted. "It could not have been mere chance!"

"Say it plainly, my boy," the wizard begged.

"Resmore's demon ran for us," Luthien replied. "He was but five paces from me when the storm broke, a sting of lightning rushing down."

"Boom!" Oliver yelled. "Right on the head."

"And all that was left of A'ta'arrefi was his blackened tongue," said Luthien.

"For-ked," Oliver finished.

Brind'Amour rubbed his white beard briskly. He had no idea of what the two were talking about, for he hadn't even been looking that way; Brind'Amour had been so engrossed with events in the east and south that he had no idea Luthien and Oliver had even gone into the mountains with Siobhan, let alone that they were facing a demon! Still, it seemed perfectly impossible to him that the lightning bolt was a natural accident. Luthien and Oliver were lucky indeed, but that was too far-fetched. Obviously a wizard had been involved. Perhaps it was even Greensparrow himself, aiming for Luthien and hitting Resmore's fiend by mistake. "Yes, of course," was all that he said to the two. "A fine shot, that. Demons are easy targets, though; stand out among mortals like a giant among halflings."

Luthien managed a weak smile, not convinced that Brind'Amour was speaking truthfully. The young Bedwyr had no other explanation, though, and so he let it go at that. If there was something amiss, magically speaking, then it would be Brind'Amour's concern, and not his own.

"Come," the wizard bade, moving down a side passage. "We have perhaps found the link between Greensparrow and the cyclopians, thus our treaty with Avon may be deemed void. Let us draw up the truce with King Asmund of Isenland and begin to lay our plans."

"We will fight Greensparrow?" Luthien asked bluntly.

"I do not yet know," Brind'Amour replied. "I must speak with our prisoners, and with the ambassador from Gascony. There is much to do before any final decisions can be made."

Of course there was, Luthien realized, but the young Bedwyr held faith then that he would not be battling against his brother. Greensparrow's treacherous hand had been revealed in full; Resmore was all the proof they needed. Visions of sailing the fleet up the Stratton into Carlisle beside the Huegoth longships danced in Luthien's mind.

It was not an unpleasant fantasy.

Brind'Amour entered the dimly lit room solemnly, wearing his rich blue wizard robes. Candles burned softly from pedestals in each of the room's corners. In the center was a small round table and a single stool.

Brind'Amour took his place on the stool. With trembling hands, he reached up and removed the cloth draped over the single object on the table, his crystal ball. It was with trepidation and nervous excitement that the wizard began his incantation. Brind'Amour didn't believe that Greensparrow had launched a bolt for Luthien that had accidentally destroyed Resmore's familiar demon. In lieu of that, the old wizard could think of only one explanation for Luthien's incredible tale: one of his fellows from the ancient brotherhood of wizards had awakened and joined in the effort. What else might explain the lightning bolt?

The wizard fell into his trance, sent his sight through the ball, into the mountains, across the width and breadth of Eriador, then across the borders of time itself.

"Brind'Amour?"

The question came from far away, but was insistent.

"Brind'Amour?"

"Serendie?" the old wizard asked, thinking he had at last found one of his fellows, a jolly chap who had been among his closest of friends.

"Luthien," came the distant reply.

Brind'Amour searched his memory, trying to remember which wizard went by that vaguely familiar name. He felt a touch on his shoulder, and then was shaken.

Brind'Amour came out of his trance to find that he was in his divining room at the Ministry, with Luthien and Oliver standing beside him. He yawned and stretched, thoroughly drained from his night's work.

"What time?" he asked.

"The cock has crowed," Oliver remarked, "has eaten his morning meal, put a smile on the beaks of a few hen-types, and is probably settled for his afternoon nap!"

"We wondered where you were," Luthien explained.

"So where were you?" Oliver asked.

Brind'Amour snorted at the halfling's perceptive question. He had been physically in this room—all the night and half the day it would seem—but in truth, he had visited many places. A frown creased his face as he considered those journeys now. The last of them, to the isle of Dulsen-Berra, central of the Five Sentinels, haunted him. The vision the crystal ball had given him was somewhere back in time, though how long ago he could not tell. He saw cyclopians scaling the rocky hills of the island. Then he saw their guide: a man he recognized, though he was not as fat and thick-jowled as he was now, a man Brind'Amour now held captive in the dungeons of this very building!

In the vision, Resmore carried an unusual object, a forked rod, a divining stick. So-called "witches" of the more remote villages of Avonsea, and all across wild Baranduine, used such an object to find water. Normally a divining rod was a form of the very least magic, but this time, Resmore's rod had been truly enchanted. Guided by it, Resmore and his one-eyed cronies had found a secret glen and the blocked entrance to a cave. Several wards exploded, killing more than a few cyclopians, but there were more than enough of the brutes to complete the task. Soon enough, the cave mouth was opened and the brutes rushed in. They returned to Resmore in the grassy glen, dragging a stiff body behind them. It was Duparte, dear Duparte, another of Brind'Amour's closest friends, who had helped Brind'Amour in the construction of the Ministry and had taught so many Eriadoran fisherfolk the ways of the dangerous dorsal whales.

All the long night Brind'Amour had suffered such scenes of murder as his fellows were routed from their places of magical sleep. All the long night he had seen Resmore and Greensparrow, Morkney and Paragor, and one other wizard he did not know, flush out his helpless, sleeping fellows and destroy them.

Brind'Amour shuddered visibly, and Luthien put a comforting hand on his shoulder.

"They are all dead, I fear," Brind'Amour said quietly.

"Who?" Oliver asked, looking around nervously.

"The ancient brotherhood," the old wizard replied—and he truly seemed old at that moment! "Only I, who spent so long enacting magical wards against intrusion, seem to have escaped the treachery of Greensparrow."

"You witnessed all of their deaths?" Luthien asked incredulously, look-

ing at the crystal ball. By Brind'Amour's tales, many, many wizards had
gone into the magical slumber those centuries before.

"Not all."

"Why did you look?" Oliver asked.

"Your tale of the encounter with Resmore," Brind'Amour replied.

"You did not send the lightning," Luthien reasoned. "Thus you believed that one of your brothers had awakened, and had come to our aid."

"But that is not the case," Brind'Amour said.

"You said you did not find them all," Oliver reminded.

"But none are awake; of that I am almost certain," Brind'Amour
replied. "If any of them were, my divining would have revealed them, or
at least a hint of them."

"But if you did not send the lightning . . ." Luthien began.

Brind'Amour only shrugged, having no explanation.

The old wizard sighed and leaned back in his chair. "We erred, my
friends," he said. "And badly."

"Not I," Oliver argued.

"The ancient brotherhood?" Luthien asked, pausing only to shake his
head at Oliver's unending self-importance.

"We thought the land safe and in good hands," Brind'Amour explained.
"The time of magic was fast fading, and thus we faded away, went into our
slumber to conserve what remained of our powers until the world needed
us once more.

"We all went into that sleep," the wizard went on, his voice barely above
a whisper, "except for Greensparrow, it seems, who was but a minor wizard, a man of no consequence. Even the great dragons had been destroyed,
or bottled up, as I and my fellows had done to Balthazar."

Luthien and Oliver shuddered at the mention of that name, a dragon
they knew all too well!

"I lost my staff in Balthazar's cave," the wizard continued, turning to regard Luthien. "But I didn't think I would ever need it again—until after I
awoke to find the land in the darkness of Greensparrow."

"This much we knew," Luthien said. "But if Greensparrow had been
such a minor wizard, then how did he rise?"

"What a great error," Brind'Amour said to himself. "We thought magic
on the wane, and so it was, by our standards of the art. But Greensparrow
found another way. He allied with demons, tapped powers that should
have been left alone, to rebuild a source of magical power. We should have
foreseen this, and warded against it before our time of slumber."

"I do so agree!" Oliver chimed in, but then he lowered his gaze as
Luthien's scowl found him.

"You should have seen me!" Brind'Amour said suddenly, his face flashing with the vigor of a long past youth. "Oh, my powers were so much greater then! I could use the art all the day, sleep well that night, then use it again all the next day." A cloud seemed to pass over his aged features. "But now, I am not so strong. Greensparrow and his cohorts find most of their strength through demonic aid, a source I cannot, and will not, tap."

"You destroyed Duke Paragor," Luthien reminded.

Brind'Amour snorted, but managed a weak smile. "True," he admitted. "And Morkney is dead, and Duke Resmore, his demon somehow taken from him, is but a minor wizard, and no more a threat." Again he looked to Luthien, his face truly grim. "But these are but cohorts of Greensparrow, who is of the ancient brotherhood. These dukes, and the duchess of Mannington, are mortals, and not of my brotherhood. Minor tricksters empowered by Greensparrow."

Luthien saw that his old friend needed his strength at that moment. "When Greensparrow is dead," he declared, "you, Brind'Amour, king of Eriador, will be the most powerful wizard in all the world."

Oliver clapped his hands, but Brind'Amour only replied quietly, "Something I never desired."

"Leave us," Brind'Amour instructed as he entered the dungeon cell below the Ministry. The small room was smoky, lighted by a single torch that burned in an unremarkable wall sconce beside the door.

The two elvish guards looked nervously to each other, and to the prisoner, but they would not disobey their king. With curt bows, they exited, though they stubbornly took up positions just outside the cell's small door.

Brind'Amour closed that door, eyeing Resmore all the while. The miserable duke sat in the middle of the floor, hands bound behind his back and shackled by a tight chain to his ankles. He was also gagged and blindfolded.

Brind'Amour clapped his hands and the shackles fell from Resmore's wrists. Slowly, the man reached up and removed first the blindfold and then the gag, stretching his numb legs as he did so.

"I demand better treatment!" he growled.

Brind'Amour circled the room, muttering under his breath and dropping a line of yellow powder at the base of the wall.

Resmore called to him several times, but when the old wizard would not answer, the duke sat quiet, curious.

Brind'Amour completed the powder line, encompassing the entire room, and looked at the man directly.

"Who destroyed your demon?" Brind'Amour asked directly.

Resmore stuttered for lack of an answer; he had thought, as had Luthien and Oliver, that Brind'Amour had done it.

"If A'ta'arrefi—" Brind'Amour began.

"A wizard should be more careful when uttering that name!" Resmore interrupted.

Brind'Amour shook his head slowly, calmly. "Not in here," he explained, looking to the line of yellow powder. "Your fiend, if it survives, cannot hear your call, or mine, from in here, nor can you, or your magic, leave this room."

Resmore threw his head back with a wild burst of laughter, as if mocking the other. He struggled to his feet, and nearly fell over, for his legs were still tingling from sitting for so long. "You should treat your peers with more respect, you who claim the throne of this forsaken land."

"And you should wag your tongue more carefully," Brind'Amour warned, "or I shall tear it from your mouth and wag it for you."

"How dare you!"

"Silence!" the old wizard roared, his power bared in the sheer strength of his voice. Resmore's eyes widened and he fell back a step. "You are no peer of mine!" Brind'Amour went on. "You and your fellows, lackeys all to Greensparrow, are a mere shadow of the power that was the brotherhood."

"I—"

"Fight me!" Brind'Amour commanded.

Resmore snorted, but the scoff was lost in his throat as Brind'Amour launched into the movements of spellcasting, chanting heartily. Resmore began a spell of his own, reaching out to the torch and pulling a piece of fire from it, a flicker of flame to sting the older wizard.

It rolled out from the wall at Resmore's bidding, flaring stronger right in front of Brind'Amour's pointy nose, and Resmore snapped his fingers, the completion of his spell, the last thrust of energy that should have caused the lick of flame to burst into a miniature fireball. Again, Resmore's hopes were abruptly quashed as his flame fell to the floor and elongated, something he never intended for it to do.

Brind'Amour continued his casting, aiming his magic at the conjured flame, wresting control of it and strengthening it, transforming it. It widened and gradually took the shape of a lion, a great and fiery cat with blazing eyes and a mane that danced with the excitement of fire.

Resmore paled and fell back another step, then turned and bolted for the door. He hit a magical wall, as solid as one of stone, and staggered back into the middle of the room, gradually regaining his senses and turning to face the wizard and his flaming pet.

Brind'Amour reached down and patted the beast's flaming mane.

Resmore cocked his head. "An illusion," he proclaimed.

"An illusion?" Brind'Amour echoed. He looked to the cat. "He called you an illusion," he said. "Quite an insult. You may kill him."

Resmore's eyes popped wide as the lion's roar resounded about the room. The cat dropped low—the duke had nowhere to run!—and then sprang out, flying for Resmore. The man screamed and fell to the floor, covering his head with his arms, thrashing for all his life.

But he was alone in the dirt, and when at last he dared to peek out, he saw Brind'Amour standing casually near the side of the room, with no sign of the flaming lion to be found, no sign that the cat had ever been there.

"An illusion," Resmore insisted. In a futile effort to regain a measure of his dignity, he stood up and brushed himself off.

"And am I an illusion?" Brind'Amour asked.

Resmore eyed him curiously.

Suddenly Brind'Amour waved his arms and a great gust of wind hit Resmore and hurled him backward, to slam hard into the magical barrier. He staggered forward a couple of steps and looked up just as Brind'Amour clapped his hands together, then threw his palms out toward Resmore. A crackling black bolt hit the man in the gut, doubling him over in pain.

Brind'Amour snarled and brought one hand sweeping down in the air. His magic, the extension of his fury, sent a burst of energy down on the back of stooping Resmore's neck, hurling him face-first into the hard dirt.

He lay there, dazed and bleeding, with no intention of getting back up. But then he felt something—a hand?—close about his throat and hoist him. He was back to his feet, and then off his feet, hanging in midair, the hand choking the life from him.

His bulging eyes looked across to his adversary. Brind'Amour stood with one arm extended, hand grasping the empty air.

"I saw you," Brind'Amour said grimly. "I saw what you did to Duparte on the Isle of Dulsen-Berra!"

Resmore tried to utter a denial, but he could not find the breath for words.

"I saw you!" Brind'Amour yelled, clenching tighter.

Resmore jerked and thought his neck would surely snap.

But Brind'Amour threw his hand out wide, opening it as he went, and Resmore went flying across the room, to slam the magical barrier once more and fall to his knees, gasping, his nose surely broken. It took him a long while to manage to turn about and face terrible Brind'Amour again, and when he did, he found the old wizard standing calmly, holding a quill pen and a board that had a parchment tacked to it.

Brind'Amour tossed both items into the air, and they floated, as if hung on invisible ropes, Resmore's way.

"Your confession," Brind'Amour explained. "Your admission that you, at King Greensparrow's bidding, worked to incite the cyclopians in their raids on Eriadoran and dwarvish settlements."

The items stopped right before the kneeling duke, hanging in the empty air. He looked to them, then studied Brind'Amour.

"And if I refuse to sign?" he dared to ask.

"Then I will rend you limb from limb," Brind'Amour casually promised. "I will flail the skin from your bones, and hold up your heart, that you may witness its last beat." The calm way he said it unnerved Resmore.

"I saw what you did," Brind'Amour said again, and that was all the proof the poor duke needed to hear to know that this terrible old wizard was not bluffing. He took up the quill and the board and quickly scratched his name.

Brind'Amour walked over and took the confession personally, without magical aid. He wanted Resmore to see his scowl up close, wanted the man to know that Brind'Amour had seen his crimes, and would neither forget, nor forgive.

Then Brind'Amour left the room, crossing through the magical wall with a single word.

"You will no longer be needed here," Resmore heard him say to the elves. "Duke Resmore is a harmless fool."

The dungeon door banged shut. The single torch that had been burning in the place was suddenly snuffed out, leaving Resmore alone and miserable in the utter darkness.

CHAPTER 14

THE PRINCESS AND HER CROWN

SHE SAT BEFORE THE MIRROR brushing her silken hair, her soft eyes staring vacantly through space and time. The bejeweled crown was set on the dresser before her, the link to her past, as a child princess. Beside the crown sat a bag of powder Deanna used to brighten the flames of a brazier enough to open a gate from Hell for the demon Taknapotin.

She had been just a child when that bag had become more important to her than the crown, when Greensparrow had become closer to her than her own father, the king of Avon. Greensparrow, who gave her magic. Greensparrow, who gave her Taknapotin. Greensparrow, who took her father's throne and saved the kingdom after a treacherous coup by a handful of upstart lords.

That was the tale Deanna Wellworth had been told by those loyal to the new king, and repeated to her by Greensparrow himself on the occasion of their next meeting. Greensparrow had lamented that, with his ascent to the throne, she was now out of the royal line. In truth, it mattered little because Greensparrow was a wizard of the ancient brotherhood, after all, blessed with long years, and would surely outlive Deanna, and all of her children, if she had any, and all of their children as well. But Greensparrow was not unsympathetic to the orphaned girl. Mannington, a not-unimportant port city on the western shore of Avon, would be her domain, her private kingdom.

That was the story Deanna Wellworth had heard since her childhood and for all of her adult life; that was the tale the sympathetic Greensparrow had offered to her.

Only now, nearing the age of thirty, had Deanna come to question, indeed to dismiss, that story. She tried to remember that fateful night of the coup, but all was confusion. Taknapotin had come to her and whisked her away in the dark of night; she vividly heard the screams of her siblings receding behind her.

O noble rescuer . . . a demon.

Why hadn't Taknapotin, a fiend of no small power, rescued her brothers and sister as well? And why hadn't the fiend and, more important, Greensparrow, who was easily the most powerful individual in the world, simply halted the coup? His answers, his excuses, were obvious and straightforward: there was no time; we were caught by surprise.

Those questions had often led Deanna to an impenetrable veil of mystery, and it wasn't until many years later that the duchess of Mannington came to ask the more important questions. Why had she been spared? And since she was alive after the supposed murderers had been executed, then why hadn't she been placed in Carlisle as the rightful queen of Avon?

Her stiff brush scraped hard against her head as the now-familiar rage began to mount inside of her. For several years, Deanna had suspected the betrayal and had felt the anger, but until recently she had suppressed those feelings. If what she feared had truly happened those two decades ago, then she could not readily excuse her own role in the murder of her mother and father, her five brothers and her sister.

"You look so much like her," came a call from the doorway.

Deanna looked into the mirror and saw Selna's reflection, the older woman coming into the room with Deanna's nightclothes over her arm. The duchess turned about in her seat to face the woman.

"Your mother," Selna explained with a disarming smile. She walked right over and put her hand gently against Deanna's cheek. "You have her eyes, so soft, so blue."

It was like a religious ceremony for the handmaid. Weekly at least, over the last twenty years, Selna, who had been her nanny in the days when her father ruled Avon, would brush her hand against Deanna's cheek and tell her how much she looked like her murdered mother. For so many of those years, Deanna had beamed under the compliment and begged Selna to tell her of Bettien, her mother.

What a horrible irony that now seemed to the enlightened woman!

Deanna rose and walked away, taking the nightclothes.

"Fear not, my Lady," Selna called after her. "I do not think our king will punish you for your weakness in the Iron Cross."

Deanna turned sharply on the woman, making her jump in surprise. "Has he told you that personally?" she asked.

"The king?"

"Of course, the king," Deanna replied. "Have you spoken with him since our return to Mannington?"

Selna appeared shocked. "My Lady," she protested, "why would his most royal King Greensparrow deem to talk with—"

"Have you spoken with him since we left the Iron Cross?" Deanna interrupted, speaking each word distinctly so that Selna could not miss the implications of the question.

Selna took a deep breath and lifted her jaw resolutely.

She feels safe within the protection of Greensparrow, Deanna mused. The duchess realized that her anger may have caused her to overstep her good judgment. If Selna's calls to Greensparrow were easily answered— perhaps the king had given her a minor demon to serve as courier—then Deanna's anger might soon bring Greensparrow's probing eye her way once more, something she most certainly did not want at this crucial hour.

"My apologies, dear Selna," Deanna said, moving over to put her hand on the woman's arm. Deanna dropped her gaze and gave the most profound of sighs. "I only fear that your perception of my weakness beside the cyclopians has lessened me in your view."

"Never that, my Lady," the handmaid said unconvincingly.

Deanna looked up, her soft blue eyes wet with tears. Ever since her childhood, Deanna had been good at summoning those; she called them "sympathy drops."

"It is late, my Lady," Selna said tersely. "You should retire."

"It was weakness," Deanna admitted with a slight sniffle. She noted that Selna's expression shifted to one of curiosity.

"I could not bear it," Deanna went on. "I hold no love for Eriadorans, and certainly none for dwarfs, but even the bearded folk seem a high cut above those ghastly one-eyes!"

Selna seemed to relax somewhat, even managed a smile that appeared sincere to Deanna.

"I only fear that my king and savior has come to doubt me," Deanna lamented.

"Never that, my Lady," Selna insisted.

"He is all the family that I have," Deanna said, "except for you, of course. I could not bear to disappoint him, and yet, that, I fear, is exactly what I have done."

"It was a task for which you of princessly temperament were not well-equipped," Selna said.

Princessly temperament. Selna often used that curious phrase when speaking to Deanna. Often the young woman wanted to yell in the face of it. If she was so attuned to royalty, then why was Greensparrow, and not she, who was of rightful blood, sitting on Carlisle's throne?

Deanna forced the angry thoughts deep within her. She let the tears come then, and wrapped Selna in a tight hug, holding fast until the woman remarked that it was time for her to go.

The duchess dashed those tears away in the blink of an eye as soon as Selna was safely out of the room. The hour was late, and she had so much to do this night! She spent a long moment looking at the dresser, at the crown and the bag, gathering her strength.

The hours passed. Deanna moved out of her room to make sure that all those quartered near her were asleep. Then she went back to her private chamber, closed and magically sealed the door, and went to her wardrobe, producing a small brass brazier from a secret compartment she had fashioned in its floor.

Not long after that, Taknapotin sat comfortably on her bed.

"A'ta'arrefi was not so formidable," the cocksure demon remarked.

"Not with the power of the storm I sent to you," Deanna replied coolly.

"Not so difficult a thing to channel the energy," Taknapotin admitted. "And so A'ta'arrefi is gone, poof!"

"And Resmore is out of the way, dead or in the dungeons of Caer MacDonald or DunDarrow," Deanna said.

"And we are one step closer to the throne," Taknapotin said eagerly.

Deanna still could not believe how easy this part of her plan had been. She had merely dangled the carrot of supreme rulership in front of Taknapotin and the fiend had verily drooled at the thought of overthrowing Greensparrow. This was the weakness of evil, Deanna realized. In alliance with such diabolical creatures, one could never securely hold any trust.

Not if one was wise.

Deanna walked over to the dresser and took up the crown, the link to her heritage, the one item that Greensparrow had managed to retrieve after the defeat of the usurpers. The one item that Greensparrow had given to her personally, begging her to keep it safe as a remembrance of her poor family.

"I do not think that any others need die," Taknapotin remarked. "Surely you are closest now, with Paragor and Resmore gone."

"Ah, but what of Duke McLenny of Eornfast in Baranduine?" Deanna asked. "He is wise to the world, my pet. So wise." The duchess chuckled silently at the irony of that statement.

"He suspects?"

Deanna shrugged. "He watches everything from the privacy of that wild land," she said. "Removed from the scene, he might better judge the players."

"Then he is a danger to us," the demon reasoned.

Deanna shook her head. "Not so." She turned from the mirror, holding the delicate crown in both hands. "Not to us."

Taknapotin looked at her curiously, particularly at the way her hands were clenched about that all-important crown.

Deanna's voice changed suddenly, dropping a complete octave as she began her chant. *"Oga demions callyata sie,"* she recited.

Taknapotin's eyes blazed brighter as the beast felt the impact of the chant, a discordant recital that pained any creature of Hell to its black heart. "What are you doing?" the fiend demanded, but it knew all too well. Deanna was issuing the words of banishment, a powerful enchantment that would send Taknapotin from the world for a hundred years!

She continued her chant, bravely, for the fiend rose up powerfully from the bed, fangs gleaming. The enchantment was powerful, but not perfect. Deanna couldn't be sure that it would work, in part because in her heart, in the heart of any wizard who has tasted such power, she could not fully desire to be rid of the demonic ally. She continued, though, and when Taknapotin, struggling and trembling, managed to take a step closer to her, she lifted high the crown that was her heritage, the gift of Greensparrow, the item that she now believed held more value than its gems or its memories. With a knowing smirk, Deanna twisted the metal viciously.

A sizzling crackle of black energy exploded from the crown, stunning Deanna and temporarily interrupting her chant. But it affected Taknapotin all the more. That crown was the demon's real tie to the world. It had been empowered by Greensparrow, the true master, and given to Deanna for reasons greater than nostalgia.

"You cannot do this!" Taknapotin growled. "You throw away your own power, your chance of ascension."

"Ascension into Hell!" Deanna yelled back, and with her strength renewed by the pitiful sight of the writhing agonized fiend, she took up her chant once more, uttering every discordant syllable through gritted teeth.

All that remained of Taknapotin was a black stain on her thickly carpeted floor.

Deanna threw down the twisted crown and stamped her foot upon it. It was the symbol of her foolishness, the tie to a kingdom—*her* kingdom—and to a family she had unwittingly brought down.

Though she had just enacted perhaps the most telling and powerful magical feat of her young life, and though Taknapotin, the demon that gave to her a great part of her power, was gone from her forever, Deanna Wellworth felt strangely invigorated. She went to her mirror and took up a vial, supposedly of perfume, but in truth, filled with a previously enchanted liquid. She sprayed the liquid generously over her mirror, calling to her closest friend.

The mirror misted over, and the fog seemed within the glass as well. Gradually the center cleared, leaving a distinct image within the foggy border.

"It is done?" asked the handsome, middle-aged man.

"Taknapotin is gone," Deanna confirmed.

"Resmore is in the care of Brind'Amour, as we had hoped," said the man, Duke Ashannon McLenny of Baranduine.

"I wish that you were here," Deanna lamented.

"I am not so far away," Ashannon replied, and it was true enough. The duke of Baranduine resided in Eornfast, a city directly across the Straits of Mann from Mannington. Their connection in spirit was even closer than that, Deanna reminded herself, and, though she was more scared than she had ever been, except of course for that terrible night twenty years before, she managed a smile.

"Our course is set," Deanna said resolutely.

"What of Brind'Amour?" Ashannon asked.

"He searches for a friend of old," Deanna replied, for she had heard the wizard's call. "He will unwittingly answer my call."

"My congratulations to you, Princess Deanna Wellworth," Ashannon said with a formal bow and the purest of respect. "Sleep well."

They broke the connection then, both of them needing their rest, especially since their respective demons were no more. Deanna was truly charmed by the man's respect, but it was she who owed the greatest debt in their friendship. Ashannon had been the one to open her eyes. It was the duke of Baranduine, who had ruled the largest clan of the island when Deanna's father was king of Avon, who had figured out the truth of the coup.

Now Deanna believed him, every word. Ashannon had told her as well the truth about her crown: that it was the key to Taknapotin, a tie in an unholy triangle that included Greensparrow and allowed the king to keep her under close scrutiny. That crown was the link that had allowed Greensparrow to call in Deanna's demon so easily that night in the Iron Cross. That crown, both by enchantment and by the subtle feelings of guilt that it incessantly forced upon poor Deanna, was the key that allowed Greensparrow to keep her locked under his spell.

"No," Deanna reminded herself aloud. "It was only one of the keys."

She walked determinedly across the room and gathered up her robe. Selna's room was only three doors down the hall.

In the duke's private room in Eornfast, Ashannon McLenny watched his mirror cloud over and then gave a great sigh.

"No turning round'about now," said a voice behind him, that of Shamus Hee, his friend and confidant.

"If ever I had meant a round'about, I'd not have told Deanna Wellworth the truth of Greensparrow," the duke replied calmly.

"Still, 'tis a scary thing," Shamus remarked.

McLenny didn't disagree. He, above perhaps any man in the world, understood Greensparrow's power, the network of spies, human and diabolical. After the coup in Avon, Ashannon McLenny had thought to break Baranduine free of the eastern nation's clutches, but Greensparrow had put an end to that before it had ever begun, using Ashannon McLenny's own familiar demon against him. Only the duke's considerable charm and wits had allowed him to survive that event, and he had spent the subsequent decade proving his value and his loyalty to the Avon king.

"I'm still not knowing why Greensparrow ever kept the lass alive," Shamus mumbled. "Seems a cleaner thing to me if he had just wiped all the Wellworths from the world."

"He needed her," McLenny answered. "Greensparrow didn't know how things would sort out after the coup, and if he could not cleanly take the throne, then he would have put the lass there, though he would have been in the shadows behind her, the true ruler of Avon."

"Wise at the time, but not so much now, so it seems," remarked Shamus with a chuckle.

"Let us hope that is the case," said McLenny. "Greensparrow has slipped, my friend. He has lost a bit of his rulership edge, perhaps through sheer boredom. Events in Eriador are proof enough of that, and, perhaps, a precursor to our own freedom."

"A dangerous course," said Shamus.

"More dangerous to Deanna by far than to us," said McLenny. "And if she can succeed in her quest, if she can even wound Greensparrow and steal his attention long enough, then Baranduine will at long last know independence."

"And if not?"

"Then we are no worse off, though I will surely lament the loss of Deanna Wellworth."

"You can break the ties to her and her little plan that easily, then?"

Ashannon McLenny nodded, and there was no smile upon his face as he considered the possibility of failure.

Shamus Hee let it go at that. He trusted Ashannon's judgment implicitly; the man had survived Greensparrow's Avon coup, after all, whereas almost all of the other sitting nobles at the time had not. And Shamus understood that McLenny, whatever his personal feelings for Deanna (and they did indeed run deep), would put Baranduine first. He had seen the man's face brighten with hope when they had first learned from Deanna Wellworth that Brind'Amour of the ancient brotherhood was alive and opposing Greensparrow.

Yes, Shamus understood, McLenny was a man for the ages, more concerned with what he left behind than with what he possessed. And what he meant to leave behind was a free Baranduine.

CHAPTER 15

DRESSED FOR BATTLE

*Y*ES, MY DEAR DEJULIENNE," Brind'Amour said absently, leaning back in his throne, chin resting heavily in his palm. "DeJulienne," he muttered derisively under his breath. The man's name was Jules!

The other man, dressed all in lace and finery, and spending more time looking at his manicured fingernails than at Brind'Amour, continued to spout his complaints. "They utter such garish remarks," he said, seeming horrified. "Really, if you cannot keep your swine civilized, then perhaps we should put in place a wide zone of silence about the wall."

Brind'Amour nodded and sat up straighter in his throne. The argument was an old one, measuring time from the formation of the new Eriadoran kingdom. Greensparrow had sent Praetorian Guards to Malpuissant's Wall to stand watch on the Avon side, and from the first day of their arrival, bitter verbal sparring had sprung up between the cyclopians and the Eriadorans holding the northern side of the wall.

"Uncivilized," Brind'Amour replied casually. "Yes, deJulienne, that is a good word for us Eriadorans."

The fop, Avon's ambassador to Caer MacDonald, tilted his head back and struck a superior pose.

"And if you ever speak of my people again as 'swine,' " Brind'Amour finished, "I will prove your point exactly by mailing your head back to Carlisle in a box."

The painted face drooped, but Brind'Amour, seeing his friends enter the throne room, hardly noticed. "Luthien Bedwyr and Oliver deBurrows," the king said, "have you had the pleasure of meeting our distinguished ambassador from Carlisle, Baron Guy deJulienne?"

The pair moved near to the man, Oliver bobbing to stand right before him. "DeJulienne?" the halfling echoed. "You are Gascon?"

"On my mother's side," the fop replied.

Oliver eyed him suspiciously, not buying a word of it. It had become common practice among the Avon nobles to alter their names so that they sounded more Gascon, a heritage that had become the height of fashion. To a true Gascon like Oliver, imitation did not ring as flattery. "I see," said Oliver, "then it was your father who was a raping cyclopian."

"Oliver!" Luthien cried.

"How dare you?" deJulienne roared.

"A true Gascon would duel me," Oliver remarked, hand on rapier, but Luthien grabbed him by the shoulders, easily lifted him off the ground, and carried him to the side.

"I demand that the runt be punished," deJulienne said to Brind'Amour, who was trying hard not to laugh.

"With my rapier blade I will write my so very long name across your puffy Avon breast!" Oliver shouted.

"He suffers from the war," Brind'Amour whispered to deJulienne.

"Phony Gascon-type!" Oliver yelled. "If you want to be truly important, why do you not stand on your knees and pretend you are a halfling?"

"I should strike him down," deJulienne said.

"Indeed," replied the king, "but do have mercy. Oliver killed a hundred cyclopians personally in a single battle and has never quite gotten over it, I fear."

DeJulienne nodded, and then, as the impact of the statement hit him fully, blanched even paler than his chalky makeup. "I will spare him then," the man said quickly.

"I trust our business is finished?" Brind'Amour asked.

The Avon ambassador bowed curtly, spun on his heel, and stalked from the room.

"Jules!" Oliver called after him. "Julie, Julie!"

"Did you really see that as necessary?" Brind'Amour asked when Oliver and Luthien came to stand before him once more.

Oliver tilted his head thoughtfully. "No," he answered at length, "but it was fun. Besides, I could tell that you wanted the fool out of here."

"A simple dismissal would have sufficed," Brind'Amour said dryly.

"Baron Guy deJulienne," Luthien snorted, shaking his head in disbelief. Luthien had tasted more than his fill of the foppish Avon aristocracy, and he had little use for such pretentious fools. The woman who had sent him on the road from Dun Varna in the first place, the consort of yet another self-proclaimed baron, was much like deJulienne, all painted and perfumed. She had used the name of Avonese, though in truth her mother had titled her "Avon." Seeing the ambassador of Avon only reaffirmed to Luthien that he had done well in giving the throne over to Brind'Amour. After the war, the Crimson Shadow could have likely claimed the throne, and many had called for him to do just that. But Luthien had deferred to Brind'Amour, for the good of Eriador— and, the sight and smell of deJulienne pointedly reminded him, for the good of Luthien!

"I should have sticked him in his puffy Avon breast," Oliver muttered.

"To what end?" Brind'Amour asked. "At least this one is harmless enough. He is too stupid to spy."

"Beware that facade," Luthien warned.

"I have fed him information since he arrived," Brind'Amour assured the young man. "Or should I say, I have fed him lies. DeJulienne has already reported to Greensparrow that nearly all of our fleet is engaged in a war with the Huegoths, and that more than twenty Eriadoran galleons have been sunk."

"Diplomacy," Luthien said with obvious disdain.

"Government, ptooey!" Oliver piped in.

"On to other matters," Brind'Amour said, clearing his throat. "You have done well, and I offer again my congratulations and the gratitude of all Eriador."

Luthien and Oliver looked to each other curiously, at first not understanding the change that had come over Brind'Amour. Then their faces brightened in recognition.

"Duke Resmore," Luthien reasoned.

"The wizard-type has admitted the truth," Oliver added.

"In full," Brind'Amour confirmed. The king clapped his hands twice then, and an old man, dressed in brown robes, moved out from behind a tapestry.

"My greetings, once more, Luthien Bedwyr and Oliver deBurrows," he said.

"And ours to you!" Luthien replied. Proctor Byllewyn of Gybi! The mere presence of the man told Luthien that the treaty with the Huegoths had been drawn.

Brind'Amour stood up from his throne. "Come," he bade the others. "I have already spoken with Ethan and Katerin and word has gone out to the Dorsal Sea. King Asmund should have arrived in Chalmbers by now, thus I will open a path that he and Ethan might join with us."

And Katerin, Luthien hoped, for how he missed his dear Katerin!

It was no small feat convincing suspicious Asmund to walk through the magical tunnel that Brind'Amour erected between Caer MacDonald's Ministry and the distant city of Chalmbers. Even after Katerin and Brother Jamesis had gone through, even after the Huegoth king had agreed, Ethan practically had to drag him into the swirling blue lights.

The walk was exhilarating, spectacular, each step causing a mile of ground to rush under their feet. Chalmbers was fully three hundred miles from Caer MacDonald, but with Brind'Amour's enchanted gate, the six men (including two strong Huegoth escorts, none other than Rennir and Torin Rogar) stepped into the Ministry in mere minutes.

"I do not approve of your magics!" Asmund said, defeating any greetings before they could even be offered.

"Time is pressing," Brind'Amour replied. "Our business is urgent."

Rennir and Torin Rogar grumbled.

"Then why did you not walk through the blue bridge to us?" Asmund asked suspiciously.

"Because Avon's ambassador is in Caer MacDonald," was all that Brind'Amour would reply. "This is the center, whether the Huegoths choose to join with Eriador's cause or not."

Luthien looked at the old wizard with true surprise; Brind'Amour's stern demeanor hardly seemed a fitting way to greet the Huegoths, especially since they were proposing an alliance that went opposite the traditions of both peoples!

But Brind'Amour did not back down, not in the least.

"I am weary," Asmund declared. "I will rest."

Brind'Amour nodded. "Take our guests to their rooms in the northeastern wing," he said to Luthien, nodding in that direction to emphasize the area. Luthien understood; deJulienne was quartered in the southeastern wing, and Brind'Amour wanted to keep the Avonese ambassador and Asmund as far apart as possible.

"I will do it," Oliver offered, cutting in front of Luthien. He turned and winked at Luthien, then whispered, "You show Lady Katerin to her room."

Luthien didn't argue.

"You are sure that all is well with you?" Luthien asked softly.

Katerin rolled over, facing away from the man. "You need to ask?" she said with a giggle.

Luthien wasn't joking. He put a hand on Katerin's shoulder and gently, but firmly, turned her back to face him. He said not a word, but his expression stole the mirth from teasing Katerin.

"Ethan was with me the whole time," she replied in all seriousness. "He is still your brother, despite his claims, and still my friend. He would have aided me, but in truth, I needed no protection or assistance. As rough as they might be, the Huegoths are honorable enough, by my eyes."

"You would not have agreed with that when we were on Colonsey," Luthien reminded her, and she had to admit that to be true. When they had first been captured, when *The Stratton Weaver* had been sent under the waves, Katerin was quite sure that her life would become a miserable thing, enslaved in the worst possible way by the savage Isenlanders.

"I am not for understanding them," she admitted. "But their demeanor changed as soon as the treaty was proposed by Asmund. I spent much time with Ethan and the Huegoths in Chalmbers, many hours out on the longship, and I was not threatened, not even insulted, in the least. No, my love, the Huegoths are fierce enemies, but loyal friends. I hold all confidence in the alliance, should it come to pass."

Luthien rolled onto his back and lay quiet, staring at the ceiling. He trusted fully in Katerin's judgment, and was filled with excitement.

But also with trepidation—for the war, if it came, would be brutal, far worse than the battles Eriador had fought to win its tentative freedom from Avon. Even with Huegoth allies, the Eriadorans would be sorely outnumbered by the more prosperous kingdom to the south. Even with the Huegoth longships and the captured Avon galleons, the Eriadoran fleet would not dominate the seas.

Luthien chuckled softly as he considered the irony of his current fears. When Princetown had fallen, that same spring only a few short months before, Luthien had wanted to press the war all the way to Carlisle. Brind'Amour had warned against such a desperate course, reminding his young friend of Greensparrow's power.

"Find your heart, my love," Katerin said, shifting so that her face was above Luthien's, her silken red hair cascading over his bare neck and shoulders.

Luthien pulled her down to him and kissed her hard. "You are my heart," he said.

"As is Eriador," Katerin quickly added. "Free of Greensparrow and free of war."

Luthien put his chin on her shoulder. Gradually a smile widened on his face; gradually the fires came again into his cinnamon eyes.

"It is all but done," Luthien remarked as he and Brind'Amour left the table after a long and private session with Asmund and Ethan.

"Your brother shows wisdom far beyond his thirty years," Brind'Amour said. "He has led Asmund down this road of alliance."

"It was Asmund who first proposed the treaty," Luthien reminded.

"And since that time, Ethan has taken the lead in making Asmund's wish a reality," replied Brind'Amour. "He is loyal to his king."

That remark stung the young Bedwyr, who did not like to think of Ethan as a Huegoth, whatever Ethan might claim. He stopped in the corridor, letting Brind'Amour get a couple of steps ahead of him. "To both his kings," he replied when his friend turned back to regard him.

Brind'Amour thought on that a moment, considered Ethan's work in the discussions, and nodded his agreement. Ethan's actions on behalf of Eriador had been considerable in the sessions; on several occasions he had openly disagreed with Asmund, and had even managed to change the Huegoth's mind once or twice.

Brind'Amour's nod set Luthien moving again. He caught up to his king, and even swept Brind'Amour up in his wake, taking the lead the rest of the way to the war room, where Siobhan, Katerin, Oliver, and Shuglin waited anxiously.

"It will be finished and signed this night," Brind'Amour confided.

Smiles were exchanged all about the oval table, on which was set a map of Avonsea. The mirth fell away when it reached Oliver, though, the halfling standing solemnly atop a stool.

"What is your pain?" Luthien asked bluntly. "An alliance with the Huegoths gives us a chance."

"Do you know how many innocent Avon people-types the Huegoth barbarians will destroy?" the halfling asked, reminding them of the reality of their newfound friends. "How many now work the oars of their longships? How many would they have thrown into the sea when we were captured, had not the one called Rennir recognized Luthien as one owed a debt?"

True enough, they all had to admit. They were about to get into bed with the devil, it seemed.

"We cannot change the Huegoth ways," Brind'Amour said at length. "We must remember that Greensparrow is the most immediate threat to our independence."

"To Eriador whole," Oliver replied, not backing down. "But do not be so quick to tell that to the next man sent bob-bobbing in the deep waters because his life with Asmund's people has taken his strength."

Katerin slammed her fist on the table in frustration; Shuglin, who had no experience with Huegoths and considered their slaves as unfortunate people too far removed for consideration at that point, glared at Oliver.

Luthien, though, nodded at his little friend, somewhat surprised by Oliver's enlightened view of things. Oliver had never been one to hesitate from separating a wealthy merchant from his purse, but Oliver, Luthien silently reminded himself, was the one who used to buy many winter coats, then find some minuscule complaint with them that he might justify throwing them out in the street—where the homeless orphans promptly found them and gathered them up.

Siobhan, too, saw the truth in Oliver's words and she walked up beside him, and, in front of everyone, kissed him.

Oliver blushed and swayed, nearly toppling from the stool. As was his way, the halfling quickly regained his dignity.

"The Huegoths are not the best moral choice as allies," Katerin agreed, "but we can trust them to keep their part in the alliance."

"But should we accept them at all?" Siobhan asked.

"Yes," Brind'Amour replied immediately, in a tone that showed no room for debate. "I, too, despise many of the Huegoth customs, slavery highest among them. Perhaps we might do something about that at another time. But for now, the foremost problem is Greensparrow and his cyclopians, who, even Oliver must agree, are far worse than the Huegoths."

Everyone looked to Oliver, and, feeling important, he nodded for Brind'Amour to continue.

"We cannot defeat Greensparrow without Huegoth aid," the Eriadoran king went on. Even with that aid, Brind'Amour doubted the outcome, but he kept that unsettling thought private. "Once Eriador is truly free, once Greensparrow is thrown down, then our power and influence will increase many times over."

"We war for freedom, not power," Luthien had to say.

"True freedom will grant us power beyond our borders," Brind'Amour explained. "Then we might properly deal with the Huegoths."

"You cannot go to war with an ally," Oliver retorted.

"No," Brind'Amour agreed, "but as allies, our influence upon Asmund will be much greater. We'll not change the Huegoth ways, any way short of complete war, and I do not think that any of us has the heart to take battle all the way to Isenland." He paused to watch the shaking heads, confirming his proclamation.

"I, too, would choose differently than the Huegoths as allies if any choice was to be made," Brind'Amour went on. "Your own Gascony, Oliver, cannot be counted on for any overt aid, though Lord de Gilbert has promised Eriador a lenient credit line should war come."

"A promise he probably has also extended to Avon," a snickering Oliver admitted, and the tension broke apart.

"Then we are agreed?" Brind'Amour asked when the nervous laughter subsided. "Asmund is our ally."

Luthien seconded the call, just beating Shuglin to the mark. Katerin came next, followed by Siobhan and finally, with a great and dramatic sigh, Oliver. There was one other voice to be heard in this debate, Brind'Amour knew, but he would have to deal with that problem later.

Brind'Amour moved up to the table's edge and took up a pointer. "Ethan has helped," remarked the wizard, who suddenly did not seem so old to Luthien. "He, too, understands the benefit of keeping the Hue-goths as far from land as possible."

"Ethan knows the truth of Eriador now," Luthien put in.

"Thus, and Asmund has tentatively agreed, the Huegoth ships will sail in formation east of the Eriadoran Dorsal fleet, which itself will sail east of the Five Sentinels." Brind'Amour ran the pointer down the eastern shores of the island line.

"What of Bangor, Lemmingburg, and Corbin?" Katerin wanted to know, referring to three Avon coastal towns, clearly marked on the wiz-ard's detailed map. "And what of Evenshorn, on the northern fringes of the Saltwash? If the ships are to sail *outside* the Five Sentinels, how are we to wage war with all the eastern towns of Avon?"

"We are not," Brind'Amour replied without hesitation. "Avon is Greensparrow. Avon is Carlisle. When Carlisle falls, so shall Avon!" He banged the pointer's tip on the point where the twin rivers both known as Stratton joined, in the southwestern section of the southern kingdom.

"The Five Sentinels are a long way from Carlisle," Siobhan remarked. "A roundabout route, and certainly longer and more dangerous than simply sailing along the Avon coast."

"But this course will keep the Huegoths offshore," Oliver piped in.

"And," said Brind'Amour slyly, "it will lessen the chance of an engage-ment with Avon's fleet."

"I thought that was the point," Shuglin said, looking confused.

Brind'Amour shook his head and waved his free hand, running the pointer down the wide channel between the Five Sentinels and the east-ern shore of Avonsea. "If we battle with Avon's fleet here," he explained, "and they are victorious, they will still have time to sail all the way around to the south, to do battle with our second fleet before it enters the River Stratton."

All the others moved closer to the table as the wizard spoke, his tone making it clear that he had thought this out completely and carefully.

"Also," the king explained, "let us keep our alliance with Asmund se-cret from Greensparrow. Surely the presence of Huegoth longships so close will make him nervous. And nervous leaders make mistakes!"

Brind'Amour again paused to consider the affirming nods, drawing strength from the others. It was clear that the wizard was doing a bit of gambling here, and a bit of praying.

"The attack will be four-pronged," he explained. "Half our fleet and the Huegoths will sail outside the Five Sentinels, securing the outer islands, and then swinging to the west for the mouth of the Stratton. A second fleet, already on its way to Port Charley from Diamondgate, will go south, through the Straits of Mann, and come into the Stratton from the east."

Luthien and Katerin exchanged nervous glances at that. Both understood the danger of this second move, for the fleet would be caught in narrow waters between the two strongholds of Mannington and Eornfast.

"The largest land force," Brind'Amour went on, moving the pointer appropriately, "will strike out from Malpuissant's Wall, securing Princetown, then sweeping down the open farmlands between Deverwood and the southern spurs of the Iron Cross, a straight run for Carlisle."

"Might they be held up at Princetown?" Oliver asked.

"By all reports, the city remains virtually defenseless," Brind'Amour said with confidence. "Neither the wizard-duke nor the garrison has been replaced."

"And the fourth prong?" Luthien asked impatiently, guessing that this last, and perhaps most important, move would likely be his to lead.

"Straight south from Caer MacDonald," Brind'Amour answered. "Collecting King Bellick's dwarfs and pressing straight through the mountains."

Luthien eyed that intended line. The Iron Cross was no easy traverse, even with a dwarvish army leading the way, and worse, it was widely accepted that the bulk of Greensparrow's cyclopian allies, including the highly trained and well-armed Praetorian Guards, were encamped along that same route. Even if those obstacles were overcome, it wouldn't get much easier for the Eriadoran army once the mountains were crossed, for that pocket of Avon, tucked into the nook between the Straits of Mann and the southern and western reaches of the Iron Cross, was the most populous and fortified region in all of Avonsea. Towns dotted the banks of all three rivers that ran from the mountains into Speythenfergus Lake, culminating with mighty Warchester, the second city of Avon, with walls as high as those of Carlisle itself!

Finally, a resigned Luthien looked to Katerin and shrugged, managing a smile.

The woman only shook her head; now that the true scope of their undertaking had been laid out before them, it seemed a desperate, almost impossible attempt.

CHAPTER 16

THE DECLARATION

THE GROUP WAS BACK in the war room later that afternoon, this time joined by Proctor Byllewyn and Brother Jamesis. The two men of Gybi talked excitedly about the prospects of war with Avon, but both of them, particularly Proctor Byllewyn, seemed to Luthien to be holding some serious reservations. The young Bedwyr didn't know how much Brind'Amour had told them of the previous meetings, but he could guess what was troubling them.

All eyes went to the door as Brind'Amour entered, his features locked. "This will be our last meeting," he said with all confidence, "until we rejoin at Carlisle's gates."

Murmurs of approval rolled about the table. Luthien kept his eyes on the men of Gybi—Proctor Byllewyn's wide smile showed that he was more than a little intrigued.

"I will entertain the ambassadors from Gascony and Avon presently," Brind'Amour explained. "The charges will be openly declared."

"War should not be declared until our armies are ready to march," Byllewyn interjected.

"But they are," Brind'Amour insisted. "Even the force from Gybi."

Byllewyn's expression turned dour. "You and I still have much to discuss," he protested quietly, calmly.

"Not so," replied Brind'Amour. "With all deference to your position, good proctor, and with all understanding that I am in desperate need of your influential cooperation, I cannot undo what has been done."

"You have signed a treaty with Asmund?" Byllewyn asked, his tone growing sharp.

There it was, Luthien realized. The men of Gybi, so recently under siege by the Huegoths, were not thrilled at the prosect of an alliance with King Asmund.

Brind'Amour shook his head fiercely, his huge white beard flopping from shoulder to shoulder. "Of course not," he replied. "My signature will not be penned until that of Proctor Byllewyn is in place on the document."

"You presume—" the proctor began.

"That you have the best intent of Eriador in mind," Brind'Amour interrupted.

Byllewyn rested back in his chair, not knowing how to respond.

Brind'Amour turned and whistled and the door opened immediately. In strode a tall, powerful-looking woman, handsome but fierce, with black hair and black eyes and the assured gait of a true warrior.

"Kayryn Kulthwain, the leader of the Riders of Eradoch," Brind'Amour explained, though she needed no introduction. She was well-known to the people in the room, particularly to the two men of Gybi.

"My greetings," Byllewyn extended, standing in salute to this warrior, a close ally of the folk of Bae Colthwyn. Byllewyn had met with Kayryn many times in Mennichen Dee for the great trading carnivals, and the two shared great respect and great friendship.

"Kayryn Kulthwain," Brind'Amour said again, "the duchess of Eradoch."

The title brought a moment of stunned silence.

"Duchess?" Katerin echoed incredulously.

"It is time for us to put our kingdom in line," Brind'Amour explained. "Wouldn't you agree, Duke Byllewyn, who is second in line to the throne of Eriador?"

Byllewyn slumped back down in his seat, overwhelmed. Brother Jamesis, beaming from ear to ear, put a comforting hand on his shoulder. All about the oval table, expressions shifted from ecstatic to confused, encompassing every emotion in between.

"A logical choice, would you not agree?" Brind'Amour asked them all. "Who in the land is more experienced in matters of state than our dear Proctor Byllewyn of Gybi?"

"False flattery to seal a necessary alliance?" Byllewyn asked slyly.

"Well-earned respect," Brind'Amour assured him, "though I admit that the alliance is necessary."

"None in this room, none in all of Eriador, would dispute the choice," Luthien piped in, and those words were indeed important from this man, the Crimson Shadow, perhaps the only man in all of Eriador whose claim as second in line for the throne of Eriador was greater than Byllewyn's. Luthien understood the importance of this as did Brind'Amour, for Gybi was viewed by most of northern Eriador as the spiritual center of the kingdom.

"I demand that the Huegoths be kept in close check," the proctor said at length. "I'll not have them slaughtering and enslaving innocents, Eriadoran or Avonese!"

"We have formulated our plans with exactly that in mind," assured Brind'Amour, who was happy to have Gybi serve as his moral conscience. "They will be kept offshore as much as is possible, and when they do come to land, they will be escorted by an Eriadoran force of at least equal strength."

Byllewyn chewed on that information for many seconds. "We will meet with Asmund when this is concluded," he finally agreed. "My folk will not sail beside the Huegoths, though!"

Brind'Amour was already nodding. "My hope is that the militia of Gybi will run with the Riders of Eradoch to lead the charge from Malpuissant's Wall," Brind'Amour explained. "With both Byllewyn and Kayryn Kulthwain to guide them, the march to Carlisle will go smoothly."

Byllewyn nodded his approval, and both Brind'Amour and Luthien sighed, realizing that the major obstacle in properly launching this war had just been overcome. Without the support of Gybi, the support from Eradoch would have been tentative indeed. Now, with Proctor Byllewyn and Kayryn Kulthwain in agreement and fully in the fold, northeastern Eriador's proud and independent folk would take part in the campaign with all their hearts.

"Ethan will be my link to the Huegoths," Brind'Amour explained, "and to the eastern Eriadoran fleet."

"I am thinking that you put much stock in a man who has proclaimed his allegiance to King Asmund," Oliver interjected.

Brind'Amour conceded the point. "He is Bedwyr," the Eriadoran king replied, as though that alone should suffice.

"I will go with the Huegoths," Brother Jamesis unexpectedly volunteered. "I understand their ways," he said in the face of the doubting expressions. "And their honor."

Brind'Amour looked to Byllewyn, who nodded his agreement.

"Very well, then," the king said. "My two eastern arms are thus secured." He paused, his gaze settling on Katerin. The woman understood what he was asking of her. In the previous war, Katerin had served well as emissary to Port Charley. She among them best understood the seafolk of western Eriador. Katerin was of that same stock.

"I will ride out for Port Charley this day," she agreed, ignoring the crestfallen expression that came over Luthien at the proclamation.

"I will get you there more quickly than any horse," Brind'Amour said with a smile.

"I will go with her," came Luthien's not-unexpected call.

Brind'Amour smiled and did well to hide his chuckle. "You will strike due south," the king replied. "At my side, with Shuglin and Bellick and the dwarfs, with Siobhan and the Fairborn, and with the militia of Caer MacDonald. Praetorian Guards await us, my young friend, and their hearts will surely sink at the knowledge that the Crimson Shadow, the man who outmaneuvered legendary Belsen'Krieg, has come against them."

Luthien couldn't deny the logic, or dismiss the call of his country. "Then Oliver will go with Katerin," he decided, and it made sense, for the halfling had been with Katerin during her first mission as ambassador to Port Charley.

Oliver started to protest, but Siobhan, sitting beside him, kicked him in the ankle. He looked to her and went silent, realizing that this one's heart was for Eriador first, for him second.

"I hate boats," was all the complaint the halfling offered, though his blue eyes, so obviously full of longing, locked on to the fair Siobhan as he spoke.

"Then it is settled," Brind'Amour said. "Now let us turn our discussion to the meeting I must soon hold with the ambassadors. We each will have a role to play."

Felese Raymaris de Gilbert was a tall and slender man with soft gray eyes and dark hair, neatly coiffed, and a clean-shaven, unblemished face. His posture was perfect, but he did not appear rigid; his dress was fashionable and rich, but he did not appear foppish. And unlike many Gascon (and Avonese) lords, he did not reek from an overabundance of perfume. His hands, though manicured, were not soft from luxury.

Felese had been chosen by the Gascon lords to represent them to the tough Eriadorans for just these reasons. The man had a lord's appearance, but a workingman's sensibilities, a rare combination that had set him in good standard in the court of Brind'Amour.

He stood now beside puffy Guy deJulienne in Brind'Amour's audience room, facing the grim-faced king of Eriador. DeJulienne's gaze was more centered on the king's companions standing behind the throne, particularly on the gaily dressed halfling who stood beside the fair half-elf named Siobhan.

Oliver eyed the foppish Avonese as well, winking and blowing kisses at the man.

It was a strange scene for the two ambassadors, and Felese was worldly enough to know that something important was brewing. Brind'Amour sat in his customary throne, but a second seat had been brought in and placed beside the first. It was empty, and Felese, suspicious and wary, hoped that Brind'Amour meant to announce that he would soon wed, or something as innocuous as that.

Judging from the king's companions, standing with perfect posture in a line behind the chairs, he didn't think so. Anchoring the line to Brind'Amour's left stood the tough dwarf with the bushy blue-black beard, Shuglin by name. Beside him stood Proctor Byllewyn of Gybi, a most important man in Eriador, and next to him, a fierce-looking black-haired woman, obviously a warrior. Then, at the king's left shoulder, stood Katerin O'Hale, a fiery woman Felese longed to know better. Looking to Brind'Amour's right, the ambassador was reminded of the impossibilities of such a tryst, though, for there stood Luthien Bedwyr, the famed Crimson Shadow, slayer of Duke Morkney and hero of the last war.

And also, Katerin's lover.

Beside Luthien came Oliver deBurrows, a fellow Gascon, that most curious of fellows. Felese liked Oliver quite a bit, mostly because of the way the halfling unnerved deJulienne, whom Felese did not like at all. Anchoring the line on Brind'Amour's right stood the half-elf Siobhan, a former slave, leader of the notorious Cutters, a band of Fairborn who had ever been a thorn in the side of those who would unlawfully rule Eriador.

Felese looked them over carefully, trying to guess the intent. It was the presence of Kayryn Kulthwain, the one he did not know, who finally tipped him off. This was no announcement of a future queen of Eriador, Felese realized, for these were Brind'Amour's generals!

"I do appreciate your coming here on such short notice," Brind'Amour said casually.

"We are entertaining a great guest?" deJulienne asked, nodding to the empty chair.

"A fellow king," Brind'Amour replied.

"Huegoth?" Felese asked hopefully, for news that the war on the eastern shores was at its end would have been most welcome to the Gascon.

Brind'Amour didn't miss that excited smile, and he also noticed that deJulienne didn't seem so pleased.

The Eriadoran king shook his head. "No," he replied. "Not Huegoth." Then, without dragging out the suspense, Brind'Amour motioned to one of the guards standing in front of a side door. The man opened the door and an orange-bearded dwarf, regally attired in a flowing purple tabard hanging loosely over gleaming silver mail, strode confidently into the room.

Both ambassadors went down to one knee as the orange-bearded dwarf walked past to take his seat beside Brind'Amour.

"I trust that you two are familiar with King Bellick dan Burso of

DunDarrow?" Brind'Amour asked, and he did well to hide his smile at the hint of a frown tugging at the edges of Guy deJulienne's mouth.

"I am honored, good King Bellick," said Felese sincerely.

"My friend Brind'Amour has spoken well of you," Bellick answered, and neither ambassador missed the importance of the fact that Bellick had not referred to Eriador's leader as "King Brind'Amour."

"I, too, am honored," said deJulienne.

Bellick snorted derisively and looked to Brind'Amour.

"I have summoned you here to announce a truce," Brind'Amour explained, then looked to his dwarvish friend. "More than a truce," he corrected. "Know you that the kingdoms of Eriador and DunDarrow are now one."

Felese wore a grin, though he realized that the situation in Avonsea might soon deteriorate. DeJulienne, though, openly gawked, obviously displeased by the prospect of taking such unwelcome news to his merciless king!

"Under Eriador's flag?" Felese asked.

Brind'Amour looked to Bellick, and both shrugged. "Perhaps we will design a new flag," Brind'Amour said with a laugh, for they hadn't even thought of such minor details.

"But you, Brind'Amour, will speak for DunDarrow in Eriador's dealings with Gascony?" Felese pressed, thinking that this might work out well for his merchant kingdom.

"Well-reasoned," replied Brind'Amour.

Guy deJulienne could hardly contain himself; he knew by the fearful flutter of his heart that something bigger would be revealed here.

Brind'Amour saw his discomfort, and so he played along, enjoying the spectacle. "All goods traded between Gascony and DunDarrow will flow through Port Charley," he explained. "Port Charley to Caer Mac-Donald, and then distributed to the dwarvish encampments in the Iron Cross."

Guy deJulienne was trembling.

"And what of the east?" Felese pressed. "When will Chalmbers be opened to Gascon trade?"

"The fighting in the east is ended," Brind'Amour announced, and it seemed to him as if deJulienne was having trouble drawing breath. How the Eriadoran king was enjoying this! "The men of Isenland will not fight in the face of Eriador's fleet."

"A stolen fleet!" deJulienne blurted before he could help himself.

Brind'Amour shrugged and chuckled, willing to concede that irrelevant point. "However gotten, the fleet flies under Eriador's flag, and the fierce

Huegoths will not battle with these ships, for they have no desire to give aid to Greensparrow, who is Eriador's enemy."

The words sent a shock ripple through the gathering, sent murmurs along the line behind the Eriadoran king and even from the guards standing at the room's three doors. All of those waves seemed to gather heavily on the shoulders of the foppish diplomat from Avon.

Baron Guy deJulienne worked very hard to control himself, to steady his breathing. Had Brind'Amour just declared war with Avon?

"Surely we have not come together on this glorious occasion to hurl insults," said Felese, trying to soothe things. The news of the Caer Mac-Donald–DunDarrow alliance was marvelous, the news of cessation of hostilities with the Huegoths even better, and Felese didn't want the continuing animosity between Eriador and Avon to put a damper on this bright situation. From Gascony's greedy perspective, it was better for all if the two kingdoms of Avonsea were at peace.

"Insults?" deJulienne managed to stammer. "Or threats?"

"Neither," Brind'Amour said sternly, coming out of his seat to stand tall over the foppish man. Felese tried to intervene, but the powerful wizard simply nudged him aside. "Know you that there will be no peace between Eriador and Avon as long as Greensparrow sits on Avon's throne," Brind'Amour proclaimed, as overt a gesture of war as could be made.

"How dare you?" deJulienne said breathlessly.

"My good King Brind'Amour," soothed the shocked Gascon ambassador.

Brind'Amour relaxed visibly, but did not sit down and did not let the scowl diminish from his face. "We asked for peace," he explained. "In good faith earlier this same year, we signed in Princetown with Duchess Deanna Wellworth, who spoke for King Greensparrow of Avon, a binding document for peace."

"Binding!" echoed deJulienne loudly, pointing an accusing finger and seeming to gain a fleeting moment of momentum.

Oliver blew him a kiss and the distraction gave Brind'Amour the upper hand.

"Broken!" the Eriadoran king roared, coming forward, and the stunned deJulienne skittered backward and nearly tumbled. Brind'Amour did not pursue him physically, but his verbal tirade continued the assault. "Broken by cyclopians, working for your treacherous king! Broken by the spilled blood of Eriadoran innocents in hamlets along the Iron Cross!

"Broken," shouted Brind'Amour, motioning to his stern-faced fellow sitting calmly in the second throne, "by the spilled blood of DunDarrow's dwarfs."

"Be not a fool!" deJulienne pleaded. "We have Huegoths to contend with, and so many other . . ."

Brind'Amour waved his hand and the terrified man fell silent. "We of Eriador have a more pressing enemy." Then, responding with his trump card, Brind'Amour motioned again to the two guards standing at the door over to the side of the room. Again the door was opened and a miserable Resmore was dragged in by two elven escorts.

Felese stood back in thoughtful posture, his hand stroking his fashionable goatee.

"Now you know your enemies, foolish pawn of Greensparrow," Brind'Amour said to deJulienne. "Go to your king. War is at your door!"

The man of Avon, horrified, ran from the room, but Felese remained, seeming truly intrigued. "A friend of Greensparrow's?" he asked, indicating Resmore, who was in a crouch on the floor, seeming barely conscious.

"The duke of Newcastle," Brind'Amour replied. "Sent into the mountains by Greensparrow to incite the cyclopians into war against Eriador and DunDarrow. I will furnish Duke Resmore's complete confession for you to take to your lords."

The man nodded. He had no intention of committing Gascony to the war, and Brind'Amour didn't ask for, or expect, such a pledge. All that the king of Eriador needed was for Gascony to stand with him in spirit or, at the least, to remain neutral.

"I will send my messengers at once," Felese replied, and bowed and turned to leave. He looked back at Brind'Amour and nodded, all the confirmation the king of Eriador needed. Then he left the room, his mind whirling with the possibilities. For the Gascons, this situation might well prove profitable. No matter the outcome, both sides would soon need tons of supplies.

Back in the audience room, Brind'Amour motioned to the guard at the door on the opposite side of the room, and when they unlocked it, it nearly burst apart as King Asmund and Ethan stormed in.

"You did not introduce your other ally," Ethan explained. "My king feels slighted."

"I did not reveal the most potent of my weapons," Brind'Amour replied, bidding Asmund to take the unoccupied throne at Bellick's side, Brind'Amour's own.

The proud Huegoth puffed out his chest and accepted the seat of honor, satisfied with the gesture and with the description of his warriors as Brind'Amour's "most potent" of weapons.

CHAPTER 17

OPENING MOVES

"I WILL KEEP ASMUND and my people from bloodlust," Ethan assured Luthien quietly. The two of them stood along the side wall of a small, unfurnished chamber. A few feet away, Brind'Amour worked his magic, opening a tunnel through the stone and across the miles, a fast run to Chalmbers. King Asmund, Proctor Byllewyn, and Brother Jamesis stood beside the old wizard, the two men of Gybi waiting patiently, but the Huegoth king obviously anxious.

Ethan looked to Asmund and couldn't suppress a grin. It had taken him a long time to convince Asmund to come through the tunnel to Caer MacDonald. Now, though Asmund desperately wanted to get back to the Dorsal Sea and his fleet, it seemed as though another battle would have to be fought.

Luthien was too busy scrutinizing Ethan to take note of the sight that had brought a smile to his brother's face. The younger Bedwyr was encouraged by Ethan's continuing shift back toward their family. Ethan's unsolicited promise to keep the Huegoths in line during the war showed that the man cared deeply about Eriador. How deeply? Luthien had to ask himself, and as yet he had no answer. In that same promise, Ethan had referred to the Huegoths as "my people," a notion that Luthien was finding harder to dispute.

The two walked over to the others as Brind'Amour, clearly growing weary from his extensive use of magic over the last few days, completed the passage. This was the old wizard's second magical tunnel this day, having earlier delivered Kayryn Kulthwain back to Eradoch, where she would gather her forces.

"My folk will join with me in Chalmbers," Proctor Byllewyn explained.

"They have sailed from Gybi already," Jamesis added. "Escorted by the thirty galleons of Eriador's Dorsal fleet."

"Our fishing boats will remain in dock there," the proctor went on.

"It is not so far a march from Chalmbers to Malpuissant's Wall, where my folk of Gybi will meet with the forces of Dun Caryth and Glen Albyn, as well as Kayryn Kulthwain and her fierce riders."

"Out with you then," insisted Brind'Amour. "Captain Leary leads the Eriadoran fleet and anticipates your return."

Proctor Byllewyn and Brother Jamesis bowed curtly and said their farewells, promising victory, then entered the tunnel without hesitation.

"One of your longships awaits you at Chalmbers's dock," Brind'Amour said to the nervous Huegoth king.

"Will it wait long enough for me to walk?" Asmund asked, managing a slight chuckle. Rennir followed suit, laughing exuberantly, but the king's other Huegoth escort was distracted at that moment.

"Luthien Bedwyr," Torin Rogar called, joining Luthien and Ethan at the side of the room. "We never found chance to speak of my kin who was your friend."

"We will meet again," Luthien promised.

"In celebration," said Torin determinedly. He clapped Luthien on the shoulder, then nodded to Ethan and moved back to join his king. He and Rennir stepped into the swirling blue mists together, paving the way for Asmund.

"I look forward to our meetings when this is at its end, King Brind'Amour," said Asmund. "We have much to learn from each other."

Brind'Amour took the huge man's wrist in a firm and sincere clasp. Luthien and Ethan exchanged hopeful looks at the encouraging words.

"Do not tarry," Asmund ordered Ethan, and with a deep breath to steady his nerves, the Huegoth king went into the magical tunnel.

"Eriador free," Luthien said as he and Ethan walked to the spot.

Ethan turned to him, curiously at first, but his expression gradually and surely changed to one of excitement. "Eriador free," Ethan offered, "my brother."

They hugged each other tightly, and for that short moment, Luthien felt as close to Ethan as he had through all their years together in Dun Varna. At that moment, Luthien understood that Ethan could proclaim whatever heritage he desired, but the truth of it was that he and Luthien were of the same blood, were indeed, as Ethan had just generously offered, brothers.

"Until we meet again," Ethan said.

"At the gates of Carlisle!" Luthien called as his brother disappeared from sight, lost in the fast pace of the swirling blue mists.

"A pity there weren't more of you," Brind'Amour snickered under his breath. Luthien looked at him curiously, not understanding the comment.

"Your father sired two fine sons," the old wizard explained. "A pity there weren't more of you." Brind'Amour walked past Luthien, patting him comfortingly on the shoulder, then exited the room, heading for his bed and some much-needed rest.

Luthien stood for a long while watching the wizard's tunnel diminish and then disappear altogether. He missed Ethan already! The last year or so, since he and Oliver had stumbled into Brind'Amour's secluded mountain cave, then into a revolt against Duke Morkney that quickly degenerated into open rebellion against Avon, had been such a wild ride for the young Bedwyr that he had hardly given his absent brother much thought. Ethan, to his knowledge, had been far away in the Kingdom of Duree, fighting with Greensparrow's loaned troops beside the Gascon army.

Only when Luthien had finally returned to Dun Varna and seen Gahris on his death bed, had he found time to focus attention on his past, on his lost brother and his redeemed father.

Then, suddenly, Ethan had been thrown back into Luthien's life. Luthien's emotions swirled as had Brind'Amour's tunnel, moving along at a pace no less swift, but with a destination far less clear. Ethan was returned, perhaps, but Gahris was dead. That much was certain.

Luthien's father was dead.

The young Bedwyr bit his lip hard, trying to hold the tears in check. Eriador needed him, he reminded himself. He was the Crimson Shadow, the hero of the last war and destined to lead this war. He could not stand facing a blank wall in an empty room and weep for what had gone before. He could not . . .

But he did.

"I will deliver Brind'Amour's head unto you," the woman promised.

King Greensparrow rested back comfortably in his plush throne, throwing both his legs over one arm of the great chair and studying closely the fingernails of one hand. The pose did little to diminish Deanna's suspicion that the king was greatly agitated. He had called to her through an enchanted mirror, a call she had at first decided not to answer. The urgency of his tone, though, could not be ignored, and Deanna had concluded quickly that if she did not go to her own enchanted mirror in her private quarters, Greensparrow would likely show up in Mannington, something the duchess most definitely did not want to see!

"Where is Taknapotin?" Greensparrow asked, the question Deanna had feared all along.

Deanna put on a perplexed look. "Where should the fiend be?" she replied.

"I want to know."

"In Hell, I would suppose," Deanna answered. "Where Taknapotin belongs." Greensparrow didn't believe any of her explanation, Deanna realized by his sour expression. He was indeed closely tied to the fiend he had given to her, as she had suspected. Now the king had her backed into a corner because he could not contact his demonic spy.

Deanna silently congratulated herself on the power of her dismissal of Taknapotin. Her enchantment and the breaking of the crown had apparently blasted the fiend from the world and put him beyond even Greensparrow's considerable reach.

Unless the king was bluffing, Deanna suddenly feared. Unless Taknapotin was sitting in Greensparrow's throne room, out of view, sharing a diabolical joke with the merciless king of Avon.

Deanna understood that her fears showed clearly on her face. She quickly composed herself and used that involuntary expression to her benefit.

"I have not been able to contact him since . . . since Selna . . ."

Greensparrow's eyes widened—too much, Deanna realized, for the name of Selna had struck him profoundly, confirming to the duchess that her handmaid was indeed yet another of Greensparrow's spies.

". . . since Selna broke my crown," Deanna lied. "I fear that Taknapotin took offense, for the demon has been beyond my call—"

"Broke your crown?" Greensparrow interrupted, speaking each word slowly and evenly.

For a moment, Deanna expected the man to fly into a fit of rage, but he composed himself and relaxed in his chair, settling comfortably.

He is angry about Selna and the crown, Deanna told herself, but he is relieved, for he believes the lie, and now thinks that I am still his willing puppet.

"The crown was indeed a link between you and your demon," Greensparrow confirmed.

And between you and my demon, Deanna silently responded.

"I enchanted it those years ago, when first you came into your power," Greensparrow said.

When you murdered my family, came Deanna's angry thoughts.

"I will find another way back to Taknapotin," the king offered. "Or to another fiend, equally malicious."

Deanna wanted to divert him from that course, but she realized that she would be walking dangerous ground. "I will not wait," she said. "I can destroy Brind'Amour without Taknapotin, for I have my brother wizards and their fiends at my call."

"You must not fail in this!" Greensparrow said suddenly, forcefully, coming forward in the throne, so close to his mirror that his appearance became distorted, his pointy nose and cheeks looming larger and more ominous. "It will all dissolve when Brind'Amour is dead. Eriador's armies will fall into disarray that we might destroy them one by one."

"Brind'Amour will die within the week," Deanna promised, and she feared that she might be correct.

A wave of Greensparrow's hand broke the contact then, to Deanna's ultimate relief.

Back in Carlisle's throne room, the king motioned for the two huge and ugly one-eyed cyclopians holding the enchanted mirror to be gone, then turned to Duke Cresis. DeJulienne, returned from Caer MacDonald, stood beside the brute, twitching nervously. He had been the bearer of ill tidings, after all, not an enviable position in Greensparrow's court!

Greensparrow's laugh put the ambassador at ease; even militant Cresis seemed to relax somewhat.

"You do not trust her?" Cresis reasoned.

"Deanna?" Greensparrow answered lightly. "Harmless Deanna?" Another burst of laughter followed, and deJulienne chimed in, but stopped and cleared his throat nervously when Greensparrow sat up abruptly, his face going stern. "Deanna Wellworth is too filled with guilt to be a threat," Greensparrow explained. "And rightly so. To turn against me, she must explore her own past, wherein she will discover the truth."

Cresis was nodding at every word, deJulienne noticed, and he realized that the brutish duke of Carlisle had obviously heard all of this before. DeJulienne had not, though, and he was perplexed as to what his king might be hinting.

"Deanna was my link to the throne," Greensparrow said bluntly, looking deJulienne right in the eye. "She unwittingly betrayed her own family, giving me personal items from each of them."

DeJulienne started to ask the obvious question, but stopped short, realizing that if what Greensparrow was hinting at was the truth of Avon's past, then his king was a usurper and murderer.

"All that I feared from Deanna was the loss of Taknapotin," Greensparrow explained, looking back to Cresis. "But if that fool handmaid broke the crown, then I understand why I have not been able to make contact, a situation that should be easily rectified."

"What of the coming war?" Cresis asked. "The Eriadorans will soon march, and sail."

"Fear Eriador?" Greensparrow scoffed. "The ragtag farmers and fisherfolk?"

"Who won the last war," deJulienne reminded, and he regretted the words as soon as he spoke them, as soon as he saw the dangerous scowl cross Greensparrow's hawkish features.

"Only because of my absence!" the king roared angrily. Greensparrow sat trembling, his bony knuckles turning white as he clasped the edges of his throne.

"Indeed, my mighty King," deJulienne said with a submissive bow, but it was too late for the man.

Greensparrow snapped a fist into the air, then extended his long fingers. Beams of light, a rainbow of hues, shot out from each of them, joining and swirling into one white column, roughly the length and breadth of a sword blade.

The king sliced his arm down, the magical blade following.

DeJulienne's left arm fell to the floor, severed at the shoulder.

The man howled. "My King!" he gasped, clutching at the spurting blood.

With a growl, Greensparrow brought his hand in a straight-across cut down low.

Off came deJulienne's left leg and the man toppled to the floor, his lifeblood gushing out from the garish wounds. He tried to call out again, but only managed a gurgle. He did lift his remaining arm in a feeble attempt to block the next strike.

It was taken off at the elbow.

"My absence was the cause of our defeat," Greensparrow said to Cresis, ignoring the squirming, shivering man on the floor. "That, and the incompetence of those I left in charge!

"And because of Gascony," Greensparrow reasoned. "The Gascons thought a free Eriador would profit them greatly; little did they realize the importance of Carlisle's protection from Huegoths and other such troubles.

"This time," Greensparrow went on, coming right out of his seat and pointing a finger to the air, "this time, the Gascons understand the truth of pitiful Eriador and will not ask that we make peace." The king gingerly stepped over the now-dead deJulienne. He noticed Cresis then, noting particularly the worried look on the ugly face of his duke.

"This is exactly what we wanted!" Greensparrow yelled, and howled with laughter. "We prodded Eriador and foolish Brind'Amour declared war."

Cresis relaxed somewhat, remembering that this was indeed the outcome that he and Greensparrow had plotted when they had sent the cyclopian tribes into raiding actions against Eriador and DunDarrow.

"They have perhaps fifty of our ships remaining," Greensparrow went on, accounting for the twenty the Huegoths had reportedly sent to the bottom. "The mere fact that so many of our fine warships were lost to those savages only confirms that the Eriadoran fisherfolk can hardly sail the great galleons." Greensparrow flashed Cresis a wild, maniacal look. "Yet we have more than a hundred, crewed by experienced sailors and cyclopian warriors. Half the Eriadoran fleet will soon enter the Straits of Mann. I have a like number of warships waiting to scuttle them."

"It could be a costly battle," pragmatic Cresis dared to interrupt.

"Not so!" yelled Greensparrow. "When the ships of Baranduine join in, another hundred strong, then that threat is ended."

The eager king grew more excited with every word, savoring the anticipation of complete victory. "Brind'Amour will then think himself vulnerable on his western shore and he will have to turn his forces about for Montfort before he ever gets out of the mountains."

It seemed perfectly easy and logical, and so Cresis again allowed himself to relax. Greensparrow came right up to him, put a hand on his shoulder.

"That is assuming that the old wizard is even alive at that time," he whispered in the cyclopian's ear. Then he leaped away, taking care to avoid the gore that had been his ambassador to Caer MacDonald.

"Do not underestimate Deanna Wellworth, my one-eyed friend," Greensparrow explained. "With the powers of my dukes and their demons at her bidding, Deanna will catch the old wizard and show him that the time of his magics are long past."

Greensparrow stopped suddenly and went silent. He had to find a way to contact Taknapotin once more. Or to get Deanna another demon, if that was his only choice.

"Easy enough!" he shouted, though Cresis had no idea what he was talking about.

The cyclopian was comforted anyway. Cresis had been with Greensparrow all the score-and-two years of the king's reign. In fact, Cresis, once an ambassador from the cyclopian tribes to Avon's rightful king, had been an instrument of Greensparrow's rise. The brute had personally murdered four of the five sons of the king, Deanna Wellworth's brothers. His reward had been a position as Carlisle's duke, and in the years of his service, Cresis had learned to trust in Greensparrow's merciless power. Well-advised were those who feared the king of Avon.

DeJulienne was yet another testament to that truth.

*   *   *

The next time Luthien saw Brind'Amour, the wizard was again at work evoking a magical tunnel. This time the destination was due west, not east, to Port Charley.

This parting would be no less difficult for Luthien than the last. Oliver and Katerin stood patiently by as the gray wall transformed into a bluish fog and gradually began to swirl. To Luthien's surprise, Oliver held Threadbare's reins in hand, the ugly yellow pony standing quietly.

Oliver's gaze kept drifting to the back of the room, where stood Siobhan, the half-elf seeming cool and impassive. It took Oliver a long while to even get her attention. Then, he merely offered her a resigned look, and lifted his hand, in which he held both of his green gauntlets, to the tip of his wide brim in salute.

Siobhan nodded slightly, and Oliver's heart skipped a beat as he caught a glimpse of the true pain in Siobhan's green eyes. She was sad that he was leaving!

Bolstered by that thought, the romantic halfling stood tall—relatively speaking—and stared resolutely at the widening passageway.

Katerin caught it all, and managed a slight, confused smile. She moved away from Oliver and over to Luthien, sweeping him up in her wake and going to the furthest corner from the others.

"Oliver and Siobhan?" she whispered incredulously.

"I know nothing," Luthien answered truthfully.

"The way she looked at him," Katerin remarked.

"The way I look at you," Luthien added.

That gave Katerin pause. She had been so caught up in the tumultuous events preceding the war, she hadn't even realized the pain her lover was feeling. Studying Luthien's expression now, she finally understood. He had found Ethan, only to lose Ethan again, and now she, too, was going from his side—and all of them were walking into danger.

"You needn't go," Luthien pleaded. "Oliver could serve as Brind'Amour's eyes."

"Then all that our king will see is a ship's rail and the water below it," Katerin quipped, a not-so-subtle reminder that the halfling wasn't the most seasoned of sailors.

A long moment of silence passed between them as they stood, staring deeply at one another. They could find another emissary for Brind'Amour, they both knew that, and Katerin could remain at Luthien's side. But it was not to be. Among Brind'Amour's tight court, Katerin was best suited for this most-important mission. These few had been the leaders of the revolution, and now were taking their rightful places as the generals of the war. Their duty was to Eriador, and personal feelings would have to wait.

Both Luthien and Katerin came to this complete understanding together, silently and separately.

"Perhaps I could go with you, then," Luthien offered on a sudden impulse. "I, too, am of Isle Bedwydrin, and familiar with the ways of the sea."

"And then again I would have a Bedwyr son by my side, protecting me," Katerin remarked, a bit of sarcasm creeping into her soft tone. "Perhaps Brind'Amour could recall Ethan, for he, too, is of our island home."

A twang of jealousy came over Luthien, showing clearly on his face.

"And Ethan's surely the cuter," Katerin continued.

Luthien's eyes widened; he didn't even realize that he had been taken until Katerin burst out in laughter and kissed him hard on the cheek.

Her face grew serious once more as she moved back from the man, though. "Your place is with our king," she explained firmly. "You are the Crimson Shadow, the symbol of Eriador free. In truth, I believe that Oliver, your most-noted sidekick, should remain with you and Brind'Amour as well, but perhaps his absence will not detract from your presence, and his presence on the ships should help me keep the coastal folk from forgetting their king."

Her words ended the debate once and for all, clearly spelling out to Luthien the duty before him, and before Katerin. As she went on, though, Katerin's face grew grim, and she offered more than one glance at Siobhan, standing still by the door at the back of the room.

"You will march across the land in the company of Siobhan," Katerin said.

Luthien sighed and tried to empathize with the emotions he knew Katerin must be feeling. Siobhan was his old lover, after all, and Katerin knew that all too well. But Luthien had thought that painful situation a thing of the past, had thought that he and Katerin had resolved Siobhan's rightful place as their common friend.

He started to protest, gently, but again Katerin burst out in laughter and kissed him hard, this time staying close and moving her lips to his.

"Let us hope you are not so gullible when facing an emissary of Greensparrow's," the woman whispered.

Luthien held her all the tighter, squeezed her close until Brind'Amour announced that the tunnel was complete, that it was time for Oliver and Katerin to go.

"You mean to take the pony?" Brind'Amour asked Oliver, and from his weary tone it seemed to Luthien that he had asked that question many times already.

"My Threadbare likes boats," Oliver replied. He looked to Luthien and snapped his fingers in the air. "And you did not believe me when I said that I rode my horse all the way from Gascony!" he declared. Then he motioned and whispered to the yellow pony, and Threadbare knelt down so that little Oliver could climb up into the saddle. With one last look to Siobhan, Oliver entered the tunnel, and with one last look to Luthien, Katerin followed.

And so it began, that same day, the gathering clouds, moving into their respective positions east of the Five Sentinels, along Malpuissant's Wall, outside of Caer MacDonald's southern gate, and along the docks of Port Charley.

The proper declarations had been sent; the invasion of Avon began.

CHAPTER 18

FRONT-RUNNERS

OF ALL THE PATHS to be taken by Eriador's forces, the one looming before Luthien's group was by far the most uncertain. In the east and the west, the army moved by sea, along routes often traveled and well-defined. From Malpuissant's Wall, the Riders of Eradoch and Proctor Byllewyn's militia swept across open, easy terrain. But within the hour of departing Caer MacDonald's southern gate, the forerunners of Luthien's group, including Luthien, Siobhan, and the other Cutters, were picking their careful way among boulder tumbles and treacherous trails, often with a sheer cliff on one side, rising high and perfectly straight, and a drop, just as sheer, on the other.

The force, nearly six thousand strong, could not move as a whole in the narrow and difficult terrain, but rather, as a plodding mass flanked by a series of coordinated patrols. Organization was critical here; if the scouting patrols were not thorough, if they missed even one unremarkable trail in the crisscrossing mountains, disaster could come swiftly. The main group, nearly a third of the soldiers with their king among them, all of the supply carts and horses, including Luthien's shining stallion, Riverdancer, would be vulnerable indeed to ambush. Most of the soldiers were more concerned with getting their supplies and horses through the impossible trails and with building impromptu bridges and shoring up the crumbling trails than with watching for enemies. Most of them carried shovels and hammers, not swords, and if some of the cyclopian enemies, particularly the highly trained Praetorian Guards, managed to slip through the front groups unopposed, the march of the entire force might be suddenly stalled.

It was Luthien's job to make sure that didn't happen. He had dispersed the remaining four thousand into groups of varying sizes. Five hundred spearheaded the main group's march, marking the trails Brind'Amour would follow; five hundred others followed the plodding force, leaving open no back door. In the rougher terrain off the main trail, things were less structured. Patrol groups ranged from single scouts (mostly reclusive men who had lived for many years in these parts of the Iron Cross) to supporting groups of a hundred warriors, sweeping designated areas, improvising as they learned each section of these rarely traveled mountains. Luthien and Siobhan moved together, along with a dozen elven Cutters. Sometimes the pair were in sight of all their twelve companions, other times they felt so completely alone in the vast and majestic mountains.

"I will feel all the better when we have met with Bellick's folk," Luthien remarked as they traveled along one open area, picking their way across the curving sides of great slabs of stone. Looking above him, a hundred feet higher on the face of the mountain, Luthien saw two elves emerge from a small copse of trees, nimbly running along the steep stone. He marveled at their grace and wished, as he stumbled for the hundredth time, that he had a bit of the elvish blood in him!

Siobhan, following the young Bedwyr's steps, didn't disagree, but her response was halfhearted at best, and made Luthien turn about to regard her. She, too, stopped, matching his stare.

The nearly two hundred elves accompanying Caer MacDonald's army had made no secret of their trepidations concerning the route that might come before them when they linked with the dwarvish army. King Bellick had explained that his dwarfs were hard at work in trying to open tunnels to get the force more easily through the Iron Cross. While elves and dwarfs got along well, the Fairborn had little desire to stalk through deep and dark tunnels. That simply was not their nature.

Siobhan had argued that point during the final preparations—successfully, Luthien had thought. Even if Bellick's folk could open a tunnel, it was decided that only the main group, laden as they were with carts and supplies, would go underground, while the rest continued their overland sweep to the south. So it confused Luthien now, for just a moment, that Siobhan appeared so glum.

"Oliver?" the young Bedwyr reasoned.

Siobhan didn't answer, just motioned with her delicate chin that Luthien should move along. He complied, satisfied that he had hit the mark. He knew the pain that he was feeling at his separation from Katerin, especially since he understood that his love was sailing into great danger. Might it be that Siobhan was feeling much the same about her separation from Oliver?

The notion brought a giggle to Luthien's lips. He cleared his throat, even faked a stumble to help cover the laughter, not wanting to deride the half-elf.

Siobhan understood the ruse, though, understood that Luthien's giggle was a fair indication of what she might expect from others. She took it stoically and continued on without a word.

Shadows came fast and deep with the setting sun, and though the month of August was not yet gone, the night air was much cooler, a chilling reminder to all the soldiers that they could not afford to get bogged down in the mountains, or get chased back into the Iron Cross once they broke free into the northern fields of Avon.

Luthien and Siobhan made contact with the other Cutters in their area, determining how they might set a perimeter to ensure that every passable trail in this region was well watched. Just a few hundred yards behind their line, a group of nearly seventy warriors was setting camp.

Siobhan found a hollow for her and Luthien, surrounded by high stones on three sides and partially capped by an earthen overhang. Within it they were sheltered from the wind. Luthien even dared to set a small fire in one deep nook, knowing that any light which spilled out of the deep hollow would be meager indeed.

It was a bit awkward for the young Bedwyr—and for his companion, too, he realized—to be so alone together on this quiet summer's eve. They had been lovers, passionate lovers, and there remained an undeniable attraction between them.

Luthien sat against the wall near to the opening, pulling his crimson cape tight about him to shield him from the nipping wind. He tried to lock his gaze on the dark line of the trail below, but kept glancing back at beautiful Siobhan as she reclined near to the glowing logs. He remembered some of the times he and Siobhan had shared in Caer MacDonald, back when the city had been called Montfort, when Morkney had been duke and life had been simpler. A smile widened on Luthien's face as he thought of his initial meeting with Siobhan.

He had gone to rescue her, thinking her a poor, battered slave girl, only to find out that she was one of the leaders of the most notorious thieving band in all of Montfort! The mere recollection of his image of Siobhan as a helpless creature made Luthien feel the fool; never in his life had he met a person less in need of rescuing!

She was his friend now, as dear to him as anyone could ever be.

Just his friend.

"They'll not come out this late," Siobhan remarked, drawing him from his thoughts.

Luthien agreed. "The mountain trails are too dangerous at night, unless the one-eyes carried such a blaze of torches that would alert all the soldiers of Eriador. We can consider our watch at its end."

Siobhan nodded and turned away.

Sitting against that cold stone, Luthien Bedwyr realized how fortunate he truly was. Katerin knew that he and Siobhan would travel together, and yet she had gone out to Port Charley willingly, saddened to be separated from Luthien, but with not a word to him concerning his relationship with his traveling companion. Katerin trusted him fully, and Luthien understood in his heart that her trust was not misplaced. Feelings for Siobhan remained strong within him; he could not deny her beauty, or that his love for her had, in many ways, been real. But Siobhan was a friend, a dear and trusted companion, and nothing more. For Katerin O'Hale was the only woman for Luthien Bedwyr.

He knew that, felt that, without any regrets, and Katerin knew him well enough to trust him completely.

Indeed, sitting there that night, with only the occasional crackle from the fire and the groaning of the wind through the stones, with the beauty of the stars and Siobhan to keep him company, Luthien Bedwyr fully appreciated the good fortune that had come into his life. With warm thoughts of his Katerin filling his mind, he drifted off to sleep.

Siobhan was not as comfortable. She kept a quiet watch over Luthien and when she was certain that he was asleep, she drew out a folded parchment from a pocket. Still watching Luthien, the half-elf eased it open and leaned near to the fire, that she might read it once more.

To my dearest half-elven-type Siobhan,
From this halfling so gallant and true,
The wind blows of war, thus I must be gone,
The fairest rose no more in my view.

But fear not, for not miles nor sea,
Not mountains nor rivers nor one-eyes,
Can block our thoughts, me for you, you for me,
Or blanket our hearts with disguise.

With summer-type breezes tickling my hairy chin,
Upon my palm rested to gaze at your beauty.
Would that I were not so needed now
Alas for hero-bound duty!

I go, but not for long!
Oliver

The half-elf closed the letter carefully and replaced it in her pocket. "Foolish Oliver," she whispered with a shake of her head, wondering what she was getting herself into. She took up a stick and prodded the embers, managing to stir forth a small flicker of fire from the nearly consumed logs.

What might Oliver be thinking, she wondered, and she sighed deeply, realizing that the halfling's amorous advances might make her seem quite ridiculous. Oliver carried a well-earned reputation as a charmer among the scullery maids and other less-worldly women, but those who better understood the ways of the wide world, who recognized the truth of the halfling's boasts and stolen finery, saw that side of Oliver as more than a bit of a joke. His fractured poems, like the one in the letter, could make quite an impression on a young girl, or a woman locked in drudgery, who did not read the works of the accomplished bards, but Siobhan was no tittering schoolgirl. She saw the halfling clearly.

Why, then, did she miss Oliver so damned much?

The half-elf looked across the way to Luthien and managed a chuckle at his mounting snores. The flame was gone now, the fire nothing more than a pile of orange-glowing embers, but its heat was considerable, and comfortable, and so Siobhan settled back and, with a final look to make sure the trail remained clear, let sleep overtake her.

A sleep filled with thoughts of a certain highwayhalfling.

The next day was dreary and cold, threatening rain. A heavy fog enshrouded the mountains, rising up from the river valleys to meet with the low-hanging clouds so that all the world seemed gray. Sound was muffled almost as much as sight, and it took Luthien and Siobhan some time to locate those Cutters camped nearby.

One of the elves suggested a delay, waiting until the fog had lifted, but Luthien couldn't agree to that.

"The ships are sailing," he reminded. "And the riders have gone out from Malpuissant's Wall. Even as we sit here talking they are likely closing in on Princetown."

There came no further arguments, and so the group carefully plotted their lines of probing forays, and split apart, with two elves waiting at the spot on the main trail for the lead runners of the rear supporting force.

Luthien and Siobhan moved steadily, their fellow scouts lost to them almost as soon as they had set out. They felt alone, so very alone, and yet, they knew they were not. They were deep into the Iron Cross now, many miles farther than they had been on the occasion of Luthien's capture of Duke Resmore. The other scouting bands were near, they knew, and so, likely, were cyclopians.

It wasn't long before the pair's fears were confirmed. Luthien led the way up a rocky bluff, creeping to its ridge and peering over.

Below him, down a short and steep decline, in a clearing edged by rocks, lay a cyclopian camp. A handful of the brutes milled about the blackened remains of the previous night's fire, gathering together their supplies. One of them polished a huge sword, another sharpened the tip of its heavy spear, while a pair of the brutes off to the side pulled on their heavily padded silver and black uniforms—regalia that Luthien and Siobhan knew all too well.

"Praetorian Guards," the young Bedwyr whispered when Siobhan, bow in hand, was in place beside him. "A pity it wasn't this easy when we sought proof of Greensparrow's involvement. Better than facing a wizard!"

"Praetorian Guards in the neutral mountains proves nothing," Siobhan reasoned. She went silent, crouching a bit lower as one of the brutes moved toward her and Luthien, carrying a bucket of dirty water. Oblivious to the pair, the one-eye splashed the water against the rocks at the bottom of the decline and turned back to camp.

Luthien nodded, conceding the point to Siobhan, then eyed the half-elf slyly. "But now we are formally at war," he remarked, "and an enemy is before us."

Siobhan scrutinized the camp carefully. "Seven of them, at least," she replied. "And we are but two." She looked all about, and Luthien did as well, but none of their allies were apparent.

Their gazes eventually met, melting into a communal smile and shrug. "Kill them quick," was all the advice that Siobhan offered.

Luthien drew out *Blind-Striker* and studied the moves of the brutes. One was near the fire, collecting warm embers in a pouch, but the others were all about the perimeter of the stony clearing, appearing as no more than gray shadows in the fog.

"Soon to be six," the young Bedwyr promised, and over the ridge he went, slipping fast and silent down the decline.

A brute to the right yelled out, and Luthien broke into a full charge. He bore down on the cyclopian; it came up and drew out a sword to meet the charge.

An arrow whistled right over the young Bedwyr's shoulder, startling him, forcing him to lurch to the left. The stunned cyclopian threw up its arms wildly, dodged and yelled, and caught the arrow deep in its shoulder. Worse for the brute, Luthien deftly followed the momentum of his reaction. The young Bedwyr went down to one knee in a complete spin and came across, both hands clinging tightly to *Blind-Striker*. The fine sword gashed the brute in the side of the ribs and tore across its chest, opening a wide wound.

It fell away dying, but Luthien hardly noticed. He put his feet under him and rushed out to the side, a few running steps to the right, lifting his sword high to defeat the chopping axe of yet another cyclopian. Luthien quickly shifted his blade diagonally, pushing the brute's weapon out wide, then punched straight ahead, slamming *Blind-Striker*'s crafted hilt into the one-eye's face. The fabulous crosspiece, sharp-edged sculptures of dragon wings, cut a deep gash along the side of the brute's single eye, and the cyclopian retreated a couple of staggering steps, red blood washing away its vision.

Luthien had no time to follow, for yet another one-eye came in hard, forcing him to pivot fast and half-turn to the left, swiping down desperately with his sword to pick off a thrusting spear.

Siobhan, another arrow set and ready, followed Luthien's rush to the right, thinking to lead him in with a killing shot. She caught movement out of the corner of her eye, though, and halted her swinging bow, leaving it locked steady in the wake of her companion. A cyclopian had circled out of the rocks and now bore down on Luthien from behind.

It crossed into view and the half-elf let fly, knowing she had to be perfect, knowing that she had but one shot to save her friend.

The arrow plunged deep into the brute's head, dropping it straight to the ground without so much as a grunt.

Her arms moving in perfect harmony, Siobhan put up another arrow and let fly, this time grazing the chest of the staggered brute Luthien had punched in the face. It fell back another few steps, buying Luthien precious time.

But Siobhan's aid was at an abrupt end. She wheeled back across the encampment to the left, taking a bead on a pair of cyclopians crossing the clearing for the rocky climb to her position. Off flew the arrow, slamming one in the belly and doubling it over.

Siobhan barely had time to grin, watching its companion dive desperately behind the cover of some rocks, when she realized that another brute had slipped out of the mist and was standing right over her, its axe up high.

"Eight," the half-elf lamented.

The speartip rushed ahead in three rapid thrusts, but Luthien managed to parry and dodge, shifting his hips out of harm's way each time. He had his back to Siobhan now, but guessed that she could not help him as yet another one-eye came rushing in at his back.

Luthien measured the footsteps and twirled aside at the very last moment, barely avoiding being skewered. The off-balance brute lurched past, nearly taking out its companion.

The young Bedwyr put his feet back under him quickly and charged in, hoping to score some hits amidst the confusion, but these were Praetorian Guards, well-trained veterans. While its stumbling companion regained its footing the other brute stepped in front, spear whipping across to pick off Luthien's series of attacks.

Luthien kept up the barrage, then cut hard down and to the side, defeating a spear thrust from the second one-eye. He rushed back to the left, forcing the first to retreat, then pivoted back, swinging his sword about.

The thrusting spear slipped past him, in front of him, and Luthien went right around the other way in a complete circle, going down low, trying to come in under the one-eye's defenses.

In response, the cyclopian thrust its speartip straight to the ground and ran out behind the blocking weapon.

Luthien rolled right under the defense, using his sword to keep the brute's weapon-arm extended. The other cyclopian was fast returning and so the young Bedwyr struck out hard and fast with his free hand, crunching the brute's nose.

Then Luthien had to leap back and break, squaring up once more against the pair. On they came, showing more respect this time, offering measured attack routines that Luthien could easily defeat, but keeping up their common defense, keeping the young Bedwyr at bay.

Gradually the cyclopians increased their tempo, working in unison, giving Luthien no opportunities and inevitably putting him back on his heels.

Purely on instinct, Siobhan tossed her bow into the air and caught it in both hands down low on one end. She snapped it out like a snake, stepping into the swing and smacking the brute across the face, staggering it backward. Again without thinking, the lightning-fast half-elf tossed her bow once more, catching it in one hand while her other went to her quiver and pulled out an arrow.

Before the axe-wielding cyclopian could even take a step forward to get near to her, she pulled back and let fly, point-blank.

The brute fell away into the fog.

Siobhan wheeled back to see the other cyclopian out from behind the rocks and in full charge. Behind it came its companion, holding its belly still, and crawling in a futile attempt to keep up.

No time for another arrow, Siobhan realized, so she dropped the bow and rushed ahead, drawing her short and slender sword as she went. She came to the lip of the ridge and leaped high and far, over the slashing sword of her adversary. She stuck her own sword down as she flew past, scoring a hit on the one-eye's shoulder, but since she was sailing past, there was little force behind the strike and the cyclopian was not badly wounded.

Siobhan hit the ground running, skipping gingerly down the treacherous slope. So fast had she moved that the crawling one-eye never realized the danger, and Siobhan finished it with a single stroke to the back of its neck as she skittered past.

The other brute came on in a fast, but respectful, pursuit, following Siobhan as she ran out of the clearing to the left, away from Luthien's continuing battle.

Luthien realized that he had to do something dramatic, and quickly, for the third one-eye, dazed and bloody, but not down, would soon join in. He launched *Blind-Striker* into a series of cunning and vicious thrusts and slashes, all parried, but Luthien used the momentum to break contact and run ahead toward the back end of the small clearing. He scrambled up the side of a waist-high boulder, then leaped out far to the side, narrowly avoiding the lumbering thrust of one pursuing brute. Luthien came down at the one-eye's side, facing away and with open ground before him. He threw himself backward—exactly the opposite of what the turning cyclopian expected. The brute didn't question the luck, though, and swung its spear about, thinking to skewer the man.

Then it understood the ruse, for Luthien snapped in a counter-clockwise spin as the spear thrust harmlessly past. Down the young Bedwyr went and across came *Blind-Striker,* scoring a wicked hit on the cyclopian's hip. The brute leaped out to the side, sprawling across the same boulder Luthien had climbed, and rolling off its side, thinking that the wicked sword would soon come in for the killing blow.

But Luthien couldn't follow the attack, for the second one-eye was back in, forcing the young Bedwyr into a defensive posture once more.

None in all of Avonsea could navigate without their sight as well as the Fairborn, who spent so many dark nights dancing among the trees. Thus, the thick mists aided Siobhan as she outdistanced the pursuing cyclopian. She took a roundabout route, smiling grimly as she came upon the body of the cyclopian she had shot point-blank, her bow on the ground just a few feet away.

The half-elf heard the grunts of the out-of-breath one-eye closing. She skittered to the bow and scooped it up and when the brute came out of the fog, it saw its doom.

The cyclopian lifted its thick arms defensively, calling out for mercy, and if the fight had been over, if Luthien had not been in desperate straits just a few yards away, Siobhan might have held her shot. Not now, though; not with the certainty that if she took her attention away from this "prisoner," the one-eye would waste no time in tackling her and choking the life out of her.

The arrow zipped between the upraised arms, bounced off the cyclopian's heavy breastplate, and ricocheted at an upward angle, driving through the brute's throat. The cyclopian stood for a moment longer, waving its arms stupidly, but gradually it sank to its knees, its dying words no more than indecipherable gurgles.

Siobhan immediately turned her attention to Luthien, engaged with two, soon to be three, cyclopians. She considered dropping her bow and drawing out her sword once more, charging to his side, but she feared she didn't have the time.

"Down!" she yelled, praying that her friend would understand.

Luthien, not sure, but without any real options, threw himself into a backward roll. He was barely halfway down when the arrow sliced the air over his head, right in front of his face, thudding solidly into the chest of one cyclopian. The brute ran backward a few steps, weirdly, flapping its arms like a dying chicken before falling into the dirt.

The other cyclopian, following Luthien's move, made the mistake of taking note of its faltering companion. That instant of hesitation gave the young Bedwyr all the room he needed. As he came around in his roll, he tucked his feet under him and reversed direction, staying low, his leading sword crossing under the defenses of the distracted brute. *Blind-Striker* dove into the one-eye's belly, running at an upward angle, through the brute's diaphragm and into its lungs.

The cyclopian tumbled backward and Luthien couldn't help but follow, coming to rest atop the dead brute.

An arrow just to the side alerted the young Bedwyr that the one remaining cyclopian had rejoined the fight. Siobhan had missed, he noted with some concern, but fortunately the arrow had come close enough to force the cyclopian into a desperate, off-balance dodge. Luthien tugged hard on *Blind-Striker,* but to no avail, for the blade was truly stuck. With a frustrated growl, Luthien scrambled out from the tangle barehanded.

Regaining its balance, the one-eye tried a halfhearted chop, but Luthien brought his arm against the side of the heavy axe and pushed it out wide. Then he waded in with a series of heavy blows, left and right, left and right, and the brute staggered away.

Stubbornly the cyclopian put up its axe defensively, fending off Luthien's pursuit, and shook its head, fast regaining its senses. A wicked grin crossed its face as soon as it realized that the man had no weapon.

Luthien didn't see the shot, didn't hear a whistle in the air or the crack of bone at the impact. As though it simply appeared from nowhere, the butt of an arrow was sticking out from the side of the cyclopian's knee. With a howl, the cyclopian dropped and Luthien waded in, again easily turning out the axe. Grunting with every heavy blow, Luthien pounded the brute into the dirt.

Siobhan was beside him then, grinning as she surveyed the battleground.

"Six dead and one captured," Luthien remarked, offering a wink and draping an arm across the shoulder of his slender companion.

Siobhan wriggled away. "Seven dead," she corrected, indicating the ridge line, "for one came out of the mist."

Luthien nodded his admiration.

"Four clean kills for me," Siobhan announced, "and you must share all three of yours, and the capture."

Luthien's smile disappeared.

"That makes six for me," the half-elf figured, "and but two for the legendary Crimson Shadow!" She skipped away then, quite pleased with herself.

A dumbfounded Luthien watched her as she searched through the camp. Gradually his smile returned. "Challenge accepted!" he called, confident that in the course of this campaign he would be given ample opportunity to catch up.

The captured cyclopian was ferried back along the lines to the main group, where Brind'Amour had no trouble in hypnotizing the brute and garnering valuable information. Other skirmishes along the line brought in more prisoners, who only confirmed what the first one-eye had revealed: a large force of cyclopians, mostly Praetorian Guards, was making its way into a wide valley some twenty miles or so to the south.

With that general description in hand, Brind'Amour then used his crystal ball to send his eyes far ahead. He located the force and was pleased. The Eriadorans would meet up with Bellick's dwarvish army halfway to the one-eyes, and then the brutes would be in for a warm welcome indeed!

Luthien and Siobhan were brought forward to speak for Brind'Amour when contact with Bellick's army was finally made. They came in sight of their allies—five thousand grim-faced dwarfs, armored in glittering mail and shining shields, and with an assortment of weapons, mostly axes and heavy hammers—on a wide and fairly open stretch of windblown stone. Bellick was there, along with their friend Shuglin.

Luthien and Siobhan could hardly catch their breath at the sight of the spectacle. Hope flooded through the young Bedwyr; with such allies as these, how could Eriador lose?

"Surely the one-eyes are in for a nasty surprise," Siobhan whispered at his side.

"Dwarvish fighters," Luthien replied, imitating Oliver's thick Gascon accent. "But, oh, how bad they smell!"

He turned to offer a wink to his half-elven companion, but lost it in the face of the forlorn look Siobhan threw his way.

Luthien cleared his throat and let it go, wondering again just how much was going on between Siobhan and Oliver.

CHAPTER 19

THE VALLEY OF DEATH

*T*HEIR LEADER IS WISE," Brind'Amour remarked, surveying the rough and broken terrain to the south.

The others gathered about the old wizard offered no arguments to the observation. The cyclopians had made haste long after sunset, not setting their camp until the steep walls of the valley were behind them.

Brind'Amour sat down on a stone, rubbing his thick white beard, trying to improvise a plan of attack.

"Not so many," the dwarf Shuglin offered. "We counted campfires, and unless they're fifty to one about the flames, they're not more than half our number."

"Too many, then," Luthien interjected.

"Bah!" snorted the battle-hungry dwarf. "We'll run them down!"

Brind'Amour listened to it all distantly. He had no doubt that his fine force, with two-to-one odds in their favor, would overwhelm the Praetorian Guards, but how expensive might an open battle be? Eriador could not afford to lose even a quarter of its force while still in the mountains, not with so much fortified ground to cover before they ever got near Carlisle.

"If we hit them hard straight on and on both flanks," Siobhan asked, "spreading our line thin so that they believe we are greater in number than we truly are, how might they react?"

"They will break ranks and run," Shuglin replied without hesitation. "Ever a coward was a one-eye!"

Luthien was shaking his head; so was Bellick. Brind'Amour spoke for them. "This group is well-trained and well-led," the old wizard answered. "They were wise enough, and disciplined enough, to get out of the valley before setting camp. They'll not run off so readily."

A sly sparkle came into the man's blue eyes. "But they will fall back," he reasoned.

"Into the valley," Siobhan added.

"Using the valley walls to tighten our lines," agreed Bellick, catching on to the idea.

"Into the valley," Luthien echoed, "where groups of archers will be waiting."

A long moment of silence passed, all the gathered leaders exchanging hopeful smiles. They knew that the cyclopians were well-disciplined, but if they could force a retreat into the vale, then make the one-eyes think they had walked into an ambush, the resulting chaos might just send them into full retreat—and fleeing enemies inflicted little damage.

"If they do not break ranks from our initial attack, then we will be dangerously thin," Brind'Amour had to put in, just a reminder that this might not be so easy as it sounded in theory.

"We will overrun them anyway," stern Shuglin promised, slapping a hammer across his open palm to accentuate his point. Looking at that grim expression, Brind'Amour believed the dwarf.

All that was left was to divide the forces accordingly. Luthien and Siobhan would collect most of the scouting groups, including all of the elvish Cutters, and filter south in two quiet lines, slipping past the cyclopian encampment and moving over the valley rims to take up defensible positions on the slopes. Bellick and Shuglin were charged with ordering the frontal line, nine thousand strong, more than half of them dwarfs.

Brind'Amour begged out of the detail planning, for the wizard understood that he would have to find a place to fit in. Magic would be a necessary ingredient, particularly in the initial assault, if they wanted to get the one-eyes moving. But the wizard knew that he had to be careful, for if he revealed himself too fully, any cyclopians who got out of the mountains would begin a whirlwind of talk that would stretch all the way to Carlisle.

The old wizard had just the enchantment in mind, subtle, yet devilishly effective. He just had to figure out how best to pull it off.

The two flanking lines, five hundred in each, set out that night, quiet archers moving swiftly. Luthien and Siobhan stayed together, spearheading the line that passed the cyclopian encampment on the east. They came over the rim of the valley shortly before dawn, picked their careful way down the slopes, searching out positions even as they heard the first rumbles of battle to the north.

Nearly two thousand Eriadoran soldiers flanked the charge on the right, another two thousand on the left, but it was the center of that line, the rolling thunder of five thousand grim-faced, battle-hungry dwarfs, that sent the Praetorian Guards into a frenzy. The leading groups of cyclopians were simply overwhelmed, buried under the weight of stomping boots, but as Brind'Amour had reasoned, the force was well-trained and they regrouped accordingly, ready to make a determined stand.

Then Brind'Amour went to work. The cyclopians recognized that they were outnumbered, but apparently had the notion to stand and fight. Holding two mugs filled with clear water, the wizard swept one arm out to the left, and one to the right, chanting all the while and dancing slightly, moving his feet in prescribed fashion.

The water flew out of the mugs and seemed to dissipate in mid-air, but in truth, it merely spread so thin as to be nearly invisible.

The curtain widened as Brind'Amour injected more of his magical energy, encompassing all of the dwarvish and Eriadoran line. In the dust and tumult, the enchanted liquid took shape as an indistinguishable mirror, effectively doubling the image of the charging force.

The cyclopian leaders were not fools. They had no specific head count, of course, but it quickly became clear to them that this raging army outnumbered them three or four to one, and they would simply be overrun. As expected, as hoped for, the call went through the cyclopian ranks to break and retreat to the narrower ground of the valley to the south.

Those cyclopians who did not turn and run fast enough found themselves quickly engaged with fierce dwarfs, usually two or three at a time.

But the bulk of the Praetorian Guard force did get out, heads bent and running swiftly. Orders continued to filter from group commander to group commander, efficiently, just the way Brind'Amour and his cohorts had expected. As the one-eyes came to the steep-walled entrance of the valley, the plan shaped out in full. Two-thirds of the cyclopian force would form a delaying line across the valley mouth, slowing their furious enemies, while the rest of the one-eyes scrambled up the slopes, east and west, finding high, defensible ground that would put the Eriadorans and their dwarvish allies at a sore disadvantage.

From their concealed perches, Luthien, Siobhan, and a thousand other archers waited patiently, letting the one-eyes charge in, letting the delaying line stretch out, and letting those others begin their ascent.

A fierce battle began almost immediately at the valley mouth, as the three groups of the Eriadoran charge converged. Still the furious dwarfs led the way, pounding the much larger cyclopians fearlessly. A dwarf fell dead for every one-eye, but the sheer weight of the line forced the Praetorian Guards slowly backward.

A one-eyed general stood on the slopes not so far below Luthien, barking out orders, calling for his soldiers to bolster a rocky outcropping that would serve as their first blocking point on this, the eastern wall.

Luthien unfolded his bow and pinned it; the general would be his first kill of the day.

"Eriador free!" he shouted, the signal, and off flew his arrow, unerringly, taking the cyclopian in the back and launching the brute into a headlong dive down the side of the valley. All around Luthien, and all along the higher ground across the way, the Eriadoran archers popped up from their concealment, letting fly a rain of deadly arrows on the surprised cyclopians.

"Eriador free!" Luthien cried again, scrambling up from behind a stone ridge, drawing out his sword and leaping down to the next lower footing. Siobhan, letting fly her second arrow, and killing her second cyclopian, started to yell out to him, to ask him where he was going, but she let it go, actually finding it within her to laugh aloud at her excited companion.

The arrow volley continued; in several spots, cyclopians and Eriadorans came into close melee. The Eriadorans held the higher ground, though, and with the archery support, most of those skirmishes ended with several cyclopians dead and the rest leaping fast to get away.

But the valley floor was no better a place for the surprised one-eyes. The delaying line held for a short while, but as it was pushed inevitably back by the dwarfs and Eriadorans pouring into the valley, all semblance of order broke down into a melting pot of sheer chaos. Clouds of dust rose from the floor, rocks tumbled away from the valley walls thunderously, and cries of victory and of agony echoed from stone to stone.

Siobhan soon found herself out of targets, her vision limited by the thick dust, and the cyclopians falling back down the valley wall. She took up her bow and scrambled over the ridge, picking her way carefully down and calling for Luthien.

She spotted a group of cyclopians stubbornly coming up, just a few yards to the side and a dozen or so yards below her. Immediately, her bow came up and she drew out an arrow, but she hesitated for just a moment, looking ahead of the one-eyes in a desperate attempt to find Luthien. Surely they were moving along the same path he had descended; surely they had come upon him, or soon would!

The leading one-eye, a huge, three-hundred pound, muscular brute, put a hand on an outcropping and threw up a leg, then heaved itself to stand atop the high stone. The cyclopian overbalanced forward, and screamed out, and Siobhan understood its frenzy as, out of the hollow below that ridge, came the blade of a familiar sword. *Blind-Striker* went right through the brute, tearing out its back, and Luthien came up fast, retracting the sword and shoulder-blocking the cyclopian right back over the outcropping.

It fell atop the next in line, and that one, in turn, tumbled atop the third.

Up came the young Bedwyr, dropping his bloody sword to the stone and taking up his bow. One, two, three, went his arrows, each scoring a hit, each nudging on the falling tumble.

"Damn you," Siobhan muttered, and she managed to get one arrow away, nailing one of the cyclopians who had moved out of the line. Then the half-elf watched, amazed and inspired, as Luthien took up his sword once more, called out for "Eriador free!" and leaped down from the outcropping, quickly catching the bouncing jumble of one-eyes and hacking away with abandon.

Siobhan quickly surmised that her reckless young friend had that situation well under control, so she moved off, looking for more targets. Not an easy proposition, the half-elf discovered when she was only fifty feet above the valley floor, for the rout was on in full. Both lines had broken apart, but Bellick's skilled dwarvish warriors formed into tight battle groups, most resembling wedges, that sliced any attempted cyclopian formations apart. Cyclopian stragglers, separated from their ranks, were immediately overwhelmed by the supporting Eriadorans, buried under a barrage of hacking swords and axes, stuck by spears from several directions at once, or simply tackled and crushed under the weight of the rolling army.

At the valley mouth, Brind'Amour watched it all with satisfaction. He had done well—they all had—for now those cyclopians who managed to escape the ambush would flee all the way back to Avon with word of an invading army twice its actual size.

Several times as large, the wizard mused, for he knew that panicking, retreating soldiers had a way of making the enemy even greater than it truly was, even greater than a simple wizard's trick had made it appear!

The wizard spotted one skirmish, on the lower slopes of the western valley wall, where a handful of cyclopians had taken cover within a protective ring of huge stones. A group of elves were trying to get at them, but the ground favored the one-eyes.

Brind'Amour began to chant once more, lifted his arms out to the side and, as his words brought forth the magical energy, swept his arms together, clapping his hands.

The stones of the cyclopians' defensive ring rolled together suddenly, squeezing the brutes, crushing a couple, and leaving the rest out in the open.

The elves were on them immediately, slender swords darting through the desperate defenses of the scrambling brutes, laying them low in a matter of seconds. One of the elves stood tall on the closed stones, shaking his head. He looked to the east, saw Brind'Amour standing quietly, and saluted the old wizard.

Then he and his fellows ran off, for there remained more cyclopians yet to kill.

Brind'Amour sighed and walked into the valley, reciting an old religious verse that he knew from his younger days those centuries before, when he had used his magics to help construct the fabulous Ministry cathedral.

"The Valley of Death," the verse was called, and barely a few feet in, the wizard began to step across the corpses of cyclopians, dwarfs, and humans.

A fitting title.

Luthien ran along a narrow ledge higher up the valley wall, looking for some alternate route, or some wider spot, for a group of fleeing cyclopians were close behind. The one-eyes didn't know that he was there, but they would figure it out soon enough. Luthien glanced left, up the steep wall, a climb he could not even attempt. Then he looked right, down toward the valley floor, hoping to see Siobhan or some other friendly archer taking a bead on those trotting behind him. All that he saw was a thick dust cloud; he would find no allies that way.

The path wound on, narrow and dangerous.

Luthien didn't know how many cyclopians were back there, but there were several, at least, and he had no desire to fight against unfavorable odds up here, with so little ground for maneuvering. He resigned himself to do just that, though, and he considered his resources and how he might strike hard and fast to better even the odds. A bow shot might kill the first in line—if he was lucky enough, that falling one might take the second with it, or at least slow the others so that Luthien could let fly a couple of more arrows. But what if he missed, or if his first shot didn't drop the leading cyclopian, but only slowed the brute?

Luthien went around another bend, resolved to use his sword alone, and not his bow. He would turn and make his stand, he decided. As he came around, he saw that the ledge widened in this one area, a depression in the cliff wall several feet deep.

With a sigh of relief, Luthien skipped to the back wall, pulled the hood of his magical cape over his head and stood very still. Only seconds later, he could hear the closing cyclopians, lumbering on and talking of climbing to the valley rim and escaping.

The one-eyes came around the bend; peeking out from under the hood, Luthien counted as they passed. The seventh, and last, came into view as the first moved on past the wider area.

The notion flitted through Luthien's mind that he had been wise to run ahead, and not to stop and fight this desperate crew. That wise thought was abruptly washed away, though, as the daring young Bedwyr realized that the back end of this cyclopian line might make for easy targets. Hardly conscious of the move, Luthien rushed out from the wall, shouldering the trailing cyclopian right over the ledge. Luthien stopped, facing the drop, then pivoted a complete turn, coming around hard with *Blind-Striker* to smash the next cyclopian across the hip as the startled brute spun about to register the attack.

Luthien dug in hard, clenched tightly on his blade with both hands, and forced that second brute over the ledge as well. The third, already on the narrower path, howled and turned about, sword at the ready. Luthien rushed right up to it, keeping it out of the wider area so that its friends could not flank him. Two of those one-eyes, thinking they had been caught from behind by the nasty Eriadorans, only increased their pace, running off as fast as they could manage along the narrow ledge. The other two stopped and turned, calling to their battling companion.

Luthien worked his blade furiously, not letting the cyclopian off its heels for a moment. "I have them!" the man yelled, looking over his shoulder as though expecting reinforcements.

His cavalier attitude and his dress told the brute fighting him much. "The Crimson Shadow!" the foolish cyclopian yelled out. That was all its companions needed to hear. With typical cyclopian loyalty, they bid their engaged friend farewell and ran off.

Terror drove the cyclopian fighting Luthien to daring, reckless attack routines. It dropped one foot back, retreating half a step, then came forward in a rush, lowering its shoulder, hoping that the bold tactic would catch its opponent off his guard.

It didn't. Luthien merely dropped back a step and slipped to the side, around the wall into the wider area. *Blind-Striker* slid easily through the cyclopian's ribs as it stumbled past.

Luthien was fast to withdraw the blade, jumping back to defensive posture. The cyclopian stood perfectly still, groaning, trying to turn about to face the swordsman squarely. It finally managed to do so, just in time to see the bottoms of Luthien's feet as the young man leaped out and double-kicked, blasting the wounded brute from the ledge.

Luthien was up in an instant. "The Crimson Shadow, true enough," he called to the tumbling cyclopian. He took a breath and ran off along the narrow path in pursuit of the four who had fled. Confident that they would not stop to wait for the pursuit, Luthien slid *Blind-Striker* back into its scabbard and pulled his folding bow from his back, extending and pinning it as he ran.

The frightened cyclopians were reckless on the treacherous path and Luthien gained little ground. He did get one shot, though, and made the most of it, nailing the trailing one-eye in the back of the calf as it rounded one bend. It stumbled out of sight, but Luthien knew it could not escape. Out came his sword and on he charged, slowing to a determined stalk as he neared that bend.

He found the brute leaning heavily against the wall, crouching low, holding a sword in one hand and its bleeding calf with the other. Its companion, a dozen feet further along the ledge, waited anxiously.

Luthien casually strode forward and whacked at the injured one-eye. It picked off the straightforward attack, but nearly toppled for the weight of the blow. Its companion howled and started forward, but Luthien put an end to that, sent the one-eye running off, merely by shifting *Blind-Striker* to his left hand, then reaching back with his right to pull the bow off his shoulder.

"Your friend has fled," he said to the injured cyclopian. "I'll accept your surrender."

The brute lowered its sword and started to straighten, then came ahead suddenly in a rush, thrusting boldly.

In a single movement, Luthien brought the tip of his bow straight across, right to left, then turned the bow tip up and swept it back across, taking the thrusting sword out wide. Out came *Blind-Striker* to stick the off-balance brute through the heart. It fell heavily against the wall and slowly sank to the ground, its lifeless eye staring coldly at Luthien.

The young Bedwyr looked ahead and could tell that the narrow ledge didn't go on much further, spilling out into wider terrain. There was no way that he could get to the fleeing cyclopians before they reached that area. With a sigh, Luthien looked back to the valley floor, then scanned the route that would get him back there. A noise quickly turned him back to the ledge, though, where, to his surprise, two of the fleeing brutes were running back toward him with all speed!

And they were both looking more over their shoulder than ahead.

Luthien skittered back from the last kill and held tight to the wall, again using the magical camouflage of his magnificent cape. Peeking out from under the cowl, he saw the trailing cyclopian stumble, then, an instant later, go down on its face.

The remaining brute put its head down and howled in terror, running full out, skipping past the companion it had deserted, lying dead against the wall.

Out jumped Luthien; the one-eye broke stride for just an instant, then rambled ahead.

Both hands clenching tight to *Blind-Striker*, Luthien thrust out and dropped his back leg out from under him, falling low as the pierced cyclopian came right over him, turning a somersault and sliding back from the bloodied blade as it passed. It slammed down on its back onto the ledge, too dazed to rise in time, for Luthien came up and about, his blade diving into cyclopian flesh to finish the task.

It was no surprise to Luthien when his unseen ally came running along the ledge, bow in hand.

"I scored eight kills this day," Siobhan announced proudly.

"Then you have fallen behind," an exhausted Luthien informed her, holding aloft his dripping sword. "Fourteen, and that makes it sixteen to fourteen in my favor."

The half-elf eyed the young man sternly. " 'Tis a long way to Carlisle," she said grimly.

The friends shared a smile.

"They are in full retreat," Shuglin informed the two kings, Bellick and Brind'Amour, when he found them among a group of Eriadorans and dwarfs near the middle of the long valley.

"In no formation," another dwarf added. "Running like the cowards they are!"

"A true rout, then," reasoned Bellick, and there was no disagreement. Losses to the joined human and dwarvish armies were amazingly light, but all reports indicated that the cyclopian dead would number near two thousand.

The dwarf king turned to Brind'Amour. "We must pursue with all speed," Bellick said. "Catch them while they are disorganized, and before they can find defensible ground."

The old wizard thought it over for a long while. There were many considerations here, not the least of which being the fact that the vast bulk of their supplies were still a couple of miles north of the valley. Bellick's reasoning made sense, though, for if they allowed the terror of the rout to dissipate, the Praetorian Guards would fast regroup, and would not likely be caught so unawares again.

"I follow your word in this," Bellick assured Brind'Amour, the dwarf recognizing the wizard's turmoil. "Yet I beg of you to allow my dwarfs to complete what they have begun!"

Every dwarf in the area cheered out at those words, and Brind'Amour realized that holding the eager warriors of DunDarrow back now would cause simmering feelings that his army could ill-afford at that time. "Go with your forces," he said to Bellick. "But not so far. Keep the one-eyes running. My soldiers will collect our wounded and our supplies, and set our camp there." Brind'Amour pointed to the southern end of the valley. "Return to us this night, that we might resume our joined march in the morning."

Bellick nodded, smiling widely beneath the bright hair of his orange beard. He reached up to clap Brind'Amour on the shoulder as he walked past, as he walked into a gathering mob of his eager subjects.

"All the way to Carlisle," began the chant, starting low and growing to a roar.

CHAPTER 20

VISIONS

*L*UTHIEN COMMANDED the main group of Eriadoran soldiers that day, setting the camp, tending the wounded, burying the dead. Though he doubted that the cyclopians would regroup and come back at them, he preferred to err on the side of caution. Scouts were sent up over the rim of the valley; archers were put in place on the valley walls, overlooking the encampment.

Brind'Amour spent the remainder of the day in his tent, alone, though soldiers venturing near to the tent often heard the wizard speaking in whispered tones. He emerged after sunset, to find Luthien and Siobhan organizing the nighttime perimeter. Many of Bellick's dwarfs, including Shuglin, had returned, all with tales of further punishment inflicted on their fleeing enemy.

"It all goes well," Brind'Amour remarked to Luthien and Siobhan when the three found a rare quiet moment.

Luthien eyed the wizard curiously, suspecting that Brind'Amour had spent the day in magical contact with the other arms of the invasion, a fact the wizard confirmed a moment later.

"Proctor Byllewyn and his force have swept down from the wall and encircled Princetown," the wizard said, "and the beleaguered folk, still without a garrison from the last war, and still without a wizard-duke to lead them, are close to surrender. This very night, the proxy mayor of Princetown meets with Proctor Byllewyn and Kayryn Kulthwain to discuss the terms."

Luthien and Siobhan exchanged satisfied nods; that was just what they had been hoping for. Princetown could have become a major obstacle to the eastern ground forces. If they had been held up for even a few days, they would have had no chance of getting to Carlisle on time.

"The eastern fleet has made the shores of Dulsen-Berra," Brind'Amour went on, "third of the Five Sentinels."

"Losses?" Siobhan asked.

"None to speak of," the wizard replied. "It seems that more of the independent islanders have joined our cause than have taken up arms against us."

"To the dismay of the Huegoths, no doubt," Siobhan quipped.

Luthien glared at her, not willing to hear such pessimism, but the half-elf remained steadfast. "Slaves must be replaced," she said matter-of-factly.

She was echoing Oliver, the young Bedwyr realized. Oliver deBurrows, my moral conscience, Luthien mused, and he shuddered at the thought.

"Not so," Brind'Amour answered to Siobhan's concerns. "The Huegoths remain far offshore, shadowing our vessels, and hopefully beyond the notice of Greensparrow. They have not joined in any of the limited action thus far, and have registered no complaints with Captain Leary."

The news was welcome, if surprising. Even Luthien, holding faith in the truce, had not expected the Huegoths to behave so well for this long.

"Your brother knows the truth, of course," Brind'Amour went on. "He understands our desires to keep the brutal Isenlanders away from innocents. But Ethan has assured King Asmund that the distant course determined for the longships is only to keep Greensparrow oblivious to Eriador's newest allies."

"Asmund believes him?" Luthien asked, somewhat skeptical.

"The Huegoths are behaving," Brind'Amour replied, and nothing more needed to be said.

"What of the western fleet?" Siobhan asked, and her concerns were clear in her voice, though she tried to hide them. That brought a sly smile from Luthien as he tried to imagine the half-elf and Oliver side by side. That vision was lost before it ever took form, though, for the mere mention of their fleet in the west sent Luthien's thoughts to Katerin. Luthien promptly reminded himself of his duty and squared his shoulders, but he could not dismiss his fears for his love. Never would Luthien demand that Katerin stay out of battle, not when the cause was this important, but he wished that she was by his side at least, that he might know every minute that she was all right. It struck Luthien then that perhaps Brind'Amour had arranged for Katerin to go far from him purposefully. And perhaps it was a good thing, the young Bedwyr had to admit. How well would he fight, how willing would he be to commit his forces to a daring battle, if he knew that Katerin was among those soldiers? She was as capable a warrior as anyone Luthien had ever known, and needed no looking after, yet with his heart so stung how could Luthien not hover over her?

"All the forces have come down from the northeastern reaches and from the three islands," Brind'Amour informed them. "They have gathered in full and will sail out from Port Charley in the morning, when the tide is high."

Better for both of them to be apart at this time, Luthien admitted, but that did little to calm his fears.

"All is in place, a most splendid start to the campaign!" Brind'Amour said cheerfully, his white teeth beaming from his hairy face.

With that proclamation, the meeting ended. As he and Siobhan walked away, Luthien noticed the expression on the half-elf's face and understood that she was harboring the same anxiety for her distant friend as he. No doubt, though, Siobhan was more tentative in her thoughts about Oliver. Luthien didn't mention their common worries; what would be the point?

"All the way to Carlisle," he said suddenly, imitating the dwarfish chant.

Siobhan looked at him, surprised, and then grateful for the reminder of the business at hand. "I will go out to the east," she announced, "and see that the watch line is secured."

"And I, to the west," Luthien said, and with a shared nod they split up.

Both were grateful for the privacy.

Brind'Amour's smile disappeared as soon as he entered his tent. Things had indeed begun full of hope and excitement, with early victories easily won. Their rout of the Praetorian Guards in the mountains exceeded even their highest expectations, as did the behavior of their Huegoth allies. But the wizard was experienced enough to temper his jubilation. Neither of the Eriadoran fleets had yet encountered Avon warships, and though Princetown was on the verge of surrender (if it hadn't already surrendered), the northern Avon city was never expected to be a factor. Eriador had already conquered Princetown, after all, before the last truce, and there was no garrison in place there, nor any of Greensparrow's wizard cohorts.

Early victories, easily won, but that had been an assumption before the invasion had ever started. It would be a foolish thing indeed for the Eriadorans and their allies to grow overly confident now that those expected victories had been realized.

Because, the wizard knew, the road ahead grew ever darker.

Brind'Amour's own central forces would soon be pressing down the Dunkery River, into the heartland of Avon, on their march to Warchester.

"Warchester," Brind'Amour said aloud. Aptly named, he knew, for he had been to the city often in times long past. The place was more a fortress than a city, with walls as high as those of Carlisle itself.

That run down the banks of the Dunkery would make this one battle with the Praetorian Guards seem as no more than a minor skirmish, for when they met organized resistance, Brind'Amour's army would likely be sorely outnumbered. Even if they struggled through, even if Warchester was taken, the weary Eriadorans would have another two hundred miles of hostile ground to cross before they ever reached the high walls of fortified Carlisle.

And the prospects for the western Eriadoran fleet seemed equally grim. Would the forty galleons and their fishing boat escorts survive their trek through the narrow Straits of Mann, right between the powers of Mannington and Eornfast? Baranduine had figured little into the preparations for war, but in truth, the wild green island to the west possessed a flotilla stronger than Eriador's, if all of Eriador's warships had been gathered together.

Even worse, by Brind'Amour's calculations, loomed the magical disadvantage. He was alone, and his type of magic, the powers gained through use of the natural elements—the fiery sun and the wind, the strength of a storm or a tree—had passed its zenith centuries before. Brind'Amour had battled Duke Paragor and Paragor's familiar demon, and had barely survived the encounter. How would he fare against Greensparrow's other allies, fresh with their hellish powers? And how would he fare against Greensparrow, who was as old as he, who had remained awake through the centuries, garnering his powers?

Indeed it seemed a desperate war to Brind'Amour, but he realized that, in truth, he had been given little choice. As he had openly proclaimed in Caer MacDonald, as long as Greensparrow sat in place on Avon's throne, there could be no peace. With Dukes Morkney and Paragor dead, Resmore broken in a dungeon in Caer MacDonald, and with Princetown still reeling and helpless from the last war, now was the time, perhaps the last true chance for Eriador to shake the lurking specter of King Greensparrow.

Brind'Amour sat on his cot and rubbed his tired eyes. He thought he was seeing things a moment later, when a great bird turned its wings perpendicular to the ground and slipped silently through the folds of his tent flap.

An owl?

The bird fluttered to a perch on the lantern holder, set halfway up the center tent pole. It eyed Brind'Amour directly, knowingly, and he understood that this was no chance meeting.

"Well, what are you about?" the wizard asked, wondering if his nemesis Greensparrow had personally come a'calling.

The owl turned its head slightly and Brind'Amour's next comment was lost by the image he saw in the owl's huge eyes. Not a reflection, but an image of a tower of stone, high and narrow and flat, set within the rugged mountains. A singular pillar of windblown rock.

Brind'Amour.

The call was distant, far removed, a whisper on the night breeze.

"What are you about?" the old wizard asked the bird again, this time breathlessly.

The owl swooped off the perch and out the flap, silent in flight.

Brind'Amour rubbed his eyes again and looked about his tent, wondering if it had been no more than a dream. He looked to his crystal ball, thinking that perhaps he might find some answers, but he shook his head. He had spent hours contacting his generals, east and west, and was too exhausted to consider sending his thoughts into the ball once again.

He lay back on his cot and soon fell into a deep slumber.

When he awoke the next morning, he was convinced that the incident with the bird had been no more than the dreaming delusions of a weary old man.

CHAPTER 21

THE SEEDS OF REVOLT

OW GOOD IT FELT to Luthien: the wind in his face, the rush of ground beneath Riverdancer's pounding hooves! They were coming out of the mountains, back onto terrain where Luthien could ride his precious Morgan Highlander.

Riverdancer, after so many miles of plodding along painful, rocky ground, seemed to enjoy the jaunt even more than his rider. Luthien constantly had to hold the powerful white stallion back, else he would have easily outdistanced the other riders coming down from the foothills beside him, mostly Siobhan and the other Cutters.

As usual, they were the lead group, the spearhead for the Eriadoran army, and the single cavalry unit. Because of the difficult mountain terrain, only two hundred horses had been brought along, and more than a third of them could not now be ridden because of problems they had developed during the difficult trek, mostly with their hooves.

Riverdancer was fine, though, ready and eager to run on. Luthien tightened up on the reins, easing the horse into a steady, solid trot as they came to one last sloping expanse. Siobhan, astride a tall and slender chestnut, caught up to him then, and wasted no time in pointing out the smoke from a village not far distant to the south. Beside it wound a great silvery snake, the Dunkery River.

"It is called Pipery, according to Brind'Amour's map," Luthien informed her. "The northernmost of a series of mill towns set along the Dunkery."

"Our next target," Siobhan said grimly. She looked to both sides, to the hundred or so riders sweeping down beside her, then turned to Luthien. "Are we to split into smaller forces, or remain as one group?"

Luthien considered the options for just a moment. He had thought to break the unit into several scouting groups, but with Pipery in sight, the line for the army seemed obvious. "Together," he said at length. "We'll go south, then cut back northeast, to meet the Dunkery where it comes out of the foothills. Then south again along the river, scouting the path all the way to the town."

Siobhan peered into the rolling southland, confirming the course, and nodded her agreement. "The cyclopians will not wait for us to get to the town," she reasoned.

The thought did not seem to bother Luthien in the least.

The group moved south for a couple of miles, coming directly to the west of Pipery. In the shade of a pine grove, they gave their mounts a much-needed break, with Luthien dispatching several riders to scout out the area, particularly the trail back to the northeast, which they would soon be riding.

Those scouts moving directly east, toward the village, returned after only a few minutes, reporting that a group of two to three hundred cyclopians, including two-score cavalry riding fierce ponypigs, were fast approaching.

"We could outrun them back to the mountains," the scout reminded.

"We could outrun them all the way to Pipery," an eager Siobhan suggested.

Luthien's thoughts were moving somewhere in the middle of the two propositions. His group was outnumbered, but held a tremendous advantage of maneuverability. Ponypigs, resembling warthogs the size of large ponies, were brutal opponents, with strong kicking legs and nasty tusks, and cyclopians could ride them well, but they were not as swift as horses.

"We cannot afford to lose any riders," Luthien said to Siobhan, "but if this is part of Pipery's militia, then better to sting them out in the open than to let them get back behind the village's fortifications."

"No doubt they think us an advance scouting unit," Siobhan replied, "with little heart for battle."

"Let us teach them differently," Luthien said determinedly.

The young Bedwyr sent nearly half of his force to the north then, on a long roundabout, while he and Siobhan led the remaining riders straight on toward the approaching cyclopians. He spread them out in a line across a ridge when the enemy force was in sight, letting the one-eyes take a full measure, while he took the measure of them.

The scouts' information was right on the mark. The cavalry groups seemed roughly equal in strength, by Luthien's design. What the cyclopians didn't know was that they were facing a force of mostly Fairborn, with a well-earned reputation for riding and for archery.

Luthien scanned the green fields to the north, but his other forces were not yet in sight. He had to hope that they had not encountered resistance, else his entire plan might fall apart.

"With the cavalry in front," Siobhan remarked, referring to the fast-forming cyclopian ranks, riders on ponypigs forming a line in front of the foot soldiers. The half-elf smiled as she spoke, for this was exactly what Luthien had predicted.

Time to go, the young Bedwyr realized, and he drew out

Blind-Striker, raising the sword high into the sky. Out came more than fifty blades in response, all lifted high.

A few quiet seconds slipped by, the very air tingling with anticipation.

Luthien jabbed *Blind-Striker* toward the sky before him and the charge from the ridge was on.

The cyclopians howled in response and the thunder of surging horses was more than matched by the thunder of charging ponypigs.

The elvish swords and *Blind-Striker* unexpectedly came down, the skilled Eriadoran riders deftly slipping them back into their sheaths. The close-melee weapons had been but a ruse, a teasing challenge to the savage cyclopians, for the Eriadorans never intended to battle in close combat. On Luthien's command, up came the bows.

A cyclopian's eye was a large and bulbous thing, and wider still seemed the eyes of the charging Praetorian Guards when they realized the ruse and understood that they would be under heavy assault before they ever got near their enemy.

Luthien Bedwyr felt like a rank amateur over the next few moments. He got his bow up and fired off a shot, barely missing, but though he was a fine horseman and a fine archer, by the time he got his second arrow in place, most of the Fairborn riding beside him had already let fly three, or even four.

And the majority of those had hit their mark.

Chaos hit the cyclopian ranks as ponypigs stumbled and fell, or reared in agony. Stinging arrows zipped through, felling rider and mount, dismantling the order of the cyclopian charge. Some one-eyes continued on; others turned about and fled.

And then a new rumble came over the field as the remaining Eriadoran riders swept down from the north, firing bows at the cyclopian foot soldiers as they charged.

Luthien drew out *Blind-Striker* again as he neared the leading cyclopian riders. He angled Riverdancer for a close pass on one, but an arrow beat him to the mark, taking down the one-eye cleanly. Luthien easily veered past the now-walking ponypig, crossing behind yet another cyclopian. The one-eye turned in its seat, trying to get its blocking sword out behind, but Luthien smacked the blade aside and stuck the brute in the kidney as he passed.

With a groan, the cyclopian slumped forward, leaning heavily on the ponypig's muscled neck.

Luthien spotted another target and charged on, his crimson cape flying out wildly behind him. The cyclopian, like most of its companions, had other ideas, though, and turned about and fled.

Luthien coaxed Riverdancer into a full gallop and ran the brute down, hacking his sword across the back of the one-eye's thick neck. He moved away quickly, not wanting to get tangled up in the ponypig as its rider slipped to the ground.

Many of the cyclopian foot soldiers turned to flee as well, but others formed up into a square, heavy shields blocking every side, long pikes ready to prod at any horsemen who ventured too near. That square marched double-time, right back the way they had come, toward Pipery.

The Eriadorans continued to nip at the one-eyes, particularly interested in running down any cyclopian rider who strayed too far from the main group, but when those Fairborn scouts watching the roads further to the east announced that a second force was coming from Pipery to reinforce the first, Luthien knew that the time had come to break off and await the approach of the larger Eriadoran army.

He eyed the field, satisfied, as he and his riders crossed back to the west. A couple of horses had been downed, with three riders injured, but only one seriously. The cyclopians had not gotten off so easily. More than a dozen ponypigs lay dead, or quickly dying, on the grass, and another twenty wandered riderless. Less than a quarter of the two-score cyclopian cavalry had escaped unscathed, with nearly half lying dead on the field, along with a handful of the foot soldiers.

More important than the actual numbers, Luthien's group had met the enemy again, on the enemy's home ground this time, and had sent them running in full flight. Luthien would continue with the scouting mission now, but he held few doubts that the larger Eriadoran army would roll through this part of their course. The road to Pipery, at least, would be an easy march.

Brother Solomon Keyes knelt in prayer, hands clasped, head bowed, in the small chapel of Pipery. A far cry from the tremendous cathedrals of the larger cities of Avonsea, the place had but two rooms: a common meeting room, and Solomon Keyes's private living area. It was a square, stone, unremarkable place; the pews were no more than single-board benches, the altar merely a table donated after the death of one of Pipery's more well-to-do widows. Still, to many in the humble village, that chapel was as much a source of pride as the great cathedrals were to the inhabitants of Princetown or Carlisle. Despite the fact that Greensparrow's cyclopian tax collectors, including one particularly nasty old one-eye named Allaberksis, utilized the chapel as a meeting house, Solomon Keyes had worked hard to preserve the sanctity of the place.

He hoped, he prayed, that his efforts would be rewarded now, that the invading army rumored to be fast approaching would spare the goodly folks of his small community. Keyes was only in his mid-twenties. He had lived practically all of his life under the court of King Greensparrow, and thus he, and most of the people of Pipery, had never before met an Eriadoran. They had heard the stories of the savage northlanders, though, of how Eriadorans had been known to eat the children of conquered villages right before parents' eyes. Keyes had also heard of the wicked dwarfs—the "head-bashers," they were called in Avon—for their reputed propensity for using their boots to cave in the heads of enemy dead and wounded. And he had heard of the elves, the Fairborn, the "devil's-spawn," disguising their horns as ears, running naked under the stars in unholy tribute to the evil gods.

And Keyes had heard whispered tales of the Crimson Shadow, and that one, most of all, had the people of his village trembling with terror. The Crimson Shadow, the murderer who came silently in the night, like Death itself.

Solomon Keyes was wise enough to understand that many of the rumors he had heard of his king's hated foes were likely untrue or, at least, exaggerations. Still, it was widely reported that somewhere around ten thousand of these enemies were nearing Pipery, whose militia, including the few Praetorian Guards who had come down from the mountains, numbered no more than three hundred. Whatever monster this force of combined enemies might truly be, Pipery was in dire trouble.

Keyes was rocked from his contemplations as the chapel door burst open and a handful of one-eyes stormed in. Praetorian Guards, the priest realized immediately, and not Pipery's regular militia.

"All is in place for the hospital," the priest said quietly, looking down to the floor.

"We have come for tithes," replied Allaberksis, coming in on the heels of the burly guards. The group never slowed, crossing the room and kicking aside benches.

Solomon Keyes looked up incredulously, staring at the withered old cyclopian, the oldest and most wrinkled one-eye anyone in these parts had ever known. Its eye was bloodshot and grayish in hue, its general luster long gone. There was a particular sparkle in the eye of Allaberksis now, though, one that Solomon Keyes recognized as pure greed.

"I have bandages," Keyes pleaded after a stunned pause. "Of what use is money?"

One of the Praetorian Guards stepped right up and shoved the priest to the floor.

"There is a box at the back of the altar," instructed Allaberksis. "And you," he said to another of the brutes, "check the fool priest's private room."

"That is the common grain money!" Keyes roared in protest, leaping to his feet. He was met by another of the brutes and pounded down, then kicked several times as he squirmed on the floor.

Solomon Keyes realized the truth of the intruders. This group, like so many of the Praetorian Guards who had come down from the Iron Cross, was planning to flee to the south, probably on wretched Allaberksis's orders.

Keyes could not fight them, and so he lay very still, praying again for guidance. He breathed a profound sigh when the group swept back out of the chapel.

That relief was short-lived, though, for it didn't take the priest long to understand the implications of Allaberksis's actions.

Pipery was being deserted as a sacrifice. King Greensparrow's elite soldiers did not consider the small village worth saving.

The Eriadoran army camped within sight of Pipery, swinging lines far to the east and west, even launching cavalry patrols across the ground south of the village to make sure that very few one-eyes escaped. Brind'Amour had no intention of allowing Greensparrow's disorganized northern army to run all the way back to Carlisle, or to Warchester, perhaps, where they might regroup behind the protection of the city's high walls.

On one such expedition, Luthien's swift cavalry group had come upon a curious band of Praetorian Guards, led by the oldest one-eye the young Bedwyr had ever seen. The cyclopians were summarily routed, and in picking through their bodies, Luthien had found a purse clearly marked as contributions for the town's common good.

The young Bedwyr thought that significant, and was beginning to discern a possibility here, a hope for an easier march. He said nothing about it on his return to the camp, though, wanting to sort things out more fully before presenting his suspicions to Brind'Amour, who, for some reason that Luthien couldn't discern, seemed more than a bit distracted this evening.

"You fear the coming battle?" Luthien asked, prodding his old friend, as the pair walked across the central area of the large camp.

Brind'Amour scoffed at that notion. "If I feared Pipery, I never would have come south, knowing that Warchester and Carlisle lay ahead!" the wizard replied. He stopped by a water trough then and bent low to splash his face. He paused before his hand touched the water, and stood very still, for in that trough, Brind'Amour saw a curious scene, a now-familiar narrow and tall, flat-topped pillar of stone.

Brind'Amour.

The call floated in on the wind. Brind'Amour glanced all about, looking for the rocks that might have made such a reflection in the water, but no such tower loomed anywhere near.

"What is it?" Luthien asked, concerned. He, too, glanced all about, though he had no idea what he might be looking for.

Brind'Amour waved his hand in the empty air, all the answer Luthien would get from him at that time. The wizard considered the call, the subtle and personal call, considered the owl and now the trough, and suddenly thought that he had sorted out the answer.

And hoped that he did, for if his guess was correct, these curious events might well alter the course of the coming battle.

"Keep a good eye to the perimeter," the old wizard instructed as he briskly walked away from Luthien.

Luthien called after him, but it was useless; Brind'Amour would not even slow his swift pace.

Back in his tent, the wizard wasted no time in taking out his crystal ball. The image of the strange rock formation was clear in his mind, and after nearly an hour of exhausting divining, he managed to replicate it in the crystal ball. Then Brind'Amour let the conjured image become a true scene and he slowly altered the perspective within the ball, searching out landmarks near the tower that might guide him. Soon he was convinced that the formation was in the Iron Cross, not so far to the north and west, closer to the coast, surely.

The wizard released the image from the ball and relaxed. He considered his course carefully, realizing that this might well be a trap. Perhaps it was one of his peers from that long-past age, awake again and ready to join in with Eriador's just cause. Perhaps it was Greensparrow, luring him to his doom that Eriador continue without a king, and without a wizard to counter the magics of the dukes and duchess and king of Avon.

"Now is not the time for caution," Brind'Amour said aloud, bolstering his resolve. "Now is not the time for cowards!"

Brind'Amour considered again the desperation of this war, the complete gamble that had been accepted by all the brave folk of Eriador with the prize of true freedom dangling before them.

The old wizard knew what he must do.

CHAPTER 22

TRAPPING THE TRAPPERS

BRIND'AMOUR SLIPPED quietly from his tent later that night. The moon had already set and the stars were crisp, in those spots where they showed through the broken canopy of rushing black clouds. The wizard, energized by thoughts of the crucial task before him, walked spryly across the encampment, past the rows of sleeping soldiers, beyond the rolling thunder of several thousand snoring dwarfs, and beyond the perimeter line, enacting a minor spell so that even the acute senses of the Fairborn sentries could not detect him. Brind'Amour had neither the time nor the desire to answer questions now.

He walked another half mile, coming to an area of stony ground, a small clearing sheltered by thick rows of maple, elm, birch, and pine. He noted that many of the leaves of the deciduous trees were already beginning to turn a light brown; autumn was fast approaching.

With a deep, steadying breath, Brind'Amour brought the enchantment—no minor spell this time—into mind. Then he began to dance, slowly, each step perfectly placed, each twirl symbolic of what he was to become. Soon his arms remained out wide as he spun more quickly, dipping and rising through each turn, his arms waving now gracefully—too gracefully for a human, it seemed.

The darkness seemed to lift then, from Brind'Amour's perspective, as the wizard's eyes became suddenly sensitive; the landscape became distinct and surreal. He heard a mouse rustle through the grass, perhaps twenty feet away, heard the cricket songs as loudly as if they were resounding through the massive pipes of the Ministry's choir organ.

He felt a series of pinlike pricks along both his arms, and looked there to see his voluminous robes melting away into overlapping lines of soft feathers. The stings were gone in an instant, as the rest of the wizard's body began its change, as the feathers became a natural part of his new anatomy.

The ground went away in a rush as the great owl flew away, soft-feathered wings beating the air without a whisper of sound.

Brind'Amour knew freedom then, true freedom. How he loved this transformation! Particularly at night, when all the human world was asleep, when it seemed as no more than a wonderful dream.

Hardly registering the move, the wizard turned sidelong, wing tips perpendicular to the ground, as he sliced between a pair of close trees.

He rose as he came out the other side, working his wings hard, then felt the warm air on his belly as he crossed near the first real mountains of the Iron Cross. Wings widespread, the wizard rose slowly into the night air, tingling from the mixture of currents and air temperatures. He soared through the night-blanketed range, weaving through valleys and riding the warm updrafts. Into the northwest he flew, to where the mountains were more rugged, impassable by foot, but merely a majestic wave for an owl to ride.

He flew for an hour, easily, wonderfully, then came into a region of sheer drops and broken, windblown pillars. He knew this region, had seen it clearly in his crystal ball.

Now the wizard slowed and took care to move closer to the sheltering cliffs. The landscape was exactly as he had viewed it in the crystal ball, and so he was not surprised when he turned around one bend, lifted up to clear a high jag, and came in sight of the singular, flat-topped rock pillar. It resembled the limbless trunk of an old, gnarled tree, except that its angles, twists, and turns through all of its five hundred feet were sharper and more distinct, seeming unnatural, as though some tremendous force had pulled it right up from the ground.

Brind'Amour flew past the pillar at about half its height, preferring to make his first run in view of the plateau from the other direction. Up he rose, in a gradual bank, coming about much higher, almost level with the pillar's flat top.

He saw a single figure atop the stone, sitting near the center of the roughly fifty-foot-diameter plateau. The person was huddled under robes, the hood pulled low, facing the glowing embers of a dying fire.

Brind'Amour passed barely thirty feet above the huddled figure, but the person made no move, took no note.

Asleep? the old wizard mused. And why not? Brind'Amour told himself. What would someone in a place so very inaccessible have to fear?

This time, the wizard's bank was sharper, nearly a spinning mid-air pivot. Brind'Amour came in even lower, not sure of whether he would make another scouting pass.

No time for such caution, he decided, and so he mustered his courage and swooped to the stone, landing across the fire from the figure, halfway between the huddled person and the plateau's edge.

"Well done, King Brind'Amour," said a familiar female voice even as the wizard began the transformation back into his human form. The figure looked up and pulled back the tremendous hood of her robes. "I knew that you would be resourceful enough to find me."

Brind'Amour's heart sank at the sight of Duchess Deanna Wellworth.

He was not truly surprised, for he had been fairly certain that none of his wizard companions from that time long past had survived. Still, the fact that he had flown so willingly into such a ruse, and the reality that he was indeed alone, weighed heavily on his shoulders.

"My greetings," Deanna said casually, and her tone gave Brind'Amour pause. Also, he realized, she had referred to him as "King Brind'Amour." The old wizard didn't know what to make of it. He glanced all about, thinking that he should resume his owl form and rush away on the winds.

No, he decided. He would trust in his powers and let this meeting play out. It had to come to this, after all; perhaps it would be better to be done with it before too many lives were lost.

"And the greetings of Duke Ashannon McLenny of Eornfast in Baranduine," Deanna went on. "And those of Duke Mystigal of Evenshorn, and Duke Theredon Rees of Warchester." As she spoke each name, the appropriate man stepped into view, as though walking from behind a curtain of night sky.

Brind'Amour felt a fool. Why hadn't he seen them through such a simple magical disguise? Of course, he could not have enacted such divining magics in owl form, but he should have flown to a nearby ledge and resumed his human shape, then scanned the plateau top more carefully before coming down. His eagerness, his desire to believe that one of his ancient brothers had returned to his side, had caused him to err.

The three dukes were evenly spaced about the plateau top. Brind'Amour scanned them now, seeking the weakest link where he might escape. Deanna Wellworth surprised him, though, and her three companions as well, when she lifted a round beaker of blue liquid before her, spoke a single word and threw it down. It smashed into the fire, which erupted into a burst of white, then went low, blowing a thick wave of fog from its sizzling embers. The wave rolled out in all directions, right past the four startled men. When it reached the edge of the plateau, it swirled upward, turning back over the stone.

Then the fog was no more, replaced by a blue-glowing canopy, a bubble of energy, that encompassed the plateau. All the plateau was bathed in the eerie light.

Brind'Amour was truly impressed; he realized that Deanna must have spent days, perhaps even weeks, in designing such a spell. He wasn't sure of the nature of the globe, but he guessed that it was some sort of a barrier, anti-magic or anti-flesh, designed to prevent him from leaving. Whether it would prove effective might be a different thing altogether, though, for the wizard was confident that he could counter anything one of Greensparrow's cohorts could enact.

But how much time did he have?

"You resort to treachery?" Brind'Amour scoffed, his tone showing his clear disdain. "How far the honor of wizards has fallen. Common thieves, is that what you have become?"

"Of course your ancient and holy brotherhood would never have done such a thing," Theredon Rees of Warchester replied sarcastically.

"Never," Brind'Amour answered in even tones. The old king stared long and hard at the upstart wizard. Theredon was a stocky, muscular man, nearing middle age. His hair was thick and black and curly, his dark eyes full of intensity. In truth, the man seemed more a warrior than a wizard, in appearance and likely in temperament, something Brind'Amour figured he might be able to turn against Theredon.

He shifted his gaze to Mystigal—Mystigal! What pretensions of power had caused this one to change his name? And of course he had changed his name, for no child in the age following the demise of the brotherhood would have been given the name of Mystigal! He was older than Theredon, slender and cultured, with hawkish and hollow features, worn away by the overuse of magic. A "reacher," Brind'Amour discerned, remembering an old term his brotherhood had used to describe those wizards who aspired to greater powers than their intelligence allowed. Any attacks from this one would likely be grandiose in nature, seeming mighty, but with little real power to support them.

The duke of Baranduine appeared as the most comfortable, and thus likely to be the most difficult of the three men. Ashannon McLenny was a handsome man, his eyes well-balanced with emotion, eager and calm. A clear thinker; perhaps this one would have been a candidate for the brotherhood in ages past. Brind'Amour let his measuring gaze linger on Ashannon for a while, then shifted it to regard Deanna. Brind'Amour knew her well enough to respect her. Deanna was a complete package: cultured, intelligent, beautiful, dangerous, and the wizard held no doubts that this one would have aspired to, and achieved, magical prowess in that time long past. She might prove to be the most formidable of all, and it was no coincidence that Brind'Amour's attack plans for Eriador had purposely avoided sending forces against Deanna's city of Mannington.

During those few moments he spent in scanning his adversaries, Brind'Amour whispered under his breath, enacting minor magical defenses. A coil of wire appeared in one hand and gradually unrolled beneath his sleeve, then under his robes until its tip poked forth beside his boot, securing itself against the stone. Next the wizard quietly gathered all the moisture from the air near to him, called it in but didn't concentrate it. Not yet. Brind'Amour set up a conditional spell to finish what he had started, and he had to hope that his magic would be quick enough to the conditional call.

"And where is Greensparrow?" Brind'Amour asked suddenly, when he noted that the others, particularly Theredon and Mystigal, were exchanging nods, as if preparing their first assault.

Theredon snorted derisively. "Why would we need our king to pluck such a thorn as the pretender king of Eriador the wasteland?"

"So said Paragor," Brind'Amour calmly replied. That set cocky Theredon back on his heels a bit.

"We are four!" snarled Mystigal, bolstering Theredon, and himself, with the proclamation.

Now Brind'Amour called up a spell to shift his vision subtly that it might record magical energies. The strength of Deanna's globe surprised him once more when he realized the tightness of its magical weaving, but the other thing that surprised the wizard was that there apparently were no other magical curtains behind which other enemies might hide. No Greensparrow and, curiously, no demons.

He caught a sly look in Deanna Wellworth's eyes then that he did not quite understand. "There is no escape," she said, and then added, as if reading his mind, "No magic, not even a creature magically summoned, can pass through the blue barrier. You are without escape and without allies."

As if to accentuate Deanna's point, a horrid figure pressed its insect-like face against the top of the bubble then, leering down at the gathering on the plateau.

Brind'Amour recognized the thing as a demon, and he scratched his beard curiously, considering that the fiend was on the *outside*.

"Deanna!" cried Mystigal suddenly.

Brind'Amour looked from the fiend to the hawkish wizard. "Friend of yours?" he asked, a smile widening on his face.

Both Mystigal and Theredon squirmed a bit, an indication to Brind'Amour that the two suspected that their lead conspirator had erred, bringing up the shield before their allies, their true connections to power, had joined with them.

"Demon of Hell," Deanna answered Brind'Amour. "My fellows have come to greatly rely on such evil fiends."

We are not friends of King Greensparrow, nor can we any longer accept the truth of our ill-begotten powers, came a telepathic message in Brind'Amour's mind. He looked to Ashannon, the duke of Eornfast, recognizing the man as the sender, and then he understood that Deanna had not erred! Indeed the woman had used treachery, but her prey was not as Brind'Amour had first assumed.

A second fiend, two-headed and lizardlike, arrived beside the first, and both pressed and clawed wildly, but futilely, at the resilient bubble shield.

"Their mistake," Brind'Amour answered Deanna grimly.

Mystigal looked up to the dome, his expression showing deep concern. "What is this?" he demanded of Deanna, who now stood swaying, shoulders slumped and head down, as though her casting of the powerful globe had drained her.

The end of the question was snuffed out under the sizzling roar of Theredon's blue-streaking lightning bolt, the most common attack form offered by any wizard.

And one Brind'Amour had fully anticipated. The old wizard threw out his arm toward Theredon as the bolt began, felt the tingle in his fingers as his defensive magics countered the spell, catching Theredon's bolt on the edge of the conjured coil and running it down under Brind'Amour's robes to the stone beneath his feet. Brind'Amour felt all the hairs on his body dancing from the shock; his heart fluttered several times before its beat evened out. But in truth, the bolt wasn't very powerful, more show than substance.

"A tickle, nothing more," Brind'Amour said to Theredon. The old wizard looked up to the dome. "It would seem that the duchess of Mannington's spell is quite complete. You cannot access the powers of your fiend, or else your fiend is not so powerful!

"Yet I am of the old school, the true school," Brind'Amour went on, striding determinedly toward Theredon. He gave a few sidelong glances at Ashannon and Deanna, wondering what they might do next. "I need no diabolical allies!"

"Deanna!" Theredon growled, skipping quickly to the side, trying to keep as much ground between himself and dangerous Brind'Amour as possible.

The old wizard stopped and closed his eyes, chanting softly.

"Deanna!" screamed a terrified Theredon, knowing to his horror that Brind'Amour was about to hit him with something.

No energy came forth when Brind'Amour opened his eyes, but the old wizard's sly grin brought no comfort to Theredon. The muscular man backed to the far end of the globe. He saw his demon ally, both its grotesque heads pressed against the unyielding bubble. Theredon put his hands up to it, tried to touch it, to gather its power, but after only a few futile seconds, the frustrated wizard began pounding on the magical shield.

Brind'Amour took a step toward Theredon, shimmered and disappeared, then came back into view suddenly right behind the muscular wizard. The king of Eriador grabbed Theredon by the shoulder and roughly spun him about, then, before the younger and stronger man could even cry out, clasped a hand over Theredon's face. Crackling red sparks instantly erupted from Brind'Amour's fingers, lashing at his foe. Theredon cried out and reached up with trembling hands, clawing at Brind'Amour's arm.

Theredon's two-headed demon flew off, then returned at full speed, slamming the bubble with tremendous force, but merely bouncing away.

Behind him, above the screams of the demon and of Theredon, Brind'Amour could hear Mystigal chanting, and a moment later a ball of fire exploded in the air right between Brind'Amour and Theredon.

Fire, the single condition set upon Brind'Amour's waiting spell, was among the most predictable of wizardly attacks. At the instant the fireball blew, all the moisture Brind'Amour had gathered rushed out from him, blanketing him in a protective seal. When the flames of the not-so-powerful fireball disappeared, the old wizard was hardly singed, though wisps of smoke rose up from several places on poor Theredon's body, melting into the misty vapors that now engulfed the pair.

Brind'Amour looked back over his shoulder to see Deanna and Ashannon converging on poor Mystigal. The older, hawkish man scrambled away, crying out repeatedly to Deanna.

From the corner of his eye, Brind'Amour caught the movement as the buglike demon rushed at the bubble, then dove low, apparently boring right into the stone. A moment later, the ground under Deanna's feet heaved and the woman stumbled to the side, allowing Mystigal some running room. Theredon's frantic demon followed suit, and soon the floor of the plateau was rumbling and dancing, great rolling waves keeping all five within the globe struggling to hold their balance.

But Deanna's spell was well-constructed, the protective shield complete, even under their feet, and the demons could do little real mischief.

Theredon was on his knees by this point, grabbing weakly at Brind'Amour's arm, offering little resistance to the much more powerful, true wizard. Knowing that he had this one fully under control, Brind'Amour turned his sights on Mystigal, who was still calling out frantically to Deanna to come to her senses, and working hard to keep away from her and Ashannon.

Brind'Amour began another chant and lifted his free hand in Mystigal's direction.

Deanna and Ashannon worked in unison now, shifting so that they soon had the man cornered, then slowly closing in, Ashannon on the hawkish man's right, Deanna on his left.

The ground heaved under Ashannon's feet, knocking him toward Deanna, and Mystigal, with a shriek, ran out to the right, behind the stumbling duke. He only got a couple of steps, though, before Brind'Amour completed his spell and snapped his fingers. As though he were fastened to an overstretched cord, Mystigal rushed forward suddenly, his feet barely scraping the ground. He went right between Deanna and Ashannon, knocking them to the stone, and continued his impromptu flight all the way across the plateau, coming face-first into Brind'Amour's waiting grasp.

Red sparks came from that hand, too, and Brind'Amour wasted no time in bending the weakling man over backward, forcing him right to his knees.

Deanna and Ashannon collected themselves and eyed the spectacle of Brind'Amour's bared power from a safe distance. Ashannon motioned questioningly toward the trio, but Deanna shook her head and would not approach.

The old wizard tilted his head back and closed his eyes, concentrating fully on the release of power. Theredon's hands were tight about one arm, but the muscular man's grip seemed not so strong anymore. Mystigal offered no resistance whatsoever, just flailed his arms helplessly as the red sparks bit at his skull.

Brind'Amour attuned himself to his opponents' magic, that inner area of wizardly power. He felt the line of power there, the connection to the frenzied fiends. He felt the line bending, bending, and then, in Mystigal first, it snapped apart.

With a resounding whining buzz, the insect demon was hurled back to Hell and the ground under Deanna's bubble was quieter. As though he gained some resolve from that, Theredon growled and forced himself back to his feet.

Brind'Amour let go of Mystigal, who fell over backward to the stone, and put his full concentration on the stronger Theredon. The two held the pose for a long while, but then Theredon's core of power, like Mystigal's, snapped apart. Brind'Amour released him and he stood, precariously balanced, staring at the old wizard incredulously. Then, with all his strength, physical and magical, torn from his body, Theredon fell to the ground, facedown.

The stone beneath the old wizard's feet was quiet suddenly, as the two-headed demon joined its buglike companion in banishment, their ties to the world cleanly severed.

Brind'Amour spun about, facing the duke and duchess, not sure what any of this was about. He tried to look threatening, but in truth feared that either Ashannon or Deanna, or both, would come at him now, for he had little strength remaining with which to combat them.

The two looked to each other, then began a cautious approach, Deanna's hands held high and open, unthreatening.

On the ground, Mystigal groaned. Theredon lay very still.

"He will not awaken," Brind'Amour said firmly. "I have torn his magic from him, destroyed the minor wizard that he was!" Brind'Amour tried to sound threatening, but Deanna only nodded, as though she had expected that all along.

"We are not your enemy," she said, reading the old wizard's tone and body language. "Our common enemy is Greensparrow, and he, it would seem, has lost two more of his wizard-dukes."

With a sizzle and a puff, the blue-swirling globe vanished.

"Good spell," Brind'Amour congratulated.

"Years in perfecting," replied Deanna, "in preparation for the day that I knew would come."

Brind'Amour looked at her curiously. "Yet you performed the powerful magic without aid of your demon," he remarked suspiciously.

"I have no demon," she answered evenly.

"Nor do I," added Ashannon.

Brind'Amour eyed the duke of Eornfast skeptically, sensing that the man was not so certain of, or comfortable with, his position as was Deanna.

"I prefer the older ways," said Deanna. "The ways of the brotherhood."

Brind'Amour found that he believed her, though he could not have done much if he didn't. He was too tired to either attack the pair or flee the plateau. Deanna, too, seemed exhausted. She walked over slowly, bending low to inspect the pair of fallen dukes.

"Theredon is dead," she announced without emotion as she looked back to Ashannon, "but Mystigal lives."

Ashannon nodded, walked to the edge of the plateau, and leaped off into the night sky. Brind'Amour caught the flutter as the man transformed into some great nightbird, and then was gone.

Brind'Amour looked to Deanna. "Talkative fellow," he said.

"Duke McLenny knows that he has sacrificed much for this day," she replied. "Too much, perhaps, and so you must be content in the knowledge that he did not join with Theredon and Mystigal against you."

"But neither did he join with me," Brind'Amour pointed out.

Deanna didn't answer, just walked back to the center of the plateau and dropped some liquid on the dying fire. Immediately the flames roared back to life, bathing Deanna in their warm, orange glow.

"Bring Mystigal near to the warmth," she instructed Brind'Amour. "He does not deserve a cold death in such a remote, nameless place."

Those were the last words she spoke that night. She sat watching the fire for a long while, not even seeming to notice Brind'Amour, who, after laying Mystigal beside the flames, sat directly across from her.

The old wizard didn't press the point. He understood Deanna's dilemma here, understood that the young woman had just cast off the beliefs that had sustained her for most of her life.

CHAPTER 23

To Know Your Enemies

*L*UTHIEN AND BELLICK went to Brind'Amour's tent together in the cool darkness before the dawn. The pair were full of enthusiasm, ready for battle once more. A lantern burned low on the pole just outside the entrance, but inside the tent was dark. The pair entered anyway, thinking to rouse Brind'Amour. The dawn attack was the customary course, after all, giving the armies all the day for fighting.

Little light followed them in, but enough for them to discern that the wizard was not inside.

"Must be out and about already, readying the plans," Bellick remarked, but Luthien wasn't so sure. Something was out of place, he realized instinctively.

Luthien moved to the wizard's bed and confirmed his suspicions that it hadn't been slept on the previous night. That was curious enough, but Luthien held a nagging suspicion that there was something more out of place. He glanced all about, but saw nothing apparent. All the furniture was in order, the table in the middle of the room, the stool beside it, the crystal ball atop it. Brind'Amour's small desk sat against the tent side opposite the bed, covered in parchments, maps mostly, and by several bags filled with all sorts of strange potions and spell components.

"Come along," Bellick called from the tent flap. "We've got to find the old one and get the line formed up."

Luthien nodded and moved slowly to follow, looking back over his shoulder, certain that something was wrong. He got outside the tent, under the meager light of the low-burning lantern, Bellick several strides ahead of him.

"The crystal ball," Luthien said suddenly, turning the dwarf about.

"What?"

"The crystal ball," the young Bedwyr repeated, confident that he had hit on something important. "Brind'Amour's crystal ball!"

"It was in there to be sure," said Bellick. "Right in plain sight on the table."

"He never leaves it so," said Luthien, moving swiftly back into the tent. He heard Bellick groan and grumble, but the dwarf did follow, coming in just as Luthien settled on the stool, peering intently into the ball.

"Should you be looking into that?" Bellick asked. Like most of his race, Bellick was always a bit cautious where magic was concerned.

"I do not understand why it isn't covered," Luthien answered. "Brind'Amour . . ."

Luthien's words fell away as an image, a familiar, cheery old face, thick with a tremendous white beard, suddenly appeared within the ball. "Ah, good," said the illusionary Brind'Amour, "it is morning then, and you are preparing to take Pipery. All speed, my friends. I doubt not the outcome. I do not know how long I will be gone, and I go only with the knowledge that Eriador's forces are secure. Righteous speed!"

The image faded away as abruptly as it had appeared. Luthien looked back to Bellick, just a stocky silhouette framed by the open tent flap.

"So the wizard's gone," the dwarf said. "On good business, I do not doubt."

"Brind'Amour would not leave if it wasn't urgent," Luthien agreed.

"The Huegoths, probably," reasoned Bellick, and the thought that there might be trouble involving Ethan put a sour turn in Luthien's stomach. Or perhaps the trouble was from the other way, from the west, where Oliver and Katerin sailed. Luthien looked again to the empty crystal ball. He reminded himself many times over that Brind'Amour's demeanor had been cheerful, not dour.

"No matter," the dwarf king went on. "We ever were an army led by two!"

Luthien understood that Bellick had just assumed control of all the forces, and he really couldn't argue with the dwarf, who surely outranked him. There was an issue, though, which Luthien had wanted to discuss with Brind'Amour before the assault began. At the end of the previous war with Avon, when he had wanted to press on to Carlisle, Luthien had held the conviction that victory would be possible because many of the folk of Avon might see the truth of the situation, might realize that the army of Eriador wasn't really their enemy. Luthien had come to agree that his expectations were likely overblown, but still, he couldn't accept the notion that all of Avon's folk, men and women much like the Eriadorans, would desire war against Eriador.

Bellick grunted and turned to go.

"Can you muster the lines yourself?" Luthien asked. The dwarf wheeled about, and though he couldn't see the details of Bellick's face, Luthien could sense his surprise.

"You're going to look for Brind'Amour?" Bellick asked incredulously.

"No, but I had hoped to secure King Brind'Amour's permission to go into Pipery, before the dawn, before the battle," Luthien replied.

Bellick glanced over his shoulder, then stepped into the tent, obviously concerned.

"To scout out their defenses," Luthien explained immediately. "With the crimson cape, I can get in and out, and not a cyclopian will be the wiser."

Bellick stood staring at the young Bedwyr for a long while. "That is not why you wish to go," the dwarf reasoned, for he had heard Luthien talking about the folk of Avon as potential allies many times in the last few weeks.

Luthien sighed. "We may have friends within Pipery's walls," he admitted.

Bellick offered no response.

"I came to ask permission of King Brind'Amour," Luthien said, standing straight. "But King Brind'Amour is not to be found."

"Thus you will go as is your pleasure," said Bellick.

"Thus I ask permission to go from King Bellick dan Burso, who rightfully leads the army," Luthien corrected, and the show of loyalty did much for Bellick as the dwarf stood straighter.

"You may be disappointed," Bellick warned.

Luthien shrugged. "At the least, I will scout out their defenses," he replied.

"And at the most?"

"Justice for the Avon populace," Luthien replied without hesitation.

"Go, and quickly," Bellick bade him. "We've less than two hours to the dawn, and I plan to eat my noontime meal in Pipery!"

*   *   *

Luthien didn't really know what he would do as he used the cover of darkness and his magical cape to slip silently over Pipery's wall, which was little more than a collection of ramshackle pilings.

He picked his way from darkened house to house, amazed at how few cyclopians were up and about. By all reports, and by his last encounter on the field, Luthien believed that the small village's garrison had swelled in number with the addition of those Praetorian Guards fleeing the rout in the mountains. But where were they?

The riddle was solved as Luthien crossed the town's main road, deep gouges cut into it from the passage of a huge caravan. Heading south, Luthien noted by the tracks, and not more than two days before. Across the road, the young Bedwyr came upon the town's stables, two buildings connected by long fences. The doors of the barn were thrown wide, but no nickers or whinnies came from within, and the corral was empty, save for a few horse carcasses that had been butchered for meat.

Luthien took a deep and steadying breath, not thrilled by the reality of war's dark threat. He wondered what other hardships the folk of Pipery, unwitting pawns in Greensparrow's grand game, might have suffered these last few days.

He composed himself immediately, reminding himself that he could not afford to waste even a second of time. He trotted from shadow to shadow along the side of the main road, then paused when he came to a fork, east and southwest. Directly across from him, Luthien spied the first light he had seen since entering the village, a candle burning in the window of a large structure, which appeared to be the town's chapel.

With a hopeful nod, Luthien darted across the road to the building's side. He considered the Ministry in Caer MacDonald, a place of spirituality, but also the chosen headquarters for Greensparrow's wretched Duke Morkney. Might that be the pattern even in the smaller villages? Within this chapel, might there be an eorl, or a baron, loyal to the king of Avon and holding Pipery under his iron-fisted rule?

A quick glance to the eastern sky reminded Luthien once again that he had little time to ponder. He slipped up to a side door, peeked in through a small window set in its middle, then, seeing no obvious enemies nearby, slowly turned the handle.

It wasn't even locked, and Luthien eased it open, fully aware that he might find the bulk of the cyclopian garrison within.

To his surprise, and relief, the place seemed empty. He quietly closed the door behind him. He had come in to a small side room, the personal quarters of the place's priest or caretaker, perhaps. The one other door lay open to the main prayer area. Luthien adjusted his shielding cape to ensure that he was fully covered, then moved up to the door jamb, peering around the corner.

A solitary figure was in the place, kneeling on a bench at the front of the chapel, facing away from Luthien. The man's white robe revealed him as a priest.

Luthien nodded and padded in softly, moving from bench to bench and stopping often, blending with the wall in case the man turned back. As he neared the front of the chapel, he quietly slipped *Blind-Striker* from its sheath, but held it low, under the cape.

He could hear the priest then, whispering prayers for the safety of Pipery. Most telling of all was when the man asked God to "keep little Pipery out of the struggles of kings."

Luthien pulled off his hood. "Pipery lays on the road to Carlisle," he said suddenly.

The priest nearly toppled, and scrambled furiously to stand facing the intruder, eyes wide, jaw slack. Luthien noted the bruises on the man's face, the split lip and the puffy eyes. Given the number of cyclopians who had come through the town recently, it wasn't hard for the young Bedwyr to guess where those had come from.

"Whether it is friend or enemy to Eriador is Pipery's own choice," Luthien finished.

"Who are you?"

"An emissary from King Brind'Amour of Eriador," Luthien replied. "Come to offer hope where there should be none."

The man eyed Luthien carefully. "The Crimson Shadow," he whispered.

Luthien nodded, then held up a calm and steady hand when the priest blanched white.

"I have not come to kill you or anyone else," Luthien explained. "Only to see the mood of Pipery."

"And to discover our weaknesses," the priest dared to say.

Luthien chuckled. "I have five thousand battle-hungry dwarfs on the field, and a like number of men," he explained. "I have seen your wall and what is left of your garrison."

"Most of the cyclopians fled," the priest confirmed, his gaze going to the floor.

"What is your name?"

The man looked up, squaring his shoulders defiantly. "Solomon Keyes," he replied.

"Father Keyes?"

"Not yet," the priest admitted. "Brother Keyes."

"A man of the church or of the crown?"

"How do you know they are not one and the same?" Keyes answered cryptically.

Luthien smiled warmly and pushed aside his cape, revealing his bared sword, which he promptly replaced in its scabbard. "They are not," he replied.

Solomon Keyes offered no argument.

Luthien was pleased thus far with the conversation; he had the distinct feeling that Keyes did not equate God with Greensparrow. "Cyclopians?" he asked, motioning toward the priest's bruised face.

Keyes lowered his gaze once more.

"Praetorian Guards, likely," Luthien went on. "Come from the mountains, where we routed them. They passed through in a rush, stealing and slaughtering your horses, taking everything of value that we Eriadorans would not find it, and ordering the folk of Pipery, and probably the village cyclopian militia as well, to defend to the last."

Keyes looked up, his soft features tightening, eyes sharp on the perceptive young Bedwyr.

"That is the way it happened," Luthien said finally.

"Do you expect a denial?" Keyes asked. "I am no stranger to the brutish ways of cyclopians, and was not surprised."

"They are your allies," Luthien said, his tone edging on accusation.

"They are my king's army," Keyes corrected.

"That speaks ill of your king," Luthien was quick to respond. Both men went silent, letting the moment of tension pass. It would do neither of them any good to get things worked up here, for both of them were fast coming to the conclusion that something positive might come from this unexpected meeting.

"It was not only the Praetorian Guards of the Iron Cross," Keyes admitted, "but even many of our own militia. Even old Allaberksis, who has been in Pipery since the earliest—"

"Old?" Luthien interrupted. Aged cyclopians were a rarity.

"The oldest one-eye ever I have seen," said Keyes, and the sharpness of his voice told Luthien that this Allaberksis was likely in on the beating he had received.

"Old and withered," Luthien added. "Running south with a small band of Praetorian Guards."

Keyes expression told him that he had hit the mark.

"Alas for Allaberksis," Luthien said evenly. "He could not outrun my horse."

"He is dead?"

Luthien nodded.

"And what of his purse?" Keyes asked indignantly. "Common grain money for the villagers, money rightly earned and needed—"

Luthien held up his hand. "It will be returned," he promised. "After."

"After Pipery is sacked!" Keyes cried.

"That needn't happen," Luthien said calmly, defeating the priest's outburst before it ever truly began.

Another long silence followed, as Keyes waited for the explanation of that most intriguing statement, and Luthien considered how he might broach the subject. He guessed that Keyes held quite a bit of influence over the village; the chapel was well-maintained and the villagers had trusted him, after all, with their precious grain money.

"We of Eriador and DunDarrow have not come to conquer," Luthien began.

"You have crossed the border in force!"

"In defense," Luthien explained. "Though a truce was signed between our kings, Avon's war with Eriador did not end. All along the Iron Cross, our villages were being destroyed."

"Cyclopian raiders," Keyes reasoned.

"Working for Greensparrow," Luthien replied.

"You do not know this."

"Did you not see Praetorian Guards coming out of the mountains?" Luthien countered. "Had they just gone into the Iron Cross, in defense against our march, or had they been there all along, prodding Eriador to war?"

Keyes didn't answer, and honestly didn't know the answer, though no Praetorian Guard caravans had been reported heading north in the few weeks before the onset of war.

"Greensparrow prodded us to march south," Luthien insisted. "He forced the war upon us if we truly desired our freedom."

Keyes squared his shoulders. His expression showed that he believed Luthien, or at least that he didn't consider the words a complete lie, but his stance became defiant anyway. "I am loyal to Avon," he informed the young Bedwyr.

"But Greensparrow is not," Luthien answered without hesitation. "Nor is he loyal to our common God. He allies with demons, I say, for I have battled with more than one of the hellish fiends myself, have felt their evil auras, have seen such a creature occupy the body of one of Greensparrow's henchmen dukes!"

Keyes winced; he had heard the rumors of diabolical allies, Luthien realized, and could not dispute the claims.

"How am I to know that you are not murderous invaders?" Keyes asked.

Luthien drew out his sword, looked from its gleaming blade to the blanching priest. "Why are you not already dead?" he asked.

The young Bedwyr was quick to replace the sword, not wanting to cause any more discomfort to the beleaguered man. "Pipery's fate is its own to decide," he said. He looked to the eastern windows then, and saw that the sky was beginning to brighten. "I do not demand your alliance or your fealty to my king, and on my word, your village will not be destroyed and your money will be returned. But if you oppose us, we will kill you, do not doubt. Eriador has come for war, and so we shall wage it with any who hold loyalty to evil King Greensparrow!"

With that, Luthien bowed and swept away.

"What am I to do?" Keyes called, and Luthien stopped and turned to face him from across the room.

"How am I to prevent my people from defending their own homes?" he asked.

"There is no defense," Luthien said grimly, and turned once more.

"Nor is there time!" Keyes pleaded. "Dawn is almost upon us!"

Luthien stopped at the doorway to the side room. "I can delay them," he promised, though he doubted his own words. "I can buy you the hours until noon. The chapel offers sanctuary, to all but one-eyes."

"Go then to your army," Keyes said in a tone that assured Luthien that the man would at least try.

More people, more cyclopians, were out and about as Luthien left the chapel, forcing him to alter his course several times. He made the wall before the dawn, though, and in the increasing light could see just how truly hopeless was Pipery's position. The wall was in bad disrepair—in many places it was no more than piled stones. Even at its strongest points, the wall loomed no higher than eight feet, and was not thick enough to slow the battering charge of Bellick's stone-crushing dwarfs.

"Do well, Solomon Keyes," Luthien prayed as he crossed out of the village, running fast across the open fields. For the sympathetic young Bedwyr, the image of the coming carnage was not acceptable.

A calm had settled over the fields between the Eriadoran encampment and Pipery, both sides waiting for the attack they knew would come this day.

And what a fine day it was! Too fine for battle, Luthien lamented. The sun dawned bright, the wind blew crisp and clean, and all the birds and animals were out in full, chirping and leaping.

Riverdancer, too, was in high spirits, snorting and pawing the ground when Luthien approached with his saddle. The white stallion leaped away as soon as Luthien had mounted.

Luthien could not ignore the nausea churning in his stomach. He always felt anxious before battle, but this time it was not the same. In every fight previous, Luthien had charged in with the knowledge that his was the just cause, and in the wider picture of Eriador's freedom, he considered the invasion of Avon a necessary and righteous thing. That did little to comfort him, though, when he thought of Pipery sacked, of men like Solomon Keyes lying soaked in their own blood.

Killing evil cyclopians was one thing, killing humans, Luthien now understood, was something altogether different.

He paced Riverdancer swiftly along the ranks, coming up to King Bellick and Shuglin as they reviewed the dwarven line.

"Good that you got back," Bellick remarked. "It would not do for you to be standing among them Avon and cyclopian dogs when we run them down!"

"We must hold our line," Luthien said bluntly.

The dwarf king turned about so abruptly that his wild orange beard slipped out of his broad belt.

"Until the hour of noon," Luthien explained.

"The day is not long enough!" Bellick roared. "They will see us now, and discover our strengths and weaknesses, and alter their defenses . . ."

"There is nothing that Pipery can do," Luthien assured the king. He saw Siobhan and several of the other Cutters approaching, along with a group of leaders of the Eriadoran army.

"They are helpless against our strength," Luthien finished, loud enough so that the newcomers could hear.

"That is fine news," replied Bellick. "Then let us go in and finish the task quickly, then march on to the next town."

Luthien shook his head determinedly, and Bellick responded with an open glare.

The young Bedwyr sat up straight in his saddle, looked all about as he spoke, for he was now addressing all who would listen. "Pipery will offer little defense," he said, "and less still if we delay through the morning."

A chorus of groans met that proposition.

"And consider our course carefully," Luthien went on, undaunted. "We will run through a dozen such villages before we ever see the walls of Warchester, with Carlisle still far beyond that. There are seeds of support for us; I have witnessed them with my own eyes."

"You have spoken with men inside Pipery's walls?" Bellick asked, not sounding pleased.

"With only one man," Luthien confirmed. "With the priest, who fears for his town's safety."

"And rightly so!" came a cry from the gathering, a call that was answered and bolstered many times over.

"How long?" Siobhan asked simply, quieting the crowd.

"Give them the morning," Luthien begged, speaking directly to Bellick once more. "They can make few adjustments to bolster their meager defenses, and we have the village surrounded that none may escape."

"I fear to delay," Bellick replied, but his tone was less belligerent. The dwarf king was no fool. He recognized the influence that Luthien Bedwyr held over the Eriadorans, the Cutters, and even a fair number of his own dwarfs, who remembered well that it was Luthien who had led the raid to free so many of their kin from the horrors of the Montfort mines. While Bellick wasn't sure that he agreed with Luthien's reasoning, he understood the dangers of openly disagreeing with the young man.

"We will lose six hours at the outset," Luthien admitted. "But much of that time will be regained in the battle, unless I miss my guess. And even if the hours are not regained, I will ask that my folk march more swiftly beside me on the way to the next village." Luthien rose up in his saddle again and addressed all the crowd. "I ask this of you," he shouted. "Will you grant me this one thing?"

The response was unanimous, and Bellick realized that it would be folly to try and resist the young Bedwyr. He hated the thought of keeping his anxious dwarfs in check, and hated the thought of wasting so fine a morning. But Bellick hated more the notion of open disagreement between himself and Luthien, a potential split in an army that could afford no rifts.

He nodded to Luthien then, but in his look was the clear assumption that Luthien owed him one for this.

Luthien's responding nod, so full of gratitude, made it clear that he would repay the favor.

"Besides," Luthien offered with a wink to Bellick and to Siobhan as the ranks broke apart around them. "I now know where Pipery's wall is weakest."

As the hopeful word spread about Pipery, Solomon Keyes rushed to the wall and peered out across the open fields.

"They are standing down!" one gleeful man yelled right in the young priest's face.

Keyes managed a smile, and was indeed grateful, but it was tempered with the knowledge that he had but a few hours to do so very much. He looked up to the sky as though he might will the sun to hold in place for a while.

Bellick, Luthien, Siobhan, and all the other commanders of the army were not idle that long morning. With Luthien's information about the physical defenses and about the emotional turmoil within Pipery, a new battle plan was quickly drawn, analyzed, and polished, each segment run over and over until it became embedded in the thoughts of those who were charged with carrying it out.

They were back on the field before noon, ten thousand strong, speartips and swords gleaming in the light, polished shields catching the sun like flaming mirrors.

All of the cavalry was together this time, more than a hundred strong and sitting in formation directly north of the town. Luthien on shining Riverdancer centered the line, along with Siobhan. On command, all heads turned to face east of that position, where stood King Bellick dan Burso in his fabulous battle gear.

A lone rider galloped out to the town's north gates.

"Will you yield, or will you fight us?" he asked simply of the growling cyclopians gathered there.

Predictably, a spear came soaring out at him, and just as predictably, it came nowhere near to hitting the mark. King Bellick had his answer.

As soon as the rider returned to his place in the ranks, all eyes again went to the dwarvish commander. With one strong arm, Bellick lifted his short and thick sword high into the air, and after a moment's pause, brought it sweeping down.

The roar of the attack erupted all along the line; Luthien and his fellow cavalry kicked their mounts into a thunderous charge.

Not all the line followed, though. Only those dwarfs directly behind the cavalry began to run ahead, the charge filtering to the east, sweeping up the line like the slow break of a wave.

Luthien brought his forces to within a few running strides of Pipery's wall, then broke left, to the east, apparently belaying the line. Out of the dust cloud on the heels of the cavalry came the leading dwarfs, straight on for Pipery, and so it went as Luthien's group circled the city, every pounding stride opening the way for another grim-faced soldier. Luthien had named the maneuver "opening the sea gates," and so it seemed to be, the riders moving like a blocking wall and the foot soldiers pouring in like a flood behind them.

As soon as the pattern became apparent to the defenders, it was reversed, with those infantry to the west coming on in a synchronous charge. Luthien's cavalry by this time had swung far around to the southeastern section of the village, trading missile fire, elvish bow against cyclopian spear. None of the cavalry had been hit, though, a testament to the fact that cyclopians simply could not judge distance, and to Luthien's hopes that few, if any, humans were among Pipery's obviously thin line.

The young Bedwyr spotted the desired section of wall, a pile of boulders, wider than it was high. Luthien swung Riverdancer away from the village, then turned abruptly and came straight in for the target, Siobhan right beside him and the elven line slowing and widening behind the pair.

Luthien saw the cyclopian spearmen and pikemen come up to defend, waited until the last moment, then pulled hard on Riverdancer's reins, yanking the steed up short and skittering out to the left, while Siobhan skipped out to the right.

Opening the way for the elvish volley. Dozens of stinging arrows rushed in, most skipping off the stones, several hitting the mark. The defenders fell away, either dead, wounded, or simply in fear, and Luthien and Siobhan called out to their kinfolk and kicked their mounts into the charge once more.

Luthien tightened his legs and posted hard, heels low, the balls of his feet pressed in tight to the stirrups. He bent low and coaxed Riverdancer on, aiming the mount straight for the center of the boulder pile. Up sprang the mighty horse, easily clearing the four-foot obstacle, bringing Luthien into Pipery.

Siobhan came in right beside him, and they turned together, thundering down the road. Luthien spied two fleeing cyclopians and ran them down, Riverdancer crushing one of them, *Blind-Striker* cutting down the other. The young Bedwyr turned about to Siobhan, grinning as he started to call out his new total. He stopped short, though, for he found Siobhan similarly running down a pair of one-eyes.

Cyclopians huddled in terror at the base of that low wall as the riders streamed over it, twenty, fifty, ninety, coming into Pipery. None of them paused at the wall, and at last the brutes managed to stand up, thinking they had been spared, thinking to go out over the wall and run away.

Before they got atop the first stones, Pipery's barrier seemed to heighten by several feet as the human wall of Eriadoran foot soldiers greeted the cyclopians.

Chaos hit the streets of Pipery, riders rushing every which way, cyclopians trying to form into defensive groups, only to find, more often than not, that half of their number were dead before they ever joined in the formation. There were some pockets of stiff resistance, though, particularly in the north, where Luthien, Siobhan, and three-score other riders charged off in support.

Trapped between such forces, the cyclopian defenses quickly evaporated, each brute thinking to save itself. One by one, the one-eyes were slain.

It was Luthien himself who finally threw wide Pipery's north gate, and King Bellick dan Burso who stood right outside, ready to greet him. Luthien jumped back astride Riverdancer, then held out his hand to help the short dwarf climb up behind him. The fighting was fast diminishing, more a matter of chasing down single brutes than any real battles, and so Luthien and the dwarf trotted off to survey the battle scene.

"Not much of a defense," the dwarf king snorted, seeing how truly thin the line had been. Cyclopian bodies—almost exclusively cyclopian, Luthien noted hopefully—were strewn about in a long line, but in most places were no more than one or two deep.

"Where are they all?" the dwarf asked. "Did more of the folk get out than we figured?"

Luthien didn't think that to be the case, and he was pretty sure that he could guess where the rest of Pipery's defenders had gone. He called his cavalry into formation behind him and trotted south along the main road, to the fork facing the town's chapel.

When all the soldiers came into place around that structure and finally quieted, they could hear the soft singing of many voices emanating from within.

Bellick slid down then to put his dwarfs and the Eriadoran foot soldiers in place, and to manage the prisoner groups being escorted into the area. Luthien, meanwhile, took a slow circuit of the chapel, calming his battle-hungry companions on all sides. The dwarf king was waiting for him when he came back around to the fork in the road, and Bellick was not surprised by the plan Luthien had devised.

"You have guessed right thus far," the dwarf remarked, not of the mind to overrule the young Bedwyr.

Luthien slid down from Riverdancer, handing the reins to a nearby soldier. He dusted himself off and strode directly for the chapel's main door, motioning and calling orders as he went.

Without hesitation, without bothering to knock, Luthien entered to find several hundred sets of eyes staring back to regard him, expressions showing too great a mix of emotions for the young man to possibly sort through. He scanned the gathering, finally settling his gaze on Solomon Keyes, who stood at the pulpit at the front of the chapel.

"It is done," the young Bedwyr announced. "Pipery is free."

A woman jumped up from the edge of a pew and charged at Luthien, but several arms caught her before she had gone two steps, pulling her screaming back into the throng.

"Many had kin out there," Keyes explained evenly.

Luthien glanced back over his shoulder and nodded and a long line of human prisoners walked into the chapel, breaking away, running to their relieved families.

"There may be others," Luthien explained. "We have not sorted it all out as of yet."

"What penalty?" Keyes started to ask.

"No penalty," Luthien replied without the slightest hesitation. "They were defending their homes and their kin, so they believed." He paused, letting the surprised murmurs quiet. "We are not your enemy," he declared. "This much I have told you before."

As one, the crowd swung about to regard Keyes, who stood nodding.

"Pipery is free," Luthien went on. "And out of the war. Your gates are open, north and south, and you shall not hinder our passage, or the continuing line that shall come down from Eriador. Nor shall you deny any boats we put on the river from safe travel past your docks."

The murmurs began again, and were quickly silenced by Luthien's booming voice. "But we ask nothing of you," he explained. "What you give to us, you give of your own free will."

"Thieves!" one man yelled, leaping to his feet and pushing to the center of the open aisle. "Thieves and murderers!" he proclaimed, slowly stalking toward Luthien.

He stopped short when Bellick dan Burso entered, to stand at Luthien's side. "We are not your enemies," the dwarf king declared, and the blood spattered upon him could not diminish the splendor of his crafted armor, nor the dust covering him steal the flames of his fiery beard. But the sympathy that was in his heart could not diminish the intensity of his stern gaze.

Bellick let that gaze linger all about the room, then settled it on Luthien, who nodded for the dwarf to continue. "We are not your enemies unless you make of us your enemies," Bellick promised grimly. "Then know that Pipery will be sacked, burned to the ground!"

Not a person in the room doubted the imposing dwarf's promise.

Bellick pulled two large pouches from a cord on his back. "Your grain money," he explained, tossing them to the floor at the feet of the deflated rabble-rouser. "Taken from cyclopians fleeing Pipery. Taken from your King Greensparrow's cyclopians as they left Pipery to its doom. Decide then who are your enemies and who are your allies."

"Or decide nothing," Luthien added. "And remain neutral. We ask nothing of you, save that your swords are not again lifted against us."

He looked down at Bellick, and the dwarf up at him. "We will tend our wounded," Bellick announced, "and clear our dead from the field, that they do not lie beside the rotting cyclopians. And then we shall leave." The dwarf and Luthien turned to go, but were stopped by the call of Solomon Keyes.

"You may bring your wounded in here," the priest offered, "and I shall prepare your dead for burial, as I prepare the human dead of Pipery."

Luthien turned to him, somewhat surprised.

"My God and your God," Keyes asked, "are they not one and the same?"

Luthien nodded, managed a thin smile, and walked from the chapel.

CHAPTER 24

FOR THE CAUSE OF JUSTICE

BELLICK DAN BURSO was not ignorant of the many angry and suspicious gazes that settled over him as he walked with an entourage of bodyguards through Pipery's narrow streets. Luthien held illusions of friendship with all the common folk of Avon, and one day that might come to pass, but Bellick knew better than to hope for such allies so soon after battle. Aside from the cyclopians who had been slaughtered, more than a few of Pipery's human soldiers had been killed as well, and a fair number of families in the village now had a dead relative because of the invading Eriadorans.

Such a greeting rarely led to friendship.

Still, there were others in the town who managed a smile and a nod as the honorable dwarf king passed, and when Bellick arrived at the front steps to the chapel house, he found his own soldiers, set in place to guard over the Eriadoran and dwarvish wounded, relaxing on the stairs, enjoying food and drink with a handful of Pipery's citizens. The dwarven soldiers fumbled all over themselves, trying to get up, but the king waved his hand absently. No need for formalities now, not with the army preparing once more for a long and arduous march.

Bellick walked into the chapel, leaving his escorts on the front steps with the others. As the dwarf expected, he found Luthien inside, crouched near one of the pews, talking quietly with a wounded man.

"Brandon of Felling Downs," Luthien explained when Bellick joined them.

The dwarf nodded deferentially, taking note that the man had lost an arm. He seemed comfortable enough, though, on the pew, which had been converted into three end-to-end beds.

Bellick looked all around. "Which are ours and which of Pipery?" he asked.

"All mixed together," said Luthien.

The dwarf turned a sly look on the young Bedwyr. "Your doing?"

"I'll take a bit of the credit," Luthien replied. "But it was Solomon Keyes who assigned the cots."

Bellick snorted and started away. "Partners in crime," he said quietly.

Three rows down, Bellick came upon a pew of four beds, all holding dwarfs. One lay out straight, but the other three were sitting, throwing dice and chatting easily. Their smiles came wide indeed when Bellick addressed them; one even shoved the sleeping dwarf.

"Let him rest," Bellick bade them, then to the others, "We're putting out this day, south along the river. Any of you fit to join in?"

All four moved to rise, but Bellick could see that none were ready for the road. "Keep your seats," the dwarf king instructed. He told the healthiest of the bunch that he was in charge. "We'll be running supplies through here," he explained. "Keep them watched, and come along when the four of you are ready.

"When you are ready!" Bellick reiterated more forcefully, noting the hopeful expressions that came over his eager warriors. "And not a moment before!"

Bellick moved on then, inspecting each cot, stopping to say a short prayer over those most seriously wounded, offering encouraging words to the others. He had just completed his rounds, telling Luthien not to tarry too long, when he was met at the chapel door by Solomon Keyes.

The young priest wiped his dirty hands and held one out to the dwarf king.

Bellick took it, but turned it over instead of shaking it, taking note of the mud on the fingers. "You've been burying the dead," the dwarf stated.

"I have set others to the task," Keyes replied. "I have been offering final prayers, consecrating the sites."

"What of the one-eyes?" the dwarf asked, a hint of a challenge in his gruff voice. "Have you any prayers for them?"

"We built a communal pyre," Keyes replied indignantly, "and burned them. And I did pray for their souls."

Bellick's bushy eyebrows rose.

"I prayed that they would learn the error of their ways in the afterlife, and that they would find redemption."

"You're fond of them, are you?"

Now it was Keyes who gave a very dwarvish snort. "I hold no fondness for the ways of cyclopians," he replied. "But that does not mean that I hate the individual one-eyes."

"Perhaps some things are worth hating," offered Luthien, coming to join the pair.

"Perhaps I have no hate in my heart," Keyes replied easily.

"They beat you up good," Bellick reminded him. Keyes merely shrugged.

Luthien studied the man for a long moment and found that he was a bit jealous. He admired Keyes, not only for finding the courage to trust in the Eriadorans, but for holding such a generous heart.

"You are marching this day?" Keyes asked Bellick. "Surely your soldiers are weary from the fight, and the sun will set in a mere two hours."

"We've got no time to be tired," Bellick replied. "The road ahead is long, and every moment we waste gives Greensparrow more time to set his defenses."

"I will be ready to go in twenty minutes," said Keyes unexpectedly. Both Luthien and Bellick stared at him wide-eyed.

"You shall encounter many villages lining the road to Warchester," the priest explained. "Many in Pipery have kinfolk there. We do not want them killed."

"I thought you were to help with the wounded," said Luthien.

"I have enough people, trusted people, set in place to care for the wounded here," Keyes replied. "I, and a select handful of others, see our place in the march with King Bellick." He looked to the south. "I will save more lives out there than in here."

It took Bellick a few minutes to sort out the unexpected news, but the dwarf soon agreed. If Keyes could help weaken the defenses of the other villages half as much as he had done in Pipery, the road to Warchester would be swift and without great cost.

Luthien's elation was even greater, for he saw not only the tactical advantage of having such emissaries, but the moral one as well. With the Pipery spokesmen along, the number of deaths on both sides was sure to be reduced.

The young Bedwyr's optimism was guarded, though. He didn't really know how much influence Keyes might command away from Pipery. He also realized that no matter how swift and easy the march, it would stall at Warchester, a great and fortified city, its defenses complete with its own wizard-duke.

Where, Luthien wondered again, was Brind'Amour?

Though she was completely drained from using the powerful spell she had spent so long in perfecting, Deanna Wellworth did not sleep for the rest of that night on the plateau. She sat beside the fire, which Brind'Amour enhanced with some minor magics, though he, too, was obviously exhausted. Deanna cradled Mystigal's head on her lap, watching Brind'Amour as he gradually drifted off to sleep.

What had she begun? Deanna had set events into motion that were now above her control; had gone against her king and mentor in a conspiracy that could not be hidden and could not be reversed. Even if she killed Brind'Amour this night—and the thought crossed her mind more than once—she would not be able to hide the truth from Greensparrow. Because of her, three more of Greensparrow's dukes were gone: one dead, the other two, Mystigal and Resmore, broken.

Deanna tried not to focus too tightly on the events of this night. In truth, it was but a logical continuation of the course she had started upon when she had used Taknapotin against Resmore in the mountains. Greensparrow would make contact with the banished demon, if he hadn't already, and he would learn the truth of Deanna Wellworth, and of Ashannon McLenny. In those courageous earlier decisions, Deanna's course had been set, and this night was as much about her own survival as it was about helping Brind'Amour.

The old wizard awakened soon after the first slanting rays of dawn touched his face.

"He will live, I believe," Deanna said, indicating Mystigal, who was still unconscious.

"But his magic is no more," Brind'Amour replied, ending with a profound yawn. "The cord of magic within him has snapped."

"As with Duke Resmore?"

Brind'Amour chuckled, amazed at how perceptive this Deanna could be. His smile did not last very long, though, as he considered what he feared might be potential trouble. "What of the duke of Eornfast?" he asked bluntly.

"His business here was finished, and so he left," Deanna answered simply.

There was much more to it than that, Brind'Amour believed—and feared. Ashannon's demeanor had been aloof, almost icy. The duke of Eornfast had apparently gone along with Deanna's ploy, but was it because he agreed with her decision, or did he simply have no choice? Or even worse, Brind'Amour had to fear, did he have ulterior motives?

The old wizard's doubt showed clearly on his wrinkled face.

"Trust in Ashannon McLenny," Deanna begged. "He is a difficult one at times, but he holds no love for any who might claim rulership over his beloved Baranduine, be it Greensparrow or Brind'Amour."

"I never made such a claim," Brind'Amour was quick to respond.

"But shall you if your war goes well?"

Brind'Amour had to work hard to try and see things from Deanna's desperate point of view, in order to avoid insult at the remark. "Never have I claimed rulership over Avon!" he insisted. "Nor has any of Eriador at any time. When Bruce MacDonald ruled Eriador united, and had a disorganized Avon at his bidding, he never claimed anything but friendship to his kin from Baranduine."

"It is irrelevant anyway," Deanna said quietly. "All that matters is what Ashannon believes."

"And what does he believe?"

Deanna shrugged. "He agreed to banish his demon," she said with confidence, "and he has done so. And this was as much his plan as it was mine own. He has been a friend for many years."

"But would it not be in his interest to see Greensparrow weakened?" Brind'Amour reasoned. "The more difficult the war for Avon's king, the more easily Baranduine might slip from his grasp."

Again Deanna only shrugged. "We will have our answers soon enough," she said. "Now I must get back to Mannington to make my report to Greensparrow."

Brind'Amour looked skeptically at Mystigal, wondering what Deanna might be thinking to do with the broken wizard.

"I should like it if you would accompany me," Deanna said.

Brind'Amour's surprise was genuine.

"There is much we need to discuss," the duchess went on.

"Planning for the time after Greensparrow?"

Deanna chuckled. "We have much to do before we can ever hope for that," she replied. "For now, there are things you must know, and proof I must offer of my integrity in this matter."

Brind'Amour didn't disagree. For all he knew, this entire situation was some sort of an elaborate ruse designed to entice him into the confidence of conspirators who cared nothing for Eriador. He gave a long look to the towering mountains, wondering what progress Luthien and Bellick had made, wondering if Pipery had yet fallen.

Then he rose and stretched, and he and Deanna worked together, joining their strength to open a magical tunnel to the south.

Just a short while later, Mystigal was resting comfortably on a bed in Deanna's private quarters, while Deanna took Brind'Amour to meet the living proof that she had turned against Greensparrow.

Selna seemed more than a little surprised to see her lady and the bushy-bearded man who accompanied her, and her jaw dropped low when Deanna introduced the stranger as the king of Eriador.

"Greensparrow was the savior of Avon," Deanna explained to Brind'Amour. "So it has been said for more than twenty years."

"Do not do this, my Lady," Selna begged, but when she looked into Deanna's eyes, she saw no compassion there.

"Tell King Brind'Amour the truth, dear Selna," Deanna said, her voice dripping with threat. "Else I will have to make you admit things as I did before."

Brind'Amour did not miss the blanch that came over the older woman. He put a hand on Deanna's shoulder. "Pray tell me, dear Lady Wellworth, what was it that you did to this handmaid?"

"When I banished Taknapotin, my demon, I knew that one of Greensparrow's informants had been removed from my court," Deanna explained. "But only one. Thus did I visit dear Selna here."

"It is not delicate to use magic in such a way," Brind'Amour remarked, recalling his own magical exertions over Duke Resmore.

"Not pleasant," Deanna agreed. She looked directly at Selna. "But I shall do it again, as often as necessary."

Selna was trembling visibly. "It was Greensparrow," she blurted suddenly. "He killed them; he killed them all! That night! Oh, my Lady, why do you keep forcing me to remember that horrible night?"

"Greensparrow murdered my entire family," Deanna said, her voice strangely devoid of emotion.

"All but one," Brind'Amour remarked.

"I was kept alive only because Greensparrow feared that he would not be accepted as king," Deanna explained. She looked to Selna, motioning for the woman to elaborate.

"Though she was but a child, Greensparrow meant to put Deanna on the throne if necessary," the handmaid admitted, lowering her gaze, for she could not look Deanna in the eye. "He would control her every action, of course, and then, when she came of age, he would marry her."

Brind'Amour was indeed surprised that the plan to conquer Avon had been so very devious, and had worked out so perfectly neatly. Again the wizard thought of that past time and the decision for the brotherhood to disband and go to their deserved rest.

"It never came to that, of course," Deanna added, "for the people of Avon exalted in Greensparrow. They begged him to hold their kingdom together."

"Then why was Deanna allowed to live?" Brind'Amour asked, directing his question to Selna. He saw something here between the woman and Deanna, something that Deanna, in her outrage upon learning the truth, might be overlooking.

"Ashannon McLenny of Eornfast," Deanna answered sternly. "He took personal interest in me, even willingly entered Greensparrow's court as a duke and accepted a demonic familiar, like all of Greensparrow's wizard-dukes—save Cresis the cyclopian of Carlisle, who is too stupid to deal with such fiendish creatures. Ashannon was a wizard in his own right, and a friend of my father's. While he abhorred the thought of dealing with Greensparrow, he had learned that Baranduine would be Greensparrow's next target, and he had not the forces to resist."

Everything was falling into place for Brind'Amour now. He understood the cool demeanor of Ashannon McLenny, the fire of Deanna, and something else, a player here whom Deanna did not fully appreciate.

"And how did Ashannon McLenny learn of the coming invasion?" the wizard asked.

Deanna shrugged—then gasped in surprise when Selna answered, "I told him."

Deanna's shocked expression made the older woman squirm. "I betrayed my dear Avon," she admitted openly. "But I had to, my Lady! Oh, I feared Greensparrow, and what he might do to you. I knew that I had to protect you until the events became a thing of the past, until you were no more a threat to Greensparrow."

Brind'Amour's snicker stopped the woman short, and turned both sets of eyes upon him. "No threat, indeed!" the wizard laughed.

Deanna managed a smile at that, but Selna, torn beyond reason, did not. Brind'Amour understood Selna fully now; she was the ultimate peacemaker, the wrinkle-smoother, and that could be a dangerous thing to her allies in times of political intrigue. Selna had betrayed Greensparrow to Ashannon, and would now betray Deanna to Greensparrow if given the opportunity, because in her heart she only wanted things nice and neat, peaceful and orderly. Selna would do whatever she thought best to end conflicts and intrigue, but while that was admirable, the success of such a course depended upon the mercy of kings, a trait Brind'Amour knew to be scarce indeed among the noble-born. In short, Selna was a fool, an unwitting lackey, though her heart was not black with ambition. In looking at Deanna, and measuring her stern demeanor toward the woman, it occurred to Brind'Amour that Selna had probably already spied upon Deanna for Greensparrow on other occasions, and that Deanna knew about it. Thus, Selna was no more a threat, Brind'Amour realized, not with Deanna so near and so watchful.

"My biggest fear in waging war was the balance of magical power," Brind'Amour said openly after he and Deanna left Selna's room, with Deanna pointedly locking the door from the outside and casting a minor enchantment to prevent any divining by other wizards into the room.

"Treat her with mercy," Brind'Amour advised.

"I will keep her safe and secure," Deanna replied, emphasizing the last. "When all of this is over, I will give back to her her life, though it will be one far removed from my court."

"Now only two of Greensparrow's wizards remain," Brind'Amour said, satisfied at that, "and one, at least, is on my side, while the other, I would hope, shall remain neutral."

"On your side?" Deanna asked. "That I never said."

"Then you are at least against Greensparrow," the old wizard reasoned.

"I am the rightful queen of Avon," the woman said bluntly. "Why would I not oppose the man who has stolen my throne?"

Brind'Amour nodded and scratched at his huge beard, trying to figure out exactly how much value Deanna Wellworth would prove to be.

"And do not think that the balance of magical strength has shifted so greatly," the duchess warned. "Mystigal, Resmore, and Theredon were minor spellcasters, conduits for their demon familiars rather than great powers in themselves, and neither I nor Ashannon hold much power anymore, now that our familiars have been banished."

Brind'Amour considered the barrier Deanna had enacted on the plateau and thought that she might be underestimating herself, but he held the thought private. "Still," he said, "I would rather battle Greensparrow alone than with his wizards allied beside him."

"Our powers were great because of our relationships with our familiars," Deanna explained. "If we achieved a higher symbiosis with them, even our lives could be extended."

"As Greensparrow's was obviously extended." Brind'Amour realized where Deanna's reasoning led. Brind'Amour was alive in this time because he had chosen the magical stasis, but Greensparrow had remained awake through the centuries. By now, the man should have died of old age, something even a wizard could not fully escape.

"So Greensparrow and his familiar are very close," Brind'Amour went on, prompting Deanna to finish her point. "A demon, perhaps a demon lord?"

"So we once thought," Deanna answered grimly. "But no, Greensparrow's familiar is not a demon, but another of the magical beasts of the world."

Brind'Amour scratched his beard again and seemed not to understand.

"He went into the Saltwash those centuries ago to find his power," Deanna explained. "And so he did find it, with a beast of the highest order."

Brind'Amour nearly swooned. He knew what creature had long ago dominated the Saltwash, and had thought that his brotherhood had destroyed, or at least had imprisoned, the beasts, as he had sealed the dragon Balthazar deep in a mountain cave.

"A dragon," he said, all color leaving his face.

Deanna nodded grimly. "And now Greensparrow and the dragon are one."

"Cyclopians," Luthien muttered grimly, seeing the slaughtered horses strewn about the fields. A single farmhouse, no more than a shell, stood on a hill in the distance, a plume of black smoke rising from it.

Luthien was walking Riverdancer, alongside Bellick, Shuglin, and Solomon Keyes. He reached up and stroked the horse's neck, as if offering sympathy to Riverdancer for the scene of carnage all about them.

"It might be that they're making our task all the easier," Shuglin remarked.

"The folk of Dunkery Valley have never held love for the one-eyes," Solomon Keyes explained. "We tolerated them because we were given little choice in the matter."

"You are not so different from everyone else in Avonsea, then," Luthien said.

Further ahead on the road, the line parted to let a pair of riders, Siobhan and another of the Cutters, gallop through. They pulled up in front of Bellick and Luthien.

"A village not so different from Pipery," Siobhan reported. "Four miles ahead."

"Alanshire," Solomon Keyes put in.

"How strong a wall?" Bellick asked Siobhan, but again it was Keyes who spoke up.

"No wall," he said. "The buildings in the central area of town are close together. It would not be a difficult task for the folk to pile crates and stones to connect them."

Siobhan nodded her agreement with the assessment.

"And how many soldiers?" Bellick asked.

"I can get in there and find out," Keyes answered. He looked back over his shoulder and motioned to the other men of Pipery who had come along.

Bellick regarded Luthien, and the dwarf's expression showed that he was suspicious of letting the priest go ahead of them.

"I can enter at dusk," the young Bedwyr said in answer.

"And I will be there to meet you," said Keyes. "With a full report of what we might expect from Alanshire."

"Some would call you a traitor," Bellick remarked.

Keyes looked at him directly, and did not back down in the least. "I only care that as few men are killed as possible," he stated flatly.

The Pipery contingent rode off, four men and a woman sharing three horses. Bellick and the others went about the task of spreading the Eriadoran line to encompass the village. The dwarf king's instincts told him to attack that same day, but after the situation in Pipery, he deferred to Luthien and to Keyes. If the night's wait would make the fighting easier, then the time would not be wasted.

Luthien rode out at dusk, taking Shuglin with him at Bellick's insistence. The dwarf king didn't fully trust Keyes, and said so openly, and he decided that if the priest had arranged a trap for Luthien, sturdy Shuglin would prove to be a valuable companion. Besides, the crimson cape was large enough that it could camouflage the dwarf as well as Luthien.

The pair reached the outskirts of Alanshire with ease, moving along the more open streets beyond the blockaded center; Luthien was certain that they could have made it this far even without the shielding cape. Now Shuglin came out from under it, and Luthien dared to pull back the hood. Soon after, the pair came upon Keyes and another man, an older, gray-haired gentleman with perfect posture and the sober dress of a old-school merchant.

"Alan O'Dunkery," Keyes introduced him, "mayor of Alanshire."

"It is a family name," the man said curtly, answering the obvious question before Luthien or Shuglin could ask it.

"The firstborn sons are all named Alan," Keyes added.

The gravity in the priest's tone seemed to escape Shuglin, but it was not lost on Luthien. This town was named after Alan's family; it was even possible that the whole river valley had been named for the family O'Dunkery, and not the other way around. This was an important man even beyond the borders of his small village, Luthien realized, and the fact that Keyes had convinced him to come out and meet Luthien gave the young Bedwyr hope.

"Brother Keyes has given me assurances that Alanshire will not be sacked, nor pillaged, and that none of our men will be killed or pressed into service," Alan O'Dunkery said sternly, hardly a tone of surrender.

"We'll not fight any who do not lift weapons against us," Luthien replied.

"Except cyclopians," Shuglin grunted. Luthien turned a sharp gaze on the dwarf, but Shuglin would not back down. "We're not leaving one-eyes on the road behind us," he said with a determined growl.

Luthien allowed the pragmatic dwarf the final word on that.

"You'll find few behind you," Alan said calmly. "Most have fled to the south."

"Taking much of Alanshire's livestock and supplies with them," Keyes pointedly added, reminding Shuglin that there were potential allies here, or at least noncombatants.

"How many cyclopians remain?" Luthien asked bluntly, the first information he had requested. This was a delicate moment, Luthien knew, for if Alan O'Dunkery told him outright, the man would be giving away information that would help the Eriadorans. "And if they are to make a stand at the wall, warn well any of your men or women who desire to stand beside them. Our fighters will not distinguish, human or one-eye, in the press of battle."

Alan was shaking his head before Luthien finished. "All the cyclopians that remain are in that building," he said, pointing to a tall, square structure that anchored the southeastern corner of the inner village. "In hiding, I would suppose, but in any case we will not allow them to come out."

Shuglin nearly choked on that revelation.

The Eriadoran army entered Alanshire the next day. There was no fanfare, no warm greetings from the populace, so many people who had lost so much in the cyclopian exodus. But neither was there any resistance. Bellick set up his line around the cyclopian stronghold and made only a single offer to the one-eyes: that he would accept their surrender.

The cyclopians responded with force, hurling spears and brutish threats from every window. With Alan O'Dunkery's permission, the Fairborn archers set the structure ablaze, and the one-eyes were summarily cut down as they came haphazardly charging out of the various exits.

Alan O'Dunkery and Solomon Keyes met with Luthien, Siobhan, and King Bellick that same day to discuss the next town in line, the influential woman who ran it, and the general mood of the place.

For the people of northern Avon, the purpose of this war was simply to escape with as little loss as possible. Greensparrow had erred badly, Luthien believed, by not sending his army north to meet the invaders. These people felt deserted and helpless, and it was not realistic for the king of Avon to believe that they would offer any resistance to so overwhelming an invading force.

The march to Warchester rolled along.

"Mystigal *and* Theredon?" Greensparrow asked angrily. "Both of them are dead?"

"Do not underestimate the power that Brind'Amour brought to the plateau," Deanna Wellworth replied. "Strong was the ancient brotherhood."

The skinny, foppish king leaned back on his throne, scratching at his hairless cheek and chin. "You are sure that he is destroyed?"

"I am *not* sure," Deanna replied. "It is possible that the wizard's spirit escaped, though his body was charred to ashes. I cannot understand the tricks of those ancient wizards, and have seen enough of Brind'Amour to respect him greatly. But I suspect that we will hear no more of him in the near future. I am confident, my King, that the army of Eriador is without a leader."

The news should have been welcomed in Carlisle, but Greensparrow scowled ominously. Brind'Amour ducked low behind a tapestry, fearful that the Avon king would somehow see through the fog of Deanna's divining mirror and through his own invisibility spell. The duchess of Mannington was equally nervous, the old wizard knew, judging by the amount of time she had spent in front of that mirror composing herself before mustering the courage to call to her king. When Deanna finally did cast the divination, it was in a trembling voice that only gradually steadied as she repeated the summons.

"It is possible that I will get to Resmore and free him," Deanna went on, trying to keep the king's thoughts full of information and empty of prying questions.

It didn't work. "Where is Ashannon McLenny?" Greensparrow snapped.

"Gone back to Baranduine to organize against the Eriadoran fleet," Deanna answered without hesitation.

Greensparrow's dark eyes flickered, telling Deanna that he would be quick to check on that.

"The dwarfs and men of Eriador have crossed through the northern-most villages," Deanna reported truthfully, information that Greenspar-row undoubtedly already possessed. "Their path is for Warchester, I believe. I will go there personally, in Theredon's stead, and make our stand."

No response.

"What aid will Carlisle send to me?" Deanna asked. "Cresis and the Praetorian Guards?"

Greensparrow snorted. "You have not heard?" he asked. "A second army makes its way southwest from Princetown. Even now they ap-proach the gap between Deverwood and the Iron Cross."

Behind the tapestry, Brind'Amour quietly sighed in relief.

"I will need Carlisle's garrison to deal with them," Greensparrow fin-ished. "Warchester's forces, along with your own, should prove ample to destroy whatever has come south through the mountains.

"And I must keep my eyes to the river south of Carlisle," the king ad-mitted. "The Eriadoran fleet in the west will be bottled in the straits and destroyed, without doubt, but another fleet has turned south of the Five Sentinels."

"And you have no ships left to stop them?" Deanna dared to ask, though she made sure that no trace of hope entered her voice.

Greensparrow scoffed. "I have thrice their number laying in wait," he said, "led by my finest sea captains. Still, if one or two of the rebels should slip through my galleons, I must be ready for them. Thus you are on your own, Duchess Wellworth," he said imperiously, signaling that the conversation was nearing its end. "Turn them back, or better, destroy them all. It will be far better if there are no organized defenders await-ing our triumphant return to Caer Mac—to Montfort!"

Greensparrow waved his hands and the image in the mirror clouded over and dissipated into nothingness. The glass quickly cleared and Deanna sat staring at her own reflection.

"So far, so good," Brind'Amour said hopefully, coming visible as he stepped out from behind the tapestry.

Deanna shook her head. "He will find a path to Taknapotin, who was my familiar demon," she explained. "Or he will make contact with the fiends of Mystigal or Theredon. We'll not hide the truth for long, I fear."

Brind'Amour nodded, unable to disagree, but he did walk over and put a comforting hand on Deanna's shoulder. "Long enough," he said. "You did well, Duchess, to deflect his curiosity, keeping him busy enough with the truth to have no time to unwind the lies. By the time Greensparrow understands that I live on, and that he has no remaining wizard allies in his cause, it will be too late."

"Even if he discerns such information this very night?" Deanna asked grimly.

Brind'Amour had no reply. The army was fast approaching Warchester, the fleet was sailing hard into the Straits of Mann. Mannington's many warships were already out at sea and Deanna could not possibly recall them without alerting Greensparrow to the truth. Even if Greensparrow learned the truth, even if all of Avon and a hundred dragons rose against the invaders, there was no turning back.

CHAPTER 25

THE STRAITS OF MANN

THE UGLY LITTLE YELLOW PONY skittered right, and then left, working hard to compensate for the rocking motion of the rough sea. Oliver seemed quite content up on Threadbare's back, though. His cheeks were rosy, his eyes bright, a far contrast from his last sea voyage, which he spent mostly at the rail.

"My horse, he likes the water," the halfling quipped to Katerin, whenever she happened by. She merely shook her head in disbelief.

The woman had little time to pause and consider the always-curious halfling, though, for the ship, *Dozier's Dream*, and the forty others sailing about it, would soon round a bend along the northwestern coast of Avon, moving into the narrowest part of the Straits of Mann. The stronghold of Eornfast lay less than twenty miles across the channel and Mannington just a few miles more on this side of the dark waters.

The lead ship, barely two hundred yards ahead of *Dozier's Dream*, hadn't even fully executed the turn when the enemy was revealed. Balls of flaming pitch streamed through the air, sputtering into the water all about the leading Eriadoran vessels. Crews tacked hard, turning out to the wider waters, dropping the sails to battle mast on those ships that could not escape.

"Katerin, to me!" cried old Phelpsi Dozier from the wheel.

Katerin rushed over to join with the weathered old mariner. This was his ship, the command given out of respect to Port Charley's oldest sailor, but Phelpsi was wise enough to understand and admit to his limitations. "Get 'em ready!" he said to Katerin. The old man paused when he glanced behind the woman, and like Katerin, shook his head. "And will ye get down from that stupid pony!" he yelled at Oliver.

"Horse!" Oliver corrected, and when Threadbare, as though the pony understood the old man's insults, stomped hard on the deck, the halfling promptly added, "And my Threadbare is not stupid!"

Most of the ships were turning to the west, putting out away from the coast, and as they sailed around the bend, Katerin saw the truth of their enemy. At least as many Avon sails were up to match the Eriadorans, forty to fifty war galleons, no doubt all manned by experienced crews, cyclopian and human. Katerin's fellows were skilled seaman, but only a handful in the entire Eriadoran fleet had ever waged battle upon ships of this size and caliber.

Where they were lacking in skill, though, the Eriadorans were determined to make up in sheer courage. So it was then for Katerin. She saw many ships turning out, and many Avon ships angling to intercept. The leading Eriadoran galleon on this side of the channel, though, would soon be surrounded, with nowhere to run. The ship took a flaming hit, then another, and the crew was soon too busy battling fires to consider the fast-closing Avonese warships.

Katerin called for full sail, straight on.

From his unusually high vantage point, Oliver saw what she meant to do, and recognized the risk that the woman of Hale was so willingly accepting. "Why do I always pick crazy-type peoples for my friends?" the halfling lamented.

"So says the halfling sitting on a pony on the deck of a ship," Katerin was quick to reply.

"Horse," Oliver corrected.

"If you sit up there that you might look important, then act important," Katerin scolded. "Put the archers in line, port side, and tell them to hold their shots until we're close enough to jump across. Same for the catapult crew!"

Oliver nodded, then paused, staring blankly at Katerin.

"The left side," the woman explained.

"I knew that," Oliver remarked, gingerly turning Threadbare about and clip-clopping off down the deck.

"Left," Katerin said again after him.

The lead Eriadoran exchanged heavy fire—catapult, ballista, and bow—with two Avon ships, one on either side. None of the three were sailing; none dared unfurl a sail in that barrage of bolt and flame. The rough tide battered the outer Avon ship the hardest, that one being to the starboard of the Eriadoran and thus the farthest out from the coast. Waves rolled against the Avonese relentlessly, driving both it and the Eriadoran toward shore and forcing all three of the ships even closer together.

Katerin tried to gauge her distance, and the speed of the drifting trio. She honestly didn't know if she could get between the Eriadoran and the Avon ship closest to shore.

"Ye've got the courage of a cuda fish," old Phelpsi Dozier remarked in her ear. "Or the brains!" he added with a snicker.

Katerin truly liked the old man, was even coming to love him. She had met Dozier on her first trip to Port Charley, when she was serving as an emissary for Luthien in the days when the revolution loomed no larger than the city walls of Caer MacDonald. Anyone looking at Phelpsi would think him frail, and perhaps simple, and yet he had managed to trap both Katerin and Oliver in the hold of his private boat, and now, with death staring them all in the face, he was as strong a shoulder as Katerin had ever known.

He continued to chuckle aloud, even when the Avon ship, realizing what *Dozier's Dream* meant to do, began firing at them, even when one crossbow quarrel cracked into the wood of the mainmast, barely a foot over Phelpsi's head. "Cyclopians never could shoot well!" the old man howled.

Katerin gained resolve from the snickering old Phelpsi, and used that strength to focus on her task. The tide pushed her ship relentlessly to port, and Katerin had to continually correct the course. Some rigging tore free and one of the sails began flapping wildly, but the damage could not slow the ship's momentum.

With only twenty yards separating them, it became apparent that *Dozier's Dream* simply would not fit between the vessels.

"Pull the reins!" Oliver cried to Katerin. "Or pull whatever a ship might have!"

"Get down from the pony," Katerin warned. She turned more to port, not wanting to clip the other Eriadoran, though the new angle put them even more in line with the Avon galleon.

"I am safer up here!" Oliver cried.

A barrage of arrows led the way for the charging Eriadoran ship; the catapult let fly, skipping a heavy stone across the Avon ship's decking, and *Dozier's Dream* crashed in, skimming the length of the Avon galleon. Rigging on both ships tangled and fell. Mast crosspieces smacked together and splintered.

Threadbare went into a short hop, landed firmly, and Oliver sailed over the pony's head, diving into a somersault, then a second, a third, even a fourth, along the deck, before he finally managed to stagger to his feet. He immediately turned toward Katerin, but overbalanced and fell headlong to the planks.

"Do not even speak it!" the halfling warned, but Katerin was paying him no heed, had no time to think of Oliver. Arrows buzzed the air all about the woman, and though *Dozier's Dream* was still moving forward, still crunching wood before the two ships settled in a tangled mess, the cyclopians were already coming over their rail.

Bolstered by the grateful cheering of the other Eriadoran crew, the crew of *Dozier's Dream* met the cyclopian charge, first with a volley of arrows, then with swords. Oliver regained his seat on Threadbare and plowed into a trio of one-eyes, knocking one into the churning water between the vessels.

One of the brutes recovered quickly, but hesitated before it rushed in at Oliver, obviously stunned to see someone riding on a ship! "Hey," the brute bellowed, "why is you up on that ugly yellow dog?"

In response, Oliver kicked Threadbare into a short hop, knocking the brute to the deck. Threadbare came on immediately, trampling the cyclopian, finally stopping with its back legs straddling the brute.

"Horse!" Oliver corrected. "But I am sure that you can see that now, from your better angle."

The cyclopian uncovered its face long enough to reach for its fallen sword. Before its hand ever got close, though, it had to cover once more, as Oliver placed his hat over Threadbare's rump, a signal he had long ago taught the pony, and the intelligent mount responded by kicking out, and then trampling the unfortunate cyclopian once again.

"A pretty horse, would you not agree?" Oliver asked.

"Ugly dog!" howled the cyclopian.

"They are so very stubborn," Oliver lamented, putting his hat back over Threadbare's rump, prompting the pony to action.

"Pretty horse!" the cyclopian yelled repeatedly, whenever it could seize a breath. It was too late for the brute to exact mercy from Oliver, though. The halfling kept his hat in place long enough for Threadbare to silence the cyclopian forever.

Those precious moments had put the halfling in a tenuous position, though. Glancing all about, Oliver soon realized that more cyclopians had come over to his ship than remained on the other. With his typical logic guiding the way, the halfling prodded the wonderful pony into a leap over the rails.

Threadbare hit the deck of the Avonese ship running, turning at Oliver's bidding toward the door of the cabin under the high rear deck, a door that had been smashed in by the catapult shot.

A huge and fat cyclopian came out of that hole, shaken and wounded, but still ready for battle, holding a gigantic mallet across its belt. Its bulbous eye widened even more, though the one-eye showed no fear when it took stock of Oliver and his pony thundering across the deck. The fat brute braced itself, legs wide apart, and smiled wickedly.

Oliver sincerely wondered if this had been a wise course. Considering the damage caused by the bouncing catapult ball, the halfling had figured the cabin to be empty—of living cyclopians, at least—offering him a fine place to relax, perhaps even to find a bit of wine and cheese.

Now he was committed. His first instinct was to continue the charge straight on, right into the brute, but he feared that this tremendous one-eye might outweigh both him and his pony combined! He pulled Threadbare to a light trot instead, bent low, and whispered into the pony's ear.

Oliver kicked hard on Threadbare over the last few paces, gaining a sudden burst of speed. The cyclopian howled and braced itself, but as quickly as he had started the charge, Oliver stopped it, falling off to the side, then dropping into a running crouch right under the belly of his pony.

On cue—Oliver's rapier tapping the pony's chest—Threadbare reared, kicking at the one-eye. The brute was too engaged to take note of the halfling as he ran out from under the pony and scampered right between the cyclopian's wide-spread legs.

Oliver fell into a roll and turned about as he regained his feet, rushing right back in, double-sticking with rapier and main gauche. Both blades bit hard, one on each side of the cyclopian's buttocks, and the brute reflexively skipped forward, right into the yellow pony's flailing forelegs. The cyclopian threw up its burly arms and frantically ran to the side, confused and battered. Threadbare chased it every step, biting at the back of its neck.

"I do hope that you can swim," Oliver remarked dryly as the cyclopian slammed against the rail, doubling over it, but catching itself quickly.

Threadbare never slowed, lifting his head high and ramming the brute right through the rail. The victorious pony reared again and neighed excitedly, then turned about to face his halfling rider.

"Join me for a spot of tea?" Oliver asked, motioning to the empty cabin.

The yellow pony snorted.

Oliver looked about and gave a great sigh. The fight was on in full, mostly on the decks of *Dozier's Dream*, and it remained fierce, though his side was obviously winning. "Very well, my equine conscience," the halfling said.

Threadbare hopped and Oliver ducked fast, as a crossbow quarrel split the air above his head. Then the halfling dodged to the side as a cyclopian fell over the rail of the poop deck, dropping dead to the main deck at Oliver's feet. The halfling looked back to regard Phelpsi Dozier, the ancient man obviously enjoying himself, patting an old crossbow, nodding and grinning wide, though few teeth remained in his mouth.

The ring of steel echoed across the decks of all four ships for more than half an hour, and when the fighting sorted itself out at last, the cyclopians were beaten, though many Eriadorans had been lost. Out in the deeper waters, the sailors from Eriador fared even worse, being outmaneuvered by the more skilled Avonese galleon crews.

Katerin organized what was left of the two crews, enough sailors to lightly man two ships. Unfortunately, the only ship of the four that could quickly put back out to sea was the Avonese vessel on the starboard side of the outer Eriadoran. Planking was put in place, and the crew went to work, changing the colors, untangling the rigging, and sorting out their positions. They left the three tangled ships, their own dead, and more than six hundred slain cyclopians behind, caught the wind in their sails, and moved out bravely to the west, into the crossfire of wild battle.

The fighting raged for several more hours, more men and brutes falling from sheer exhaustion than from arrows. Of the eighty-seven ships that had engaged, seventeen were either sunk or sitting helplessly, colors struck in surrender, drifting on the waves and wakes of passing ships.

And more than half of those seventeen were Eriadoran.

Katerin held out hope that they still might win out, but she realized that her fleet would be far weaker when it sailed out the southern mouth of the Straits of Mann, too diminished to be much of a factor even if they ever did reach the Stratton River and the seawall of Carlisle.

But they had to fight on, the determined woman realized, because every Avon ship that slipped under the waves was one fewer raider to strike at Port Charley, or at Diamondgate, or even her own home of Isle Bedwydrin.

"The one-eyes're good," old Dozier remarked, standing between Katerin, who was at the wheel, and Oliver, who remained atop his pony.

In truth, the pilots of the Avonese vessels were almost exclusively human, but Katerin could not disagree with Phelpsi, as much as she hated giving any credit at all to wretched cyclopians.

"There is an old Gascon saying," Oliver interrupted. "My Papa halfling, he once told to me, 'A fight is first of skill, then of heart.' And he also told to me," the halfling went on, striking a heroic pose for emphasis, " 'A one-eye, his chest is big, but his heart is oh so small!' We will win."

The simple confidence in the halfling's tone as he spoke the last three words, "We will win," struck Katerin profoundly. With a determined growl, she found the angle to intercept the closest Avonese vessel and daringly called for full sail.

Katerin took care this time not to entangle; there were simply too many free Avon ships for any Eriadoran to get caught up with one. Her crew was now much larger than before, more than four hundred strong, and as the ship slipped across the prow of the Avon vessel, the barrage of arrows raking the decks of the enemy ship took a mighty toll, including a score of bolts that cleaned out the two men and one cyclopian standing near the wheel.

Katerin's crew cheered her on; the catapult got off yet another shot as the daring woman cut the ship into a sharp one-eighty turn, bringing her around before the Avonese could replace their helmsmen and properly react. This time Katerin cut across the Avonese galleon's stern, and the volley started earlier, cleaning out the cyclopians, archers, and catapult crew from the poop deck. The Eriadoran archers got off a second shot, then a third, as the ship slipped past, and the catapult waited until the optimum moment to slam a ball of flaming pitch against the Avonese mainmast, which went up like a great candle.

Again the reply from the Avonese vessel was weak and without consequence, and Katerin knew better than to give this enemy a third try at her ship with her sails so very vulnerable. She took the galleon away, sails full of wind. Fighting against so many in such tight and dangerous waters was reckless, she knew; one ball of pitch could turn her entire deck into a conflagration, one flaming arrow could destroy a mast.

"Perhaps we should drop to battle sail," Oliver offered as the speeding ship closed in on a pair of Avonese vessels.

"You are the one who always claimed that cyclopians were terrible with bows," Katerin replied. "They could not hit the side of a mountain, so you said."

Oliver looked up and it seemed to him that those stretched sails were larger targets than any mountain. He regarded stubborn Katerin and shook his head helplessly.

Katerin didn't have to look at him to understand the stare, but she accepted the look and the risk. Now was the time for daring, even desperation that bordered on recklessness. She spotted a pair of Avonese vessels and angled accordingly.

Even determined Katerin had to back off, though, when she realized that the two galleons had spotted her and were calling back and forth, coordinating their response. With a frustrated snarl, Katerin cut hard to port, turning her ship low in the water. Her crew let fly, so did the Avonese, but the vessels were still too far apart and none of the three took hits of any consequence.

Katerin's frustrated expression melted into a grin a few moments later, though, when her crew began to cheer wildly. A trio of Eriadoran ships had come in at the Avonese from the other side when they had been intent on Katerin's speeding ship, and the Avonese had not been able to react appropriately. Both tried to turn their broadsides to the new threat, but they had gone in opposite directions and had actually tangled together. Now the crews of the two Avonese vessels were more engaged in fighting flames than in fighting Eriadorans, while the three Eriadoran vessels began to circle, archers and catapults pounding away. They pumped hundreds of arrows and dozens of balls of pitch and heavy stones into the Avonese galleons before more enemy warships sailed in, forcing the three Eriadorans to flee.

So I will be the taunting mouse for the Avonese cats, Katerin thought. She would be the distraction, the daring, darting little mouse, trying hard to stay out of the cat's claws, while her companion vessels found the openings left in her speeding wake.

Of the next eight ships that struck colors or filled with water, six were Avonese.

The spirits of all the Eriadoran crews began to rise, bringing new energy to continue the fight as the sun began its western descent. Katerin's spirits were perhaps highest of all, the fearless woman full of energy, full of the fight for Eriador. She would continue her wild run until one of her sails went down, she determined, and then she would find an Avonese ship to ram, that she might keep up the fight.

Something about the tone of Oliver's groan gave her pause, though, as profound a lament as the fiery young woman had ever heard. She looked to the halfling and then followed his gaze out to the north, the starboard side.

There she saw the end of the invasion, the doom of her fleet: a solid wall of sails, it seemed, lining the horizon. The vessels were not galleon size, but neither were they little fishing boats. "How many?" Katerin gasped. A hundred?

"Green flag!" cried a crewman straddling the mainmast, sighting the new fleet as he was trying to repair some of the rigging damage. "White-bordered!"

Katerin was not surprised. She had expected these newcomers, though not in such numbers. "Baranduine," she muttered hopelessly.

Phelpsi Dozier ambled over. "Not bad folks, the Baranduiners," he said. "Not like these damned cyclopians! I seen 'em often in the open waters. Might be they'd accept an honorable surrender."

The mere mention of the word sent Katerin's teeth to grinding. How could they surrender, thus laying open the entire western coast of Eriador? What would Brind'Amour and his forces do if Greensparrow walked in the back door and flattened Caer MacDonald?

There came a burst of billowing orange smoke on the deck right before the wheel, an eruption out of nowhere, it seemed, and after the initial shock, Katerin thought she might get her answer. Had Brind'Amour come personally to her ship to speak with her?

When the smoke cleared, though, the woman saw not Brind'Amour, but another man, middle-aged, but undeniably handsome. His dress was practical for the weather and rigors of the sea, but fashionable and showed that the man was not wanting.

"My greetings," he said politely, giving a sweeping bow. His eyes locked on Oliver, the halfling all in his finery—purple cape, green hose and gauntlets, and wide, plumed hat—sitting astride Threadbare. "I am Duke Ashannon McLenny of Eornfast on Baranduine."

Katerin and old Dozier stared open-mouthed.

"And I am not amused by your show of silly wizard tricks," the halfling proclaimed, never at a loss for words. "Etiquette demands that you ask permission before you board a ship."

That brought a smile to Ashannon's face. "There was little opportunity," he explained. "And in truth, yours is the third Eriadoran ship I've boarded already. I must speak with a woman, Katerin O'Hale by name, and a man of Port Charley who is called Dozier, and a halfling . . ." His voice trailed off as he continued to stare at the most-curious Oliver.

"You would be Oliver deBurrows," Ashannon reasoned, for there simply couldn't be two such halflings in all of Avonsea!

"And I am Katerin O'Hale," Katerin interrupted, finding her tongue— and her anger. Her hand went immediately for the hilt of her belted sword. This was one of Greensparrow's wizard-dukes standing before her, and considering her past experiences with these men, she figured that Ashannon's demon ally wouldn't be far away.

"Fear not," Ashannon assured her. "I have not walked into your midst as an enemy. Some consider me a fool, perhaps, but I am not."

"Why are you here?" Oliver had to ask.

Ashannon swept his hand out to the north, forcing them all to look again to the incoming fleet. "A hundred warships," he began.

"You come asking for surrender," Katerin said grimly, and she wasn't certain that she could refuse such an opportunity. The Baranduine ships were fast closing on a group of several Avonese vessels, whose mostly cyclopian crews were standing at the rail, cheering wildly.

Ashannon smiled. "You will see," he said, turning to the north.

By the end of the first volleys, balls of smoking brown earth that exploded when they landed and scores and scores of arrows, most of the cyclopians on those three Avon ships were dead and fires raged on each of the galleons.

Katerin, Dozier, and Oliver snapped blank stares on the duke of Eornfast.

"I have met with Brind'Amour," Ashannon explained. "Baranduine is no friend to King Greensparrow. Pass the word to your fleet," he instructed. "I warn you, any of my ships that are attacked will respond." With a burst of smoke, the man disappeared, and a similar puff of smoke rising from the midst of the Baranduine fleet told the three startled companions which ship Ashannon marked as his flagship.

The fight was over hours later, in the dark, with thirty Avon galleons scuttled and ten others sent running, and a weary and battered, but now tripled, invasion fleet ready to move on. The Baranduiners sent skilled seamen to aid the Eriadorans, and gently passed over some peat bombs, the brown earthen balls that would violently burst apart upon impact.

Katerin and Oliver readily accepted Ashannon's invitation to board his flagship and sail beside him, the two of them intrigued and full of hope.

The fleet, more than a hundred strong, crossed out the southern end of the Straits of Mann, past the lights of Mannington, before the dawn.

CHAPTER 26

THE NIGHT OF THREE ROUTS

THOUGH HE HAD NEVER BEEN in this region before, Luthien Bedwyr needed no map to tell him which city was next in line. The Eriadoran army had thundered across a hundred miles and a dozen villages since coming out of the mountains. Resistance had been light, even nonexistent in some places, as the cyclopians—particularly the Praetorian Guards who had been routed out of the Iron Cross—continued to flee to the south, pillaging supplies as they went. That rowdy retreat had played well into Luthien's hands, turning the populace against Greensparrow. And with the help of Solomon Keyes and Alan O'Dunkery and other important Avonese, there had been minimum loss of human life to either side.

But now . . .

Luthien walked Riverdancer to the top of a small hillock. He peered south in the waning light of the day, following the silver snakelike Dunkery until it widened and dispersed into a shining blot on the horizon. There lay Speythenfergus Lake, and on its northern banks, along the strip of land between the Dunkery and Eorn Rivers, sat high-walled Warchester, its militia no doubt swelled by the thousands of cyclopians who had forsaken the villages to the north.

Below him on his right, Luthien's army plodded along, making steady progress. They would march long after sunset, setting their camp in sight of the mighty city.

How would the Eriadorans and mountain dwarfs fare against the fortifications of mighty Warchester? Luthien and his forces had never laid siege to a city, or tried to battle their way through towering walls of stone. They had won in Caer MacDonald by fighting house to house, but they had already been inside the city's walls when the battle had begun. They had won in Princetown by deception, luring the garrison outside of the city into a killing valley known as Glen Durritch. But how would they fare against a fortified city that expected them and had prepared for their arrival?

Luthien entertained the thought of convincing Bellick to go around Warchester, flanking Speythenfergus Lake on the east and marching straight out for Carlisle. The young Bedwyr understood the folly of such a plan, of course; they could not leave an entire cyclopian army behind them!

And so they had to go to Warchester, had to lay waste to the fortified city, and perhaps even turn west to the coast and attack Mannington as well. Not for the first time, and certainly not for the last, Luthien considered the apparent folly of their march and longed for the quiet rolling hills of Isle Bedwydrin.

"When Duke Theredon is not here, I am in command," the brutish cyclopian insisted in its sputtering lisp, poking its fat and grimy thumb into its barrel-sized chest.

Deanna Wellworth scrutinized the one-eye. She had always thought cyclopians disgusting and ugly, but this one, Undercommander Kreignik, was far worse than most. Its bulbous eye dripped with some yellow liquid, caking on the side of the brute's fat, oft-broken nose. All of Kreignik's teeth were too long and crooked, jutting out at weird angles over torn and twisted lips, and the cyclopian's left cheekbone had long ago been smashed away in a fight, leaving half of Kreignik's face sunken, and giving him a tilted, uneven appearance.

"I am a duchess, equal in rank to your missing duke," Deanna reminded, but Kreignik was shaking its ugly head before she ever finished.

"Not in Warchester," the brute insisted.

Deanna knew that she could not win this verbal battle. Since her arrival through a magical tunnel the previous night, she had been treated with outright disrespect. Like all of the other rightly paranoid wizards of Greensparrow's court, Theredon had put safeguards in place against the intrusions of any other wizards. The dead duke's orders to Kreignik, and probably to every ranking cyclopian below the one-eye, were unyielding; even Greensparrow himself would have trouble prodding the brute to comply. Kreignik likely wasn't the first cyclopian to rise to the rank of undercommander of Warchester. Men such as Theredon tested their subordinates by, for example, assuming the form of another duke, then challenging the loyalty of the cyclopian officers. Failure to follow Theredon's specific orders would mean a terrible, torturous death.

Kreignik had probably witnessed more than one such event. No threats and no logic that Deanna could use would sway the stubborn one-eye.

"I told you that Undercommander Kreignik would not fail at a critical time," came a call from behind the brute. Kreignik turned, and Deanna looked beyond the massive brute, to see Duke Theredon ambling down the hall.

Deanna winced at the sight. Brind'Amour, though he had altered himself to appear as Theredon, had the mannerisms all wrong, shuffling like an older man, and not walking with the confident and powerful gait of the strong duke.

"And you feared that my soldiers would not be ready!" the fake Theredon roared, clapping Kreignik on the back—an inappropriate action that made Deanna wince yet again. "Ready?" Brind'Amour roared. "Why, with all the cyclopians that have come down from the north, we are more than ready!"

Deanna noted the skeptical look on Kreignik's face and knew she had to do something to salvage the situation. "Why my dear Duke Theredon," she said with a laugh, "you have been drinking that Fairborn vintage I gave to you!"

"What?" Brind'Amour stammered, growing serious at the sight of Deanna, her lips drawn tight again as soon as the obviously mocking chuckle had ended. "Oh, yes," the old man improvised. "But not so much."

"I warned you of its potent kick," Deanna said, and Brind'Amour understood that she would have liked to really kick him then and there. "What good will you be in the coming battle?"

"What good?" the old wizard scoffed, and he assumed a more regal posture. "With the Praetorian Guards from the Iron Cross, I estimate that we outnumber the Eriadoran fools by nearly two to one. And we have the better side of the walls in our faces!" He snapped his fingers in the air before Deanna's unblinking eyes. "They could not take Warchester in a hundred years!"

Kreignik seemed to like that proclamation, so much so that the scowl melted from the ugly brute's face. Kreignik even dared to reach over and pat the imposter duke on the back, though Brind'Amour was quick to flash a scowl at the one-eye, backing it away.

"Perhaps they will not then attack," Deanna prompted. "But lay in wait in siege."

Brind'Amour laughed, and so did Kreignik, but Deanna was not amused. The plan, after all, had been to convince the cyclopian undercommander that retaining their forces in the city would be foolish and dangerous. Brind'Amour's words were true enough; even with Deanna and Brind'Amour working their magic, the Eriadorans had little chance of crashing through Warchester's fortified gate with the city so swollen by retreating cyclopians. Even if Luthien and Bellick somehow managed to enter and win out, their army certainly would be badly wounded, and with two hundred miles still to go to Carlisle.

Deanna's skin felt prickly as a wave of anxiety crept up about her. All of this seemed suddenly foolhardy; how could they hope to win out all the way to Carlisle? How could she, even with Brind'Amour and

Ashannon, hope to defeat Greensparrow? The duchess firmly shook the thoughts away, reminding herself that Greensparrow's strength lay mostly in terror and in the hordes of cyclopians he had brought under his rule. Magic and demons and dragons were powerful weapons, but in the end measure, this war would be won by the resolve of the common soldiers and the cunning of their leaders.

Steadied once more, Deanna focused on the immediate task at hand, that of convincing Kreignik to go out from Warchester. She was about to try another course, when Brind'Amour abruptly stopped laughing.

"That is it!" the old wizard shouted in Kreignik's face.

The cyclopian backed a step, its expression twisted with confusion.

"Do you not see our opportunity?" Brind'Amour shouted, and danced about the corridor. "We can take the offensive, Kreignik," he explained. "We will go out onto the field and utterly destroy them. And we will catch this Crimson Shadow fool, and the fool Brind'Amour, too, if he is among their ranks. Oh, what gifts will King Greensparrow give to us when the Eriadorans are delivered to him!"

Kreignik didn't seem to buy it, though the brute had trouble hiding its intrigue at the possibility of such glory.

"We have no choice in the matter," Deanna quickly put in. "By all reports, there is a second Eriadoran army rounding the southern spur of the Iron Cross. If this army at our gates gets bogged on the fields outside Warchester, we can expect the second group to join up with them. Or worse, both armies will bypass Warchester altogether and march straight on to Carlisle."

"We will pursue them then," reasoned Kreignik. "We will catch them from behind and squeeze them against Carlisle's walls."

Brind'Amour draped an arm across the brute's wide shoulders. "Would you like to be the one who tells King Greensparrow that we willingly allowed the Eriadorans to get all the way to Carlisle?" he asked quietly.

The brute stood straight, as if slapped. "Catch them on the field!" he proclaimed. "Ten thousand Praetorians will go out this night!"

Brind'Amour tossed a wink Deanna's way, and the woman managed a slight nod and smile before Kreignik turned back to her. She noticed then that Brind'Amour went suddenly stiff, the grin flying from his face. He looked all about frantically, and Deanna had no idea what was so suddenly causing him such distress.

"The Fairborn wine," the old wizard stammered. "I must . . ." He gave a wail and ran off, leaving Deanna mystified.

Until a moment later, when King Greensparrow stalked around the corner at Deanna's back, flanked by an escort of five Praetorian Guards.

Deanna nearly fainted. "My King," she stuttered, dropping a respectful curtsy.

"What preparations have you made, Duchess Wellworth?" Greensparrow snapped. "And why have you not returned to Mannington, guiding the fleet against the Eriadorans?"

"I . . . I did not think so small an Eriadoran flotilla would prove a problem," Deanna explained. "My captains are more skilled . . . and Duke Ashannon will sail across the channel, no doubt." Deanna hardly knew what she was saying, was desperately trying to improvise. "The more immediate threat seemed this army. The speed and sureness of its approach has been remarkable—I could not leave Warchester unattended."

She noticed a frown grow on Kreignik's ugly face. The brute was not stupid. How could Deanna have been in on a "test" with Theredon, as the duke had claimed, yet now claim she thought Warchester had been unattended? Deanna's heart beat faster; it could all come tumbling down right here, right now. The undercommander said nothing, though, probably too afraid of Greensparrow's wrath should it speak out of turn.

Greensparrow mulled over the explanation for a moment, then nodded, though his dark eyes never blinked, and his gaze never left Deanna's eyes. "So you came into Warchester and assumed control," the king said.

"As we discussed," Deanna replied, resolutely not looking at Kreignik.

Greensparrow nodded and turned to Kreignik. "And what have you planned?"

"We will go out to destroy the enemy on the field," the undercommander replied.

Deanna held her breath, not knowing how Greensparrow would feel about such a daring move. The king, after all, understood that the Eriadorans could not possibly crush Warchester, especially since he believed that Brind'Amour was dead.

"This was Deanna's idea?" Greensparrow asked.

Deanna could tell by his suspicious tone that the king was prying for something. She wondered if Brind'Amour would reveal himself now, come out in open challenge to Greensparrow once and for all. Deanna felt faint with that possibility. Neither she nor the Eriadoran wizard had prepared for such an encounter; both were magically drained from their journey to the city, and Brind'Amour even more so from his impersonation. And to fight the Avon king in here, in the midst of an Avon stronghold, with more than fifteen thousand loyal cyclopians around him, was nothing short of foolish.

Kreignik straightened. "I only thought that . . ." it stammered. "The duchess was not . . . I mean . . ." Kreignik continued to stumble, even more so as Greensparrow's dark eyes flashed dangerously and the king began to wave his arms. Kreignik took a deep breath, visibly trying to sort out its thoughts, but before the brute got the next word out of its mouth, it was dead, lying in a smoldering heap on the floor. Deanna stared wide-eyed, and then turned her stunned gaze on Greensparrow, who stood shaking his head angrily.

Watching the action through a mirror in a side room far removed from the corridor, Brind'Amour, too, stared wide-eyed at the unexpected scene. The old wizard knew that he should break the connection—certainly he was taking a risk in divining so near to Greensparrow—but he feared that the Avon king had discovered them, that Deanna would need him. He got some relief when he glanced down to the yellow disenchanting powder he had set about the perimeter of the room the night before. Only the mirror was open to the palace, but even that was dangerous, Brind'Amour realized. He had detected Greensparrow quite by accident, by luck, and now he had to hope that the Avon king was not so fortunate. For Brind'Amour did not want a fight now, not here, not with Luthien oblivious to it all out on the field. At first he had considered throwing himself at the Avon king, in a desperate effort to finish this ugly business once and for all. That course would have gotten him killed, though, and Deanna, too, even if they managed to overcome Greensparrow. Brind'Amour lamented again the weakness of magic in these days. In times of old, if he and another wizard had fallen into a personal battle, then all the soldiers, human or cyclopian, in the area would have run for cover, would have been absolutely inconsequential in the magical fight. But now a sword could be a formidable weapon against a wizard, and those cyclopians standing defensively around Greensparrow certainly knew how to wield their swords!

So Brind'Amour could only watch and pray—pray that Deanna would make no mistakes, and that Greensparrow wouldn't happen to notice him.

"Cyclopians," the Avon king fumed. "This one's orders were explicit: only Duke Theredon Rees or myself could issue any commands concerning the Warchester garrison. Yet here he is, the fool, abiding by the requests of the duchess of Mannington."

"You disapprove of my plan?" Deanna asked, trying to keep the sincere relief out of her voice. "I thought that we had agreed—"

"Of course I do not disapprove," Greensparrow replied with a growling voice, obviously agitated. "I have Eriadorans coming at me from four sides. You destroy the middle here, while Ashannon crushes their flank in the straits, and the threat, if there ever was one, is ended.

"But do not think that your duties will be ended!" Greensparrow snapped suddenly, sharply, and Deanna jumped in surprise. "I expect the invaders to be crushed, slaughtered to the man, or dwarf, and then I charge you and Ashannon with our counterattack. Retrace Brind'Amour's own steps back to the north, while Ashannon sails to Port Charley. Your forces will meet in Montfort, which the upstarts call Caer MacDonald. Raise my pennant over the city once more, on your life!" He paused a moment, taking a full measure of the woman: recalling, Deanna knew, her failure in the Iron Cross. "Kill anyone who argues the point, and murder their children as well!" he finished, his eyes narrowing.

Deanna nodded with every word, glad that Greensparrow was still following his typically overconfident instincts, thoroughly relieved that he was too assured to suspect the treachery that she and Brind'Amour had attempted here in Warchester. Also, the king's orders left little doubt in Deanna's heart that she was following the correct course. When evil Greensparrow told her to murder children, he meant it.

He meant it as he had meant to murder Deanna's own brothers and sister that night in Carlisle.

It took all the woman's resolve and years of training for her to hold her thoughts private, and properly shield her emotions. She wanted to lash out at the evil king then and there, force Brind'Amour into the fight so that she could pay this wretched man back for the deaths of her family.

She grinned wickedly instead, nodding.

"You," Greensparrow snapped at one of his Praetorian Guard escorts. The brute immediately jumped forward, fearing a fate similar to that of Undercommander Kreignik.

"What is your name?"

"Akrass."

"Undercommander Akrass," Greensparrow corrected. "You are to follow Duchess Wellworth's commands as you would have followed those of Duke Theredon Rees."

Akrass shook its head. "I cannot," the brute replied. "My orders are to stand by you, and you alone, to the death."

Greensparrow chuckled and nodded. "You have passed the test," he assured the brute. "But the test is no more, by my own words.

"Deanna Wellworth is the duchess of Warchester," he went on, then to Deanna, he added, "Temporarily."

This caught the five Praetorian Guards by surprise, and Akrass even dared to look back to the others.

Deanna nodded. "I will not fail in this," she said with clear resolve, and she meant every word, though her intended mission was not what King Greensparrow had in mind.

Not at all.

"You are leaving?" Deanna asked as Greensparrow suddenly swept away.

"I am off to the coast to see about Ashannon," he snarled.

Deanna was glad that he turned back to the corridor before realizing how pale her face suddenly went.

"You should fly to the east instead," she blurted, stopping Greensparrow short. He turned slowly to regard her.

"New information," she stammered, searching for something to tell this tyrant. "I fear that some Huegoths have joined in with our enemies. Their western fleet . . ."

Greensparrow's face screwed up with rage.

"I wanted to search it out more before speaking with you," Deanna tried to explain. "I cannot be certain. But now, I have other duties, more important." She straightened her shoulders, finding her courage. "You should fly out to the east and determine if the information is true. Ashannon will see to the Eriadoran fleet, and I will strike back to the north. We will await you in Montfort!"

Greensparrow let his gaze linger a bit longer on the woman, then turned and pushed through the Praetorian Guards.

Deanna nearly fainted with relief.

In a room not so far away, Brind'Amour sighed.

Luthien had heard the earlier reports that a great winged creature had landed on the fields south of Warchester. The descriptions had been vague—the army was still several miles from the city, and miles further from those southern fields—but the young Bedwyr could guess at what his scouts were talking about.

This time, he, too, spotted the beast, its great lizardlike form, widespread wings, and long, serpentine tail, as it flew far off to the south and east. Some on the hillock beside him called it a bird, but Luthien knew better.

It was a dragon.

Luthien's heart sank at the sight. He was one of the very few people alive in all the world who had faced a dragon before, and only dumb luck and the work of Brind'Amour had allowed him to escape. The young Bedwyr couldn't even imagine fighting such an enemy; he wondered if his entire army could even harm the great beast if it turned suddenly to the north and attacked.

Luthien shook that thought away; if such was true, then the dragon would have come north, breathing its fire and rending man and dwarf. The young Bedwyr looked back over his troops, and took heart. Let the wyrm come north, he decided, and they would put up such a barrage of arrows that the sheer weight of the volley would bring the beast down!

The dragon continued to the east, Luthien saw as he looked back, and was now no more than a speck on the distant horizon.

"Keep going," Luthien prayed quietly. He suspected that he would see this one again, though. It had landed south of Warchester, which meant that Greensparrow's allies included more than cyclopians and a handful of wizards.

"How could you tell him?" Brind'Amour asked, comfortable in his own form again when he and Deanna were alone in the locked and magically secured room.

Deanna held up her hands.

"Of the Huegoths," Brind'Amour explained impatiently, for she knew what he meant. "How could you tell Greensparrow of the Huegoths?"

Deanna shrugged. "It seemed the lesser evil," she replied casually. "If Greensparrow had gone to the west, as he had intended, then Ashannon and our fleets would be sorely pressed—likely destroyed even, when you consider the power such a wizard might exert over the cloth and wood of sailing ships. Even worse for us all, if Greensparrow flew west, he would likely discern the truth of it all. Flying east, he will spend many days confirming the information of the Huegoths, if they are as far offshore as you believe, days that we will need if we ever hope to get to Carlisle."

Brind'Amour was upset, but he understood Deanna's reasoning. There had to be a measure of truth within a web of lies, the wizard realized, and that truth had to be convincing. Deanna had thrown Greensparrow a bit of valuable information that she might keep his trust, something that she and Brind'Amour certainly needed. It was only that confidence Greensparrow held, in himself and in those he had subjugated, that had thus far kept him oblivious to the treachery. Still, it occurred to Brind'Amour that Deanna's goals and his own were not one and the same. Both wanted Greensparrow thrown down, but Brind'Amour didn't think that the duchess would shed many tears if the Eriadoran, dwarvish, and Huegoth forces were badly diminished in the effort.

He would have to keep a close eye on Deanna Wellworth. With that in mind, the wizard closed his eyes and began his transformation once more, assuming the form of Theredon Rees.

"Have you the strength for the illusion?" Deanna asked, drawing the wizard from his contemplations.

Brind'Amour stared at her blankly.

"Dusk is nearly upon us."

Brind'Amour nodded, catching on. Akrass was busy assembling the ten thousand who would go out from Warchester under cover of darkness.

"The mantle of Duke Theredon is ready to be donned," Brind'Amour assured her.

Deanna wasn't sure if that would even be necessary—or wise, since they would have to make up yet another story to satisfy the curiosity of Akrass. Greensparrow had publicly given her power over the entire Warchester garrison, after all, and Theredon was not needed.

Brind'Amour understood the same, but he wasn't about to let ten thousand cyclopians march out of Warchester under Deanna's control with his own forces so vulnerable if things were not handled just right. Not yet.

The pair left the room soon after to meet with Akrass, Deanna explaining quickly that since Theredon had returned—and wouldn't Greensparrow be pleased to learn that his duke was indeed still alive?—she was relinquishing command to him, but also that Greensparrow's words concerning her own power still held, and she would serve as the duke's second.

Akrass believed it—what choice did the poor brute have?

They came out of the gates after sunset, the full moon rising in the east. "Theredon" and Deanna headed the procession, in step with the cyclopian Akrass, whose chest was swollen with pride. The one-eye wasted no time in beating any who ventured too near, or who showed even the least amount of disrespect.

Before they had gone very far, before the entire cyclopian line had even crossed under the huge gates, Brind'Amour put out a whistling call that was answered, a moment later, by a small owl, which flew down to the wizard's arm and cocked its head curiously.

Brind'Amour whispered into the bird's ear and sent it away, flying north with all speed.

"What do you do?" Akrass asked.

Brind'Amour scowled at him, reminding him that his newly granted power did not include questioning the duke of Warchester! The cyclopian lowered its gaze accordingly.

"Now we have eyes," Brind'Amour remarked to Deanna.

"Eyes and a plan," the duchess replied.

That plan was fairly simple: the cyclopians broke up into three groups, with three thousand going over the Dunkery River to flank the Eriadorans on the right, three thousand going over the Eorn River to flank the enemy on the left, and the remaining four thousand, including a fair amount of ponypig cavalry, going straight north, between the rivers, headlong into the Eriadoran encampment with the initial attack. The confusion caused within the Eriadoran army's ranks would turn to sheer panic, it was reasoned, as soon as the one-eyes came across the Dunkery and the Eorn, squeezing like a vise.

Of course, Brind'Amour and Deanna had other ideas.

Luthien, Bellick, and Siobhan were quick to respond when word reached them that a talking bird had entered the camp. The young Bedwyr prayed that this might be the work of Brind'Amour, even the wizard himself in a transformed body.

He was a bit disappointed when he found the owl perching on a low branch. It seemed oblivious, and though Brind'Amour often appeared that way, Luthien knew that this was not the wizard. Still there was no doubt that there was a bit of magic about the bird, for it was indeed speaking, uttering only one word: "Princetown."

"Brind'Amour has gone to Princetown?" Siobhan asked the bird.

"Princetown," the owl replied.

"At least we now know where the wizard has gone off to," Bellick remarked sourly, not thrilled to think that Brind'Amour would not rejoin them for their all-important attack against Warchester. As far as any of those in the camp knew, there was an enemy wizard ready to meet that charge.

Luthien wasn't convinced. He tried questioning the bird along different lines: "Are we to go to Princetown?" and "Has Princetown claimed allegiance with Eriador?" but all that the bird would reply was that one word.

Until Luthien and the other two turned to leave. Then the owl said suddenly, "Glen Durritch."

As one, the three turned back to the bird. "Princetown, Glen Durritch," grumbled Bellick, not catching on.

"Left, right, straight ahead," said the bird, and then, as though the enchantment put over the creature had expired, the owl silently flew off into the darkness.

Luthien's face brightened.

"What do you know?" Siobhan asked him.

"Only once have we gone against a fortified Avon city," Luthien replied. "And we won a smashing victory."

"Princetown," Bellick put in.

"But we did not actually battle against the city," Siobhan objected.

"We fought in Glen Durritch," said Luthien. Siobhan's face brightened next, but Bellick, who had come on the scene in Princetown near the end of the battle and really didn't know how things had fallen out so favorably, remained in the dark.

"Brind'Amour took the form of Princetown's Duke Paragor and sent the city's garrison out from behind the high walls," Luthien explained.

Bellick's gaze snapped to the south, toward Warchester. "You're not thinking . . ." the dwarf began.

"That is exactly what I am thinking," Luthien replied.

Siobhan called for the scouts to go out in force, and for the camp to be roused and readied for battle.

"This was a warning from Brind'Amour," Luthien insisted, joining Bellick as the dwarf continued to stare out to the south. "The garrison is coming out, and we must be ready for them."

For the three cyclopian groups, the one crossing the swift Dunkery had the most difficult time.

Even worse for the one-eyes, Bellick had realized that they would.

The cyclopian flank was split, a third already across the river, a third in the water, and the rest lining the eastern bank, preparing to cross, when the Eriadorans hit. The cavalry, led by Luthien and Siobhan, sliced down the eastern bank, while archers opened mercilessly on those brutes struggling in the water, their thrashing forms clearly illuminated by the full moon. At the same time, Bellick's dwarven charges overwhelmed those on the western bank, pushing them back into the river.

The waters ran red with cyclopian blood; even more brutes drowned in the swift current, their support lines chopped by dwarvish axes. Those one-eyes on the eastern bank were the most fortunate, for some of them, anyway, managed to run off into the night, screaming and without any semblance of order.

It was over quickly.

But though the rout was in full spate, the Eriadorans had just begun this night's work. Spearheaded by Luthien's cavalry, the force charged off to the south, determined to get to Warchester ahead of the remaining two cyclopian groups, to ambush them out on the field.

* * *

"It is empty!" Akrass roared, kicking at a bedroll—a bedroll stuffed with leaves and stones so as to appear full. Every fire in the vast encampment burned low, every blanket, every bedroll, covered nothing more than inanimate stuffing.

Before the cyclopian could even begin to express its outrage, the sounds of battle drifted in from the east, from the Dunkery.

"They have gone out to meet our flank!" yelled Brind'Amour, still in Theredon's guise but growing more weary by the moment.

Akrass called for formations, thinking to charge right off to the east and ambush the ambushers. With his duke's blessing, the undercommander did just that, so he thought.

The moon could be a curious thing when wizards were nearby. Simple spells of reflection could make the pale orb seem to shift its position. Similarly, spells of echo reflection could alter the apparent source of clear noise. And so the disoriented Akrass led his four thousand straight to the north instead of the east.

"Nice moon," Brind'Amour remarked to Deanna as they put their horses in line for the march, as the old wizard realized just how well Deanna had executed the enchantment.

"Simple trick," the woman replied humbly.

Brind'Amour was truly pleased. "Simple but effective."

The last of the Warchester formations trudged across the low and muddy Eorn without incident. They were too far away to hear the sounds of battle, or the rumble of the cyclopian thrust to the north, and so they, like Akrass's group, were caught completely by surprise when they happened upon the Eriadoran encampment, expecting to find the battle underway, but discovering nothing but empty bedrolls.

By that time, the fields to the east were quiet once more.

The cyclopian leader of this group, without Theredon or Deanna or even Akrass to guide it, ordered a full retreat, and so the force set out back down the Eorn, this time on the river's eastern bank. They looked over their shoulders every step, hoping that their comrades would come marching down behind them, but fearing that the charge from behind might come from the sneaky Eriadorans.

Their defensive posture was to the rear then, as in any good retreat.

Except that this time they got hit from the front, and then from both sides as the superior Eriadoran forces closed on them like the jaws of a hungry wolf. It took several minutes for all the one-eyes to realize that these were their enemies; many thought that they were being greeted, and then erroneously attacked, by the garrison that had remained at Warchester!

They figured out the truth eventually, those that were still alive, but by that time it was far too late. Confusion turned to panic; cyclopians ran off in every direction, though the dark silhouette of high-walled Warchester was clearly visible to the south. Some desperately called for the garrison to come out to their aid, but the one-eyes inside the high walls, with typical selfish cowardice, would not dare desert the defensible city to save their kin.

"Long enough," Brind'Amour and Deanna decided, though it was a moot point. The leading edge of the cyclopian force, Akrass riding among them, had come into a village—and recognized the place as Billingsby, a hamlet five miles north of Warchester.

Deanna trotted her horse ahead of the main group to meet with the undercommander as Akrass came thundering back from Billingsby.

"The Eriadoran wizard-king, Brind'Amour, has struck," she said in despair. "He has obviously deceived us and led us in the wrong direction!"

Akrass wanted to strike the woman; Deanna could see that.

"Greensparrow will blame me," Deanna said, intercepting the brute's intentions.

The furious cyclopian backed off immediately, figuring that if it attacked Deanna now, perhaps even killing her, Greensparrow's ire might fall squarely on its own shoulders.

"To Warchester!" the cyclopian undercommander howled, waiting for no commands from the wizards. Akrass galloped his ponypig up and down the line, sweeping up the marching cyclopians in its wake, thundering back to the south.

By the time the battle was finished, the eastern sky had turned a lighter shade of blue, dawn fast approaching. Bellick's Cutter scouts came riding hard, informing the dwarf king that the third and largest force had swung about and was double-timing it back to the south, straight for Warchester.

King Bellick stroked his fiery orange beard and considered his options. His army was tired, obviously so, for they had fought two vicious encounters already. And with the daylight, and the warning cries that would no doubt come out from Warchester, it didn't seem likely that this third group would be caught so unawares.

Bellick split his forces, east and west, marching them out of sight of the city, with orders to let the one-eyes pass, then come in hard at the back of their line.

The men and dwarfs and Fairborn, bone-weary, covered in blood of kin and enemy, eagerly agreed.

The cyclopian line came in stretched thin, with the one-eyes too concerned with getting back to the safety of Warchester to consider their defensive posture. That march turned into an all-out rout when the Eriadorans appeared, striking hard at the rear flanks, chasing and killing the brutes all the way to Warchester's gates.

That was where Bellick and Luthien had determined to turn about for some much-needed rest, but unexpectedly, a moment later, the iron gates crackled with blue lightning—and then fell open wide.

For one horrible moment, Luthien feared that the entire Warchester garrison was about to come out at them. But then, as the lightning continued to crackle, consuming many Praetorian Guards standing near those gates, the young Bedwyr recognized the truth: that Brind'Amour had opened wide the city. All weariness washed from Luthien, and from the rest of the Eriadoran forces, with the presentation of such an opportunity. To Bellick's call, they charged ahead, howling and firing bows.

CHAPTER 27

THE WALLS OF WARCHESTER

THE CAVALRY MADE THE COURTYARD inside the gates and found it surprisingly deserted—even those one-eyes who had just reentered the city had fled for better ground. And that, Luthien saw with despair, would not be difficult to find. Warchester was surrounded not by one wall, but by several, all spiraling around the city proper and offering scores of defensible positions. Cyclopians were terrible with bows and even with throwing spears, but the defenders of the city were not all cyclopian, and Luthien could see just from this one area that those archers among the Avonese ranks would have many opportunities to fire their bows at the invaders. Luthien wished that he had the luxury of proper preparation, that he and Siobhan, Bellick, and some others could sit around a fire with a map of the city's interior and lay out organized plans. The young Bedwyr had been in enough large-scale battles to know the impossibility of that. He had pointed his forces in the right direction, but now, in the helter-skelter of pitched fighting, each warrior would have to make his own choices, each group would find new obstacles and would have to discern a way around them.

Luthien hated the prospects of this city fighting with so many miles yet to go, but the Eriadorans had gained the main gate, and this was an opportunity that simply could not be passed up. Luthien prodded Riverdancer to his right, where the curving courtyard began to slope up. Most followed in his wake, some went to the left. Still others, mostly dwarfs, went straight ahead at the next wall, hoisting ladders or throwing ropes fixed with strong grappling hooks, then pulling themselves upward, fearless, seemingly oblivious to the many one-eyes who came to defend the high wall.

Luthien didn't have to go far to find a fight. Just around the bend, he came to a jag in the wall, behind which a score of cyclopians had dug in. Calling for Siobhan, he plunged ahead, cutting down the closest of the brutes with a mighty swing of his heavy sword. Riverdancer trampled yet another one, and then Luthien leaped the horse ahead, leaving the one-eyes behind to the throng coming hard in his wake.

Further around the bend, Luthien was able to gain a vantage point where he might look back to the inner wall directly across from the broken gates. He turned just as a dwarf went tumbling from its height, sliding off the edge of a cyclopian sword. But that brute, and others near it, were overwhelmed as a dozen other bearded warriors crashed in. The wall was taken.

An arrow zipped past Luthien's face, and he turned to follow its course in time to see it nail another one-eye right in the chest. The brute staggered, but was pushed aside as a wedge of cyclopians charged down the gap between the walls, heading Luthien's way.

The young Bedwyr and his cavalry unit met them and trampled them.

The central and highest area of Warchester, like all large Avonsea cities, was dominated by a tremendous cathedral, this one named the Ladydancer. Around the structure was an open plaza, which on quiet days served as a huge open marketplace. Now that plaza was swarming, the terrified populace desperate to get inside the cathedral.

But the doors were not yet open.

Deanna Wellworth, Brind'Amour, and Akrass the cyclopian stood on the balcony that opened above the cathedral's main doors. Over and over, Brind'Amour, posing still as Duke Theredon, called for quiet, and gradually the hysterical crowd did calm—enough so that the sounds of the battle raging along the outer walls of the city could be clearly heard.

That done, the old wizard stepped back, taking a place next to Akrass, and Deanna took center stage.

"You know me," the woman cried out to the crowd. "I am Deanna Wellworth, duchess of Mannington."

Several calls came back, some for the opening of the Ladydancer, others asking if Deanna's garrison would come to Warchester's support.

"What you do not know," Deanna went on, and her voice was super-humanly powerful, enhanced by magic, "is that I am the rightful heir to the throne of Avon."

The people didn't react strongly, seemed not to understand her point. Of course they knew of Deanna's lineage, at least the older folk among them did, but what did that have to do with the present situation, the impending disaster in Warchester?

"I am the rightful queen of Avon!" Deanna shouted. She looked to Brind'Amour and nodded, and before Akrass could even begin to digest that proclamation, the one-eye was dead, Brind'Amour's dagger deep into its back.

"I can no longer tolerate the injustices!" Deanna cried above the growing murmurs and open shouts. "I can no longer tolerate any alliance with filthy one-eyes, nor the truth of Greensparrow! You have heard the rumors of a dragon lighting on the fields south of the city. That was no Eriadoran ally, my people, but our own king, in his natural form!"

Like a giant wave caught between many great rocks, the crowd jostled back and forth, erupting in places, noisy everywhere.

"Hear me, my subjects of proud Warchester!" Deanna shouted. "This is no invading army, but a mercenary force hired by your rightful queen! This is my army, come from Eriador to restore the proper ruler of Avon to her throne!"

Brind'Amour heard a tumult behind him and casually turned about and threw his magical energy into the huge door of the balcony, warping the wood and sealing it tight. "You will start a riot," he stated, an obvious fact, given the level of commotion mounting below them.

"We need a riot," Deanna insisted.

Brind'Amour could not disagree. He had seen the defenses of the fortress called Warchester and knew that there remained several thousand cyclopians ready to fight in the place. Add to that the thirty thousand humans who called Warchester city their home and Bellick's forces were sorely outnumbered.

The old wizard stepped forward, dragging dead Akrass with him. Yet another enchantment—and Brind'Amour was fast exhausting the energy to cast such spells—made the cyclopian as light as a feather pillow, and Brind'Amour lifted the corpse high into the air above his head. "Take up arms against your true oppressors!" the fake Duke Theredon instructed. "Death to the one-eyes!"

That cry echoed back from a surprisingly large number of men and women, and the plaza erupted into chaos. There weren't many cyclopians about—most were down at the lower walls—but not all of the gathered people would heed Deanna's call. Thus the riot Brind'Amour had predicted began in full.

"Sort it out," he bade Deanna. "Find your allies and secure the Lady-dancer. Get the wounded and the defenseless inside."

Deanna was already thinking along those same lines, and she nodded her agreement, though Brind'Amour, in a puff of orange smoke, was already gone to find Luthien.

Deanna continued to prod on her supporters, telling them to join together, to clearly identify themselves. Her speech was interrupted, though, as a heavy spear thudded down on the balcony just beside her. Turning, Deanna saw that several brutes had gained a perch on the tower high above her.

Her response—a crackling bolt of writhing black energy—only bolstered Deanna's support as it cleared that tower of one-eyes.

Turning back to the crowd, Deanna soon discerned a large group of organized supporters, working coherently and trying to get the innocents behind them, between them and the cathedral doors. The rightful queen of Avon turned and shattered Brind'Amour's stuck doors with yet another bolt, then fried the band of surprised cyclopians standing in the anteroom just inside. Soon the cathedral doors were thrown wide, and Deanna had her growing army of Warchester rebels.

The riot raged across the plaza.

Brind'Amour knew that his magic was nearing its end for this day. Despite the adrenaline rush and the wild fighting all about him, the old wizard wanted nothing more than to lie down and go to sleep. He used his wits instead, using his disguise to break up groups of cyclopians who were holding defensible regions of the wall by ordering them off on some silly business, weakening the line with improper commands.

It was more than an hour before the old wizard finally spotted some allies, a force of nearly a hundred dwarfs battling fiercely in ankle-deep water on the edge of a small moat surrounding one of the guardhouses.

With no magical power to spare, Brind'Amour moved on. It took him another half hour to finally hear the thunder of hooves.

Coming to the edge of a high wall, Brind'Amour saw the forces squaring off on either side of a long and narrow channel: Luthien and a hundred riders, Fairborn mostly, at one end, and a like number of cyclopians on ponypigs at the other.

The charge shook the ground of all the huge city. Luthien's cavalry gained an advantage with a volley of bow shots, but unlike the encounters on the open fields, they could not strike and then turn away. This time, the forces came crashing together in a wild and wicked melee, many going down under the sheer weight of the impact, others held up in their saddles only because there was no room for them to fall.

Amidst it all, the weary old wizard spotted Luthien on that shining white stallion, his mighty sword chopping ceaselessly, his voice calling for spirit and for Eriador free.

But the cost, Brind'Amour pondered. The terrible cost.

Luthien and nearly half his force broke through, and a swarm of Eriadoran foot soldiers came into the channel behind them, finishing off the beaten cyclopians, tending the Eriadoran wounded, and running off eagerly after the Crimson Shadow.

The fighting soon got worse—by Brind'Amour's estimation, and by Luthien's—for it became, in many places, human against human.

It ended late that afternoon, except for a few pockets of fortified resistance, with another victory for Eriador, with Warchester taken. The price had been high, though, devastatingly high, the northern army taking casualties of four out of every ten. Nearly half of Bellick's fearless dwarfs were dead or wounded.

Support for Deanna Wellworth was strong among the populace, but not without question. The woman had taken credit for the attack, and every family in Warchester had suffered grievously. Still, those Avonese who came out of the Ladydancer that night spoke of the evil of Greensparrow and their common hatred of cyclopians, and, sometime later, of the mercy shown by the conquering Eriadorans, who were tending Warchester's wounded as determinedly as they tended their own.

Brind'Amour was glad to be back in his own form again, though he was so exhausted that he could hardly walk. He introduced Deanna to Luthien, Bellick, and the other Eriadoran leaders and told them all that had transpired.

"We have won the day," Siobhan declared, "but at great cost."

"We're ready to march on," a determined Shuglin was quick to respond. "Carlisle is not so far!"

"In good time," Brind'Amour said to the eager dwarf. "In good time. But first we must see what allies we have made here."

"And I must return to Mannington," Deanna added, "to find what forces I can muster for the march to Carlisle."

Brind'Amour nodded, but did not seem so encouraged. "Mannington is still a city of Avon," he reminded. "This battle might well be repeated in your own streets, but without the support of Eriador's army."

"Not so," said Deanna. "Most of my Praetorian Guards are out with the fleet, and no doubt at the bottom of the channel by now, and I have sown the seeds of revolt for some time among the most influential of my people." She managed a sly grin. "Among the bartenders and innkeepers, mostly, who have the ear of the common folk. Mannington will not be so bloody, and a large number, I believe, will follow me out to the south, to Carlisle, where we will join you on the final field."

It was encouraging news, to be sure, but for the Eriadorans, who had fought through fifty miles of mountains and a hundred miles of farmland, who had fought four battles over the course of one night and one day, the mere thought of continuing the march brought deep and profound sighs. They were tired, all of them, and they had so far yet to travel.

"Keep a transportation spell ready," Brind'Amour warned, "in case Greensparrow looks in on you and discovers the truth of it all."

"He will know soon enough," Deanna replied. "And he will not be pleased." With a comforting smile, and a pat of her hand on the old wizard's stooped shoulder, the proclaimed queen of Avon went off.

"Secure the city and our camp," Brind'Amour instructed Bellick. "We will stay five days, at the least."

"Time favors Greensparrow," the dwarf warned.

"Who could have anticipated the fall of Warchester in a single day?" Brind'Amour asked. "I had believed we would be bogged here for at least a week, perhaps even several, perhaps even leaving half our numbers behind to maintain a siege. We have the time, and need the rest."

Bellick grunted and nodded, and walked off with Shuglin and his other dwarven commanders to see to the task.

Luthien and Siobhan also went off, to determine what remained of their cavalry, and what new horses might be garnered within Warchester. They tallied their number of kills as they walked, after agreeing that they would not count, or even speak of, the men they had necessarily killed this day. Counting dead cyclopians was one thing, a relief from the pressures of the war, an incentive to keep up the good fight. Counting human kills would only remind them of the horrors of war, something that neither of them could afford.

"Sixty-three," Luthien decided for himself, and Siobhan's fair face screwed up as she admitted a total of only "Sixty-one."

Neither of them spoke it, but they both realized that the half-elf would find ample opportunity to catch up in the days, even weeks, ahead.

When the army left Warchester, six days later, they were well-rested and well-supplied, their ranks thick with soldiers indeed, for many of Warchester's folk decided to join in the fight against Greensparrow, to join in the cause for their rightful queen.

"It is as I told you it would be," a grinning Luthien said to Brind'Amour as they started out. "Avon will rise against Greensparrow in the knowledge that our cause is a just one. Perhaps we should have continued our last war from Princetown, after we together destroyed evil Duke Paragor."

"You did predict this," Siobhan admitted, riding along easily beside the pair. "Though I never would have believed that the folk of Avon would join in the cause of an invading force."

"They did not," Brind'Amour said in all seriousness. "Those who have joined have done so only because of one person. Had Deanna Wellworth not risen against Greensparrow, then our fight for Warchester would have been desperate and the army marching from Mannington would be marching against us."

It was sobering talk, a reminder of just how tentative this had all been, and would likely remain. Brind'Amour said nothing of the sea battle in the Straits of Mann, for he had not found the time or the magical energy to discern how his fleet had fared.

The old wizard could guess at the situation, though, had a good feeling about it all that he kept private until he could be sure.

The rout of Avon was on in full.

Greensparrow paced anxiously about his great throne, wringing his hands every step. He went back to the throne and sat down once more, but was standing and pacing again within a few short moments.

Duke Cresis had never seen the king so agitated, and the cyclopian, who had heard many of the reports, suspected that the situation was even more grave than it had reasoned.

"Treachery," Greensparrow muttered. "Miserable treacherous rats. I'll see them dead every one, that wretched Ashannon and ugly Deanna. Yes, Deanna, I'll take whatever pleasures I desire before finishing that traitorous dog!"

So it was true, Cresis understood. The duke of Baranduine and the duchess of Mannington had conspired with the enemy against Greensparrow. The brutish one-eye wisely held in check its comments concerning the irony, realizing that a single errant word could bring the full wrath of Greensparrow. When the king of Avon was in such a foul temper, most thinking beings made it a point to go far, far away. Cresis couldn't afford that luxury now, though, not with two Eriadoran land armies and one, possibly two, fleets converging on Carlisle.

Greensparrow went back to the throne and plopped down unceremoniously, even fell to the side and threw one leg over the arm of the great chair. His kingdom was crumbling beneath him, he knew, and there seemed little he could do to slow his enemy's momentum. If he threw himself into the battle with his full magical powers, he would be putting himself at great risk, for he did not know the full power of Brind'Amour.

There is always an escape, the king mused, and that part of Greensparrow that was the dragon longed for the safe bogs of the Saltwash.

He shook that notion away; it was too soon for thinking of abdicating, too soon to surrender. Perhaps he would have to go to the Saltwash, but only after the Eriadorans had suffered greatly. He had to find a way . . .

"The Eriadoran and Baranduine fleet approaches the mouth of the Stratton," Cresis offered. "Our warships will hit them on the river, in the narrower waters where the great catapults lining the banks can support us."

Greensparrow was shaking his head before the brute was halfway finished. "They will sail right past the river," the king explained, confident of his words, for he had seen much in his days of dragonflight. "A battle is brewing on the open waters south of Newcastle."

"Then our eastern fleet will join in, and we will catch all the Eriadoran ships and those of treacherous Baranduine in between!" the cyclopian said with great enthusiasm. "Our warships are still the greater!"

"And what of the Huegoths?" Greensparrow snapped, and fell back helplessly into his throne. That much of what Deanna had told him was true, he had confirmed. A great Huegoth fleet was sailing with the Eriadorans in the east. In his dragon form, Greensparrow had swooped low, setting one longship aflame, but the wall of arrows, spears, even balls of pitch and great stones that rose up to meet him had been too great, forcing him to turn for home.

He had gone to Evenshorn first, and there had confirmed that Mystigal was not to be found. Then, flying high and fast to the west, he had spotted the second Eriadoran army sweeping across the rolling fields between Deverwood and Carlisle, like an ocean tide that could not be thwarted. Still, it wasn't until Greensparrow had arrived back in Carlisle, his fortress home, that his spirits had been crushed. In the time the king of Avon had taken to go so far to the east and back, many had come running down from the region of Speythenfergus to report the disaster in Warchester, and word had passed along the coast and up the Stratton about Duke Ashannon's turnabout in the Straits of Mann.

Cresis appeared truly horrified. "Huegoths?" the cyclopian stammered, knowing well the cursed name.

"Evil allies for evil foes," Greensparrow sneered.

The cyclopian's eye blinked many times, Cresis licking its thick lips as it tried to sort out the stunning news. To the brutish general, there seemed only one course.

"One army at a time!" Cresis insisted. "I will march north with the garrison to meet our closest enemies. When they are finished, if time runs short, I will turn back for Carlisle to prepare the city defenses."

"No," Greensparrow said simply, for he knew that if the garrison went north, that second Eriadoran army would swing west and catch them from the side. Greensparrow was even thinking that he had better focus his vision on Mannington for a while, to see if treacherous Deanna had raised an army of her own to march south.

"Prepare the defenses now," Greensparrow instructed after a long silence. "You must defend the city to the last."

Cresis didn't miss the fact that Greensparrow had not said "We must defend the city to the last."

With a click of his booted heels and a curt bow, the cyclopian left the king.

Alone, Greensparrow sighed and considered again how fragile his kingdom had become. How could he have missed the treachery of Deanna Wellworth, or even worse, how could he not have foreseen the efforts of the duke of Baranduine against him? As soon as Deanna had reported the supposed fight with Brind'Amour, Greensparrow should have gone straight off to find Taknapotin or one of the familiar demons of the other dukes and confirmed her tale.

"But how could I have known?" the king said aloud. "Little Deanna, how surprising you have become!" He had underestimated her, and badly, he admitted privately. He had thought that her own guilt, his cryptic stories and those of Selna, and the carrot of ruling over Mannington, and perhaps soon in Warchester as well, would have held her ambition in check, would have kept Deanna bound to him for the remainder of her life. Greensparrow had long ago seen to it, using devilish potions administered by his lackey Selna, that Deanna would bear no children, thus ending the line of Wellworths, and he had sincerely believed that Deanna could prove no more than a minor thorn in his side for the short remainder of her life.

How painful that thorn seemed now!

His northern reaches had crumbled and four armies were on the move against him. Carlisle was a mighty, fortified city, to be sure, and Greensparrow himself was no minor foe.

But neither was Brind'Amour, or Deanna, or Ashannon McLenny, or this Crimson Shadow character, or the Huegoths, or . . .

How long the list seemed to the beleaguered king of Avon. Again that dragon side of him imparted images of the warm bogs of the Saltwash, and they seemed harder to ignore. Perhaps, Greensparrow considered, he had erred so badly because he had grown weary of Avon's throne, had grown weary of wearing the trappings of a mere human when his other side was so much stronger, so much freer.

The Avon king growled and leaped up from his throne. "No more of that, Dansallignatious!" he yelled, and kicked the throne.

I would have kicked it right through the wall, the dragon side of him reminded.

Greensparrow bit hard his lip and stalked away.

CHAPTER 28

CAUGHT

THEY CAME IN RIGHT between the twin tributaries that bore the name of Stratton, a scene not unlike the approach to Warchester, except that there was less ground leading to Carlisle. And the cities themselves, though both formidable bastions, could not have appeared more different. Warchester was a dark place, a brooding fortress, its walls all of gray and black stone banded with black iron, its towers square and squat, and with evenly spaced crenellations across its battlements. Carlisle was more akin to Princetown, a shining place of white polished walls and soaring spires. Her towers were round, not square, and her walls curved gracefully, following the winding flow of the Stratton. Huge arching bridges reached over that split river, east and west, joining the city proper with smaller castles, reflections of the main. She was a place of beauty, even from afar, but also a place of undeniable strength.

Luthien could feel that, even regarding the place from across two miles of rolling fields. He could imagine attacking Carlisle, the white walls turning brown from poured oil, red from spilled blood. A shudder coursed along the young Bedwyr's spine. The trek to Carlisle had been filled with terrible battles, in the mountains, across the fields, in Warchester, but none of them seemed to prepare Luthien for what he now believed would soon come, the grandfather of those battles.

"You should be afraid," remarked Siobhan, riding up beside the young man where he sat upon Riverdancer.

"It is a mighty place," Luthien said quietly.

"It will fall," the half-elf casually replied.

Luthien looked upon her, truly scrutinized the beautiful woman. How different Siobhan appeared now, all bathed and cleaned, than after the fights, when her wheat-colored tresses were matted flat to her shoulders by the blood of her enemies, when her eyes showed no sympathy, no mercy, only the fires of battle rage. Luthien admired this indomitable spirit, loved her for her ability to do what was necessary, to shut her more tender emotions off at those times when they would be a weakness.

The young Bedwyr dared to entertain an image then, of him and Katerin, Oliver, and Siobhan, riding across the fields in search of adventure.

"Do not tarry," came a call from behind, and the pair turned to see Brind'Amour's approach. "Bellick is already at work, and we must be as well, setting our defenses in place."

"Do you think Greensparrow will come out of his hole?" Siobhan asked skeptically.

"I would, if I were caught in his place," replied Brind'Amour. "He must know of the approaching fleets—he was told of the Huegoths—and his eyes have no doubt seen the charge of our sister army, sweeping down from the northeast.

"I would come out at this one force with all my strength," the wizard finished. "With all my strength."

Luthien looked back to the high walls of Carlisle, shining brightly in the afternoon sun. Brind'Amour's reasoning was sound, as usual, and the army would be better off taking all precautions.

So they dug trenches and set out lines of scouts, fortifying their perimeter and sleeping beside their weapons, particularly the tough dwarfs, who settled down for the night in full battle armor.

They didn't really expect anything until the next dawn; cyclopians didn't like to fight in the dark any more than did the men or dwarfs. The Fairborn, though, with their keen eyesight, thought little of the problems of night fighting, even preferred it.

And so did the dragon.

Greensparrow walked out of Carlisle as the midnight hour passed, quietly and without fanfare. Safely out of the city, the king called to that other half, the great dragon Dansallignatious, the familiar beast he had joined with those centuries before in the Saltwash. The king began to change, began to grow. He became huge, black and green, spread wide his leathery wings and lifted off into the night sky.

Just a few minutes later, he made his first pass over the Eriadoran encampment, spewing forth his fiery breath.

But the invaders were not caught by surprise, not with the Fairborn elves watching the night sky. A hail of arrows nipped at the swooping dragon, and Brind'Amour, who had rested through all the ten days it had taken the army to march from Warchester, and for the week before that when they had remained in the captured city, loosed his fury in the form of a series of stinging bolts of power, first blue, then red, then searing yellow, and finally a brilliant white, cutting the night sky like lightning strokes.

Dansallignatious took the hits, one, two, three, four, and flew on to the north, scales smoking, eyes burning. The beast took some comfort in the havoc he had left in his wake, a line of fire, a chorus of agonized screams. Far from the camp, he banked to the west, then turned south, preparing another pass.

Again came the hail of arrows, again came the wizard's bolts, and the dragon flew through, killing and burning the earth below him.

There would be no third run; Greensparrow was spent and battered. He went back into the city satisfied, though, for his wounds would quickly heal, but those scores he had killed on the field were forever dead.

The next day dawned gray and gloomy, fitting for the mood in the Eriadoran camp. Many had died in the dragon strafing, including more than a hundred dwarfs, and the wounds of dozens of survivors were horrible indeed.

The Eriadorans prepared for an assault, suspecting that the dragon attack had been the precursor for the full-scale attack. They expected the gates of Carlisle to swing wide, pouring forth a garrison that numbered, by most reports, more than twenty thousand.

That indeed was Greensparrow's intention, but the plan was

scratched, and the hearts of the Eriadorans were lifted high indeed, when the wide line of the Stratton south of Carlisle filled suddenly with sails! Scores of sails, hundreds of sails, stretched by a south wind and rushing to the north.

Siobhan spotted the banner of Eriador, Brind'Amour noted the green, white-bordered markings of Baranduine, and Luthien saw the froth of Huegoth oars.

"The dragon will come out against them, and leave them flaming on the river," Luthien said.

Brind'Amour wasn't so sure of that. "I do not believe that our enemy has truly revealed himself to those he commands," the old wizard reasoned. "Do you think that the folk of Carlisle know that they have a dragon for a king?"

"He could still come out," Luthien argued, "and later dismiss the event as the trick of a wizard."

"Then let us hope that we wounded him badly enough yestereve that he will not," Siobhan put in grimly.

The lead vessels never slowed, crossing under the high bridges east of Carlisle proper. Cyclopians crowded on those bridges, heaving spears, dropping stones, but the ships plowed on, returning fire, clearing large sections with seemingly solid walls of arrows. From Carlisle proper and from the smaller fortress across the river to the east, came catapult balls. One galleon was hit several times and sent to the bottom.

But the maneuverable Huegoth longships were on the spot in a moment, plucking survivors from the river, then swinging fast to the north, oars pounding to keep them in close to their companion vessels.

Despite the Stratton's sometimes formidable current, the ships passed the killing zone too quickly for the defenders of Carlisle to exact very much damage, and as if in answer to the prayers of those watching in the north, the dragon Greensparrow did not make an appearance. Nearly a third of the total fleet sailed on, their prows lifting high the water. An occasional catapult shot soared in, more often than not splashing harmlessly into the river, and even those attacks were soon enough put far behind the vessels.

Luthien took note of the wide grin that came over Siobhan's face, and he followed her shining stare to one of the lead sailing ships, a Baranduine vessel, which seemed to be in a race against a Huegoth longship. Both ships were still too far away for individuals to be discerned on the decks, even for Siobhan's keen eyes, with the exception of one remarkable silhouette.

"He is on his pony!" Luthien exclaimed.

"He always has to be the center," snickered Siobhan.

Luthien smiled widely as he considered the half-elf, once again trying to picture her with Oliver.

Lines of soldiers cheered the approach at a wide and sheltered region where the ships could drop anchor and the Huegoths and some of the smaller Baranduine vessels could even put in to shore. The ropes came flying in to them, were caught and secured, and the forces were joined.

"Luthien!" The call, the familiar voice, sent the young Bedwyr's heart fluttering. Throughout the weeks of fighting, Luthien had been forced to sublimate his pressing fears for his dear Katerin, had to trust in the woman's ability. Now that trust was rewarded as Katerin O'Hale, her skin darker from the days under the sun, but otherwise none the worse for her journey, came bounding down the gangplank of the lead Baranduine vessel, Duke Ashannon McLenny's flagship. The woman pushed her way through the crowd and threw herself into Luthien's waiting embrace, planting a deep kiss on the young man's lips.

Luthien blushed deeply at the coos and cheers that went up around him, but that only spurred Katerin on to give him an even more passionate kiss.

The cheering turned to laughter, drawing the couple from their embrace. They shifted to get a view of Oliver, still on Threadbare, coming onto the long gangplank.

"My horse, he so loves the water," the halfling explained. That may have been true, but his horse, like everyone else coming off the ships after weeks at sea, had to find its land legs. Threadbare came down two steps, went one to the side, then two back the other way, nearly tumbling from the narrow plank. Then back the other way, and back and forth, all the while making slow progress toward the shore.

Oliver tried to appear calm and collected through it all, coaxing his pony and praying that he wouldn't be thrown into the water—not in front of all these people! With some care, the halfling finally managed to get the pony onto the bank, to a chorus of cheers.

"Not a problem!" the halfling cried with a triumphant snap of his fingers, as he slid his leg over the saddle and dropped to the ground.

Unfortunately, Oliver's legs were no less used to the swaying of shipboard than were Threadbare's, and he immediately skittered to the left, then three steps back, then back to the right, then back again. He made a halfhearted grab at Threadbare's tail, but the pony was so named because of that skinny appendage, and Oliver slipped off, falling to his seat in the water.

The cheers became howls of glee and two men ran down to Oliver and scooped him up.

"I meant to do that," the halfling insisted.

That brought even louder howls, but they stopped abruptly, transforming into hushed whispers, when Siobhan moved near Oliver. Rumors about these two had been circulating and growing during the weeks and now everyone, Luthien and Katerin perhaps most of all (with the sole exception of wide-eyed Oliver!), wanted to see what Siobhan would do.

"Welcome back," she said, taking Oliver's hand, and she kissed him on the cheek and led him away.

The crowd seemed disappointed.

The time for greetings was necessarily short, with so many plans to be made and movements to be coordinated. Carlisle had not yet fallen, and the mere appearance of reinforcements did not change that situation!

The leaders met within the hour, Brind'Amour, Bellick, old Dozier, and Ashannon, along with Luthien, Siobhan, Katerin, and Oliver. Brind'Amour arranged for Ethan to keep King Asmund away for a short while, that he might first deal with his closest advisors, and with Duke Ashannon, who was still a bit of a mystery in all of this.

Ashannon and Katerin did most of the talking at first, with Oliver throwing in details of his own heroics.

"The Avonese fleet did not engage us south of Newcastle, as we expected," Katerin reported.

Brind'Amour seemed concerned, but Katerin was quick to put his obvious fears to rest.

"They were badly outnumbered and had little heart for the fight, especially when the Huegoth longships came into the lead of our eastern fleet," she explained. "They sailed south for Gascony, and there asked for refuge."

"Which the Gascons granted," Ashannon added. "But not without concessions."

Oliver conspicuously cleared his throat, and Ashannon yielded the floor.

"I met with my countrymen," the halfling explained. "The Avontypes were granted sanctuary, but only on condition that they declare neutrality. Greensparrow's fleet is out of the war."

"Most welcomed news," Brind'Amour congratulated. "Most welcomed!"

There were smiles all around, except for Katerin. "I have heard word of a force of five thousand coming down from the north," she said gravely.

"Duchess Deanna Wellworth and her garrison from Mannington," Luthien explained, and the tone of his voice told Katerin that these were not enemies.

"Deanna is a friend," Ashannon assured her. "And more important, she is a sworn enemy of King Greensparrow."

It proved to be a fine meeting, a meeting full of optimism, and now that the prongs of the invasion were closing in on Carlisle, Luthien and all the others dared to hope for victory.

Those hopes brightened with the dawn, as Deanna Wellworth's soldiers joined the line, and that same afternoon, the lead riders, Kayryn Kulthwain among them, came in from the northeast, heralding the approach of the second Eriadoran army, a force that was now larger than it had been when it left Malpuissant's Wall.

By mid-morning of the next day, Brind'Amour would have fifty thousand on the field encircling Carlisle, with supply lines stretching the breadth of Avon and the fruitful southern coast open to his warships.

Among the Eriadoran allies, there remained only one voice of dissent, a certain Huegoth leader who could not be put off any longer.

Luthien was with Brind'Amour when the king went to Asmund's longship. The younger Bedwyr hardly noticed the principals at the initial greeting, when he looked again upon his older brother. Ethan offered a hand to Luthien, but did not accompany it with a smile, nor a flicker of recognition in his cinnamon-colored eyes. Even after weeks moving in common cause, Ethan seemed as cold to Luthien as he had when the brothers had first found each other on the Isle of Colonsey.

Could it be that Ethan would never remember, or admit, who he truly was?

They had no time to discuss their personal situation, though, for Asmund descended on Brind'Amour like a great bear.

"We are warriors!" the Huegoth king roared. "And yet we have been sitting on the empty waves for weeks, our foodstuffs delivered by Eriadoran ships that have touched the shores of Avon!"

"We could not reveal—" Brind'Amour began, but Asmund cut him short.

"Warriors!" the barbarian roared again, looking for support from Torin Rogar, standing at his side. The huge Rogar nodded and grunted.

"I have not lifted my spear in many days," Torin complained. "Even the Avon warships turned from us and would not fight."

Brind'Amour tried to appear sympathetic, but in truth, after the beating his forces had taken all the way from Caer MacDonald, such eagerness for battle left a bitter taste in his mouth. The old wizard held little love for Huegoths, and for a moment seriously considered granting Asmund's desires, throwing the king and all his brutal warriors against Carlisle's high walls.

"I pain for battle," Asmund said hungrily.

"That you might replenish your slave stocks?" Luthien said bluntly. He noted Brind'Amour's scowl, and Ethan's, and he understood. Prudence told the young Bedwyr that they should keep the alliance solid at this critical juncture, but Luthien could no longer hold back his ire—at the Huegoths and at Ethan.

Asmund grabbed at the handle of the great axe that was strapped to his back; Luthien likewise put a hand to the hilt of *Blind-Striker*.

"You dare?" Asmund began. He thrust his fist into the air, a signal to his sturdy men that the meeting was at its end. Brind'Amour sucked in his breath, but Luthien did not blink.

"Perhaps Eriador would be wise to guard its coast," Asmund threatened.

"Is your pledge of honor so fragile that it might be broken by a few words spoken in anger?" Luthien asked, giving Asmund pause.

The king squared against Luthien, came very close to the young man, glaring down at him ominously. Luthien didn't back away an inch, and didn't blink.

"Friends do not fear to point out each other's faults," Luthien said in all seriousness, and he was taken aback a moment later, when Asmund suddenly bellowed with laughter.

"I do like you, young Luthien Bedwyr!" the king roared, and all his warriors stood more easily.

Luthien started to respond, again with grim confidence, but this time, Brind'Amour's scowl became an open threat and the young Bedwyr held his tongue.

The alliance was solid, for the time being, and after Asmund extracted a promise from Brind'Amour that the Huegoths could lead the charge against Greensparrow's fortress—a promise the Eriadoran king was more than happy to give—Brind'Amour and Luthien took their leave.

"When Greensparrow is properly dealt with, we will turn our eyes to the Huegoths," Luthien said as soon as he and Brind'Amour were back on land and away from Huegoth ears.

"What would you do?" Brind'Amour asked. "Wage war on all the world?"

"Promise me now that you will not let them leave the Stratton on ships rowed by slaves," Luthien begged.

Brind'Amour looked long and hard at the principled young man, wearing a stern and determined expression that the old wizard could not ignore. That dedication to principle was Luthien's strength. How could he possibly refuse to follow such an example?

"Asmund will be properly dealt with," Brind'Amour promised.

CHAPTER 29

THE SIEGE OF CARLISLE

*T*HEY STOOD ON THE FORWARD MASTS of the warships closest to Carlisle and on the hills outside of the city. Some brave ones rode their horses dangerously close to the white walls, waging a battle of words.

"We have fifty thousand on the field against you," they all said, as instructed by Brind'Amour and Deanna Wellworth. "Among our ranks is Deanna Wellworth, rightful queen of Avon. Surrender Greensparrow, the murderer of King Anathee Wellworth!"

Every hour of every day, those words were called out to the besieged people of Carlisle. Brind'Amour didn't really expect the Avonese within the city to rise up against their king, but he was looking for every possible advantage once the fighting did start. And that would take some time, the old wizard understood. An army could not simply charge the walls of a fortified bastion such as Carlisle.

They did wage a few minor battles, with the Eriadorans testing the strength of various points along Carlisle's perimeter. Asmund's Huegoths took the lead in most of these, but even the fierce Isenlanders knew when to turn about, and casualties remained light on both sides.

Meanwhile, other, more important preparations were underway, foremost among them the old wizard's work to keep Greensparrow busy. The Eriadorans could not afford to have the dragon coming out at them every night, or to have the wizard-king launching magical attacks into their ranks. Thus, Brind'Amour took it upon himself to engage Greensparrow, to test his strength, the powers of the ancient brotherhood, against this new-styled wizard. Alone in his tent the first night of the siege,

Brind'Amour created a magical tunnel, reaching from his chamber to the tower Deanna had identified as Greensparrow's. This tunnel was not like the ones the wizard had used to transport Asmund or Katerin and Oliver, but one that would take him in spirit only to face the wizard-king.

Greensparrow was surprised, but not caught off guard, to see the ghostly form of the old wizard hovering before his throne.

"Come to scold?" the Avon king snarled. "To tell me the error of my ways?"

Brind'Amour's response was straightforward, a burst of crackling red sparks that burned, not into Greensparrow's physical body, but into his soul. A moment later, Greensparrow stepped from his corporeal form, spirit leaping forward to engage the old wizard. And thus they battled, as Brind'Amour and Paragor had battled, but in spirit form alone. It went on for exhausting hours, neither truly hurting the other, but draining each other, and when Brind'Amour broke the connection the following morn, he was weary indeed, sitting on the edge of his bed, head down and haggard-looking.

Deanna found him in that position. "You met with him," she reasoned almost immediately.

Brind'Amour nodded. "And he is powerful," he confirmed. "But not compared to what we wizards once were. Greensparrow came to power through treachery because he could not gain the throne through sheer might. So it is now. He rules, iron-fisted, but that iron fist is not one of magic, nor even one of his dragon alter-form, but of allies, cyclopian mostly."

"Do not underestimate his power," Deanna warned.

"Indeed I do not," Brind'Amour replied. "That is why I went to him, and why I will go to him again this night, and the next, and the next, if need be."

"Can you defeat him?"

"Not in this manner," Brind'Amour explained, "for I go to him in spirit only. But I can keep him occupied, and weary! This battle will be one of swords."

Deanna liked that prospect far greater than the thought of waging a magical battle against Greensparrow. Five armies had joined against Carlisle, and the besieged city had no apparent prospects for reinforcement.

In this situation, the biggest advantage for the Eriadorans was their dwarvish allies. Carlisle had been built to withstand the charge of an army, most likely a straightforward cyclopian force, but the designers had not foreseen the tunneling expertise of an enemy such as the bearded folk of DunDarrow. The dwarfs worked tirelessly, taking shifts so that the digging never stopped. They went down low, right under the river, so that the people within the city would not hear their work. Ashannon worked tirelessly as well, using his magic to shield the dwarvish work from Greensparrow's prying eyes.

On the sixth day of the siege, the first decisive encounter took place, in the smaller city across the eastern branch of the Stratton from Carlisle proper. Asmund led the Huegoth charge from the north, Siobhan's cavalry and the Riders of Eradoch in strong support. Several galleons braved the catapult fire from both banks to come in at the city along the river to the west, while Shuglin led two thousand dwarfs through their crafted tunnels, popping up at various strategic points within the fortress. Even more important, the dwarvish burrowing had weakened the substructure of the walls.

The north wall, its bottom carved out, crumbled under the weight of the charge, and in poured the vicious Huegoths and the cavalry. Luthien, Oliver, and Katerin, already within the city through dwarvish tunnels, spent more time sorting out innocents and ushering them out of harm's way than in fighting, for in truth there wasn't much fighting to be found. The garrison fled the minor city, along the bridges to Carlisle proper, almost as fast as the invaders entered it. And Greensparrow, who they assumed to be weary from his nightly encounters with Brind'Amour, made no appearance.

The place was conquered within an hour, and fully secured before the day was out.

The noose around Carlisle had tightened.

That same night, Luthien and Oliver, using the crimson cape and Oliver's magical grapnel, a puckered ball that could stick to any surface, made their stealthy way into Carlisle and walked the streets of Greensparrow's domain. They ventured into taverns, met with people in alleys, always whispering the name of Deanna Wellworth, planting the rumors that the invading army was, in fact, a force raised by the rightful queen of Avon.

The pair were out of the city again long before the dawn.

Also that night, Brind'Amour went again in spirit to meet the Avon king, but he failed, finding the way blocked by a disenchantment barrier akin to the one he had used on Resmore and again in the castle at Warchester. Up to that point, Greensparrow had been more than willing to battle the old wizard, but now, Brind'Amour realized, the wily Avon king had come to understand their strategy. His engagements with Brind'Amour were in part to blame for the fall of the section across the river; he could no longer afford the distraction of a nightly stand-off with his adversary.

The realization did not greatly worry Brind'Amour. He understood his foe better now, the man's strengths and limitations, and he was confident that his forces could strike hard and decisively, and that he, along with his fellow wizards, Deanna and Ashannon, would effectively neutralize the overburdened Avon king.

As he had proclaimed to Deanna on the second morning of the siege, this would be a battle of swords, not of magic.

"He cannot come at us across the river when our ships hold the waterway," Brind'Amour explained at a strategy meeting early the next morning. "And with us so close to his walls, he would not dare open the city's gates and try to break out to the north."

"We would be in Carlisle in a matter of minutes," Katerin reasoned, and though her estimate seemed overly optimistic, the point was well-taken.

"Time favors us," Siobhan thought it would be prudent to add.

"Does it?" asked Deanna Wellworth.

"The seeds of rebellion are being sown within Carlisle," Luthien answered before Siobhan could respond. "Oliver and I found many folk willing to hear of Avon's rightful queen, and of the treachery of Greensparrow."

"Of course, that might be only because I am so convincing," added the halfling.

That brought a chuckle—from all but surly Asmund, who was fast growing weary of this siege.

"I will not sit on the field and wait for the first snows of winter," the Huegoth said. Indeed, Asmund and his forces could not wait much longer. They had a long way to sail to get home, in waters that would grow more inhospitable with the changing season. Soon the winds would shift to the north, blowing in the face of Huegoth longships trying to make their return to Isenland and Colonsey, where a fair number of their women and children waited.

Brind'Amour sat back and let the chatter continue around him. Asmund wanted action; so did Kayryn Kulthwain and especially Bellick, who assured the others that at least twenty openings would be burrowed into Carlisle that very night, and that the substructure of several key points along the eastern and southern walls had already been compromised.

"They're thinking that we'll come from the north and east," the dwarf king remarked with a wink at Brind'Amour. "But they'll be only half-right. Mannington's and Luthien's riders will fake the attack from the north, while our ships put an army in the shallows of the river delta south of the city. We'll be in so fast, the one-eyes will still be standing at the north wall, wondering when your folk will attack," he said to Deanna. "And the rest of us will poke them from behind!"

It wouldn't be quite that easy, Brind'Amour knew, but it was a good point. Carlisle was ripe for plucking, and if they attacked and were not successful, they could always retreat to their current position and take up the siege once more, this time against a city weakened by battle. The co-ordination would be tricky, though, since so many various factions were together on the field, but the old wizard, the king of Eriador, decided then and there that the time for action had come at last.

"With the dawn," Brind'Amour said unexpectedly, silencing conversation and turning all eyes upon him. "Even before the dawn," he corrected, then paused to better sort out the plan, and the emotions of all of those staring at him.

And so it began, an hour before the eighth dawn of the siege, when Shuglin the dwarf came out of a tunnel into a quiet house just east of the plaza of Carlisle Abbey. All throughout the silent city, Bellick's forces slipped into position, while on the plain north of Carlisle, Deanna Well-worth's five thousand, along with the first army of Eriador, including Luthien, Siobhan, Katerin, Oliver, and the Cutter cavalry, formed a long and deep line. South of Carlisle, Huegoths crowded into their longships, ready to storm the river fork, and in the east, Kayryn prepared her gallant riders for the mighty charge across the bridges.

The dawn was heralded by the blowing of a thousand horns—Eriadoran horns, Huegoth horns, Mannington horns—and by the thunder of cavalry in the north and on the stone of the eastern bridges, and by the roars of charging armies.

Luthien led the rush from the north, a feigned attack that kept the massive cyclopian force along Carlisle's northern wall distracted until the dwarfs within the city could organize. Then Carlisle's south wall crumbled in several places and on came the Huegoth charge, the army of Baranduine rolling in behind them. Kayryn herself led the thunder across the fortified bridges.

For more than an hour, little ground was gained, with Luthien and his forces stuck out on the northern fields, unable to find a breach in the intact and well-defended northern wall. In the south, Asmund's Hue-goths met stiff resistance just inside the wall, and the Riders of Eradoch took brutal casualties on those narrow bridges. The waters of the Stratton ran red; the white walls of Carlisle were splattered with the blood of defender and invader alike.

Five of the leaders, Brind'Amour, Bellick, Deanna, and Ashannon, along with Proctor Byllewyn of Gybi, stood watching from the captured eastern region throughout that terrible hour, wondering if they had erred. "Did I underestimate Greensparrow?" Brind'Amour asked many, many times.

But then came the turning point, as Bellick's dwarfs, led by mighty Shuglin, gained the main courtyard and threw wide Carlisle's massive northern gates. Now Luthien's charge was on for real, the young Bedwyr and his forces pouring into the city, spreading wide in every direction like the finger flames of a wildfire.

Greensparrow, too, watched it all, from a high chamber in Carlisle Abbey. Duke Cresis came to him many times over the first hour, assuring him that the city was holding strong.

Then the cyclopian came in to report that the northern gate had fallen, and Greensparrow knew that the time had come for him to act. He dismissed Cresis (and the one-eye was glad to be away from the dangerous and unpredictable tyrant!) and went alone up the stairs of the Abbey's main tower.

From that rooftop, King Greensparrow saw the ruin of his life. There was fighting in every section of the city. The north was lost, and the dwarfs were sweeping east to open the bridges, while the cavalry was thundering along the streets, winding its way to join in the fierce fighting at the south wall.

"Fools, all," the wizard-king sneered.

Greensparrow spotted a curious group of riders, noted particularly a man on a shining white stallion, a crimson cape billowing out behind him.

"At least, this," the king remarked, and his hands began weaving semicircles in the air, touching thumb to thumb, then little finger to little finger, the tempo gradually increasing as Greensparrow gathered his magical energies that he might strike dead the troublesome Crimson Shadow once and for all.

But before he could execute the spell, Greensparrow found his feet knocked right out from under him as the tower trembled under a tremendous magical assault.

Looking to the east, Greensparrow noted three forms: an old wizard in blue robes and holding an oaken staff, the duke of Baranduine, and the woman who would be queen. Brind'Amour struck repeatedly at the tower, lightning bolts reaching out from his staff to slam at the foundations beneath Greensparrow. Deanna and Ashannon were not so powerful, but still they threw every ounce of their strength at the king.

The tower swayed dangerously.

Looking back, looking all around, Greensparrow saw that he had become the focus. Even the Crimson Shadow and his cohorts had stopped their charge, were sitting astride their mounts and pointing.

"Fools, all!" the evil king cried, and then, in the daylight, before the eyes of so very many, the king of Avon revealed himself. He felt the pain, the torment, as his limbs crackled and expanded, as some bones fused while others broke apart. That horrible itch covered him head to toe, skin breaking and twisting, hardening into green and black scales. Then he was no longer Greensparrow; that part of the being that was Dansallignatious spread wide its leathery wings. And just in time, for the tower of the Abbey shuddered again and toppled.

All across the city, defender and attacker alike paused in their fighting to watch the fall, to see the king-turned-dragon hovering in the air above the cloud of rising dust.

A blue bolt of lightning reached out across the river and jolted Greensparrow, and with a howl of pain the dragon king swooped about. Cyclopian, Huegoth, Eriadoran, and dwarf—it did not matter—fell beneath the fiery breath as the great beast swept on. That part of the monster that was Greensparrow wanted to destroy the Crimson Shadow most of all, then turn east and across the river to engulf his wizard adversaries in killing fire. But that part of the monster that was Dansallignatious could not discriminate, was too taken up with the sheer frenzy of the killing.

And then, as the defense organized against the dragon, as walls of stinging arrows rose to meet his every pass, as warships sailed closer that they might launch their catapult volleys at the passing beast, and as the magical barrage from across the river only intensified, the dragon king saw the ruin and the loss and knew that it was time to flee.

Across the river Greensparrow soared, sending a last line of fire at the building where his principal adversaries stood ready. Deanna Wellworth was prepared, though, enacting a globe similar to the one she had used to trap Mystigal and Theredon on the high plateau. And though the area within grew uncomfortably hot, though Bellick's face beaded with sweat, and Byllewyn collapsed for lack of breath, when the dragon king had soared far off to the east, he left none of them truly hurt.

"Abdication!" screamed Bellick. "I know a running king when I see one!"

Tears in her blue eyes, Deanna wrapped the dwarf in a victorious hug.

Brind'Amour was not so full of glee. He started away in a great rush, bidding the others to follow. He led the way onto the nearest bridge and used his powers to their fullest to help clear the defense at the other end.

He would not explain his urgency, and the others didn't dare question him.

Somewhere far south of that point, Luthien Bedwyr was surprised when Riverdancer pulled up short so suddenly that Oliver, on Threadbare right behind him, almost wound up on his back. Siobhan and Katerin brought their mounts up a short distance ahead, looking back curiously at Luthien.

He had no answers for them, for he could not get Riverdancer to move. The shining horse held perfectly still for several moments, didn't even take notice when Threadbare bit him on the tail.

Then, despite Luthien's bidding, and fierce tugging on the bridle, Riverdancer swung about and pounded away. "Ride on to the south!" Luthien yelled, but his friends would not desert him, not when they didn't know whether his horse was taking him to allies or enemies.

Mighty Riverdancer soon outdistanced them, though, and Luthien breathed a sigh of profound relief when he turned into an alley to find Brind'Amour and the others waiting for him. The old wizard waved him down off the horse, then began whispering into Riverdancer's ear.

"What?" Luthien started to ask, but Deanna pulled him aside and shook her head.

Riverdancer neighed and bucked suddenly, and tried to pull away. Brind'Amour would not let go, though, and, his enchantment over the horse complete, he began instead to speak soothing words to the beast.

Luthien's eyes popped open wide—so did Oliver's, as the halfling led Katerin and Siobhan into the alley—when Riverdancer's sides bulged and expanded. The horse shrieked terribly, and Brind'Amour apologized and hugged the beast's head close.

But the pain passed as the bulges expanded, shaping into beautiful feathered wings.

"What have you done?" cried a horrified Luthien, for though the horse-turned-pegasus was indeed beautiful, this was his Riverdancer, his dear friend.

"Fear not," Brind'Amour said to him. "The enchantment will not last for long, and Riverdancer will bear no ill effects."

Luthien still found himself gasping at the appearance of the winged horse, but he accepted his trusted king's explanation.

"It must be finished here and now," Brind'Amour explained. "Greensparrow cannot get away!" He moved to the side of the magnificent beast, and obedient Riverdancer stooped low to help him climb into the saddle.

"The city will soon be yours," Brind'Amour said to Deanna. "Avon will soon be yours. I may miss your triumphant ascent to your rightful seat. Do not forget those who came to your aid, I beg."

"There are many wrongs to be righted," Deanna replied.

"If I do not return, then know that Greensparrow shall forever remain a problem to you. Keep your eyes to the Saltwash and your guard up high!"

Deanna nodded. "And for Eriador, whatever your fate, I promise independence," she replied. "Your army will not go north until a proper line of command has been established, be it King Bellick of DunDarrow, or Luthien Bedwyr, Proctor Byllewyn of Gybi, or Siobhan of the Fairborn."

Luthien was horrified that they were speaking so plainly of the possibility of Brind'Amour's death, but he quickly came to accept the necessity. Eriador could not be thrown into chaos again, whatever might now happen, and Luthien found that he believed Deanna's promise that Avon would no longer seek domination over his homeland. Still, given Deanna's last words, it seemed a real threat to Luthien that if Brind'Amour did not return, Eriador would split into tribal factions. Luthien could foresee trouble between Kayryn Kulthwain and Bellick, both so very proud and stubborn, perhaps trouble between both of them and Proctor Byllewyn!

Luthien's gaze went right to Brind'Amour, the brave wizard leaning low, stroking Riverdancer's muscled neck. On sudden impulse, Luthien ran to his horse, sliding Brind'Amour back almost onto Riverdancer's withers.

Brind'Amour put an arm out to stop him. "What are you about?" the wizard demanded.

"I am going with you," Luthien replied determinedly. "It is my horse, and it is my place!"

Brind'Amour looked long and hard into the young Bedwyr's cinnamon-colored eyes. He found that he could not disagree. Luthien had earned the right to join in this last and most desperate chase.

"If the horse will not carry us both, then select another as well," Luthien demanded. He looked back to Oliver, sitting, now nervously, on his yellow pony. "Threadbare," Luthien added.

"You want to grow wings on my precious horse that we might chase a dragon into a swamp?" Oliver asked incredulously.

"Yes," answered Luthien.

"No!" Brind'Amour emphatically corrected, and just as emphatic was the halfling's sigh of relief.

"Riverdancer will take us both," Brind'Amour explained, and Luthien was appeased.

"Luthien!" cried Katerin O'Hale.

The young Bedwyr slipped down from the horse and went to her at once, pulling her in a close embrace. "It is the proper finish," he said with all his heart. "It is the end of what I began when I killed Duke Morkney atop the Ministry's tower."

Katerin had meant to tell him not to go, to scold him for thinking so little of her that he would ride off on such a suicidal quest as to chase a dragon king into its swamp home. But like Brind'Amour, the young woman couldn't deny the sincerity in Luthien's eyes, the need he felt to see it through to the possibly bitter end.

"I only feared that you would go without bidding me goodbye," she lied.

"Not goodbye," Luthien corrected. "Just a kiss and a plea from me that you keep yourself safe until I can return to your side in this, the domain of Queen Deanna Wellworth."

His optimism touched Katerin, mostly because she realized that Luthien only half-believed that he had any chance of getting back to her. Still, she could not tell him to stay. She kissed him, and bit back the word "Goodbye," before it could escape her lips.

Then the gallant pair were off, Riverdancer as powerful in flight as he had been in the gallop, climbing high above the embattled city, noting the progress of their allies. Then Carlisle was far behind them, and the fields of Avon rolled along far beneath them.

The Saltwash was waiting.

CHAPTER 30

THE DRAGON KING

A GRAY AND HAZY MORNING greeted the companions as the great pegasus set down on a patch of soft and mossy turf. They had flown throughout the afternoon and the night, straight to the east, but had not caught sight of the speeding dragon.

Luthien's fears were obvious: what if Greensparrow had not really gone to the Saltwash, but had merely flown out from Carlisle to rest before resuming the battle?

Brind'Amour would hear nothing of that disturbing talk. "Greensparrow knows that all is lost," he explained. "He revealed himself openly in his true and wretched form, and the Avon populace will never accept him as king. No, the beast went home, into the swamp."

As comforting as the wizard's confidence was, Luthien understood that filtering through Greensparrow's home in search of the runaway wizard would not be an easy thing. The Saltwash was a vast and legendary marsh, its name known well even in Eriador. It covered some fifteen thousand square miles in southeastern Avon. On its eastern end, it was often unclear where the marsh ended and the Dorsal Sea began, and on the west, where Luthien now stood, the place was deep and dark, filled with crawling dangers and bottomless bogs.

Luthien did not want to go in there, and the thought of entering the swamp in search of a dragon was almost too much for the young man to bear.

Brind'Amour was determined, though. "Take your rest now," he bade Luthien. "I have spells with which to locate the dragon king, and I will strengthen the enchantment on Riverdancer. We will find Greensparrow before the sun has set."

"And what then?" the young Bedwyr wanted to know.

Brind'Amour leaned back against the winged horse, trying to find a reasonable response. "I did not want you to come," he offered quietly at length. "I do not know that you will be of much help to me against the likes of Greensparrow, and do not know that I can defeat the dragon king."

"Then why are we here, just we two?" Luthien asked. "Why are we not in Carlisle, finishing the task, helping Deanna assume her rightful throne?"

Brind'Amour didn't appreciate the young man's sharp tone. "The task will not be finished until Greensparrow is finished," he replied.

"You just said—" Luthien started to protest.

"That I may not have the power to defeat the dragon king," Brind'Amour finished for him, the old wizard's eyes flashing dangerously. "A fair admission. But at the very least, I can hurt the beast, and badly. No, my young friend, it cannot be finished in Carlisle until the true source of Avon's fall is dealt with. We could have defeated the cyclopian garrison, and roused support for Deanna—no doubt that is happening even as we stand here talking—but what then? If we packed up our soldiers and marched back to Eriador, would Deanna truly be safe with Greensparrow lurking, waiting, only a few score miles to the east?"

Luthien had run out of arguments.

"I will go into the swamp later this day," Brind'Amour finished. "Perhaps it would be better if you waited here, or even if you took the road back to the west."

"I go with you," Luthien said without hesitation. He thought of everything he had to lose after he had spoken the words. He thought of Oliver and Siobhan, his dear friends, of Ethan and the possibilities that they might live as brothers once more, and most of all, he thought of Katerin. How he missed her now! How he longed for her warmth in this cold and dreary place! All the good thoughts of how his life might be when this was ended did nothing to change the young Bedwyr's mind, though. "We have been in this together since the beginning," he said, laying a hand on the old wizard's shoulder. "Since you rescued Oliver and me off the road, since you sent me into the lair of Balthazar to retrieve your staff and gave to me the crimson cape."

"Since you started the revolution in Montfort," Brind'Amour added.

"Caer MacDonald," Luthien corrected with a grin.

"And since you slew Duke Morkney," Brind'Amour went on.

"And now we will finish it," Luthien said firmly. "Together."

They rested in silence for only a couple of hours, their adrenaline, even Riverdancer's, simply too great for them to sit still. Then they walked cautiously into the swamp. Brind'Amour hummed a low resonating tone, sending it off into the moss-strewn shadows, then listening for its echoes, sounds that might be tainted by the presence of a powerful magical force.

The Saltwash quickly closed in behind them, swallowing them and stealing the light of day.

Luthien felt the mud seeping over the tops of his boots, heard the hissing protests of the swamp creatures all about him, felt the sting of gnats. To his left, the brown water rippled and some large creature slipped under the water before he could identify it.

The young Bedwyr focused straight ahead, on Brind'Amour's back, and tried not to think about it.

The fighting in Carlisle had continued through the night. There were no recognizable lines of defense in the city anymore, just pockets of stubborn defenders holding their ground to the last. Most of these were cyclopians, and they continued to fight mainly because they knew that the Avon populace would show them little mercy after twenty years of cyclopian brutality. The one-eyes had been Greensparrow's elite police, the executioners and tax collectors, and now, with the king revealed as a dragon, and long gone from the city, the cyclopians would serve as scapegoats for all the misery that Greensparrow had brought.

Not that all the citizens of Carlisle had taken up the cause of the returning queen. Far from it. Most had taken to their homes, wanting only to stay out of the way, and though many had surrendered and even offered to fight alongside the Eriadorans, more than a few continued their resistance, particularly in the southern sections of Carlisle against the fierce Huegoths.

To Oliver, Siobhan, and Katerin, and many others who had come from Caer MacDonald, it seemed a replay of the revolt in Montfort, only on a much grander scale. The trio had witnessed this same type of building-to-building fighting, and though they had been split apart from each other during the night, they understood the inevitable outcome and where it would lead. Thus Oliver was not surprised when he galloped Threadbare through the main doors of Carlisle Abbey to find Siobhan and Katerin, each leading their respective groups of soldiers, already inside, battling the one-eyes from pew to pew. The slanting rays of morning cut through the dimly lit cathedral, filtering through the many breaks in the wall of the semicircular apse, where the tower had crumbled.

"So glad that you decided to join in!" Katerin called to the halfling as he cantered past her, his pony thundering down the center aisle of the nave.

Oliver pulled Threadbare up short, the pony skidding many feet on the smooth stone floor. "We cannot let them have the cathedral," he said, echoing the reasoning that had brought Katerin in here, and Siobhan, and many others. It was true enough; in all of Carlisle, as in every major Avonsea city, there was no more defensible place than the cathedral. If the cyclopians were allowed to retreat within Carlisle Abbey in force, it might be weeks before the invaders could roust them, and even then, only at great cost.

The leaders of the army understood that fact, though, and so it did not seem likely that any cyclopians would find refuge in here. Siobhan's Cutters had gained the triforium, and from that high ledge were already raining arrows on the cyclopians in the nave, a force that was rapidly diminishing. Katerin's force had gained two-thirds of the pews in the main nave, and the northern transept, up ahead and to the left of Oliver's position, had been taken. In the southern transept, the defense was breaking down as terrified one-eyes ran out the doors, scattering to the city's streets.

"With me!" Oliver cried, bolting Threadbare ahead, barreling into a throng of cyclopians. Several went flying, but Oliver's progress was halted by the sheer number of brutes. The halfling's rapier flashed left, poking one in the eye, then swiped across to the right, cutting a line down another's cheek.

But Oliver soon realized that his call had caught his comrades by surprise, and that he had rushed out too far ahead for any immediate support.

"I could be wrong!" the halfling sputtered, parrying wildly, trying to protect himself and his pony. Cyclopian hands grasped at any hold they could find, trying to bring both rider and beast down under their weight. Other one-eyes came out of the pews behind Oliver, cutting off those, Katerin included, who were trying to come to the halfling's defense.

"Oh, woe!" Oliver wailed, and then he remembered that Siobhan was watching him, and that most important of all, he must not die a coward. "But I must sing in my moment of sacrifice!" he proclaimed, and he did just that, taking up an ancient Gascon tune of heroics and the spoils of war.

> *We take the town and throw it down,*
> *Fighting for the ladies.*
> *Whose so sweet thorns bring out our horns,*
> *Fighting for the ladies.*
>
> *And so we kick, and punch and stick,*
> *Fighting for the ladies.*
> *And if we hurt, they bind with their shirts!*
> *Fighting for the ladies.*
>
> *Fighting for the ladies!*
> *Take off your clothes to cover our holes,*
> *Oh, won't you pretty ladies.*
> *Then run away because we won the day!*
> *Chasing naked, pretty ladies!*

As he finished, the halfling shrieked and ducked as the air about him filled suddenly with buzzing noises. For a moment, Oliver thought that he was in the middle of a swarm of bees, and when he finally figured out that these were arrows swishing right by him, he was not comforted!

But then it ended, as quickly as it had begun, and the cyclopian press around Oliver and his yellow pony was not so great anymore. And then Katerin was up to him, scolding him for such a foolish charge.

Oliver hardly heard a word she said. He looked up to the triforium, to Siobhan and her Fairborn forces, already many of them moving along to seek out the next important target.

Oliver tipped his great hat to the beautiful half-elf, but Siobhan did not smile.

"My friends, they do not shoot so well!" she yelled down, imitating Oliver's Gascon accent.

Oliver stared at her, perplexed.

"She heard your song," Katerin remarked dryly. "I think she told them to shoot you dead."

"Ah," noted the halfling, tipping his hat once again and smiling all the wider.

"Gascon pig," Katerin said with a snicker, and turned away.

"But I am so wounded!" Oliver wailed suddenly, and Katerin spun about. "May I use your shirt to bandage my wounds?"

It was among the finest bits of riding that Katerin O'Hale had ever witnessed, for as she took a single threatening stride Oliver's way, the halfling swung Threadbare to the side and hopped the pony up onto a narrow wooden pew, running along in perfect balance.

Katerin looked helplessly to Siobhan, the both of them grinning widely at their irreverent little friend.

Then it was back to business, finishing off the one-eyes on this lowest floor of the cathedral, securing the nave, the transepts, and what remained of the apse. Soon the twin front towers were taken as well, but not before the cyclopians managed one breakout, led by a huge and terrible brute, dressed in regal fashion and wielding a beautifully crafted broadsword. Duke Cresis forged along at the head of the fighting wedge, crossing through the semicircular apse at the cathedral's eastern end, then turning into the southern transept. And when Cresis found that way blocked by a wall of Eriadoran defenders, the brute swung back to the east, down a narrow passageway and then through a cleverly concealed door on the left-hand wall. Cresis and twenty of his fellows had gained the catacombs.

"Throw burning faggots down the stairs," one Eriadoran offered. "Smoke them out, or to death—let the choice be on them!"

Others seconded the call, but Siobhan held reservations. The leader of that one-eye band had been identified as Duke Cresis, and the half-elf wasn't so sure that the brute should be given any opportunity to escape. "Perhaps there is another exit from the catacombs," she reasoned. "We cannot let so powerful a cyclopian slip back onto Carlisle's streets."

"Would any want to follow the brutes into the dark catacombs?" another soldier asked bluntly.

There came several calls for the dwarfs, but Siobhan silenced them. "We have no time to find Bellick's folk," she explained. "I am going."

A score of Fairborn were quick to line up behind her.

"I hate to leave my so fine horse," Oliver lamented, but he, too, moved near to Siobhan, and Katerin was there at the same time.

"Four by three!" Siobhan ordered, and twelve archers took up positions before the closed door, four ranks of three each. "Do not wait to see," the half-elf explained, and she nodded to two men standing beside the door.

On a three-count, the men pulled the door open wide, diving out of the way as the first rank of Fairborn let fly. They dropped and rolled aside, and the second rank loosed their arrows as the first ran to the end, setting new bolts to their bowstrings. Then the third, then the fourth, let fly, and then the first again, and so it went, through two complete volleys, a score and four arrows bouncing down the stone walls and stairs.

Both Oliver and Katerin were handed lanterns, but Siobhan told them to keep the light down low. "Fairborn fight better in the dark than do one-eyes," she explained, and then she paused, studying closely her two friends, who were not of the elvish race.

"We're going down there beside you," Katerin said determinedly, ending the debate before Siobhan could even begin it. And so they did, three abreast, eight ranks in all, moving slowly and cautiously down the rough and uneven stairs.

They passed several dead cyclopians, the unfortunate first line of defense that had taken the brunt of the missile barrage, and then they came into the lower level.

Oliver's lantern seemed a tiny thing in here. The ceilings were low and close; Katerin and some of the taller elves had to stoop to avoid clunking their heads. The massive archways were even lower, their stones so thick that the whole of this area, built to support the tremendous cathedral above it, seemed one great winding maze.

The friends tried to stay together, but often they were forced to walk single file. Every archway presented four possible turns, and the floor was so uneven that being on the same line as a friend was no guarantee that the ally could even be seen. The torchlight did little to defeat the perpetual gloom, the cobwebs hung low and thick, and the archways were so numerous and imposing, and so low, that the area seemed more a winding, twisting nest of passageways than an open area dotted by columns.

"This was where the old abbey stood," Oliver reasoned, his voice low and muffled by the many cobwebs and blocking stones. "They built the cathedral right above it." As he spoke, the halfling turned a corner, coming upon a raised section of floor, three or four age-worn steps that led up to a stone box, an altar, or perhaps a crypt. Oliver could not be sure. He turned back to ask Siobhan's opinion, only to find that he had somehow split away from the others.

"I do so like the sky for my ceiling," the halfling whispered.

"One-eye!" came an echoing cry from somewhere in the distance, followed quickly by the ring of steel, and then a guttural grunt, followed soon by a Fairborn voice claiming, "They are in here still!"

"Siobhan!" Oliver called softly, trying hard to backtrack. He went through an archway, but every direction looked the same. "Left breast, right breast, down the middle, damn the rest," Oliver chanted, pointing in each direction. Then, as Gascon tradition demanded, the halfling went the way of the last "Damn the rest."

He heard more sounds of battle, individuals clashing but nothing large-scale. The cyclopians were indeed in here, hiding separately, looking to ambush.

Oliver went left at the next low arch, then, thinking he recognized the area as the entry foyer, came around a corner with a bright smile, expecting to see only the stairs leading back to the main floor of the cathedral.

His light was immediately swallowed by a pair of forms too large to be Fairborn, too wide to be Katerin.

The halfling squeaked and thrust forth his rapier, trying to get his lantern to the floor that he might draw out his main gauche. He thought that his slender blade would surely get the closest foe, but the form moved with the perfect balance and grace of a pure warrior, smoothly and deftly dodging.

Oliver thought he was about to die, but the shine of skin as the foe came around was ruddy and tan, not the grayish hue more common to one-eyes, and this opponent had two eyes—cinnamon-colored eyes.

"Luthien," Oliver began, but stopped short as he realized his error.

"Watch that blade, fool!" Ethan Bedwyr snarled, gingerly turning aside the still-poking rapier.

"What are you doing here?"

"I was told that Katerin had come in here," Ethan replied softly. "I promised my brother that I would watch over her."

A sly grin came over Oliver. "Your brother?" he asked.

Ethan had no time for such semantic games. He motioned to two other Huegoth companions who were still on the stairs, indicating that they should go to the right, then he and his immediate companion set off straight ahead.

Oliver bent down to retrieve his lantern and replace the main gauche on his belt, only to find himself alone once more. He looked to the stairs, tempted to go back up, but then he heard another cry from somewhere in the distance, a voice he recognized.

Siobhan and one Fairborn companion went down a dozen steps and turned a sharp corner, putting the sounds of the others far behind, then dared to crawl under a tiny door, no more than three-feet-square, barely large enough to admit a large cyclopian. The tunnel beyond was not much larger than the entrance, and the pair had to bend low, even crawling at points to continue along.

The darkness was complete, even to the sensitive eyes of the Fairborn, forcing Siobhan to light a hand lamp, a tiny lantern she had used often in her days as a housebreaker in Morkney-controlled Montfort.

She motioned for her companion, who was leading, to move on.

Finally, they came out into a higher area, the oldest catacombs in all the cathedral. Open crypts faced them from every wall, displaying the tattered skeletal remains of the first priests and abbots in Carlisle, perhaps in all of Avonsea. Most were lying on their back, but some, in more ornate crypts, were seated upon stone thrones.

Siobhan worked hard to steady her breathing as she noted one ancient corpse beside her, sitting tall and proud through the centuries, except that its skull was on the floor, probably the victim of hungry rats whose bones, too, were now likely resting in this place of death. The half-elf pulled her gaze away to see her companion bump his head hard on the curving ceiling of the next arch.

"Careful," Siobhan whispered, but then she cried out as her companion turned about and toppled.

Even in the dim light of her hand lamp, Siobhan could see the bright blood spewing from the elf's chest, which had been ripped from armpit to spinal cord.

Ahead of her stood the brutish cyclopian duke, that fabulous broadsword dripping elvish blood, Cresis's ugly face twisted with the promise of death.

There had only been a single, distant cry, and yells were becoming more frequent with each passing moment as more and more of the hunters happened upon hiding cyclopians. But Oliver had never been more focused in all his life. His mind, his soul, had locked on to that single utterance, and the maze seemed to sort itself out before him as he darted along, daring to turn up the flame in his lantern that he might better see the breaks in the uneven floor.

He paused in one wider area to jab his rapier into the butt of a battling cyclopian. Then, seeing that his prod had distracted the brute enough to give its Fairborn opponent an insurmountable advantage, Oliver ran on.

He passed through one archway without a look to either side, replaying that cry in his head, following his instincts and his heart.

Katerin spotted him and called out, and she, Ethan, and a Huegoth came in close pursuit.

But they could not keep up with Oliver in these tight quarters. They reached the top of a broken and uneven staircase, angling downward, just after the halfling had entered the little hole at its bottom.

Only the ring of steel told them that they had come the right way.

Siobhan was an archer, among the finest shots in all of Avonsea. But she was no novice with the blade, as Duke Cresis soon discovered.

The brute thought it had her by surprise, and so its first attack was straight ahead, a thrust for the half-elf's heart.

Out flashed a short sword, turning the brute's blade minutely as the half-elf turned her own body. A clean miss, and Siobhan countered lightning-fast, rolling her wrist to launch her blade in a diagonal line at Cresis's ugly face.

The brute fell back, stumbling over a block of stone into a wider area, the oldest altar in the ancient abbey.

Siobhan was fast to pursue, trying to press her advantage, but the same block of stone slowed her enough for the one-eye to steady its defenses.

"Duke Cresis?" Siobhan sneered.

Cresis snorted and did not bother to answer.

"I offer you the chance for surrender," Siobhan bluffed, and she prayed that the obviously powerful one-eye would accept. "The city is ours; you have no place to run."

"Then I will die with my sword in one hand and your head in the other!" the one-eye promised, and on Cresis came.

The broadsword flashed right, left, left again, and then straight down, the brute taking it up in both hands for the final attack. Siobhan parried and dodged, ducked low under the third swing and came up hard to meet the chop, her blade flat out over her head. She meant to catch the broadsword and turn it out wide, then step ahead, in close, and use the advantage of her much shorter sword in the tighter press.

Cresis's swing was far too powerful for that maneuver, and Siobhan found her legs nearly buckling under the weight of that vicious overhead chop. Her finely forged elvish blade held firm, though, stopping the attack short of her head, and she rolled out to the side, stabbing twice in rapid succession as she went, scoring one slight hit on the cyclopian's hip.

Cresis laughed at the minor wound and came in fast pursuit, thrusting his sword with every step. Siobhan danced desperately to keep out of the brute's reach. She came up hard against the block of stone that had once been an altar, and Cresis, thinking her caught, forged ahead.

Siobhan's balance was perfect as she went over the thigh-high block, falling prone on the other side as the cyclopian's blade swished the air above her.

Cresis leaped over, but the agile half-elf was already gone, scrambling out one end and putting her feet back under her. She reversed direction immediately, regaining the offensive, snapping her smaller blade at the brute's groin, then cutting it up so that Cresis's down-angled sword missed the parry.

The cyclopian fell back, a deep gash along its chin, its bulbous nose split nearly in half.

Siobhan could have asked again for surrender, and the brute might have agreed, but she was too far into the fight by then. She came on hard and fast, scoring again, this time putting the point of her sword deep into the brute's left shoulder, and coming in so close that she pinned Cresis's arms against the brute's torso.

But only for a moment, for Cresis howled in pain and heaved forward with all its considerable strength, launching Siobhan a dozen feet. She somehow managed to keep her balance and was ready when the brute came in at her again, with an all-too-familiar routine.

Right, left, left again, and then down, but this time, with only one hand on the sword.

Siobhan parried, dodged straight back, sucking in her belly, then ducked the third, coming up powerfully, seeing that Cresis had only one hand on the broadsword.

The blades met with a tremendous ring; Siobhan twisted with all her might, then stepped ahead, grinning in expected victory as the broadsword went out wide.

The light intensified as Oliver entered the chamber, to see his dear Siobhan in close with the huge and ugly brute. Cresis's sword was out to the side, not moving, but for some reason neither was Siobhan's readied blade diving for the one-eye.

Oliver understood when his love slipped away from the brute's chest, and more particularly, away from Cresis's left hand, which held a bloody dirk.

Siobhan managed a look at Oliver, then her sword hit the ground with a dead ring, and the half-elf quickly followed its descent.

Oliver was no match for Cresis and the mighty one-eye was hardly injured, but the halfling fostered no thoughts of retreat at that horrible moment. He roared for his love and leaped ahead, coming so furiously with his rapier, a ten-thrust routine, that Cresis could hardly distinguish each individual move, and the brute took several stinging hits along the forearm as it tried to maneuver the broadsword to block.

The cyclopian tried to square, but the enraged halfling would not relinquish the offense. Sheer anger driving him on, Oliver poked and poked, slashed at the broadsword with his main gauche, even catching the blade between the front-turned crosspiece of the crafted dagger at one point, though he had not the leverage to break the cyclopian's weapon or to tear it from Cresis's powerful grasp.

Still, it was Cresis, and not Oliver, who continued to back up, and Oliver found an opportunity before him as the cyclopian neared the altar block. Up the halfling leaped, and now Cresis had to work all the harder to parry, for Oliver's rapier was dangerously in line with the cyclopian's already-torn face.

"You are so ugly!" the halfling taunted, spitting his words. "A dog would not play with you unless you had a piece of meat tied about your fat waist!"

"I would eat the dog!" Cresis retorted, but the brute's words were cut short by yet another multiple-thrust attack.

Cresis was wise enough to understand that the halfling's rage was too great. If Cresis could keep Oliver moving, keep him sputtering and slashing wildly, the halfling would soon tire.

So the brute parried and started away from the altar, but then its one eye went wide with surprise as the main gauche came spinning, end over end. Up went the cyclopian's arm, blocking the dagger, but that wasn't the only incoming missile as Oliver ran to the edge of the altar block and threw himself at his enemy.

Cresis howled in pain again, his forearm burning from the stuck dagger. He tried to maneuver the broadsword to catch the flying halfling, but the brute's reaction was slow, its muscles torn and tightening.

Oliver crashed in hard, though the three-hundred-pound cyclopian barely took a tiny step backward. It didn't matter, for Oliver had leaped in with his rapier blade leading.

He was tight onto Cresis's burly chest then; he might have been a baby, clinging to its burly father. But that rapier had hit the mark perfectly, was stuck nearly to its basket hilt right through Cresis's bulky neck.

The cyclopian wheezed, sputtering blood from its mouth and its throat. It held on tight, tried to squeeze the life out of Oliver. But that grip inevitably loosened as the gasping brute's lungs filled with its own blood. Slowly, Cresis slumped to its knees, and Oliver was careful to get away, avoiding a halfhearted swing of the broadsword.

Cresis went down to all fours, gasping, trying to force air into its lungs.

Oliver paid the brute no more heed. He ran to his love, cradling her head in one arm and plunging his hand over the bleeding wound in the hollow of Siobhan's chest.

Ethan scrambled into the chamber then, followed closely by Katerin. "Ah my love!" they heard the halfling wail. "Do not die!"

"We cannot go on in this direction," Brind'Amour informed Luthien. The young Bedwyr pushed through some brush to join the wizard and saw the flat water, surrounding them on three sides.

They had spent nearly half an hour walking through the tangled and confusing underbrush to the end of a peninsula.

Luthien was about to suggest that they start back, but he held quiet as Brind'Amour moved behind him, the wizard staring intently at River-dancer.

"The steed is rested," Brind'Amour announced. "We will fly."

Luthien didn't argue the point; he was thoroughly miserable, his feet wet and sore, his scalp itching from a hundred bites, and his nerves frayed, and though no monster had risen up against them, every one of the Saltwash's shadows appeared as though it hid some sinister beast.

So Luthien breathed a sigh of relief, filling his lungs with clean air as they broke through the soggy canopy. He squinted for some time, trying to adjust his eyes to the dazzling sunlight whenever it found a break in the thick cloud cover that rushed overhead. Logically, Luthien knew that they were probably more vulnerable up here than they had been in the cover of the swamp; Greensparrow would spot them easily if he bothered to look to the skies above his dark home. But Luthien was glad for the change anyway, and so was Riverdancer, the horse's neck straining forward eagerly. On Brind'Amour's suggestion, Luthien kept the horse moving low over the treetops.

"Do you see . . . anything?" Luthien asked after several minutes, look-ing back to the wizard.

Brind'Amour shook his head in frustration, then, after a moment's consideration, poked his thumb upward. "We'll not find the beast through this tangle," the wizard explained. "Let us see if the dragon finds us!"

The words resonated through Luthien's mind, inciting memories of his one previous encounter with a dragon, a sight that still sometimes woke him in the night. They had come out here for Greensparrow, he reminded himself, and they would not leave until the evil dragon king had been met and defeated.

Up went Riverdancer, a hundred feet above the dark trees. Two hundred, and the swamp took on different dimensions, became a patchwork of indistinct treetops and splotches of dark water. Still higher they went, the Saltwash widening below them, every shape blending together into one great gray-green quilt.

Flattening and blending, all the sharp twists of branches smoothed and blurred together in softer edges. All except for one, a single break in the collage, as though the Saltwash, like a great bow, had shot forward this singular, streaking arrow.

Luthien hesitated, mesmerized. What propelled the dragon at such speed? he wondered dumbly, for the mighty beast flapped its wings only occasionally, one beat and then tucked them in tight, speeding upward as though it was in a stoop!

Riverdancer snorted and tried to react, but it was too late. Luthien's heart sank as he realized his error, his hesitation. He looked into the maw of the approaching beast and saw his doom.

Then the world seemed to shift about him, to warp within the blue-white swirl of a magical tunnel. It ended as suddenly as it began, and Luthien found himself looking *up* at the dragon as it sped away from him.

Brind'Amour's staff touched his shoulder and the wizard called forth a bolt of crackling black energy that grabbed the dragon and jolted it.

Out wide went Greensparrow's wings, dragging in the air, stopping the momentum.

Luthien reacted quickly this time, bringing Riverdancer up high in a steeper climb, trying to come around behind the great beast.

But Dansallignatious, Greensparrow, ducked his head as he fell, turning his serpentine neck right about.

Riverdancer folded one wing and did a complete roll as the dragon breathed its line of fire. As he came upright, fighting to hold his seat and hold control, Luthien stared incredulously, watching a green, disembodied fist rush out from behind him. It shot through the air, punching hard into the dragon's midsection, and exploding there with enough force to hurl the beast many yards away.

"Hah!" Brind'Amour snorted, and snapped his fingers in the air beside Luthien's ear.

In less confident tones, the wizard whispered, "You've got to stay near to the beast, boy. Close enough so that if Greensparrow breathes, he'll burn away his own wing."

Luthien understood the logic of the reasoning, but saying something and doing something were often two completely different things—especially when one was talking about a dragon!

A second fist of magical energy went flying out, and then a third, and Luthien prodded Riverdancer in their wake, following their course toward the beast.

Greensparrow's winding neck swerved and the next fist shot by. The last one, though, scored a glancing blow, snapping the dragon's head out to the side. Still, Greensparrow seemed perfectly focused on the third missile, the living missile of the pegasus and its two riders, and Luthien nearly swooned, thinking suddenly that he had put himself and his companions right into the path of certain death.

"Hold the course!" Brind'Amour yelled, and Luthien, screaming all the way, obeyed.

The second flying fist, the one that had missed the mark altogether, had turned about like a boomerang, and came in hard, clapping the dragon off the back of the head just before Greensparrow could loose his fire. The beast pitched forward; Riverdancer flew in right over its bending neck. Luthien tried to draw out his sword, for he was close enough, almost, to hit the monstrous thing, and Brind'Amour's staff came forward once more as another bolt, this one red in hue, streaked down, sparkling from scale to scale.

Now the dragon roared and continued to duck its head, rolling right into a dive. Brind'Amour cried out in victory, so did Luthien as he started to bank Riverdancer into pursuit, but neither of them comprehended the vast repertoire of weapons possessed by a beast such as this. The dragon was rolling down, putting its head toward the safety of the swamp, but as the great bulk came around, Greensparrow kept the presence of mind to lash out with his long and powerful tail.

Riverdancer was turning, and that surely saved the steed's life and those of its riders, but still the pegasus took a glancing blow on the rear flank.

Suddenly the trio were spinning, holding on for their lives. Brind'Amour came right off the horse's back and had to latch on with both hands to the cowl of Luthien's cape. He cried out, cursing as his staff plummeted out of sight, disappearing into the tangled background of the Saltwash.

Luthien righted the horse and wrapped one arm about the wizard as he continued to flail helplessly at Riverdancer's side.

The sun seemed to go away then, as the dragon soared past them, barely twenty feet to their right, great clawed feet reaching out. Luthien pulled hard to his left, turning the steed away, but a claw tore at Riverdancer's right wing, gashing flesh and snapping bone.

They spun over once more, this time in a roll that Luthien could not hope to control. Down they tumbled, and as they came around, Luthien saw that Greensparrow had folded his wings in a power dive and was in close pursuit, that awful fanged mouth opened wide.

But again came that blue swirl, as Brind'Amour opened a magical tunnel right below them. They were in it for only a split second, a split second that put them two hundred feet lower, barely at treetop level and several hundred yards to one side.

Falling again, too confused and surprised to even know what lay below, Luthien could only hold on and scream.

The pair and their wounded pegasus splashed hard into a muddy pool.

It seemed like minutes passed, but in truth it was but seconds before the two men and the wounded steed pulled themselves onto the soft turf at the pool's edge. Mud covered Brind'Amour's blue robes, turned Riverdancer's shining white coat a soiled brown, and coated Luthien as well— except for that magnificent crimson cape, which seemed to repel any stains, holding fast its shining crimson hue.

The companions hardly had time to take note of that, though. Riverdancer's right wing was badly broken and torn, the pained horse tucking it close to his side. Brind'Amour grabbed the bridle and led the steed into a thick copse, then cast some enchantment and motioned for Luthien to follow him.

"I cannot leave Riverdancer . . ." the young Bedwyr started to protest.

"The horse must revert to its natural form," Brind'Amour tried to explain, patting the air soothingly. "Riverdancer's wounds shall not be so great when the wings are gone, but even then, the horse will be in need of rest. And no use in trying to ride in this tangle anyway, against the likes of Greensparrow."

As if on cue, there came a deafening roar and a great shadow passed overhead.

"Come along," said Brind'Amour, and this time Luthien offered no argument.

* * *

To Oliver's surprise, and temporary relief, Siobhan opened her beautiful green eyes and managed a pained smile. "Did we get him?" she asked, her words broken by labored breathing.

Oliver nodded, too choked to respond. "Duke Cresis of Carlisle is a bad memory and nothing more," he finally managed to say.

"Half-credit for the kill," Siobhan whispered.

"All for you," Oliver readily replied.

Siobhan shook her head, which took great effort. "Only half," she whispered. "All I need."

Oliver looked back to Katerin, noting the streaks of tears on the woman's fair features.

"Half for me," Siobhan went on. "Fifteen and a half this day."

Oliver tried to respond, but couldn't understand the significance.

"Tell . . . Luthien that," Siobhan stuttered. "Fifteen and half for me this day. Final count . . . ninety-three and a half for me . . . only ninety-three for . . . Luthien . . . even if he kills . . . Greensparrow."

Oliver hugged her close.

"I win," she said, a bit of cheer somehow seeping into her voice. Then her timbre changed suddenly. "Oliver?" she asked. "Are you here?"

The light had not diminished, and Oliver knew that her eyes were not wounded. But she could not see, and the halfling realized what that foretold.

"I am here, my love," Oliver replied, hugging her, and keeping his voice steady. "I am here."

"Cold," Siobhan said. "So cold."

More than a minute passed before Katerin bent over and closed Siobhan's unseeing eyes.

"Come with us, Oliver," she bade the distraught halfling, her voice firm for she knew that she had to be strong for her friend. "There is nothing more you can do here."

"I stay," Oliver replied determinedly.

Katerin looked to Ethan, who only shrugged.

"I will finish the business in the catacombs," Ethan promised. "And return for you."

Katerin nodded and Ethan was gone, back the way they had come. The woman moved away from Oliver then, respectfully, and sat upon the altar block, her heart torn, as much in sympathy for poor Oliver as in grief for the loss of her dear half-elven friend.

"We must find my staff," Brind'Amour whispered.

"How?" Luthien balked, looking around at the endless tangles and shadows of the Saltwash. "We have no chance . . ."

"Sssh!" Brind'Amour hissed. "Keep your voice quiet. Dragons have the most excellent of hearing."

Again as if on cue, there came a great rush of wind and the canopy above the two exploded into a fiery maelstrom. Brind'Amour stood as if frozen in place, gaping at the conflagration, and only Luthien's quick reaction, the young Bedwyr tackling the wizard into a shallow pool and throwing himself, and his magical shielding cape, over Brind'Amour's prone form, saved the old man from the falling brands. Great strands of hanging moss dove down to the ground, coiling like snakes as they landed, their topmost ends burning like candle wicks. Not so far from the companions a tree, its sap superheated by the fires, exploded in a shower of miniature fireballs, hissing and sputtering as they landed on the pools or muddy turf.

"Up, and run away!" Brind'Amour cried as soon as the moment had passed, the blazing branches smoldering quickly in the dampness of the marsh.

Luthien tried to follow that command, stumbling repeatedly on the pool's slippery banks. In the distance, he heard Riverdancer's frantic neighing, and then, as he turned back in the direction of the area where he had left the horse, he saw the approach of doom.

He grabbed for Brind'Amour, thinking to pull the man back into the mud, but the wizard darted away. The cover was not so thick anymore—certainly not enough to shield them from the penetrating gaze of a dragon!—and Brind'Amour knew that to cower was to be caught.

No, the old wizard determined, they had come in here to battle Greensparrow, and so they would, meeting his charge.

Brind'Amour scrambled up to the trunk of an ancient willow, a graceful spreading mass that had accepted the first dragon pass as though it were no more than a minor inconvenience. "Lend me your strength," the wizard whispered to the trunk, and he embraced the tree in a gentle hug.

The dragon rushed overhead, looking about the area it had so brutally cleared. It let out a shrill shriek as it crossed over Brind'Amour, and immediately began its long and graceful turn.

Luthien called out a warning to the wizard, but Brind'Amour seemed not to hear. Nor did the wizard appear to take any note at all of the dragon. He stood hugging the tree, whispering softly, his eyes closed.

Luthien inched closer, not wanting to disturb the man, but keeping a watchful eye for the returning dragon. He started to call out to Brind'Amour again, but stopped, startled, when he noticed that the fingers of the wizard's hands were gone, as if they had simply sunken into the willow! Luthien looked to the man's face, was touched by the serenity there, then looked back to see that Brind'Amour's arms were in up to the wrists!

"Lend me your strength," Brind'Amour whispered again, but in a language that Luthien could not understand, a language of music, not words, of the eternal harmony that had brought the world into being, that gave the tree its strength and longevity, the language of the very powers that sustained all the world.

Luthien did not know what he should do, and when he looked back the way the dragon had flown, to see the creature speeding toward him once more, he could only cry out helplessly to his entranced friend and throw himself to the side, away from Brind'Amour and the willow, to the base of another large tree.

Greensparrow issued a deafening roar, culminating with the release of that tremendous fire. At the same moment, Brind'Amour cried out, as if in ecstasy, and a green glow engulfed the wizard, ran up his arms and to the tree, then up the tree, intensifying as it spread wide along the branches.

The hot dragon flames fell over them all; Luthien tried to dig a hole in the ground. His eyes burned and he felt as if his lungs would explode, and he could only imagine the grim fate that had befallen Brind'Amour, who was not protected by the marvelous crimson cape.

Indeed those fires did fall over the wizard, but Brind'Amour felt them not at all, no more than did the ancient willow. For Brind'Amour was a part of that tree then, and it a part of him, and while he had taken from it its ancient resilience, it had gained the wizard's sentience. Stooping, pliable limbs reached up from the swamp, swatting and entangling the dragon as it flew past.

Greensparrow was caught completely off his guard as one great limb whipped up to smack him right between the eyes and another caught fast on his left wing. Over and around the dragon spun. Wood bent and twisted and tore apart.

Now Brind'Amour did cry out in pain, and the sheer shock of the dragon hit destroyed his symbiosis with the tree, left him sitting on the wet ground, wondering why wisps of smoke were rising from his robes. He groaned as he considered the willow, many of its branches torn away, the trunk half-uprooted and tilting to the side, the whole of the ancient tree nearly pulled from the ground by the weight of its catch.

Brind'Amour wanted to go to the willow, to offer comfort and thanks, to try to lend his powers that it might better heal. He had other problems, though, for the dragon had been taken from the sky, to crash down heavily, clearing a swath a hundred yards long. But the beast was far from defeated. Greensparrow pulled himself free of the tangled and broken flora and righted himself, facing the wizard. One wing had been torn and would need time to heal; the dragon could not fly. Like a gigantic cat, Greensparrow crouched, tamping down his back legs, his yellow-green orbs locked on the puny man who had given him such pain.

A single leap brought him close enough to loose his fires once again, engulfing Brind'Amour.

But the old wizard was ready. With his magic, he reached down to the earth at his feet, drawing the moisture from it, meeting the dragon fire with a wall of water. Then he loosed his own response, a blazing line of energy that cut through the fires and slammed at Greensparrow.

Luthien huddled and trembled, blocked his ears from the thunderous roars of beast and flame. It went on and on, seconds seeming like hours. All that Luthien wanted was a single gasp of air, but that would not come. All that he wanted was to get up and run away, but his feet would not answer his call. Then the world started to slip into blackness, an endless pit, it seemed, and he was falling.

The sounds receded.

Then it ended, the fires and the energy bolt, and Greensparrow and Brind'Amour stood facing each other. Brind'Amour knew by the way the serpentine neck suddenly snapped back and by the beast's wide eyes that his resilience had surprised the beast.

"You have betrayed all that was sacred to the ancient brotherhood," the old wizard cried.

"The ancient fools!" the dragon replied in a snarling, resonating voice.

Brind'Amour was caught off guard, for the dragon's words did not come easily, every syllable stuttered and intermixed with feral snarls.

"Fools, you say," the wizard replied. "Yet that brotherhood is where you first found your power."

"My power is ancient!" the dragon answered with a roar. "Older than your brotherhood, older than you!"

Brind'Amour understood it then, recognized the struggle between the wills of this dual being. "You are Greensparrow!" he cried, trying to force the issue.

"I am Dansallignat . . . I am Greensparrow, king of Avonsea!" the beast roared.

Then the dragon flinched, an involuntary twist, perhaps, and Brind'Amour was quick to the offensive, hurling yet another bolt, this one white and streaking like lightning. The dragon roared; the wizard screamed in pain as all his energy, all his life force, was hurled into that one bolt. Magic was a power limited by good sense, but Brind'Amour had no options of restraint now, not when facing such a foe. He felt his heart fluttering, felt his legs go weak, but still he energized the bolt, launched himself into it fully, sapping every ounce of strength within him and hurling it, transformed, into the great beast.

He could hardly see the dragon, and wasn't really conscious of his surroundings anyway, but somewhere deep in his mind, Brind'Amour realized that he was indeed hurting the monster, and that it was transforming.

Finally the energy fizzled, and the wizard stood swaying, thoroughly spent. After a moment, he managed to consider his opponent, and his eyes went wide.

No longer did the dragon stand before him, nor was his foe the foppish king of Avon. Greensparrow and Dansallignatious had been caught somewhere in the middle of their dual forms, a bipedal creature half again as large as a man, but with scaly skin mottled green and black, great clawed hands, a swishing tail, and a serpentine neck as long as Brind'Amour was tall.

"Do you think you have defeated me?" the beast asked.

Luthien heard that call distantly, and the very voice of the beast, a whining, grating buzz, wounded him, stung his ears and his heart.

"You are a fool, Brind'Amour, as were all your fellow wizards," Greensparrow chided.

"And Greensparrow was among that lot," the wizard said with great effort.

"No!" roared the beast. "Greensparrow alone was wise enough to know that his day had not passed."

Brind'Amour had no response to that, for he, too, had come to believe that the brotherhood of wizards had surrendered their powers too quickly and recklessly.

"And now you will die," the beast said casually, moving a stride forward. "And all the world will be open to me."

Again, Brind'Amour could not refute the dragon king's words—at least not the first part, for he had not the strength to lift his arm against the approaching creature. He wasn't so convinced, though, that Greensparrow's claim about the world would prove true.

"They know who you are now," he said defiantly, his voice as strong and confident as he could possibly make it. "And what you are."

Greensparrow laughed wickedly, as if to question how that could possibly matter.

"Deanna Wellworth will take back her throne and her kingdom, and Greensparrow the foul will not be welcomed!" Brind'Amour proclaimed.

"If I can so easily defeat the likes of Brind'Amour, then how will the weakling queen, or any of her ill-advised allies, stand against me?" As he spoke, Greensparrow continued his advance, moving to within a few feet of Brind'Amour, who was simply too spent to retreat. "I will take back what was mine!" the beast promised, and the time for talking had passed.

Greensparrow's serpentine neck shot forward, maw opening wide. Brind'Amour let out a cry that sounded as a pitiful squeak, and threw up his arms before his face. Fangs tore his sleeves, ripped his skin, but the defensive move stopped Greensparrow from finding a secure hold, his snout butting the wizard instead and throwing Brind'Amour down to the ground.

At the same moment, the dragon king caught a movement to the side and behind, as a form uncoiled from its position at the base of a tree and rushed out at him.

Brind'Amour's companion! the dragon king realized. But how had he missed seeing that one?

Luthien took two powerful strides, bringing *Blind-Striker* in a two-handed over-the-shoulder arc that drove the blade hard against the beast's extended neck. He chopped again and again as Greensparrow tried to reorient and square himself to this newest foe. Green-black scales splintered and flew away. The beast's clawed hind feet dug trenches in the earth as it backpedaled.

Luthien, blinded by rage, screamed a dozen curses and pumped his arms frantically, refusing to give up the offensive, knowing that if he allowed the beast to gain its composure and its footing, he would surely be doomed. Again and again he launched his mighty sword, each swing culminating in a hit, sometimes solid, sometimes glancing. He kept Greensparrow backing, kept whacking at the twisting form with all his strength.

But then he slipped—a slight stumble, but one that allowed the dragon king to get out of reach, to gain its footing.

"The Crimson Shadow!" Greensparrow snarled. "How much a thorn you have been to me!"

Luthien put his feet back under him and started to charge once more, but skidded to a fast stop, realizing that to dive into that tangle of claws and fangs was certainly to die.

"For months I have been waiting for this moment," Greensparrow promised. "Waiting to pay you back for all the trouble. For Belsen'Krieg and Morkney, for Paragor of Princetown and for the ridiculous cries of 'Eriador free!' that have reached my ears."

Luthien stepped forward and swung, but found himself falling backward before the blade got halfway around, as the snakelike neck snapped out at him. He fell into the mud and scrambled backward. Greensparrow was laughing too hard to pursue.

"Watch him die, Brind'Amour," the dragon king chided. "Watch all your hopes torn apart."

Luthien glanced Brind'Amour's way, praying that the wizard was ready to join in then. But Brind'Amour could not help him, not this time. The wizard remained on the ground, barely holding himself in a sitting position. His magic was gone, expended in the enchantments, particularly that last bolt of power, his ultimate attack. It had taken much strength from the dragon, had even reduced it to this present form, but it had not destroyed Greensparrow.

Luthien studied his foe carefully. The dragon king was certainly wounded, had suffered a great beating from the tree and the energy bolts, and from Luthien's own wild attack. Large welts lined Greensparrow's neck, and his face was scored on one side. One of his wings was tucked neatly against his back, but the other hung out at a weird angle, obviously broken.

Slowly Luthien slid his foot back under him.

"Or perhaps I should not kill you," Greensparrow was saying, his gaze as much at the empty distance as at Luthien. "Perhaps I should bring you back to Carlisle, an admitted liar and enemy of the throne. Perhaps I could use you to discredit Deanna Wellworth," the beast mused, and looked back—to see that Luthien was up and charging!

Greensparrow snapped his head at the young Bedwyr, but too late. Luthien came under the descending maw, throwing up the tip of his blade, and Greensparrow's own momentum worked against him as *Blind-Striker* bit under the dragon king's bottom jaw, right through scales and skin, right through the flicking forked tongue and into the roof of his mouth.

Luthien continued forward and held on with all his strength, trying desperately to get inside the angle of the monster's flailing arms.

Greensparrow hissed and thrashed and Luthien could not hold the sword and stay in tight. His feet went out from under him as Greensparrow spun to the side, but *Blind-Striker* held fast and Luthien was pulled right from the ground.

A clawed hand swiped at his exposed ribs, tearing through his chainlink armor and the thick leather tunic below it as easily as if it was old and brittle paper. Bright lines of blood appeared, one gash so deep that Luthien's rib was visible.

Still he hung on, growling against the pain, but then the other blow came across, punching and not raking, a blow so fierce that Luthien flew away, taking his sword with him.

The dragon king's head jerked violently to the side as *Blind-Striker* tore free, and Greensparrow slumped to one knee, giving horrified Luthien enough time to scramble away into the cover of the swamp.

But the beast was fast in pursuit, sniffing and snarling, sputtering curses that rang in the ears of the young Bedwyr. Never before had he run from battle, not from Morkney, not from the demon Taknapotin. But this beast, even wounded as it was, was beyond both of them, was something too evil and too awful.

And so Luthien ran, stumbling, pressing his arm against his side in an effort to keep his lifeblood from spilling away. He heard the sniffing behind him, knew that Greensparrow was following the trail of dripping blood.

The beast was right behind him. Luthien gave a cry and ran on as fast as he could go, but caught his foot in an exposed root and went tumbling headlong.

All his sensibilities screamed at him that the trail had ended, that he was about to die!

A long moment passed; Luthien could hear the breathing of the monster, not more than a few feet behind him. Why didn't Greensparrow get it over with? he wondered.

His cape. It had to be the cape. Luthien dared to peek out from under the hood, could see the lamplight glow of those terrible dragon eyes scanning the ground. Luthien held his breath, forced himself to stay perfectly still.

He would have been found; he knew that Greensparrow would have sorted out the riddle soon enough, except that there came a crashing noise somewhere up ahead, and the white coat of Riverdancer flashed into view, running past.

Greensparrow howled, thinking that his young opponent had somehow gotten ahead of him, back to his horse. If the beast went airborne, it would be beyond his grasp!

That the dragon king could not allow, so he took up the chase, leaping forward, and stumbling over a form that he could not see.

Greensparrow hardly took note of the trip, and his heavy foot had taken the breath from Luthien. The young Bedwyr could have remained where he was, allowing the dragon king to run off in pursuit of River-dancer, while he went back to Brind'Amour.

But Luthien saw his chance before him and would not pass it up, no matter the terror, no matter the pain. With a shout of "Eriador free!" the young Bedwyr launched himself forward, catching up to the beast even as it pulled itself from the ground. *Blind-Striker's* tip bit hard, right between the wings, tearing through the scales and nicking the backbone.

Luthien kept going forward, leaped right onto Greensparrow's back, catching a firm and stubborn hold on the broken wing even as the beast tried to turn about.

Greensparrow threw himself into a roll, ducking his shoulder so that he would go right over the pitiful human. Luthien tried to leap free, got his blade out of the beast's back and pushed off the wing. He scrambled away as Greensparrow rolled, but the dragon king came up in a leap that brought him up to Luthien, and the man's breath was blasted from his lungs as Greensparrow came down heavily atop him.

He was pinned, nowhere to run, with the dragon king's terrible face barely inches away. They held the pose for several seconds, a strange expression, a look of confusion perhaps, on Greensparrow's dragon features.

Luthien knew that the torn maw could not bite at him, but his arms were pinned against his chest and he could not hope to block if Greensparrow gouged at his face with that array of horns. Desperately he struggled, to no avail. He couldn't even draw breath, and felt a pointed press against the hollow of his breast that he soon realized to be the tip of his own sword!

Luthien's eyes went wide. If that was the swordtip, then *Blind-Striker* was pointing straight out. But if the dragon king was on top of him . . .

"Foolish, wretched boy," Greensparrow said, his voice serene and his words accompanied by dripping blood. The creature managed a small, incredulous chuckle. "You have killed me."

Luthien was too stunned to reply.

"But I will kill you as well," Greensparrow promised, and Luthien had no words, and certainly no actions, to refute the claim as Greensparrow's neck lifted the horned head up high and put the sharp horns in line with Luthien's face. Even if the dragon king expired before he struck, the simple weight of the dropping horns would surely finish Luthien.

He tried to face death bravely, tried not to cry out. His concentration was shattered, though, by a thunderous roar to the side of his head, by the spray of muddy turf as Riverdancer charged up and spun about, then kicked out with his hind legs, connecting solidly with the dragon's head even as it began its descent.

Greensparrow's neck snapped out to the side violently; the head thumped hard against the ground.

The dragon king lay very still.

EPILOGUE

IT TOOK LUTHIEN SOME TIME to extract himself from under the dead beast. Even after he had squirmed clear, he spent many minutes just lying in the muck, trying to catch his breath, praying that the searing pain would abate. Somehow he managed to get to his feet. And then he nearly collapsed, fell against his precious Riverdancer, merely a horse once again and with no sign of Brind'Amour's wings, and hugged the horse tight.

Luthien looked to the fallen dragon king, to see *Blind-Striker*'s crafted pommel poking into the air out the creature's back. Guiding Riverdancer, using the horse's strength, Luthien managed to get the dead dragon king angled so that he could retrieve the sword. Then Luthien led the horse back to Brind'Amour, and the young Bedwyr was relieved indeed to see that the wizard, though he was lying on his back, apparently unconscious, was breathing steadily.

It took a long while to get Brind'Amour across Riverdancer's back. That done, and with no desire to be in the swamp when night descended over it, Luthien led the horse away, following as direct a westerly course as he could.

Luck was with him, and sometime long after sunset, Luthien emerged from the Saltwash onto the rolling fields of southeastern Avon. He meant to build a fire, but collapsed on the grass.

When he awoke to the slanting rays of dawn, he found a cheerful Brind'Amour standing over him. "This day you ride," the wizard said with a wink. "A long road ahead of us, my boy."

Brind'Amour helped him to his feet, and Luthien realized that his wounds were not so sore anymore. He looked to the one on his ribs and saw a thick muddy salve there, and he didn't have to ask to figure that Brind'Amour had added a bit of magic to the healing.

"A long road," the wizard said again, adding a wink. "But this time, the end of that road should be a better place by far!"

Indeed it was, for by the time the companions got back to Carlisle, Deanna Wellworth had assumed her rightful place as queen of Avon. Her speech to the doubting and frightened populace had been conciliatory and apologetic, but firm. She was back, by right of blood. They would have to accept that, but Deanna was wise enough to understand that the real test of her power, and the real reason for her return, was to improve the lives of those who looked to her for guidance.

Her reign, she promised, would be as her father's had been, gentle and just, for the good of all.

How much her hopes, and the hopes of those who supported her, were lifted on that morning when Luthien and Brind'Amour, both riding the healed Riverdancer, came back through Carlisle's shining gates, with news that the dragon king, evil Greensparrow, was truly dead!

That settled, Deanna acted quickly. She recognized Brind'Amour as rightful king of the free land of Eriador, and afforded the same autonomy to King Ashannon McLenny of Baranduine and to King Bellick dan Burso of DunDarrow. The four then struck a truce with Asmund of Isenland, though the subtle threat of war was needed to convince the fierce and proud Huegoth king to agree. For the three kings and one queen of Avonsea held a firm front in their demand that none of their subjects be held in slavery by Asmund's warriors.

The longships were emptied; men who thought they would never again see the light of day fell to their knees on the banks of the Stratton, giving thanks to God.

Asmund's warriors would row themselves home!

That business completed, Brind'Amour took to his own matters, arranging for the proper burial of those Eriadorans who had fallen, including the brave half-elf who had been his dear and valued friend, and who had been so instrumental in the change that had come over the land.

Luthien, too, could not hold back the tears as Siobhan was laid to rest, and only the sight of broken Oliver and the strength of Katerin gave Luthien the resolve that he, too, must remain strong for his halfling friend.

The first week after Deanna's ascent was filled with grief; the second began a celebration that the new queen of Avon declared would last for a fortnight. It began as a farewell to Asmund and the Huegoths, but seeing that the party was about to commence, the pragmatic barbarian changed his plans and allowed his rightly weary warriors to stay a bit longer.

On the first night of revelry, after a feast that left the hundred guests at Deanna's table stuffed, Brind'Amour pulled Luthien and Oliver, Kayryn Kulthwain and Proctor Byllewyn aside. "Greensparrow was right in dividing his kingdom among dukes," the king explained. "I will not be able to see the reaches of my kingdom from my busy seat in Caer MacDonald."

"We accept you as king," Proctor Byllewyn assured him.

Brind'Amour nodded. "And I name you again, and formally, as duke of Gybi," he explained. "And you, Kayryn Kulthwain, shall be my duchess of Eradoch. Guide your peoples well, with fairness and in the knowledge that Caer MacDonald will support you."

The two bowed low.

"And you, my dearest of friends," Brind'Amour went on, turning to Luthien and Oliver. "I am told that there is no duke of Bedwydrin, and no eorl, but only a steward, put in place until things could be set aright."

"True enough," Luthien admitted, trying to keep his tone in line with the honor that he expected would fall his way, though his heart was not in the assignment. Luthien had his fill of governments and duties, and wanted nothing more than a free run down a long road.

"Thus I grant you the title of duke of Bedwydrin," Brind'Amour announced. "And command of all the three islands, Bedwydrin, Marvis, and Caryth."

"Marvis and Caryth already have their eorls," Luthien tried to protest.

"Who will answer to you, and you to me," Brind'Amour replied casually.

Luthien felt trapped. How could he refuse the command of his king, especially when the command was one that almost anyone would have taken as the highest of compliments? He looked to Oliver, then his gaze drifted past the halfling, to Katerin, who was out on the floor, dancing gaily. There, in the partner of the red-haired woman of Hale, Luthien found his answer.

"This I cannot accept," he said bluntly, and his words were followed by a gasp from both Kayryn and Byllewyn.

Oliver poked him hard. "He does not mean to say what he tries to say," the halfling stammered and started to pull Luthien aside.

Luthien offered a smile to his diminutive friend; he knew that Oliver wanted nothing more than the comfortable existence that Brind'Amour's offer to Luthien would provide for them all.

"I am truly honored," Luthien said to the king. "But I cannot accept the title. Our ways are beyond the edicts of a king, are rooted in traditions that extend to times even before your brotherhood was formed."

Brind'Amour, more intrigued than insulted, cocked his head and scratched at his white beard.

"I am not the rightful heir to Bedwydrin's seat," Luthien explained, "for I am not the eldest son of Gahris Bedwyr."

That turned all eyes to the dance floor, to Katerin and to her partner, Ethan Bedwyr. Brind'Amour called the couple over, and called to Asmund as well.

Ethan's initial response to the offer was predictable and volatile. "I am Huegoth," came the expected claim.

Katerin laughed at him, and his cinnamon-colored eyes, that obvious trademark to his rightful heritage, flashed as he snapped his gaze about to regard her.

"You are Bedwyr," the woman said, not backing down an inch. "Son of Gahris, brother of Luthien, whatever your words might claim."

Ethan trembled on the verge of an explosion.

"You left Bedwydrin only because you could not tolerate what your home had become," Katerin went on.

"Now you can make of your home your own vision," added Brind'Amour. "Will you desert your people in this time of great change?"

"My people?" Ethan scoffed, looking to Asmund.

A large part of Oliver deBurrows, that comfort-loving halfling constitution, wanted Ethan to reject the offer so that Luthien had to take the seat, that Oliver could go beside him and live a life of true luxury. But even that temptation was not enough to tear the loyal halfling from the desires of his dearest friend. "Even Asmund would agree that such a friend as Ethan Bedwyr sitting in power among the three islands would be a good thing," Oliver put in, seeing his chance. "Mayhaps you have seen your destiny, Ethan, son of Gahris. You who have befriended the Huegoths might seal in truce and in heart an alliance and friendship that will outlive you and all your little Ethan-type children."

Ethan started to respond, but Asmund clapped him hard on the back and roared with laughter. "Like a son you've been to me," slurred the Huegoth king, who had obviously had a bit too much to drink. "But if you think you have a chance of claiming my throne . . . !" Again came the roaring laughter.

"Take it, boy!" Asmund said when he caught his breath. "Go where you belong, just don't you forget where you've been!"

Ethan sighed deeply, looked from Katerin to Asmund, to Luthien, and finally to Brind'Amour, offering a somewhat resigned, somewhat hopeful nod of acceptance.

It might have been simply the perception, the hope that embraced the kingdoms of Avonsea, but the ensuing winter did not seem so harsh. Even on those surprisingly infrequent occasions when snow did fall, it was light and fluffy, settling like a gentle blanket. And winter's grip was

not long in the holding; the last snow fell before the second month of
the year was ended, and by the middle of the third month, the fields
were green once more and the breeze was warm.

So it was on the bright morning that Luthien, Katerin, and Oliver set
out from Carlisle. Brind'Amour and the Eriadoran army had long ago
returned to Caer MacDonald, Ethan Bedwyr to Bedwydrin, Ashannon
McLenny and his fleet to Baranduine, and Bellick dan Burso to Dun-
Darrow, all ready to take on the responsibilities of their new positions.
But for Luthien and his two companions, those responsibilities had
ended with the fall of Greensparrow and the official coronation of
Queen Deanna Wellworth of Avon. Thus the trio had lingered in
Carlisle, enjoying the splendors of Avon's largest city. They had spent the
winter healing the scars of war, letting the grief of friends lost settle into
comfortable memories of friends past.

But even Carlisle, so huge, so full of excitement, could not defeat the
wanderlust that held the heart of all three, of Luthien Bedwyr most of
all, and so, when the snows receded and the wind blew warm, Luthien,
upon Riverdancer, had led the way to the north.

They rode easily for several days, keeping to themselves mostly,
though they would have been welcomed in any village, in any farmhouse. Their companions were the animals, awakening after winter's
slumber, and the stars, glittering bright each night above the quiet and
dark fields.

The trio had no real destination in mind, but they were moving inevitably to the north, toward the Iron Cross, and Caer MacDonald beyond that. The mountains were well in sight, Speythenfergus Lake left
far behind, before they formally spoke of their destination.

"I do not think Caer MacDonald will be so different from Carlisle,"
Luthien remarked one morning soon after they had broken camp. Again
the day was unseasonably warm and hospitable, the sun beaming overhead, the breeze soft and from the south.

"Ah yes, but Brind'Amour, my so dear friend, rules in Caer MacDonald," Oliver said cheerily, kicking Threadbare to move ahead of Katerin's
chestnut and come up alongside Riverdancer.

Katerin did not smile as Oliver moved past her; her thoughts, too,
were on Caer MacDonald, and the impending boredom promised by
such a peaceful existence.

"True enough," said Luthien.

"So," Oliver began to reason, "if we creep into the house of a merchant-
type and are caught—not that any could ever catch the infamous Oliver
deBurrows and his Crimson Shadow henchman!" Oliver quickly added

when his companions brought their mounts to an abrupt stop, both regarding him skeptically.

"Crimson Shadow henchman?" Katerin asked.

"We'll not go to Caer MacDonald as thieves, Oliver," Luthien said dryly, something the halfling obviously already knew. The halfling shrugged; Katerin and Luthien looked to each other and smiled knowingly, then urged their horses ahead once more.

"Why would we need to?" Oliver asked. "Of course, we shall live in the palace, surrounded by all pleasures, food and pretty ladies! Of course I was only joking; why would I want to steal with so much given to me?"

Luthien's next question stopped his companions short again.

"Then what shall we do?" the young Bedwyr asked.

"What must we do?" Oliver asked, not understanding.

"Are we two to build a home and raise our children?" Luthien asked Katerin, and the woman's stunned expression showed that she hadn't given that possibility any more thought than had Luthien. "Are we all to serve Brind'Amour, then," Luthien went on, "carrying his endless parchments from room to room?"

Oliver shook his head, still not catching on.

Katerin had it clear, though, and in truth, Luthien had brought up something that the young woman hadn't really considered. "What are we to do?" she asked, more to Luthien than to Oliver.

The young Bedwyr regarded her, his face skeptical as he considered that the reality of their apparent future could not match the intensity of their recent past.

"What is there for us in Caer MacDonald?" the woman asked.

"Caer MacDonald is the seat of Eriador, where our friend is king," Luthien answered, but his statement of the obvious did little to answer the woman's question.

Katerin nodded her agreement, but motioned for Luthien to continue, to explain exactly what that might mean.

"There is important . . ." the young Bedwyr started. "We will be needed . . . Brind'Amour will need emissaries," he finally decided, "to go to Gybi, to Eradoch, to Dun Caryth, and Port Charley. He will need riders to take his edicts to Bedwydrin. He will need—"

"So?" Katerin's simple question caught Oliver off his guard, and defeated Luthien's mounting duty-bound speech before it could gain any momentum—not that the young Bedwyr was trying to instill any momentum into it!

"The war is over," Katerin said plainly.

Oliver groaned, finally catching on to the course the two were walking. He started to protest, to remind them of the luxuries awaiting them, the accolades, the pretty ladies, but in truth, Oliver found that he was out of arguments, for in his heart he agreed—though the halfling part of him that preferred comfort above all else screamed a thousand thousand protests at his sensibilities. The war was over, the threat of Greensparrow ended forever. And the threat of the cyclopians had been ended as well, at least for the foreseeable future. The three kingdoms of Avonsea's largest island were at peace, a solid alliance, and any problems that might now arise would surely seem petty things when measured against the great struggle that had just been waged and won.

That was why Luthien had refused the crown of Eriador when his name had been mentioned as possible king soon after the northern kingdom had gained its independence from Greensparrow's Avon. Oliver studied his young friend, nodding as it all came clear. That was why Luthien had deferred to Ethan for the high position that Brind'Amour had offered. That was, in truth, why Luthien and Katerin had been so agreeable to the idea that they should linger in Carlisle. They had spent months waging a just war, their veins coursing with adrenaline. They were young and full of excitement and adventure; what did Caer MacDonald really have to offer to them?

"I spent many hours with Duke McLenny . . . King McLenny, on board his flagship as we sailed along Avon's western and southern coasts," Katerin said sometime later, the trio moving again, but more slowly now. "He spoke to me at length about Baranduine, wild and untamed."

Luthien looked at her, a mischievous smile crossing his face.

Oliver groaned.

"Untamed," Katerin reiterated, "and in need of a few good heroes."

"I do like the way this woman thinks," Luthien remarked, promptly turning Riverdancer to the west.

Oliver groaned again. On many levels, he wanted to convince Luthien and Katerin to accept the life of luxury, wanted them to settle down with their baby-types, while he got fat and comfortable in Brind'Amour's palace. On one level, though, Oliver not only understood, but, despite himself, agreed with the turn in direction. Wild Baranduine, rugged and unlawful, a place where a highwayhalfling might find a bit of sport and a bit of treasure. Suddenly Oliver recalled the carefree days he and Luthien had spent when first they had met, riding the breadth of Eriador at the expense of merchants along the road. Now the halfling envisioned a life on the road once more, with Luthien and that marvelous cape, and with Katerin, as capable a companion as any highwayhalfling could ever want, beside him. His vision grew into a full-blown daydream as they moved along, becoming vivid and thoroughly enjoyable—until the halfling saw an error in the image.

"Ah, my dear Siobhan," Oliver lamented aloud, for in his fantasy, the group riding about Baranduine's thick green hillocks was four, and not three. "If only you were here."

Luthien and Katerin regarded the halfling, sharing his sorrow. How much more complete they, too, would feel if the beautiful half-elf was riding alongside!

"A couple of couples we would then be!" Oliver proclaimed, his tone brightening, his dimples bursting forth as that cheery grin widened on his cherubic face. "We could call ourselves the two-two's, and let the fat merchant-types beware!"

Luthien and Katerin just laughed helplessly, a mirth tainted by the scars of a war that would never fully heal.

ABOUT THE AUTHOR

R. A. SALVATORE is the bestselling author of more than forty novels, which have sold more than 15 million copies. His works include The Icewind Dale Trilogy, The Dark Elf Trilogy, and The Cleric Quintet, and his most recent series is The Hunter's Blade Trilogy. Now he is making the jump to graphic novels, with many of his works being adapted to that format.

He lives in Massachusetts with his wife and family.

Straight from the Author

R. A. Salvatore Answers Questions from Readers About *The Crimson Shadow*

Q: Where do you get your inspiration for your characters, especially Bruenor, Drizzt, Catti-brie, and Regis? And where do you get your inspiration for the stories in general?

—Karen S., Lexington, SC

R. A. Salvatore: I think every writer will tell you pretty much the same thing: Inspiration comes from all around us. Every book I read, or movie I see, or landscape I discover, or song I hear makes an impression on me. As does every person I meet. Often I suspect that being a writer is a matter of unconsciously taking all of this information, breaking it apart, spinning all the bits into a different collage, and regurgitating them in different combinations. There are no specific people I meet who become "characters" in my books, but the characters in my books carry traits of many people I've met. For example, I've often said that Drizzt is who I wish I had the courage to be.

The same is true of the stories I craft. They come from deep inside, from the reams of information that have settled in that mass of gray matter sitting atop my shoulders, in my gut and in my heart. Everybody is a storyteller, of course. Being a working professional writer may be nothing more than having an instinctive way of telling your stories which appeals to enough people to keep publishers interested in publishing more.

Q: Does the Crimson Shadow series have any ties into the Forgotten Realms? If so, where does it fit in?

—Kris L., Dallas, TX

RAS: No, the Crimson Shadow takes place in a world I created. One that more closely resembles our own world, I might add. It's no accident that the isles look like Britain, for example.

The Forgotten Realms® book series was created by Ed Greenwood. Although dozens of authors and game designers have put their stamp on the place, in my mind it will ever be Ed's amazing world. I salute him and love him dearly and will be forever grateful that he allowed me to push the dirt around in his sandbox. The only work I've done that is in any way connected to the Forgotten Realms are my Forgotten Realms novels (twenty-three and counting). That's the way it has to be, both legally and morally.

Q: Do you think that writing is a God-given talent, or do you think that anyone can do it if they have enough determination?

—Luke G., Bismarck, ND

RAS: I think it's a little of both. Anyone can become well versed in things grammatical. Anyone can learn the "rules" of a language. It occurs to me that some people learn them too well, and lose track of the notion that grammar is something different. It's not a set of rules; it's a set of tools.

Also, as I said before, everyone is a storyteller. Every person has an "idea" for a great book. If you connect this with my previous paragraph, it seems apparent that "anyone can do it," right?

Maybe, but there's a third piece of the puzzle. We all have different ways of telling our stories, different inner voices. Being a writer means finding that voice, and being a successful writer, I believe, means having an instinctual method of telling a story that pleases many people. You won't please everyone, of course. No writer can hope for that. But maybe, just maybe, you'll please enough to make it worthwhile for you and for the publishers to print it and put it on the shelves.

That's all regarding "publishing" and not "writing," and believe me when I tell you that there's a huge gulf between the two concepts. So yes, anyone can become a writer, but not everyone can get published. And by the way, that's not always a measure of talent. Timing and luck are huge components!

Q: What sort of role do you think music plays in the creative process of writing a book?

—Wesley J. K., Wellesley, Ontario, Canada

RAS: That would depend on the author. For me, it plays a huge role. I wrote my first book, *Echoes of the Fourth Magic*, way back in 1982–1983, longhand, by candlelight, to Fleetwood Mac's amazing *Tusk* album. That music acted as a conduit to my writing "trance." When Stevie Nicks sang of the sisters of the moon, I envisioned the witch Brielle dancing on a moonlit field. I even named Brielle's daughter Rhiannon, with ties to the Welsh witch that Ms. Nicks made famous in the late '70s.

I choose my mood music carefully now. The theme from World of Warcraft makes for great scene-setting for large-scale battles, I find, and no one sets a soft wintery mood better than George Winston.

And I've still got my Fleetwood Mac, of course—only on CD and not LP.

Q: Is the Oliver deBurrows character really based on your dog?
                                                    —Neil R., King George, VA

RAS: You've got that backwards. My oldest dog, Oliver, is three years old. When we got him and began our name search, my wife decided that we should name him after one of the lesser known characters in my books, since he was, in effect, our sidekick. Well, since he's a Japanese Chin, and all of ten pounds, we considered Oliver, and as his rather strange personality became apparent, the name stuck.

The following year we lost one of our cats, who had become Oliver's best friend, and I replaced him with a gift to my wife on her birthday: another Japanese Chin. This one is even smaller and possessed of a personality that can be quite devious. His name is Artemis.

The following year, to pay me back for the curse of Artie, my wife woke me up at 4:30 on my birthday in January 2005. "Just trust me and follow me," she instructed and in a few minutes we were on the road heading for Boston's Logan Airport. When I saw that we were going to Pittsburgh, I got excited, as my beloved Patriots were playing in the AFC Championship game against the Pittsburgh Steelers that very weekend. In fact, one of our Boston sportscasters was sitting on the plane not far from us.

But no, we were going to see the Japanese Chin breeder, who met us at the airport with yet another of the little beasties. This one's the biggest and the toughest, a snarling fiery beast named Ivan (Bouldershoulder). Go figure.

Q: Oliver deBurrows, highwayhalfling, is one of the funniest characters you've come up with in my opinion. Where did his accent come from?
                                                    —Sean S., Portland, OR

RAS: Ah, Oliver again. Truly he's one of my favorite characters ever, and so much fun to write. In the very broadest terms, I consider him a cross between Inigo Montoya of *The Princess Bride* and the little French guy on the wall in *Monty Python's Holy Grail*. There's your accent—sort of a Gascon-Cockney cross, with a few Crimson-Shadow-world idiosyncrasies thrown in for good measure. If anything draws me back to this world, it'll be Oliver, that's for certain. I love the little guy, and miss him dearly.

Q: You wrote the Crimson Shadow trilogy early in your writing career and I have often heard that it helped you when you wrote Demon Wars and the Drizzt novels. What was the biggest thing you learned from writing the Crimson Shadow trilogy that reflects on your later works?
—Andy G., Austin, MN

RAS: I wrote the Crimson Shadow at the same time I was cutting my teeth on the early Drizzt and Cleric Quintet books. I wanted to create my own world more fully than I had in my previous original series, the Chronicles of Ynis Aielle and the Spearwielder's Tale, both of which were intricately attached to our world.

Unfortunately at that time, my writing schedule was such that I simply didn't have the time I needed to fully flesh out the world. So I focused on the characters most of all in Crimson Shadow.

But I did get a taste of what was involved in creating my own world, my own Forgotten Realms or Shannara or Middle-earth. This series began the process, truly.

Q: Have we heard all there is from Luthien and Oliver? Might there be more to their tale?
—Tom C., Bellflower, CA

RAS: I purposely left the ending of *The Dragon King* with possibilities for sequels. I fall for my characters (those that survive). I always want to go back and see what they're up to. Right now, my contractual obligations prevent a peek at the pair, but I never say never.

I did consider an Oliver book, but I have to tell you, he's a hard character to write. I started a file on my computer called "Good Stuff," and every time I come up with something ridiculous that Oliver might say, I add it to the note pile. When I get enough . . .

As for further exploring the world without these guys, I don't expect it. One caveat is that this world might roll into another, larger one that

I've created, and if that's the case, then of course we'll see much more on the history of the place.

Q: What role does fantasy literature play in today's world?
—Jeremy J., Boiling Springs, SC

RAS: The short answer is that fantasy literature plays the same role as the rest of literature. To expand on that, today's fantasy genre is wildly diverse, and with many authors writing for many different reasons. It would be wrong of me to speak for all of them, and I'm hardly qualified to do so.

For me, fantasy can fill several roles. First and foremost is the joy of escapism. As Peter Beagle beautifully explained in his intro to the Tolkien books many years ago, "escapism" isn't a bad word.

Fantasy can also reinforce a sense of right and wrong, for its heroes are most often men and women of conviction who have a belief in something larger than themselves. And in fantasy, of course, one hero can often make a difference, can throw Sauron's ring into Mount Doom or slay the dragon that has terrorized the countryside. That goes back to the first role of fantasy as well, because isn't it wonderful to feel like you're in a world where you can actually make a difference?

Without going too deeply into the psychology of the genre, fantasy can also deliver comfort on a higher level. There's something very spiritual about a world where not everything can be explained by science, where magic is real.

I had a fellow at a convention telling me that my audience had grown up over the last nineteen years and, thus, my books should grow up with them. He wanted them to have more "adult" themes and situations. I got the feeling he was talking about sexual situations here. (Of course, after listening to his complaint, I asked him if he had read my Demon Wars novels, and he said he hadn't.)

Here's the thing of it for me; here's the reason I write fantasy: There is no better genre for getting young people to fall in love with reading. For all the reviews and all the heartfelt stories of a reader feeling a personal affinity for one of my characters, or for someone telling me that Oliver helped him through a bad time in his life, the letters that I most enjoy are the ones from teenagers that begin, "I never read a book until . . ." or from the parent of a teen, saying, "I couldn't get my son/daughter to read until I gave him/her one of your books." That for me is the ultimate high. Tolkien did that for me during my freshman year of college. His books literally changed my life and got me into serious reading, and not because they unlocked the mysteries of the universe to me. No—they did it because they reminded me how wonderful an adventure in a book could be.

I wouldn't want to be an English teacher in a high school today. Between the video games, AIM, message boards, and all the rest, the competition for a kid's time is fierce and unrelenting. So how do you get a kid to actually sit down and read a novel? There's only one answer: Give him a novel that he enjoys. My experience has shown me that among teens, fantasy has the highest reader retention rate by far. Helping turn teenagers on to reading is something this genre is almost uniquely poised to do.